Watters • Leyh • Sotuyo • Laiho

LUMBERJANES™

TO THE MAX EDITION

VOLUME SIX

BOOM! BOX™

LUMBERJANES TO THE MAX EDITION Volume Six, March 2020. Published by BOOM! Box, a division of Boom Entertainment, Inc. Lumberjanes is ™ & © 2020 Shannon Watters, Grace Ellis, Noelle Stevenson & Brooklyn Allen. Originally published in single magazine form as LUMBERJANES No. 41-48. ™ & © 2017, 2018 Shannon Watters, Grace Ellis, Noelle Stevenson & Brooklyn Allen. All rights reserved. BOOM! Box™ and the BOOM! Box logo are trademarks of Boom Entertainment, Inc., registered in various countries and categories. All characters, events, and institutions depicted herein are fictional. Any similarity between any of the names, characters, persons, events, and/or institutions in this publication to actual names, characters, and persons, whether living or dead, events, and/or institutions is unintended and purely coincidental. BOOM! Box does not read or accept unsolicited submissions of ideas, stories, or artwork.

BOOM! Studios, 5670 Wilshire Boulevard, Suite 400, Los Angeles, CA 90036-5679. Printed in China. First Printing.

ISBN: 978-1-68415-494-4, eISBN: 978-1-64144-652-5

THIS LUMBERJANES FIELD MANUAL BELONGS TO:

NAME:_____

TROOP:_____

DATE INVESTED:_____

FIELD MANUAL TABLE OF CONTENTS

LUMBERJANES
FIELD MANUAL

For the Advanced Program

Tenth Edition • December 1984

Prepared for the

**Miss Qiunzella Thiskwin
Penniquiqul Thistle Crumpet's**
CAMP FOR  HARDCORE LADY-TYPES

"Friendship to the Max!"

A MESSAGE FROM THE LUMBERJANES HIGH COUNCIL

miss Qiunzella Thiskwin Penniquiqul Thistle Crumpet's
Camp for
HARDCORE LADY TYPES
FRIENDSHIP to the MAX!

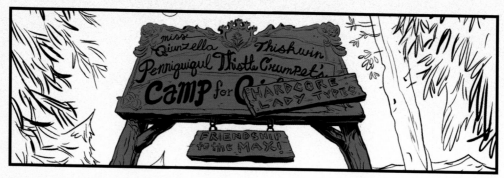

You may sometimes feel yourself being pulled in many directions all at once. Adults love to ask children what it is they would like to be when they grow up, and this is often a question children struggle to answer. There are some High Councillors who insist they knew that they wanted to become High Councillors (that is to say, professional Lumberjanes) from the age of six or seven, but there are even more of us who remember changing our ambitions as often and as lightly as the wind changes direction, or who grew up never knowing what to say when an aunt or uncle knelt before them to ask what they imagined their adult life would be.

There is often so much pressure handed down to young people to know what it is they want to do and be. Whether it comes from parents, or coaches, or teachers, or even from within yourself, there can be an intense desire to be certain when you decide upon a course of action. To know exactly what you want, and how to do it well. But there are so many ways our lives can go, and so many options we don't even know exist yet—from childhood to adulthood, and even into old age. And when you step back to look at it, in the grander scheme of your life, the question of what you want to be when you grow up presupposes that there is just one answer. The truth of the matter is that the answer to that question may be a constantly evolving, constantly blossoming array of possibilities.

We hope that your days as a Lumberjane scout will feel free and open, as they bloom like wildflowers. We hope that the time you spend making friendship bracelets and s'mores, or singing songs around the campfire will be time for you, the current version of you. Not your future self, or a version of yourself that someone else wants or expects you to be. We hope that you will come to understand that there is no right or wrong answer here, no 'should', no 'must'. Climb trees as they branch off into the future, and sail down minor tributaries on the great river that is your life. Follow your interests, whether they shift with the breeze, or with the rising sun, or with the phases of the moon. Your future is still there, waiting for you to come and fill it up with glorious things, but you needn't rush toward it with every step you take. Enjoy the trip, and take the time to get lost. It's the best way to learn where you want to go, after all.

THE LUMBERJANES PLEDGE

I solemnly swear to do my best
Every day, and in all that I do,
To be brave and strong,
To be truthful and compassionate,
To be interesting and interested,
To pay attention and question
The world around me,
To think of others first,
To always help and protect my friends,
[redacted]
And to make the world a better place
For Lumberjane scouts
And for everyone else.

THEN THERE'S A LINE ABOUT GOD, OR WHATEVER

LUMBERJANES™
TO THE MAX EDITION

Created by **Shannon Watters, Grace Ellis, Noelle Stevenson** *&* **Brooklyn Allen**

Written by
Shannon Watters & Kat Leyh

Illustrated by
Ayme Sotuyo

Colors by
Maarta Laiho

Letters by
Aubrey Aiese

Collection Designer
Jillian Crab

Badge Designs by
Kelsey Dieterich & Kara Leopard

Associate Editor
Sophie Philips-Roberts

Series Editor
Dafna Pleban

Collection Editor
Jeanine Schaefer

Special thanks to **Kelsey Pate** *for giving the Lumberjanes their name.*

LUMBERJANES FIELD MANUAL

CHAPTER FORTY-ONE

Lumberjanes "Out-of-Doors" Program Field

TIME AFTER CRIME

"Time is an illusion, never waste it!"

What did you have for breakfast this morning? What about yesterday? Three weeks ago? Six months? If you're anything like us, the further you go back, the more difficult it is to recall details, particularly for events as small and everyday as breakfast. Now imagine that effect across the vast span of history, and imagine how many little details have been forgotten or erased over the years. There are so many historical ideas and implements that we view through a skewed lens, or misunderstand, or simply don't know!

History, the long stretch of time that came before you, is unfathomably vast. There are countless ways to work on remembering or relearning the things that have been lost, via archaeology, paleontology, genealogy, anthropology, or any other number of "ologies" (like the most vital of all: apology), but it can sometimes seem that this work is all being done by adults, like scientists and researchers and librarians, and that there is little room for children. In the Time After Crime badge, we hope that you will take part in uncovering the history all around you and become a time traveler through memory!

Perhaps your mother has told you about how her parents grew up in houses that didn't have electricity, or how their parents didn't have so much as running water, maybe in a country far away from here. Perhaps you have thought about these distant relatives, so long ago and far away, and wondered if your life bears any resemblance to theirs. Did they like to play games, like you do? Did they eat the same foods as you? Did they read books that you like to read, or make crafts like you like to? Asking your parents and grandparents about their childhoods is a great way to get started, and if you're lucky, they may even have diaries, photos, or toys, to help give you a fuller picture of what their lives were like!

From there, you may decide to take this badge in a few different directions. Learning more about your family's history and creating a family tree can be a fun second step, but you may also enjoy grouping up with your troopmates to talk about your families' histories: where they came from, what traditions they hold dear. How does your family's history and culture compare and contrast to your friends? What can you discover about the past, and about yourselves?

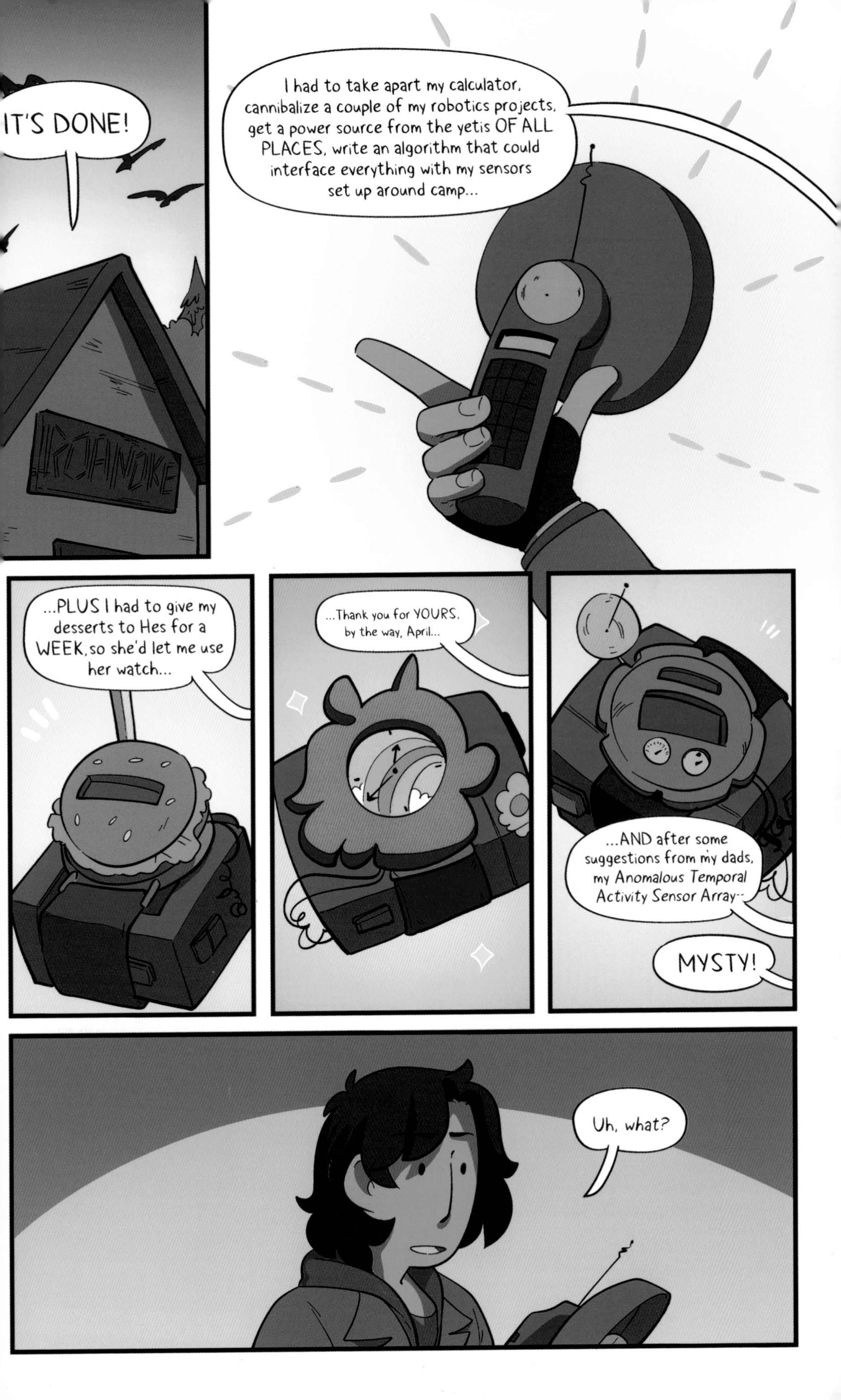
IT'S DONE!
I had to take apart my calculator, cannibalize a couple of my robotics projects, get a power source from the yetis OF ALL PLACES, write an algorithm that could interface everything with my sensors set up around camp...
ROANOKE
...PLUS I had to give my desserts to Hes for a WEEK, so she'd let me use her watch...
...Thank you for YOURS, by the way, April...
...AND after some suggestions from my dads, my Anomalous Temporal Activity Sensor Array--
MYSTY!
Uh, what?

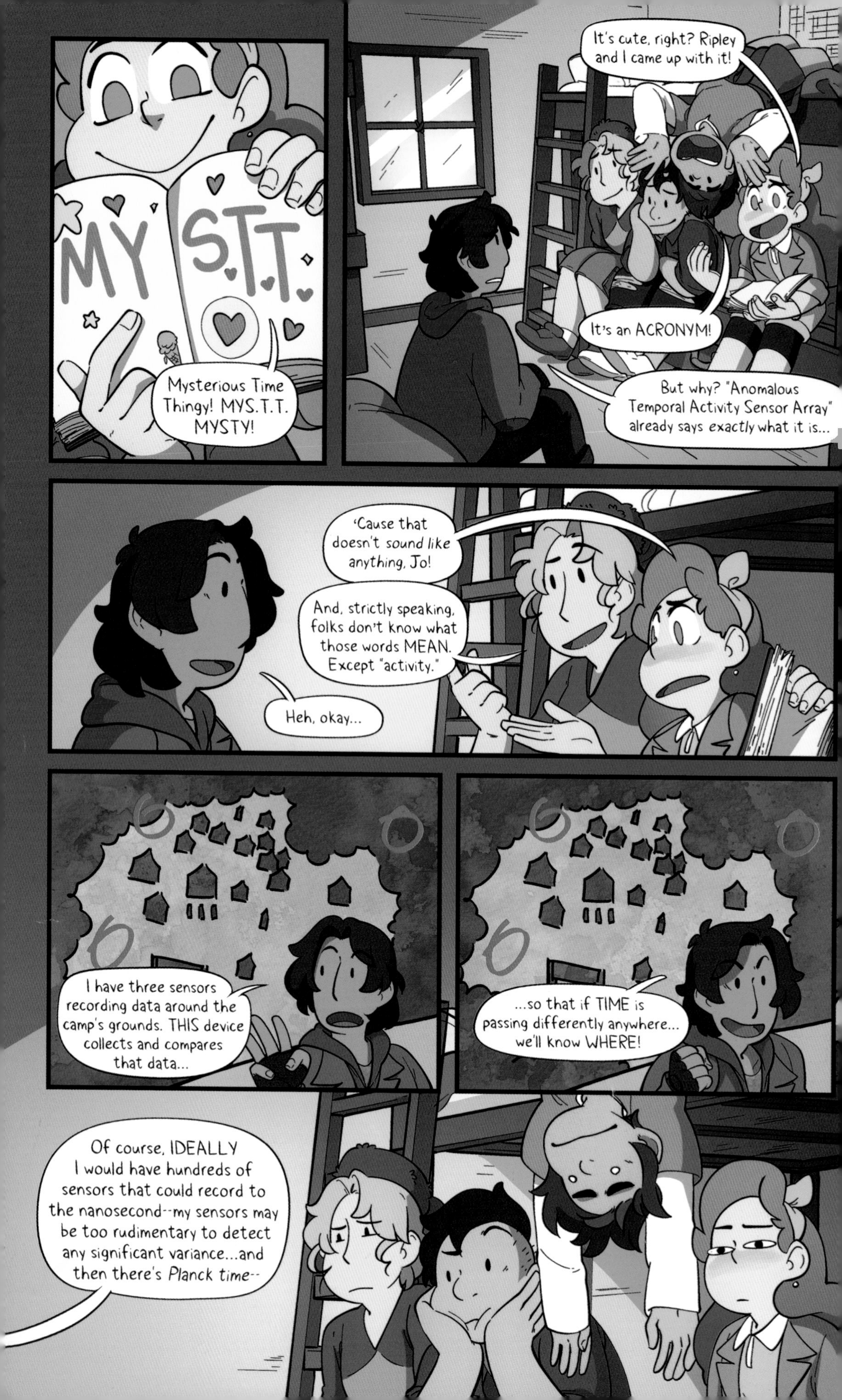
MY S.T.T.
Mysterious Time Thingy! MYS.T.T. MYSTY!
It's cute, right? Ripley and I came up with it!
It's an ACRONYM!
But why? "Anomalous Temporal Activity Sensor Array" already says *exactly* what it is...
'Cause that doesn't *sound* like anything, Jo!
And, strictly speaking, folks don't know what those words MEAN. Except "activity."
Heh, okay...
I have three sensors recording data around the camp's grounds. THIS device collects and compares that data...
...so that if TIME is passing differently anywhere... we'll know WHERE!
Of course, IDEALLY I would have hundreds of sensors that could record to the nanosecond--my sensors may be too rudimentary to detect any significant variance...and then there's *Planck time*--

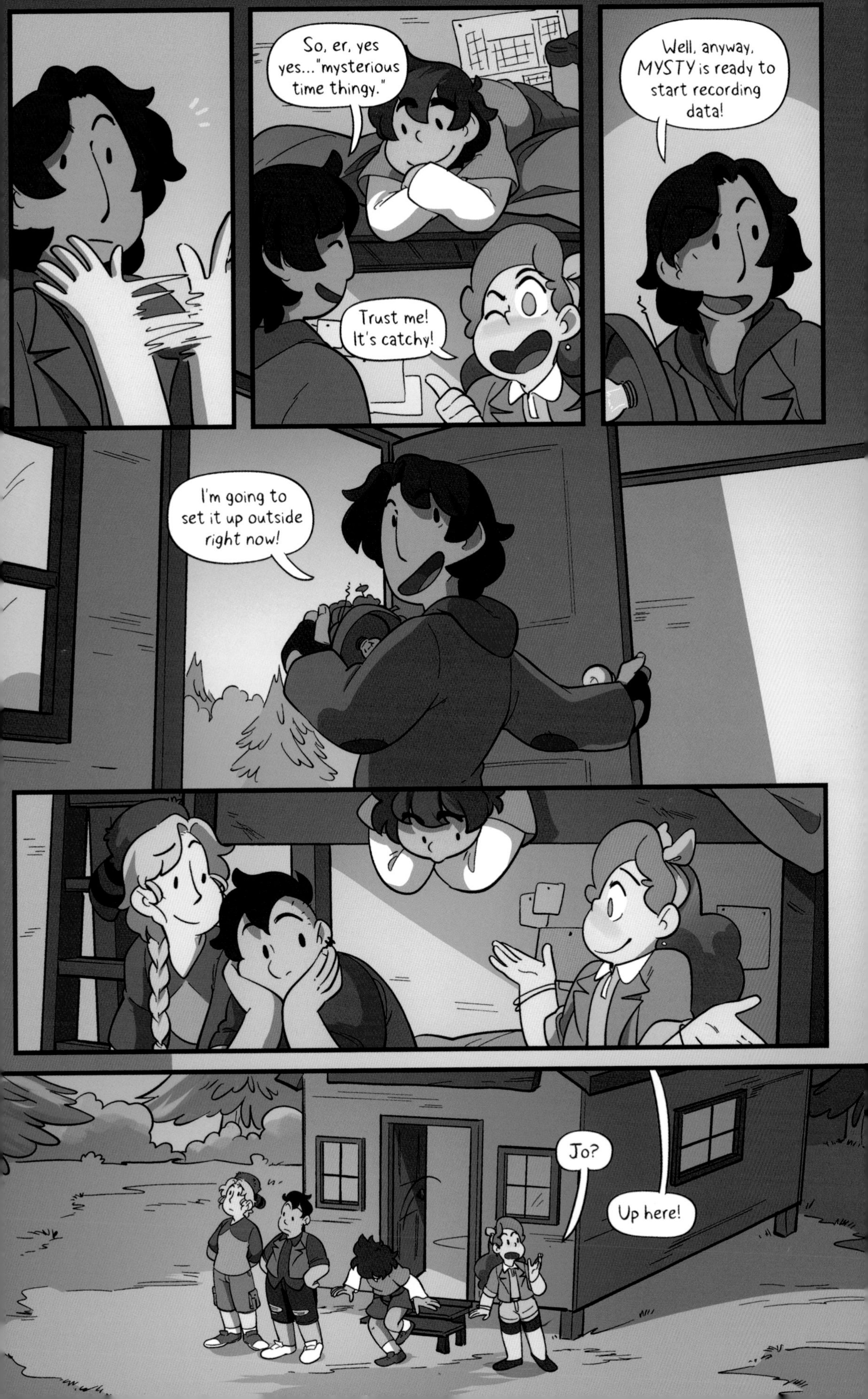
So, er, yes yes... "mysterious time thingy."
Trust me! It's catchy!
Well, anyway, MYSTY is ready to start recording data!
I'm going to set it up outside right now!
Jo?
Up here!

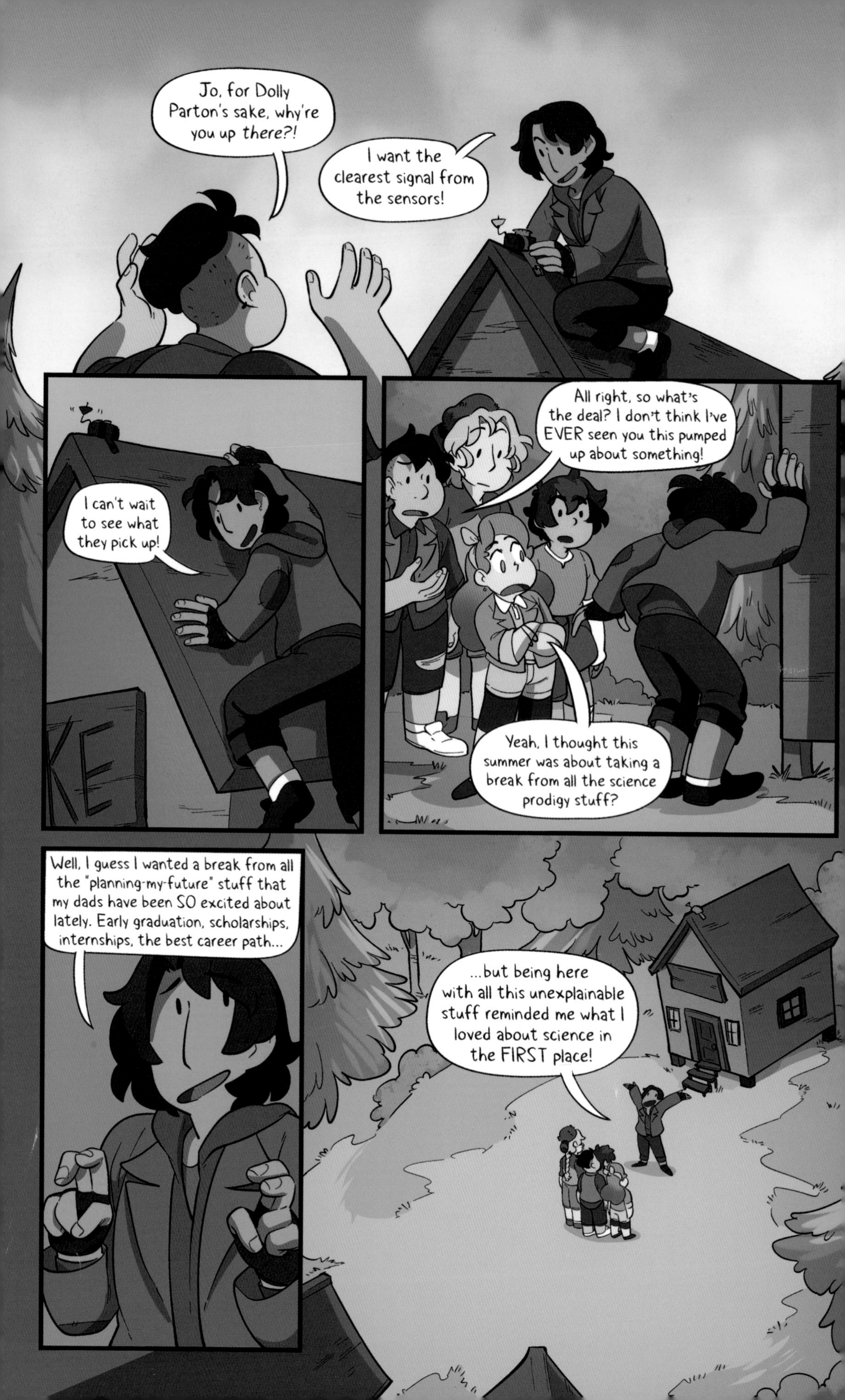
Jo, for Dolly Parton's sake, why're you up there?!
I want the clearest signal from the sensors!
I can't wait to see what they pick up!
All right, so what's the deal? I don't think I've EVER seen you this pumped up about something!
Yeah, I thought this summer was about taking a break from all the science prodigy stuff?
Well, I guess I wanted a break from all the "planning-my-future" stuff that my dads have been SO excited about lately. Early graduation, scholarships, internships, the best career path...
...but being here with all this unexplainable stuff reminded me what I loved about science in the FIRST place!

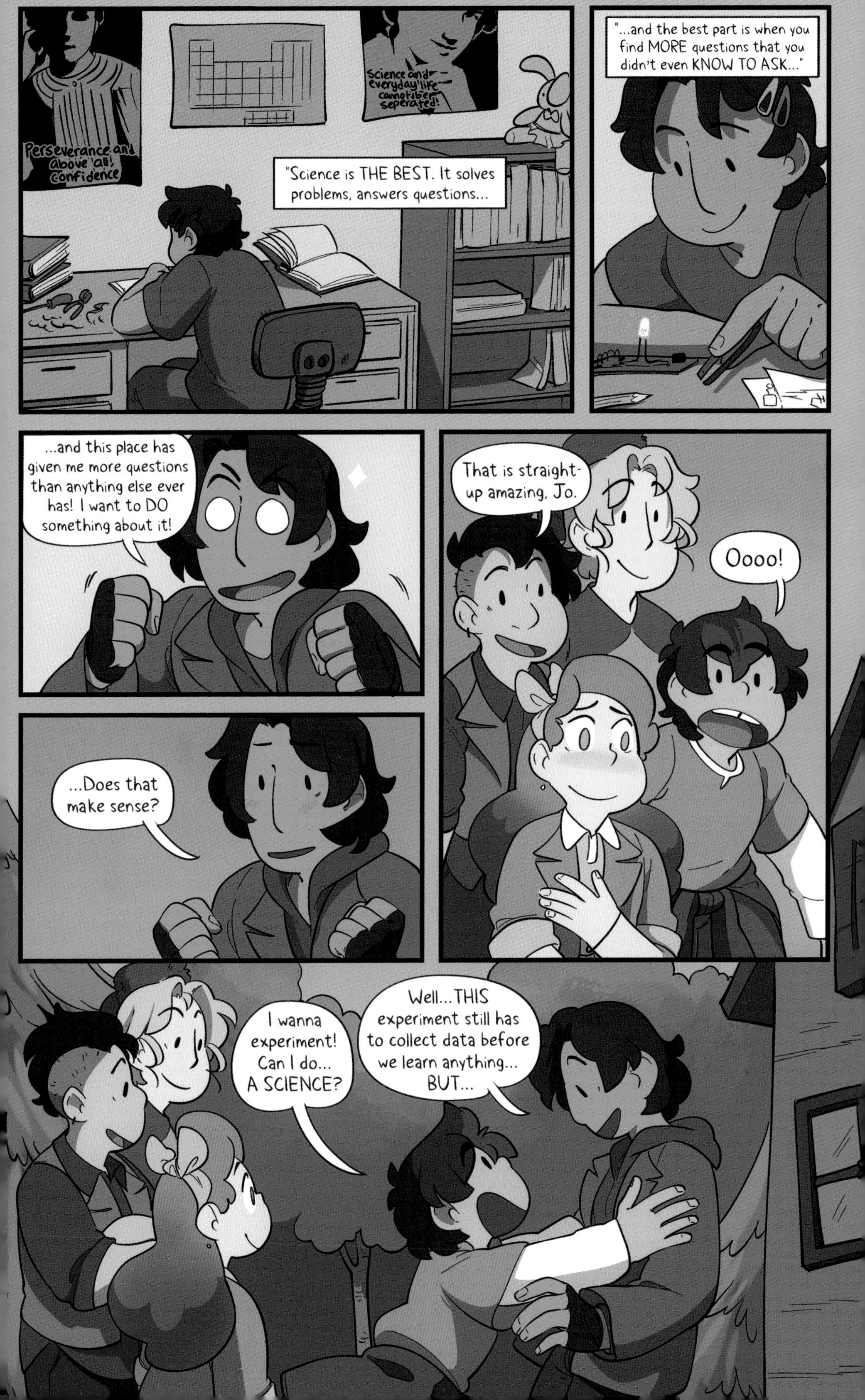
Perseverance and above all, confidence
Science and everyday life cannot be seperated!
"Science is THE BEST. It solves problems, answers questions...
"...and the best part is when you find MORE questions that you didn't even KNOW TO ASK..."
...and this place has given me more questions than anything else ever has! I want to DO something about it!
...Does that make sense?
That is straight-up amazing, Jo.
Oooo!
I wanna experiment! Can I do... A SCIENCE?
Well... THIS experiment still has to collect data before we learn anything... BUT...

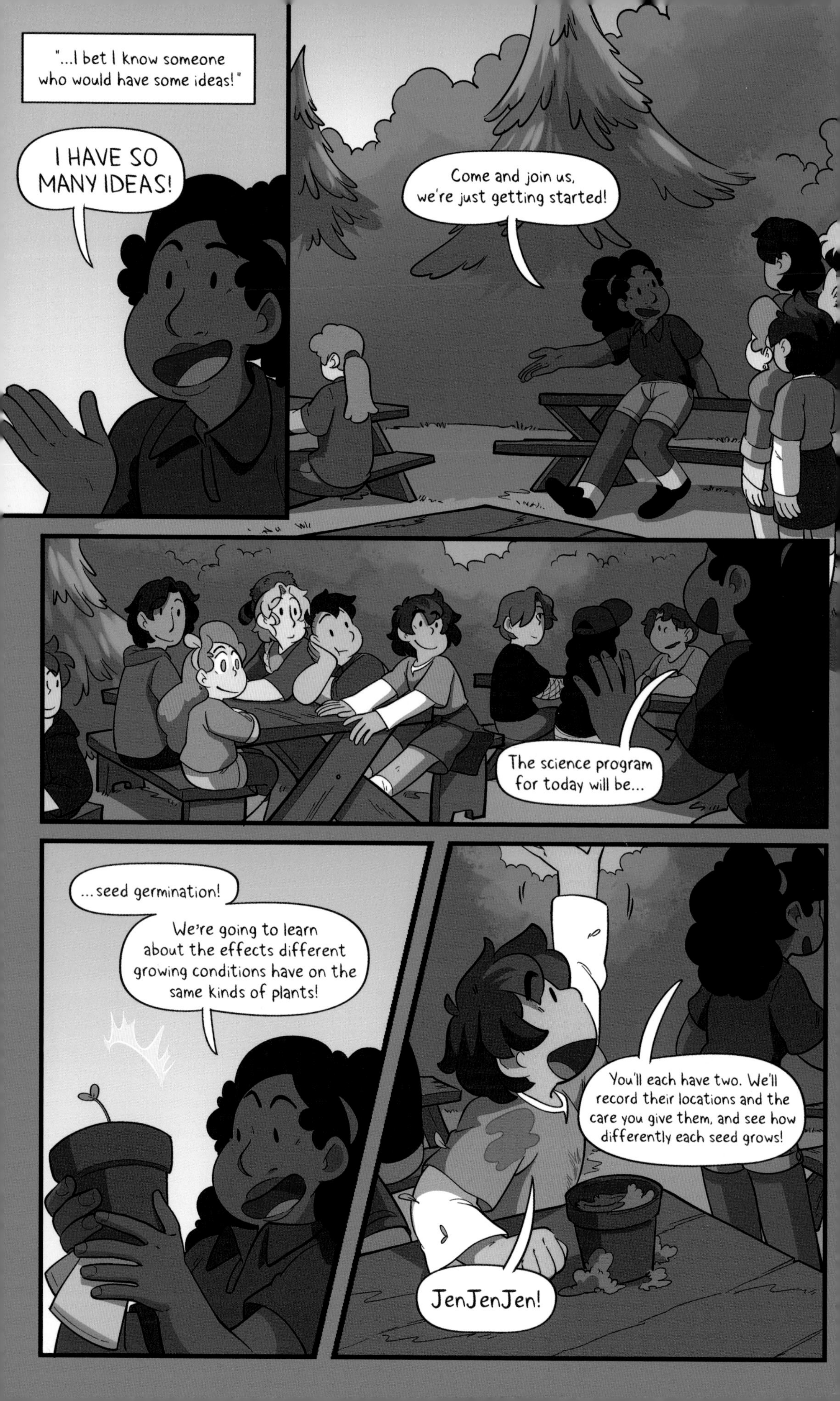
"...I bet I know someone who would have some ideas!"
I HAVE SO MANY IDEAS!
Come and join us, we're just getting started!
The science program for today will be...
...seed germination!
We're going to learn about the effects different growing conditions have on the same kinds of plants!
You'll each have two. We'll record their locations and the care you give them, and see how differently each seed grows!
JenJenJen!

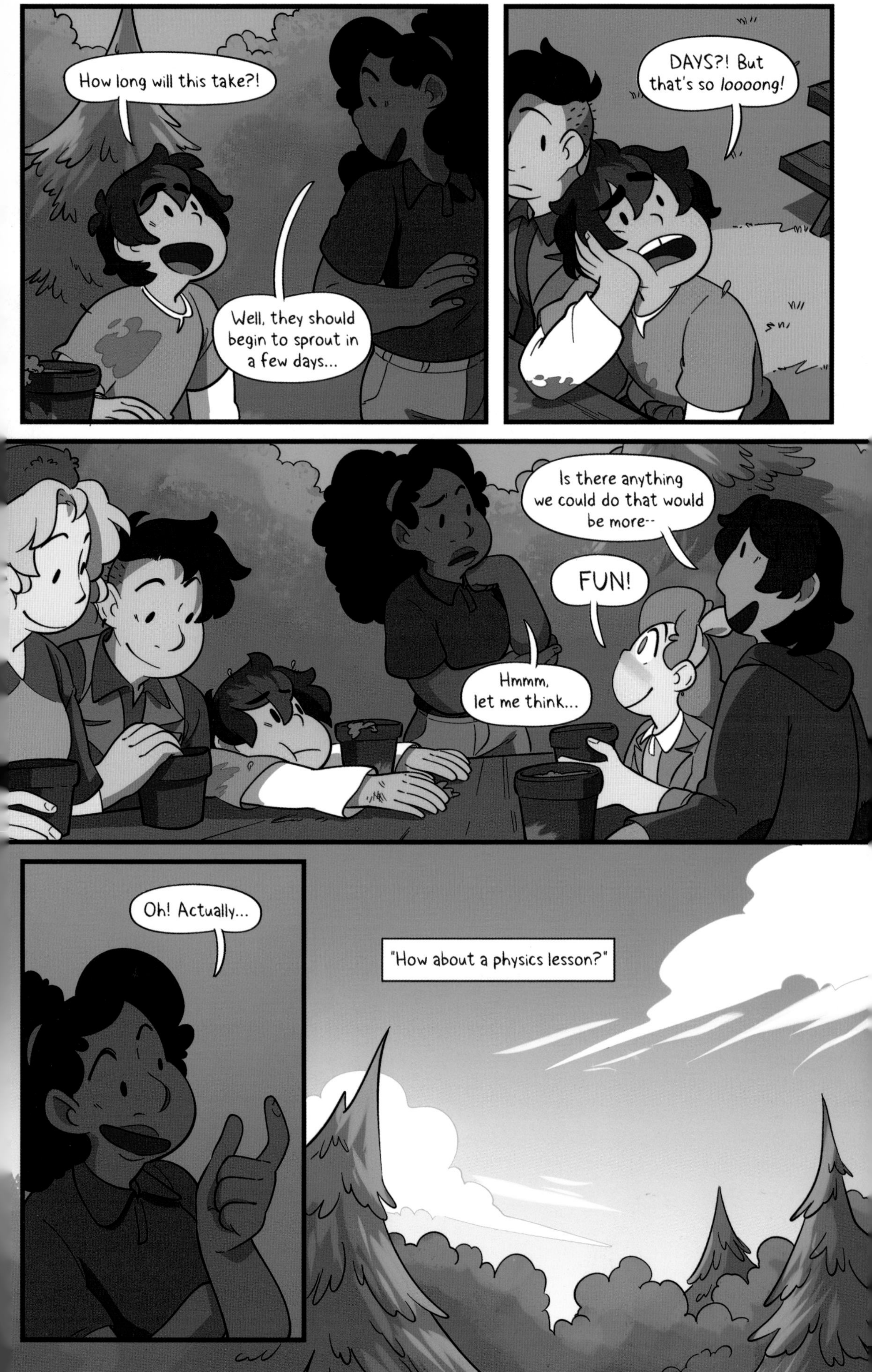
How long will this take?!
Well, they should begin to sprout in a few days...
DAYS?! But that's so *loooong*!
Is there anything we could do that would be more--
FUN!
Hmmm, let me think...
Oh! Actually...
"How about a physics lesson?"

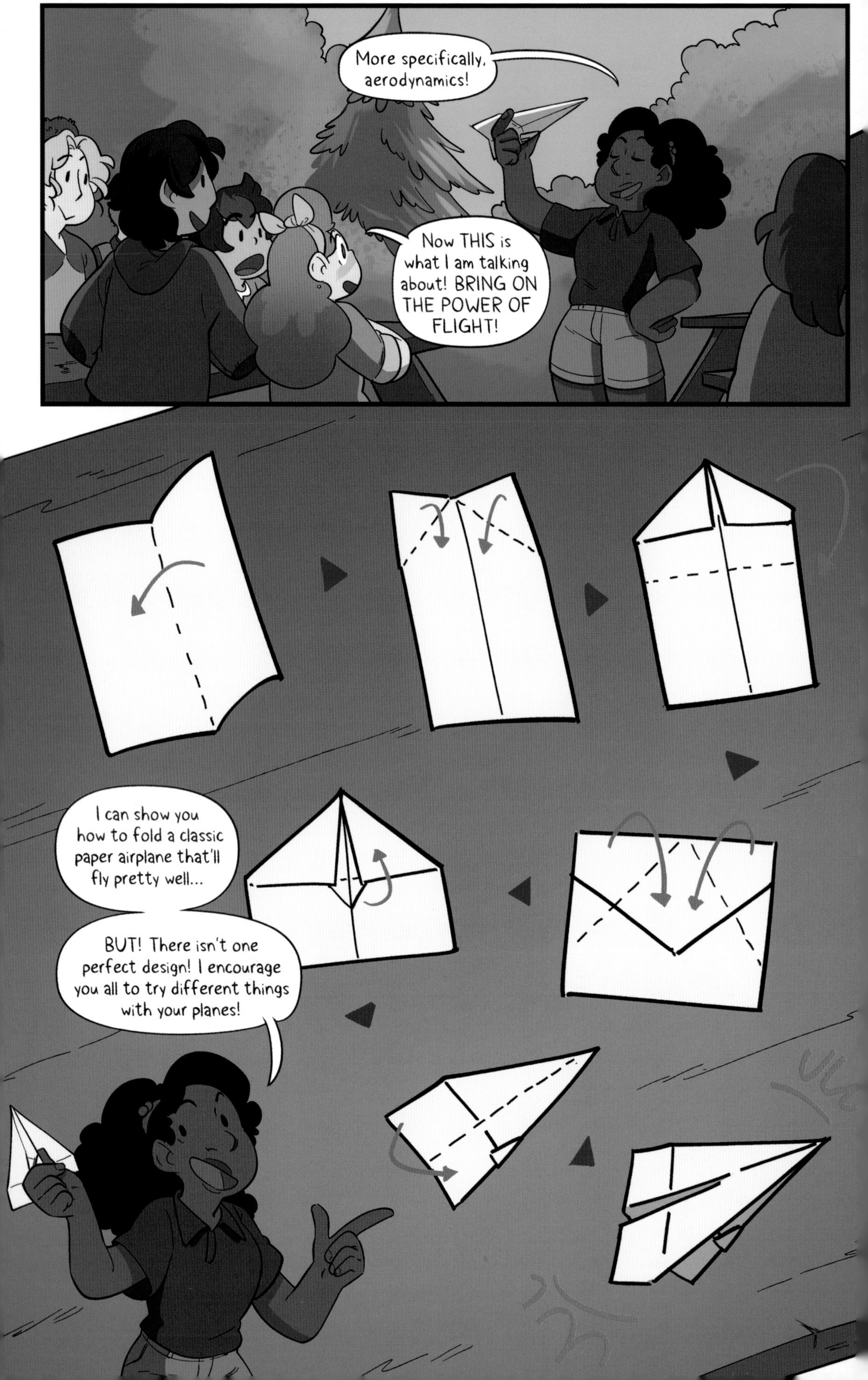
More specifically, aerodynamics!
Now THIS is what I am talking about! BRING ON THE POWER OF FLIGHT!
I can show you how to fold a classic paper airplane that'll fly pretty well...
BUT! There isn't one perfect design! I encourage you all to try different things with your planes!

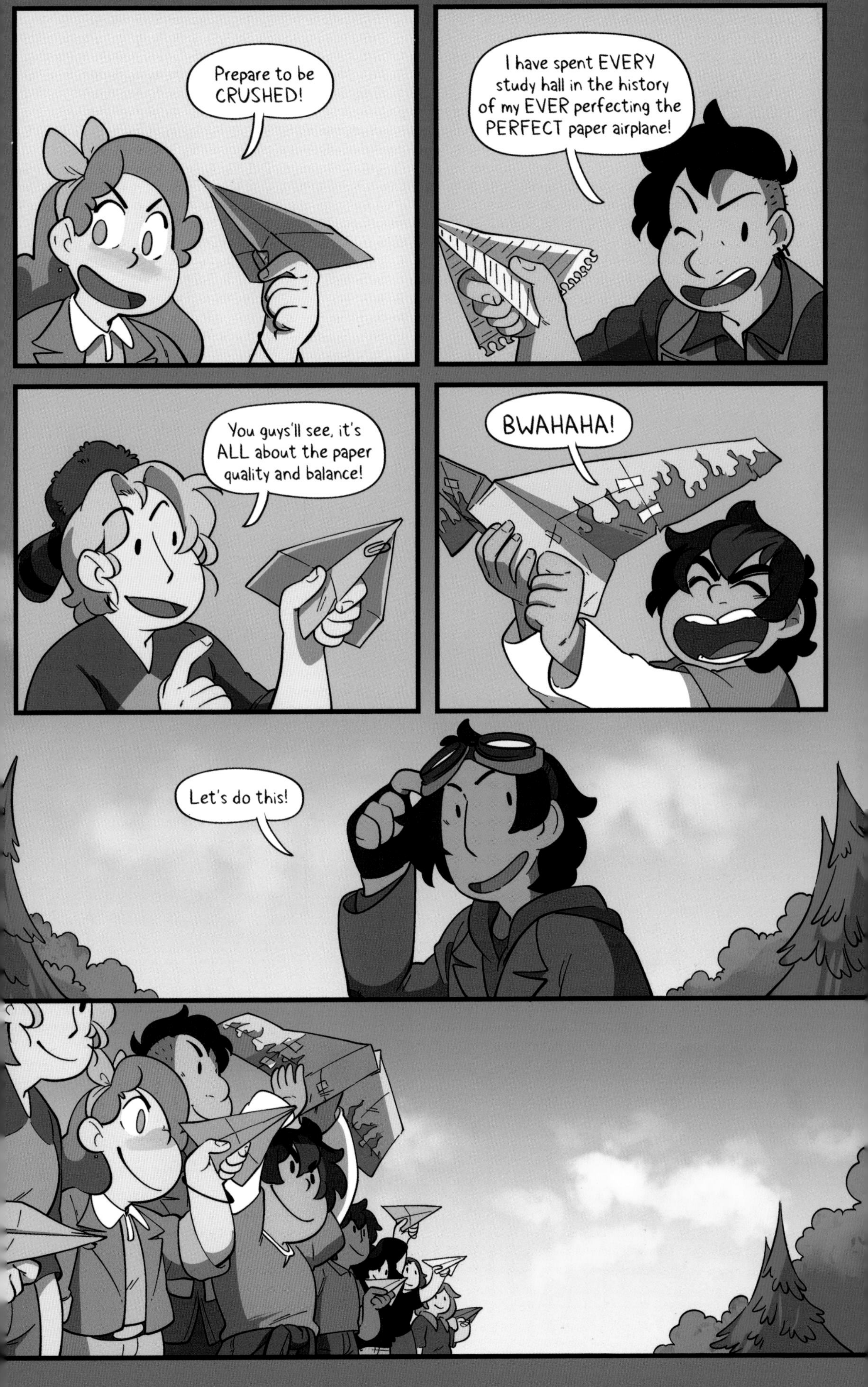
Prepare to be CRUSHED!
I have spent EVERY study hall in the history of my EVER perfecting the PERFECT paper airplane!
You guys'll see, it's ALL about the paper quality and balance!
BWAHAHA!
Let's do this!

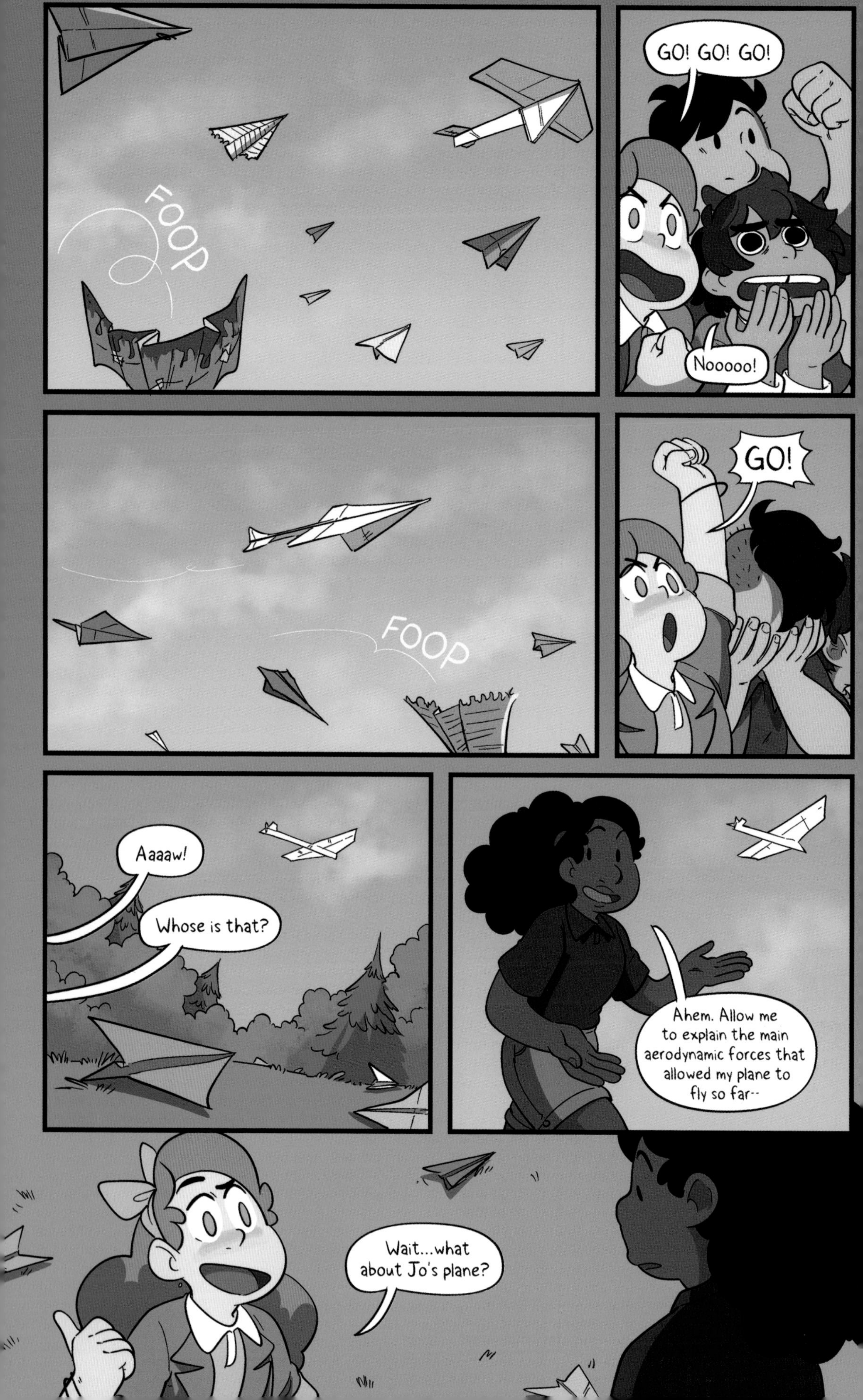
FOOP
GO! GO! GO!
Nooooo!
FOOP
GO!
Aaaaw!
Whose is that?
Ahem. Allow me to explain the main aerodynamic forces that allowed my plane to fly so far--
Wait...what about Jo's plane?

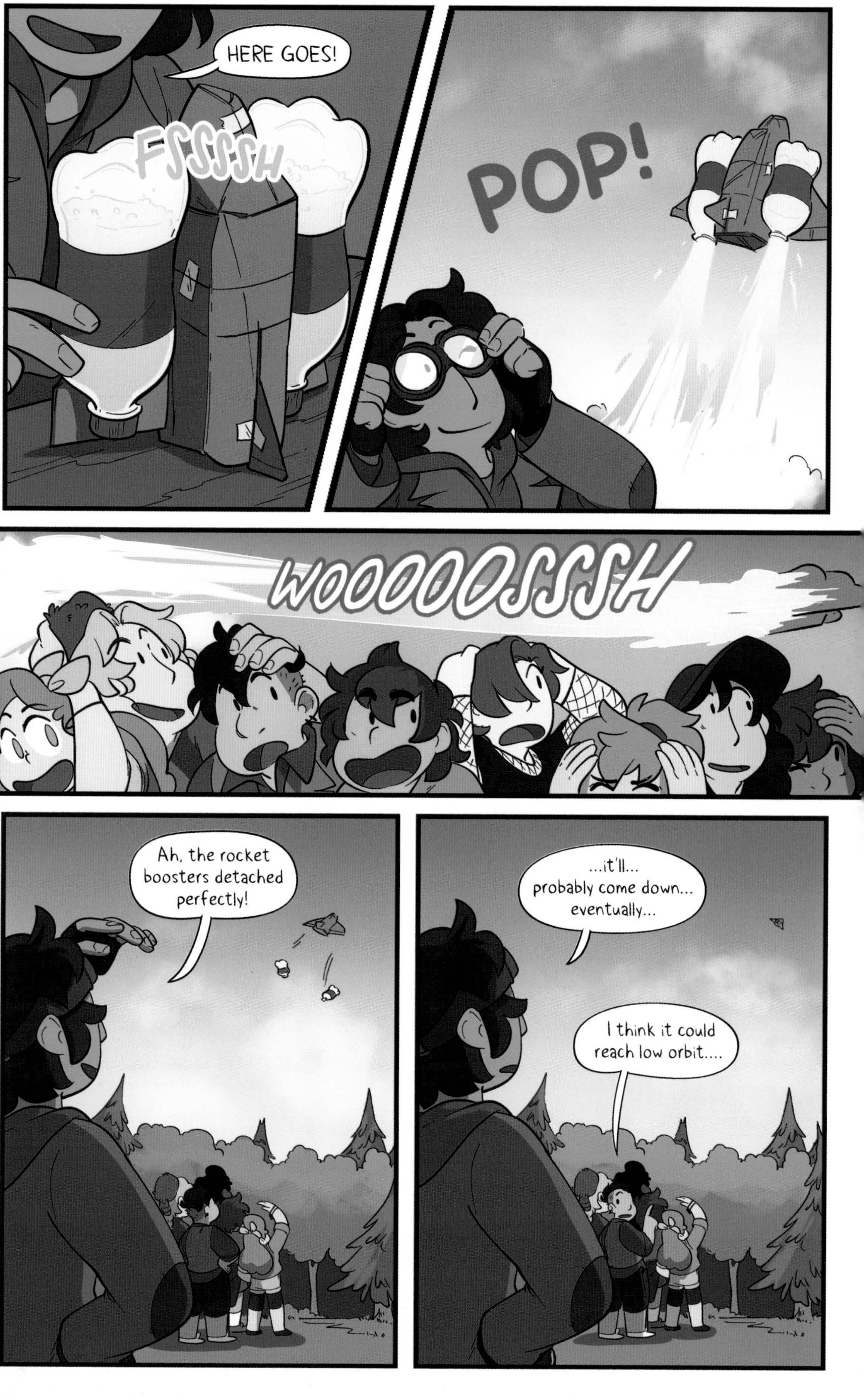
HERE GOES!
FSSSSH
POP!
WOOOOOSSSH
Ah, the rocket boosters detached perfectly!
...it'll... probably come down... eventually...
I think it could reach low orbit....

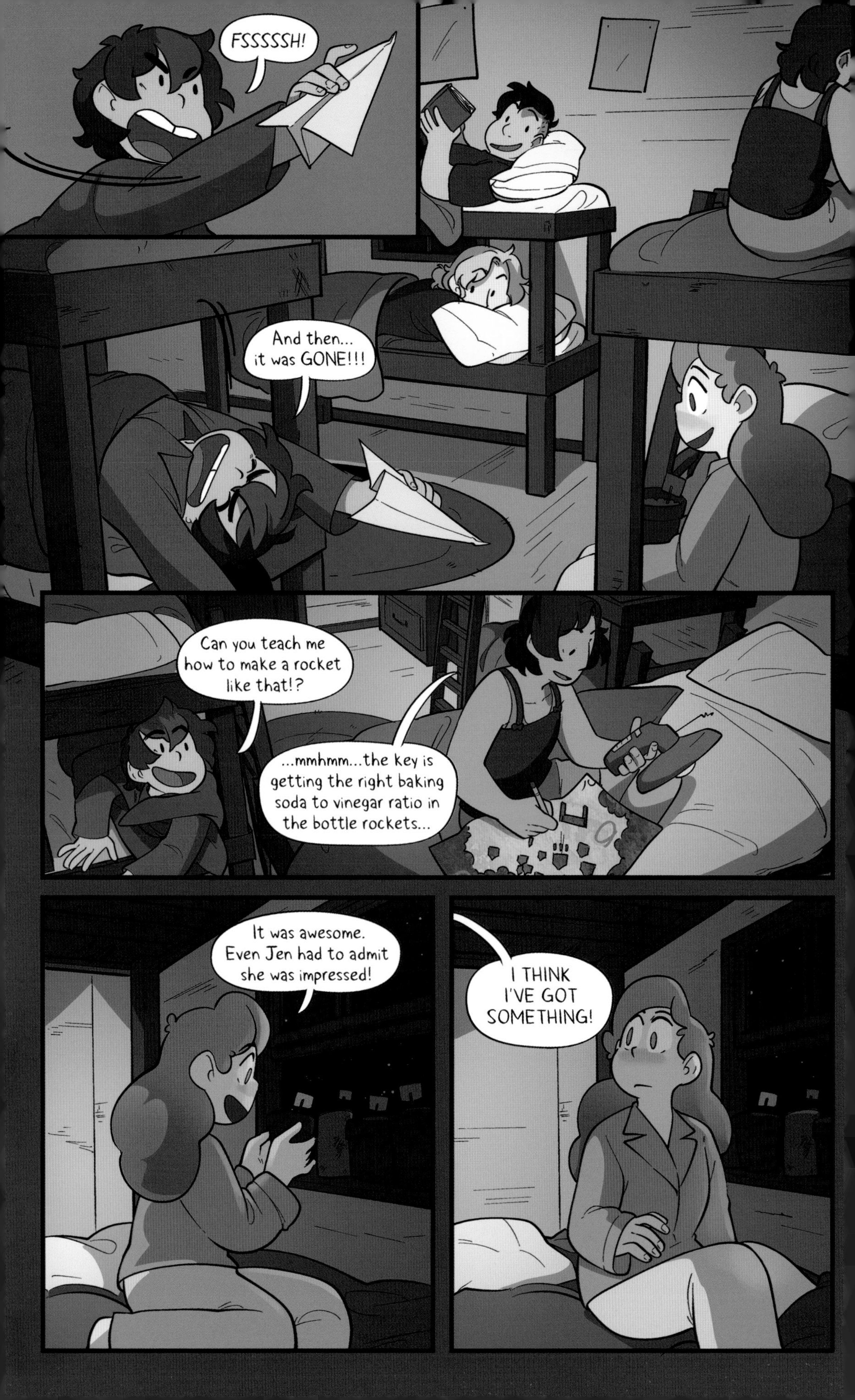
FSSSSSH!
And then... it was GONE!!!
Can you teach me how to make a rocket like that!?
...mmhmm...the key is getting the right baking soda to vinegar ratio in the bottle rockets...
It was awesome. Even Jen had to admit she was impressed!
I THINK I'VE GOT SOMETHING!

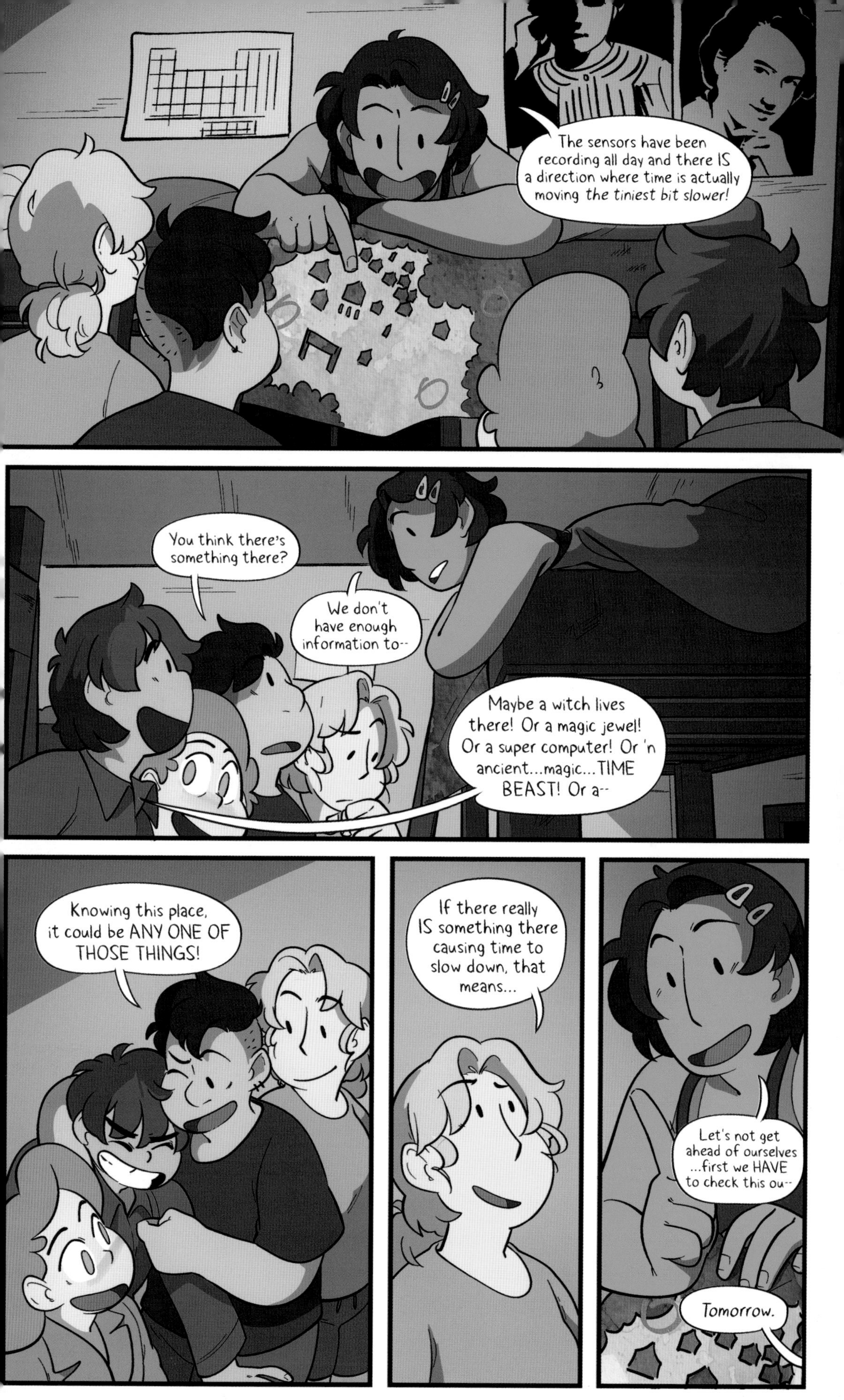
The sensors have been recording all day and there IS a direction where time is actually moving *the tiniest bit slower!*
You think there's something there?
We don't have enough information to--
Maybe a witch lives there! Or a magic jewel! Or a super computer! Or 'n ancient...magic...TIME BEAST! Or a--
Knowing this place, it could be ANY ONE OF THOSE THINGS!
If there really IS something there causing time to slow down, that means...
Let's not get ahead of ourselves ...first we HAVE to check this ou--
Tomorrow.

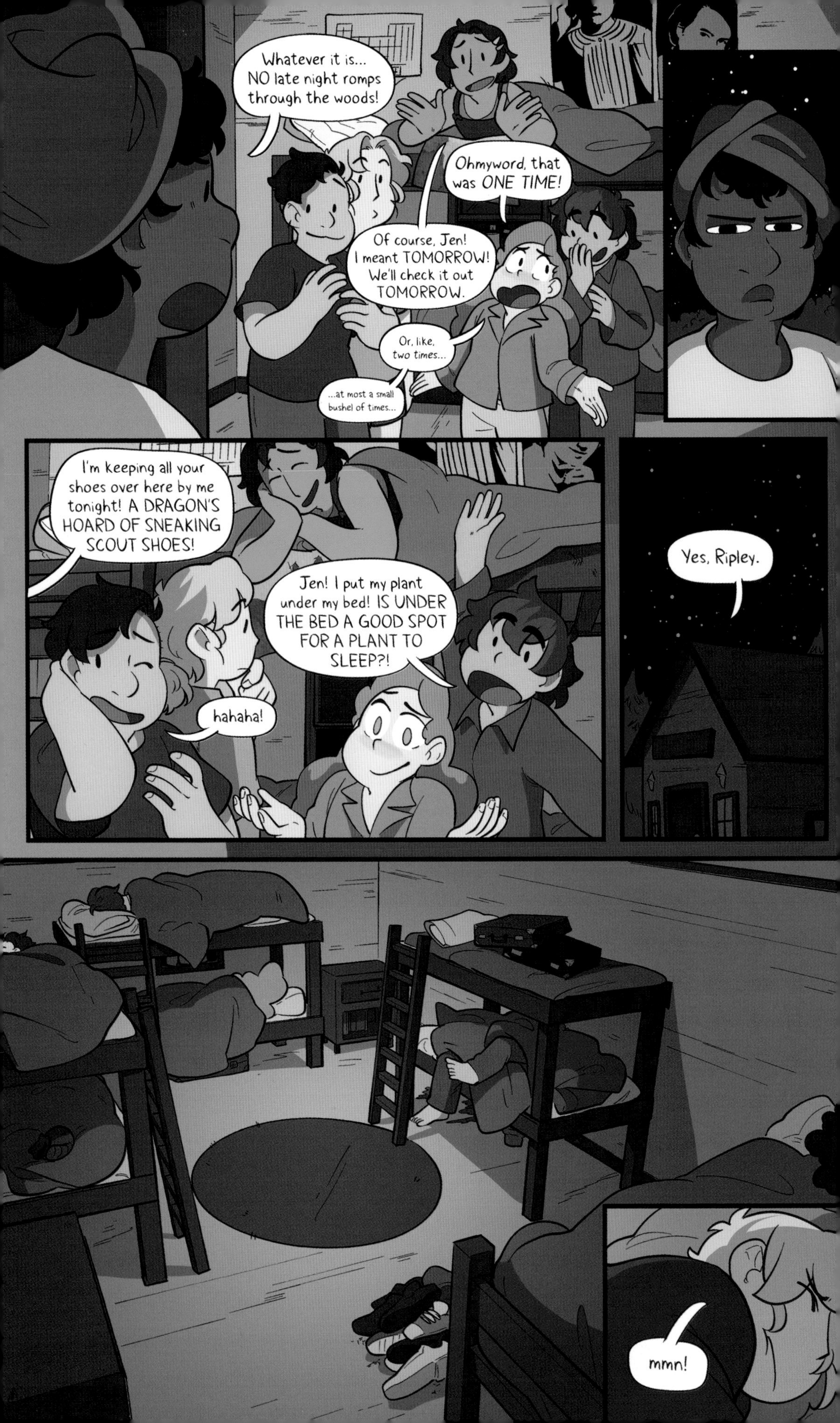
Whatever it is... NO late night romps through the woods!
Ohmyword, that was ONE TIME!
Of course, Jen! I meant TOMORROW! We'll check it out TOMORROW.
Or, like, two times...
...at most a small bushel of times...
I'm keeping all your shoes over here by me tonight! A DRAGON'S HOARD OF SNEAKING SCOUT SHOES!
Jen! I put my plant under my bed! IS UNDER THE BED A GOOD SPOT FOR A PLANT TO SLEEP?!
hahaha!
Yes, Ripley.
mmn!

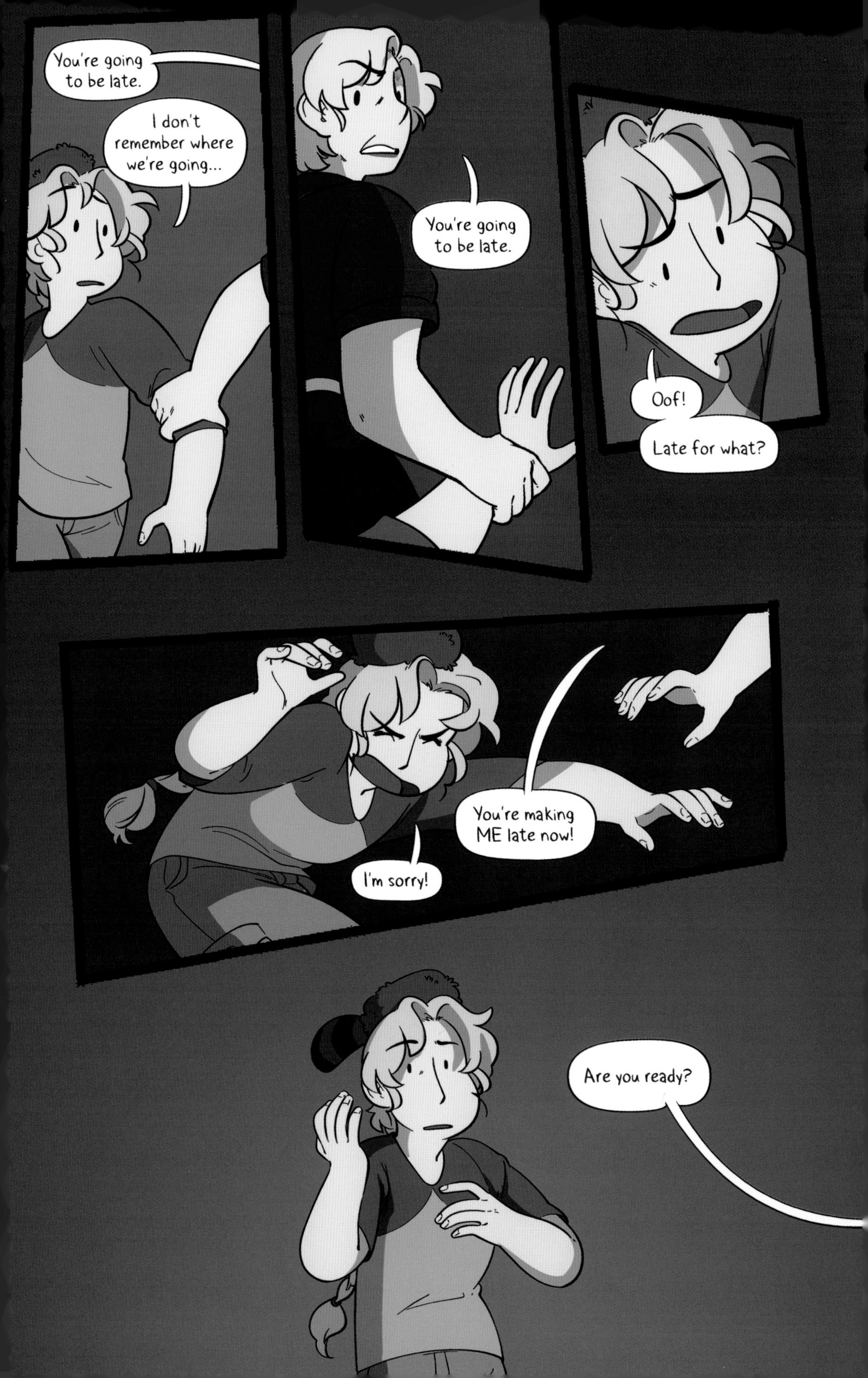
You're going to be late.
I don't remember where we're going...
You're going to be late.
Oof!
Late for what?
You're making ME late now!
I'm sorry!
Are you ready?

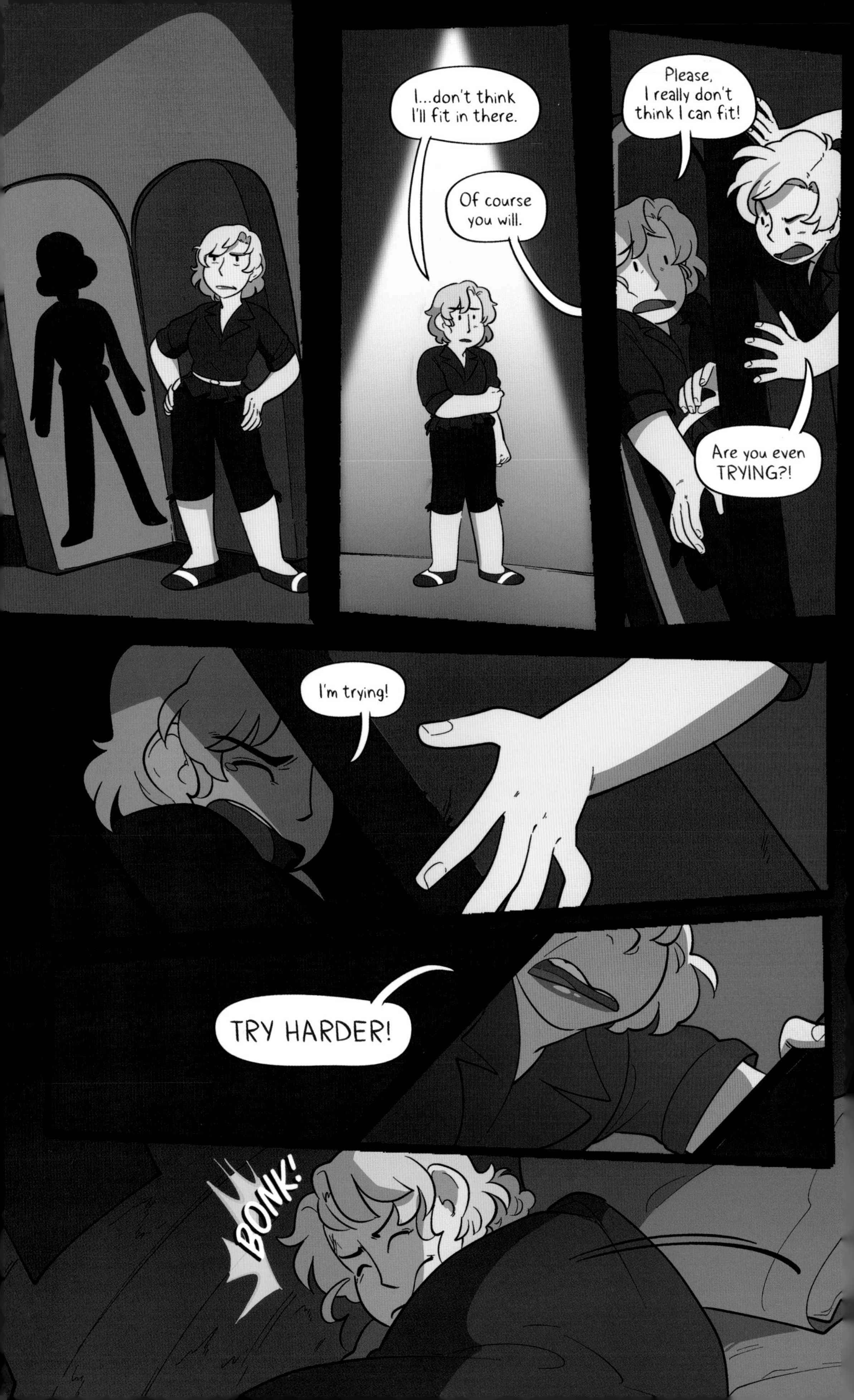
I...don't think I'll fit in there.
Of course you will.
Please, I really don't think I can fit!
Are you even TRYING?!
I'm trying!
TRY HARDER!
BONK!

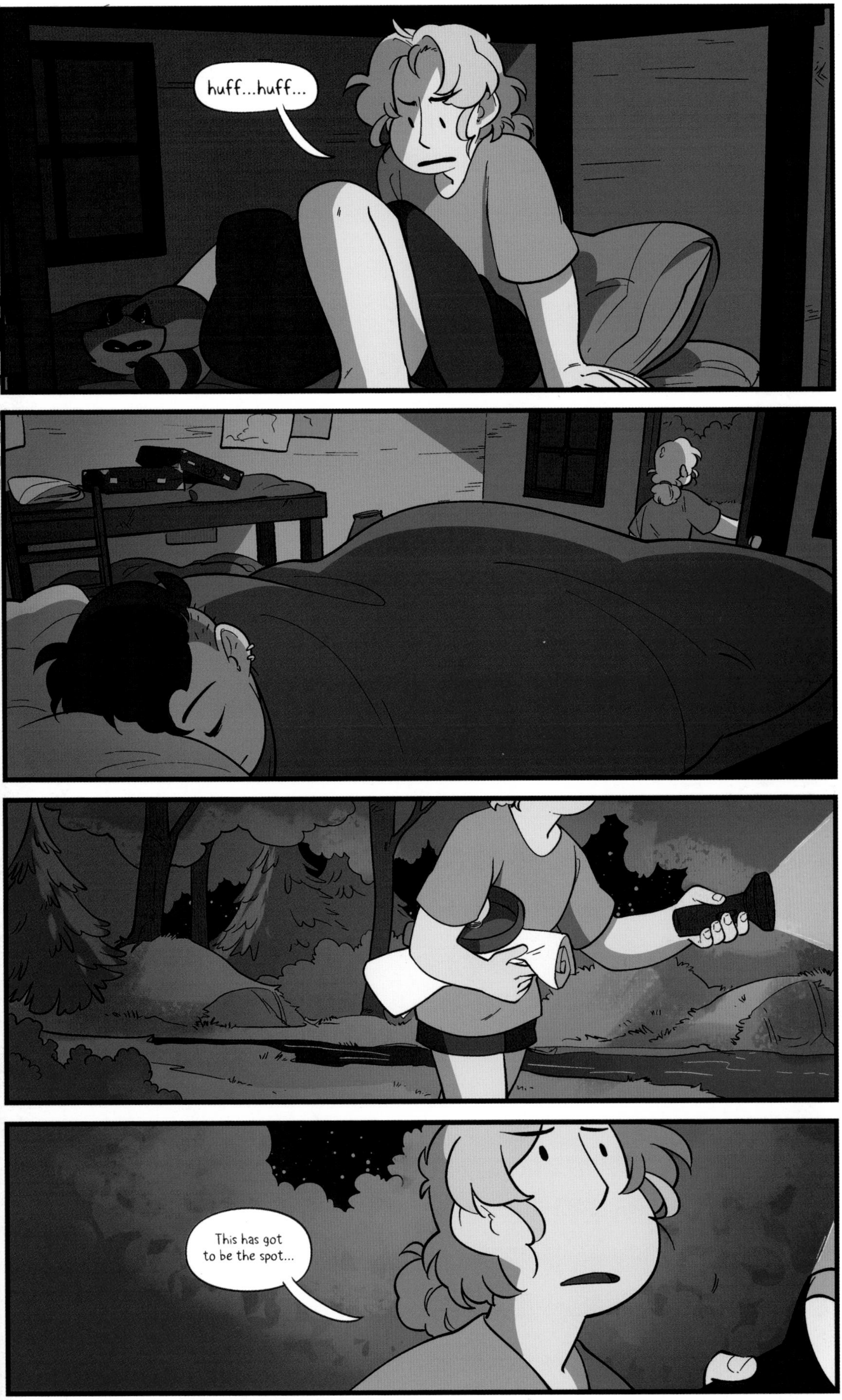
huff...huff...
This has got to be the spot...

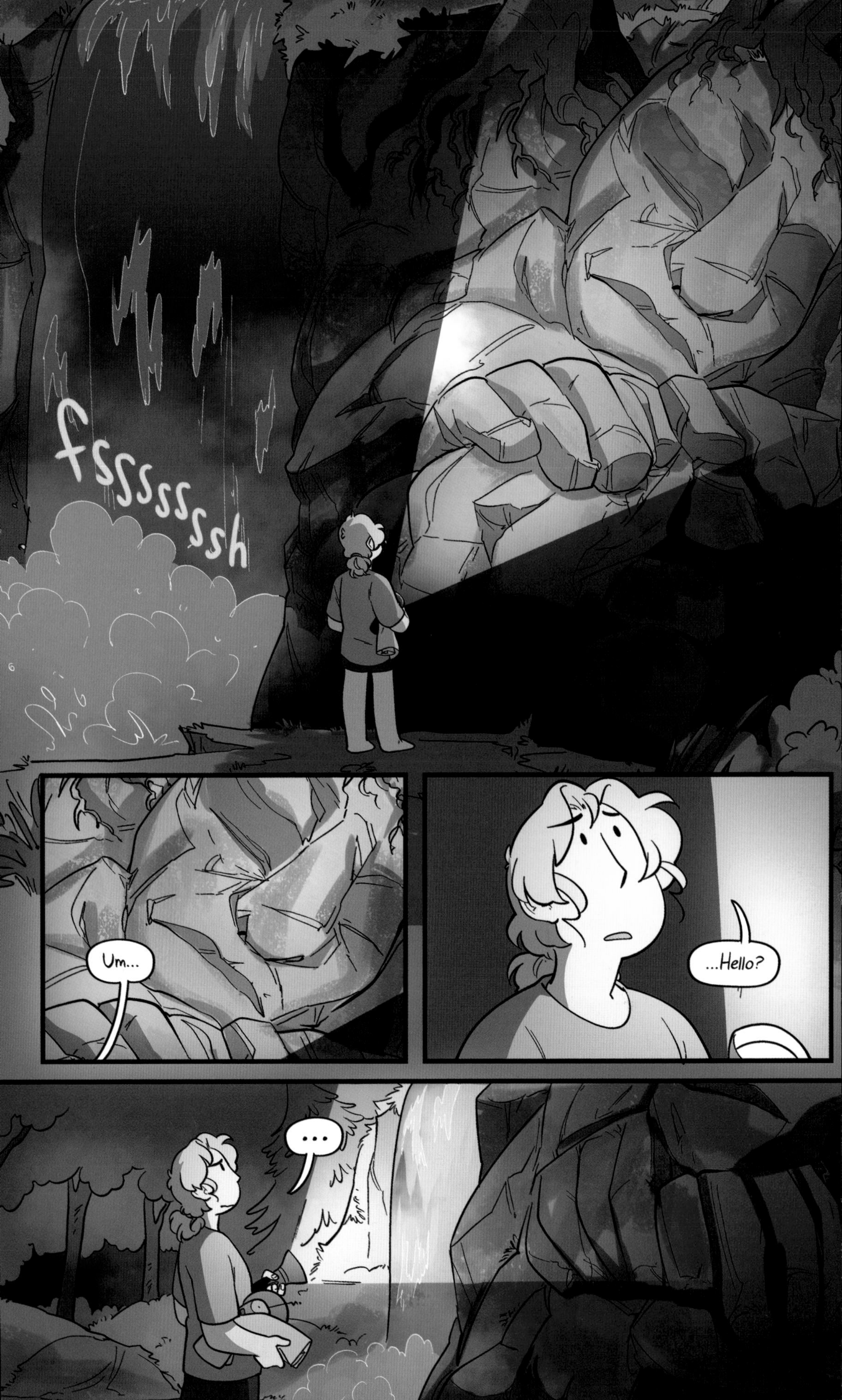
fssssssh
Um...
...Hello?
...

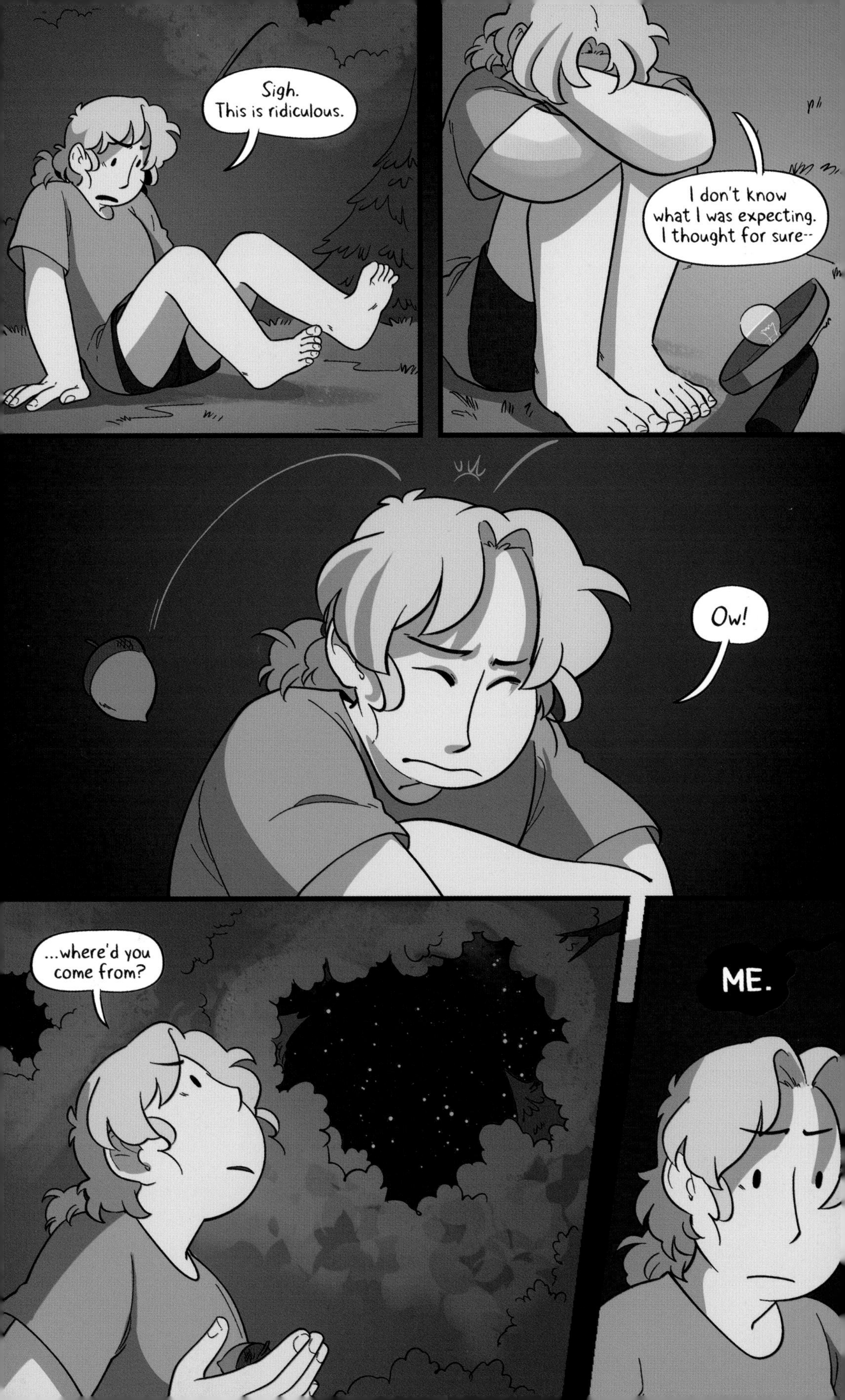
Sigh.
This is ridiculous.
I don't know what I was expecting. I thought for sure--
Ow!
...where'd you come from?
ME.

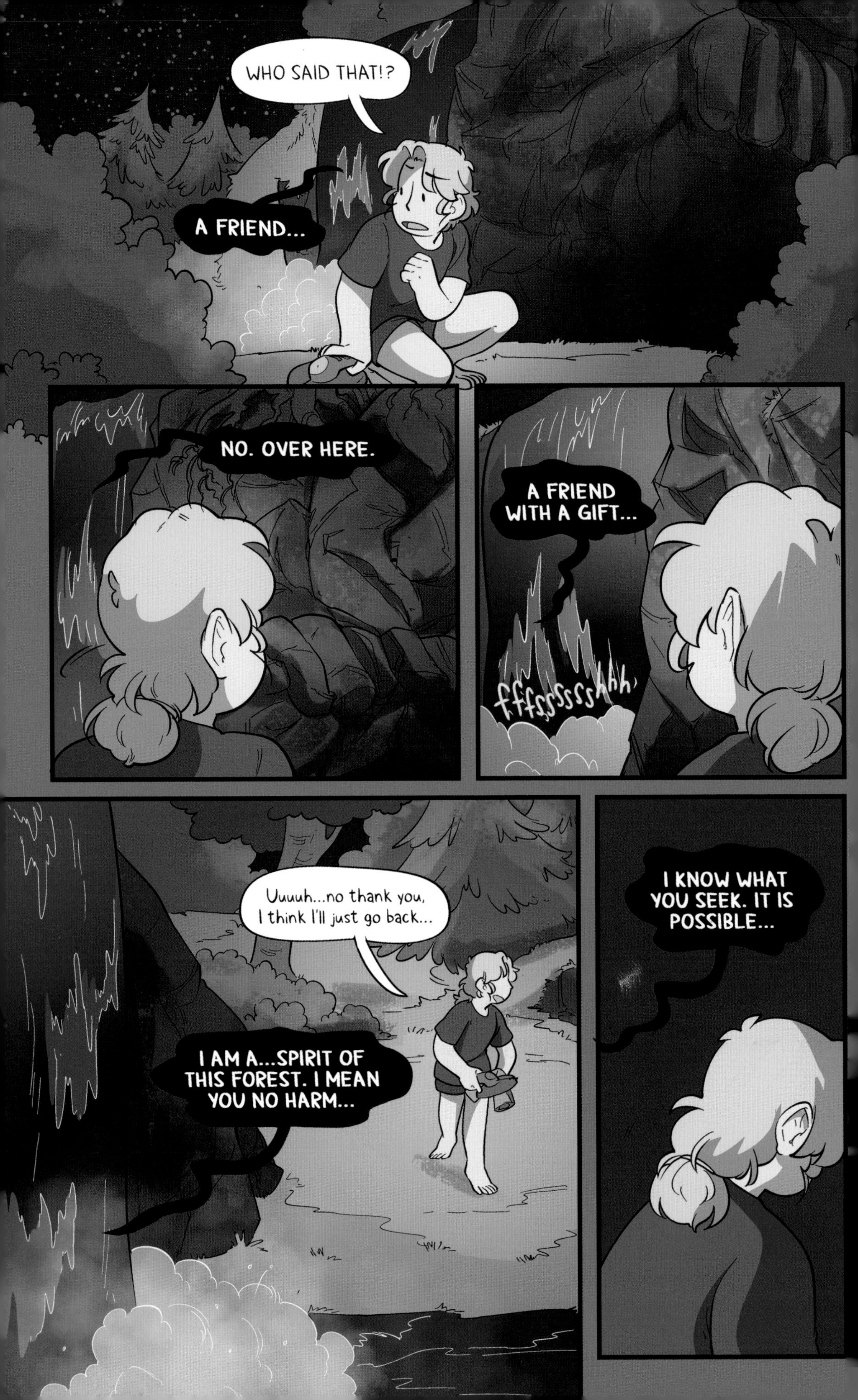
WHO SAID THAT!?
A FRIEND...
NO. OVER HERE.
A FRIEND WITH A GIFT...
ffffsssssshhh
Uuuuh...no thank you, I think I'll just go back...
I AM A...SPIRIT OF THIS FOREST. I MEAN YOU NO HARM...
I KNOW WHAT YOU SEEK. IT IS POSSIBLE...

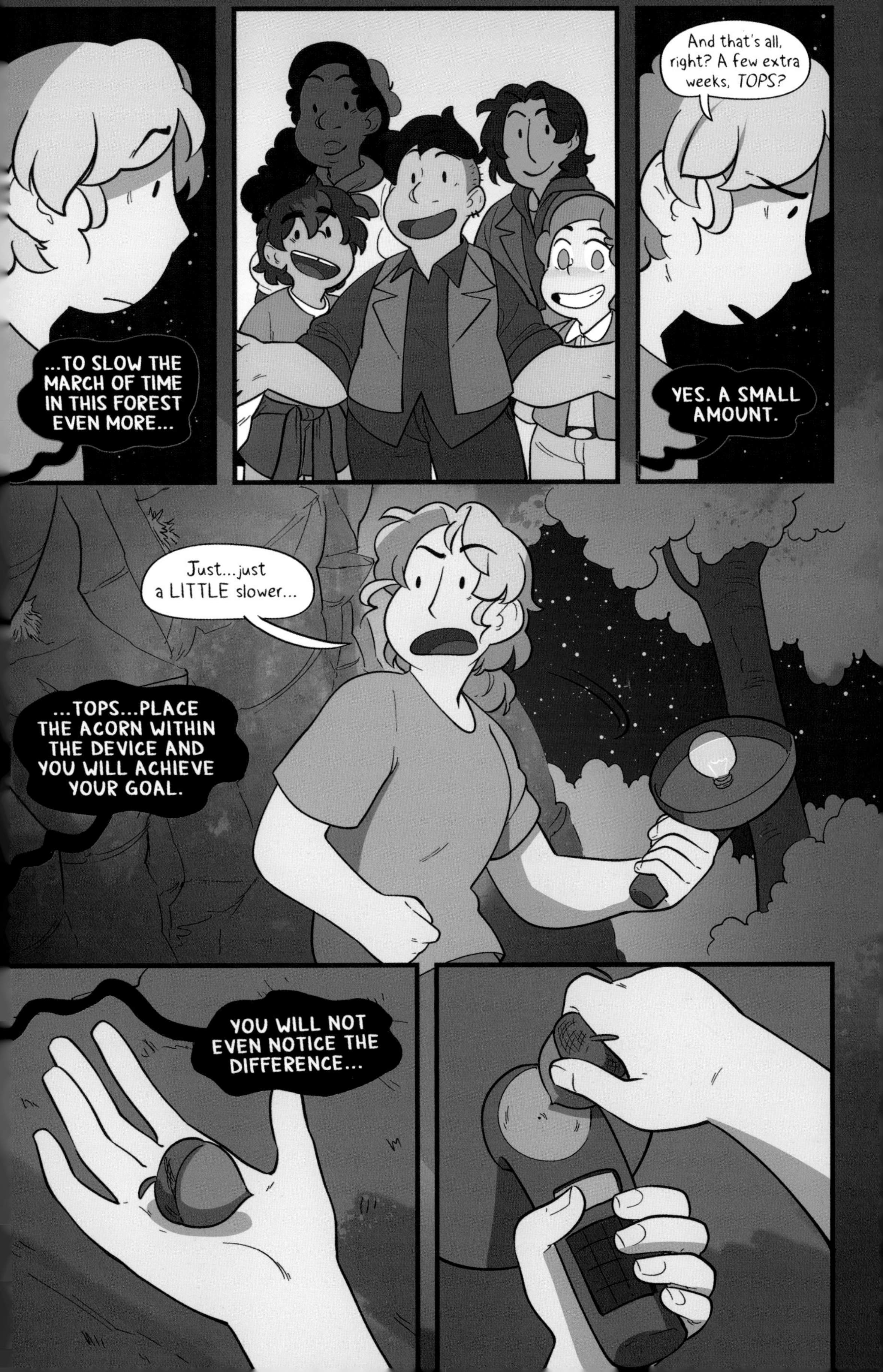
...TO SLOW THE MARCH OF TIME IN THIS FOREST EVEN MORE...
And that's all, right? A few extra weeks, TOPS?
YES. A SMALL AMOUNT.
Just...just a LITTLE slower...
...TOPS...PLACE THE ACORN WITHIN THE DEVICE AND YOU WILL ACHIEVE YOUR GOAL.
YOU WILL NOT EVEN NOTICE THE DIFFERENCE...

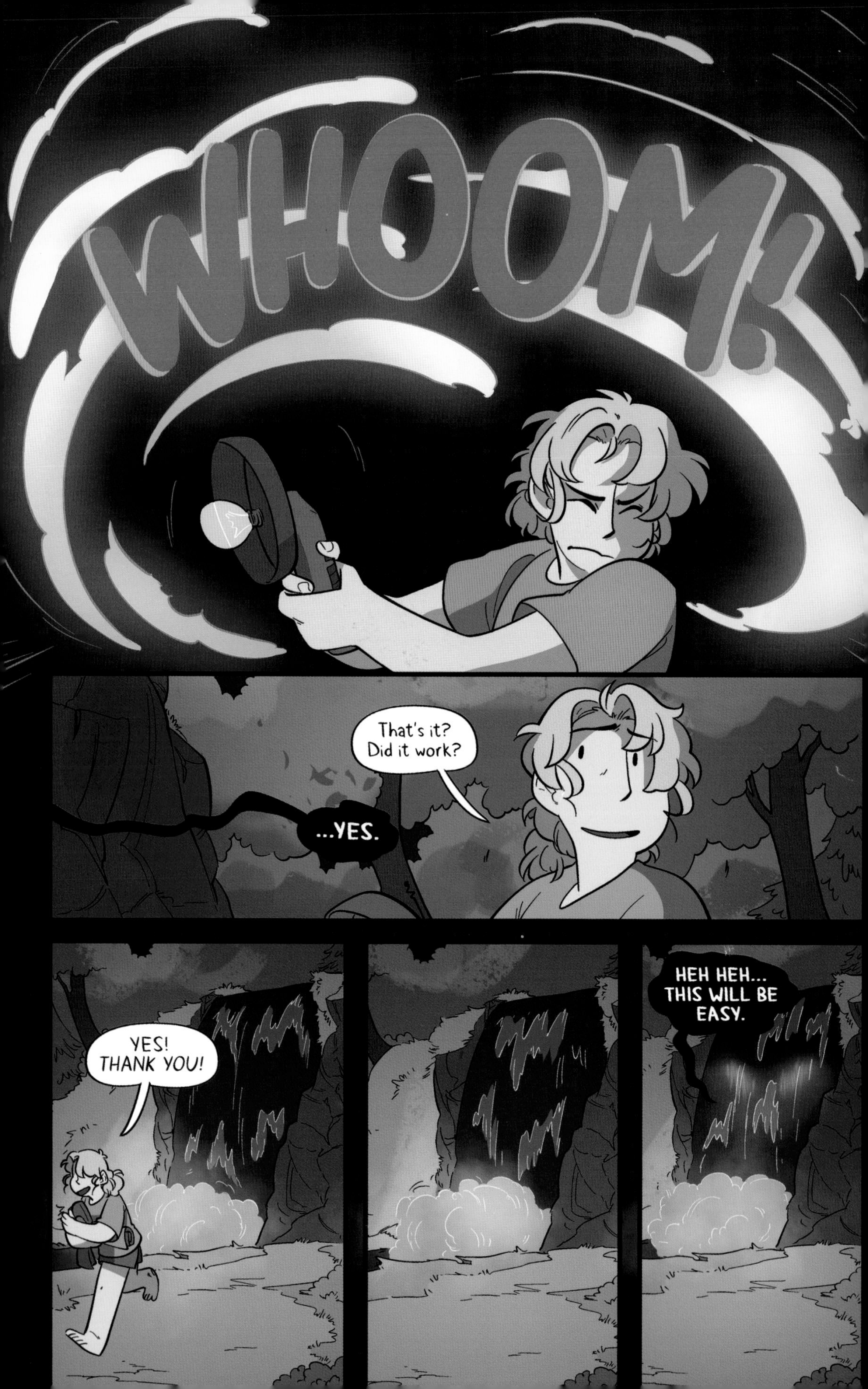
WHOOM!
That's it? Did it work?
...YES.
YES! THANK YOU!
HEH HEH... THIS WILL BE EASY.

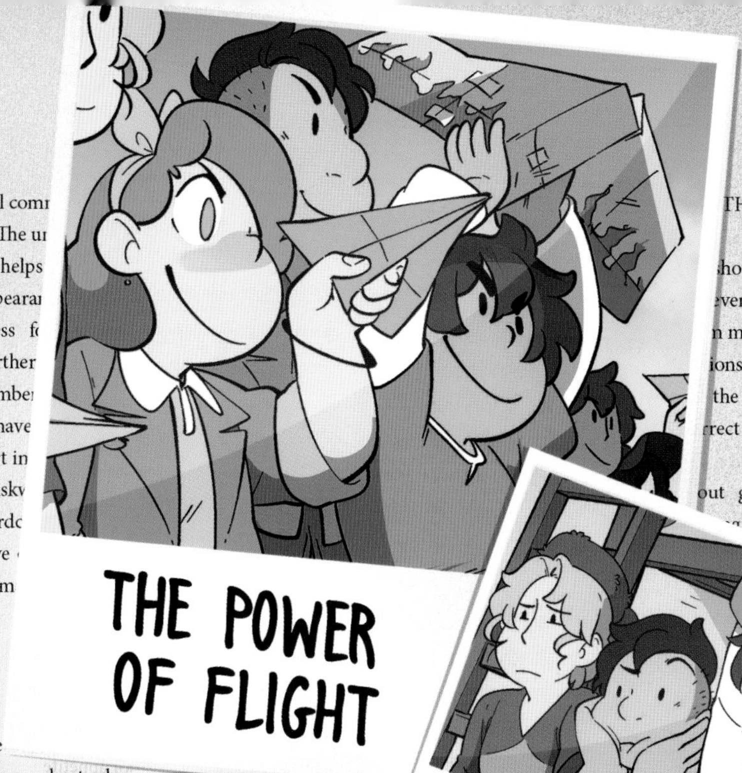
THE POWER OF FLIGHT

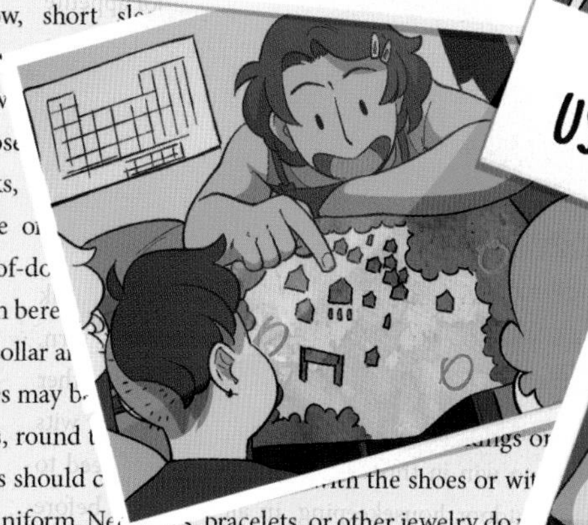

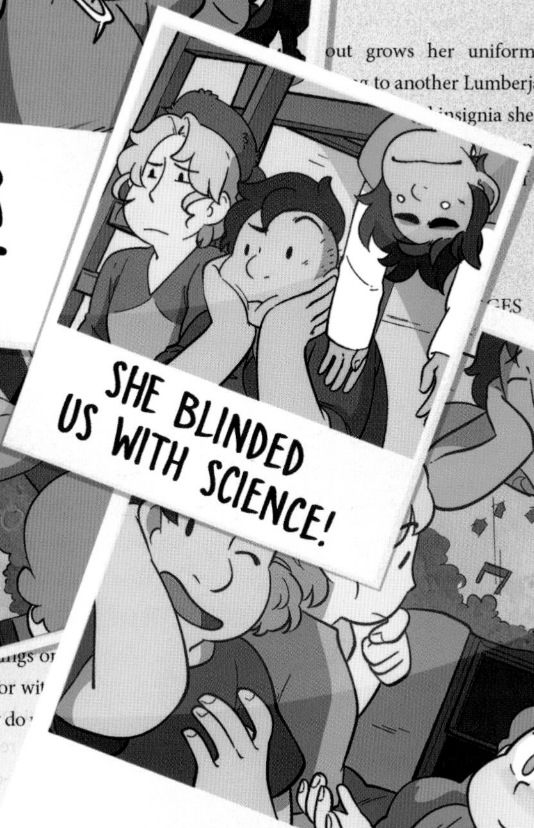
SHE BLINDED US WITH SCIENCE!

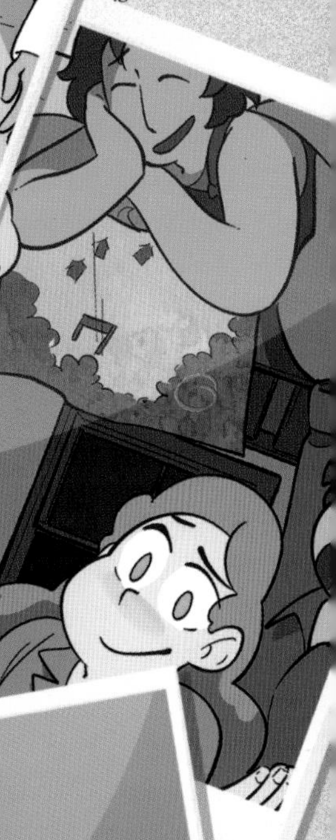

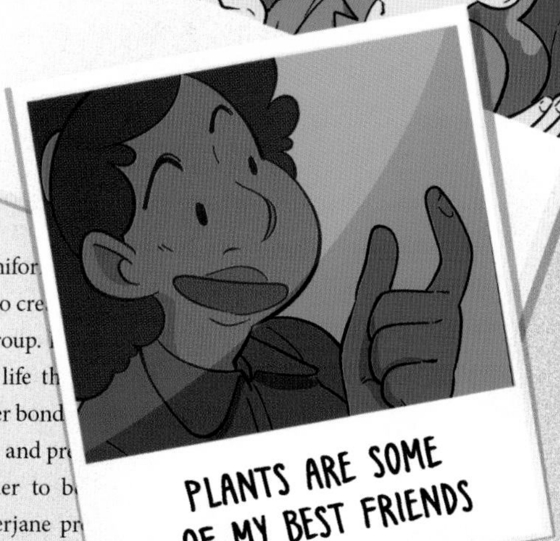
PLANTS ARE SOME OF MY BEST FRIENDS

will comr
The ur
It helps
appearar
dress fo
Further
Lumbe
to have
part in
Thiskv
Hardc
have
them

THE UNIFORM

should be worn at camp events when Lumberjanes n may also be worn at other ions. It should be worn as a the uniform dress with rrect shoes, and stocking or

out grows her uniform or to another Lumberjane. insignia she has her her

The ... GES
yellow, short sle
emb
the w
choose
slacks,
made o
out-of-do
green bere
the collar a
Shoes may b
heels, round t ... kings or
socks should c ... with the shoes or wit
the uniform. Ne... ces, bracelets, or other jewelry do
belong with a Lumberjane uniform.

HOW TO WEAR THE UNIFORM

To look well in a uniform demands first of ... uniform be kept in good condition—clean ... pressed. See that the skirt is the right length for your own height and build, that the belt is adjusted to your waist, that your shoes and stockings are in keeping with the uniform, that you watch your posture and carry yourself with dignity and grace. If the beret is removed indoors, be sure that your hair is neat and kept in place with an inconspicuous clip or ribbon. When you wear a Lumberjane uniform you are identified as a member of this organization and you should be doubly careful to conduct yourself in a way that will show everyone that courtesy and thoughtfulness are part of being a Lumberjane. People are likely to judge a whole nation by the selfishness of a few individuals, to criticize a whole family because of the misconduct of one member, and to feel unkindly toward an organization because of the

The unifor
helps to cre
in a group.
active life th
another bond
future, and pr
in order to b
Lumberjane pr
Penniquiqul Thi ... core Lady
Types, but most ... janes will wish to have one. They can either buy the uniform, or make it themselves from materials available at the trading post.

LUMBERJANES FIELD MANUAL

CHAPTER
FORTY-TWO

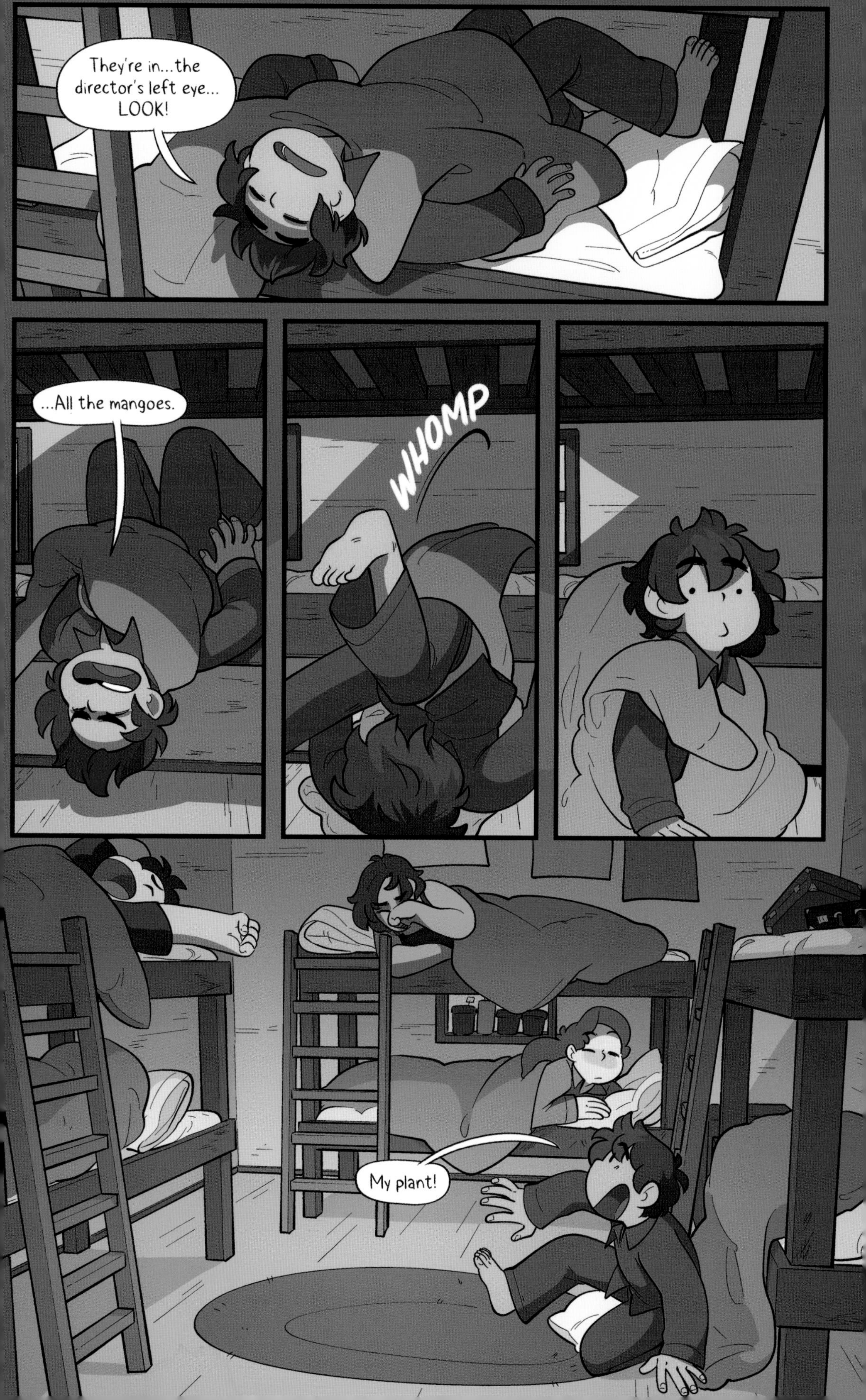
They're in...the director's left eye... LOOK!
...All the mangoes.
WHOMP
My plant!

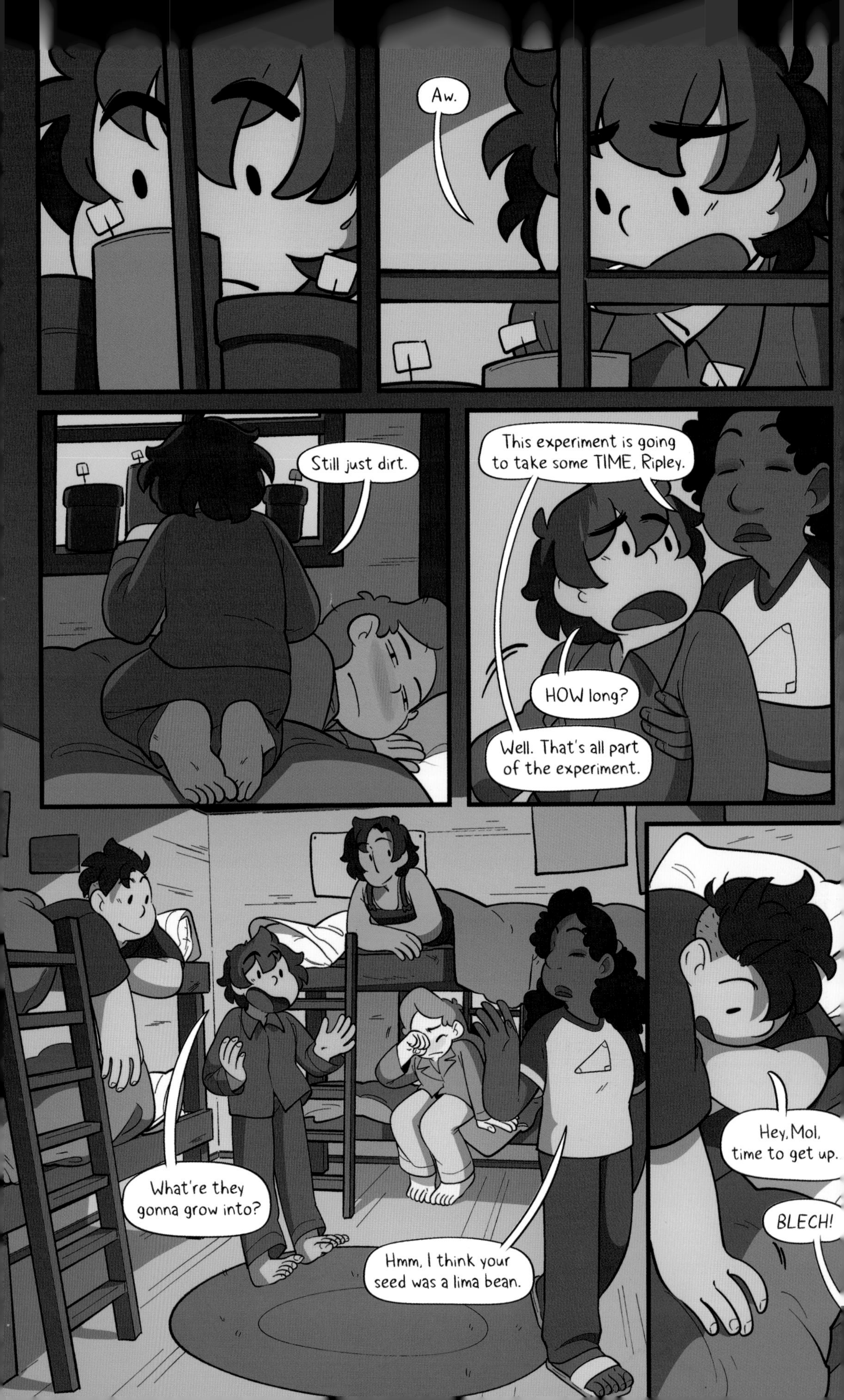
Aw.
Still just dirt.
This experiment is going to take some TIME, Ripley.
HOW long?
Well. That's all part of the experiment.
What're they gonna grow into?
Hmm, I think your seed was a lima bean.
Hey, Mol, time to get up.
BLECH!

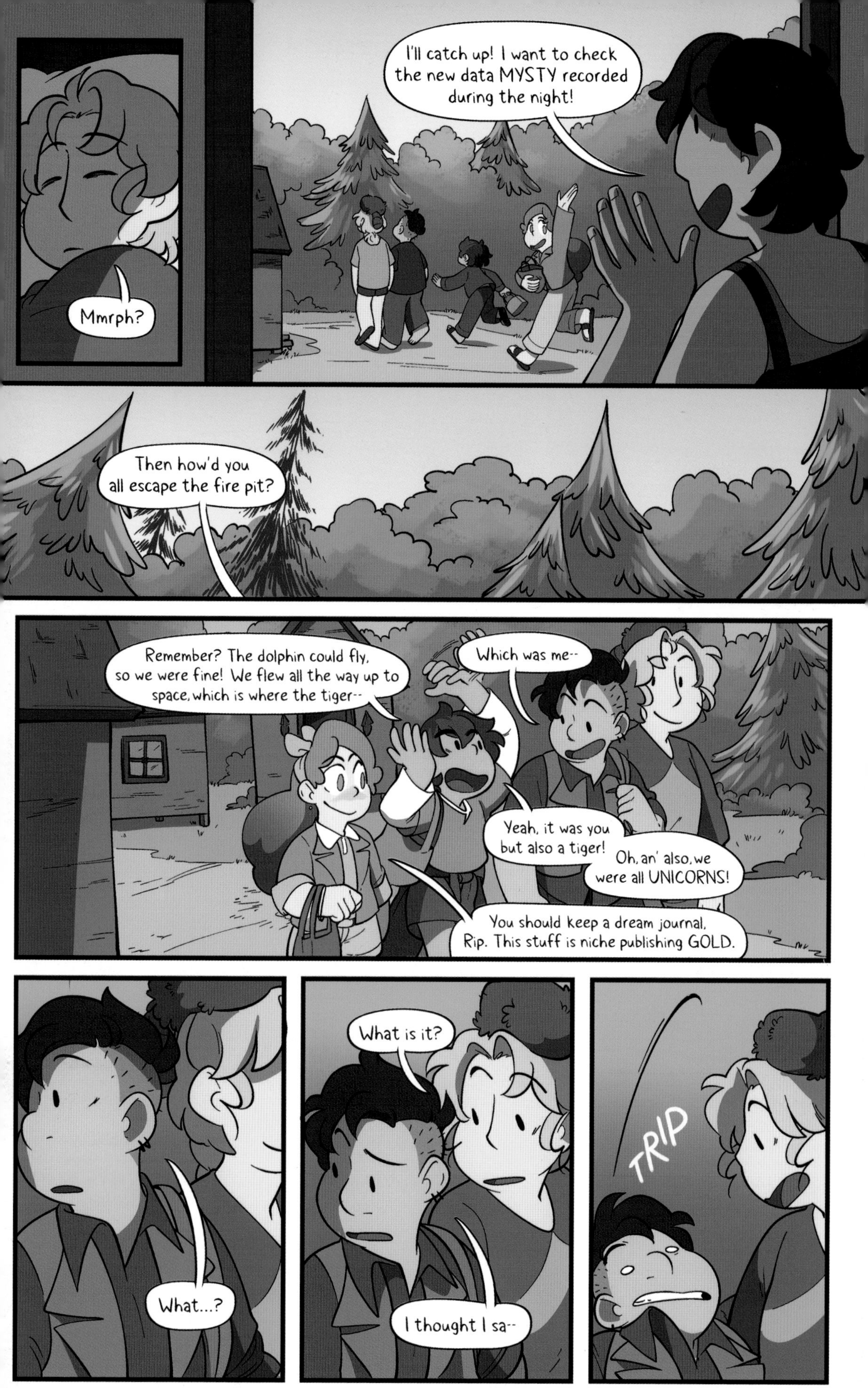
Mmrph?
I'll catch up! I want to check the new data MYSTY recorded during the night!
Then how'd you all escape the fire pit?
Remember? The dolphin could fly, so we were fine! We flew all the way up to space, which is where the tiger--
Which was me--
Yeah, it was you but also a tiger!
Oh, an' also, we were all UNICORNS!
You should keep a dream journal, Rip. This stuff is niche publishing GOLD.
What...?
What is it?
I thought I sa--
TRIP

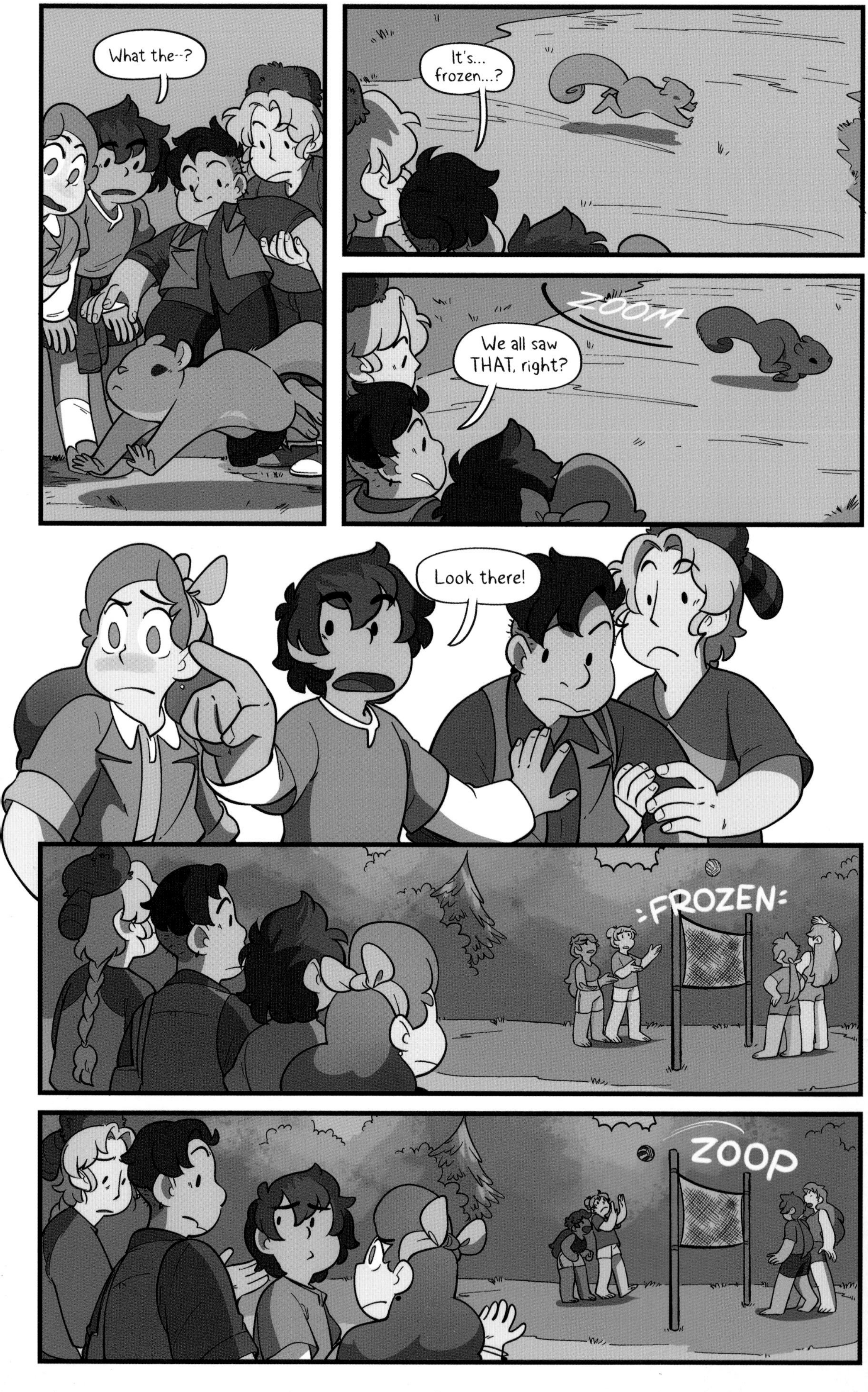
What the--?
It's... frozen...?
ZOOM
We all saw THAT, right?
Look there!
FROZEN
ZOOP

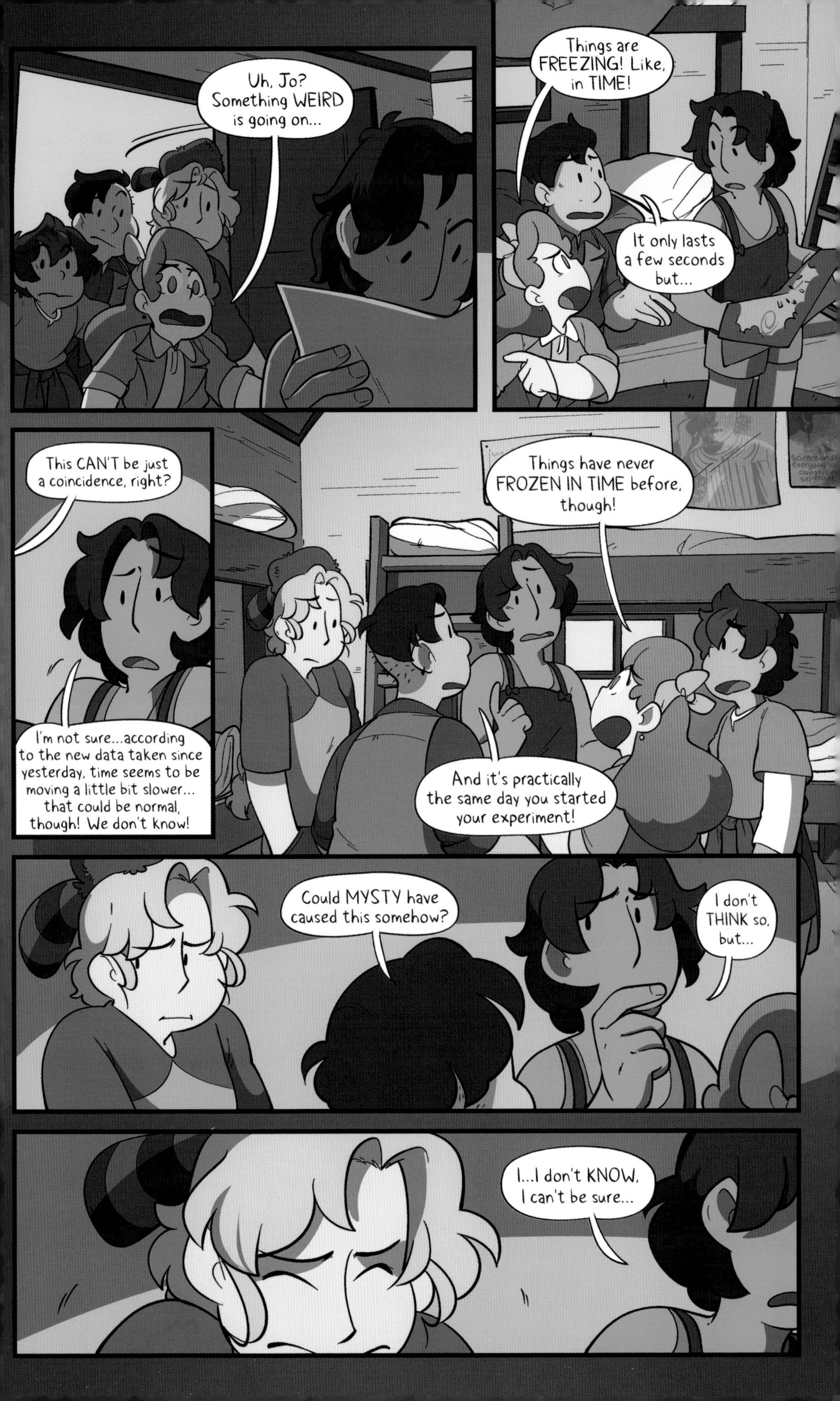

Uh, Jo? Something WEIRD is going on...
Things are FREEZING! Like, in TIME!
It only lasts a few seconds but...
This CAN'T be just a coincidence, right?
I'm not sure...according to the new data taken since yesterday, time seems to be moving a little bit slower... that could be normal, though! We don't know!
Things have never FROZEN IN TIME before, though!
And it's practically the same day you started your experiment!
Could MYSTY have caused this somehow?
I don't THINK so, but...
I...I don't KNOW, I can't be sure...

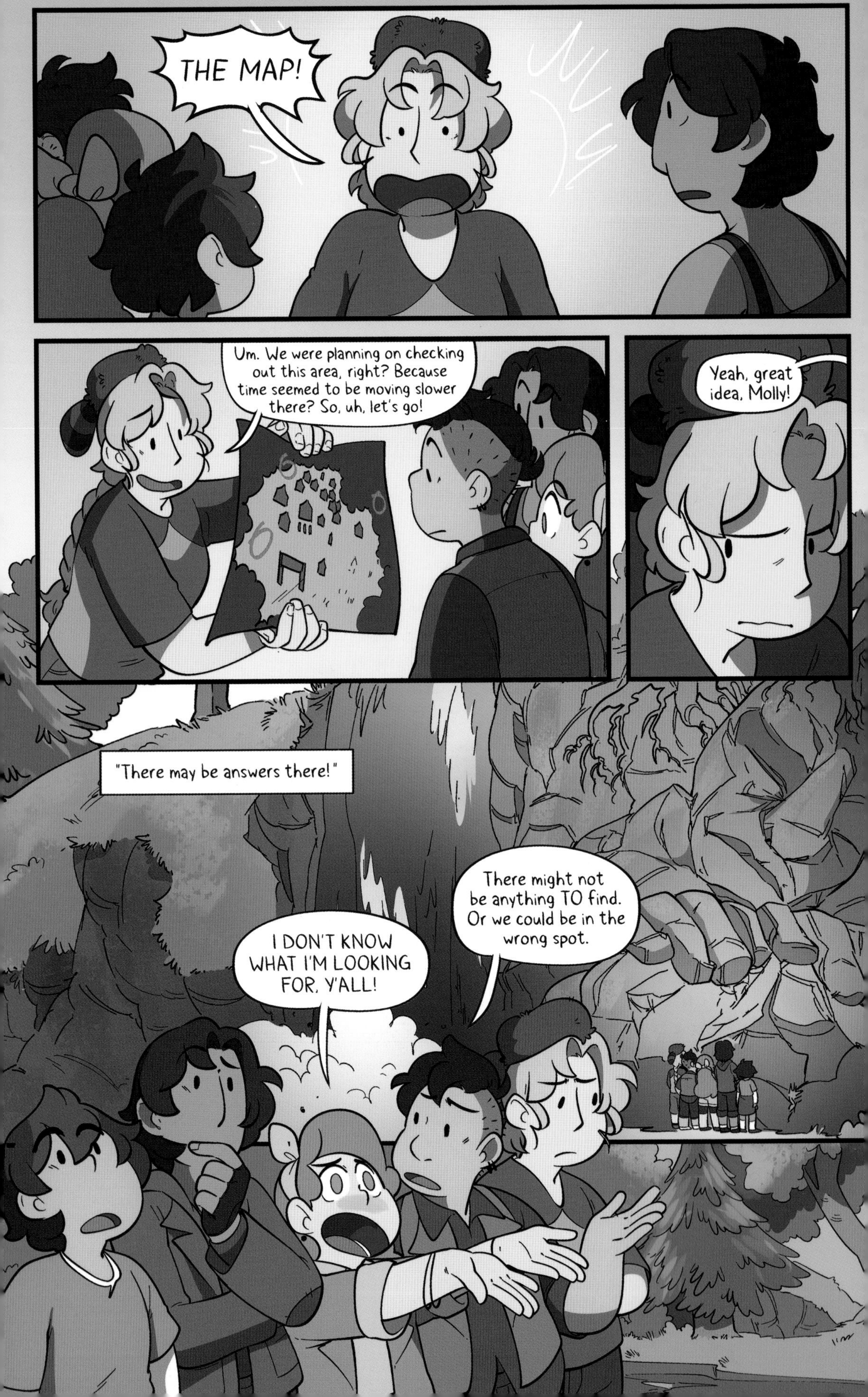
THE MAP!
Um. We were planning on checking out this area, right? Because time seemed to be moving slower there? So, uh, let's go!
Yeah, great idea, Molly!
"There may be answers there!"
I DON'T KNOW WHAT I'M LOOKING FOR, Y'ALL!
There might not be anything TO find. Or we could be in the wrong spot.

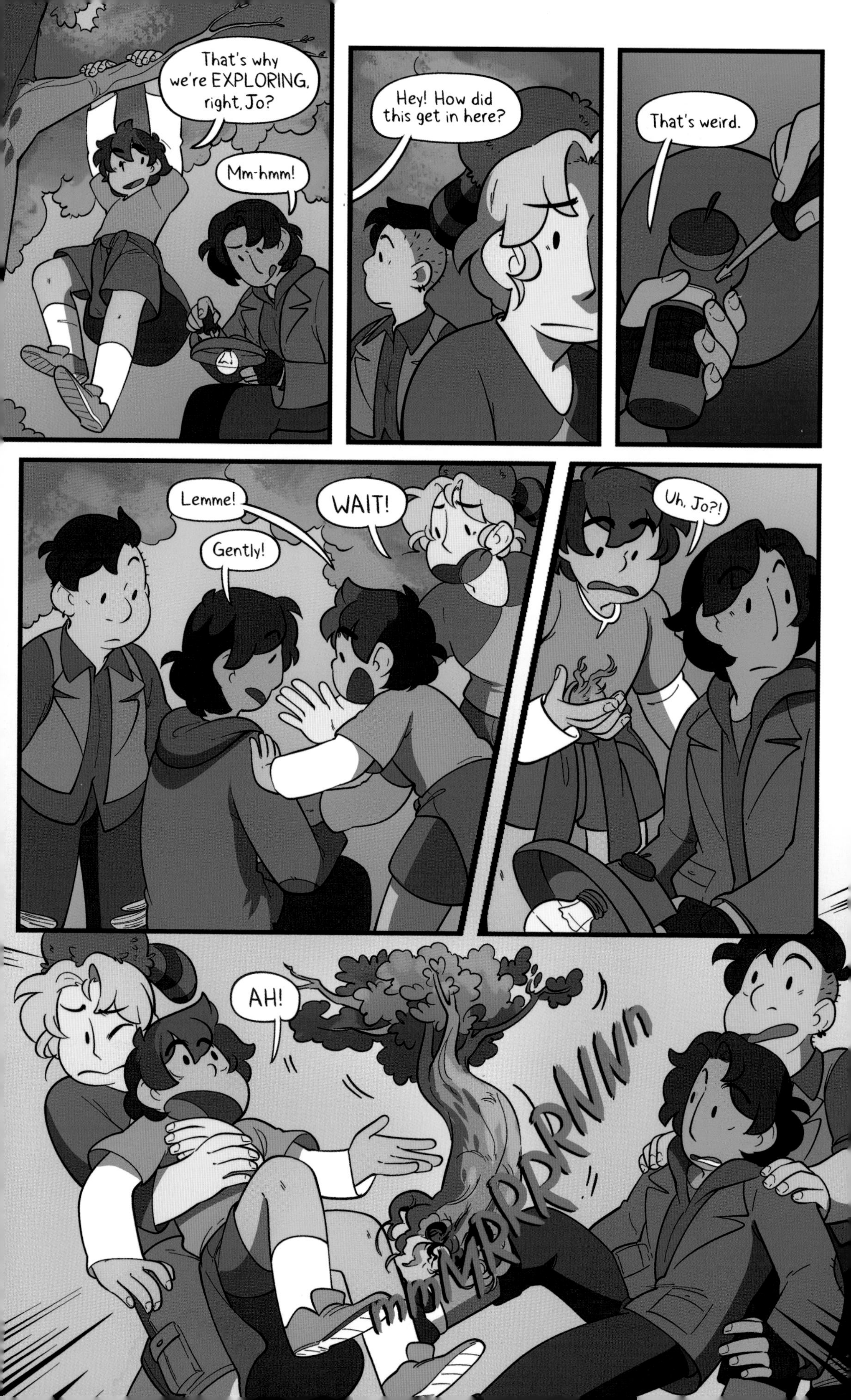
That's why we're EXPLORING, right, Jo?
Mm-hmm!
Hey! How did this get in here?
That's weird.
Lemme!
WAIT!
Gently!
Uh, Jo?!
AH!
mmMRRRRNNn

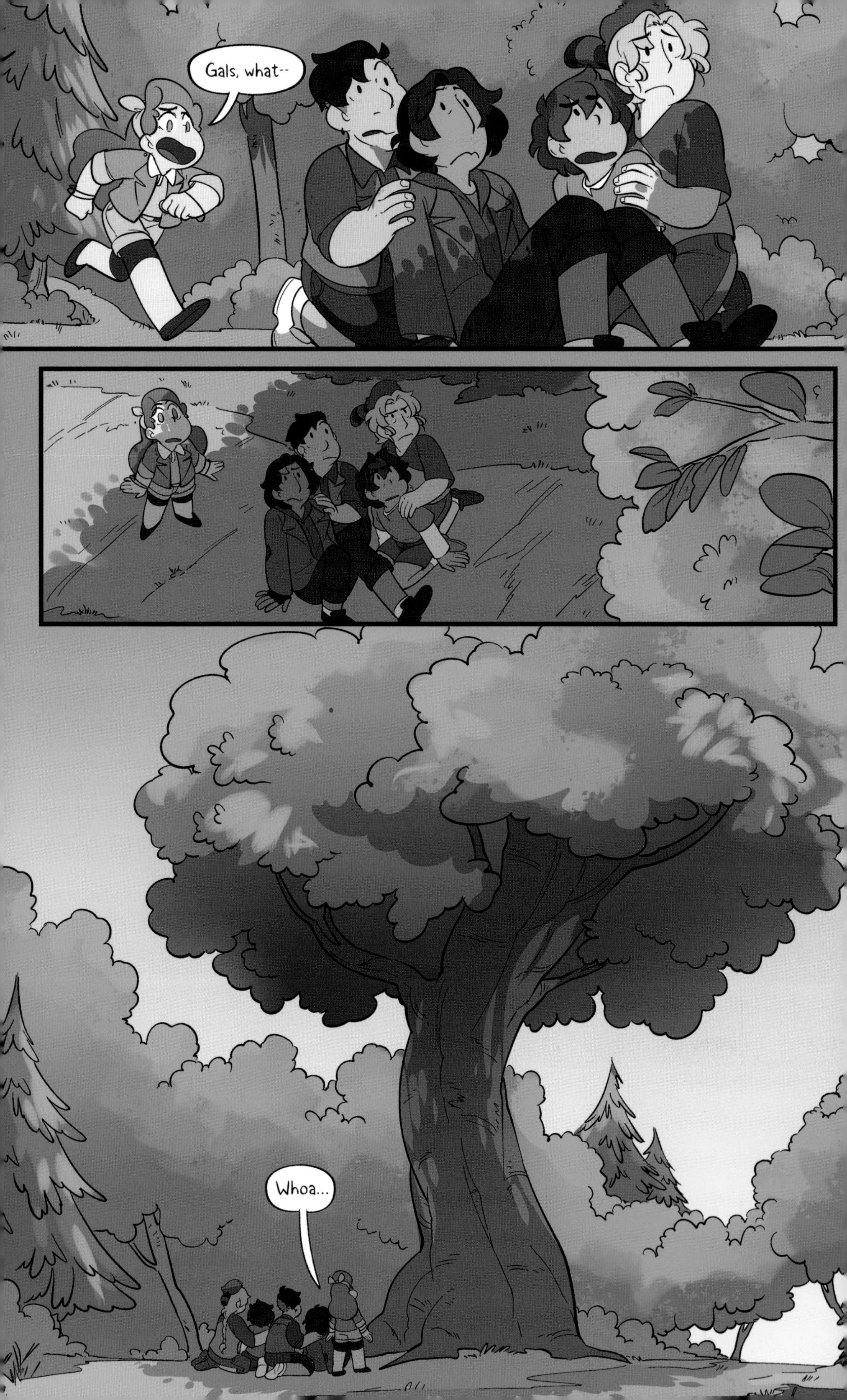
Gals, what--
Whoa...

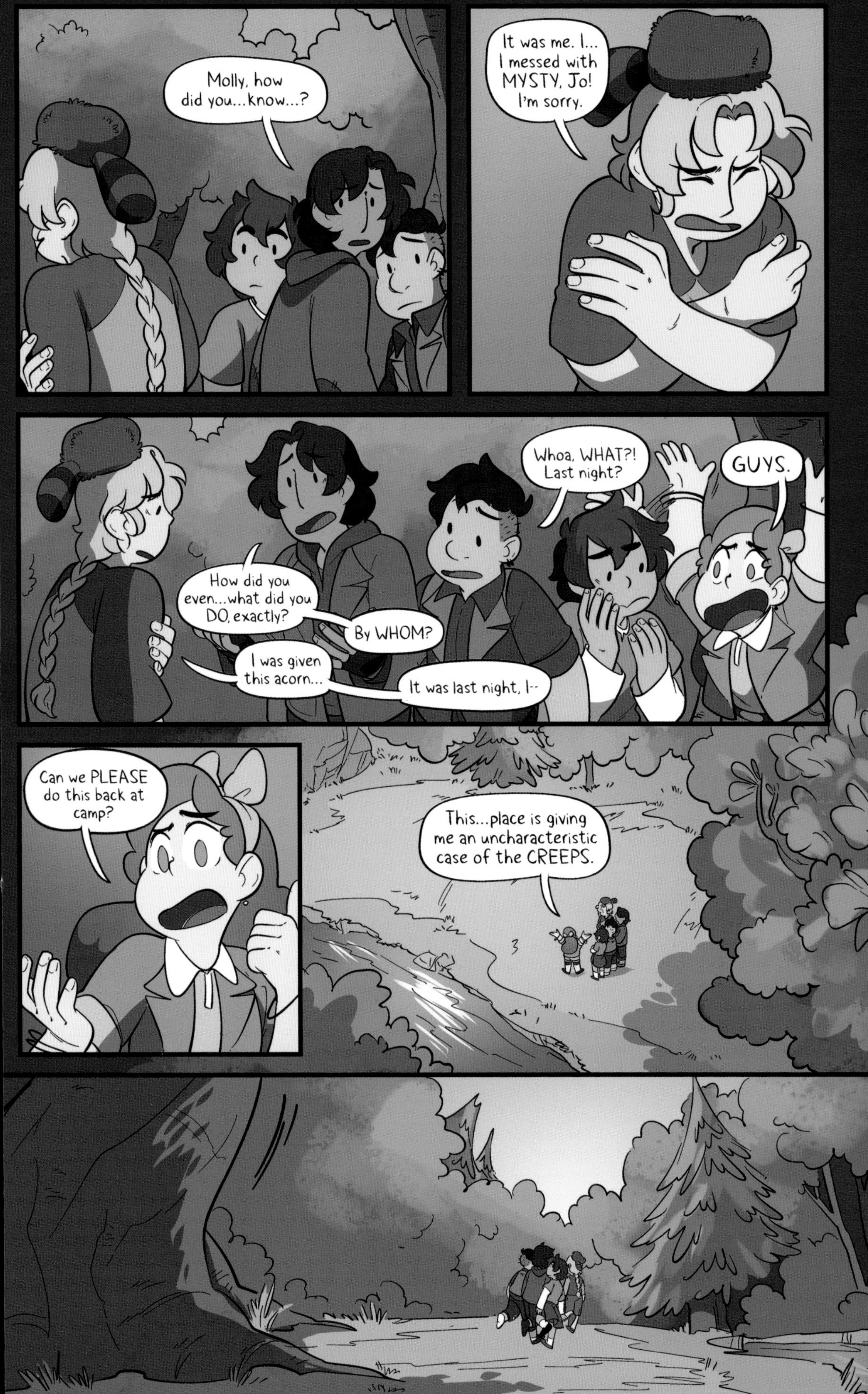
Molly, how did you...know...?
It was me. I... I messed with MYSTY, Jo! I'm sorry.
How did you even...what did you DO, exactly?
By WHOM?
I was given this acorn...
It was last night, I--
Whoa, WHAT?! Last night?
GUYS.
Can we PLEASE do this back at camp?
This...place is giving me an uncharacteristic case of the CREEPS.

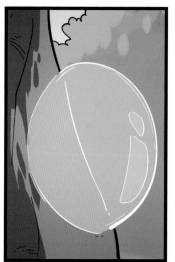
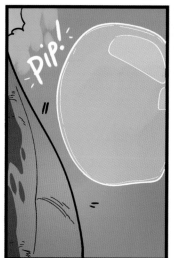

"Mysterious voice"? Mol, why would you trust a mysterious voice coming from NOWHERE?

It seemed...nice? Helpful, I guess.

I know, I'm jus--

C'mon, Jo, give her a break, it's not like we all haven't been tricked before.

Uuuuuh, pals?

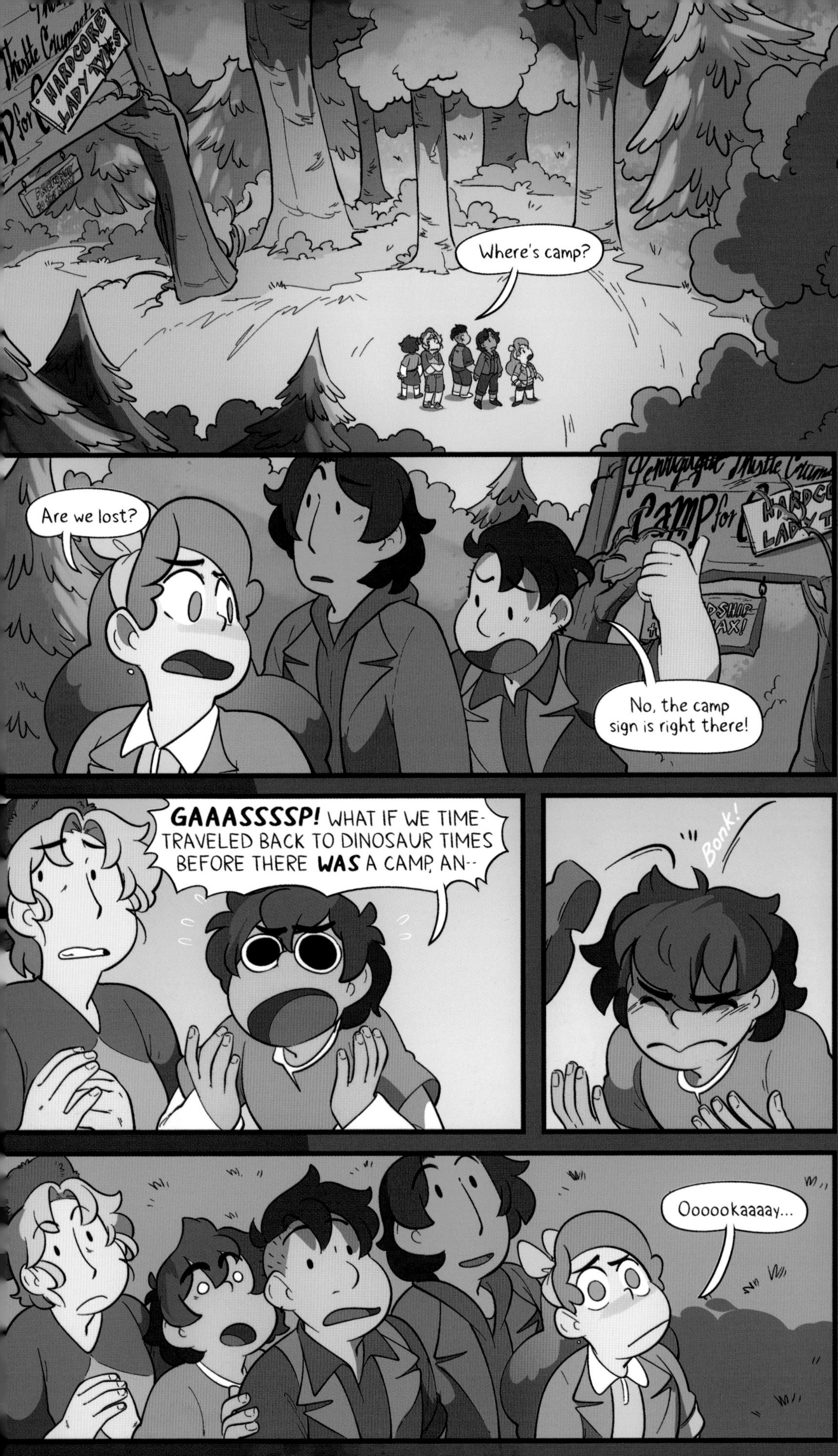
HARDCORE LADY TYPES
Where's camp?
Are we lost?
No, the camp sign is right there!
GAAASSSSP! WHAT IF WE TIME-TRAVELED BACK TO DINOSAUR TIMES BEFORE THERE WAS A CAMP, AN--
Bonk!
Oooookaaaay...

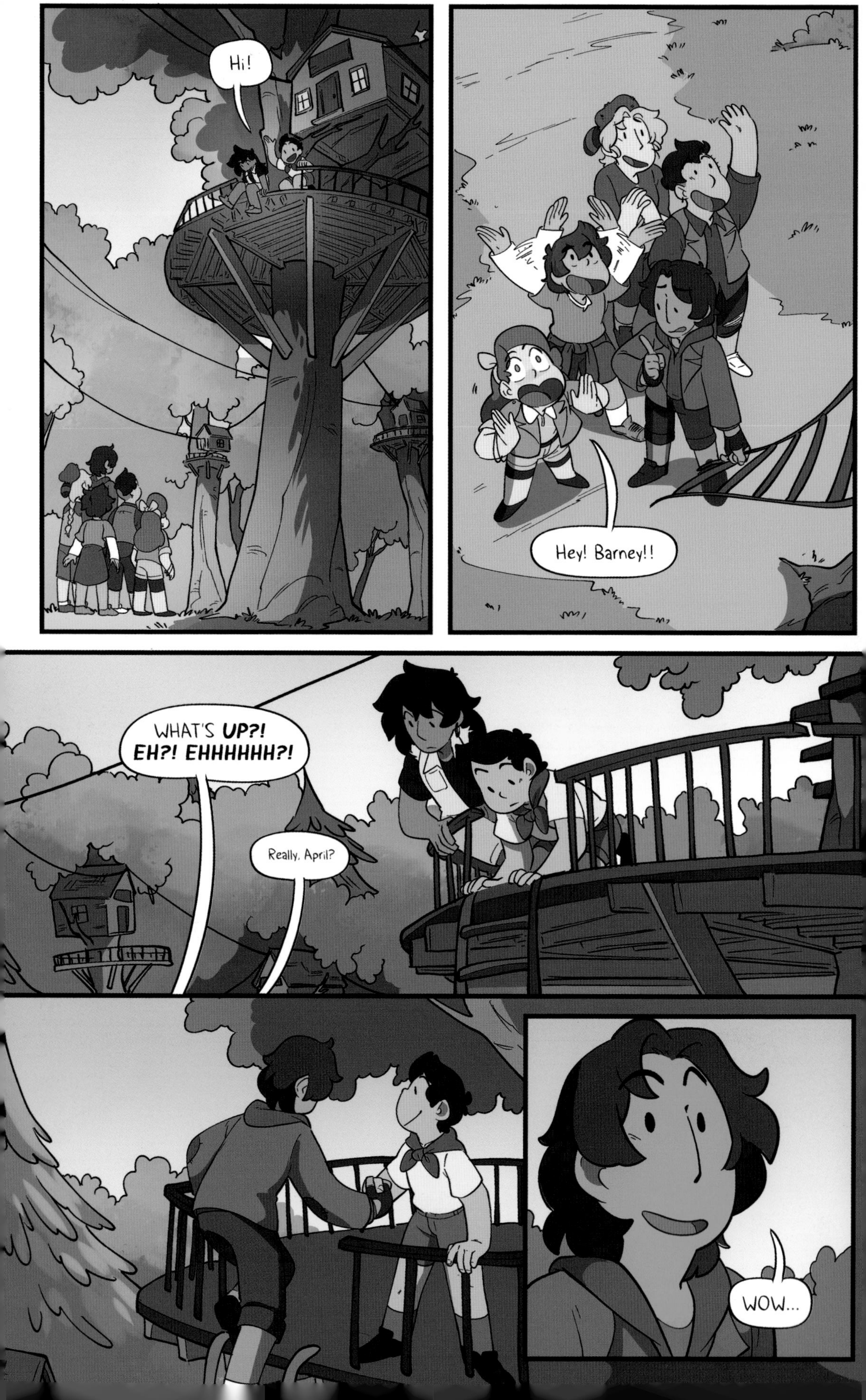
Hi!
Hey! Barney!!
WHAT'S **UP?! EH?! EHHHHHH?!**
Really, April?
WOW...

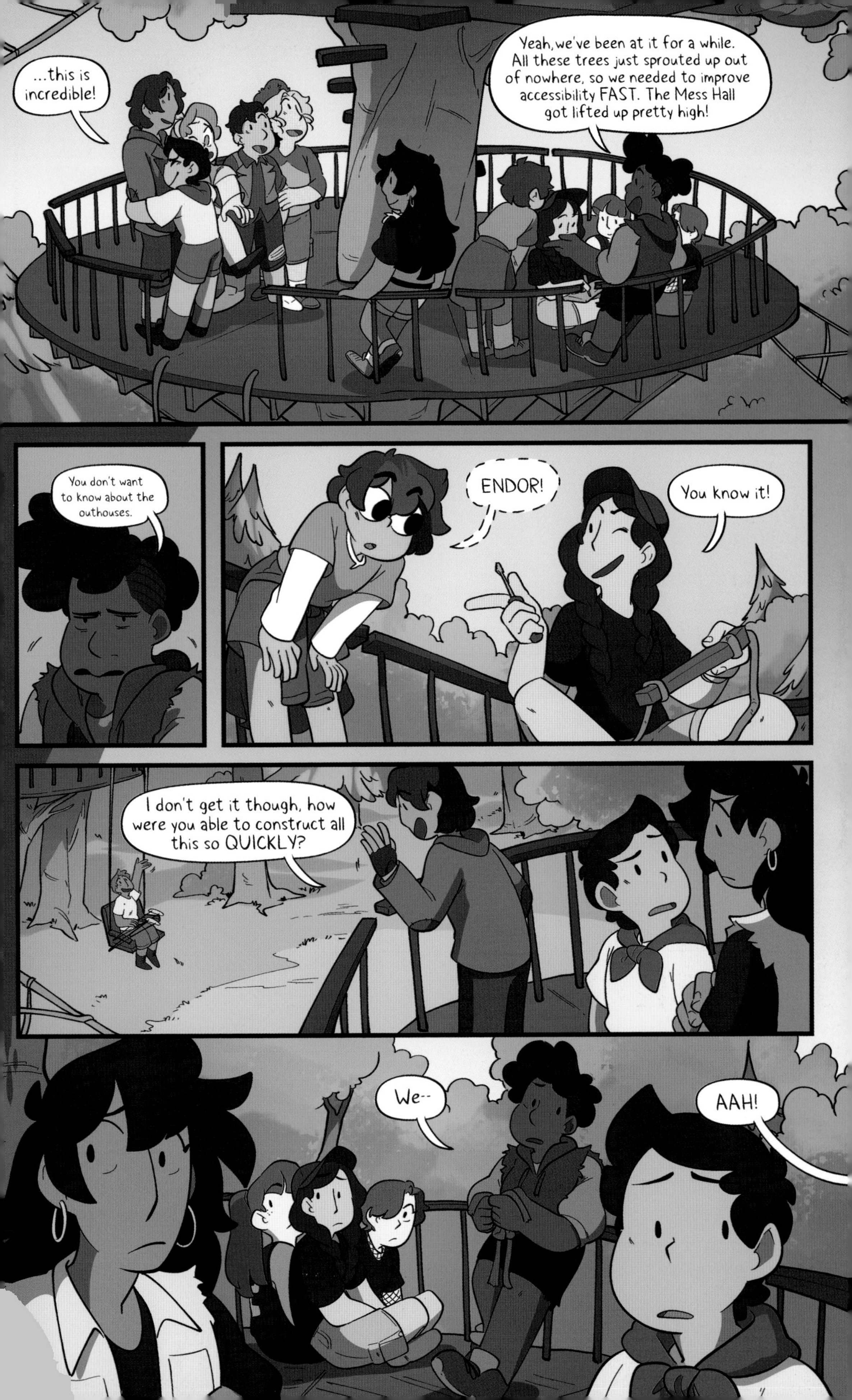
...this is incredible!
Yeah, we've been at it for a while. All these trees just sprouted up out of nowhere, so we needed to improve accessibility FAST. The Mess Hall got lifted up pretty high!
You don't want to know about the outhouses.
ENDOR!
You know it!
I don't get it though, how were you able to construct all this so QUICKLY?
We--
AAH!

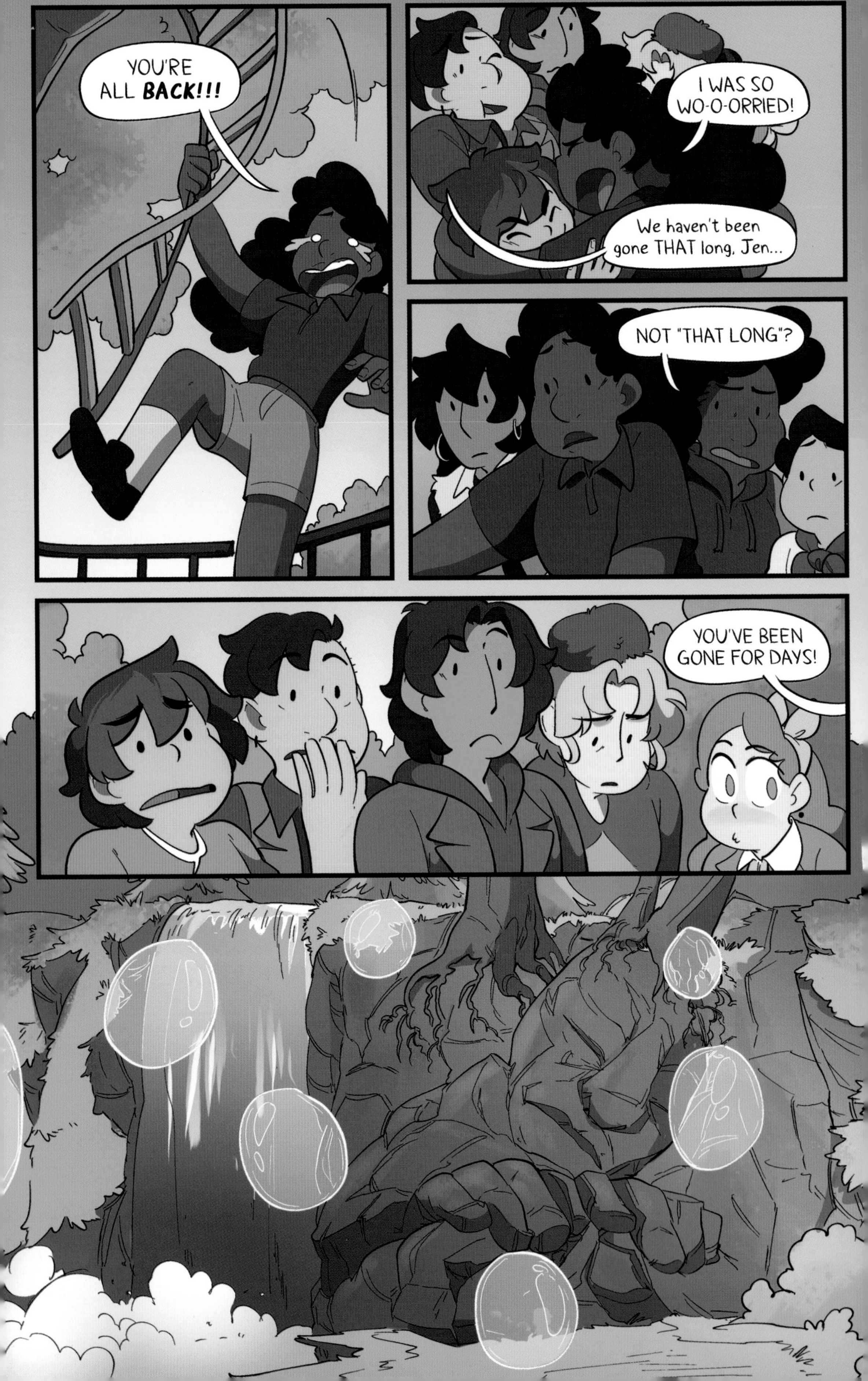
YOU'RE ALL BACK!!!
I WAS SO WO-O-ORRIED!
We haven't been gone THAT long, Jen...
NOT "THAT LONG"?
YOU'VE BEEN GONE FOR DAYS!

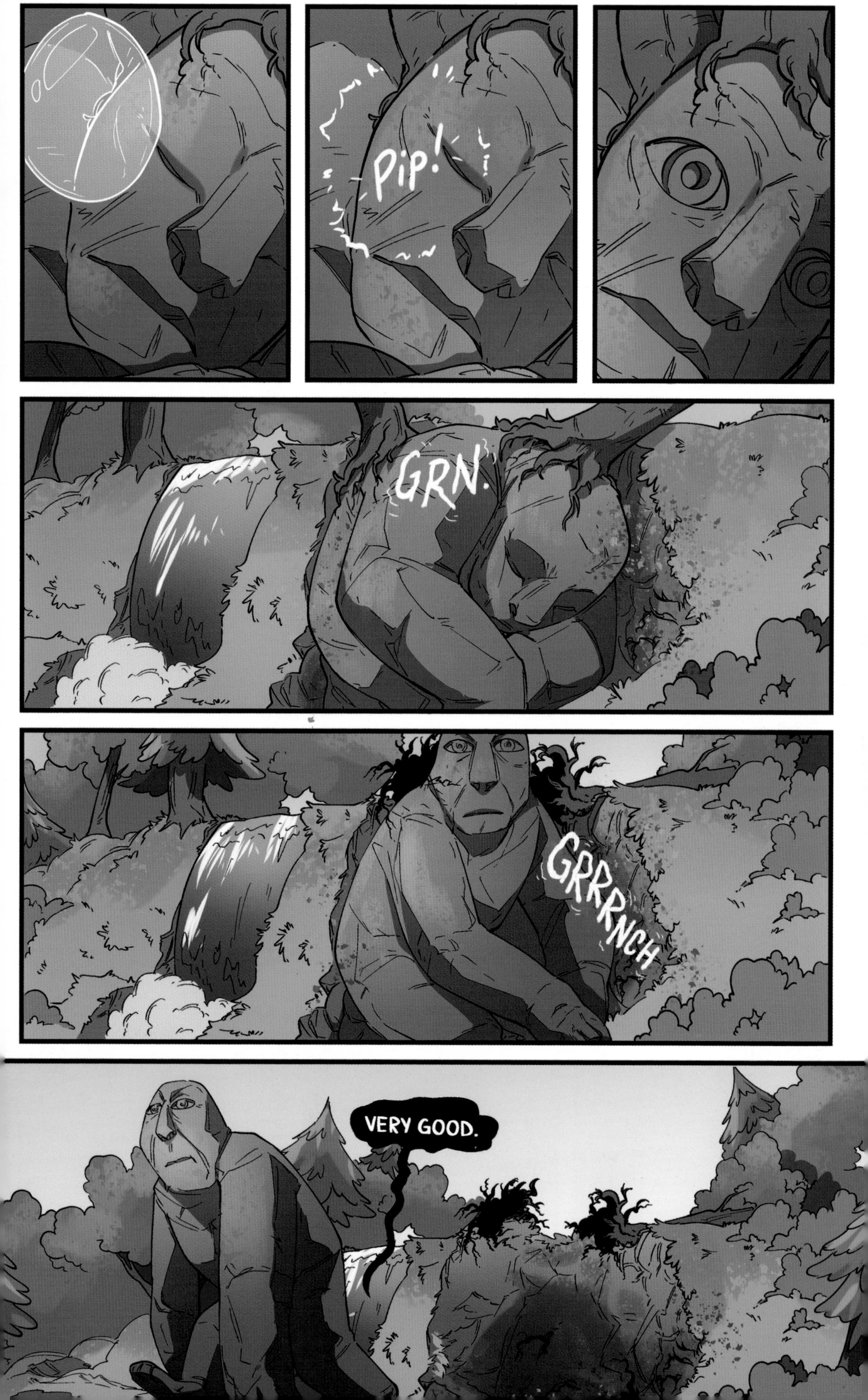
PIP!
GRN.
GRRRNCH
VERY GOOD.

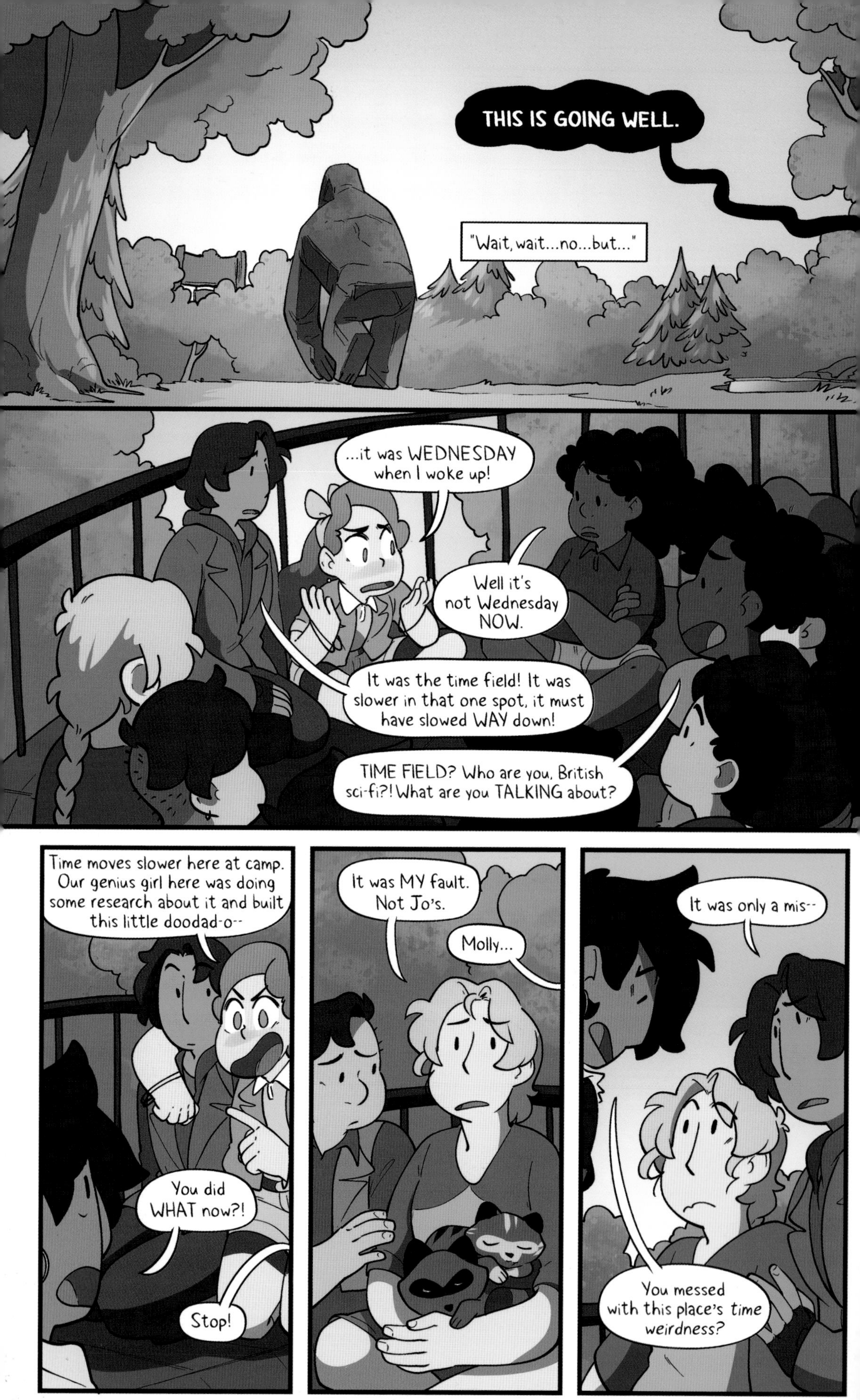
THIS IS GOING WELL.
"Wait, wait...no...but..."
...it was WEDNESDAY when I woke up!
Well it's not Wednesday NOW.
It was the time field! It was slower in that one spot, it must have slowed WAY down!
TIME FIELD? Who are you, British sci-fi?! What are you TALKING about?
Time moves slower here at camp. Our genius girl here was doing some research about it and built this little doodad-o--
You did WHAT now?!
Stop!
It was MY fault. Not Jo's.
Molly...
It was only a mis--
You messed with this place's time weirdness?

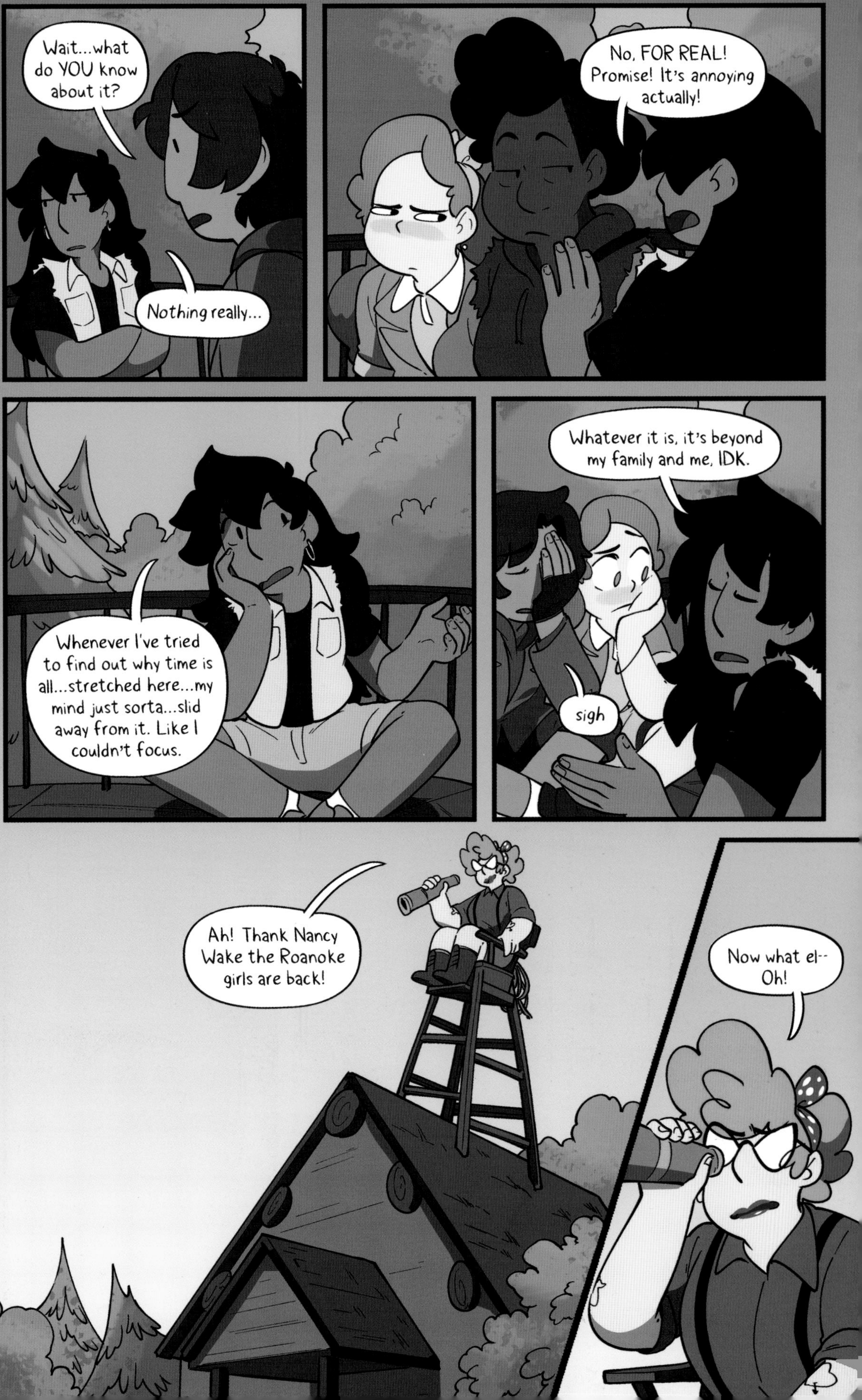

Wait...what do YOU know about it?
Nothing really...
No, FOR REAL! Promise! It's annoying actually!
Whenever I've tried to find out why time is all...stretched here...my mind just sorta...slid away from it. Like I couldn't focus.
Whatever it is, it's beyond my family and me, IDK.
sigh
Ah! Thank Nancy Wake the Roanoke girls are back!
Now what el-- Oh!

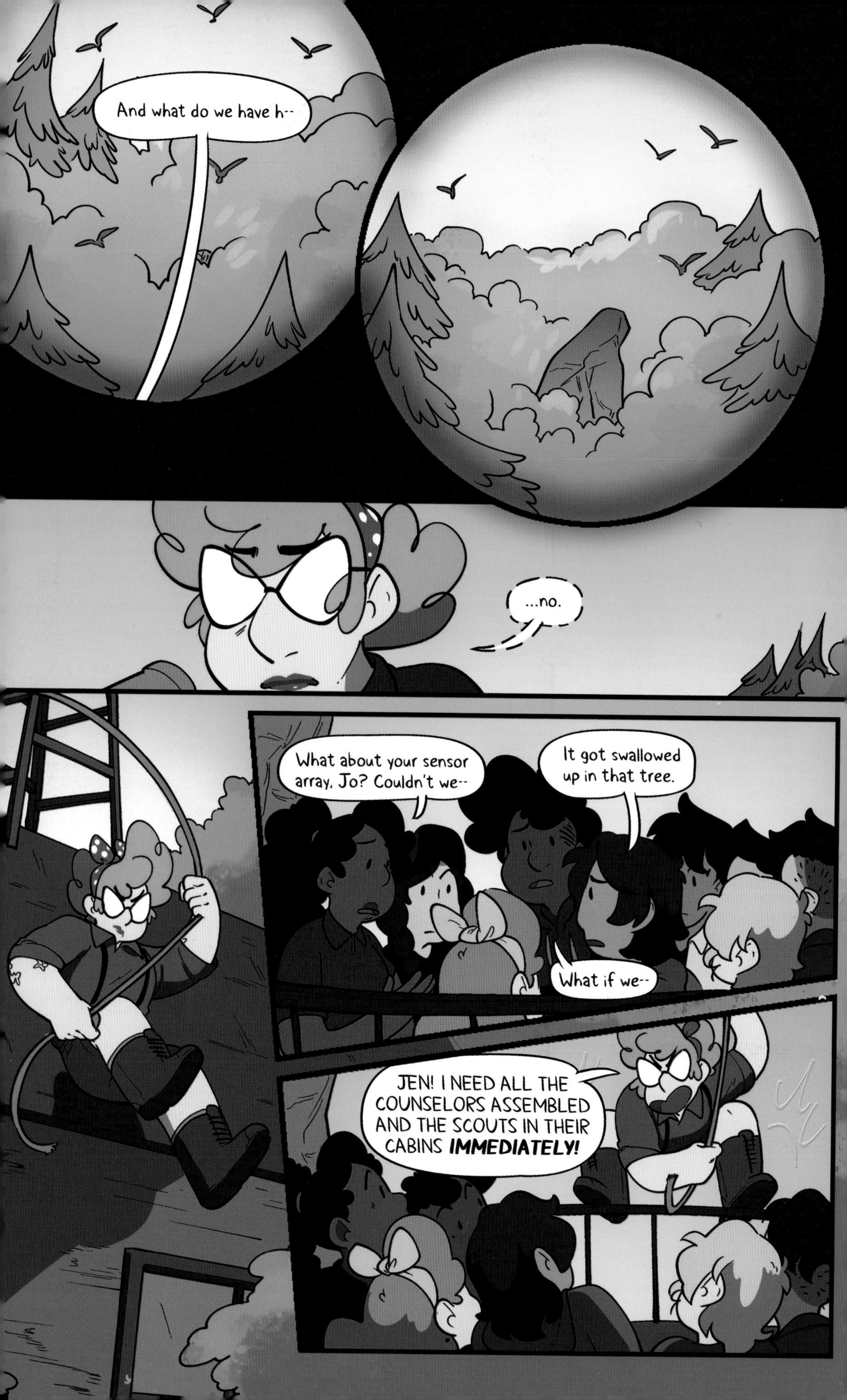
And what do we have h--
...no.
What about your sensor array, Jo? Couldn't we--
It got swallowed up in that tree.
What if we--
JEN! I NEED ALL THE COUNSELORS ASSEMBLED AND THE SCOUTS IN THEIR CABINS **IMMEDIATELY!**

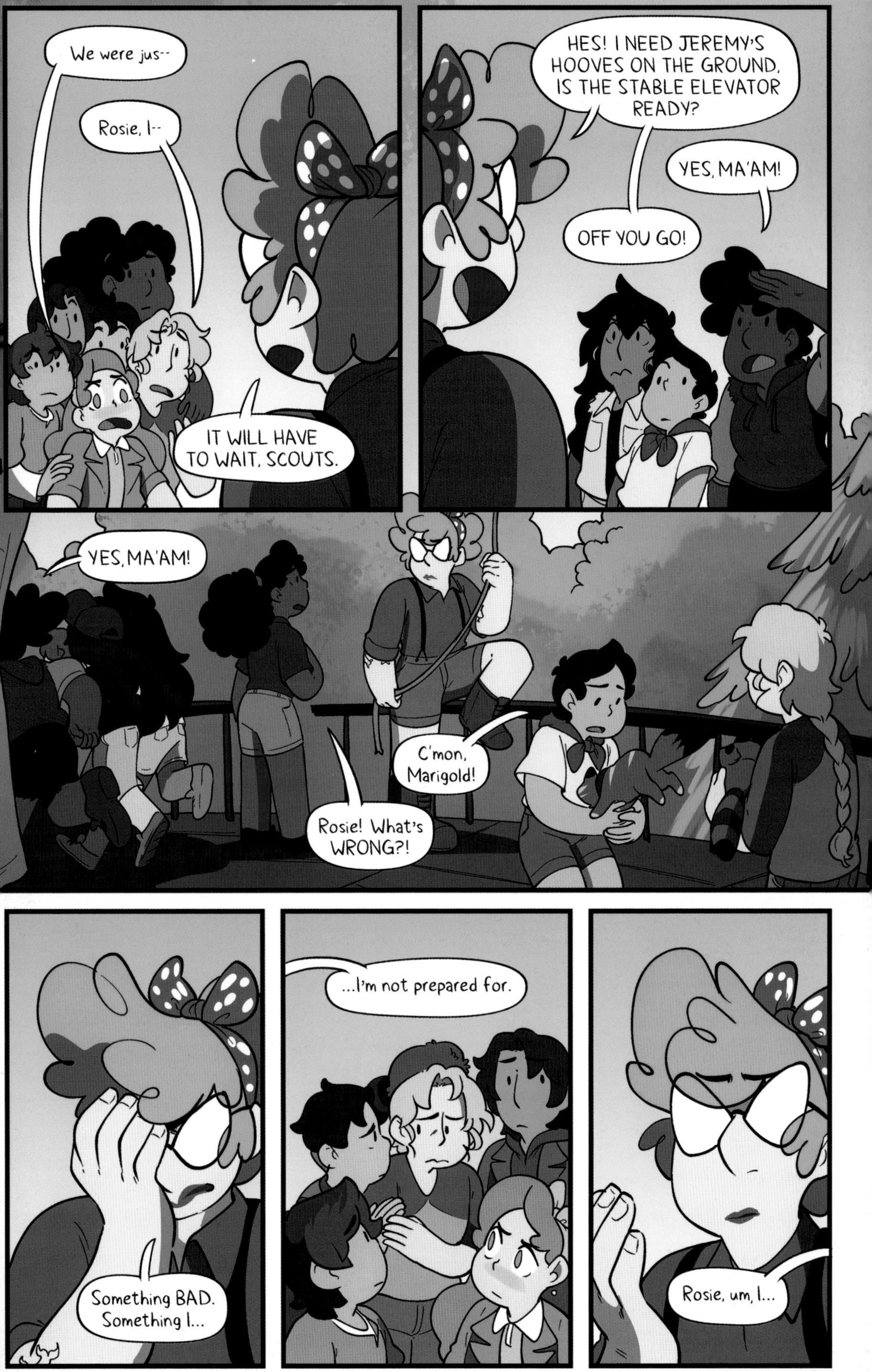
We were jus--
Rosie, I--
IT WILL HAVE TO WAIT, SCOUTS.
HES! I NEED JEREMY'S HOOVES ON THE GROUND, IS THE STABLE ELEVATOR READY?
YES, MA'AM!
OFF YOU GO!
YES, MA'AM!
C'mon, Marigold!
Rosie! What's WRONG?!
Something BAD. Something I...
...I'm not prepared for.
Rosie, um, I...

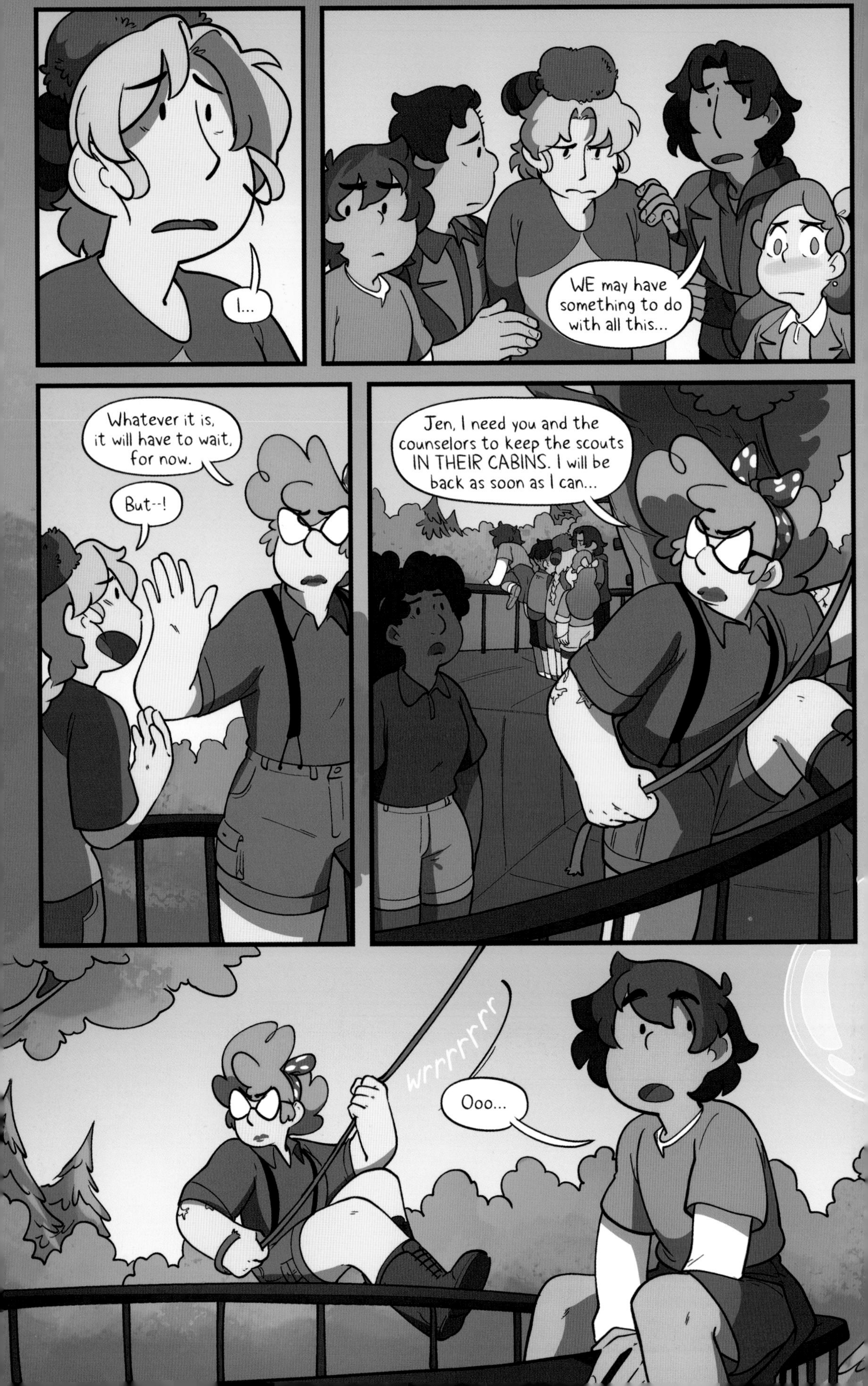
I...
WE may have something to do with all this...
Whatever it is, it will have to wait, for now.
But--!
Jen, I need you and the counselors to keep the scouts IN THEIR CABINS. I will be back as soon as I can...
wrrrrrr
Ooo...

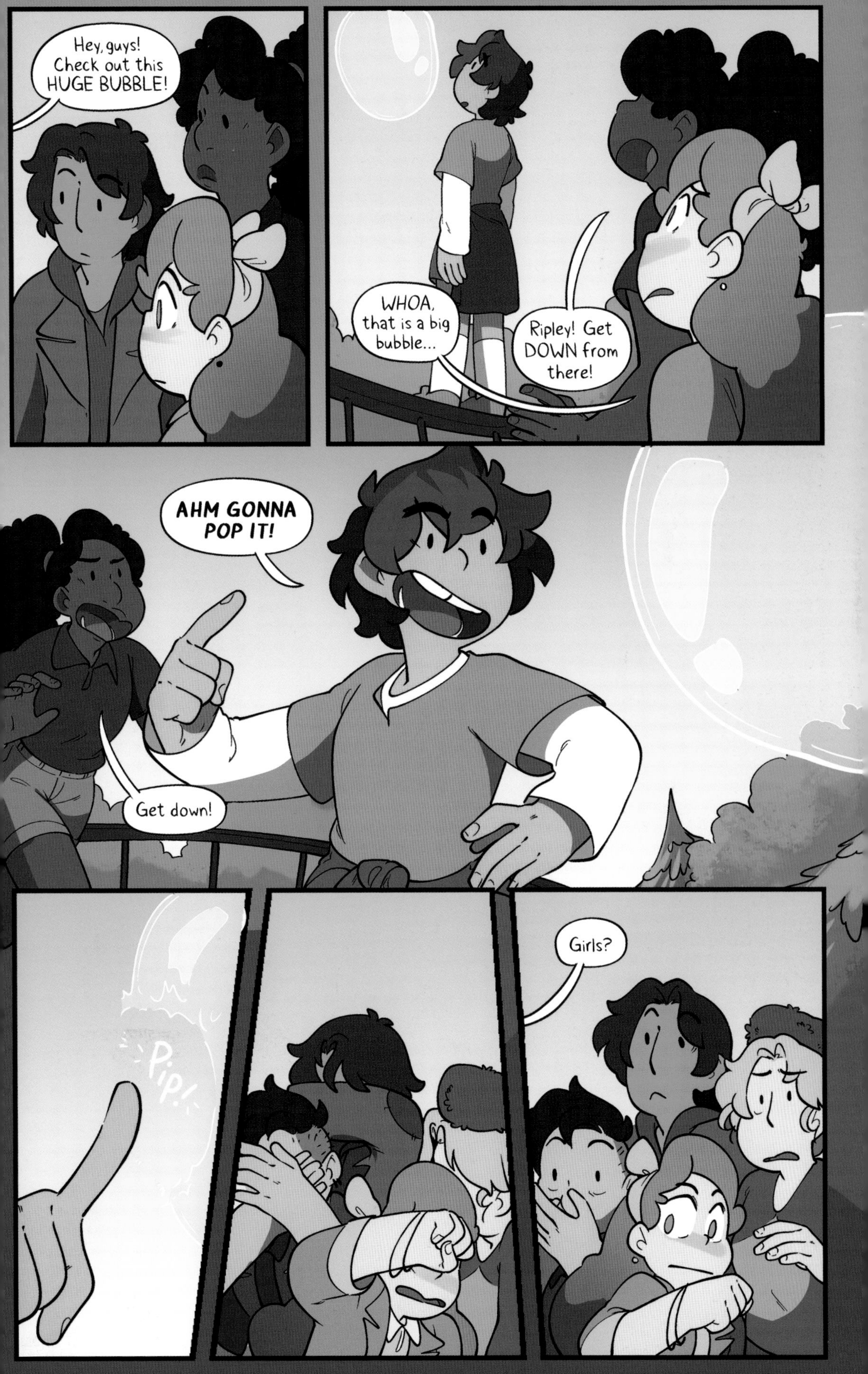
Hey, guys! Check out this HUGE BUBBLE!
WHOA, that is a big bubble...
Ripley! Get DOWN from there!
AHM GONNA POP IT!
Get down!
Pip!
Girls?

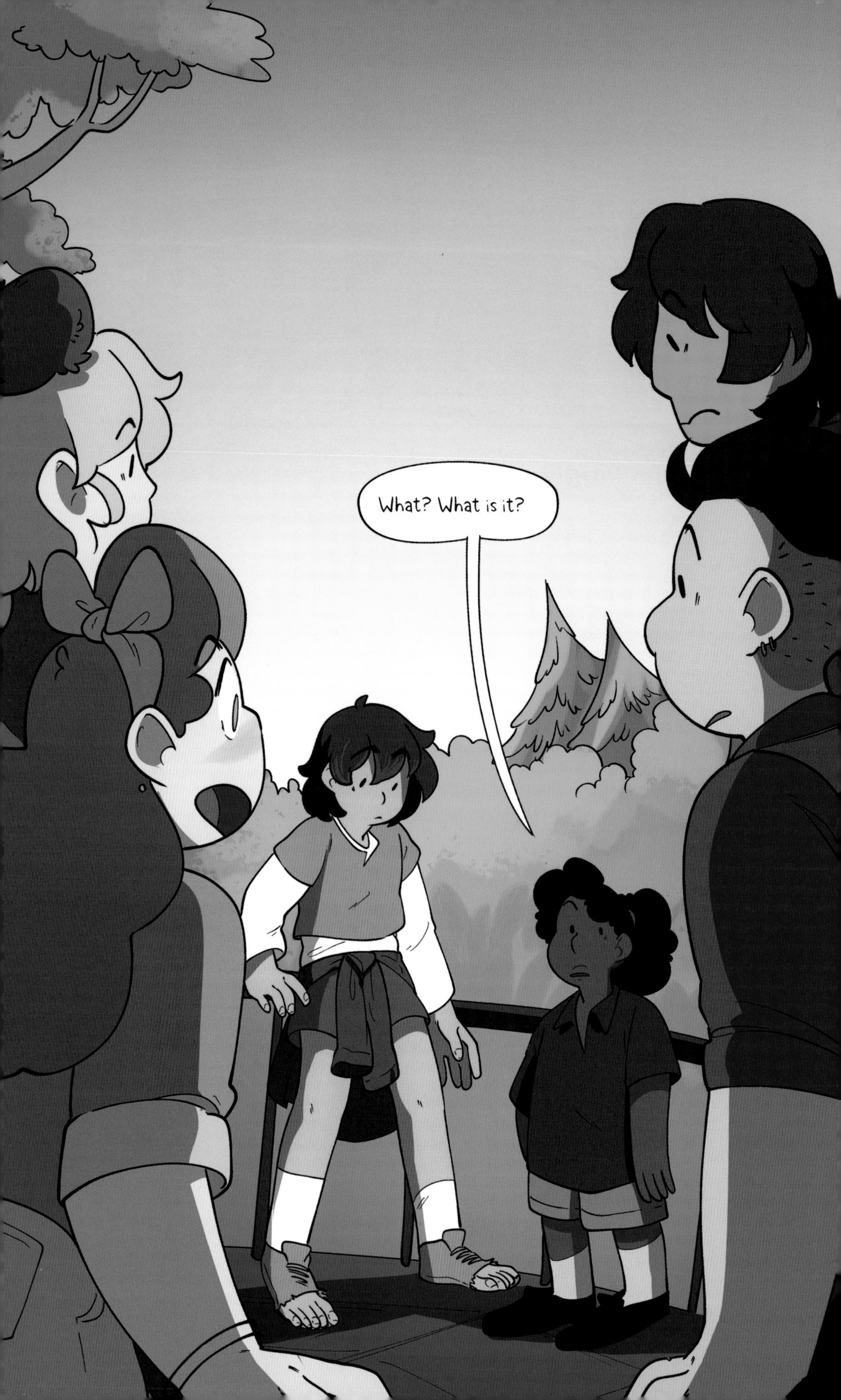
What? What is it?

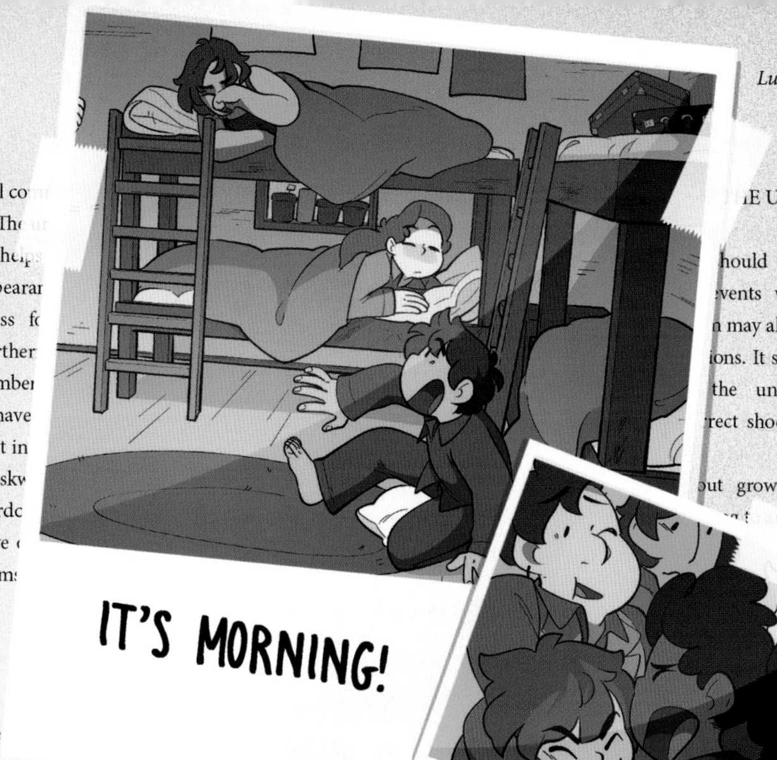
IT'S MORNING!

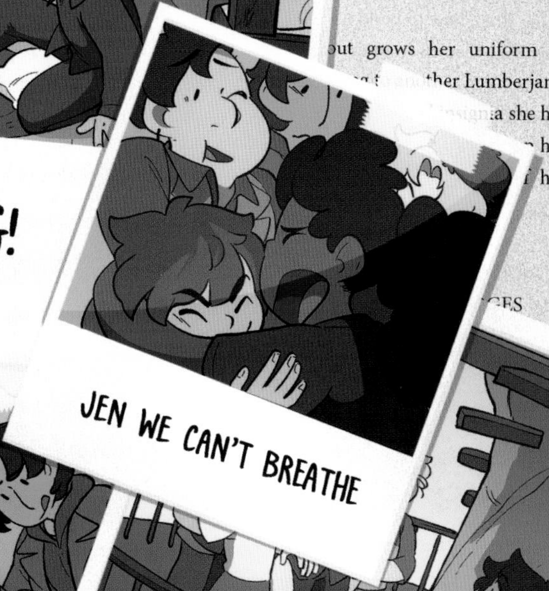
JEN WE CAN'T BREATHE

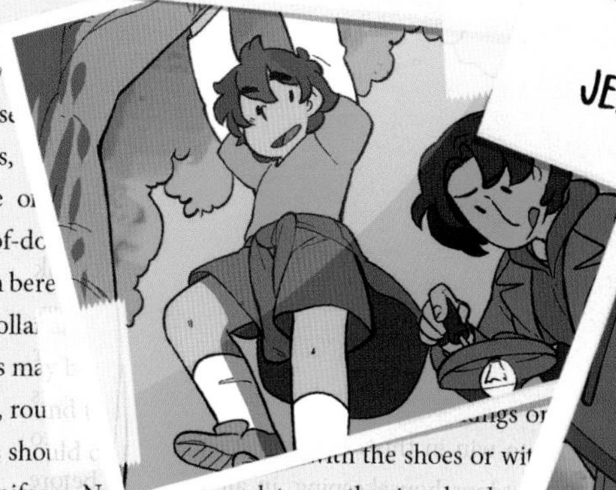

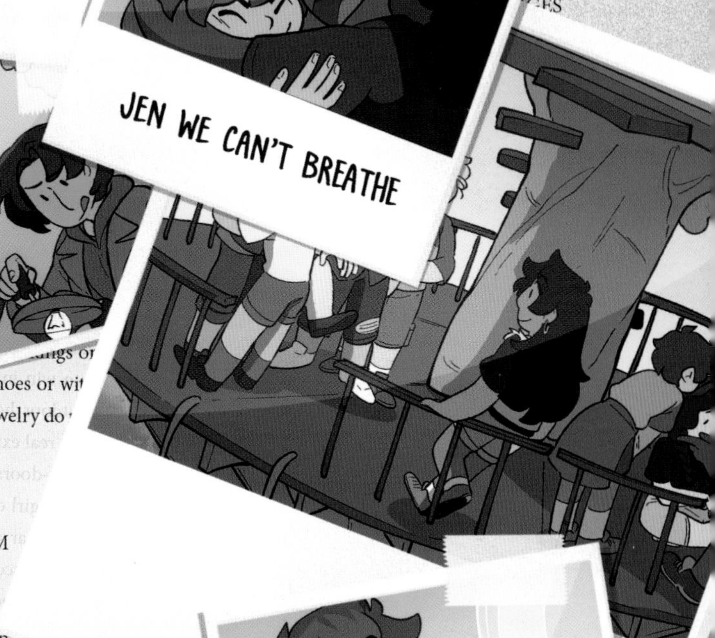

will co…

The…

It h… appearar… dress f… Further… Lumber… to have… part in… Thiskv… Hardc… have… thems…

…E UNIFORM

…hould be worn at camp …vents when Lumberjanes …n may also be worn at other …ions. It should be worn as a … the uniform dress with …rrect shoes, and stocking or …

…out grows her uniform or …ther Lumberjane. …ia she has … her … her

The … yellow, … emb… the w… choos… slacks, … made o… out-of-dc… green bere… the colla… Shoes ma… heels, roun… …ings or socks shou… …ith the shoes or wi… the uniform. Ne… …es, bracelets, or other jewelry do … belong with a Lumberjane uniform.

HOW TO WEAR THE UNIFORM

To look well in a uniform demands first of … uniform be kept in good condition—clean … pressed. See that the skirt is the right length for your own height and build, that the belt is adjusted to your waist, that your shoes and stockings are in keeping with the uniform, that you watch your posture and carry yourself with dignity and grace. If the beret is removed indoors, be sure that your hair is neat and kept in place with an inconspicuous clip or ribbon. When you wear a Lumberjane uniform you are identified as a member of this organization and you should be doubly careful to conduct yourself in a way that will show everyone that courtesy and thoughtfulness are part of being a Lumberjane. People are likely to judge a whole nation by the selfishness of a few individuals, to criticize a whole family because of the misconduct of one member, and to feel unkindly toward an organization because of the

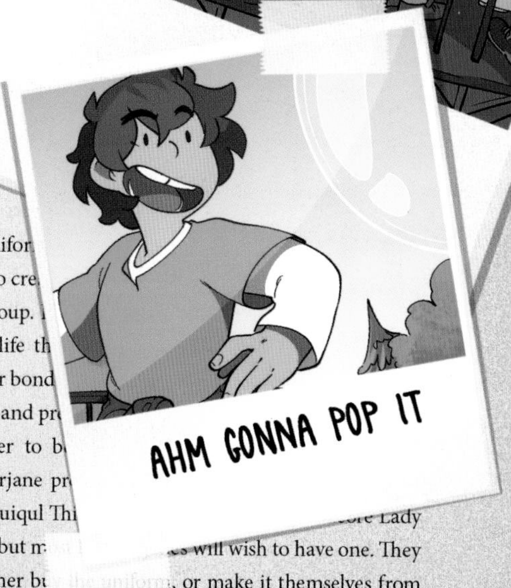
AHM GONNA POP IT

The unifor… helps to cre… in a group. … active life th… another bond… future, and pr… in order to b… Lumberjane pr… Penniquiqul Thi… …ore Lady Types, but m… …s will wish to have one. They can either bu… …uniform, or make it themselves from materials available at the trading post.

LUMBERJANES FIELD MANUAL

CHAPTER
FORTY-THREE

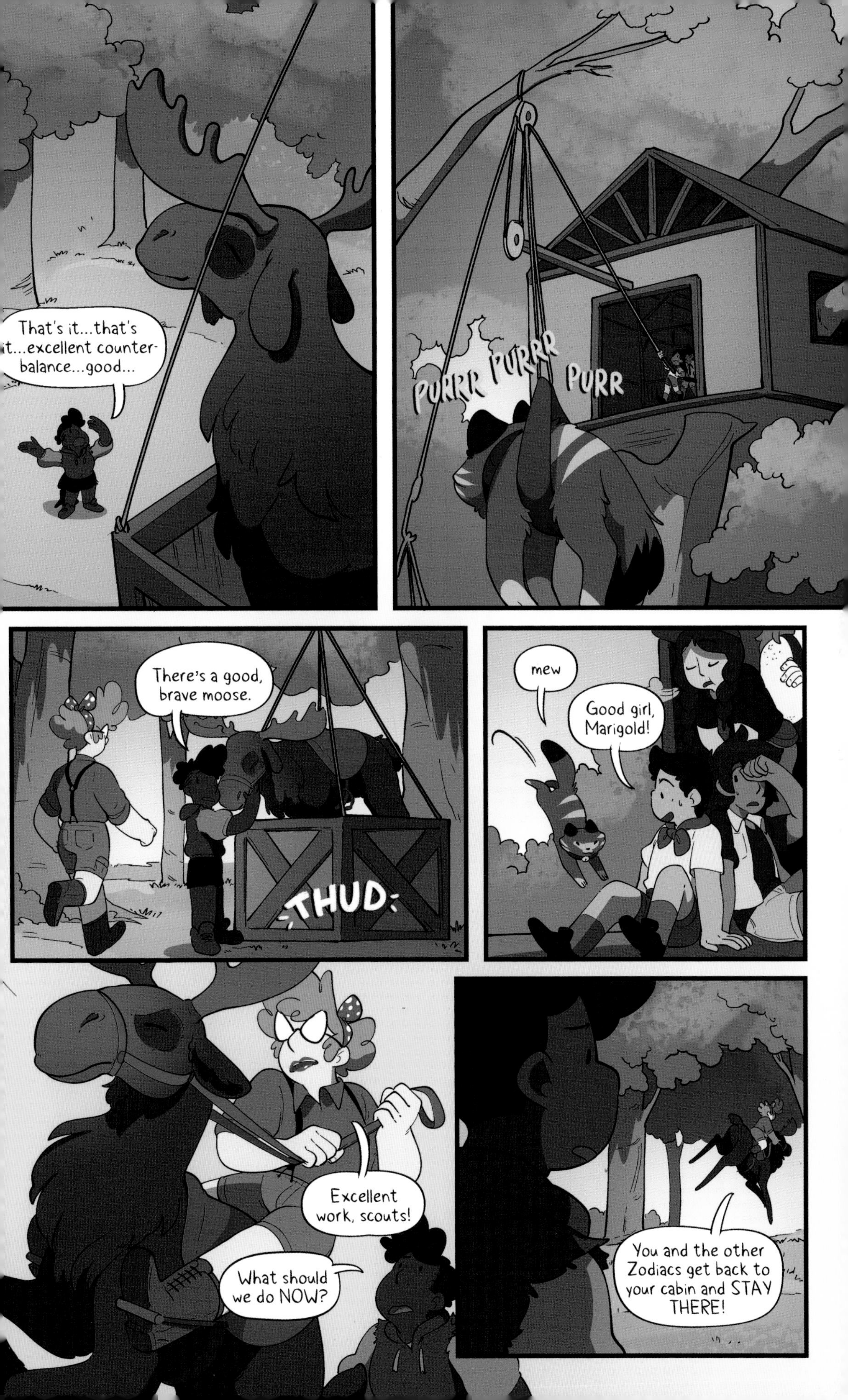
That's it...that's t...excellent counter-balance...good...
PURRR PURRR PURR
There's a good, brave moose.
THUD
mew
Good girl, Marigold!
Excellent work, scouts!
What should we do NOW?
You and the other Zodiacs get back to your cabin and STAY THERE!

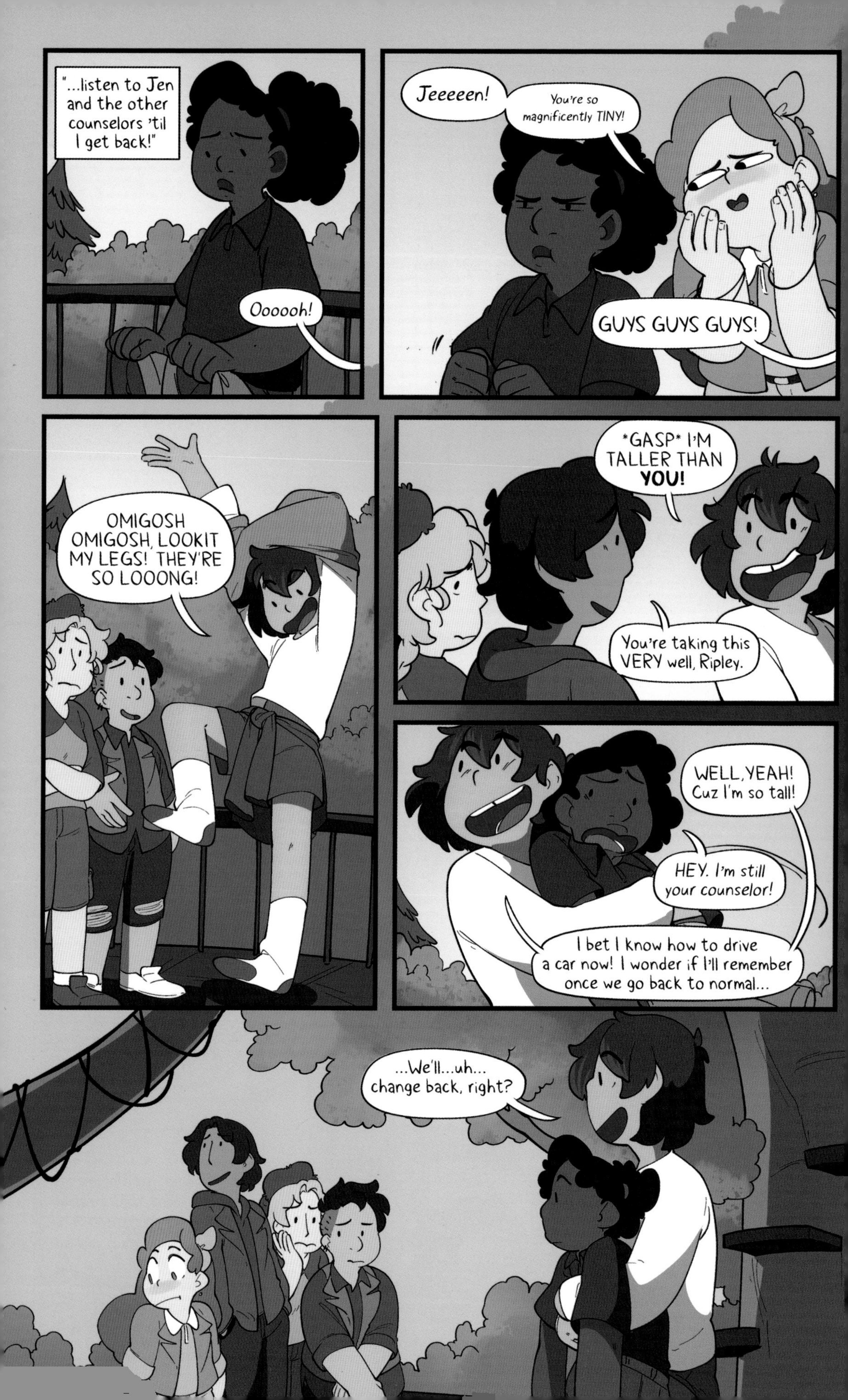
"...listen to Jen and the other counselors 'til I get back!"
Oooooh!
Jeeeeen!
You're so magnificently TINY!
GUYS GUYS GUYS!
OMIGOSH OMIGOSH, LOOKIT MY LEGS! THEY'RE SO LOOONG!
GASP I'M TALLER THAN YOU!
You're taking this VERY well, Ripley.
WELL, YEAH! Cuz I'm so tall!
HEY. I'm still your counselor!
I bet I know how to drive a car now! I wonder if I'll remember once we go back to normal...
...We'll...uh... change back, right?

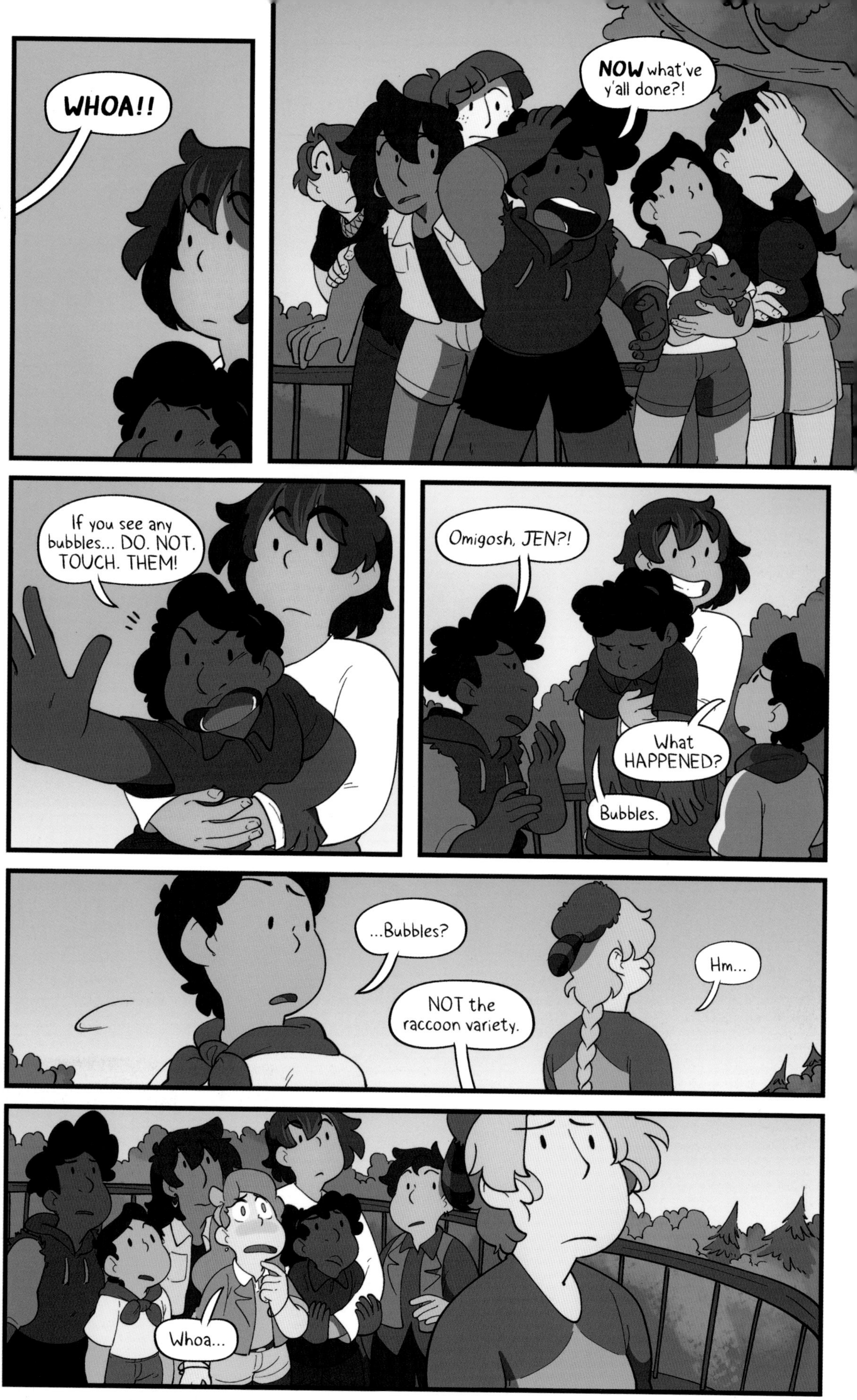
WHOA!!
NOW what've y'all done?!
If you see any bubbles... DO. NOT. TOUCH. THEM!
Omigosh, JEN?!
What HAPPENED?
Bubbles.
...Bubbles?
NOT the raccoon variety.
Hm...
Whoa...

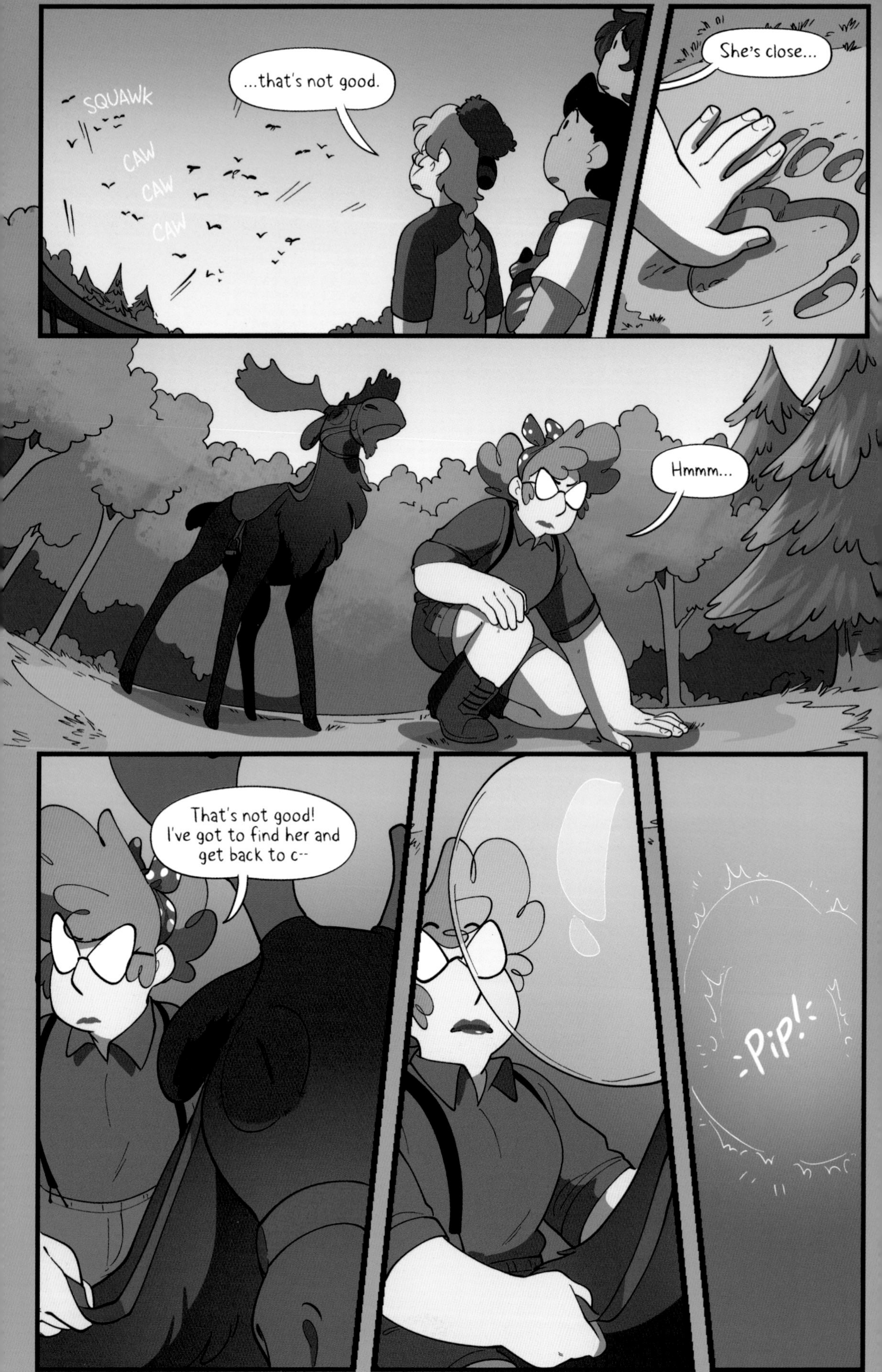
SQUAWK
CAW
CAW
CAW
...that's not good.
She's close...
Hmmm...
That's not good!
I've got to find her and
get back to c--
PIP!

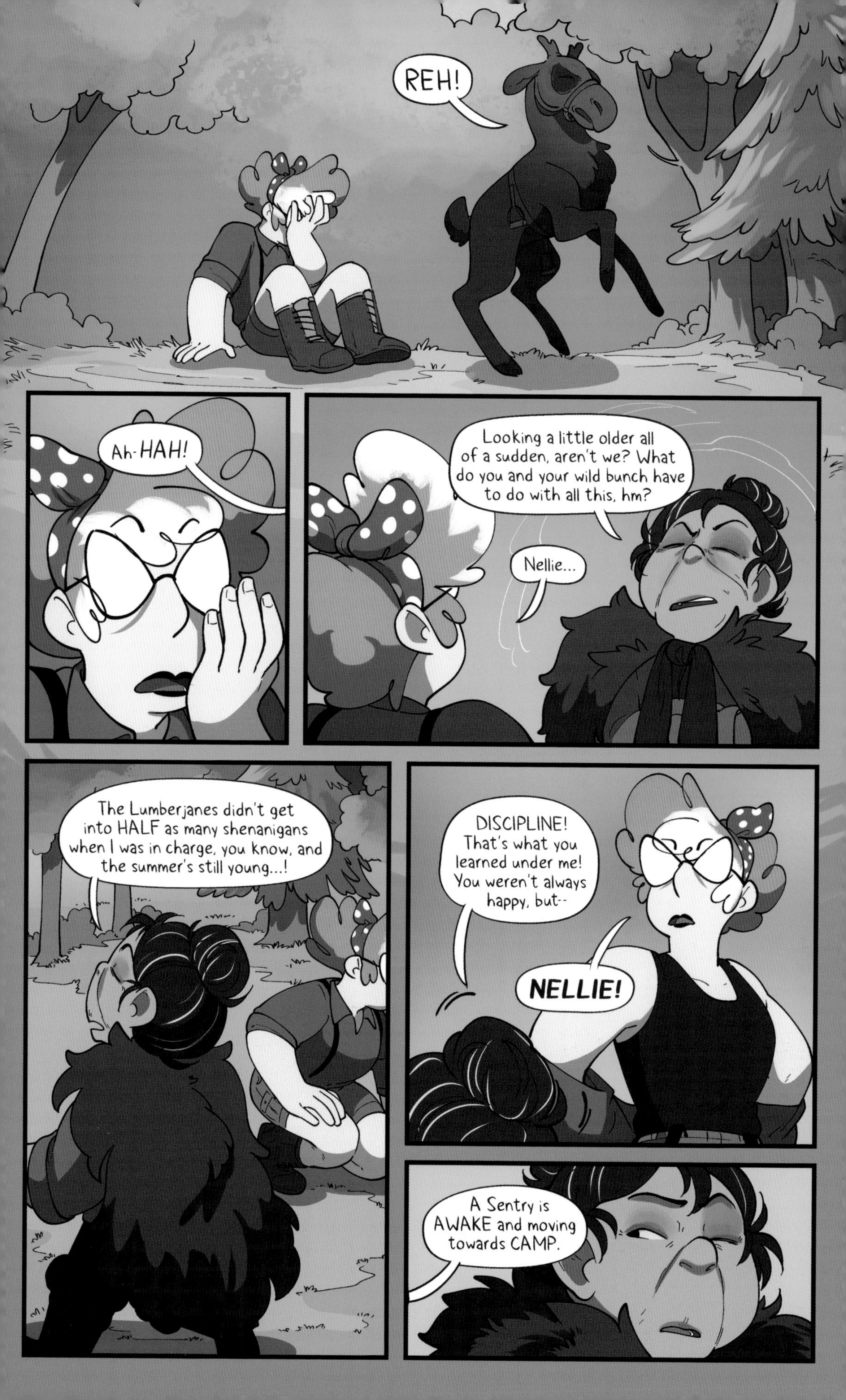
REH!
Ah-HAH!
Looking a little older all of a sudden, aren't we? What do you and your wild bunch have to do with all this, hm?
Nellie...
The Lumberjanes didn't get into HALF as many shenanigans when I was in charge, you know, and the summer's still young...!
DISCIPLINE! That's what you learned under me! You weren't always happy, but--
NELLIE!
A Sentry is AWAKE and moving towards CAMP.

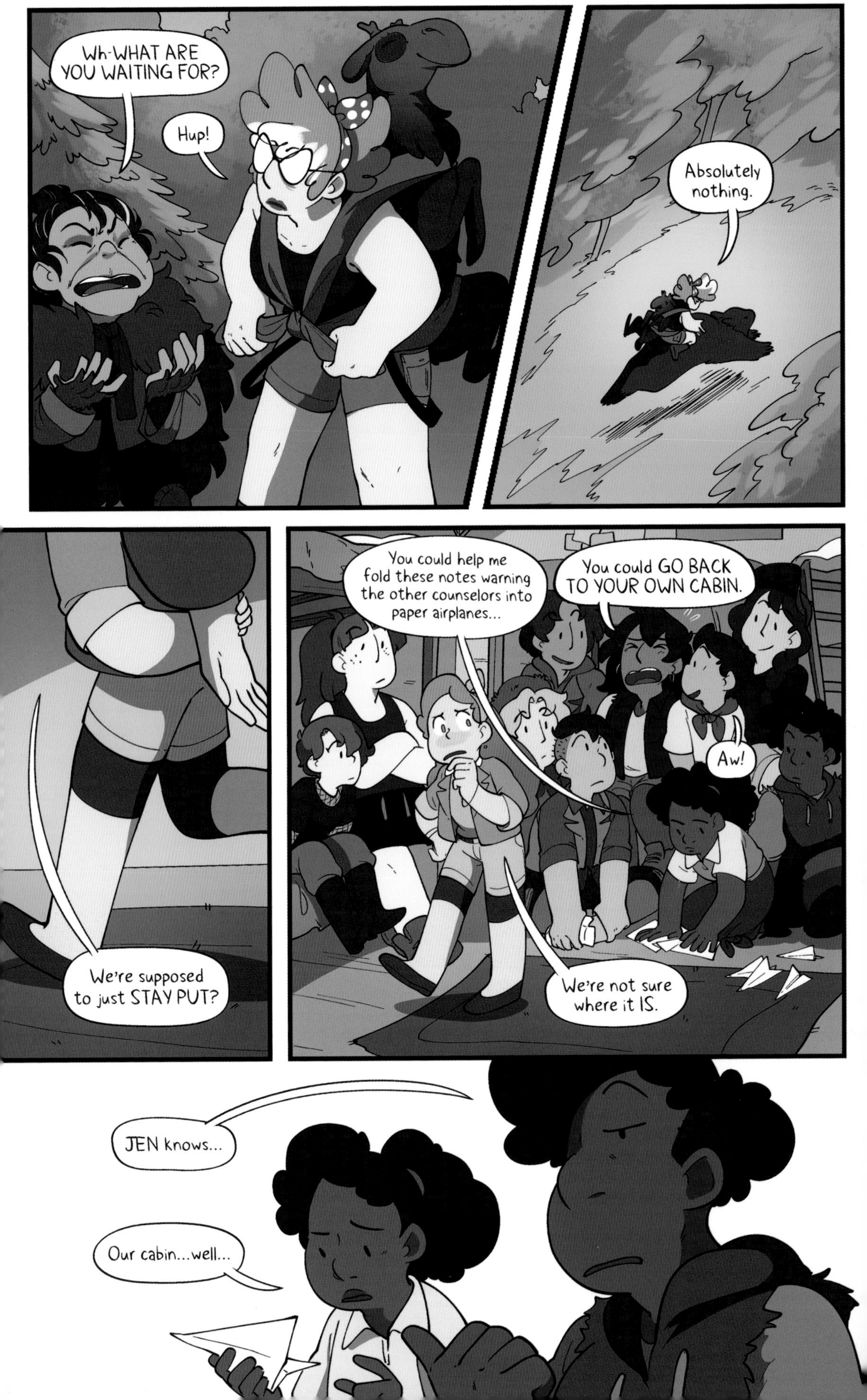

Wh-WHAT ARE YOU WAITING FOR?
Hup!
Absolutely nothing.
We're supposed to just STAY PUT?
You could help me fold these notes warning the other counselors into paper airplanes...
You could GO BACK TO YOUR OWN CABIN.
Aw!
We're not sure where it IS.
JEN knows...
Our cabin...well...

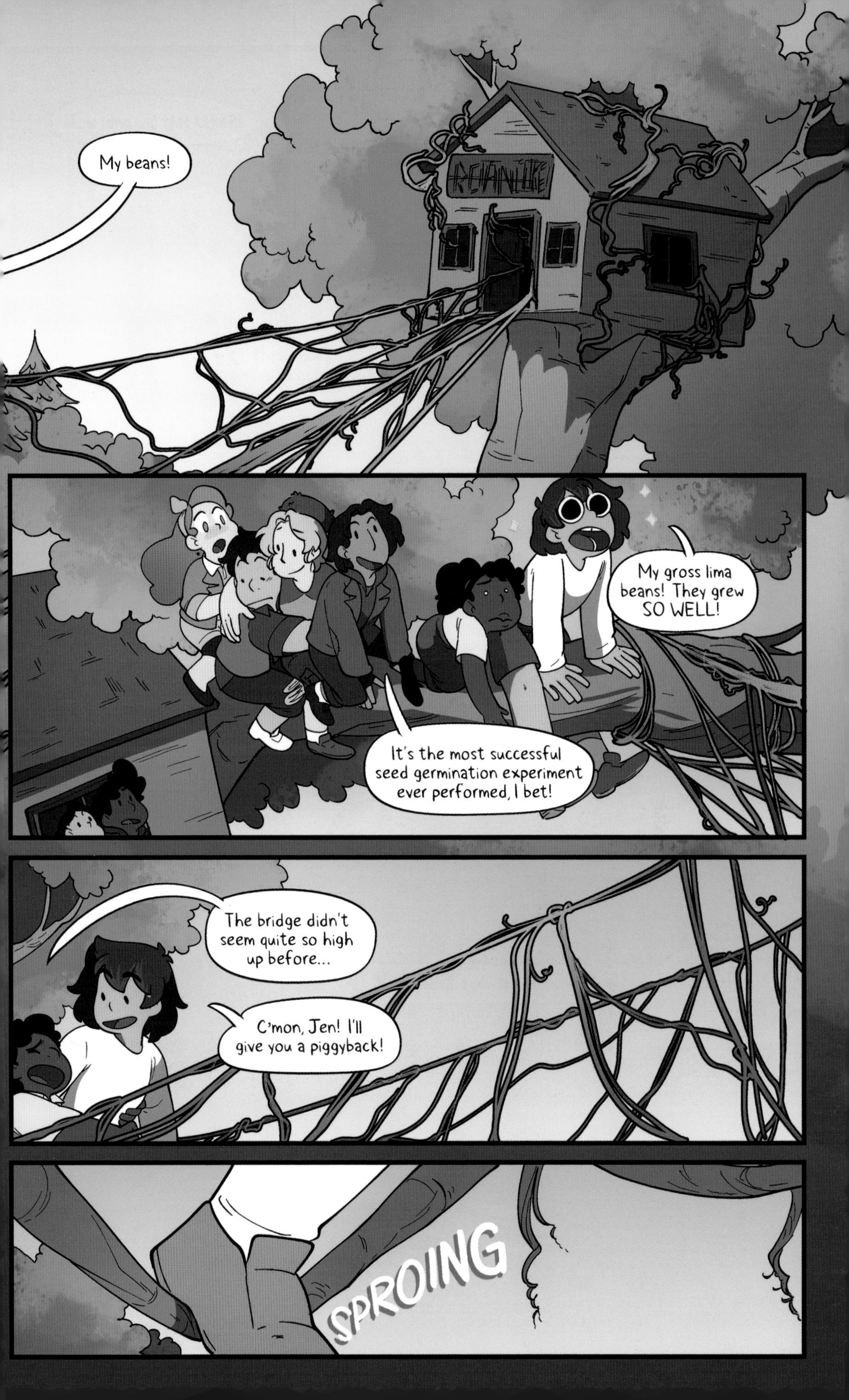
My beans!
My gross lima beans! They grew SO WELL!
It's the most successful seed germination experiment ever performed, I bet!
The bridge didn't seem quite so high up before...
C'mon, Jen! I'll give you a piggyback!
SPROING

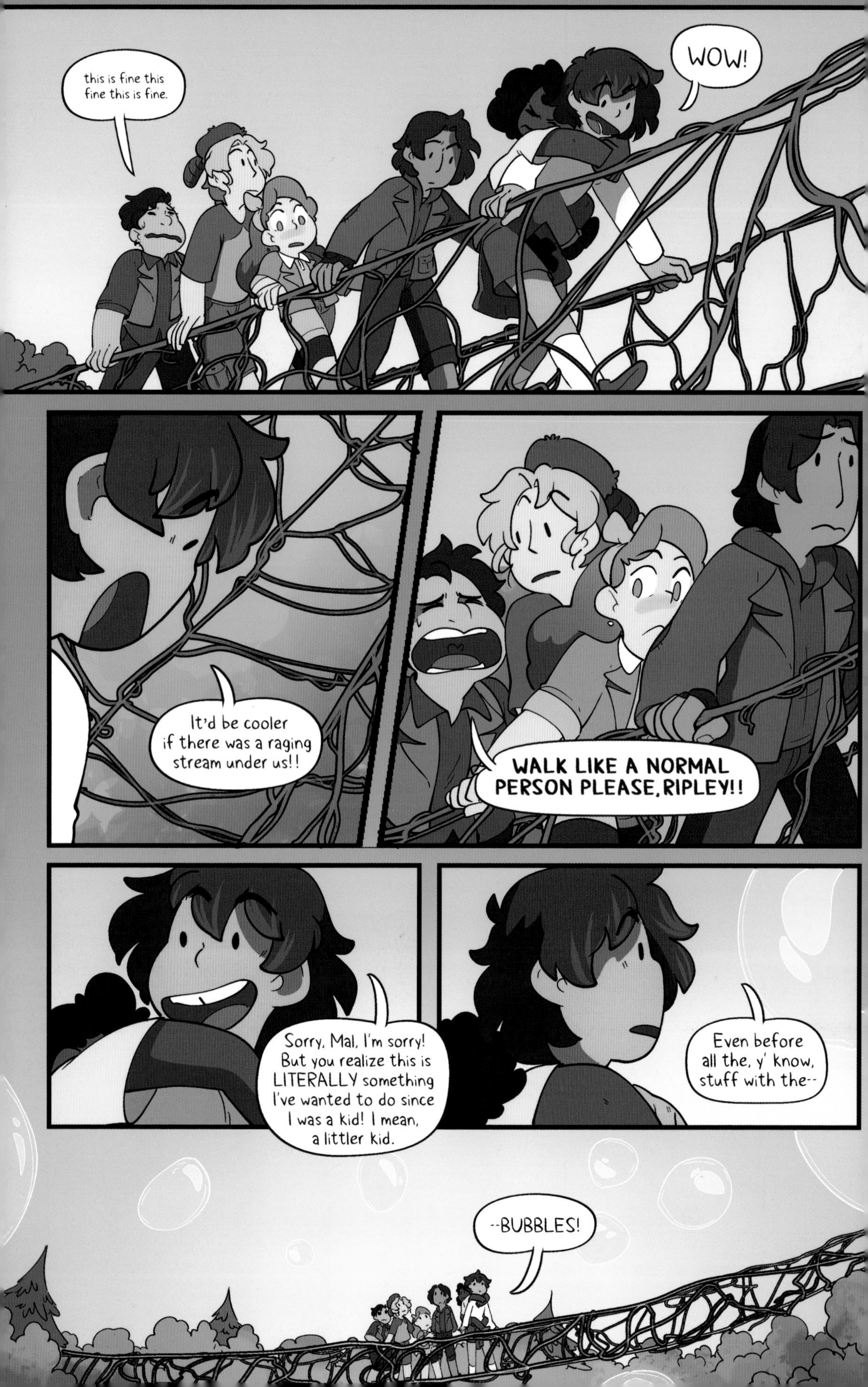
this is fine this fine this is fine.
WOW!
It'd be cooler if there was a raging stream under us!!
WALK LIKE A NORMAL PERSON PLEASE, RIPLEY!!
Sorry, Mal, I'm sorry! But you realize this is LITERALLY something I've wanted to do since I was a kid! I mean, a littler kid.
Even before all the, y' know, stuff with the--
--BUBBLES!

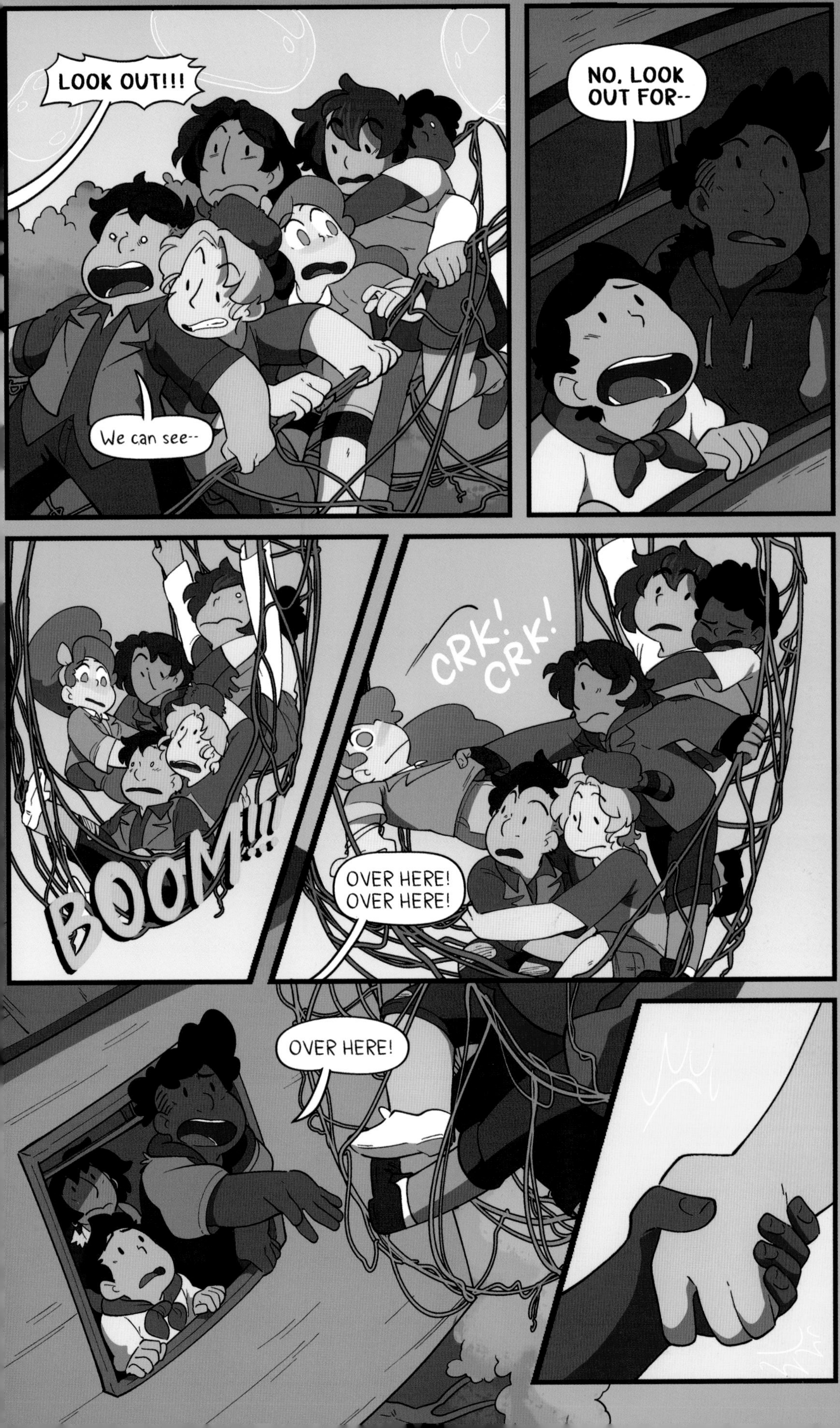
LOOK OUT!!!
We can see--
NO, LOOK OUT FOR--
BOOM!!!
CRK! CRK!
OVER HERE! OVER HERE!
OVER HERE!

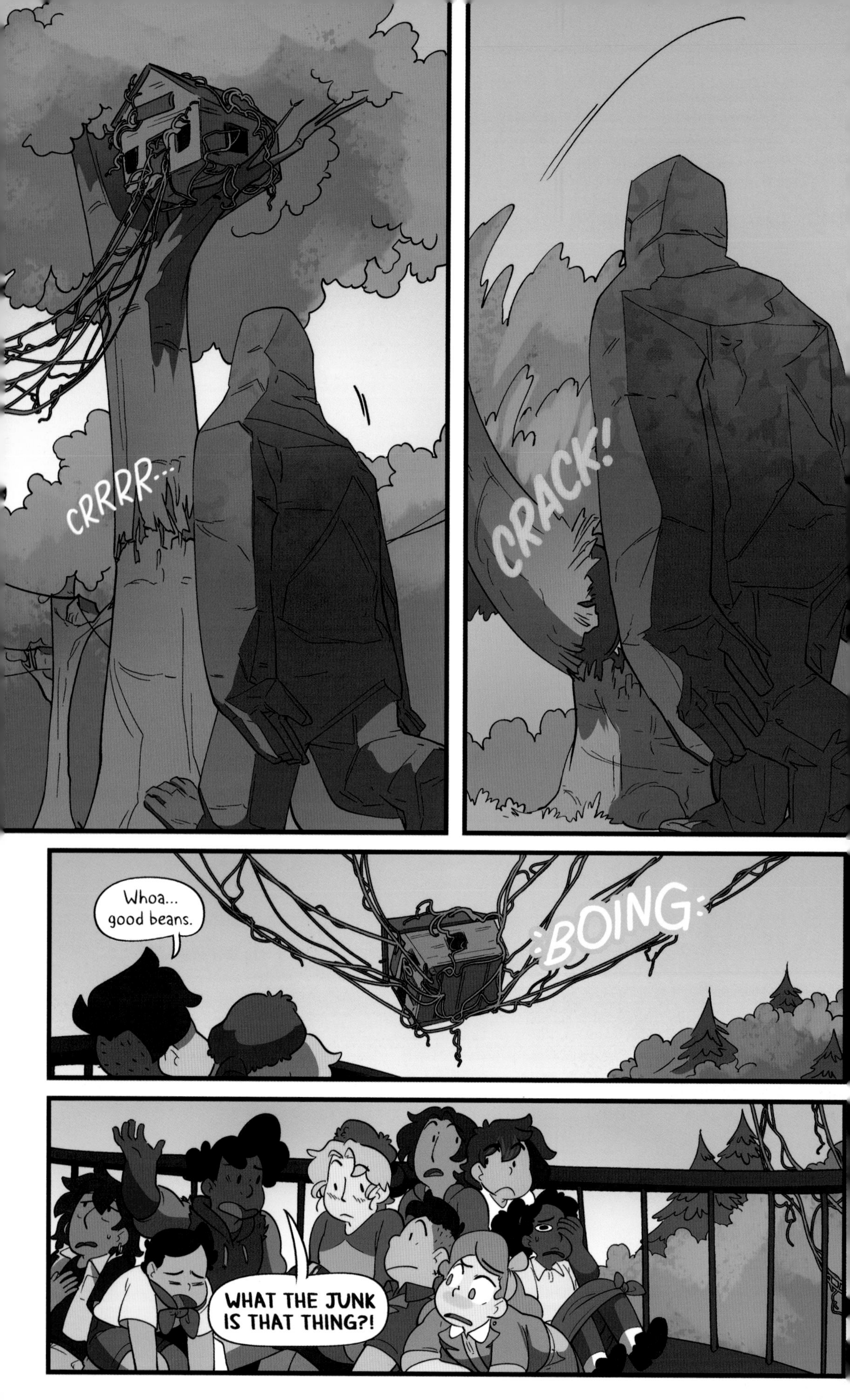
CRRRR...
CRACK!
Whoa... good beans.
BOING
WHAT THE JUNK IS THAT THING?!

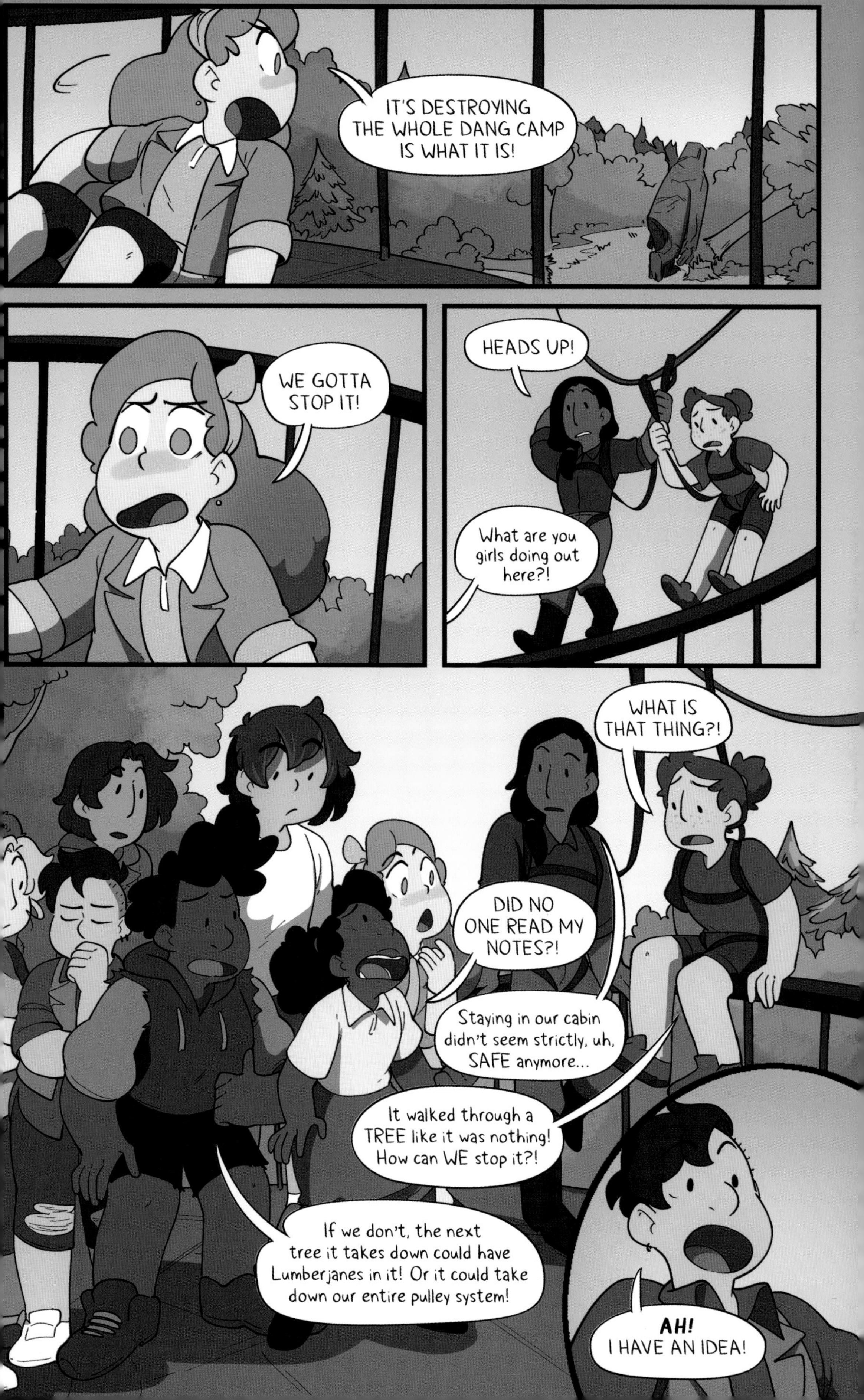
IT'S DESTROYING THE WHOLE DANG CAMP IS WHAT IT IS!
WE GOTTA STOP IT!
HEADS UP!
What are you girls doing out here?!
WHAT IS THAT THING?!
DID NO ONE READ MY NOTES?!
Staying in our cabin didn't seem strictly, uh, SAFE anymore...
It walked through a TREE like it was nothing! How can WE stop it?!
If we don't, the next tree it takes down could have Lumberjanes in it! Or it could take down our entire pulley system!
AH! I HAVE AN IDEA!

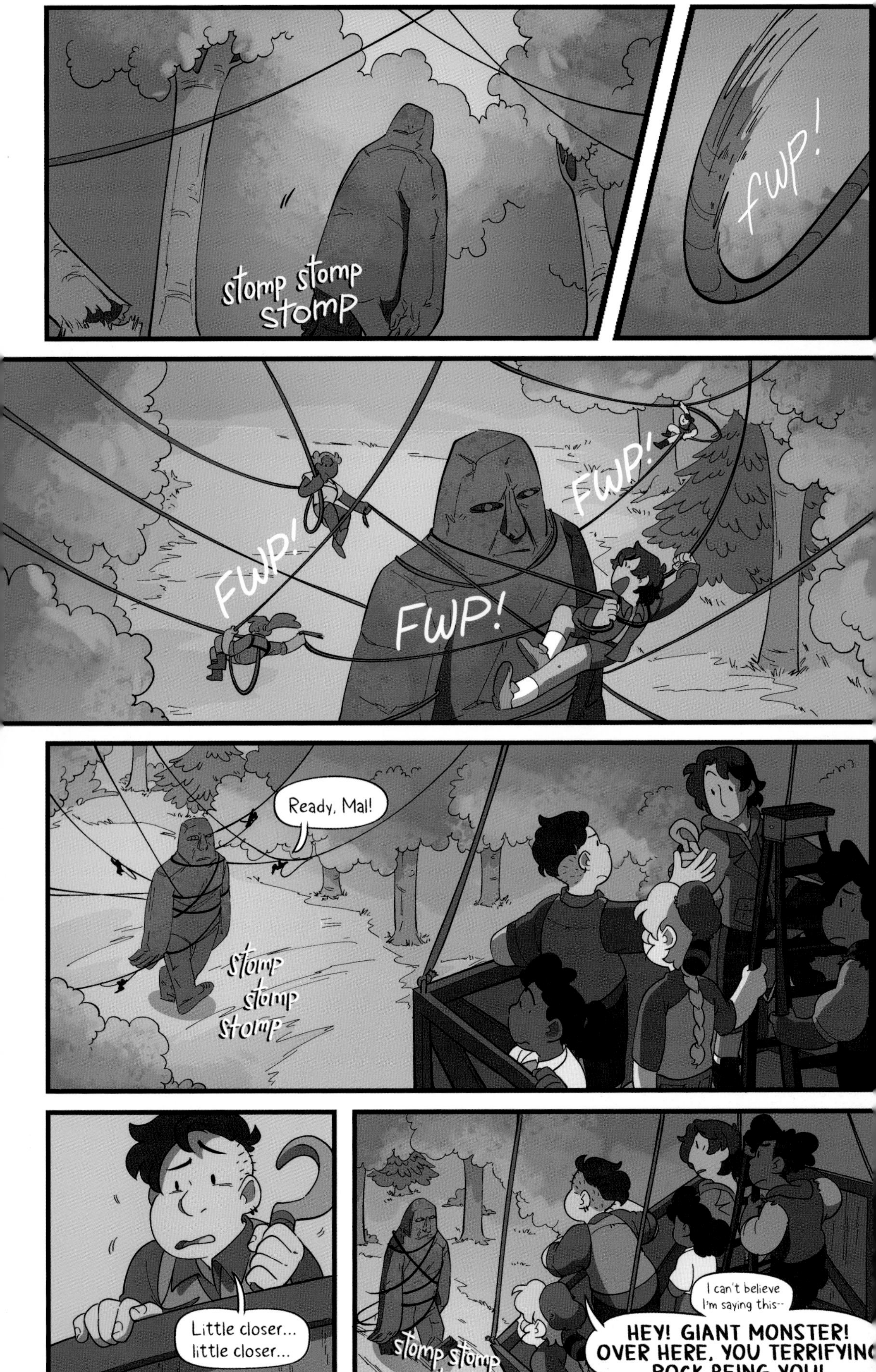
stomp stomp
stomp
fwp!
FWP!
FWP!
FWP!
Ready, Mal!
stomp
stomp
stomp
Little closer...
little closer...
stomp stomp
stomp
I can't believe
I'm saying this--
HEY! GIANT MONSTER!
OVER HERE, YOU TERRIFYING
ROCK BEING, YOU!

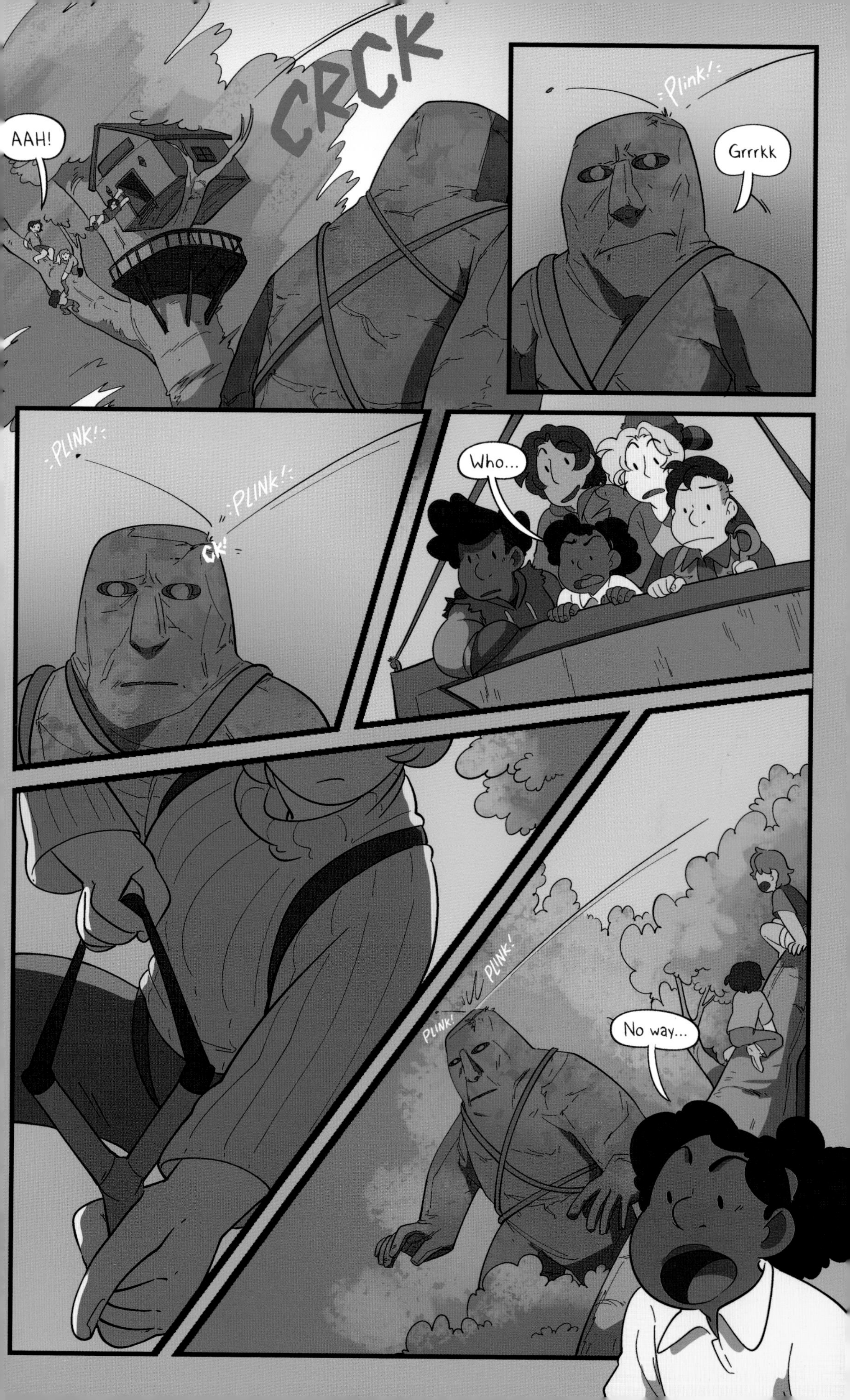
CRCK
AAH!
Plink!
Grrrkk
PLINK!
PLINK!
CK!
Who...
PLINK!
PLINK!
No way...

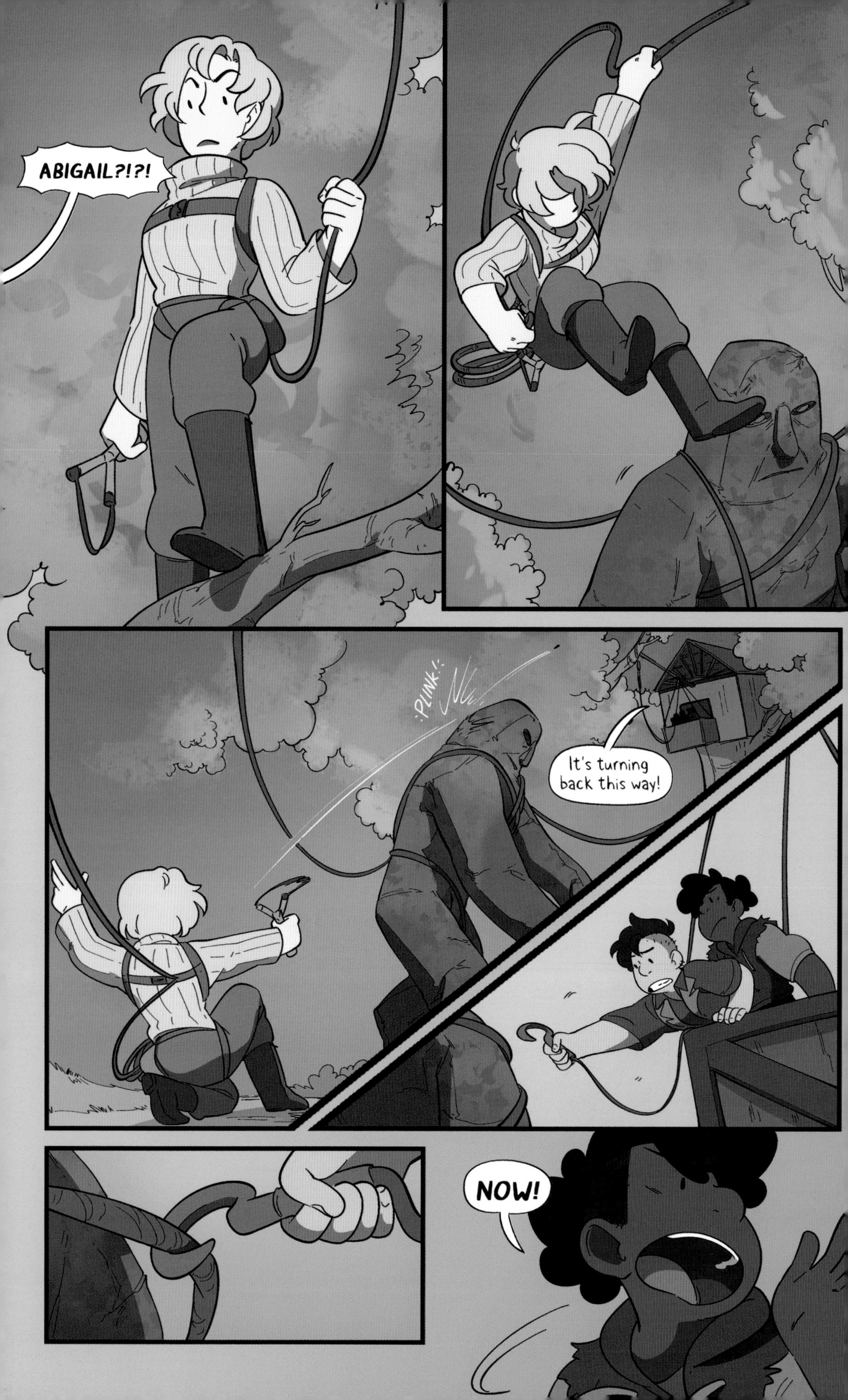
ABIGAIL?!?!
:PLINK!:
It's turning back this way!
NOW!

ptoo!
Make like Sarah Robles and PULL! Use your legs!
SWOOP

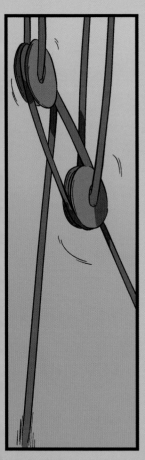

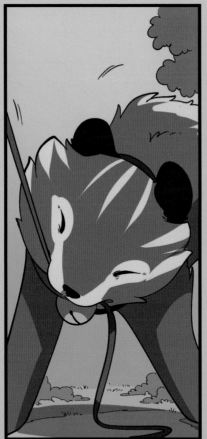

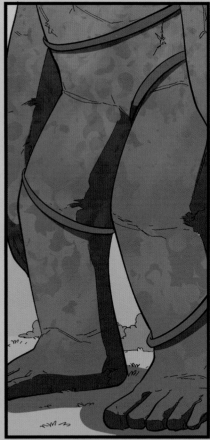

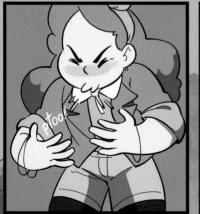

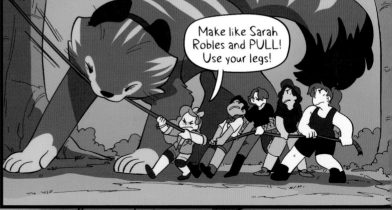

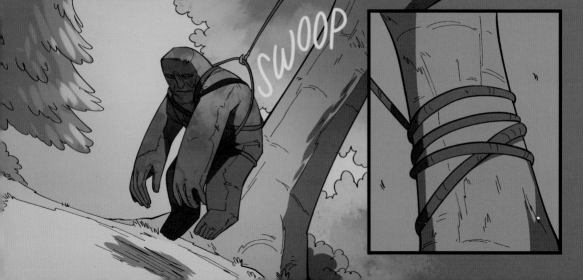

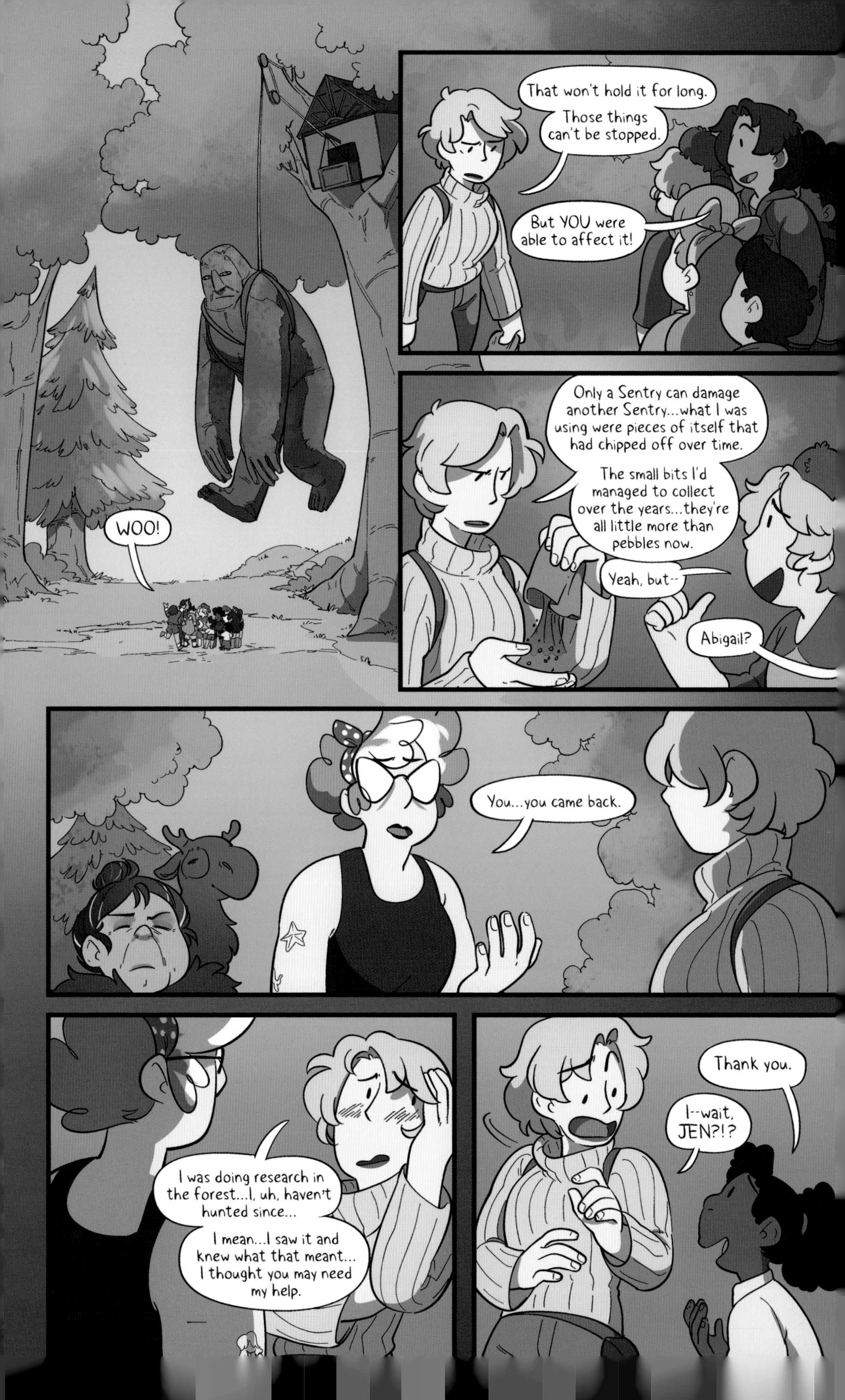
That won't hold it for long.
Those things can't be stopped.
But YOU were able to affect it!
WOO!
Only a Sentry can damage another Sentry...what I was using were pieces of itself that had chipped off over time.
The small bits I'd managed to collect over the years...they're all little more than pebbles now.
Yeah, but--
Abigail?
You...you came back.
I was doing research in the forest...I, uh, haven't hunted since...
I mean...I saw it and knew what that meant... I thought you may need my help.
Thank you.
I--wait, JEN?!?

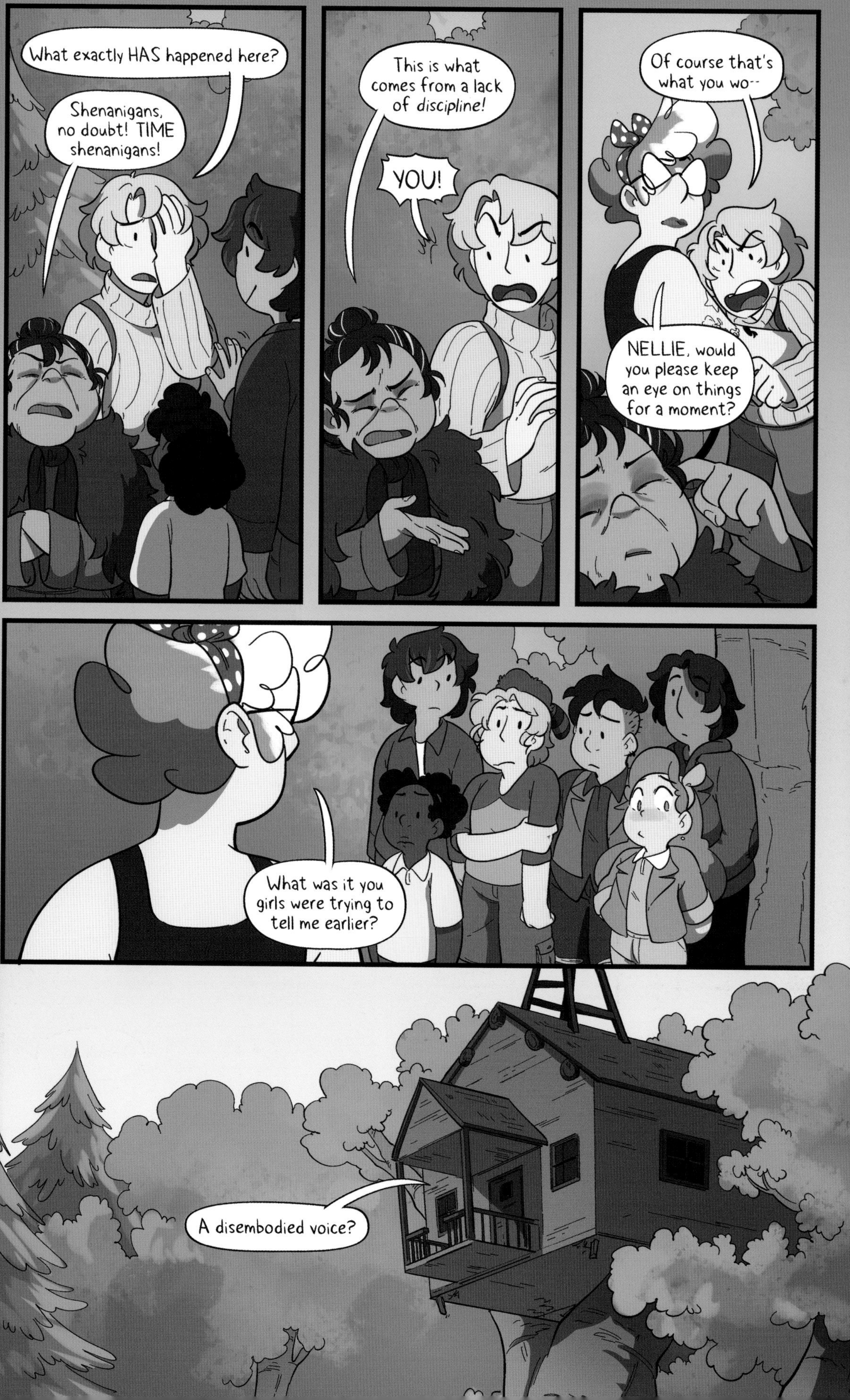
What exactly HAS happened here?
Shenanigans, no doubt! TIME shenanigans!
This is what comes from a lack of *discipline*!
YOU!
Of course that's what you wo--
NELLIE, would you please keep an eye on things for a moment?
What was it you girls were trying to tell me earlier?
A disembodied voice?

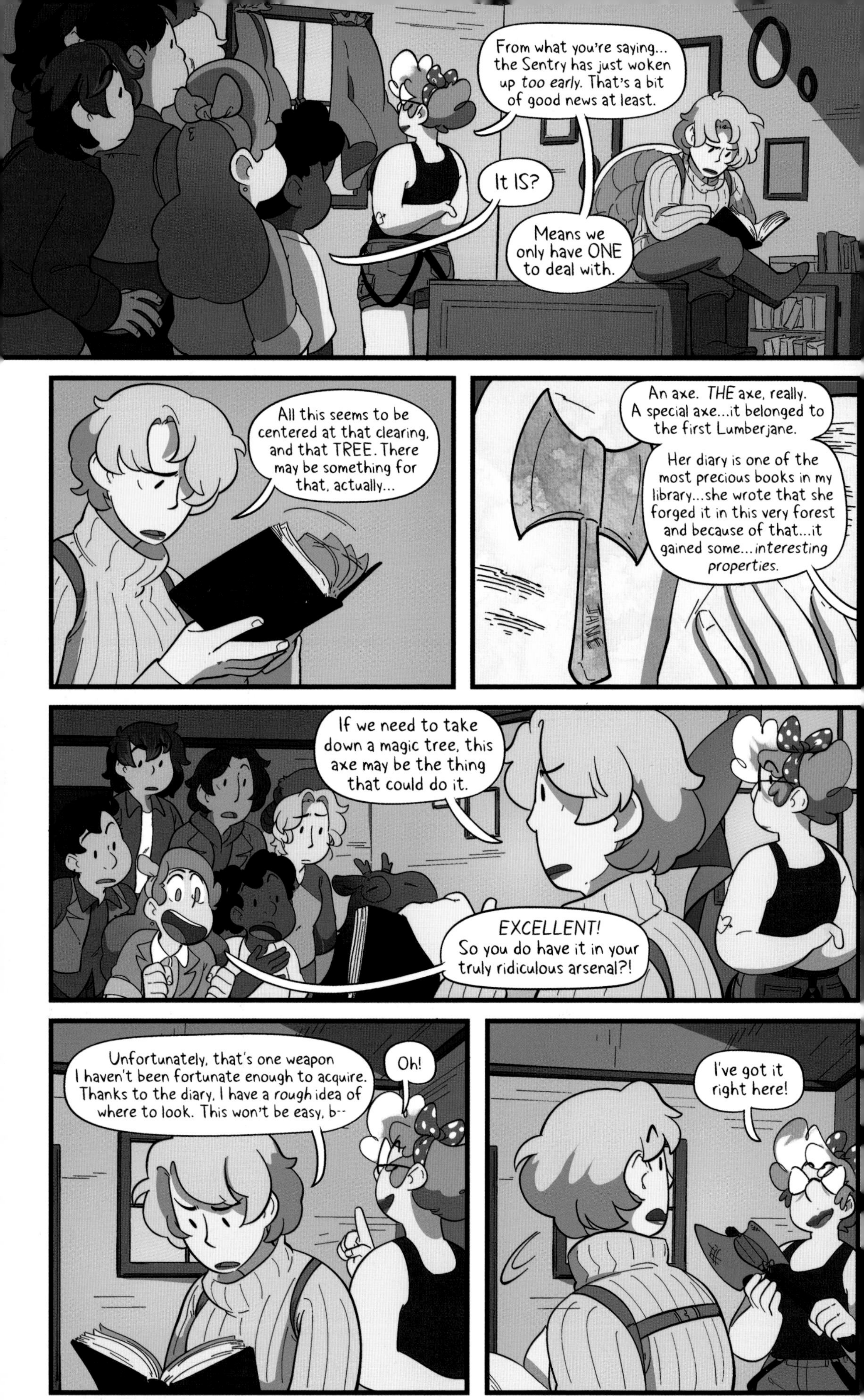
From what you're saying... the Sentry has just woken up *too early*. That's a bit of good news at least.
It IS?
Means we only have ONE to deal with.
All this seems to be centered at that clearing, and that TREE. There may be something for that, actually...
An axe. *THE* axe, really. A special axe...it belonged to the first Lumberjane.
Her diary is one of the most precious books in my library...she wrote that she forged it in this very forest and because of that...it gained some...*interesting properties*.
If we need to take down a magic tree, this axe may be the thing that could do it.
EXCELLENT! So you do have it in your truly ridiculous arsenal?!
Unfortunately, that's one weapon I haven't been fortunate enough to acquire. Thanks to the diary, I have a *rough* idea of where to look. This won't be easy, b--
Oh!
I've got it right here!

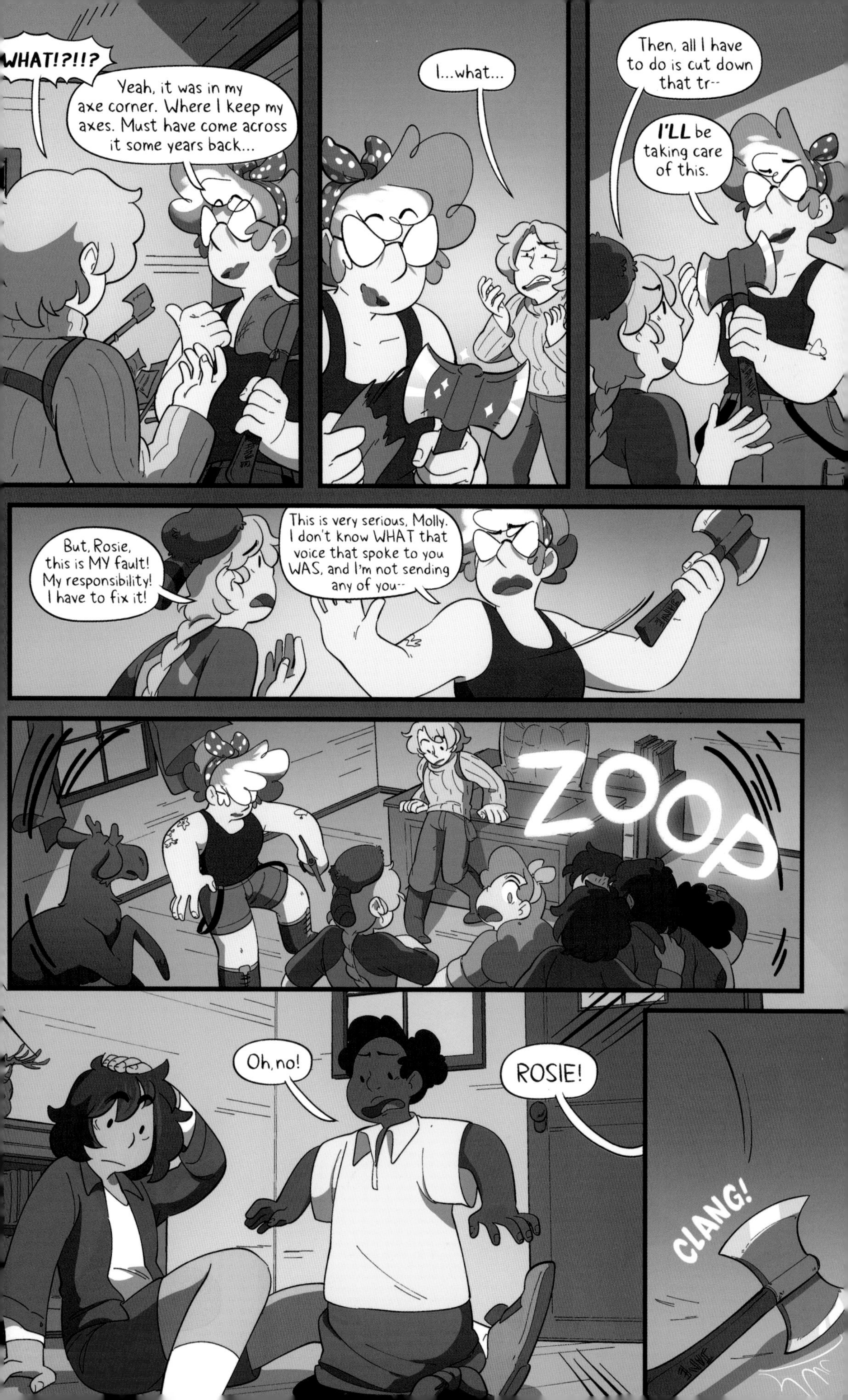
WHAT!?!!?
Yeah, it was in my axe corner. Where I keep my axes. Must have come across it some years back...
I...what...
Then, all I have to do is cut down that tr--
I'LL be taking care of this.
But, Rosie, this is MY fault! My responsibility! I have to fix it!
This is very serious, Molly. I don't know WHAT that voice that spoke to you WAS, and I'm not sending any of you--
ZOOP
Oh, no!
ROSIE!
CLANG!

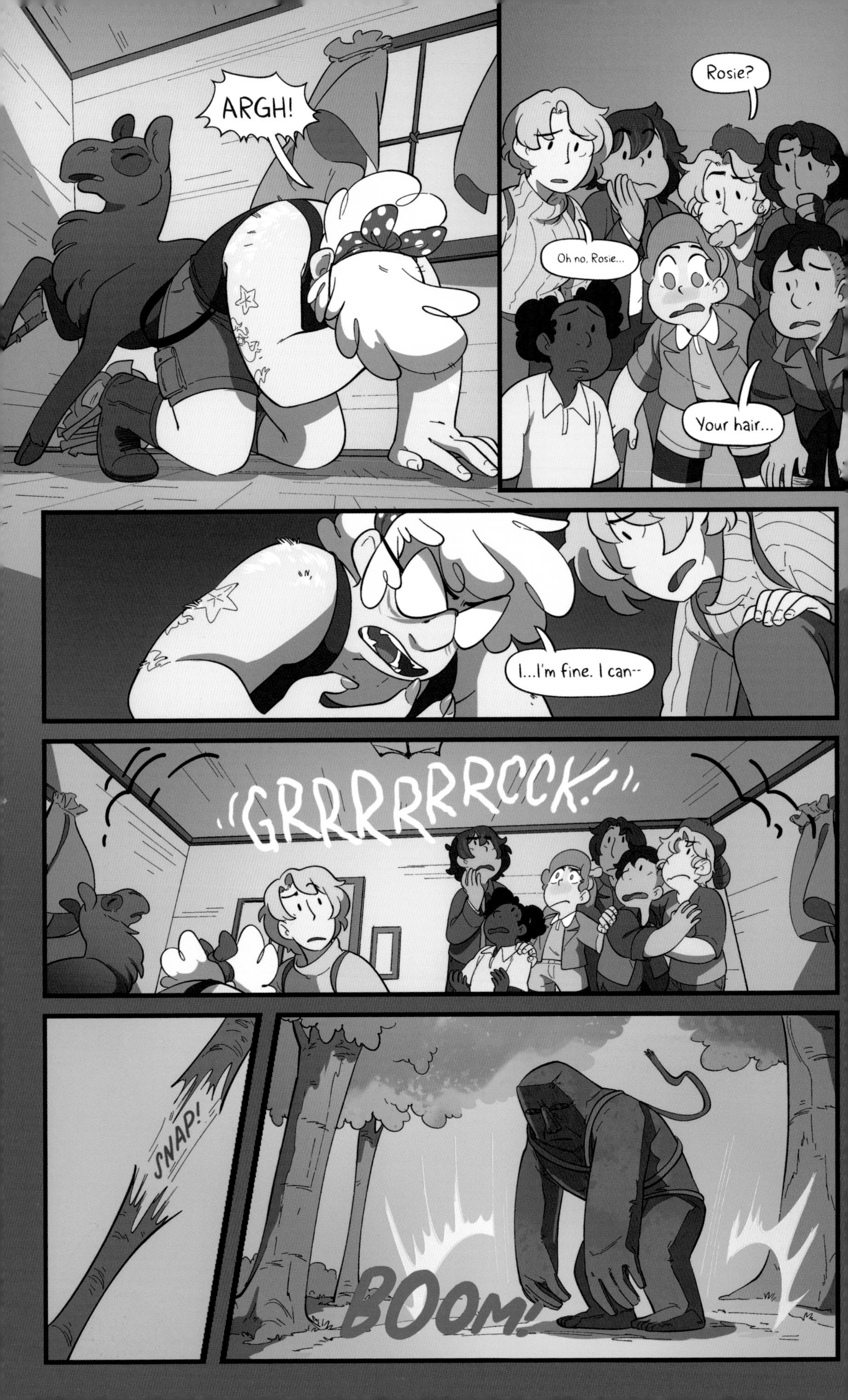
ARGH!
Rosie?
Oh no, Rosie...
Your hair...
I...I'm fine. I can--
GRRRRRRCCK
SNAP!
BOOM!

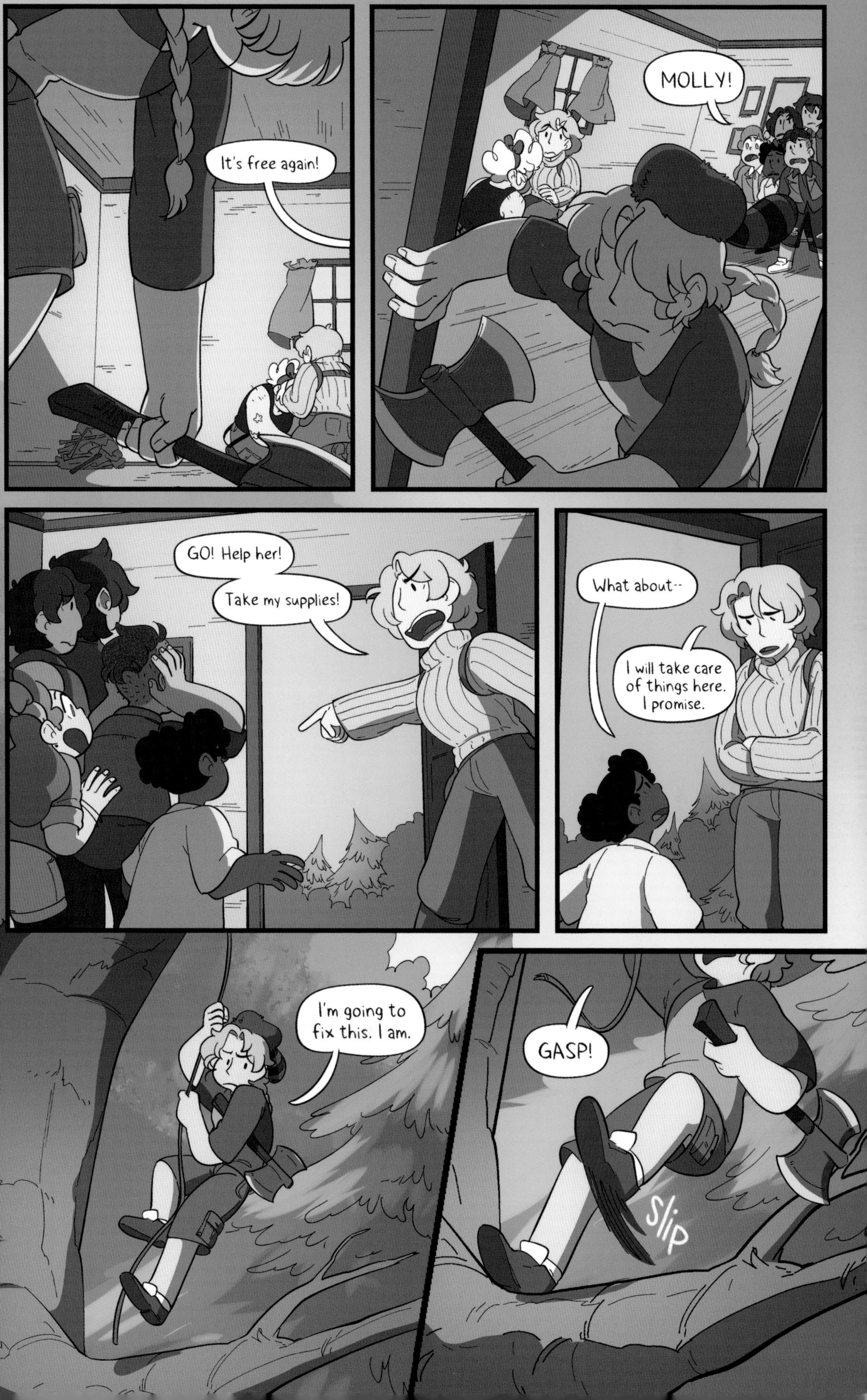
It's free again!
MOLLY!
GO! Help her!
Take my supplies!
What about--
I will take care of things here. I promise.
I'm going to fix this. I am.
GASP!
Slip

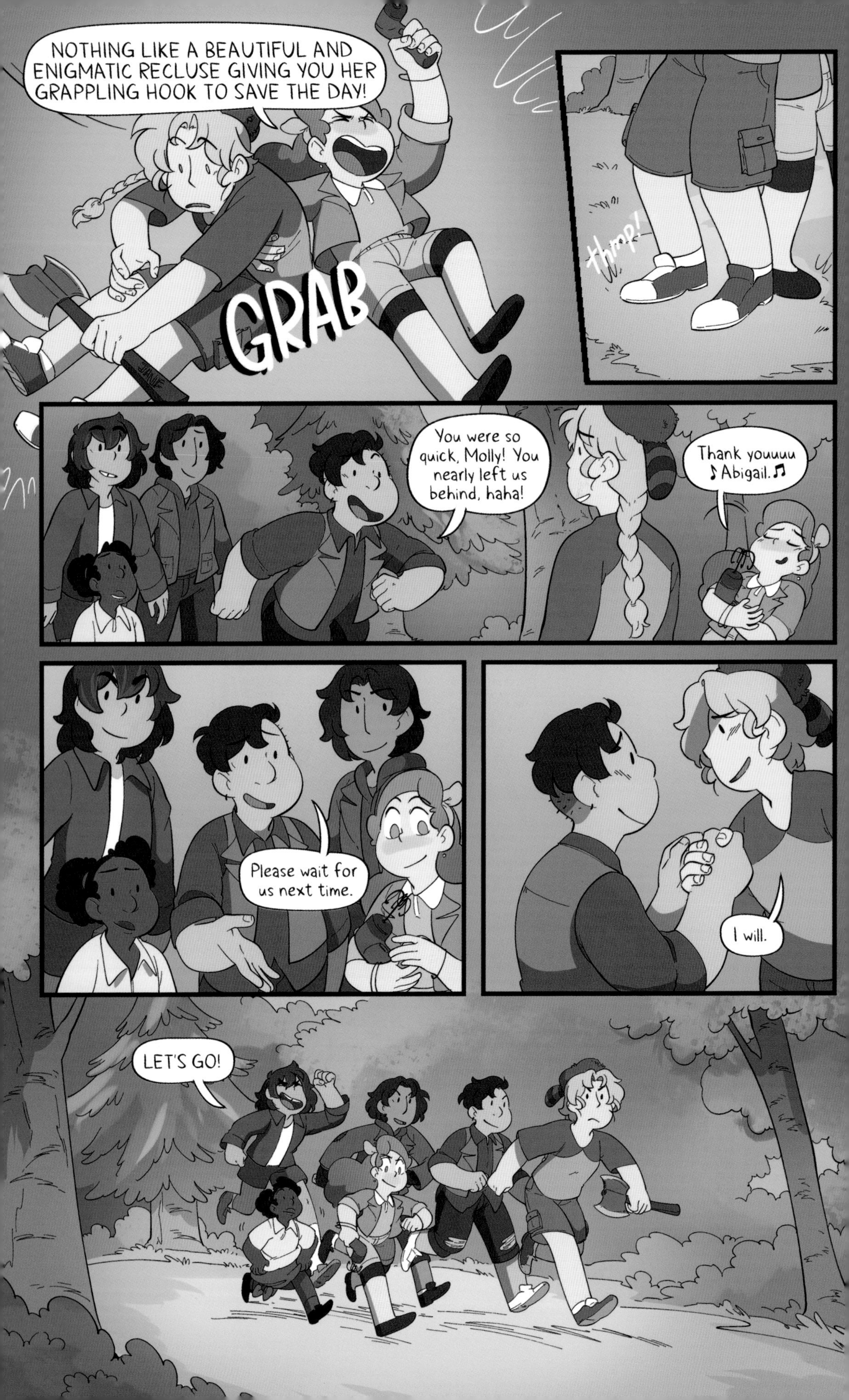
NOTHING LIKE A BEAUTIFUL AND ENIGMATIC RECLUSE GIVING YOU HER GRAPPLING HOOK TO SAVE THE DAY!
GRAB
thump!
You were so quick, Molly! You nearly left us behind, haha!
Thank youuuu ♪ Abigail. ♫
Please wait for us next time.
I will.
LET'S GO!

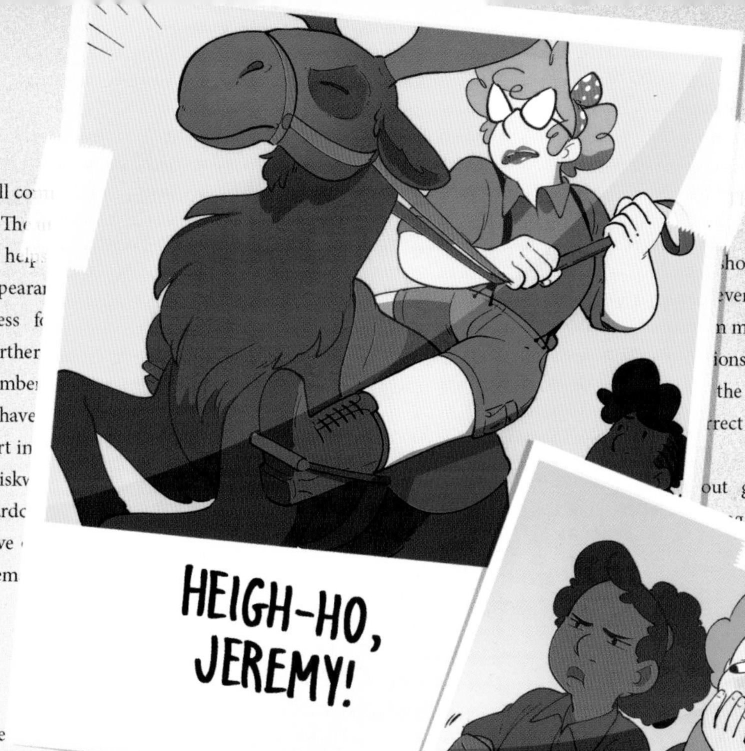
HEIGH-HO,
JEREMY!

will co...

The...
It help...
appeara...
dress f...
Further...
Lumbe...
to have...
part in...
Thiskw...
Hardc...
have...
them...

...HE UNIFORM

...hould be worn at camp
...events when Lumberjanes
...n may also be worn at other
...ions. It should be worn as a
... the uniform dress with
...rrect shoes, and stocking or

... out grows her uniform or
...other Lumberjane.
...a she has
... her
... her

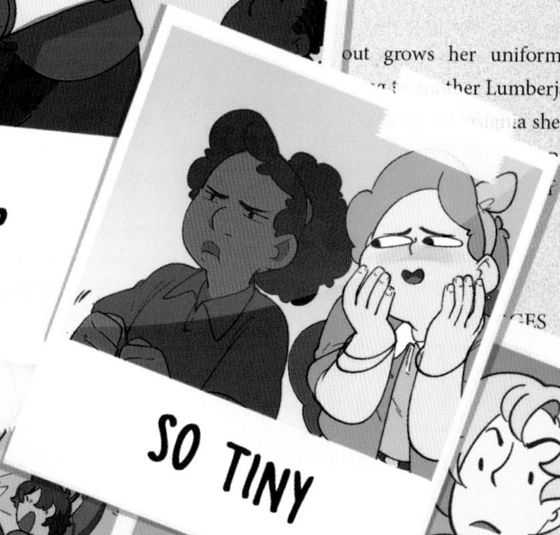
SO TINY

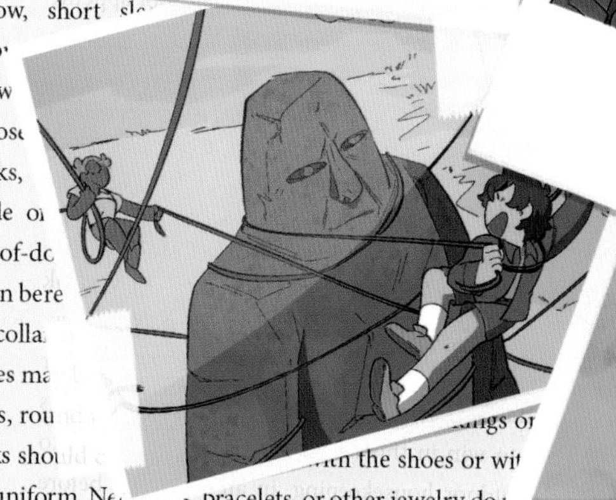

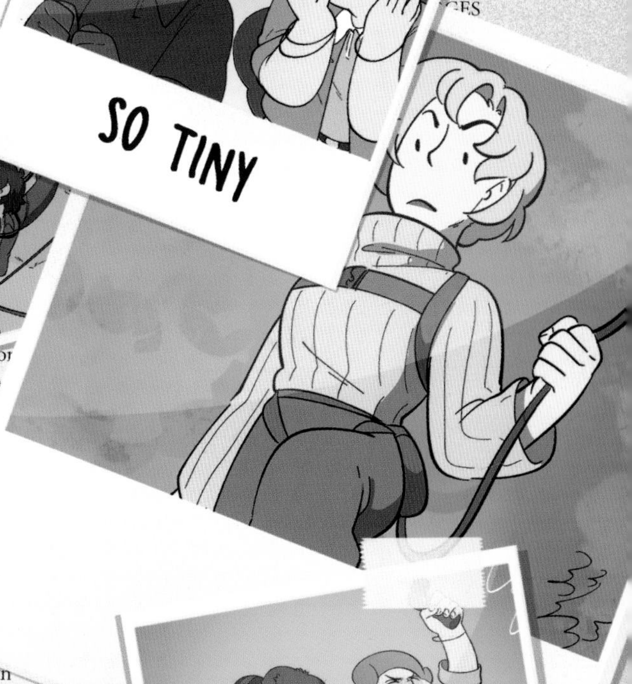

The...
yellow, short sl...
emb...
the w...
choose...
slacks,...
made o...
out-of-do...
green bere...
the colla...
Shoes ma...
heels, rou... ...ings or
socks shou... ...with the shoes or wi...
the uniform. Ne... ...es, bracelets, or other jewelry do...
belong with a Lumberjane uniform.

HOW TO WEAR THE UNIFORM

To look well in a uniform demands first of ... uniform be kept in good condition—clean ... pressed. See that the skirt is the right length for your own height and build, that the belt is adjusted to your waist, that your shoes and stockings are in keeping with the uniform, that you watch your posture and carry yourself with dignity and grace. If the beret is removed indoors, be sure that your hair is neat and kept in place with an inconspicuous clip or ribbon. When you wear a Lumberjane uniform you are identified as a member of this organization and you should be doubly careful to conduct yourself in a way that will show everyone that courtesy and thoughtfulness are part of being a Lumberjane. People are likely to judge a whole nation by the selfishness of a few individuals, to criticize a whole family because of the misconduct of one member, and to feel unkindly toward an organization because of the

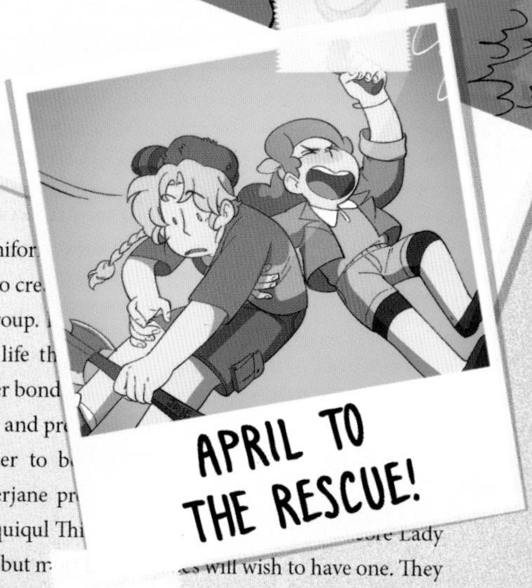
APRIL TO
THE RESCUE!

The unifor...
helps to cre...
in a group. ...
active life th...
another bond...
future, and pr...
in order to b...
Lumberjane pr...
Penniquiqul Thi... ...ore Lady
Types, but m... ...s will wish to have one. They
can either bu... ...uniform, or make it themselves from
materials available at the trading post.

LUMBERJANES FIELD MANUAL

CHAPTER
FORTY-FOUR

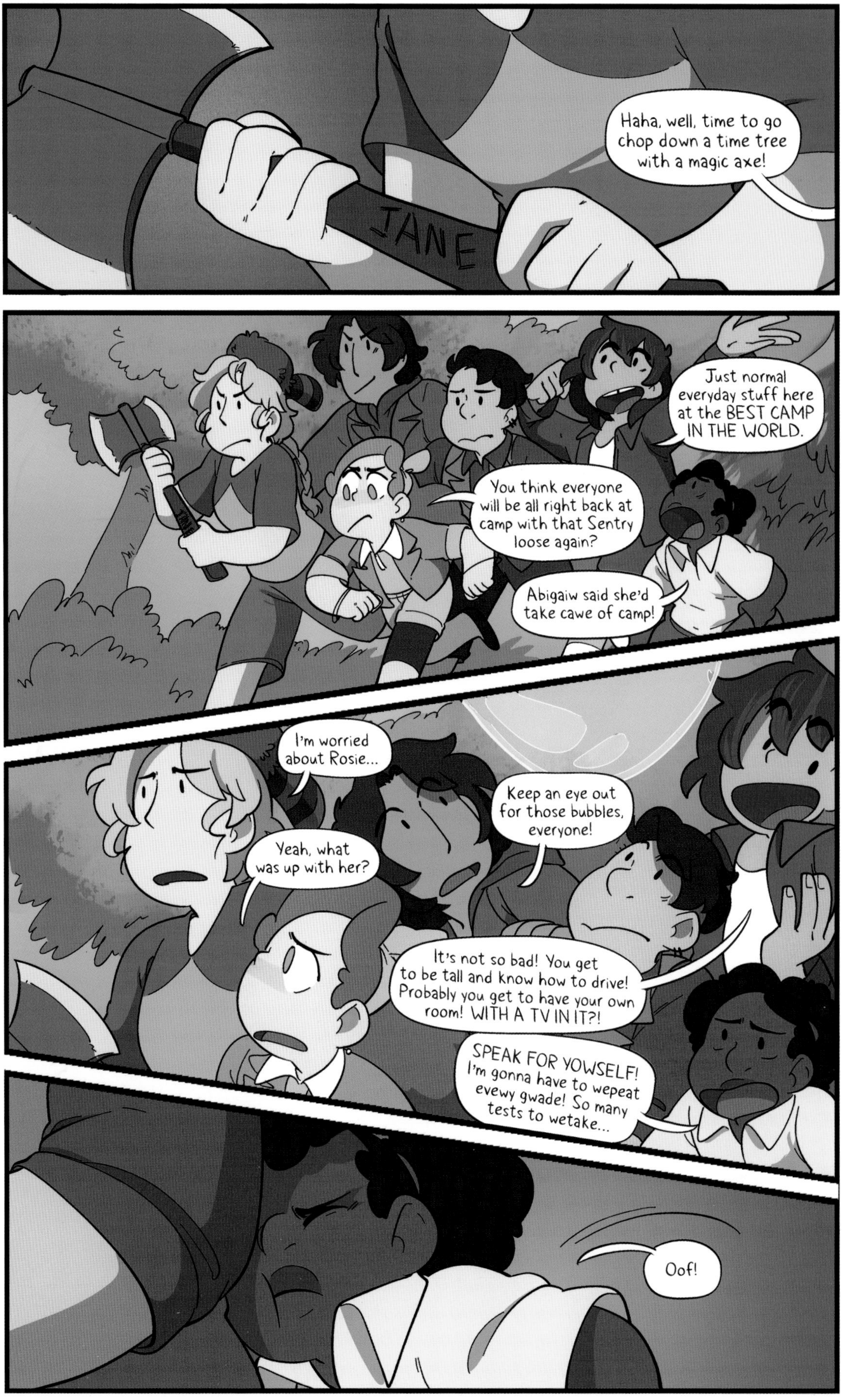
Haha, well, time to go chop down a time tree with a magic axe!
JANE
Just normal everyday stuff here at the BEST CAMP IN THE WORLD.
You think everyone will be all right back at camp with that Sentry loose again?
Abigaiw said she'd take cawe of camp!
I'm worried about Rosie...
Keep an eye out for those bubbles, everyone!
Yeah, what was up with her?
It's not so bad! You get to be tall and know how to drive! Probably you get to have your own room! WITH A TV IN IT?!
SPEAK FOR YOWSELF! I'm gonna have to wepeat evewy gwade! So many tests to wetake...
Oof!

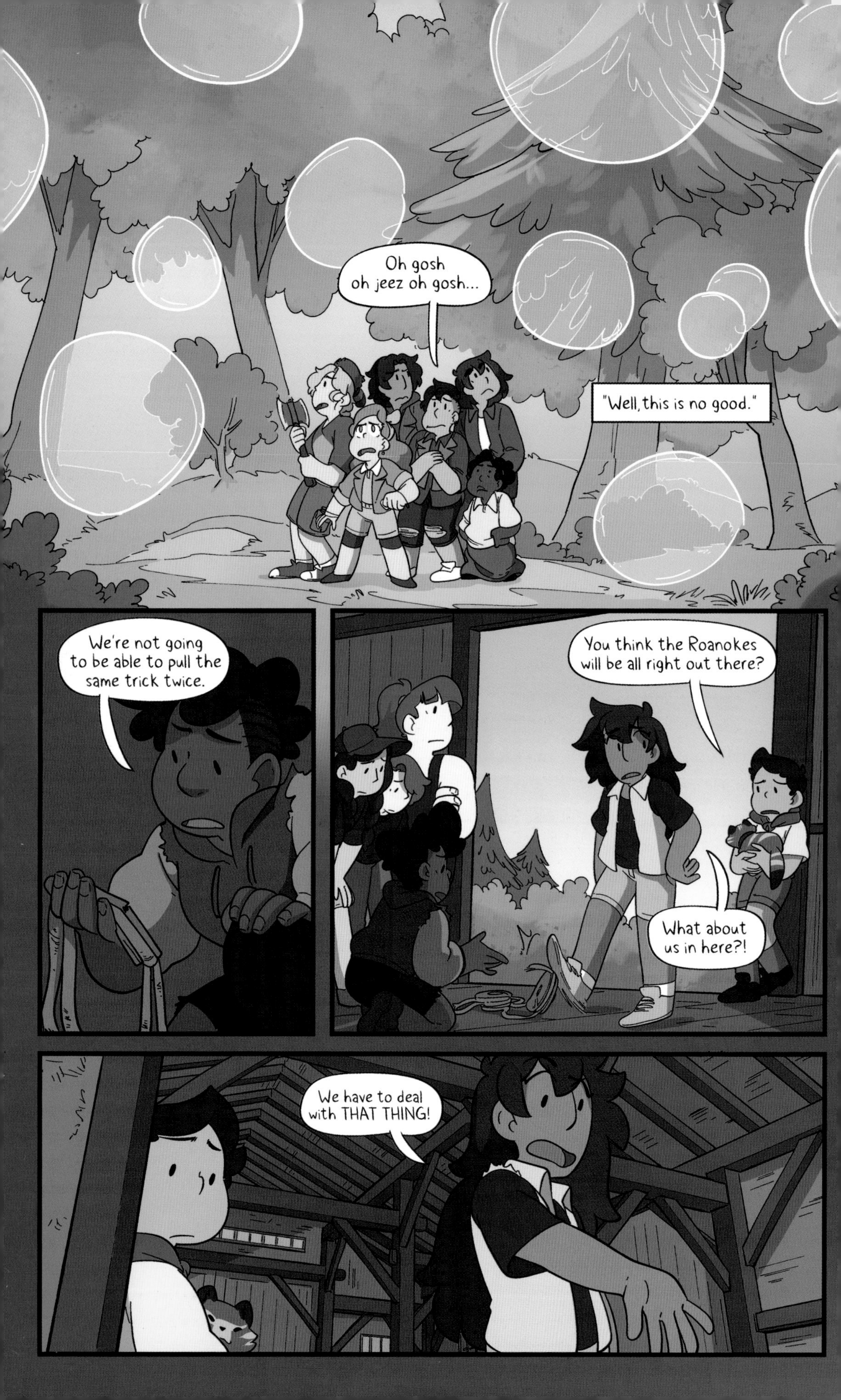
Oh gosh oh jeez oh gosh...
"Well, this is no good."
We're not going to be able to pull the same trick twice.
You think the Roanokes will be all right out there?
What about us in here?!
We have to deal with THAT THING!

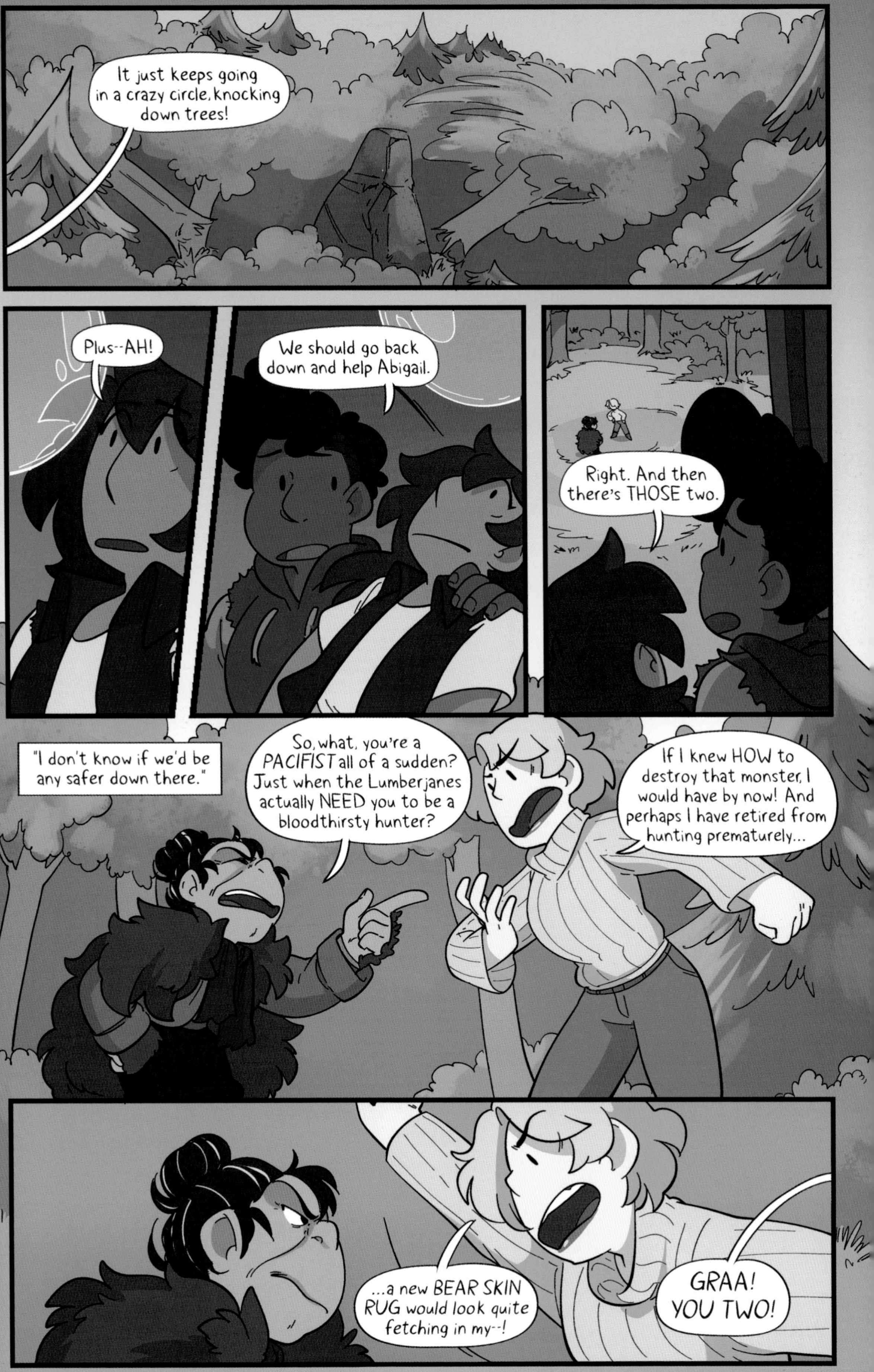
It just keeps going in a crazy circle, knocking down trees!
Plus--AH!
We should go back down and help Abigail.
Right. And then there's THOSE two.
"I don't know if we'd be any safer down there."
So, what, you're a PACIFIST all of a sudden? Just when the Lumberjanes actually NEED you to be a bloodthirsty hunter?
If I knew HOW to destroy that monster, I would have by now! And perhaps I have retired from hunting prematurely...
...a new BEAR SKIN RUG would look quite fetching in my--!
GRAA! YOU TWO!

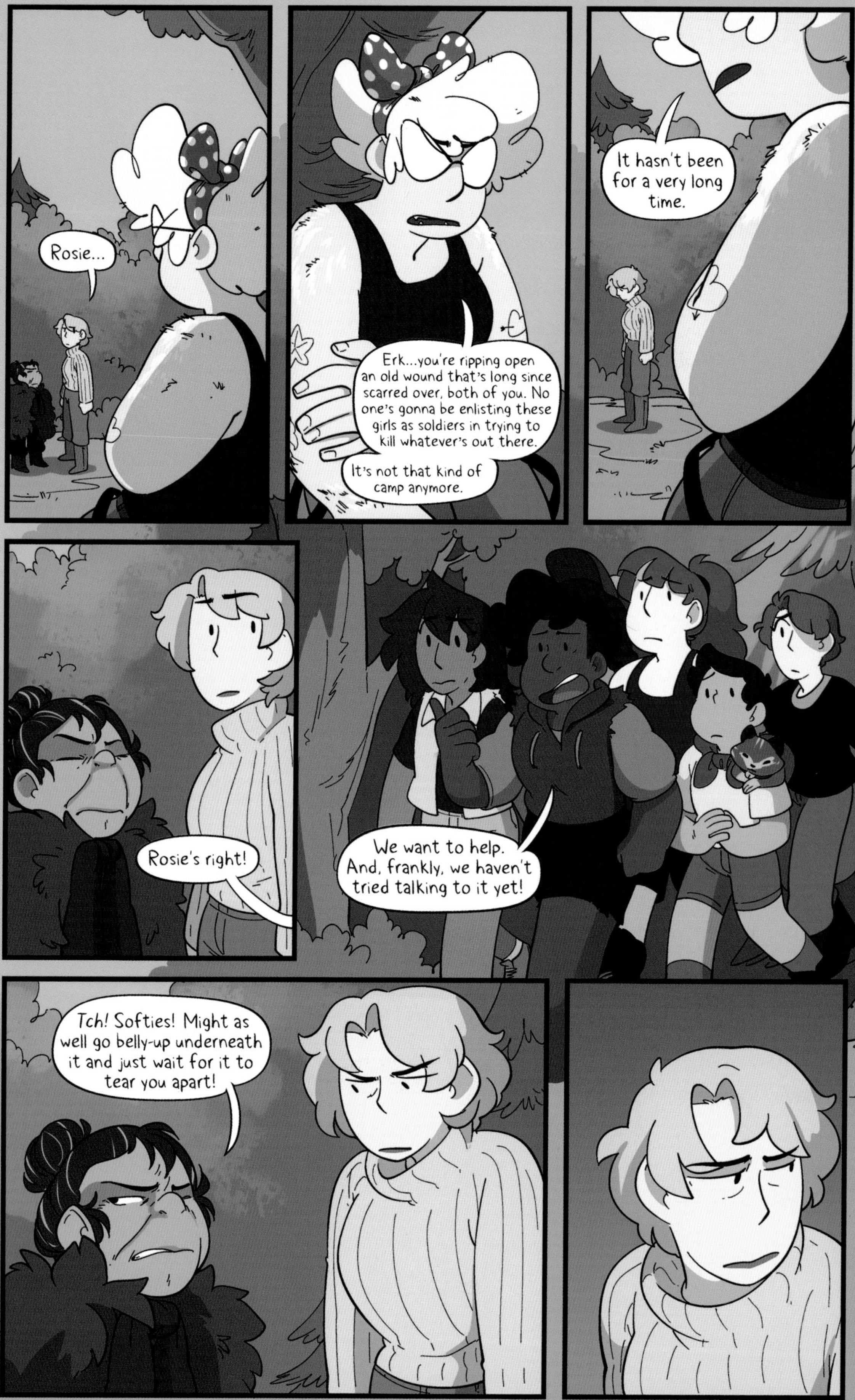
Rosie...
Erk...you're ripping open an old wound that's long since scarred over, both of you. No one's gonna be enlisting these girls as soldiers in trying to kill whatever's out there.
It's not that kind of camp anymore.
It hasn't been for a very long time.
Rosie's right!
We want to help. And, frankly, we haven't tried talking to it yet!
Tch! Softies! Might as well go belly-up underneath it and just wait for it to tear you apart!

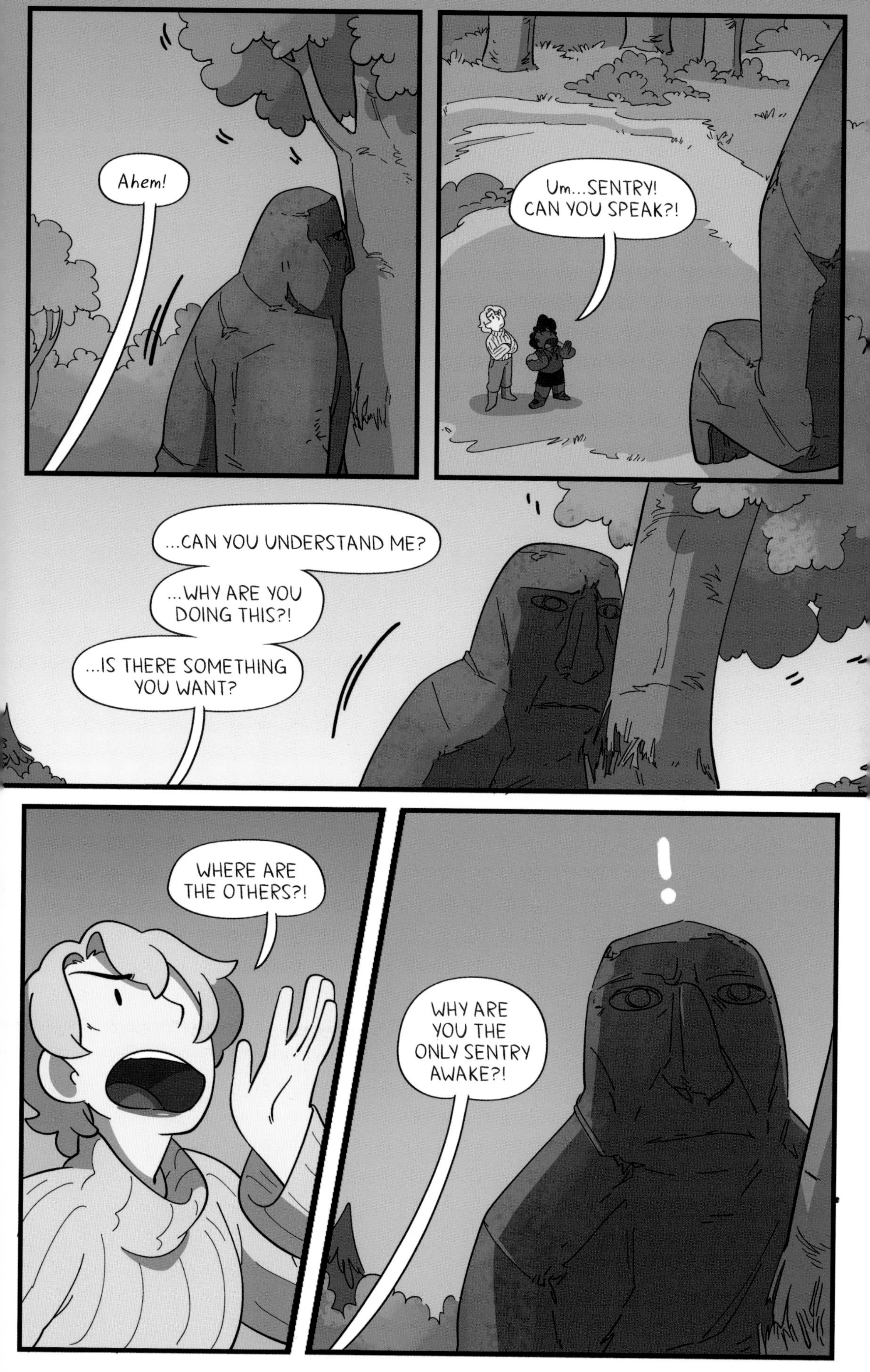
Ahem!
Um...SENTRY! CAN YOU SPEAK?!
...CAN YOU UNDERSTAND ME?
...WHY ARE YOU DOING THIS?!
...IS THERE SOMETHING YOU WANT?
WHERE ARE THE OTHERS?!
!
WHY ARE YOU THE ONLY SENTRY AWAKE?!

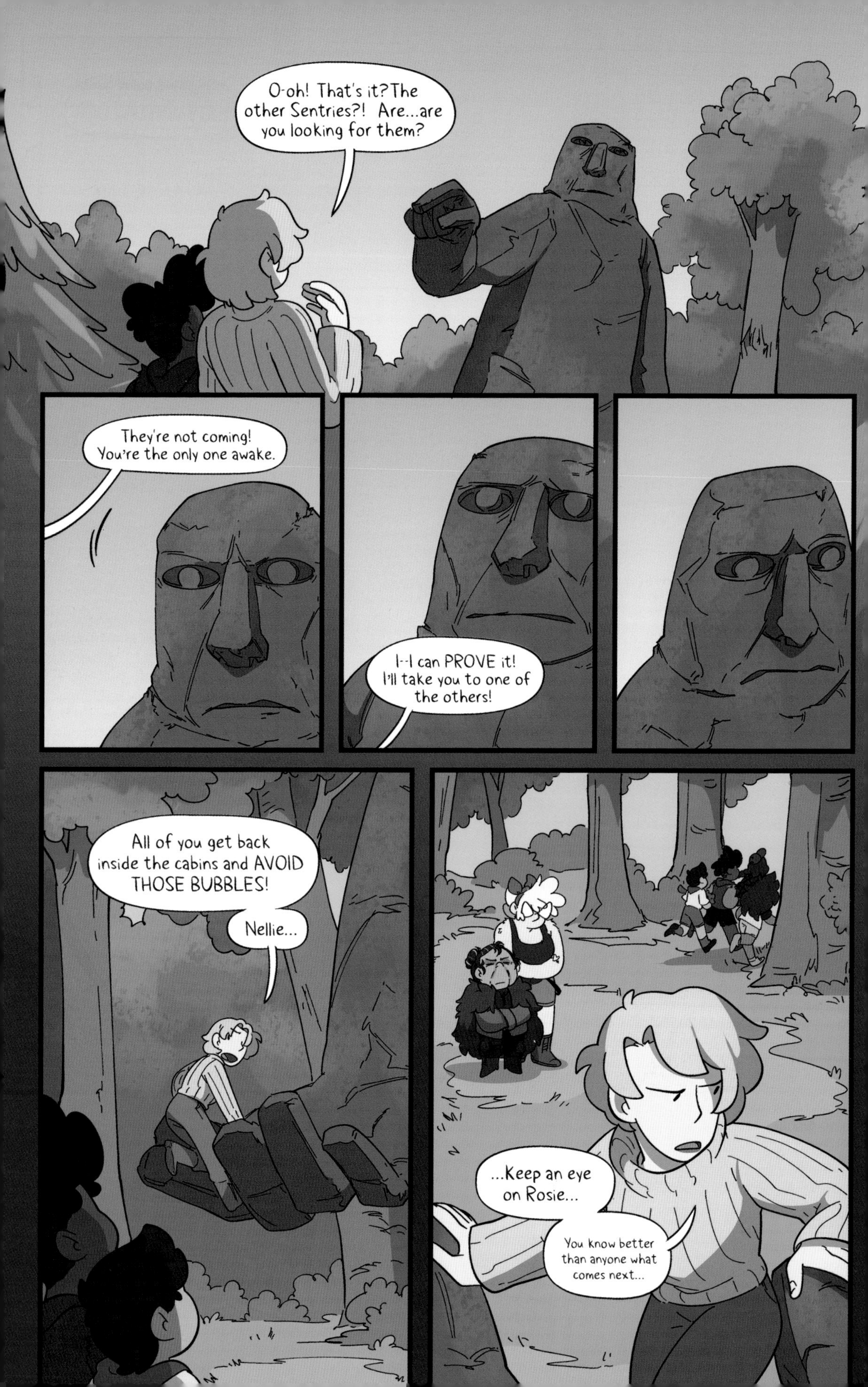
O-oh! That's it? The other Sentries?! Are...are you looking for them?
They're not coming! You're the only one awake.
I--I can PROVE it! I'll take you to one of the others!
All of you get back inside the cabins and AVOID THOSE BUBBLES!
Nellie...
...Keep an eye on Rosie...
You know better than anyone what comes next...

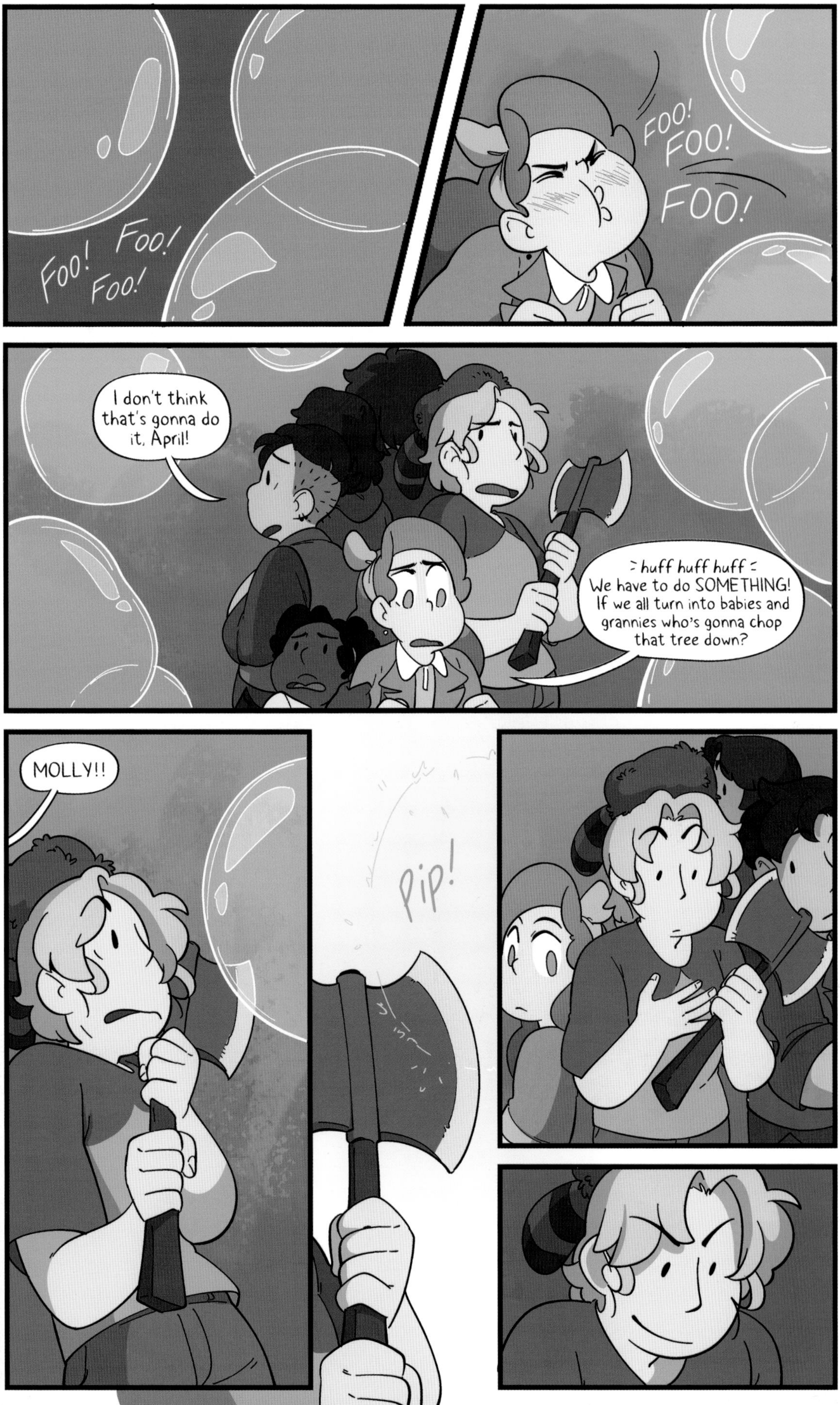
Foo! Foo!
Foo!
FOO!
FOO!
FOO!
I don't think that's gonna do it, April!
= huff huff huff =
We have to do SOMETHING! If we all turn into babies and grannies who's gonna chop that tree down?
MOLLY!!
Pip!

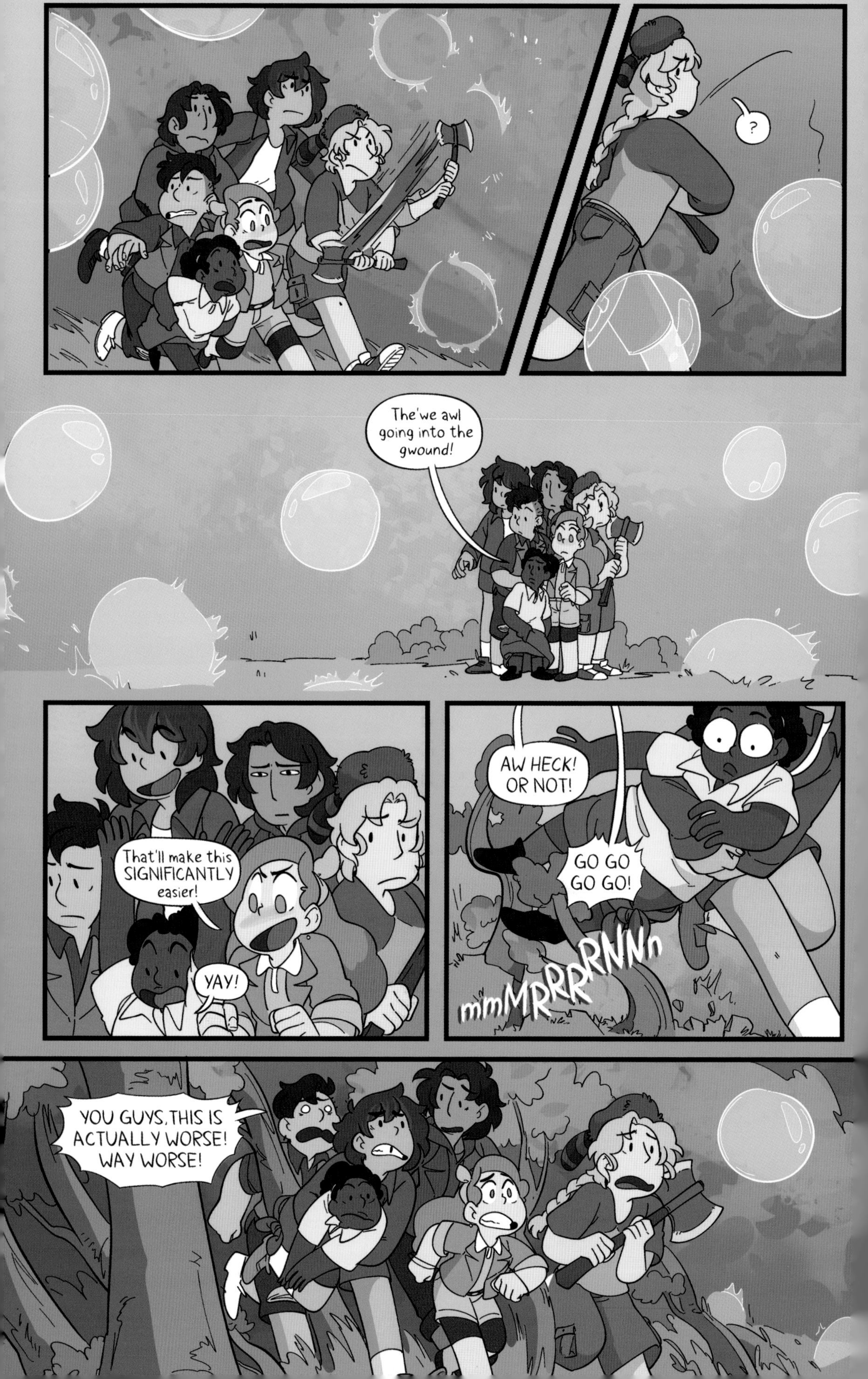
?
The'we awl going into the gwound!
That'll make this SIGNIFICANTLY easier!
YAY!
AW HECK! OR NOT!
GO GO GO GO!
mmMRRRRNNn
YOU GUYS, THIS IS ACTUALLY WORSE! WAY WORSE!

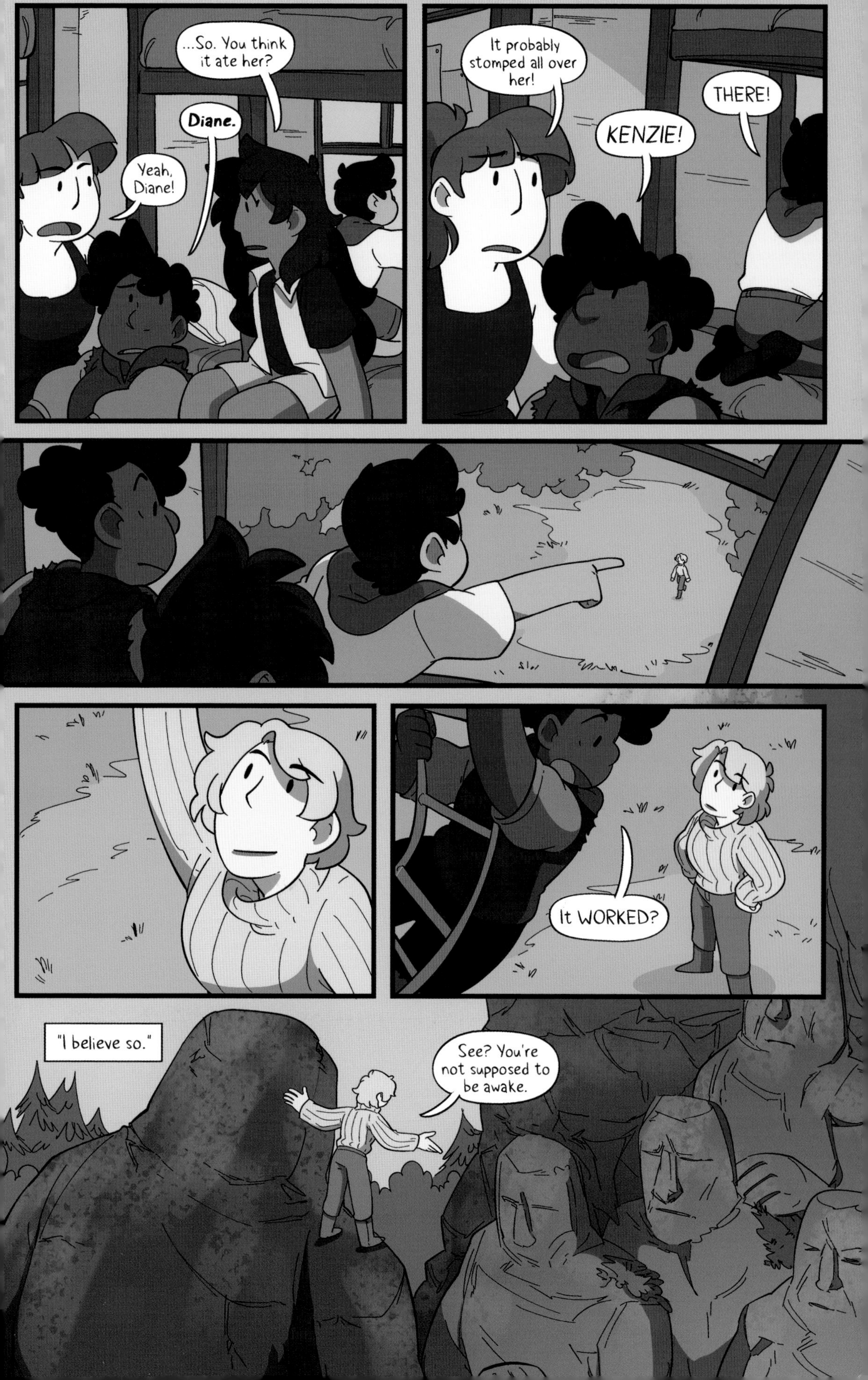
...So. You think it ate her?
Diane.
Yeah, Diane!
It probably stomped all over her!
KENZIE!
THERE!
It WORKED?
"I believe so."
See? You're not supposed to be awake.

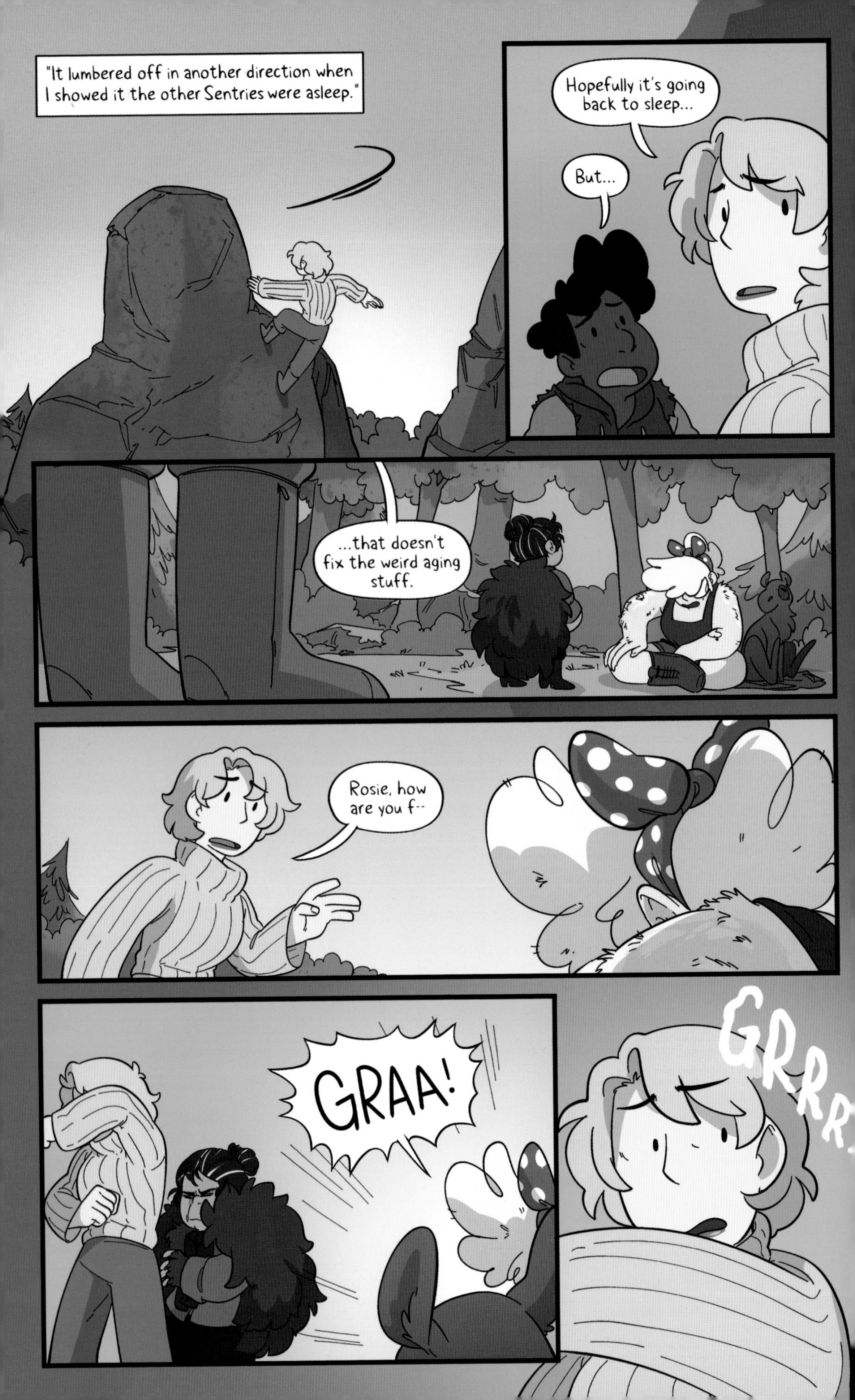
"It lumbered off in another direction when I showed it the other Sentries were asleep."
Hopefully it's going back to sleep...
But...
...that doesn't fix the weird aging stuff.
Rosie, how are you f--
GRAA!
GRRR.

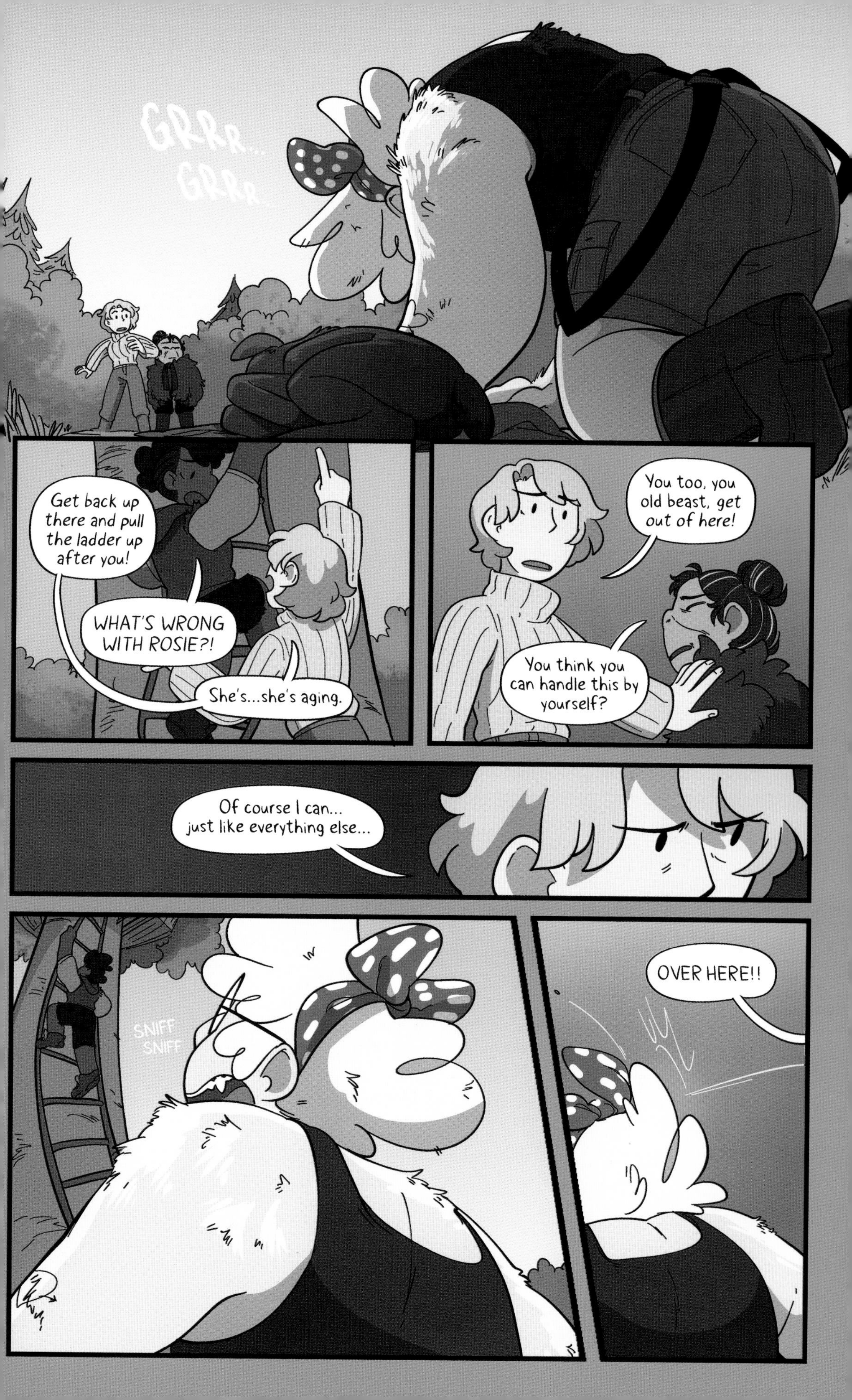
GRRR...
GRRR...
Get back up there and pull the ladder up after you!
WHAT'S WRONG WITH ROSIE?!
She's...she's aging.
You too, you old beast, get out of here!
You think you can handle this by yourself?
Of course I can... just like everything else...
SNIFF SNIFF
OVER HERE!!

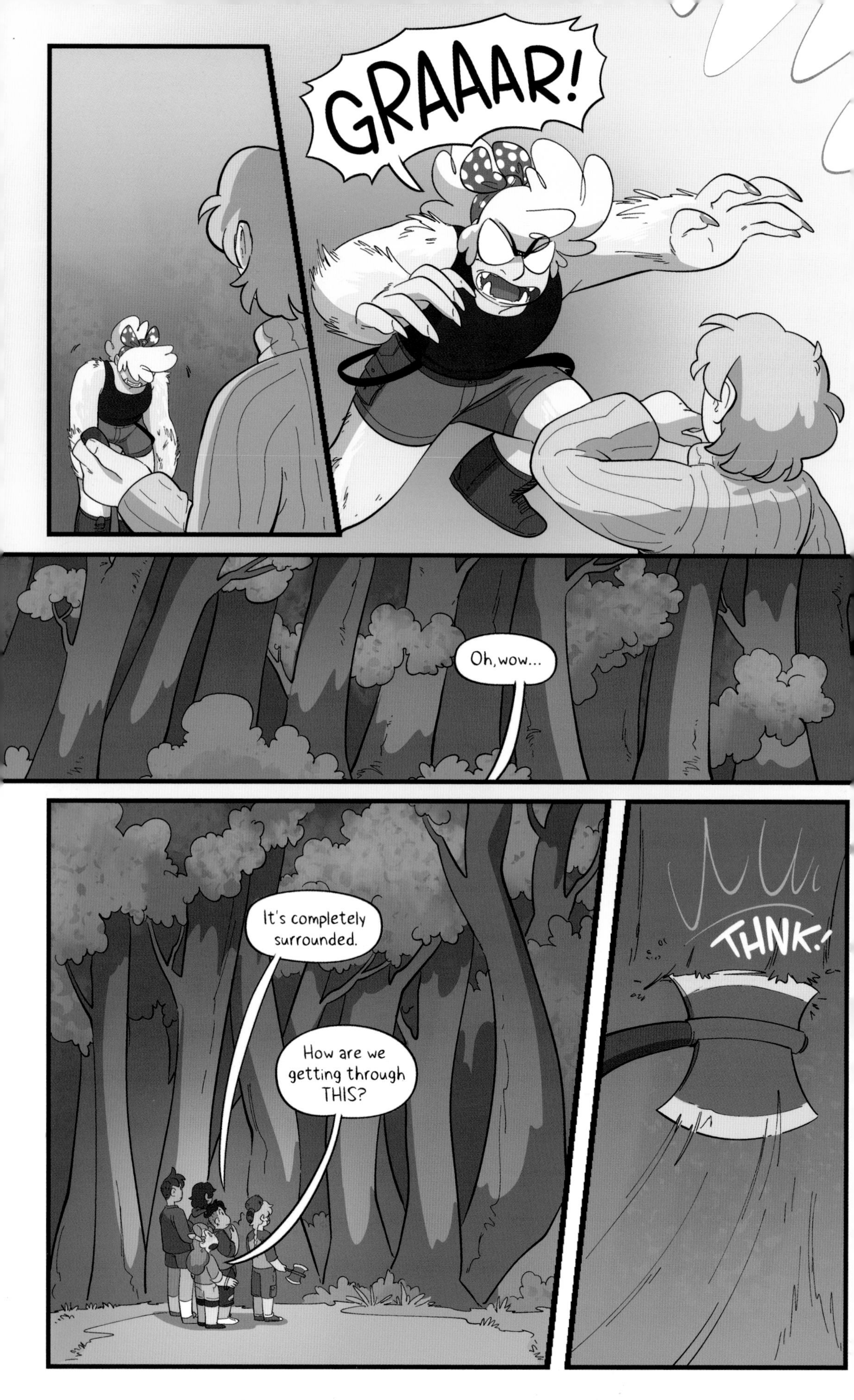
GRAAAR!
Oh, wow...
It's completely surrounded.
How are we getting through THIS?
THNK!

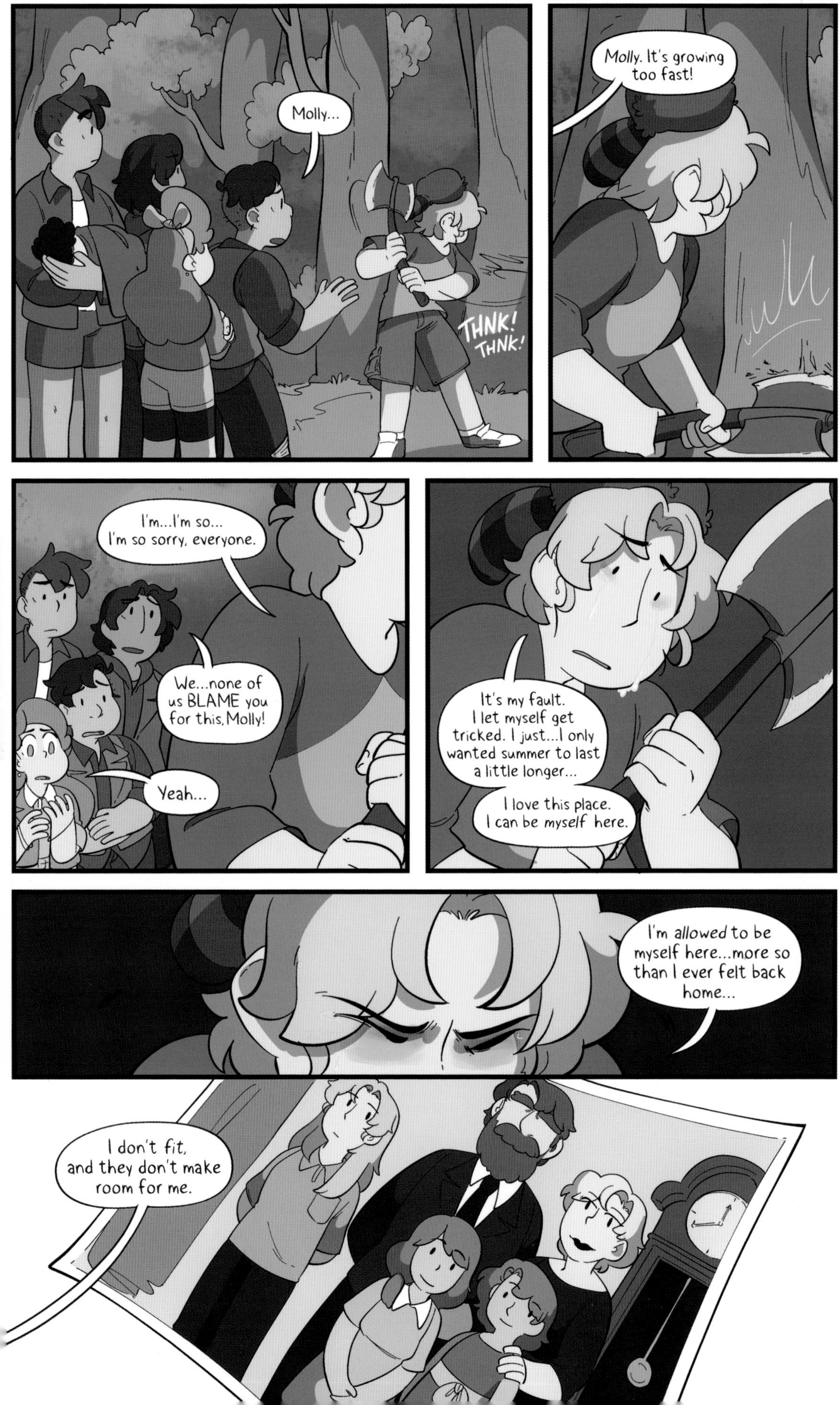
Molly...
THNK! THNK!
Molly. It's growing too fast!
I'm...I'm so... I'm so sorry, everyone.
We...none of us BLAME you for this, Molly!
Yeah...
It's my fault. I let myself get tricked. I just...I only wanted summer to last a little longer...
I love this place. I can be myself here.
I'm allowed to be myself here...more so than I ever felt back home...
I don't fit, and they don't make room for me.

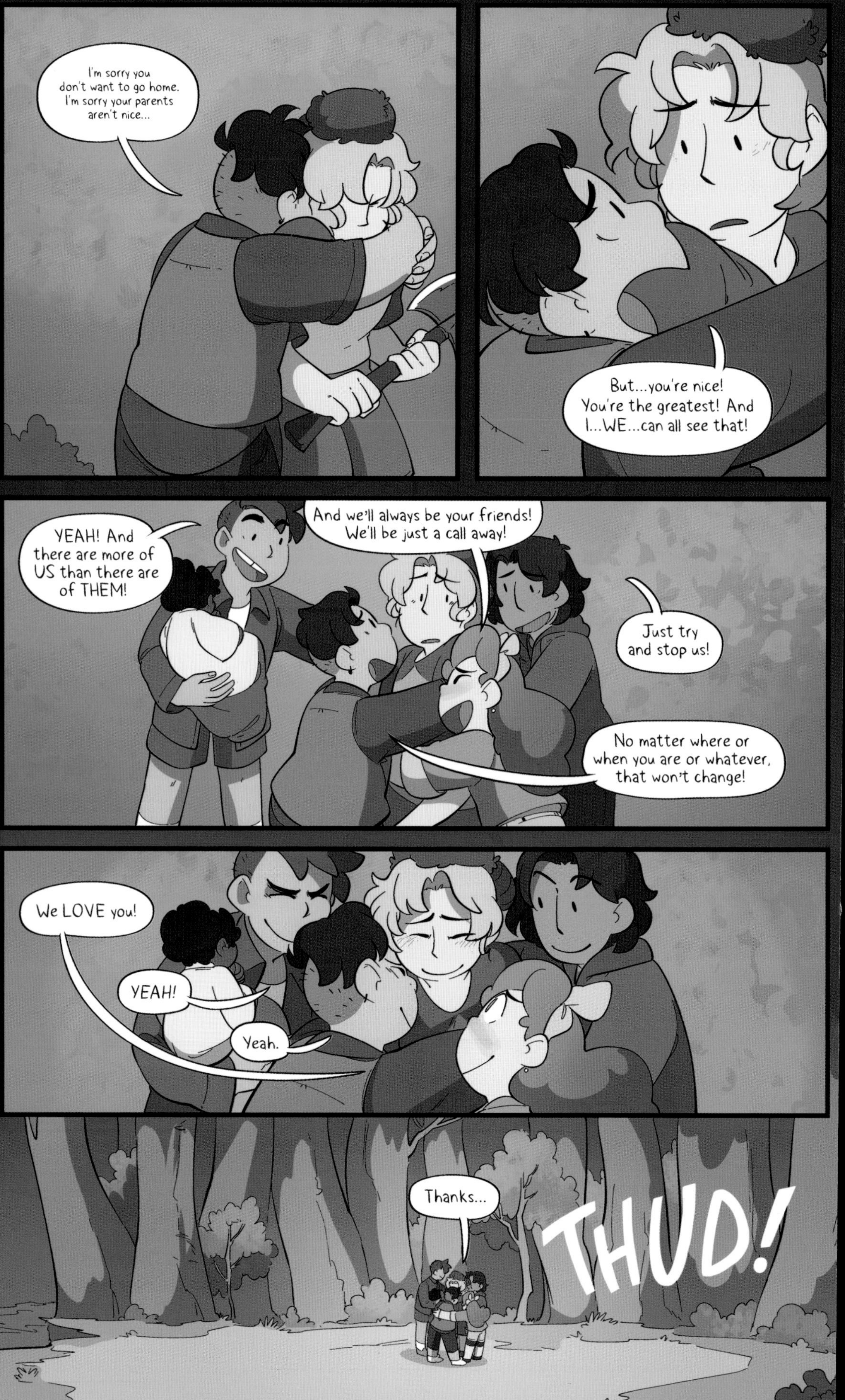
I'm sorry you don't want to go home. I'm sorry your parents aren't nice...
But...you're nice! You're the greatest! And I...WE...can all see that!
YEAH! And there are more of US than there are of THEM!
And we'll always be your friends! We'll be just a call away!
Just try and stop us!
No matter where or when you are or whatever, that won't change!
We LOVE you!
YEAH!
Yeah.
Thanks...
THUD!

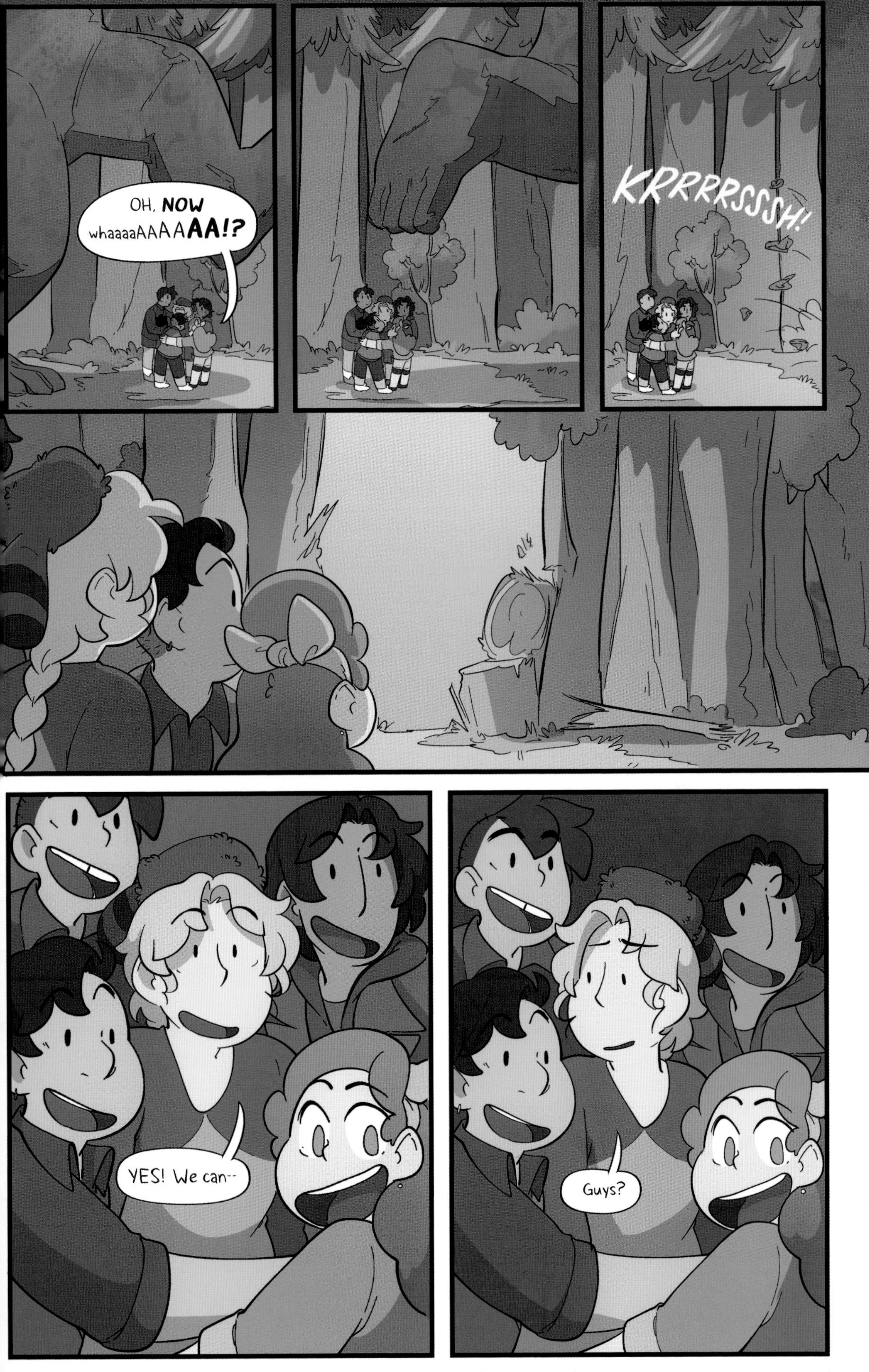
OH, NOW whaaaaAAAAAA!?
KRRRRSSSH!
YES! We can--
Guys?

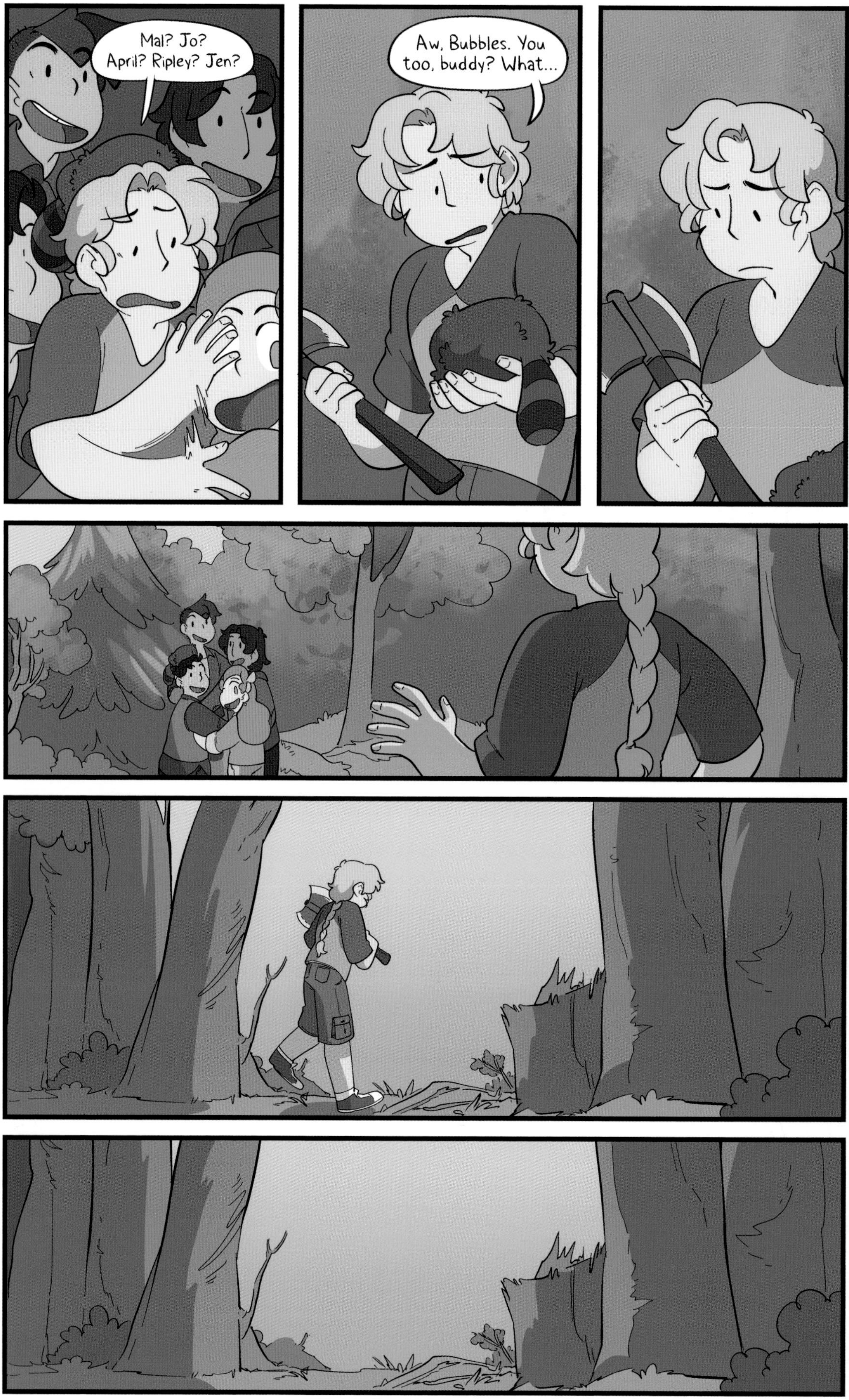
Mal? Jo?
April? Ripley? Jen?
Aw, Bubbles. You
too, buddy? What...

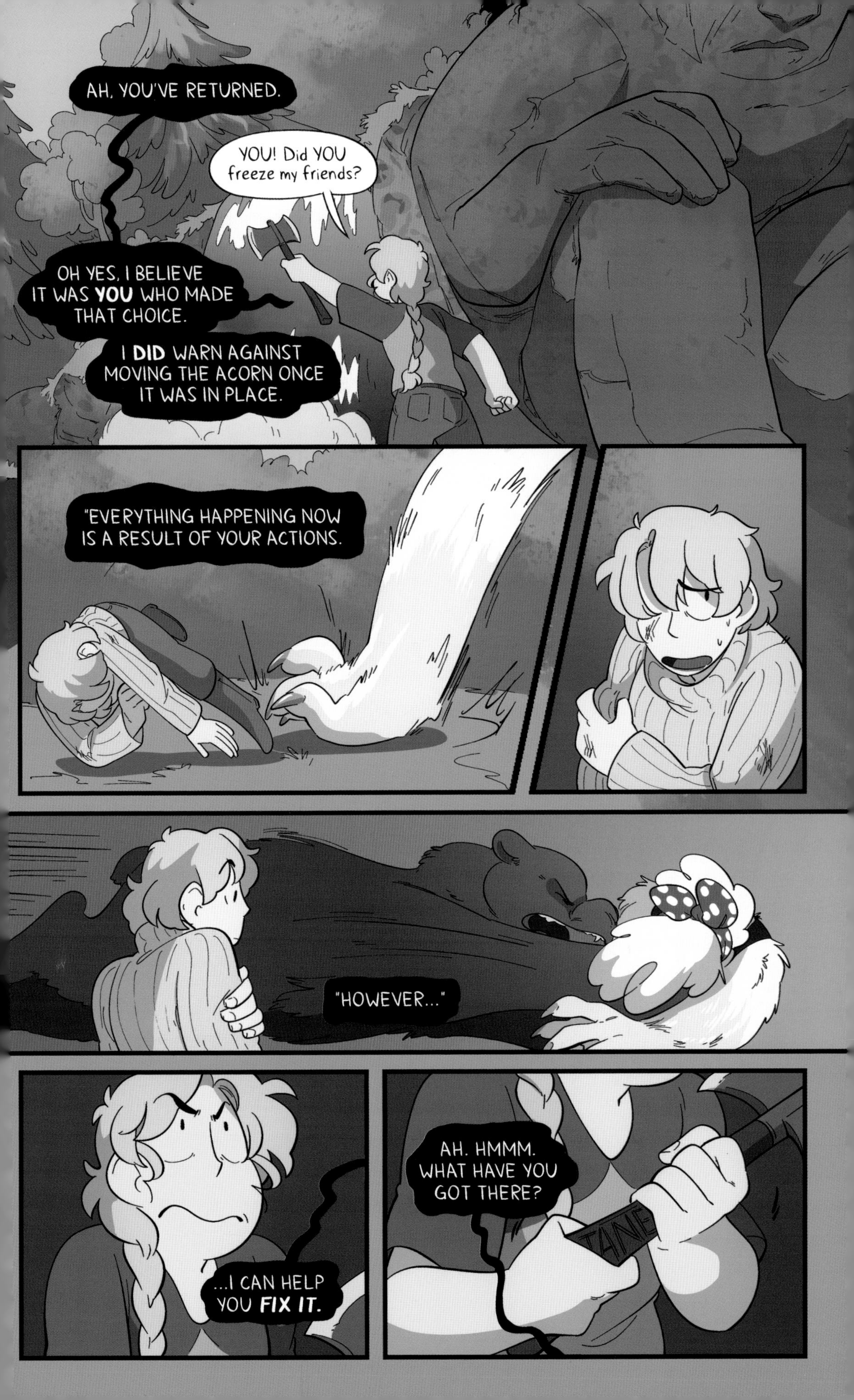
AH, YOU'VE RETURNED.
YOU! Did YOU freeze my friends?
OH YES, I BELIEVE IT WAS YOU WHO MADE THAT CHOICE.
I DID WARN AGAINST MOVING THE ACORN ONCE IT WAS IN PLACE.
"EVERYTHING HAPPENING NOW IS A RESULT OF YOUR ACTIONS.
"HOWEVER..."
...I CAN HELP YOU FIX IT.
AH. HMMM. WHAT HAVE YOU GOT THERE?
JANE

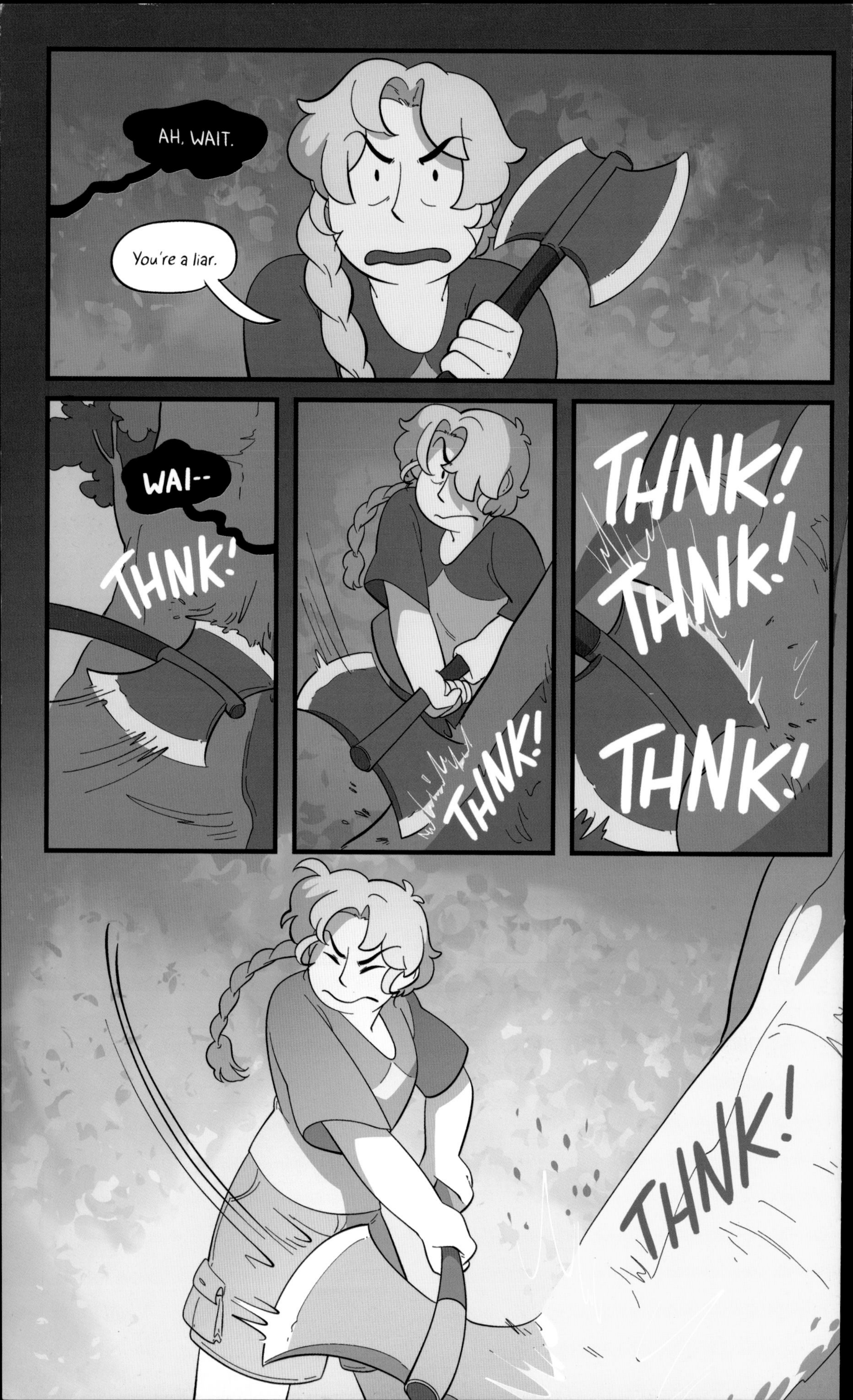
AH, WAIT.
You're a liar.
WAI--
THNK!
THNK!
THNK!
THNK!
THNK!
THNK!

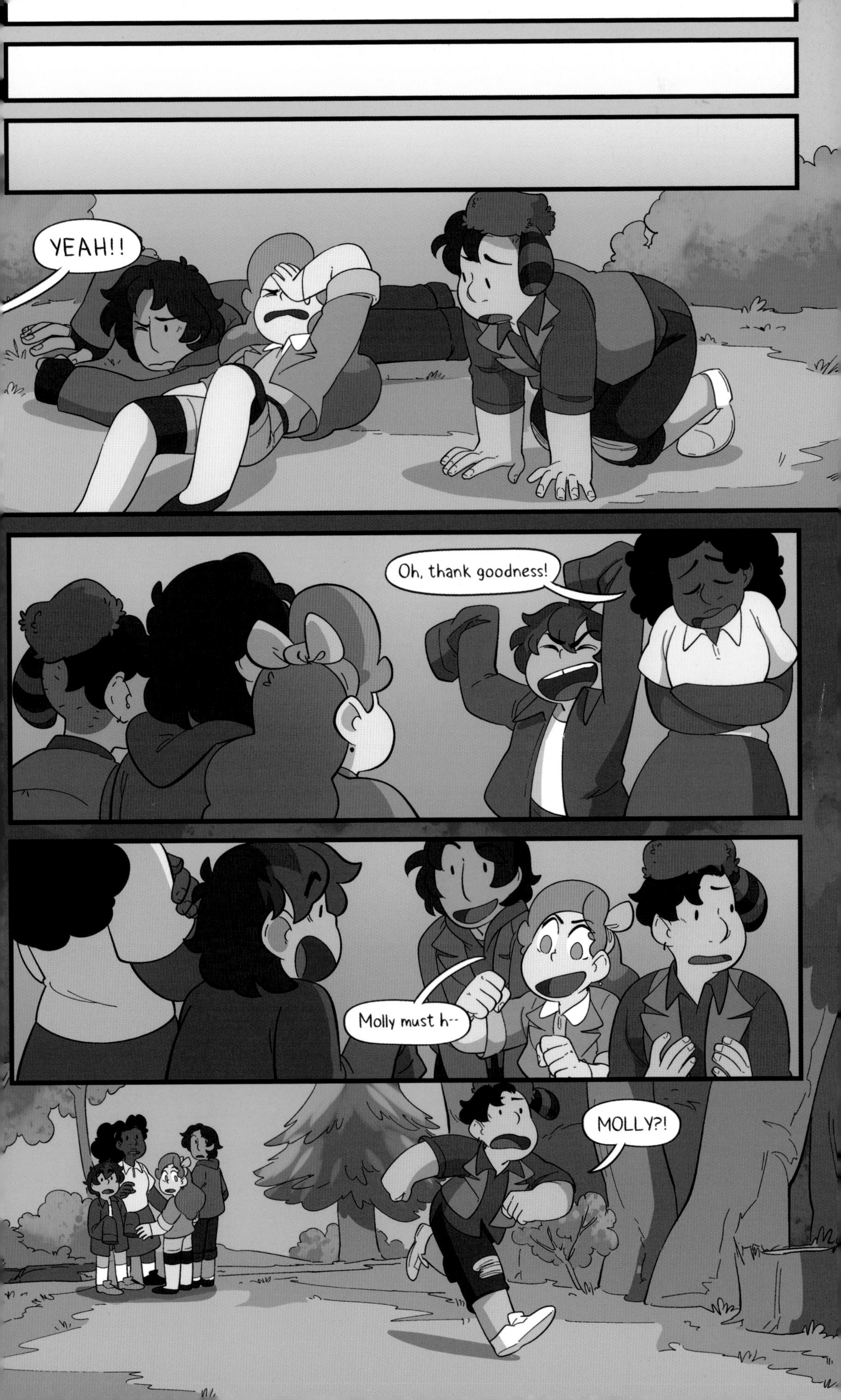
YEAH!!
Oh, thank goodness!
Molly must h--
MOLLY?!

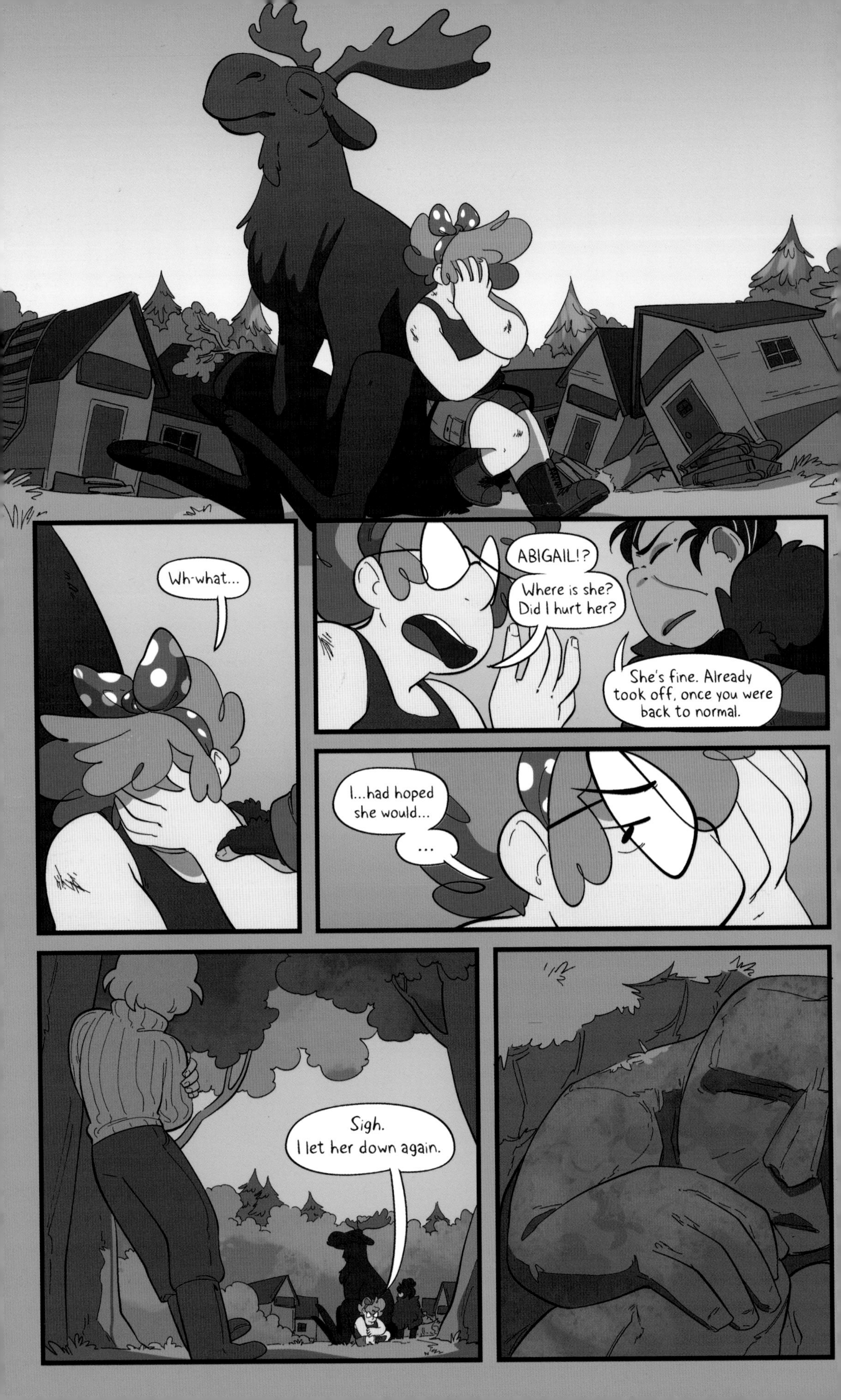
Wh-what...
ABIGAIL!?
Where is she? Did I hurt her?
She's fine. Already took off, once you were back to normal.
I...had hoped she would...
...
Sigh. I let her down again.

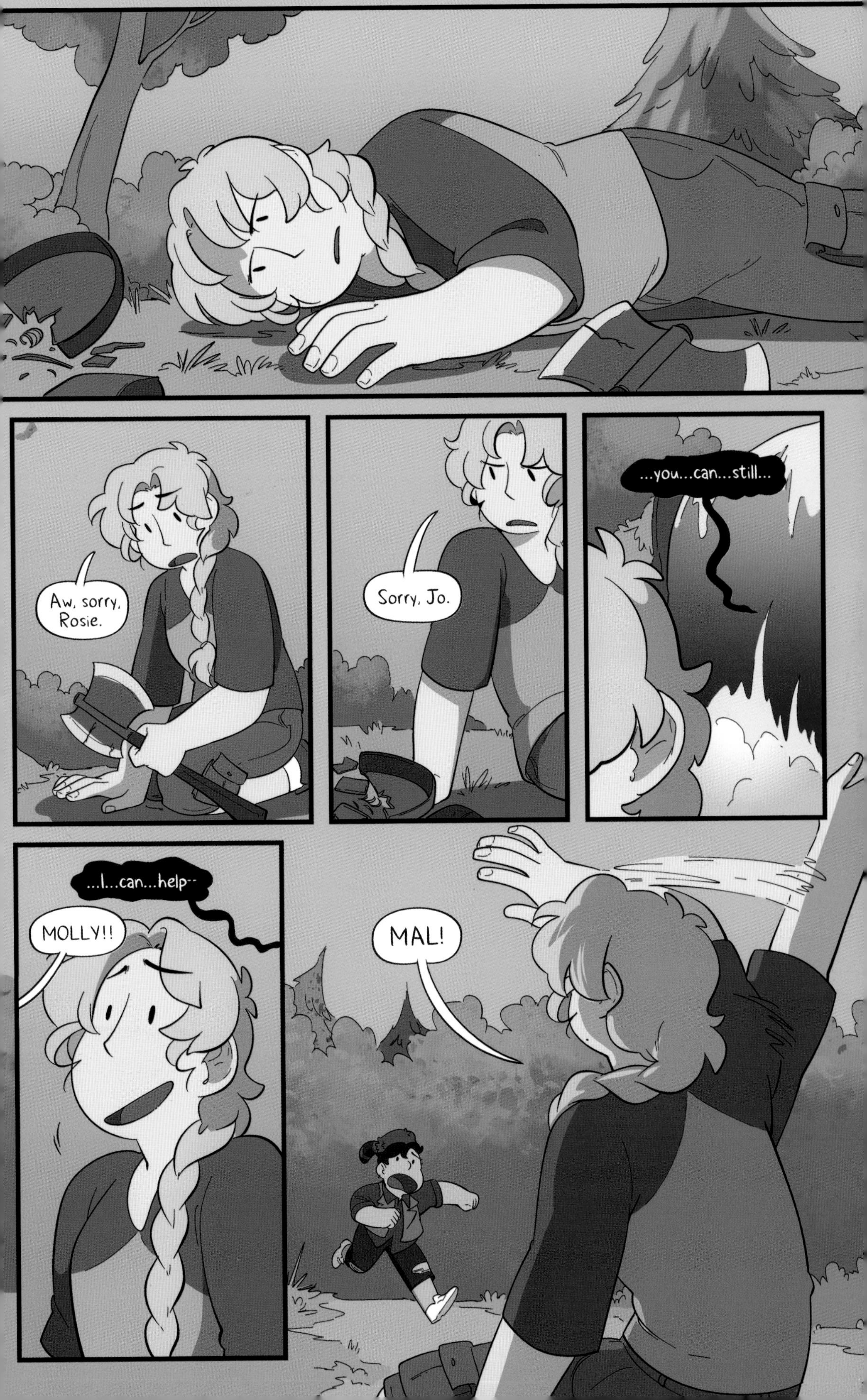
Aw, sorry, Rosie.
Sorry, Jo.
...you...can...still...
...I...can...help--
MOLLY!!
MAL!

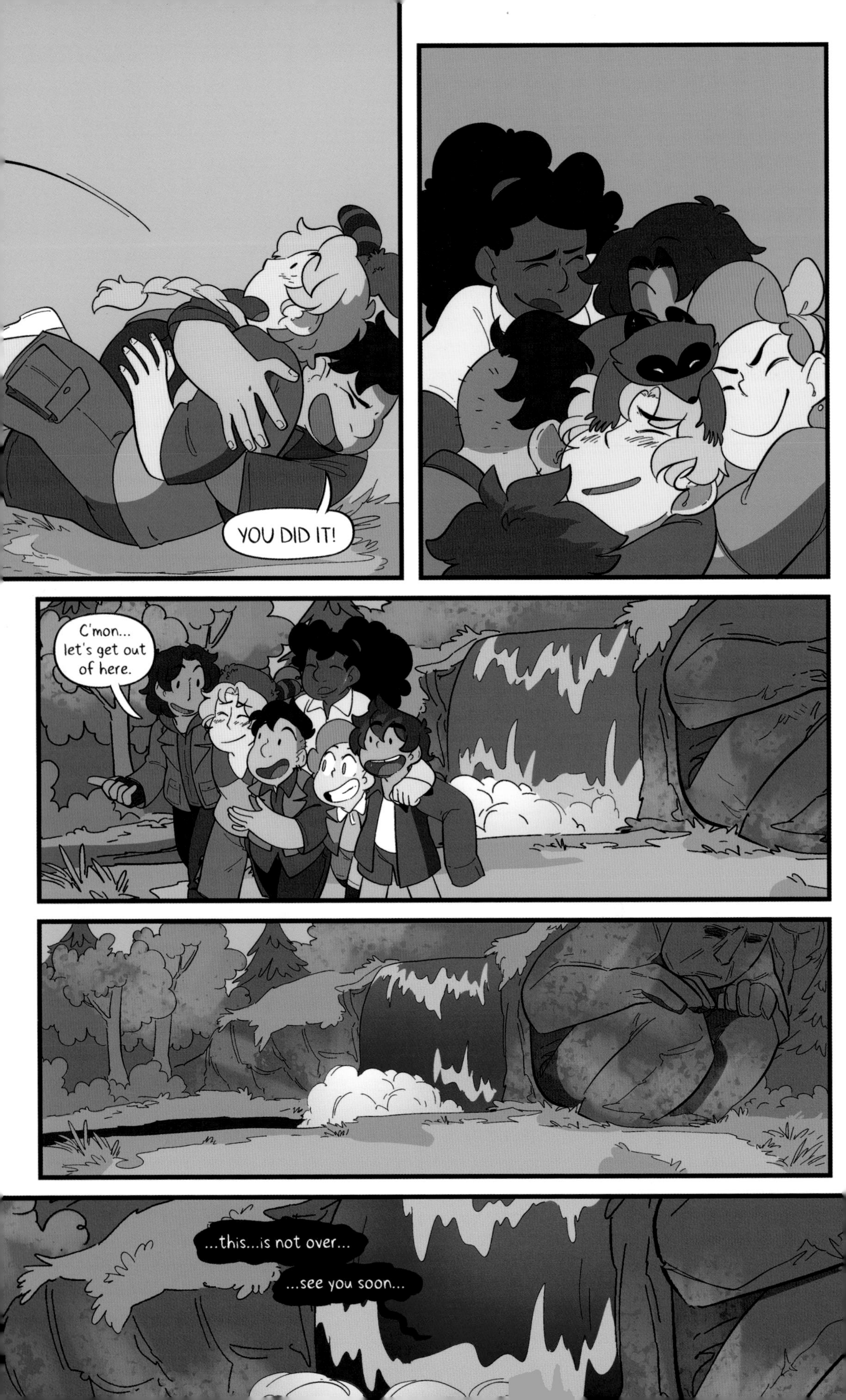
YOU DID IT!
C'mon... let's get out of here.
...this...is not over...
...see you soon...

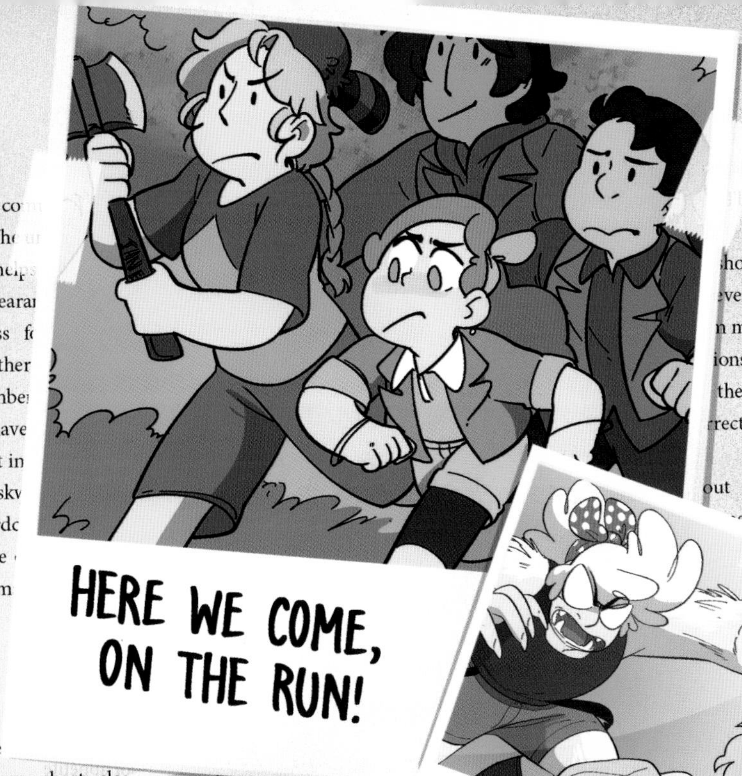
HERE WE COME,
ON THE RUN!

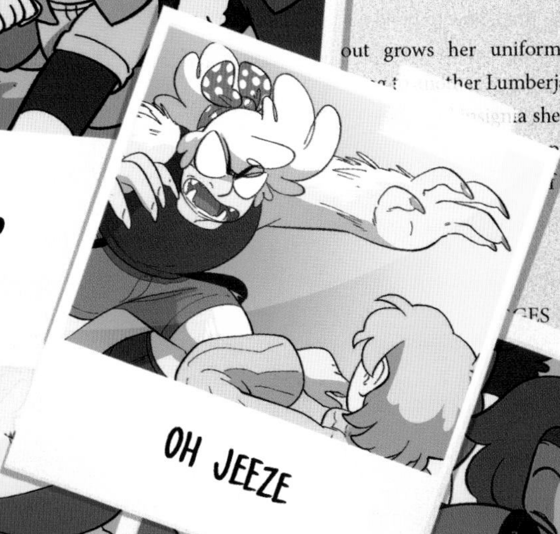
OH JEEZE

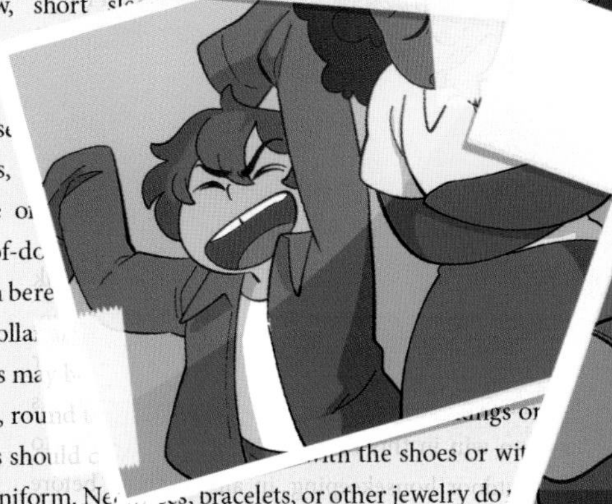

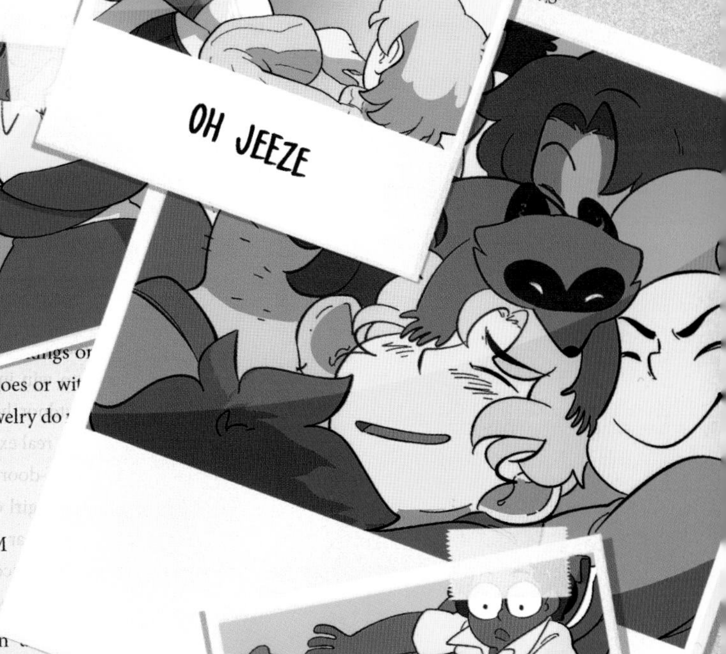

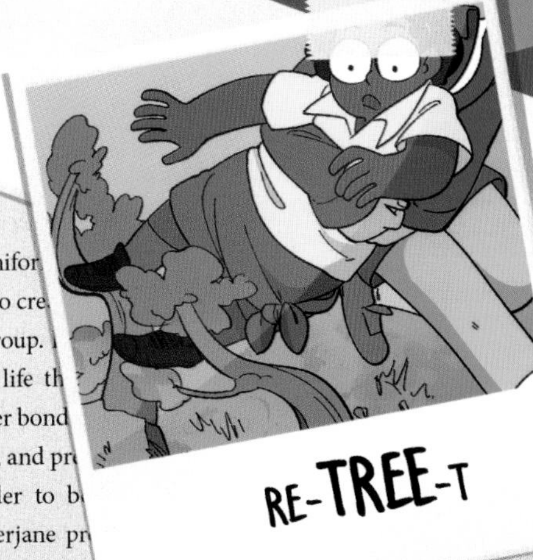
RE-TREE-T

will co
The u
It hel
appeara
dress f
Further
Lumbe
to have
part in
Thiskv
Hardc
have
them

...HE UNIFORM

...should be worn at camp
...events when Lumberjanes
...n may also be worn at other
...ions. It should be worn as a
...the uniform dress with
...rrect shoes, and stocking or

...out grows her uniform or
...ther Lumberjane.
...insignia she has
...her
...her

...GES

The
yellow, short sl...
emb...
the w
choose
slacks,
made o
out-of-do
green bere
the colla
Shoes ma
heels, rou ...ings or
socks should c... ...with the shoes or wit
the uniform. Ne... ...es, bracelets, or other jewelry do...
belong with a Lumberjane uniform.

HOW TO WEAR THE UNIFORM

To look well in a uniform demands first of ...
uniform be kept in good condition—clean ...
pressed. See that the skirt is the right length for your own height and build, that the belt is adjusted to your waist, that your shoes and stockings are in keeping with the uniform, that you watch your posture and carry yourself with dignity and grace. If the beret is removed indoors, be sure that your hair is neat and kept in place with an inconspicuous clip or ribbon. When you wear a Lumberjane uniform you are identified as a member of this organization and you should be doubly careful to conduct yourself in a way that will show everyone that courtesy and thoughtfulness are part of being a Lumberjane. People are likely to judge a whole nation by the selfishness of a few individuals, to criticize a whole family because of the misconduct of one member, and to feel unkindly toward an organization because of the

The unifor...
helps to cre...
in a group. ...
active life th...
another bond...
future, and pr...
in order to b...
Lumberjane pr...
Penniquiqul Thi... ...ore Lady
Types, but m... ...es will wish to have one. They
can either bu... ...uniform, or make it themselves from
materials available at the trading post.

LUMBERJANES FIELD MANUAL

CHAPTER FORTY-FIVE

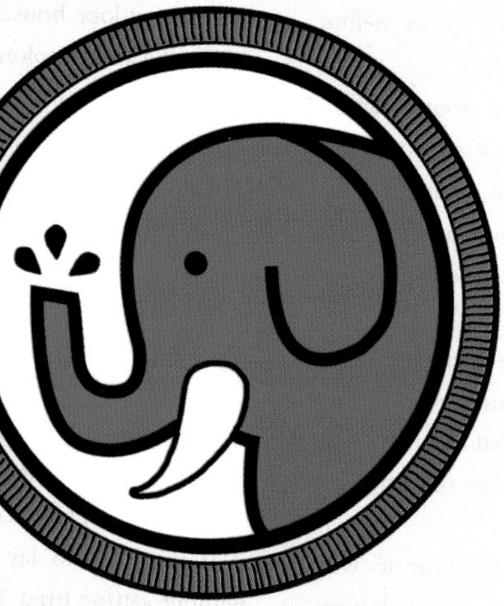

Lumberjanes "Out-of-Doors" Program Field

ZOO IT YOURSELF

"You can always trust a wet nose and toe beans."

Whether they're tiny tadpoles, or elephants the size of your house, the animals we share our homes and world with are all important in their own, unique ways, and the desire to care for animals is one that many young scouts share. As children, we are so used to being cared for and looked after, that having an opportunity to nurture something else, be it a goldfish or a puppy, is often our first chance at true autonomy. So whether you have one pet or a menagerie, or even if you're simply pet-sitting, we hope that you will enjoy earning your Zoo It Yourself badge.

A major goal of modern zoos is conservation, public education, and ensuring that the animals in their care live the happiest, healthiest lives possible. And while you might not have a chance to look after or interact with lemurs, giraffes, or other wild creatures, keeping those values in mind when you are spending time with pets makes an excellent first step!

Consider the unique needs and personalities of different types of animals, and work with your troop or counselors to learn what they require and how best to read their moods and preferences. A good place to start is meeting the pets your fellow Lumberjanes have at home, or volunteering at an animal shelter! You will quickly come to find out that each pet prefers different food, toys, and bonding activities, and that the best thing to do is to give to each according to their needs. What makes a dog happy may not suit a cat, a horse, or even a different dog!

Think about what a zoo run by you would look like. Draw a map to plan the sizes of enclosures and the layout, or put together a menu that reflects each animal's dietary needs and place in the food chain. Try your hand at writing descriptions of habits and habitats, to think about how you would like to teach the public about the incredible animals in your care!

And remember, no matter how interested we are in them, not every creature is meant to be kept, whether in a home or in a zoo. Just as we try to respect our pets' wishes when it comes to playtime and petting, we should also strive to respect that some creatures are simply not meant to be kept away from the wild, and instead do our best to create a world that will be hospitable to them.

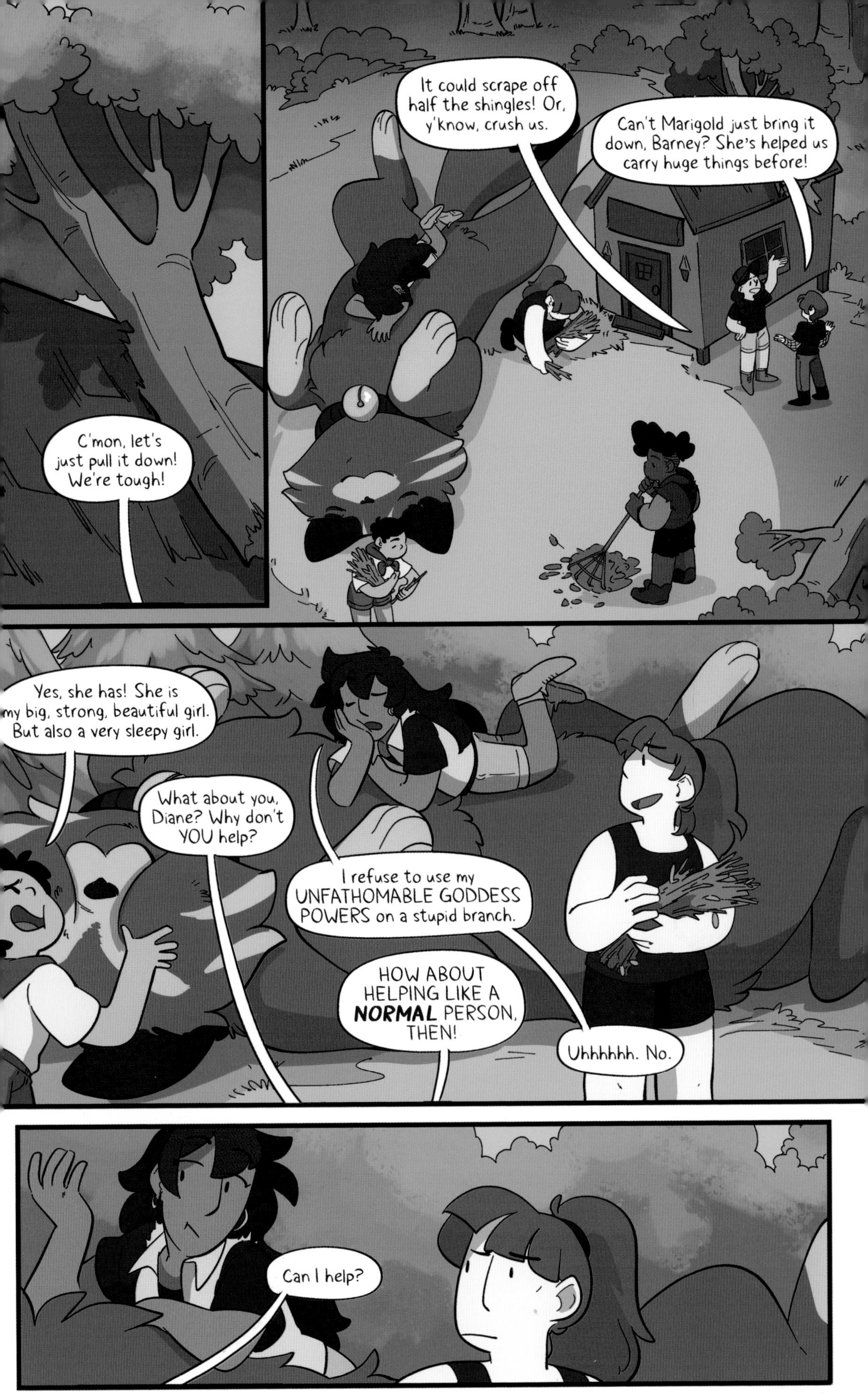
C'mon, let's just pull it down! We're tough!
It could scrape off half the shingles! Or, y'know, crush us.
Can't Marigold just bring it down, Barney? She's helped us carry huge things before!
Yes, she has! She is my big, strong, beautiful girl. But also a very sleepy girl.
What about you, Diane? Why don't YOU help?
I refuse to use my UNFATHOMABLE GODDESS POWERS on a stupid branch.
HOW ABOUT HELPING LIKE A NORMAL PERSON, THEN!
Uhhhhhh. No.
Can I help?

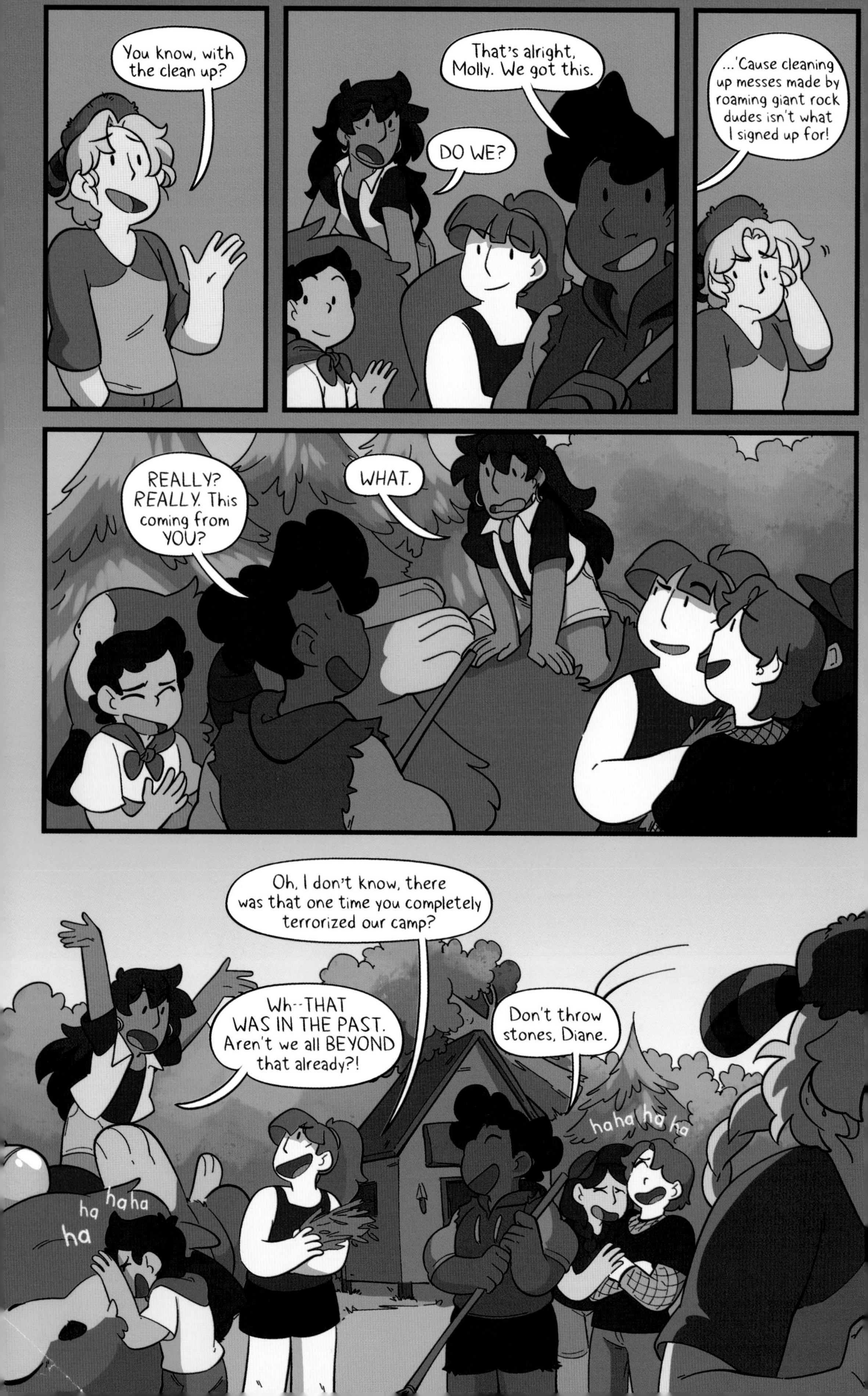
You know, with the clean up?
That's alright, Molly. We got this.
DO WE?
...'Cause cleaning up messes made by roaming giant rock dudes isn't what I signed up for!
REALLY? REALLY. This coming from YOU?
WHAT.
Oh, I don't know, there was that one time you completely terrorized our camp?
Wh--THAT WAS IN THE PAST. Aren't we all BEYOND that already?!
Don't throw stones, Diane.
haha ha ha
ha haha ha

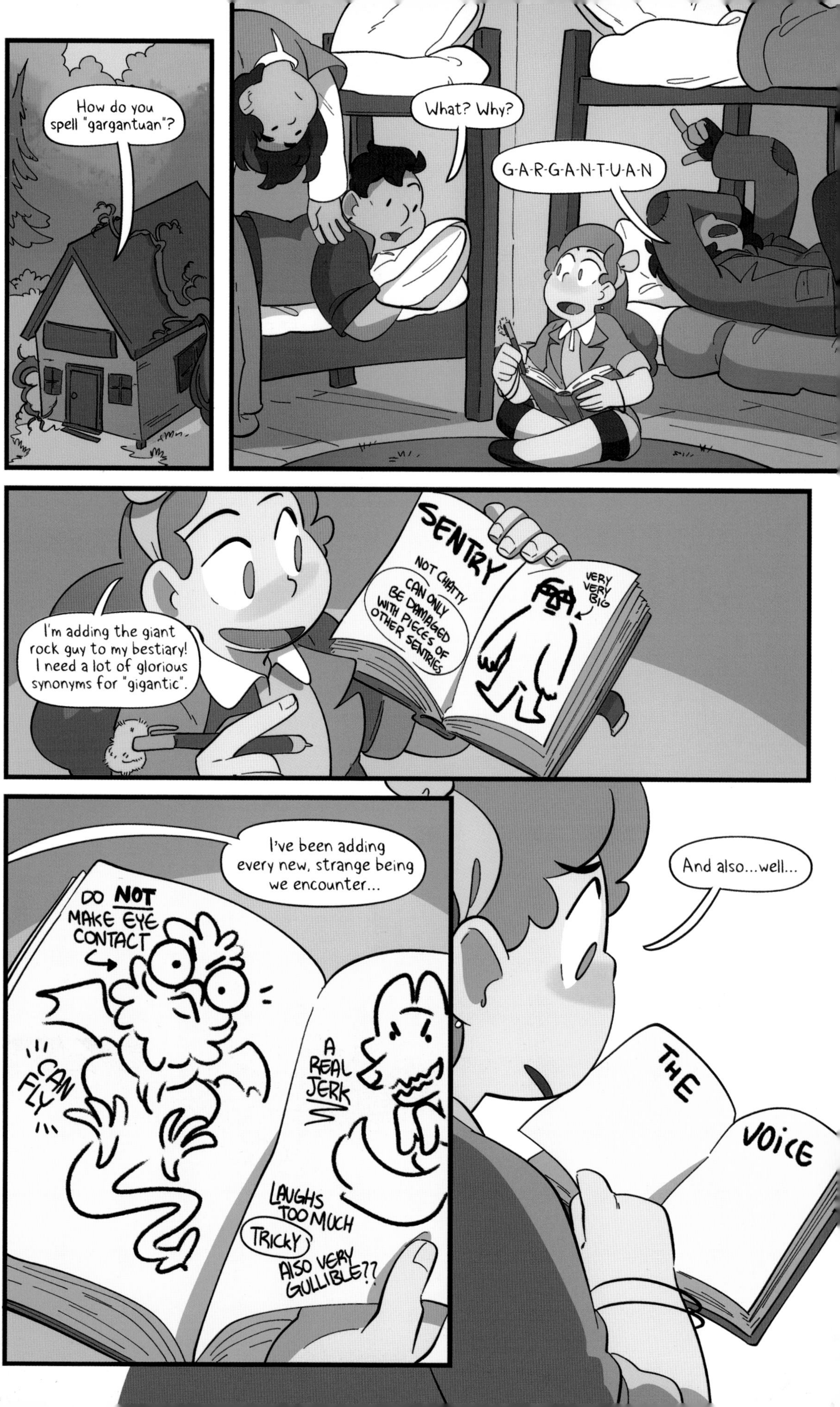
How do you spell "gargantuan"?
What? Why?
G-A-R-G-A-N-T-U-A-N
I'm adding the giant rock guy to my bestiary! I need a lot of glorious synonyms for "gigantic".
SENTRY
NOT CHATTY
CAN ONLY BE DAMAGED WITH PIECES OF OTHER SENTRIES
VERY VERY BIG
I've been adding every new, strange being we encounter...
DO NOT MAKE EYE CONTACT
CAN FLY
A REAL JERK
LAUGHS TOO MUCH
TRICKY
ALSO VERY GULLIBLE??
And also...well...
THE VOICE

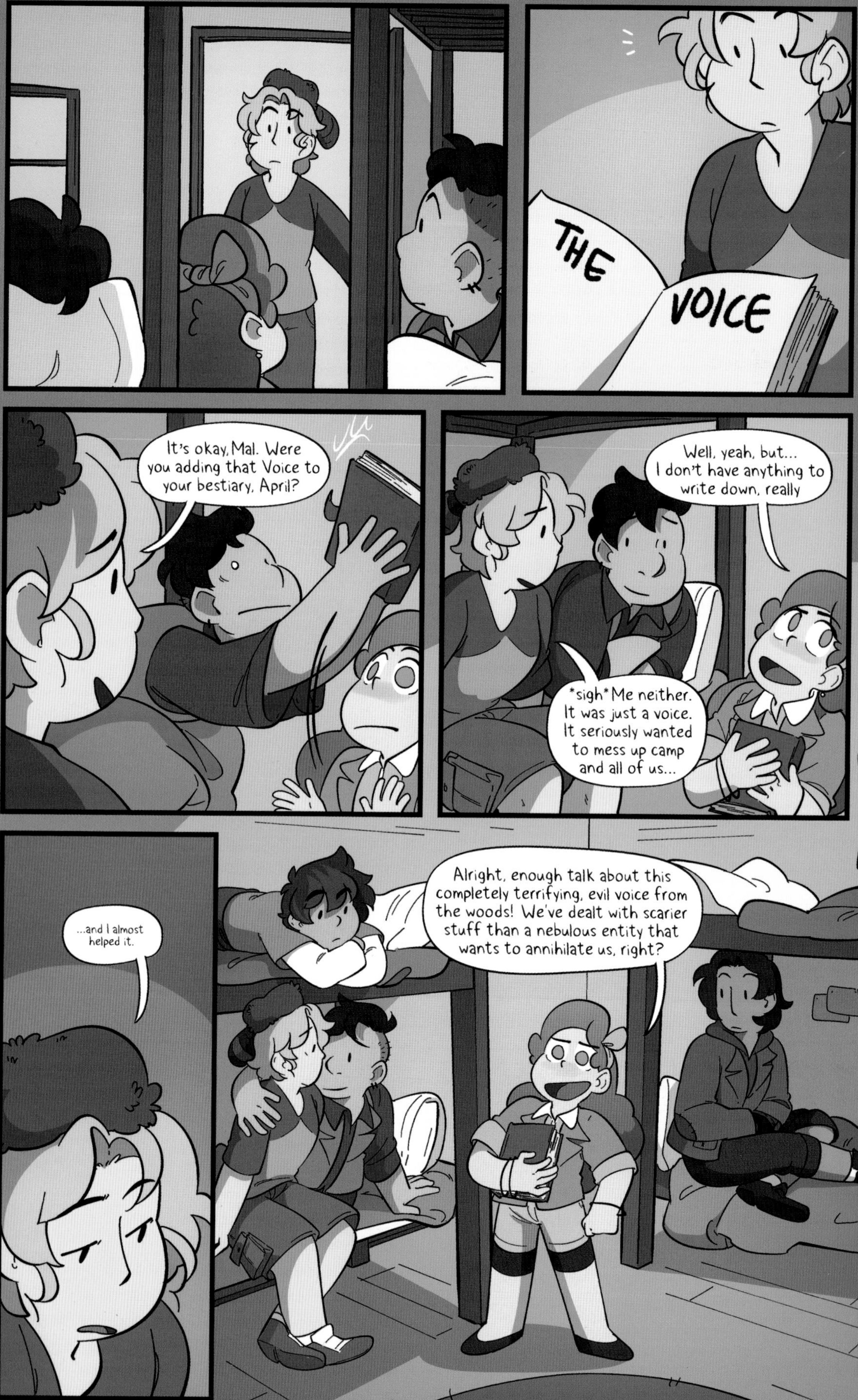
THE VOICE
It's okay, Mal. Were you adding that Voice to your bestiary, April?
Well, yeah, but... I don't have anything to write down, really
sigh Me neither. It was just a voice. It seriously wanted to mess up camp and all of us...
...and I almost helped it.
Alright, enough talk about this completely terrifying, evil voice from the woods! We've dealt with scarier stuff than a nebulous entity that wants to annihilate us, right?

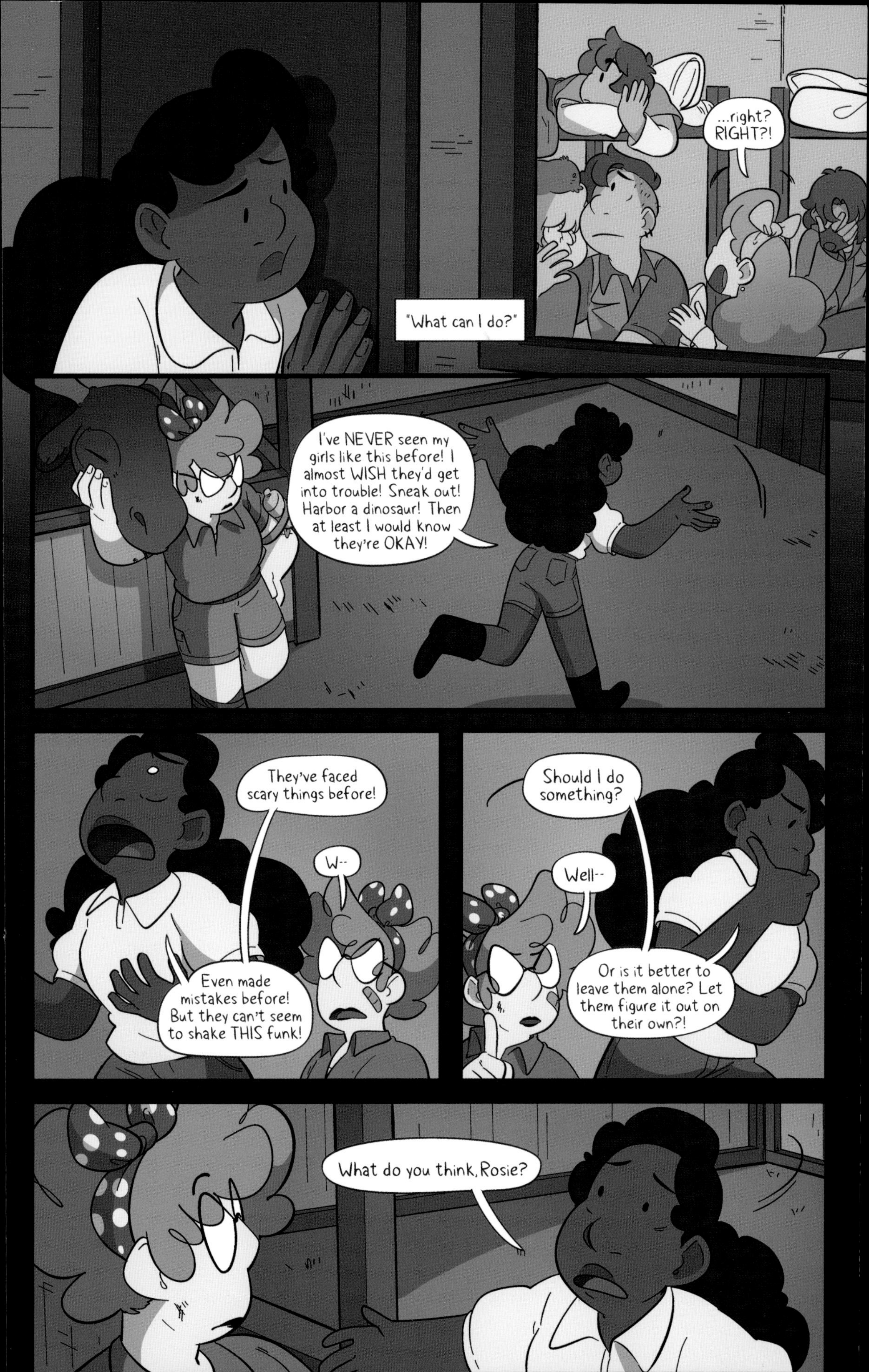
...right? RIGHT?!
"What can I do?"
I've NEVER seen my girls like this before! I almost WISH they'd get into trouble! Sneak out! Harbor a dinosaur! Then at least I would know they're OKAY!
They've faced scary things before!
W--
Even made mistakes before! But they can't seem to shake THIS funk!
Should I do something?
Well--
Or is it better to leave them alone? Let them figure it out on their own?!
What do you think, Rosie?

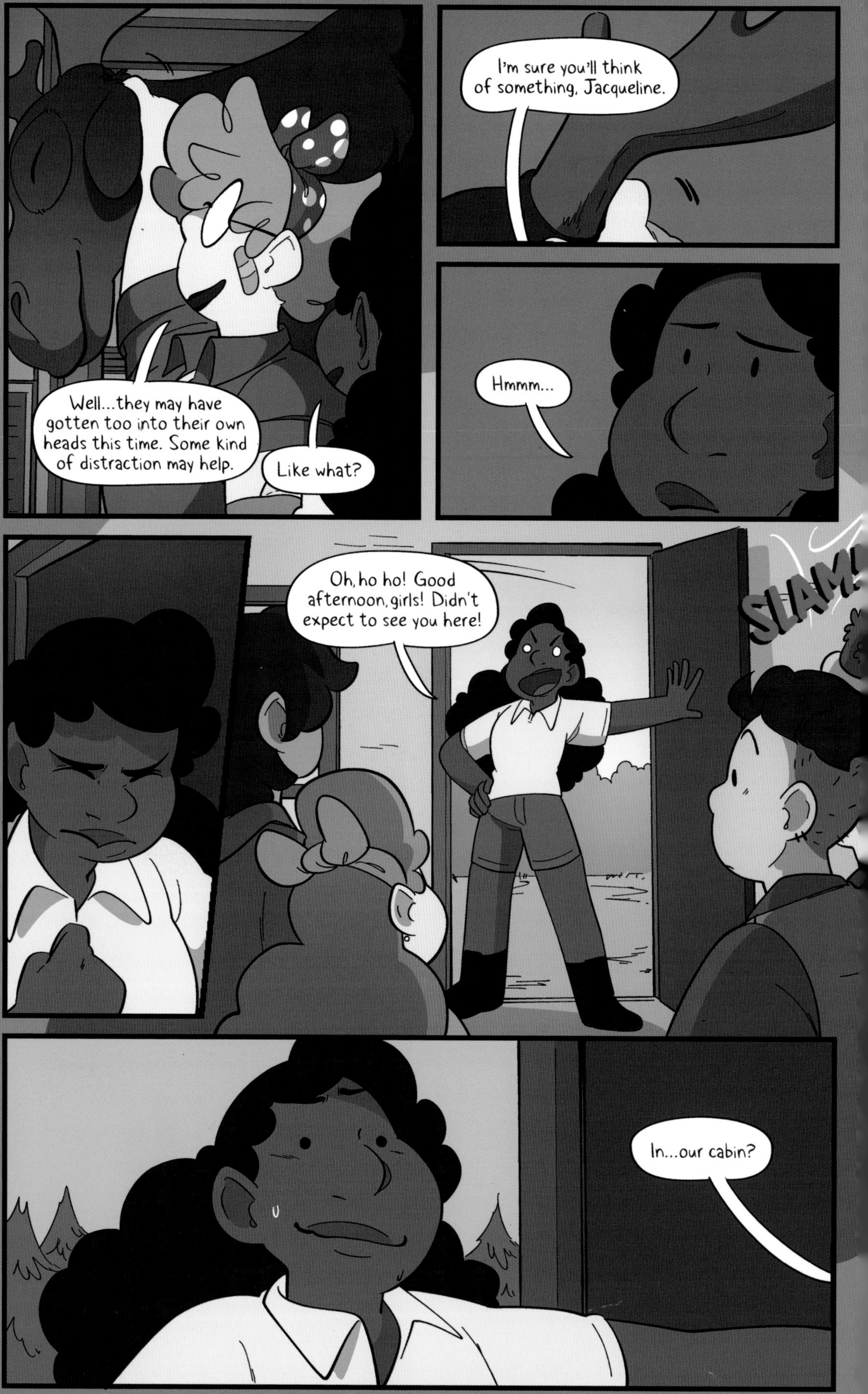
Well...they may have gotten too into their own heads this time. Some kind of distraction may help.
Like what?
I'm sure you'll think of something, Jacqueline.
Hmmm...
Oh, ho ho! Good afternoon, girls! Didn't expect to see you here!
SLAM!
In...our cabin?

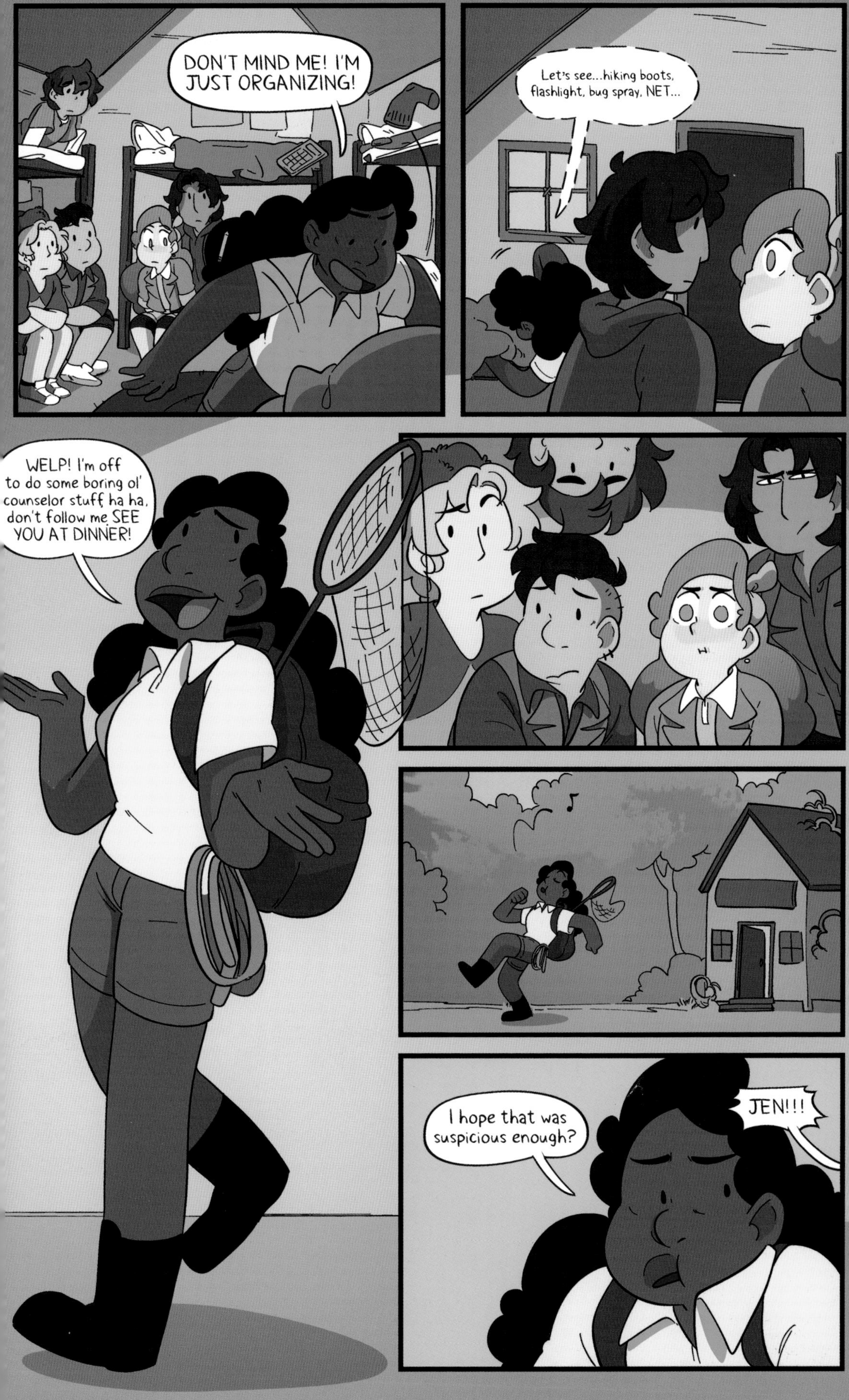
DON'T MIND ME! I'M JUST ORGANIZING!
Let's see...hiking boots, flashlight, bug spray, NET...
WELP! I'm off to do some boring ol' counselor stuff ha ha, don't follow me SEE YOU AT DINNER!
I hope that was suspicious enough?
JEN!!!

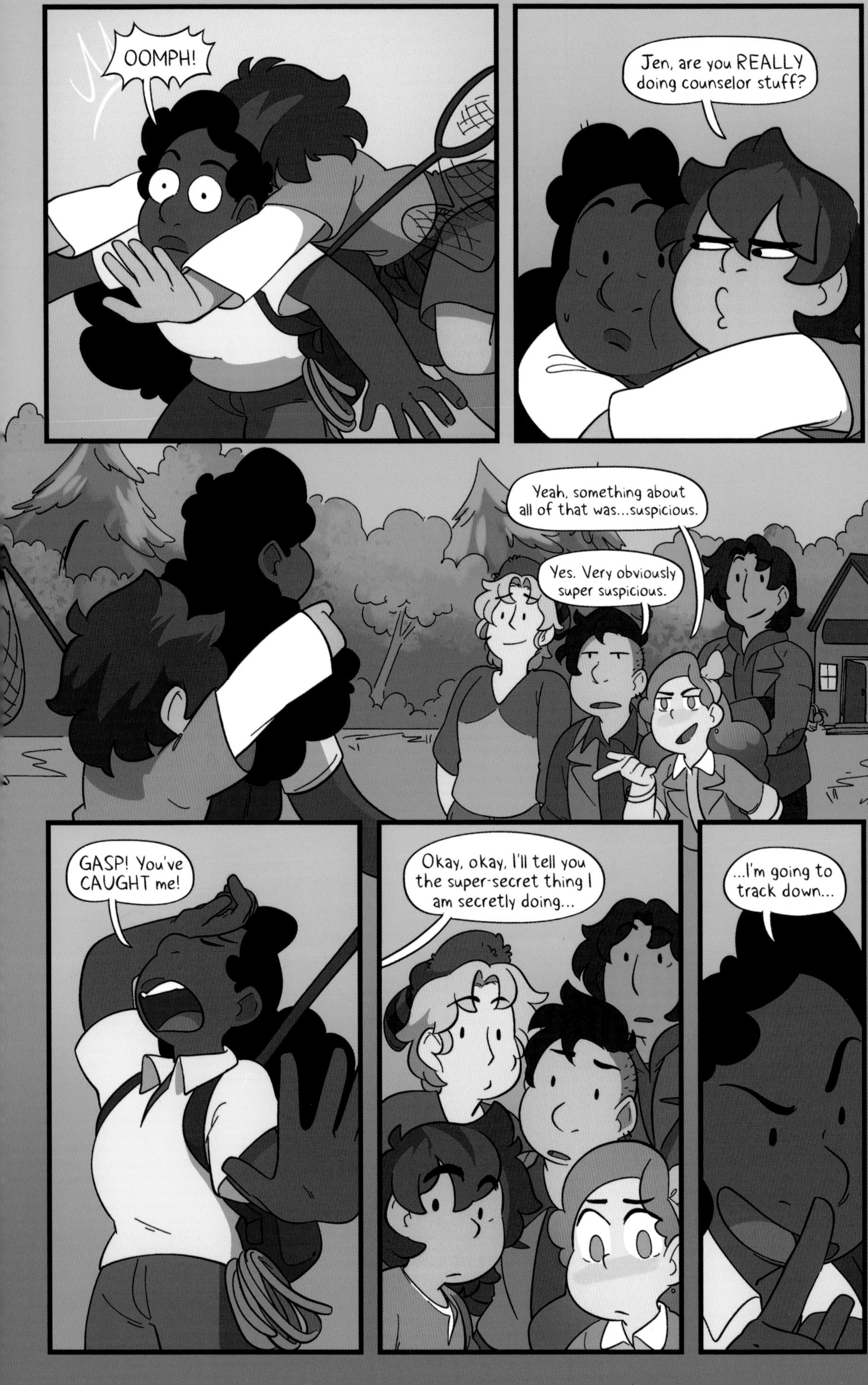
OOMPH!
Jen, are you REALLY doing counselor stuff?
Yeah, something about all of that was...suspicious.
Yes. Very obviously super suspicious.
GASP! You've CAUGHT me!
Okay, okay, I'll tell you the super-secret thing I am secretly doing...
...I'm going to track down...

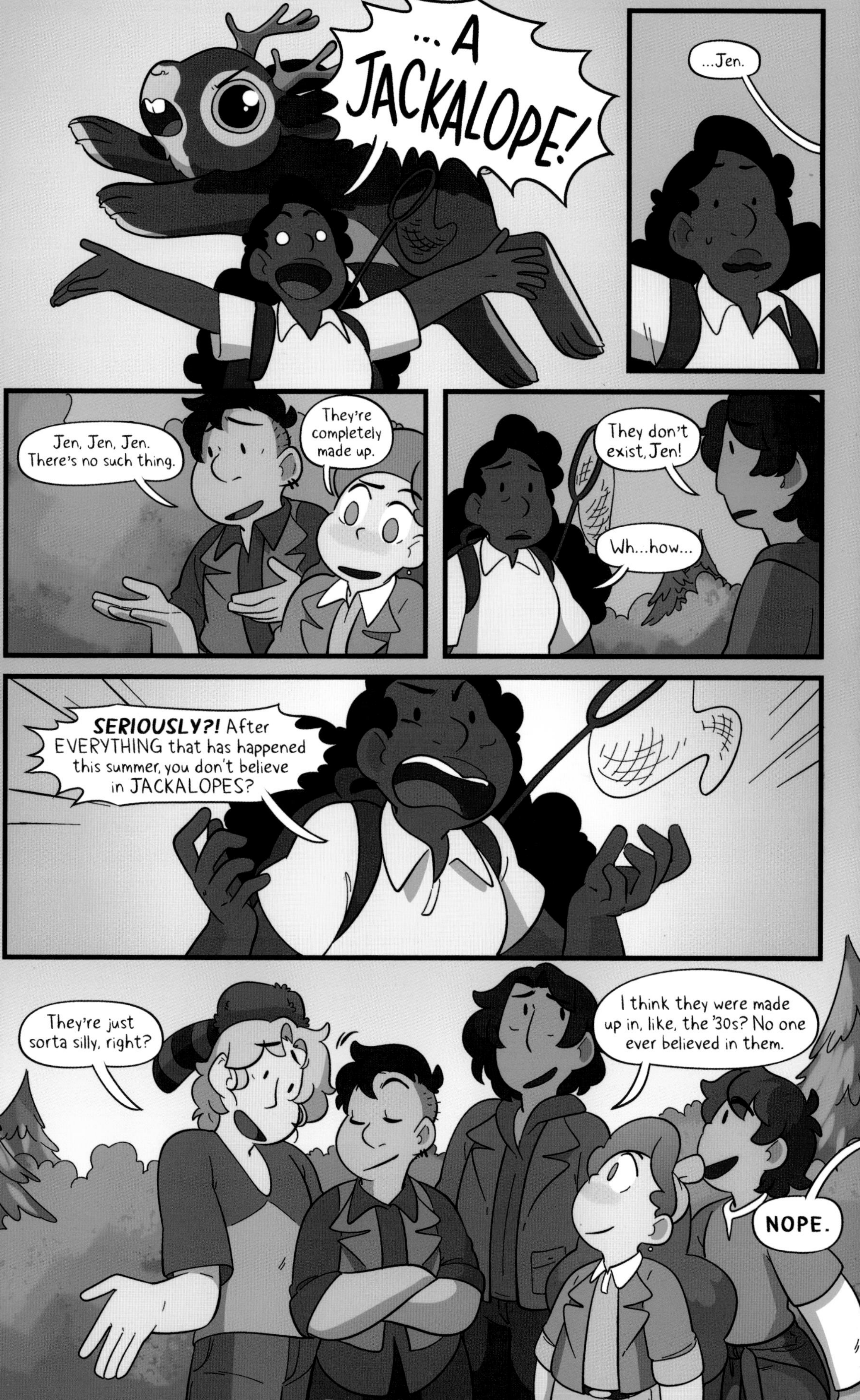
...A JACKALOPE!
...Jen.
Jen, Jen, Jen. There's no such thing.
They're completely made up.
They don't exist, Jen!
Wh...how...
SERIOUSLY?! After EVERYTHING that has happened this summer, you don't believe in JACKALOPES?
They're just sorta silly, right?
I think they were made up in, like, the '30s? No one ever believed in them.
NOPE.

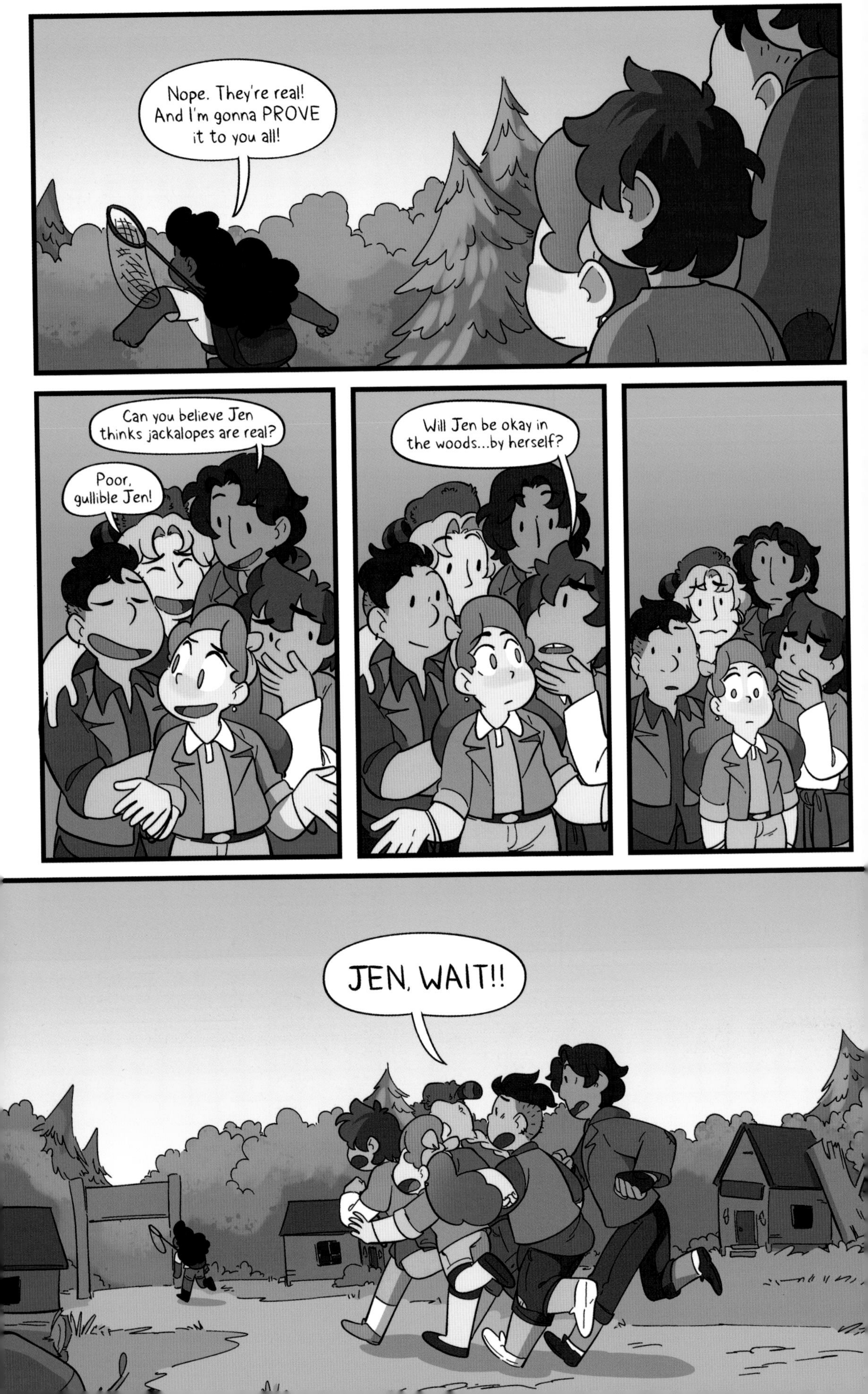
Nope. They're real! And I'm gonna PROVE it to you all!
Can you believe Jen thinks jackalopes are real?
Poor, gullible Jen!
Will Jen be okay in the woods...by herself?
JEN, WAIT!!

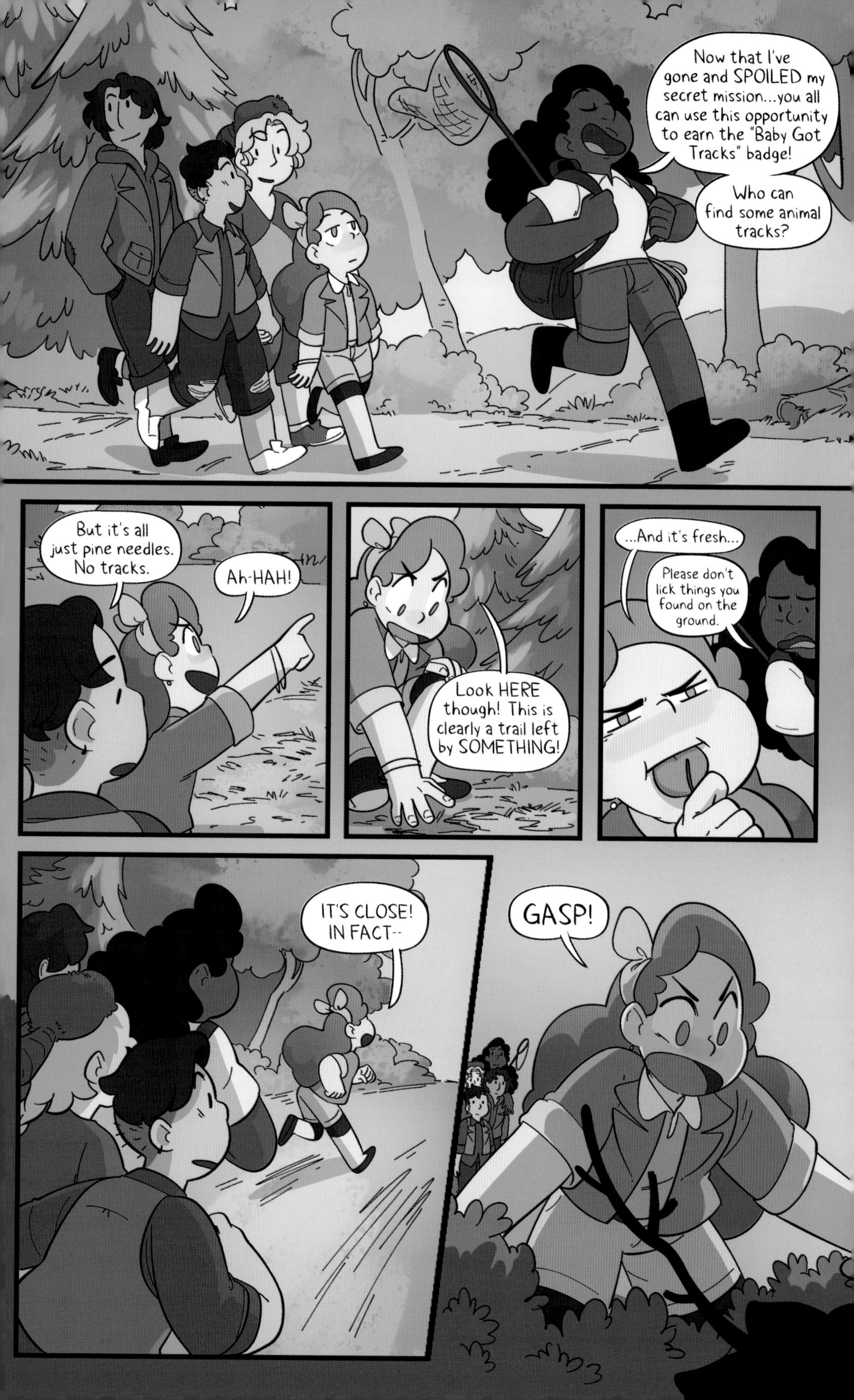
Now that I've gone and SPOILED my secret mission...you all can use this opportunity to earn the "Baby Got Tracks" badge!
Who can find some animal tracks?
But it's all just pine needles. No tracks.
Ah-HAH!
Look HERE though! This is clearly a trail left by SOMETHING!
...And it's fresh...
Please don't lick things you found on the ground.
IT'S CLOSE! IN FACT--
GASP!

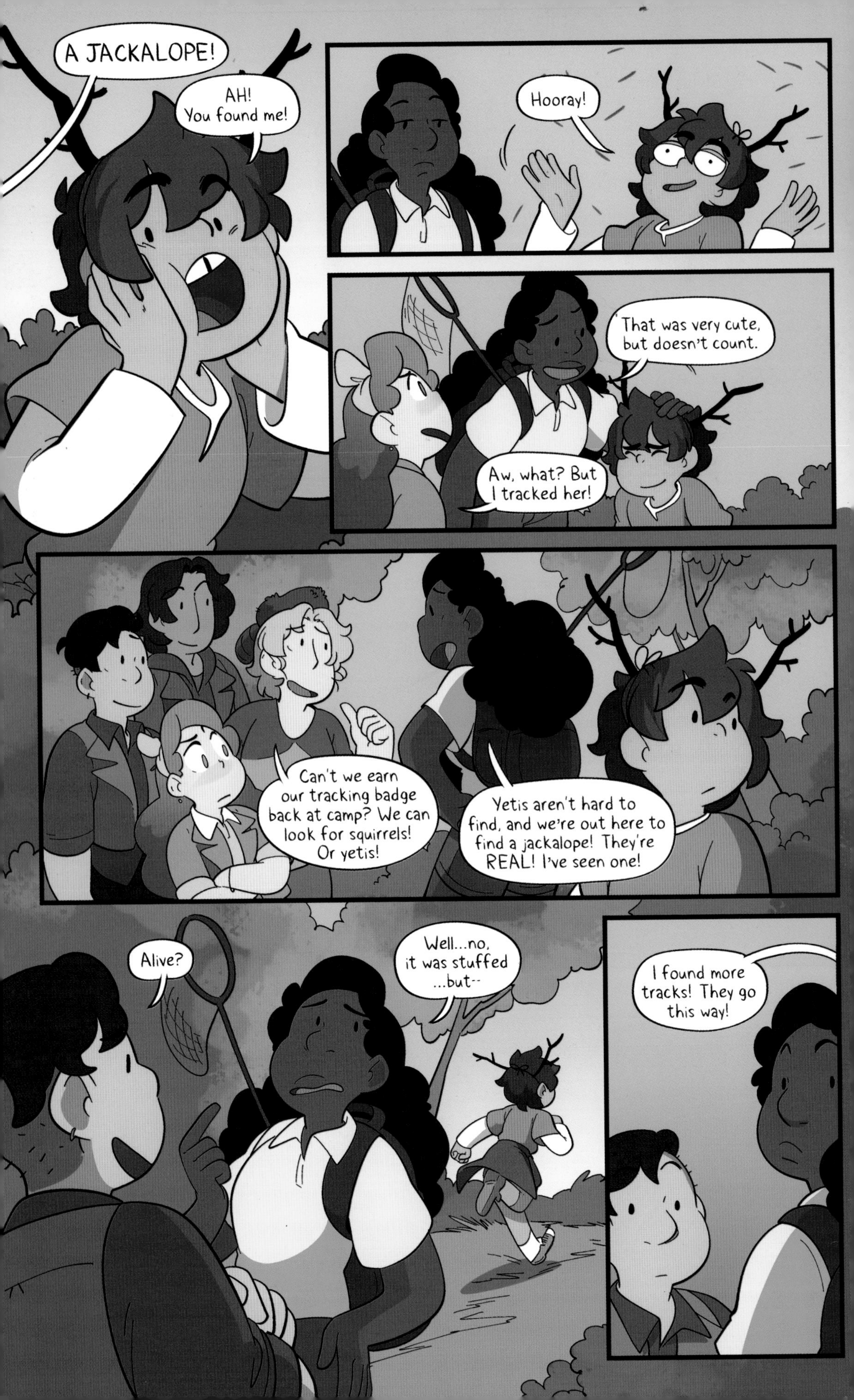
A JACKALOPE!
AH! You found me!
Hooray!
That was very cute, but doesn't count.
Aw, what? But I tracked her!
Can't we earn our tracking badge back at camp? We can look for squirrels! Or yetis!
Yetis aren't hard to find, and we're out here to find a jackalope! They're REAL! I've seen one!
Alive?
Well...no, it was stuffed ...but--
I found more tracks! They go this way!

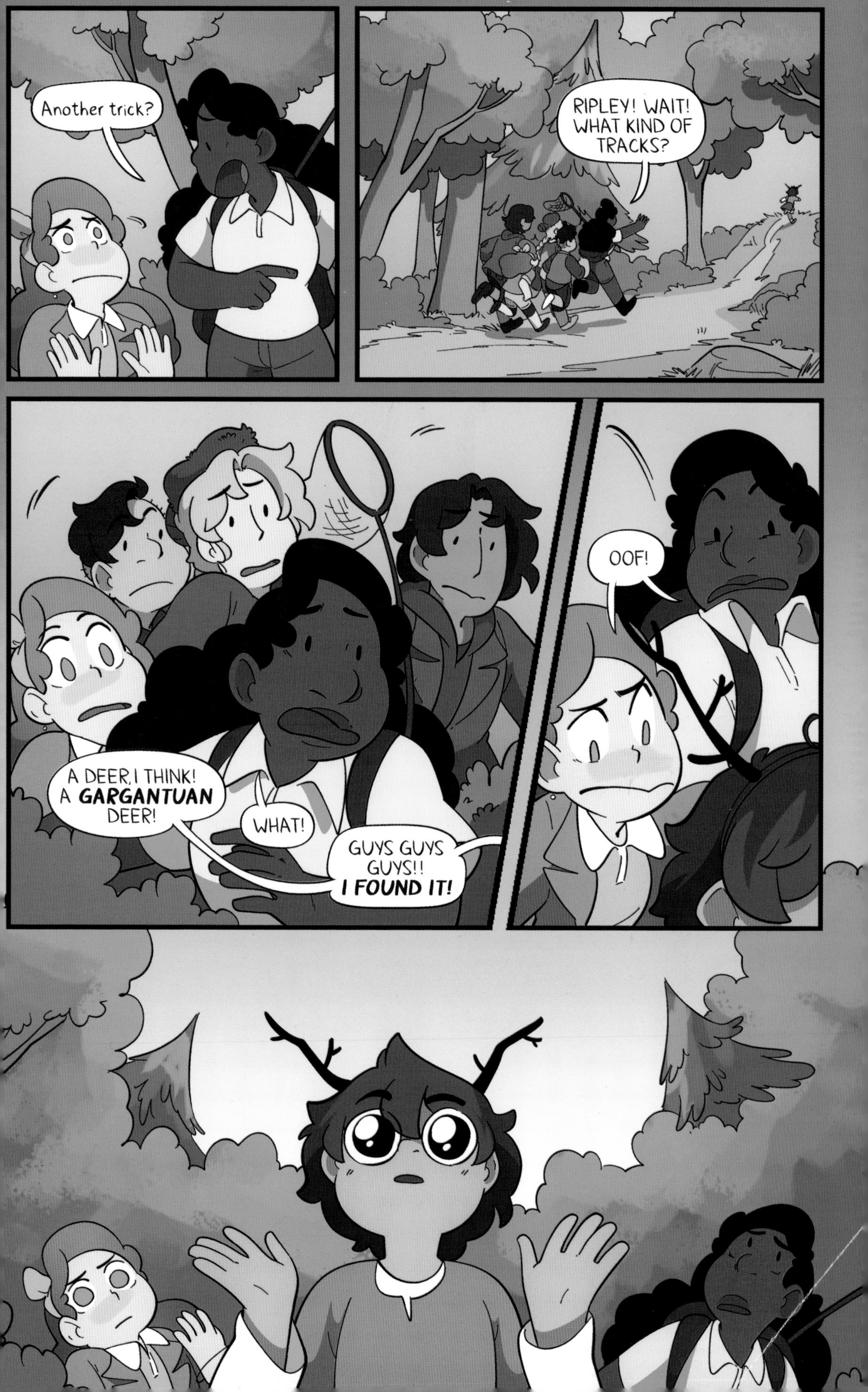
Another trick?
RIPLEY! WAIT! WHAT KIND OF TRACKS?
A DEER, I THINK! A GARGANTUAN DEER!
WHAT!
GUYS GUYS GUYS!! I FOUND IT!
OOF!

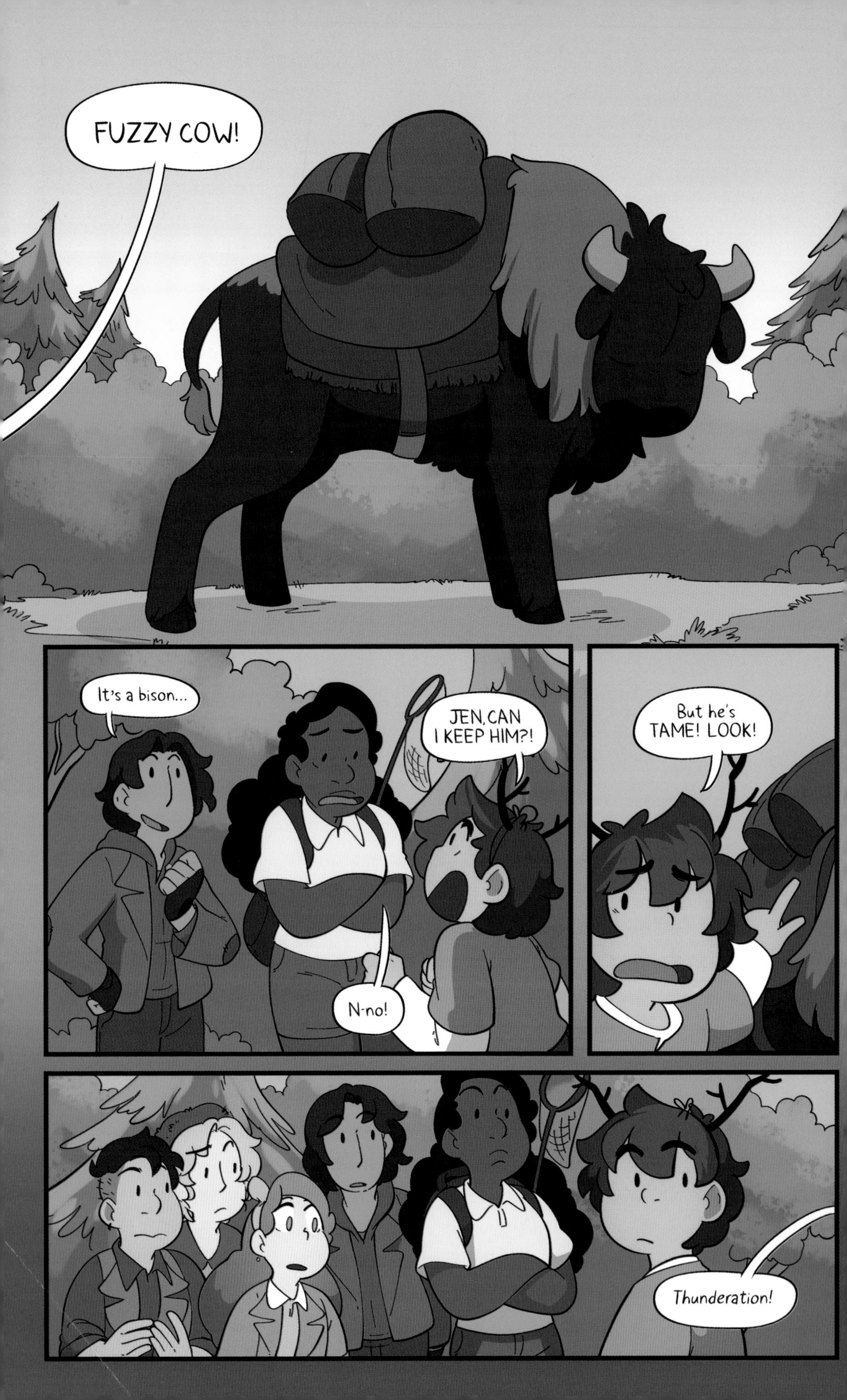
FUZZY COW!
It's a bison...
JEN, CAN I KEEP HIM?!
N-no!
But he's TAME! LOOK!
Thunderation!

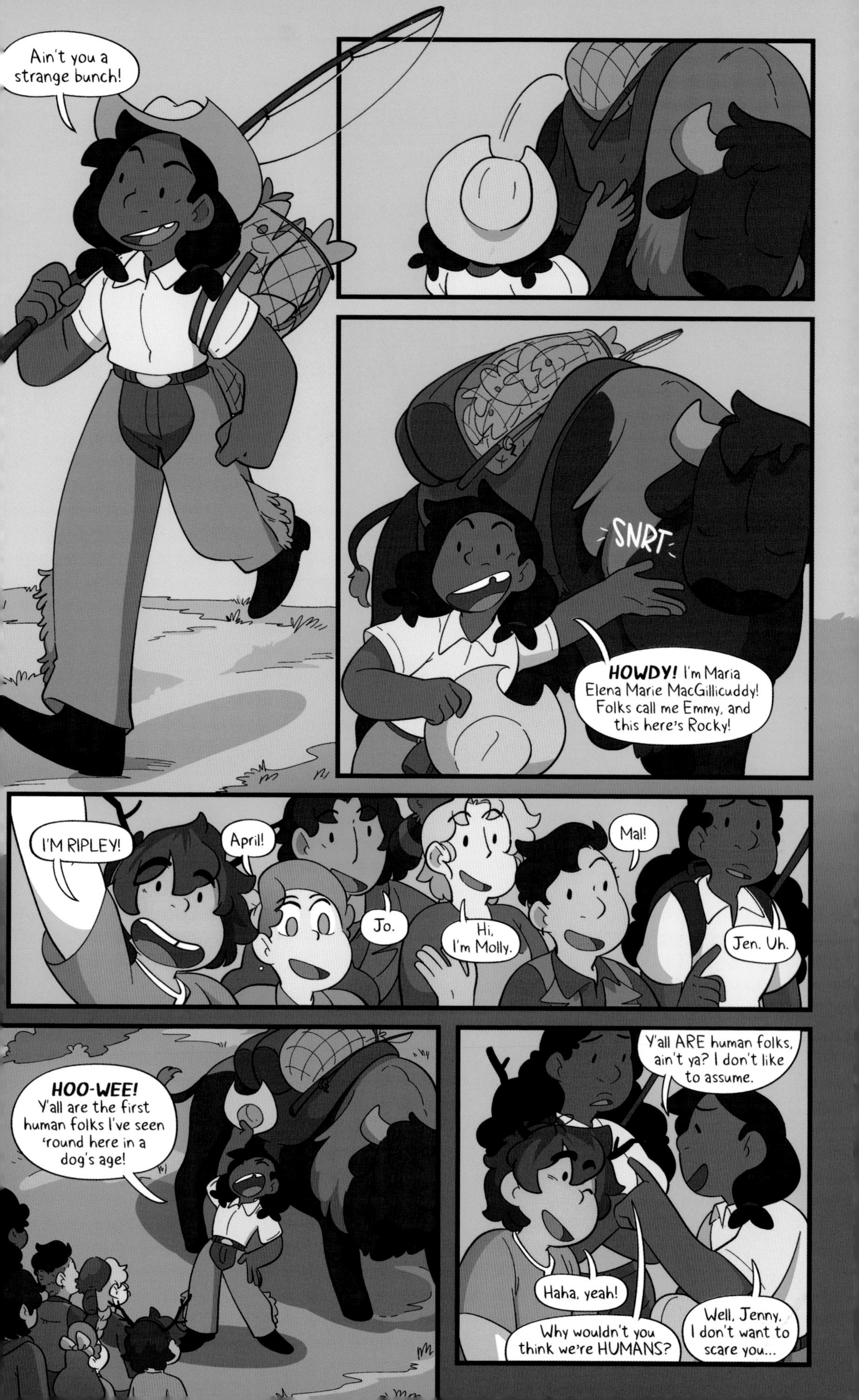
Ain't you a strange bunch!
SNRT
HOWDY! I'm Maria Elena Marie MacGillicuddy! Folks call me Emmy, and this here's Rocky!
I'M RIPLEY!
April!
Jo.
Hi, I'm Molly.
Mal!
Jen. Uh.
HOO-WEE! Y'all are the first human folks I've seen 'round here in a dog's age!
Y'all ARE human folks, ain't ya? I don't like to assume.
Haha, yeah!
Why wouldn't you think we're HUMANS?
Well, Jenny, I don't want to scare you...

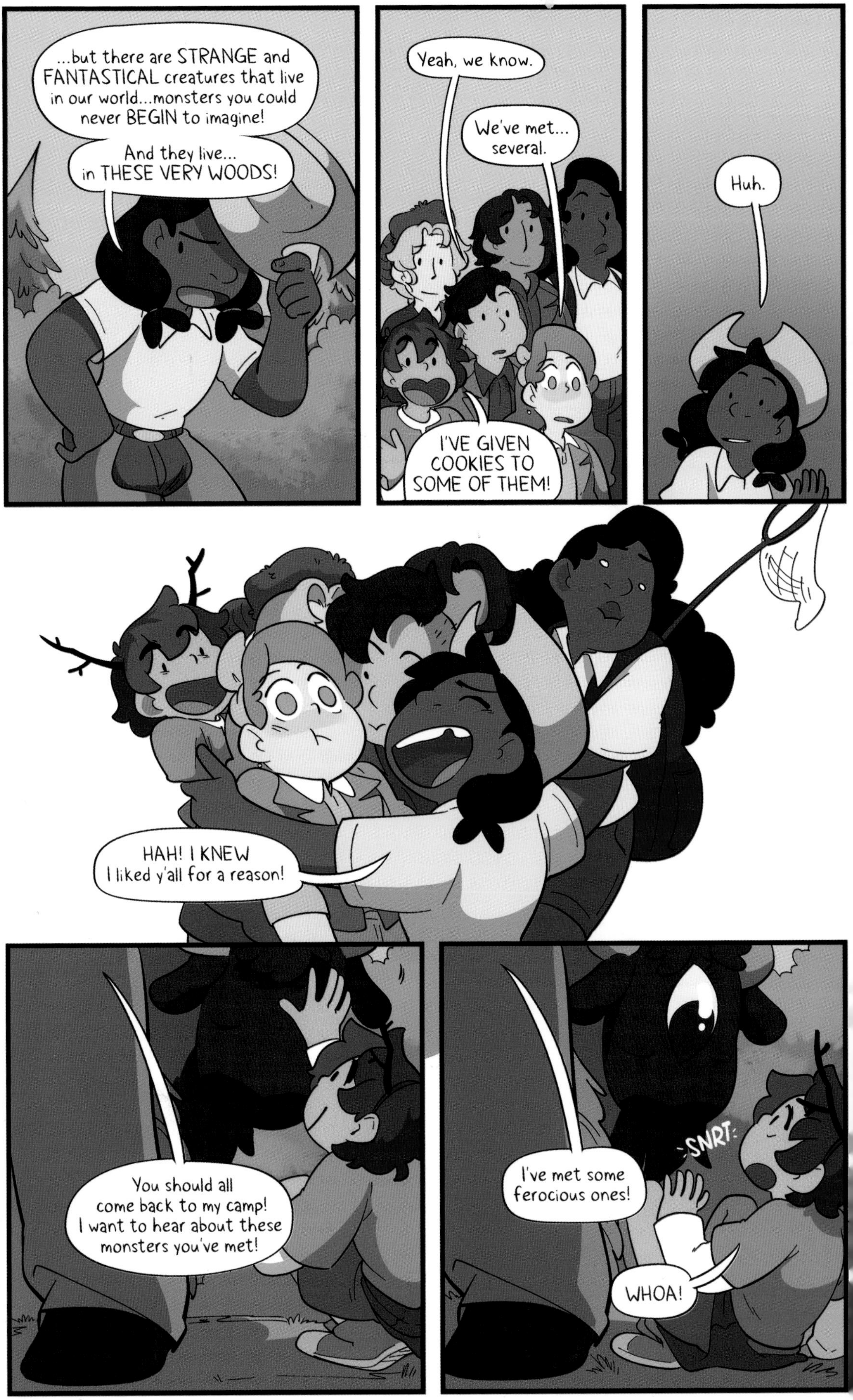
...but there are STRANGE and FANTASTICAL creatures that live in our world...monsters you could never BEGIN to imagine!
And they live... in THESE VERY WOODS!
Yeah, we know.
We've met... several.
I'VE GIVEN COOKIES TO SOME OF THEM!
Huh.
HAH! I KNEW I liked y'all for a reason!
You should all come back to my camp! I want to hear about these monsters you've met!
SNRT
I've met some ferocious ones!
WHOA!

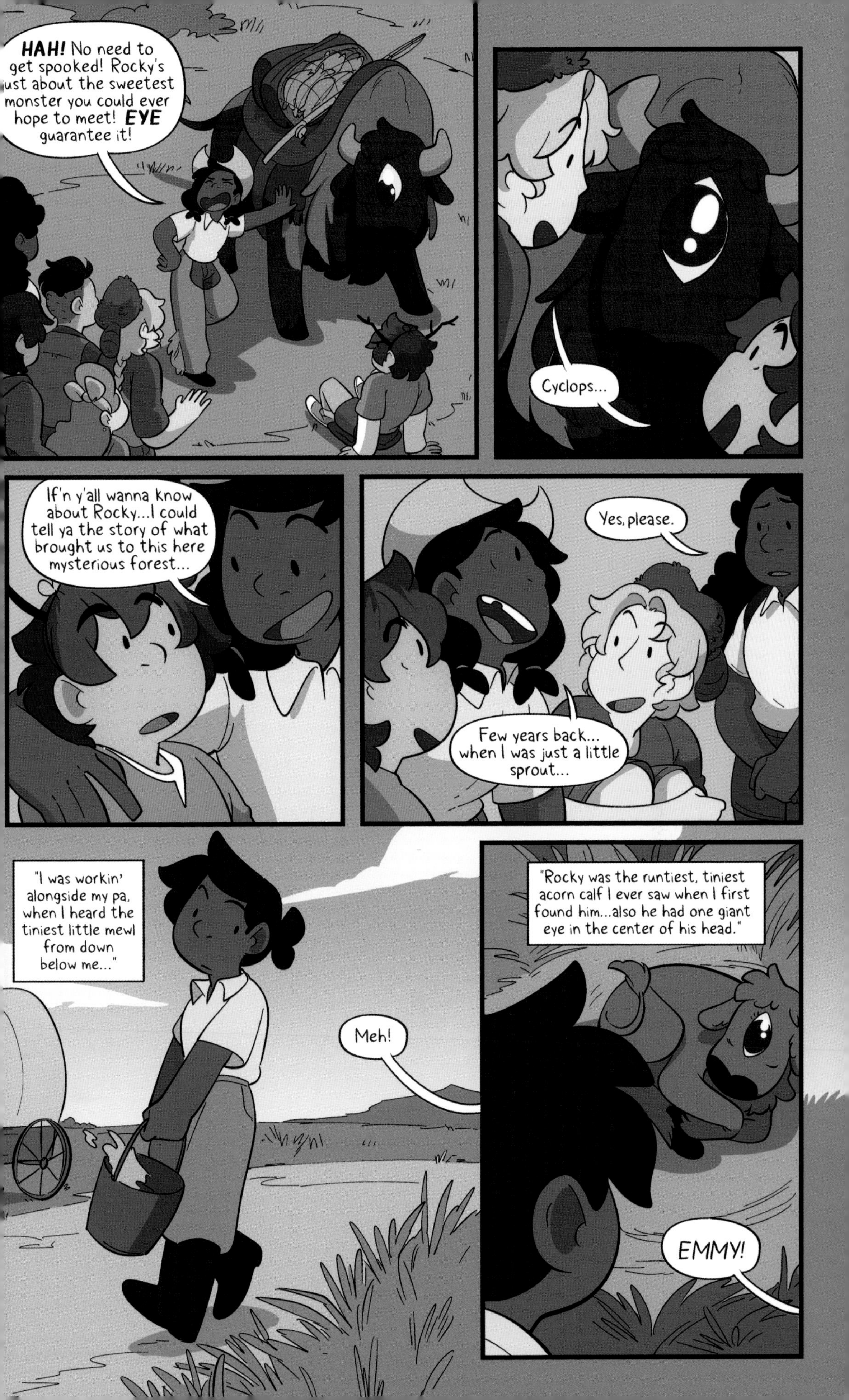
HAH! No need to get spooked! Rocky's just about the sweetest monster you could ever hope to meet! ***EYE*** guarantee it!
Cyclops...
If'n y'all wanna know about Rocky...I could tell ya the story of what brought us to this here mysterious forest...
Yes, please.
Few years back... when I was just a little sprout...
"I was workin' alongside my pa, when I heard the tiniest little mewl from down below me..."
Meh!
"Rocky was the runtiest, tiniest acorn calf I ever saw when I first found him...also he had one giant eye in the center of his head."
EMMY!

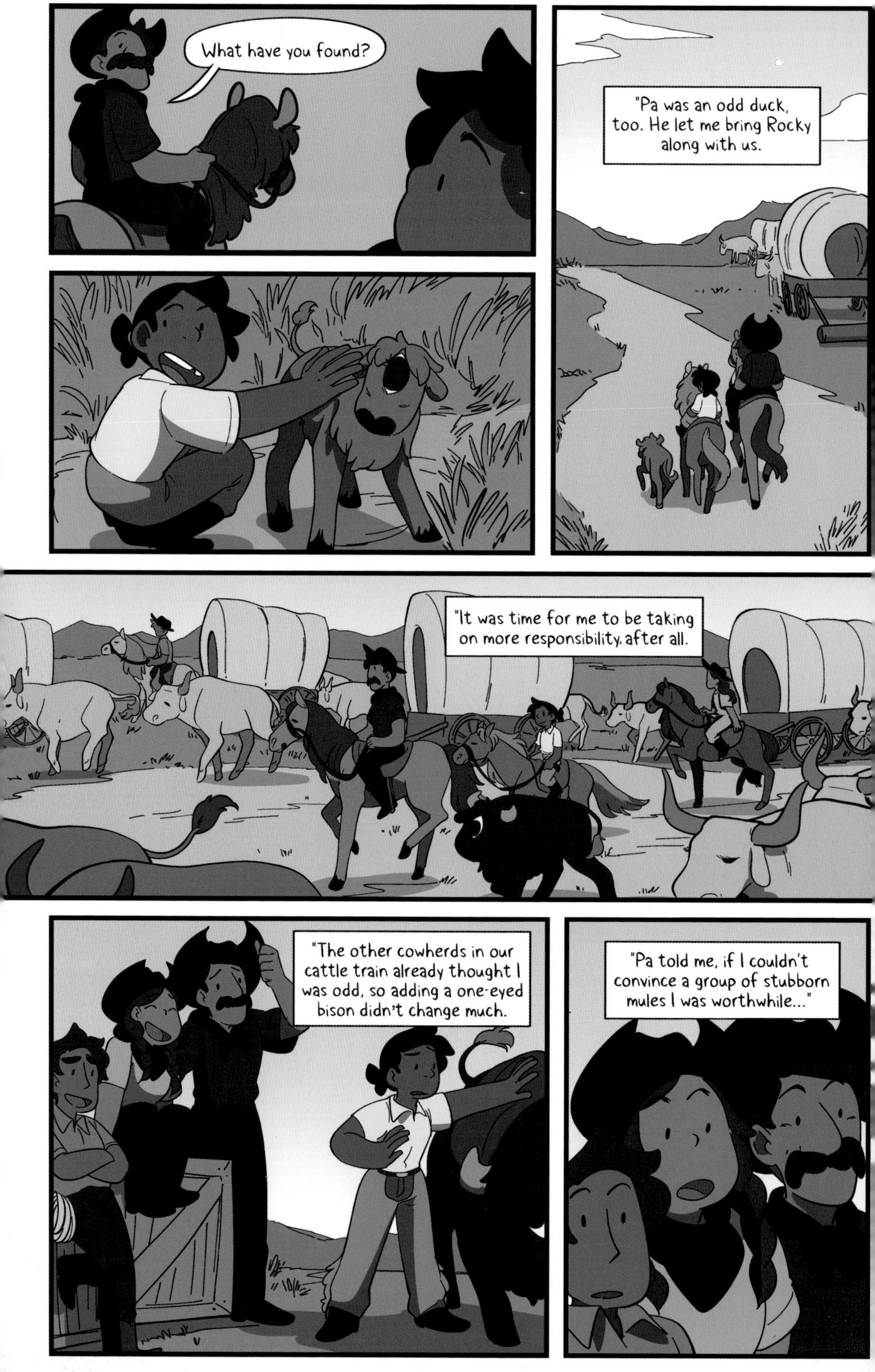
What have you found?
"Pa was an odd duck, too. He let me bring Rocky along with us.
"It was time for me to be taking on more responsibility, after all.
"The other cowherds in our cattle train already thought I was odd, so adding a one-eyed bison didn't change much.
"Pa told me, if I couldn't convince a group of stubborn mules I was worthwhile..."

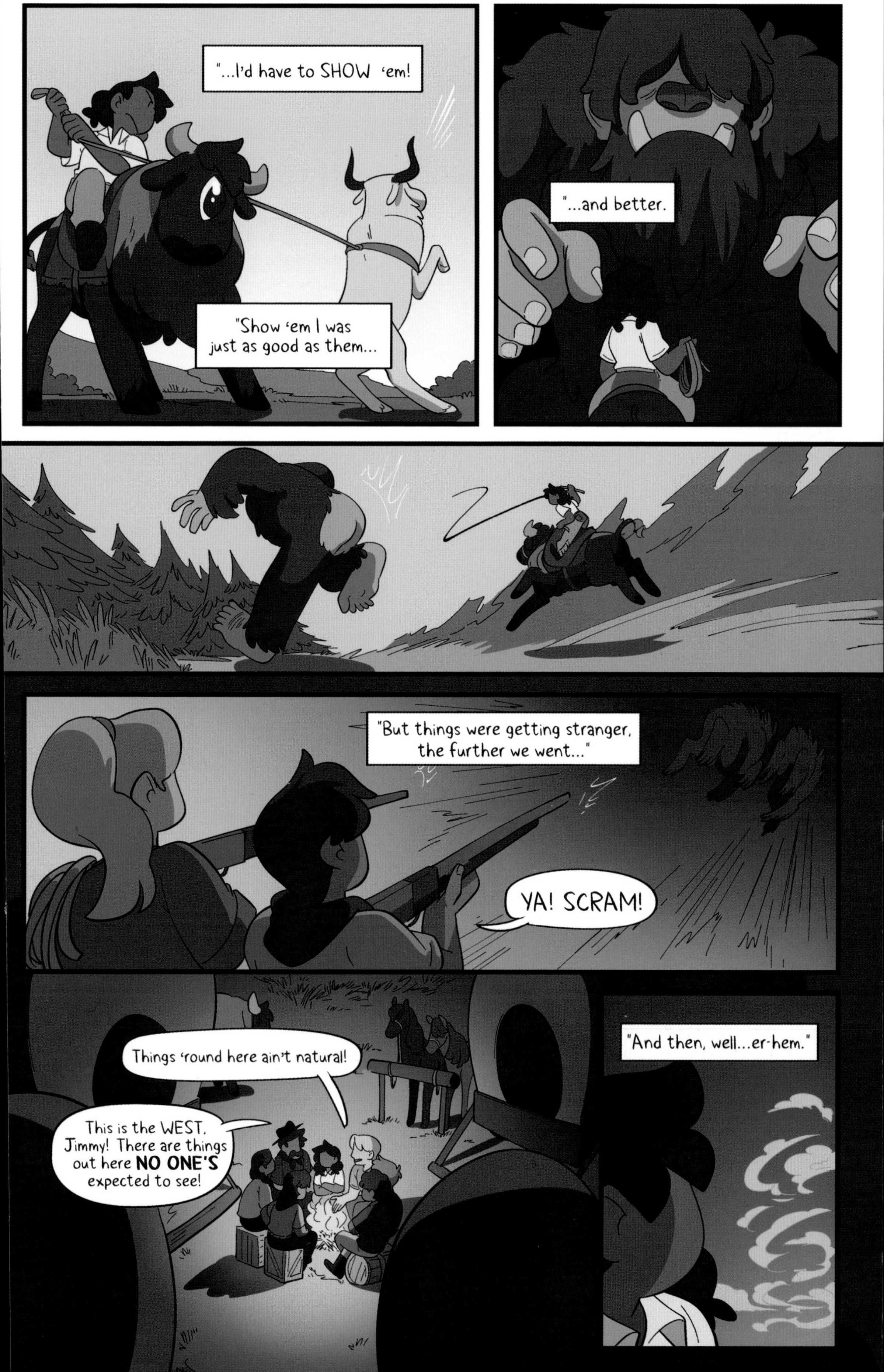
"...I'd have to SHOW 'em!
"Show 'em I was just as good as them...
"...and better.
"But things were getting stranger, the further we went..."
YA! SCRAM!
Things 'round here ain't natural!
This is the WEST, Jimmy! There are things out here **NO ONE'S** expected to see!
"And then, well...er-hem."

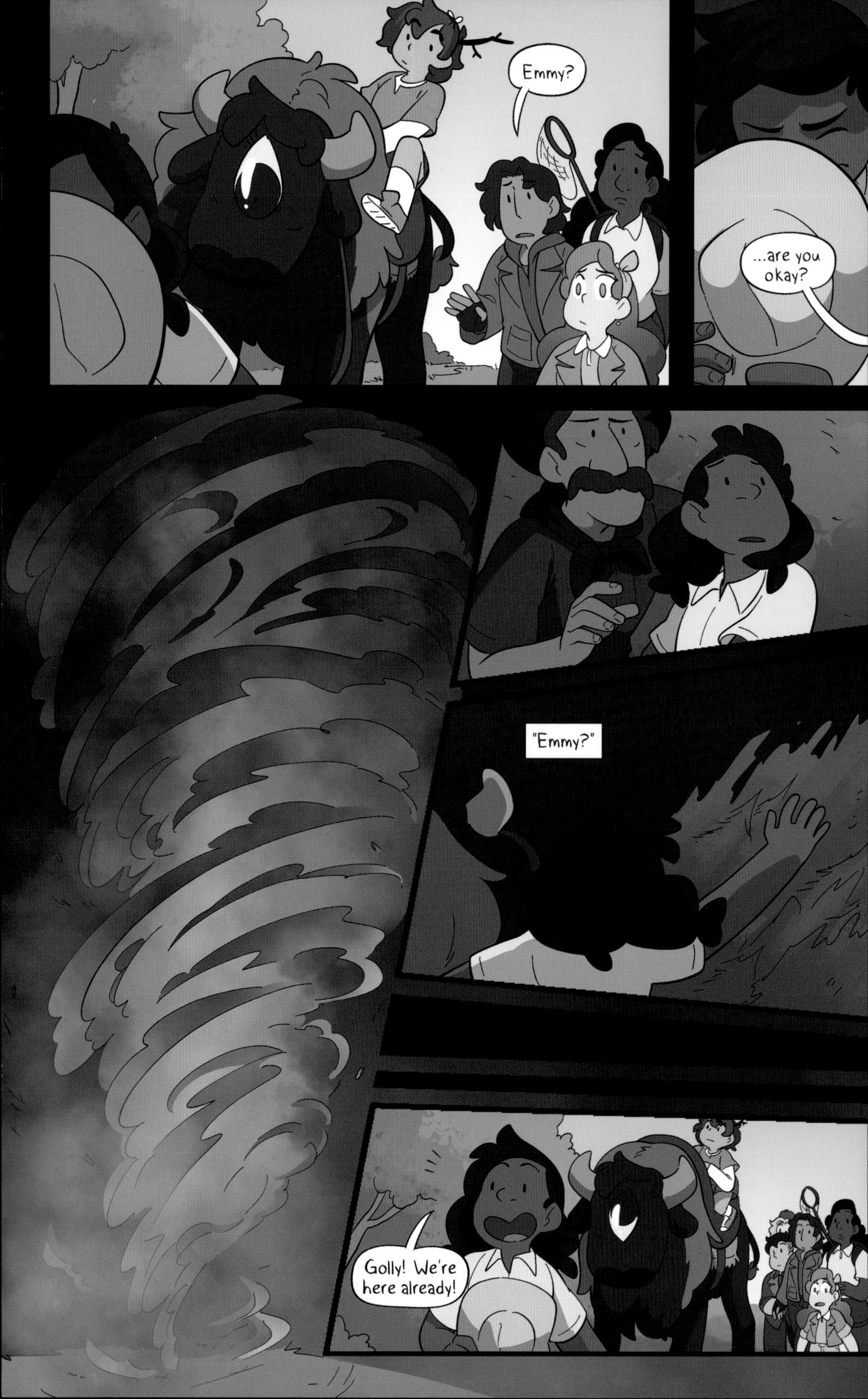
Emmy?
...are you okay?
"Emmy?"
Golly! We're here already!

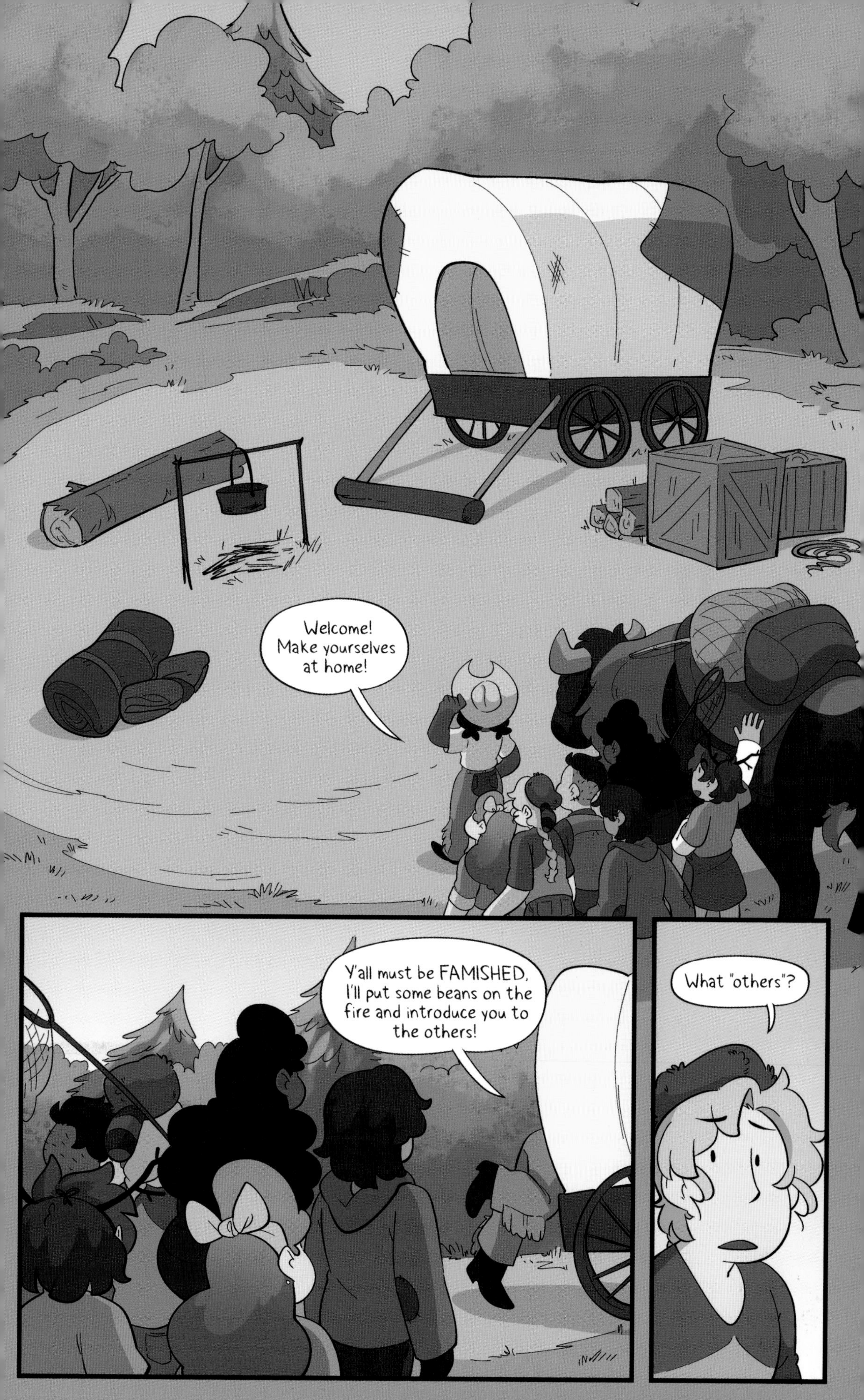
Welcome! Make yourselves at home!
Y'all must be FAMISHED, I'll put some beans on the fire and introduce you to the others!
What "others"?

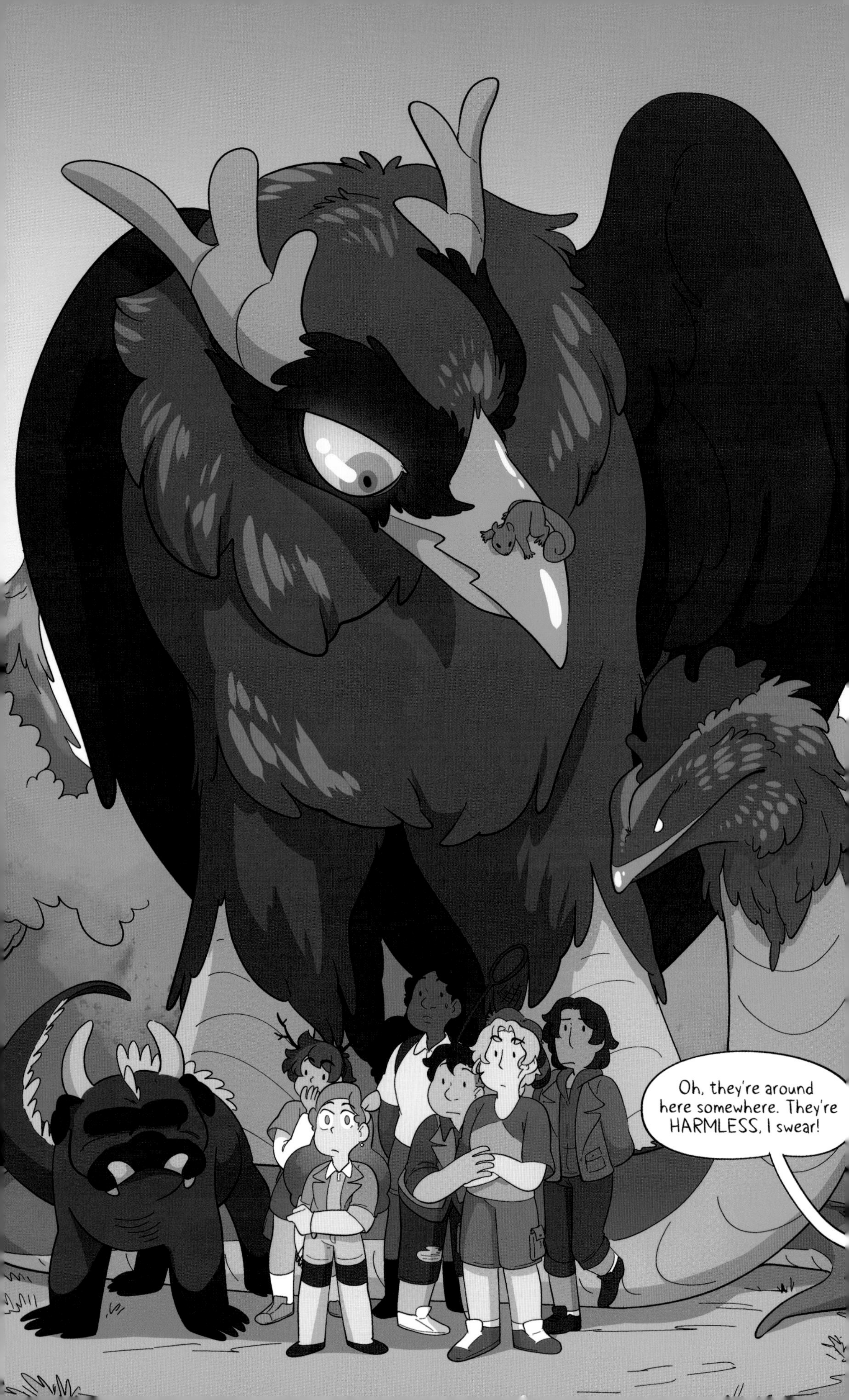
Oh, they're around here somewhere. They're HARMLESS, I swear!

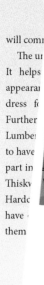

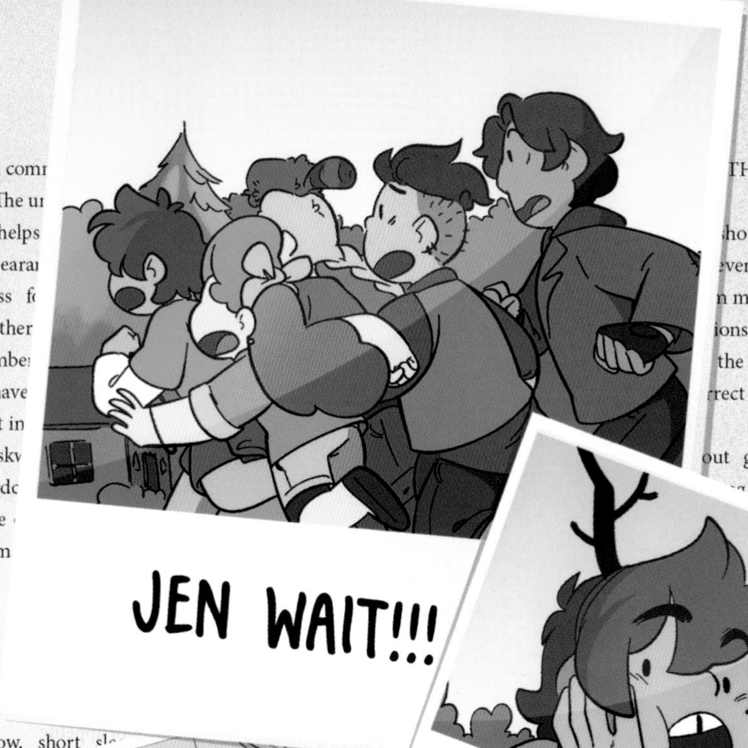
JEN WAIT!!!

will comm

The ur

It helps

appeara

dress f

Further

Lumbe

to have

part in

Thisk

Hard

have

them

THE UNIFORM

should be worn at camp

events when Lumberjanes

n may also be worn at other

ions. It should be worn as a

the uniform dress with

rrect shoes, and stocking or

out grows her uniform or

g to another Lumberjane.

insignia she has

her

her

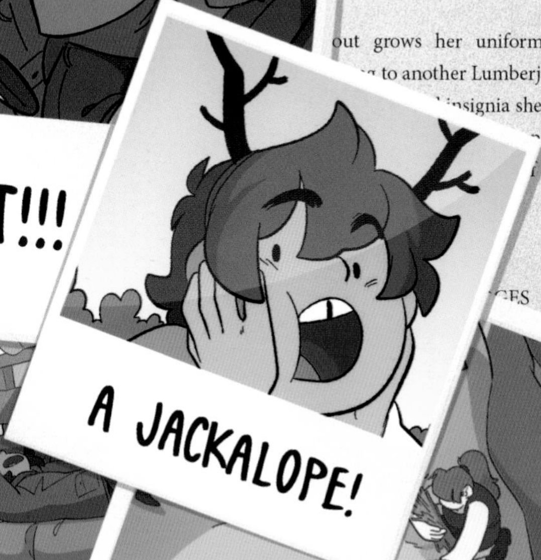
A JACKALOPE!

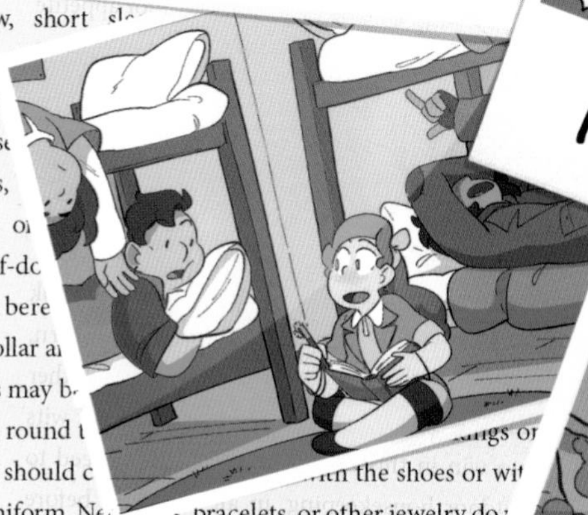

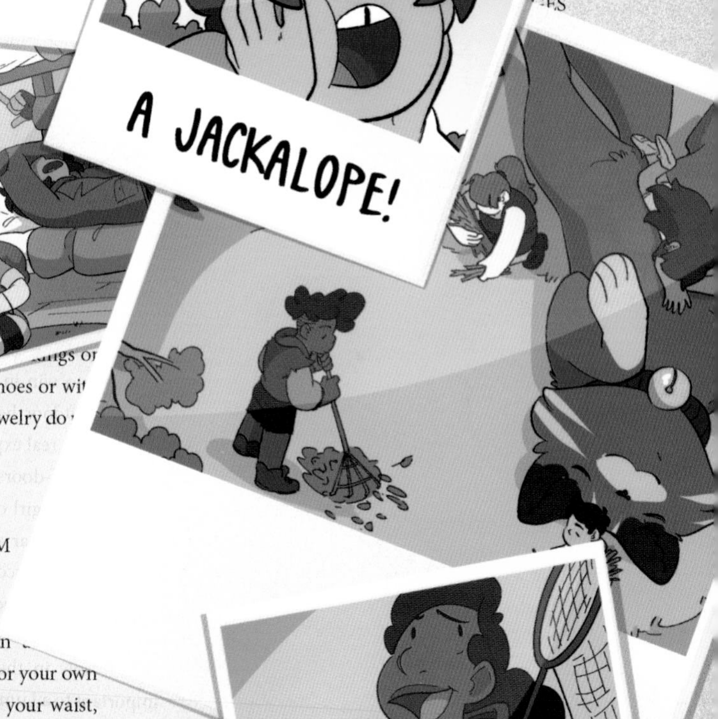

The

yellow, short sl

emb

the w

choose

slacks,

made o

out-of-do

green bere

the collar a

Shoes may b

heels, round t ... ings or

socks should c ... with the shoes or wi

the uniform. Ne... ces, bracelets, or other jewelry do

belong with a Lumberjane uniform.

HOW TO WEAR THE UNIFORM

To look well in a uniform demands first of ... uniform be kept in good condition—clean ... pressed. See that the skirt is the right length for your own height and build, that the belt is adjusted to your waist, that your shoes and stockings are in keeping with the uniform, that you watch your posture and carry yourself with dignity and grace. If the beret is removed indoors, be sure that your hair is neat and kept in place with an inconspicuous clip or ribbon. When you wear a Lumberjane uniform you are identified as a member of this organization and you should be doubly careful to conduct yourself in a way that will show everyone that courtesy and thoughtfulness are part of being a Lumberjane. People are likely to judge a whole nation by the selfishness of a few individuals, to criticize a whole family because of the misconduct of one member, and to feel unkindly toward an organization because of the

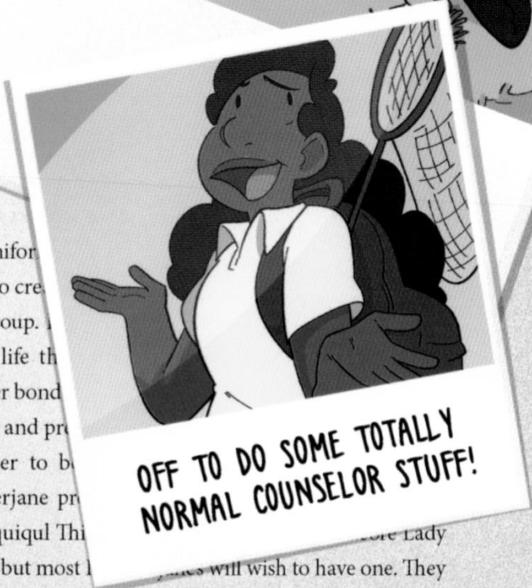
OFF TO DO SOME TOTALLY
NORMAL COUNSELOR STUFF!

The unifor

helps to cre

in a group.

active life th

another bond

future, and pr

in order to b

Lumberjane pr

Penniquiqul Thi ... ore Lady

Types, but most ... janes will wish to have one. They can either buy the uniform, or make it themselves from materials available at the trading post.

LUMBERJANES FIELD MANUAL

CHAPTER
FORTY-SIX

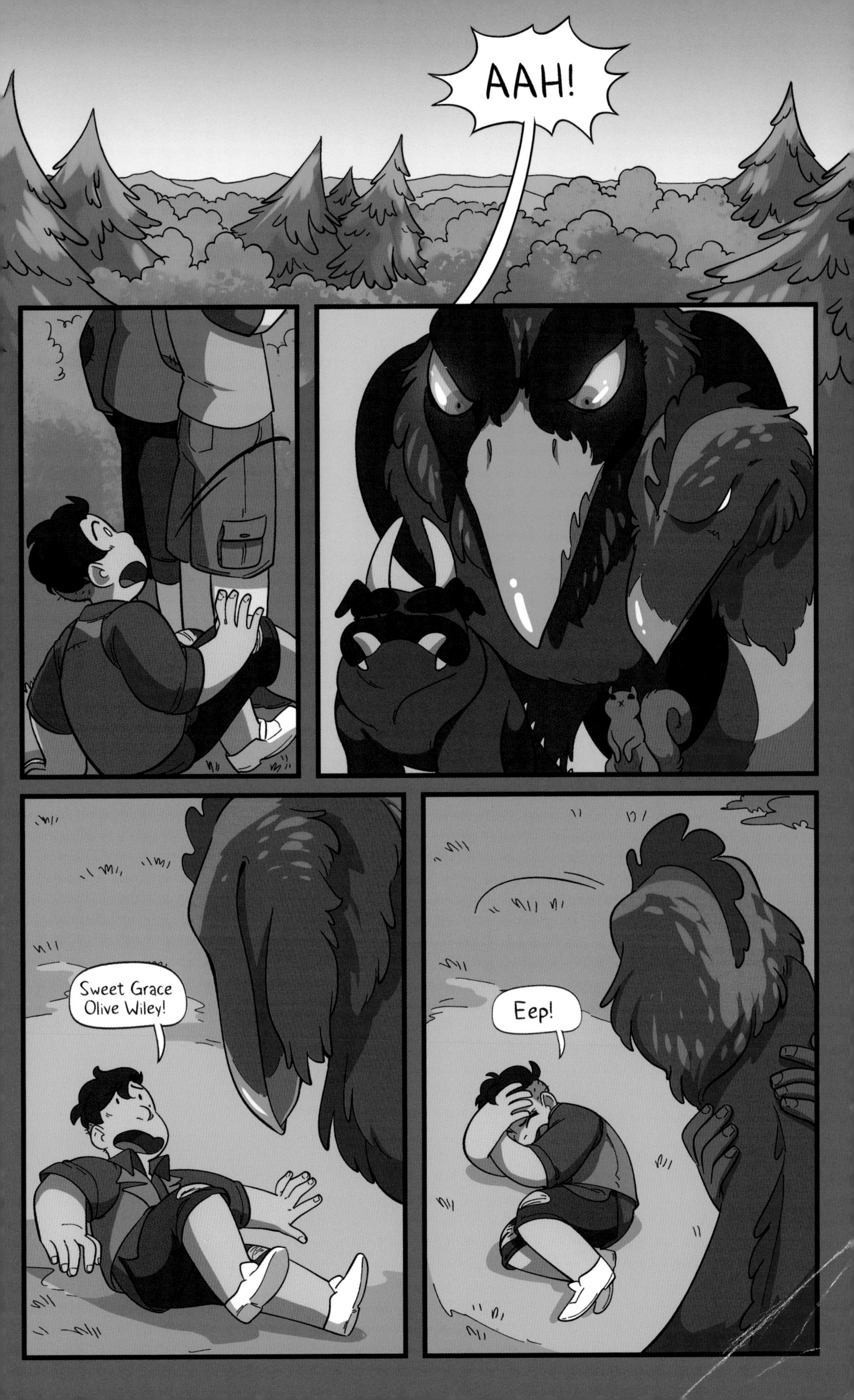
AAH!
Sweet Grace Olive Wiley!
Eep!

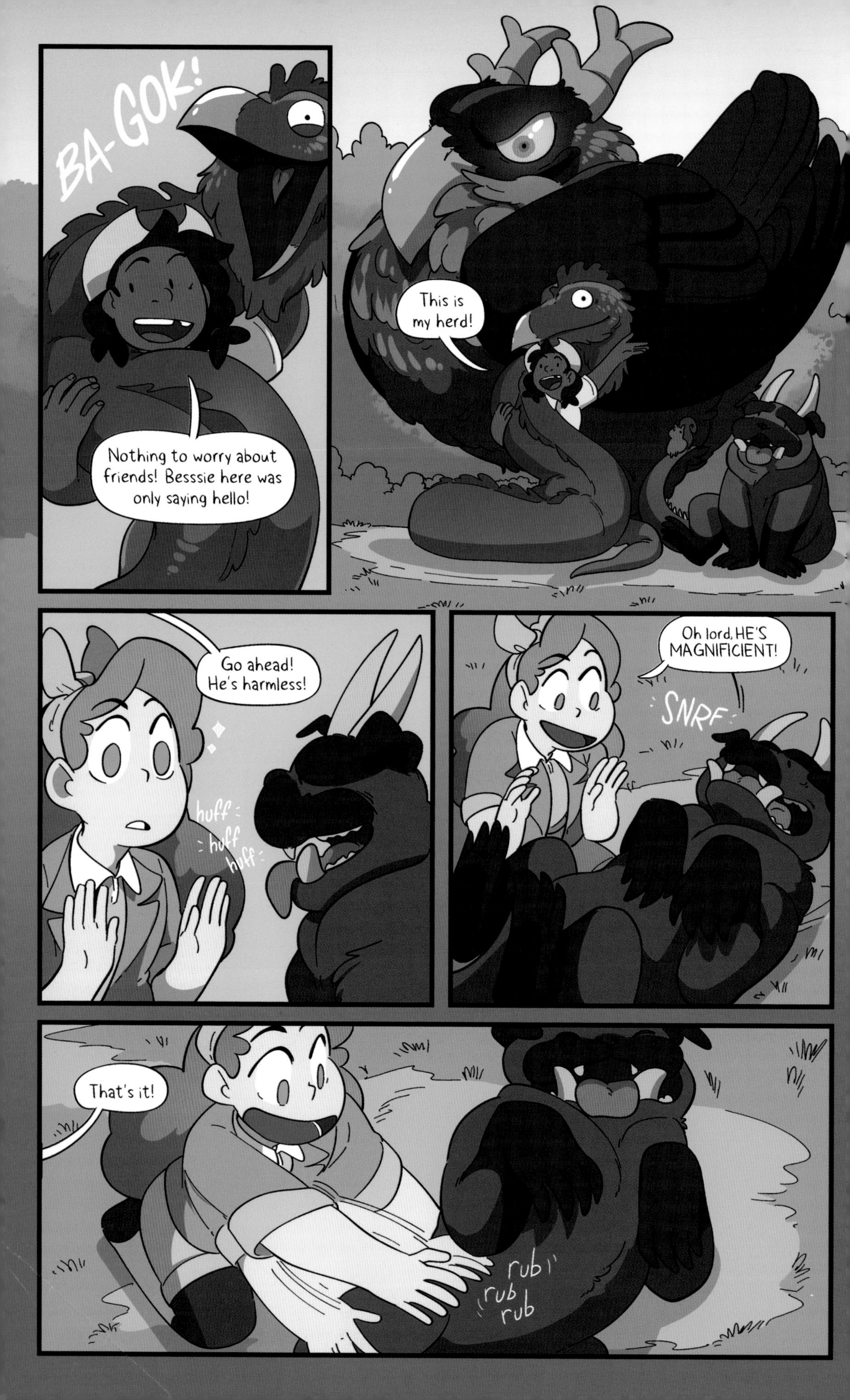
BA-GOK!
Nothing to worry about friends! Besssie here was only saying hello!
This is my herd!
Go ahead! He's harmless!
huff huff huff
Oh lord, HE'S MAGNIFICIENT!
SNRF
That's it!
rub rub rub

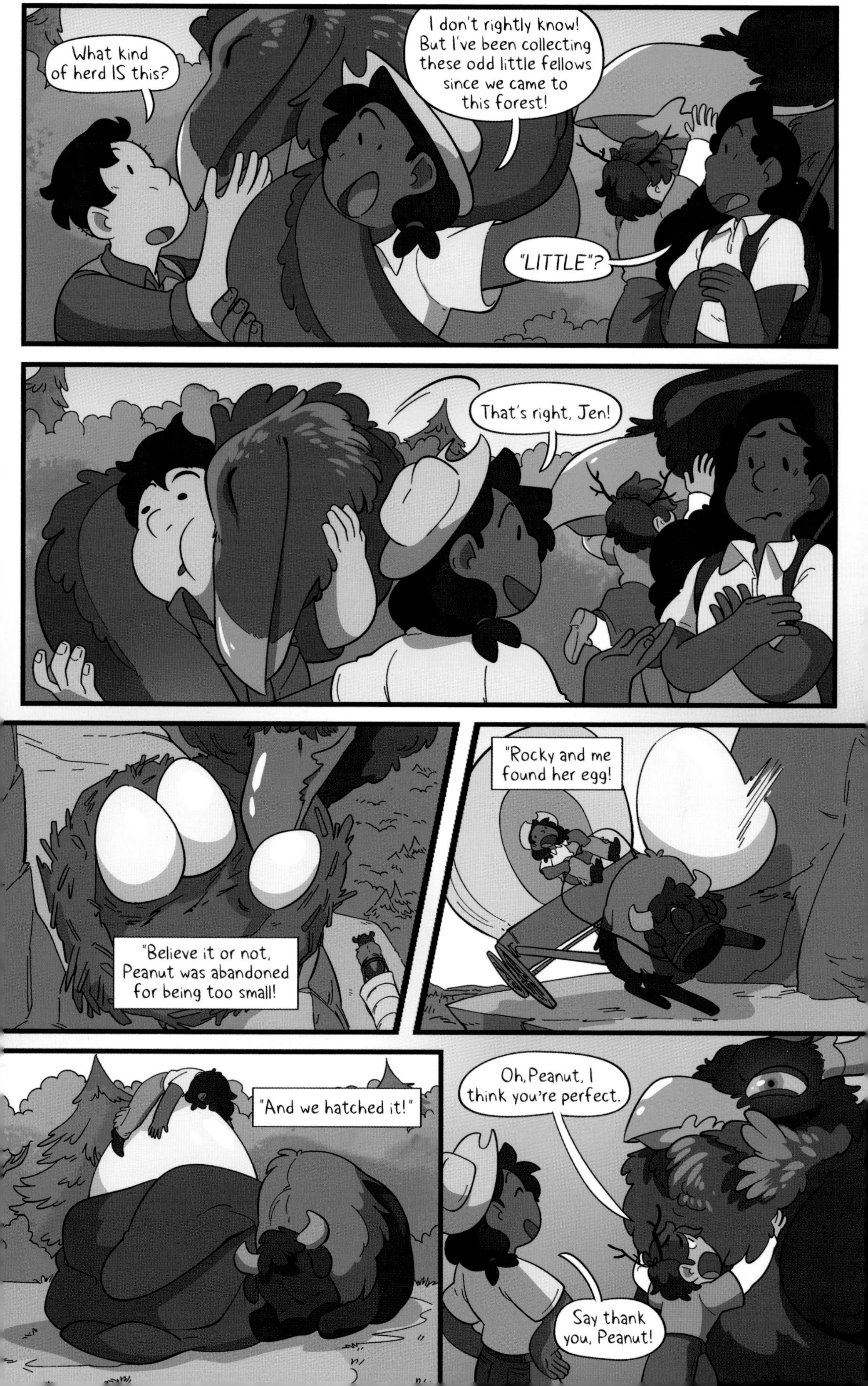
What kind of herd IS this?
I don't rightly know! But I've been collecting these odd little fellows since we came to this forest!
"LITTLE"?
That's right, Jen!
"Believe it or not, Peanut was abandoned for being too small!
"Rocky and me found her egg!
"And we hatched it!"
Oh, Peanut, I think you're perfect.
Say thank you, Peanut!

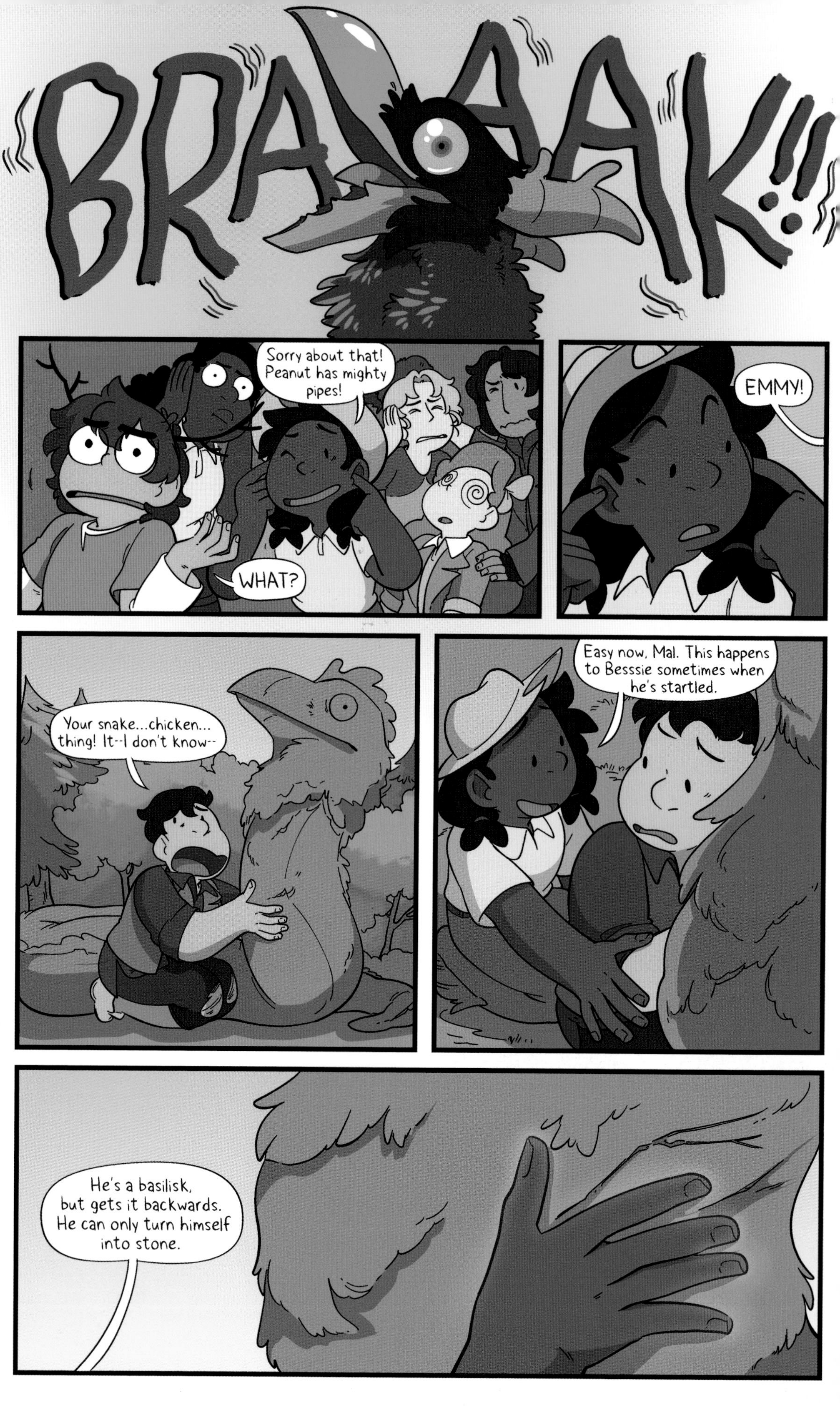
BRAAAK!!!
Sorry about that! Peanut has mighty pipes!
WHAT?
EMMY!
Your snake...chicken... thing! It--I don't know--
Easy now, Mal. This happens to Besssie sometimes when he's startled.
He's a basilisk, but gets it backwards. He can only turn himself into stone.

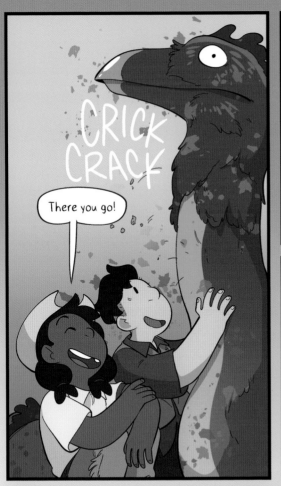

CRICK CRACK

There you go!

Hey, Emmy! What about, uh, this one?

The squirrel?

Ah! Good eye, Jo! This is Eggy! A perfectly normal looking squirrel, right?

BUT...

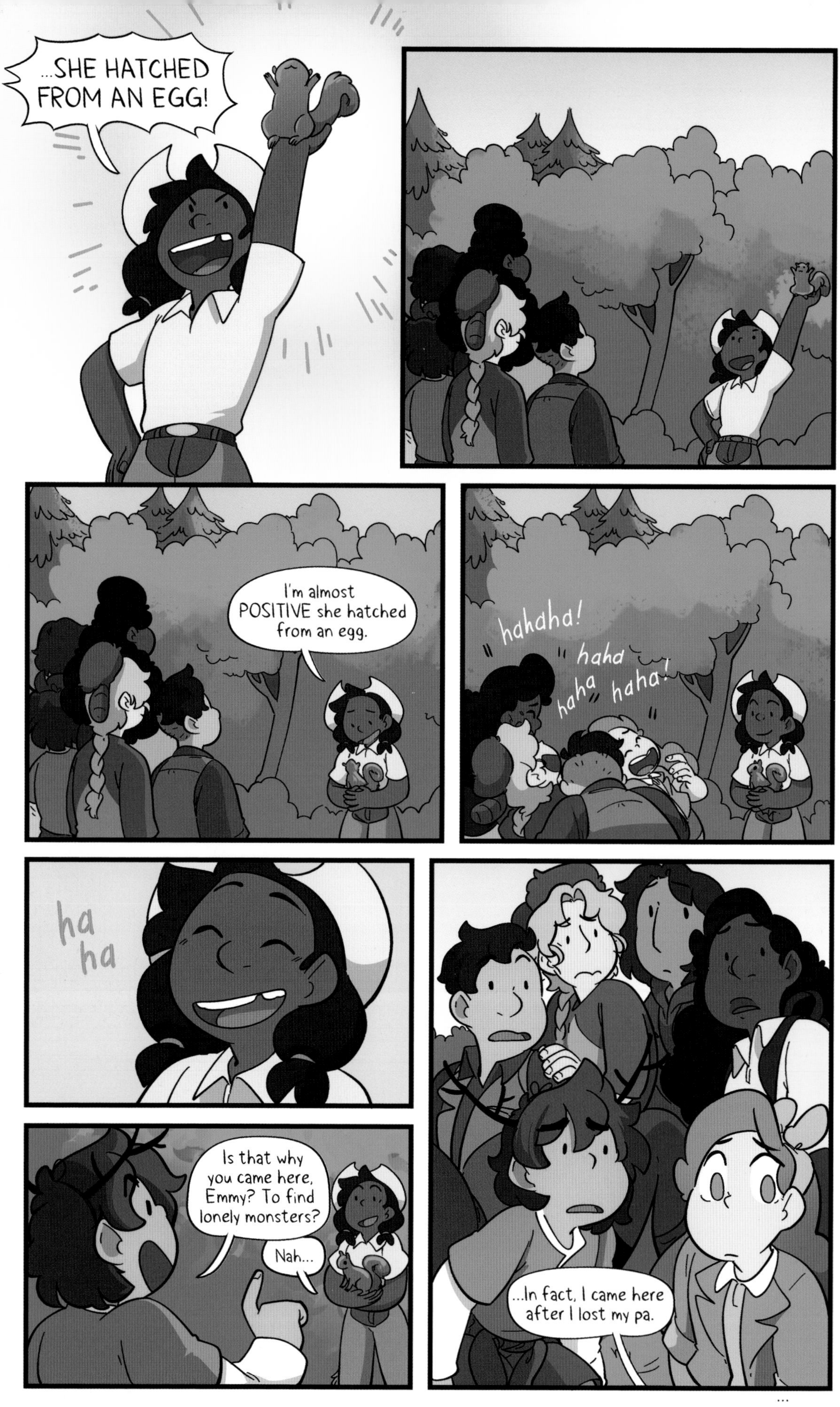
...SHE HATCHED FROM AN EGG!
I'm almost POSITIVE she hatched from an egg.
hahaha!
haha
haha
haha!
ha ha
Is that why you came here, Emmy? To find lonely monsters?
Nah...
...In fact, I came here after I lost my pa.
...

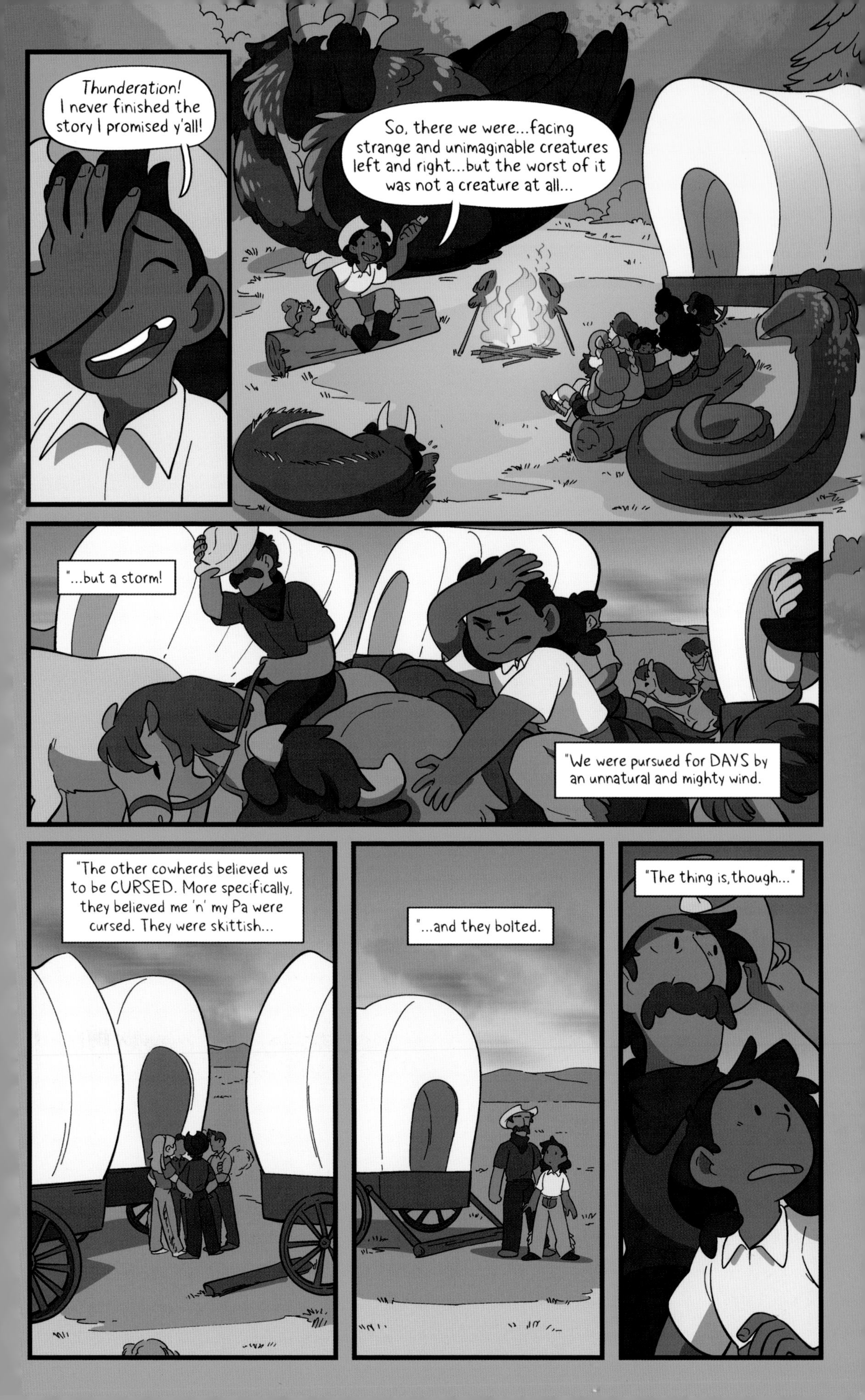
Thunderation! I never finished the story I promised y'all!
So, there we were...facing strange and unimaginable creatures left and right...but the worst of it was not a creature at all...
"...but a storm!
"We were pursued for DAYS by an unnatural and mighty wind.
"The other cowherds believed us to be CURSED. More specifically, they believed me 'n' my Pa were cursed. They were skittish...
"...and they bolted.
"The thing is, though..."

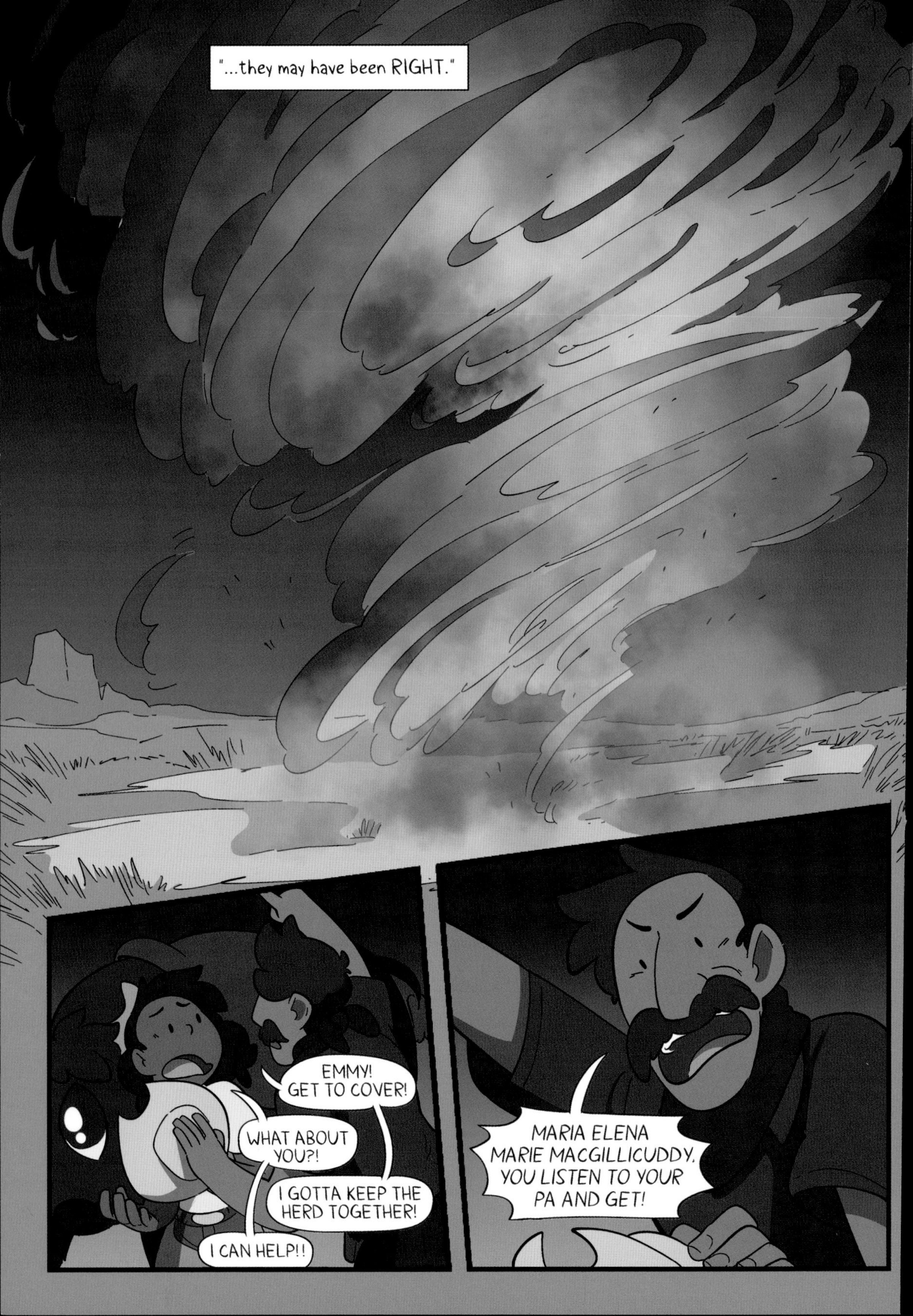
"...they may have been RIGHT."
EMMY! GET TO COVER!
WHAT ABOUT YOU?!
I GOTTA KEEP THE HERD TOGETHER!
I CAN HELP!!
MARIA ELENA MARIE MACGILLICUDDY. YOU LISTEN TO YOUR PA AND GET!

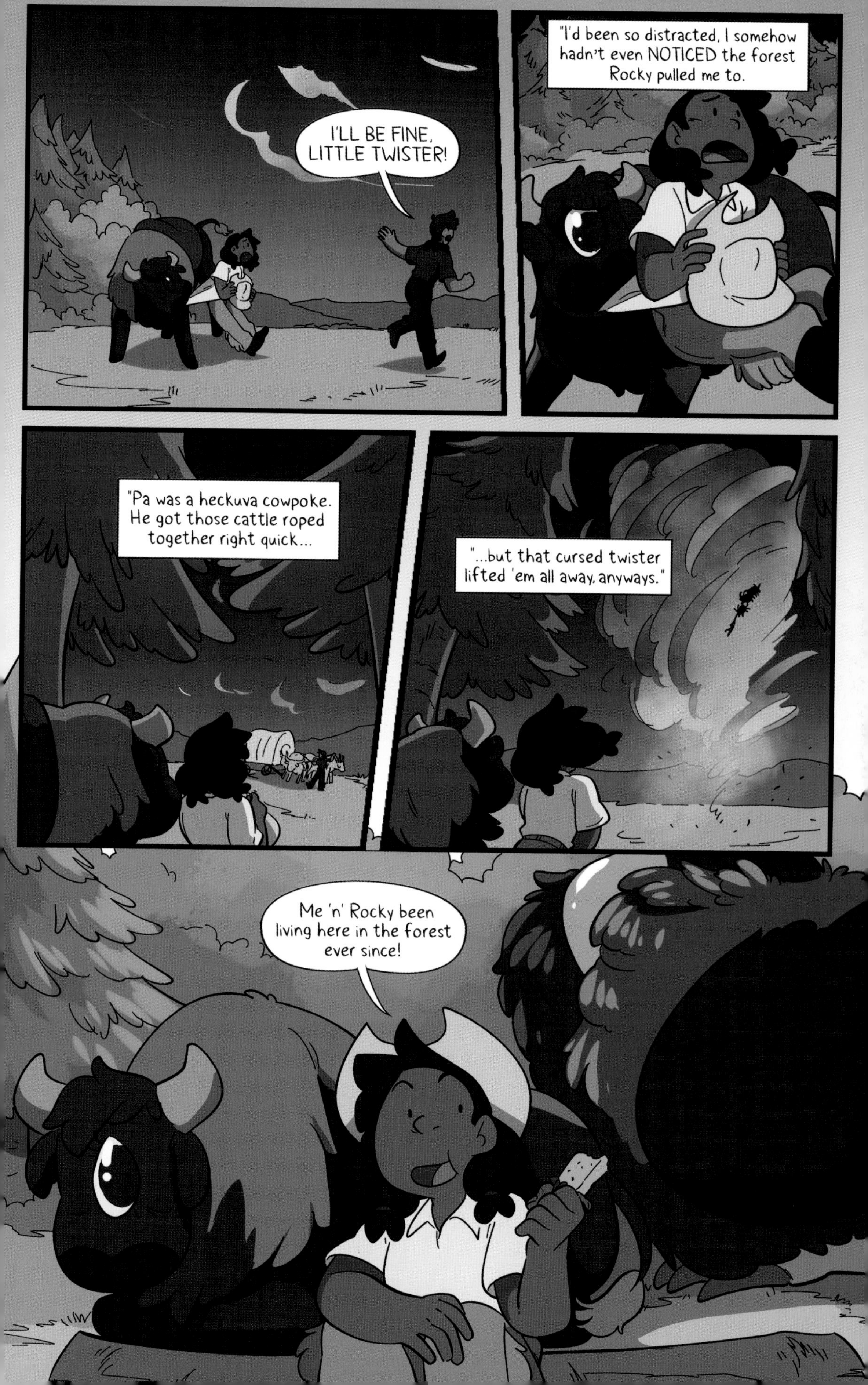
I'LL BE FINE, LITTLE TWISTER!
"I'd been so distracted, I somehow hadn't even NOTICED the forest Rocky pulled me to.
"Pa was a heckuva cowpoke. He got those cattle roped together right quick...
"...but that cursed twister lifted 'em all away, anyways."
Me 'n' Rocky been living here in the forest ever since!

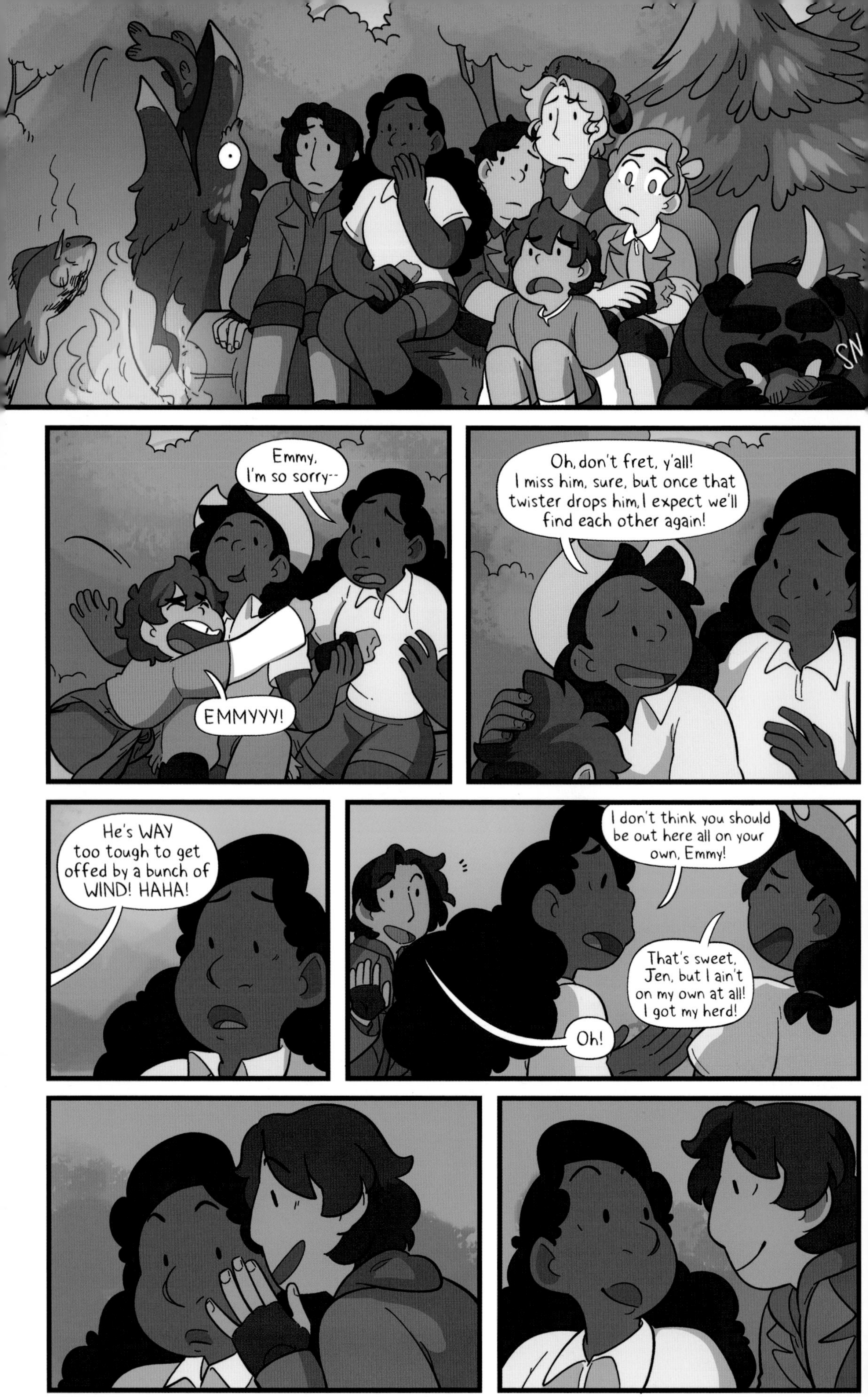
Emmy, I'm so sorry--
EMMYYY!
Oh, don't fret, y'all! I miss him, sure, but once that twister drops him, I expect we'll find each other again!
He's WAY too tough to get offed by a bunch of WIND! HAHA!
I don't think you should be out here all on your own, Emmy!
That's sweet, Jen, but I ain't on my own at all! I got my herd!
Oh!

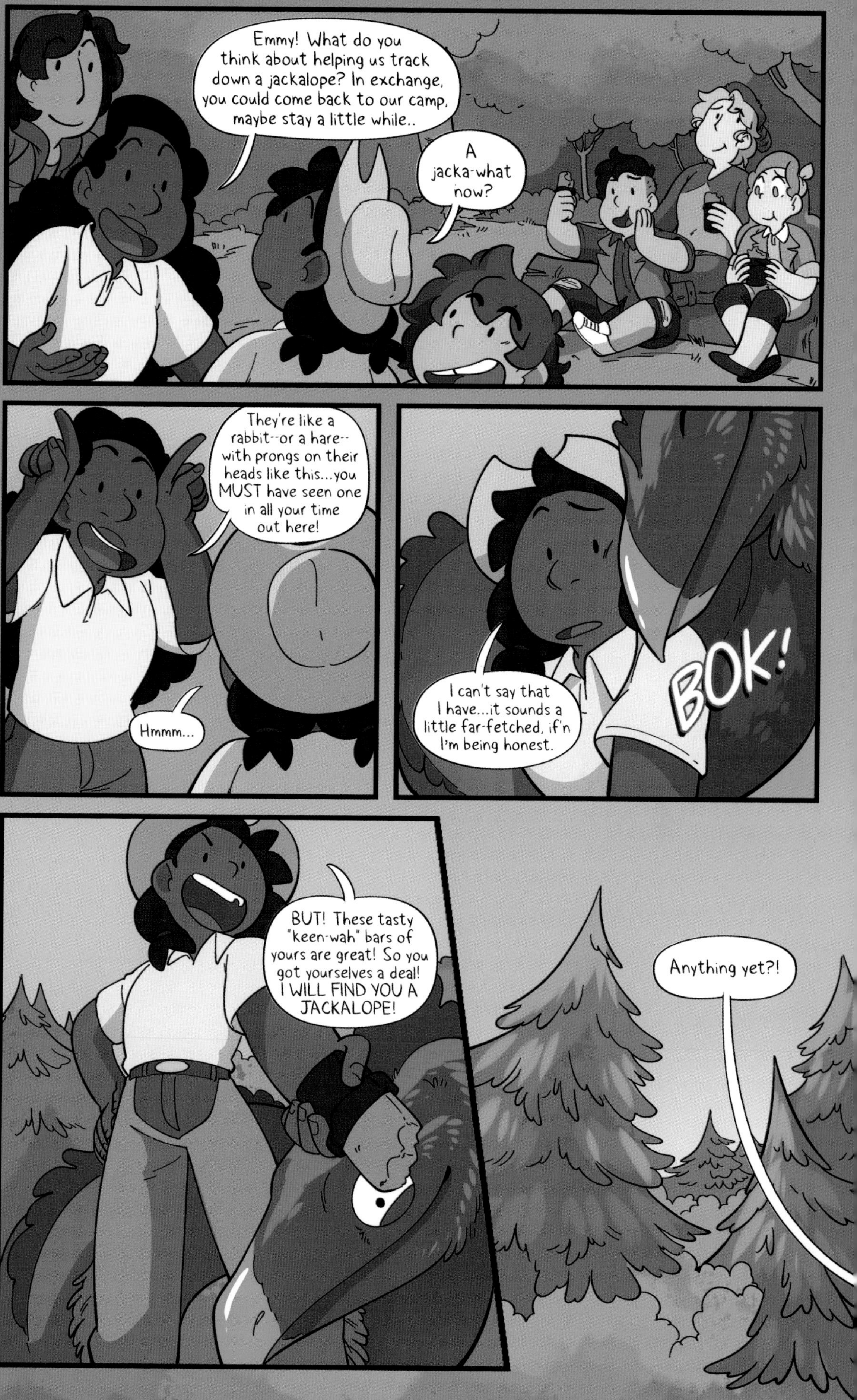
Emmy! What do you think about helping us track down a jackalope? In exchange, you could come back to our camp, maybe stay a little while..
A jacka-what now?
They're like a rabbit--or a hare--with prongs on their heads like this...you MUST have seen one in all your time out here!
Hmmm...
I can't say that I have...it sounds a little far-fetched, if'n I'm being honest.
BOK!
BUT! These tasty "keen-wah" bars of yours are great! So you got yourselves a deal! I WILL FIND YOU A JACKALOPE!
Anything yet?!

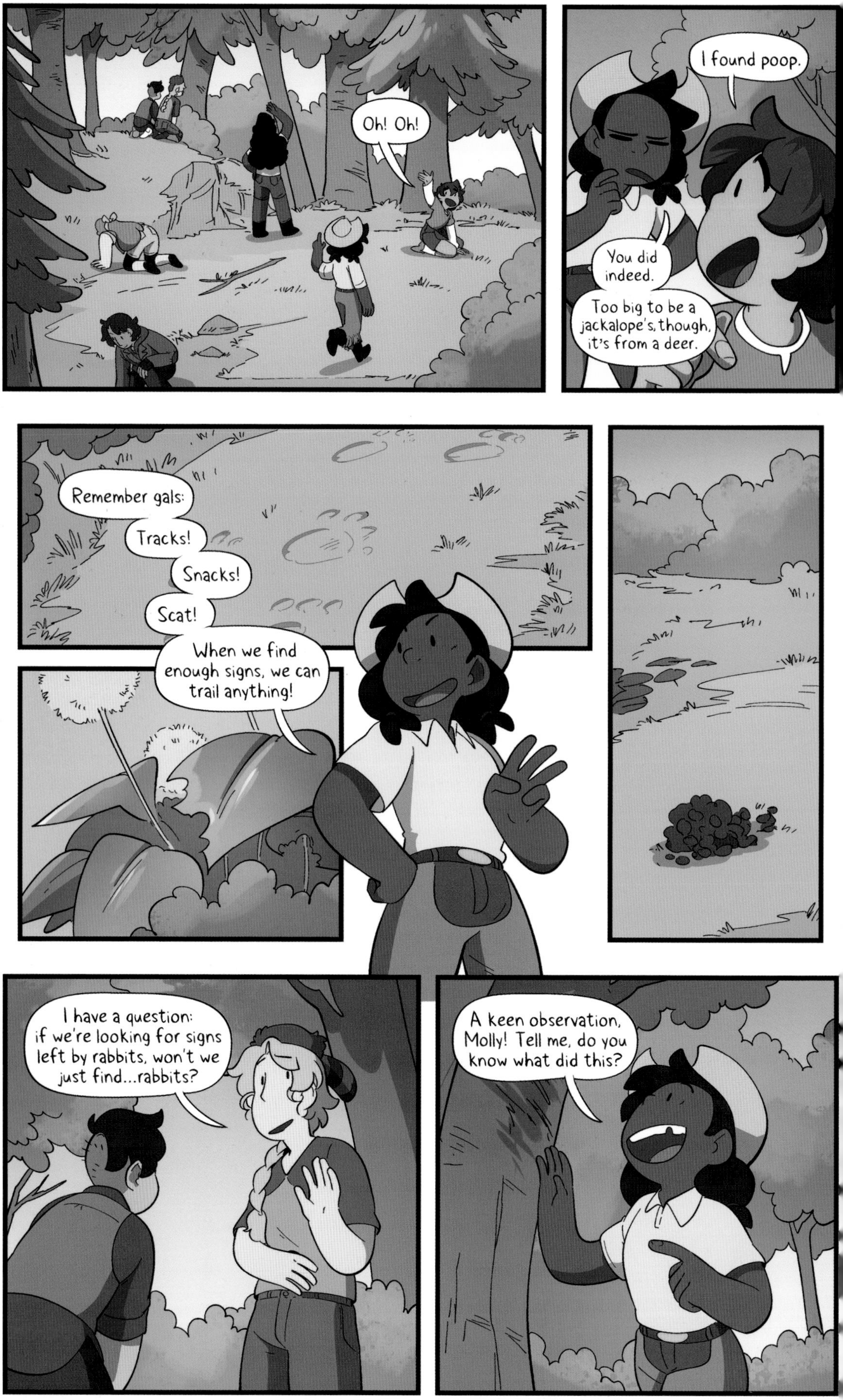
Oh! Oh!
I found poop.
You did indeed.
Too big to be a jackalope's, though, it's from a deer.
Remember gals:
Tracks!
Snacks!
Scat!
When we find enough signs, we can trail anything!
I have a question: if we're looking for signs left by rabbits, won't we just find...rabbits?
A keen observation, Molly! Tell me, do you know what did this?

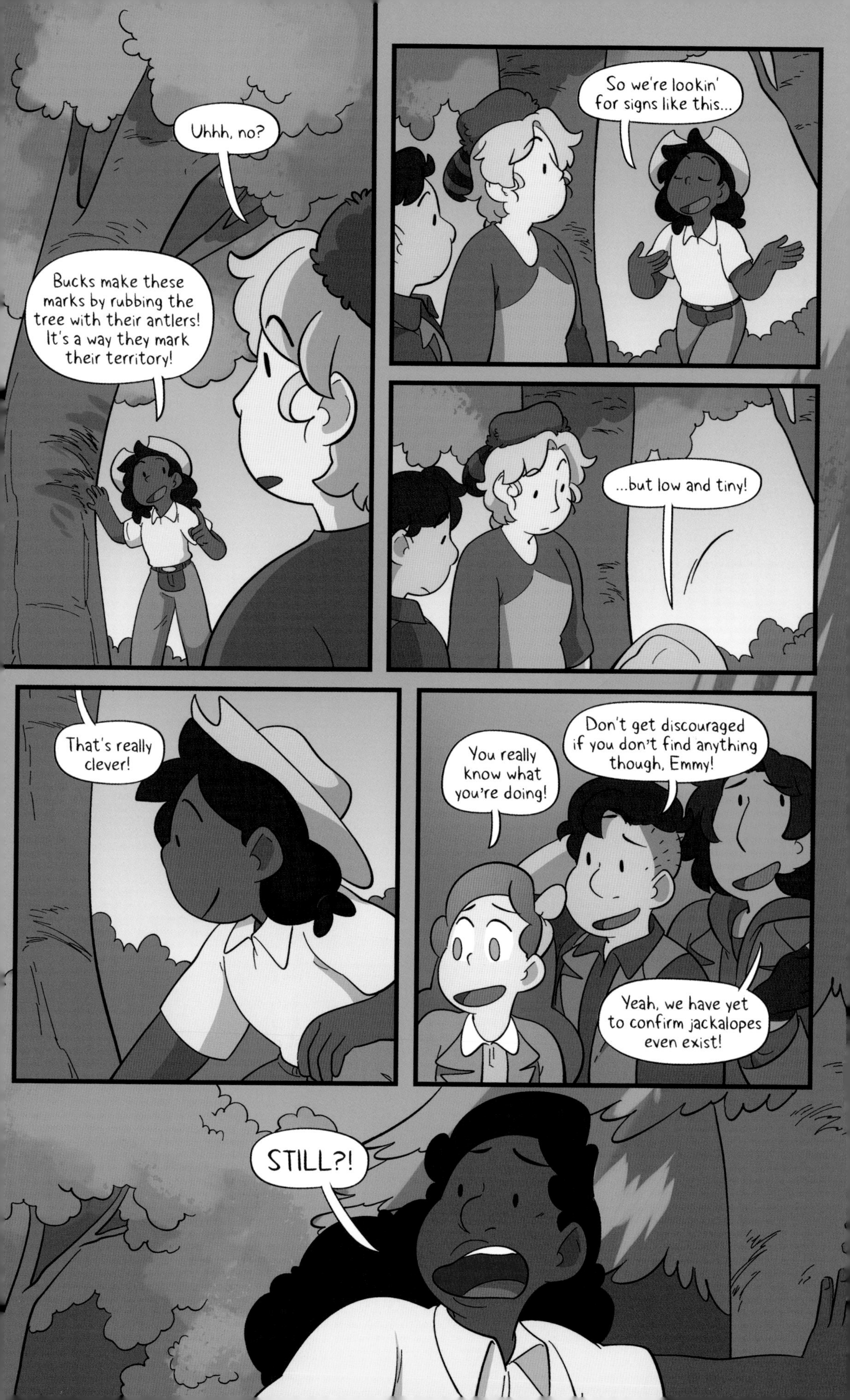
Uhhh, no?
Bucks make these marks by rubbing the tree with their antlers! It's a way they mark their territory!
So we're lookin' for signs like this...
...but low and tiny!
That's really clever!
You really know what you're doing!
Don't get discouraged if you don't find anything though, Emmy!
Yeah, we have yet to confirm jackalopes even exist!
STILL?!

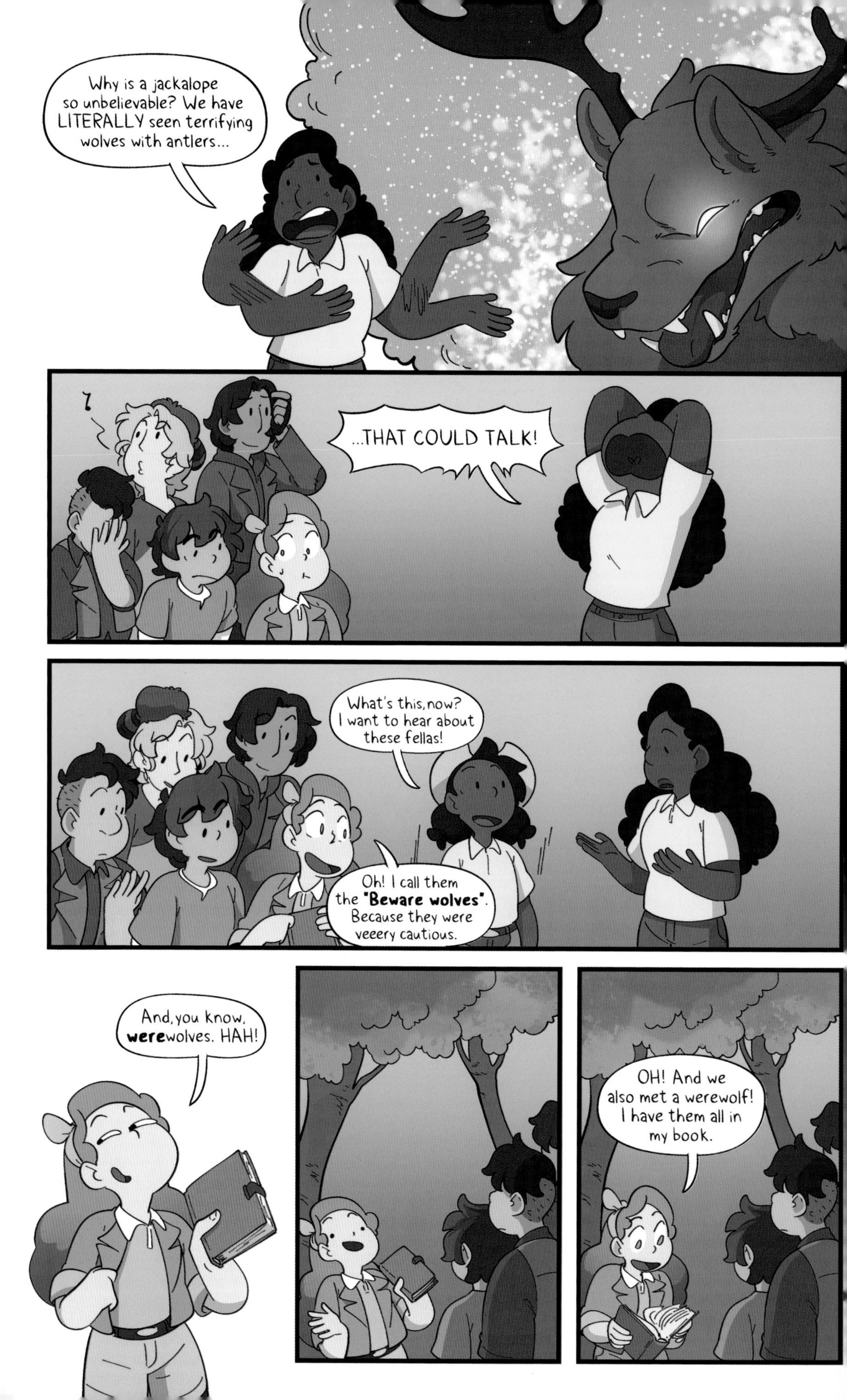

Why is a jackalope so unbelievable? We have LITERALLY seen terrifying wolves with antlers...
...THAT COULD TALK!
What's this, now? I want to hear about these fellas!
Oh! I call them the "Beware wolves". Because they were veeery cautious.
And, you know, werewolves. HAH!
OH! And we also met a werewolf! I have them all in my book.

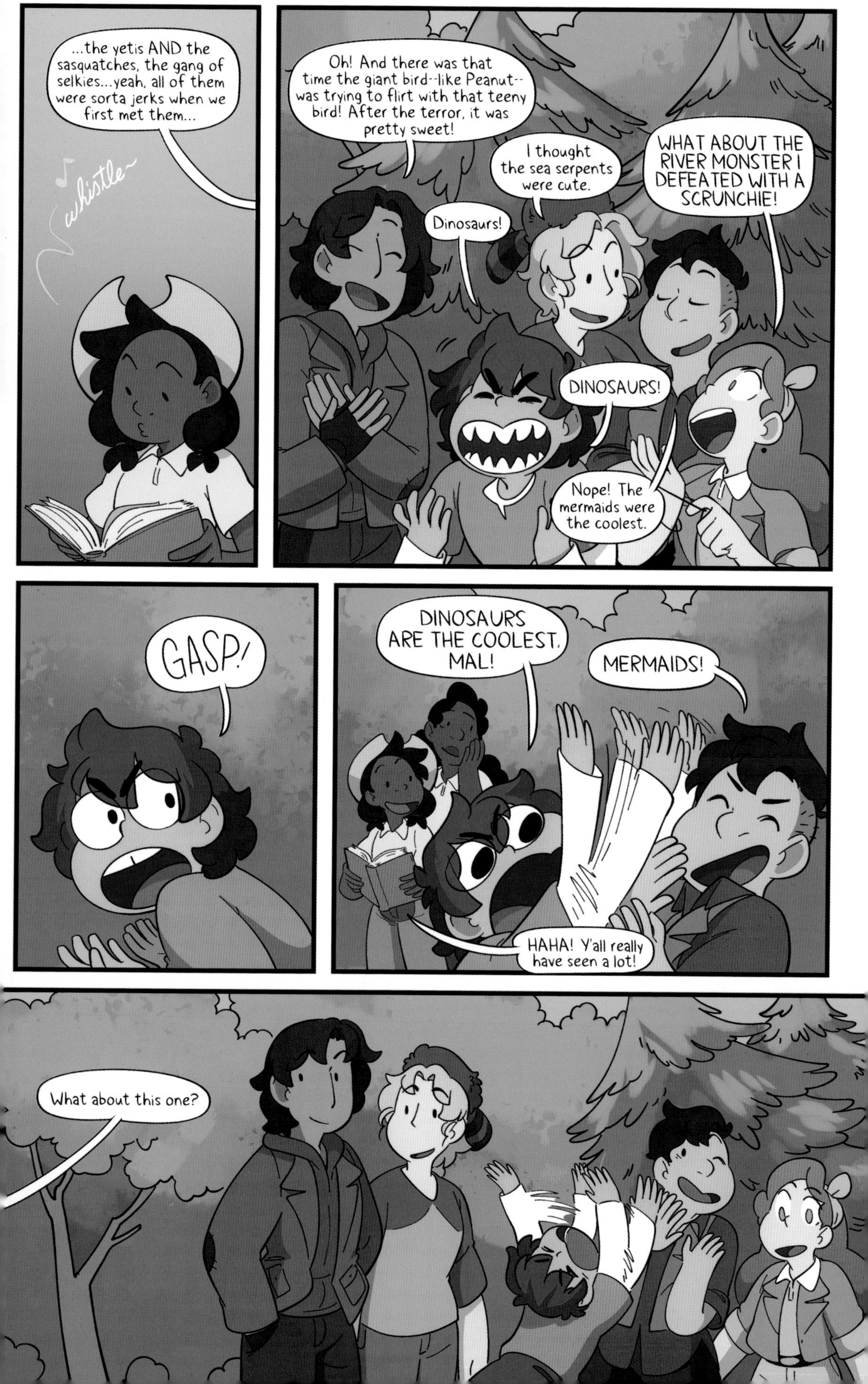
...the yetis AND the sasquatches, the gang of selkies...yeah, all of them were sorta jerks when we first met them...
whistle~
Oh! And there was that time the giant bird--like Peanut--was trying to flirt with that teeny bird! After the terror, it was pretty sweet!
I thought the sea serpents were cute.
WHAT ABOUT THE RIVER MONSTER I DEFEATED WITH A SCRUNCHIE!
Dinosaurs!
DINOSAURS!
Nope! The mermaids were the coolest.
GASP!
DINOSAURS ARE THE COOLEST, MAL!
MERMAIDS!
HAHA! Y'all really have seen a lot!
What about this one?

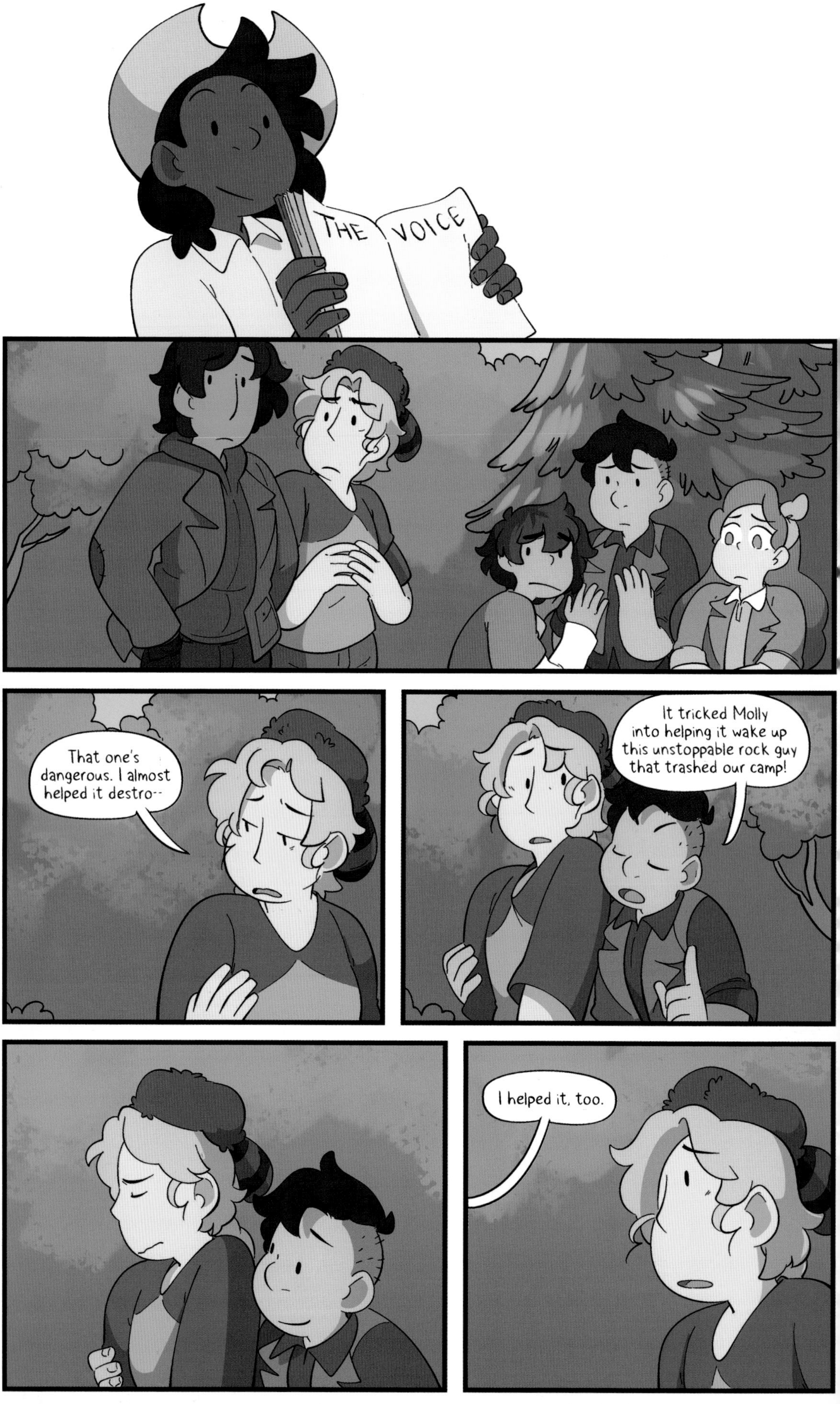
THE VOICE
That one's dangerous. I almost helped it destro--
It tricked Molly into helping it wake up this unstoppable rock guy that trashed our camp!
I helped it, too.

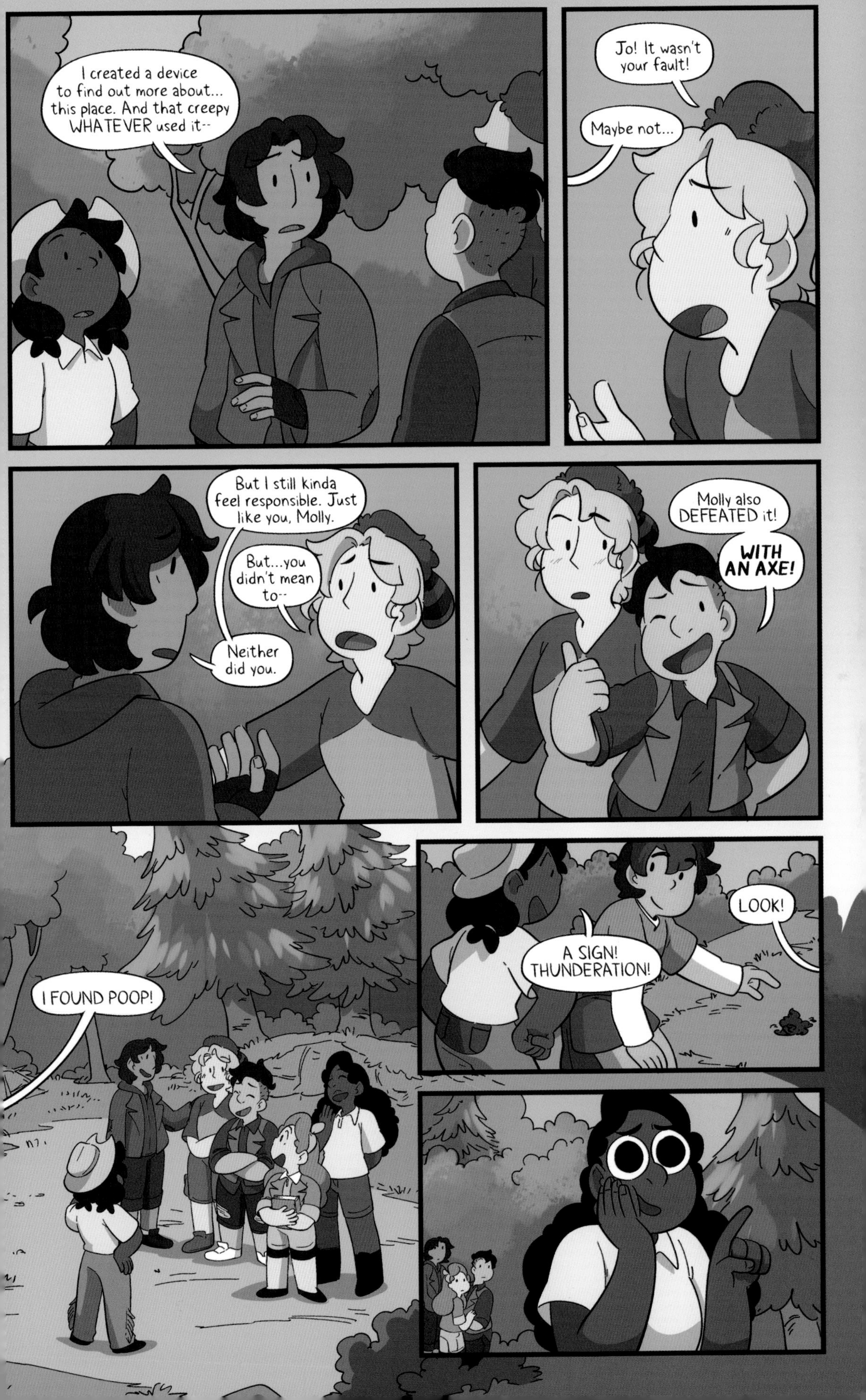
I created a device to find out more about... this place. And that creepy WHATEVER used it--
Jo! It wasn't your fault!
Maybe not...
But I still kinda feel responsible. Just like you, Molly.
But...you didn't mean to--
Neither did you.
Molly also DEFEATED it!
WITH AN AXE!
I FOUND POOP!
LOOK!
A SIGN! THUNDERATION!

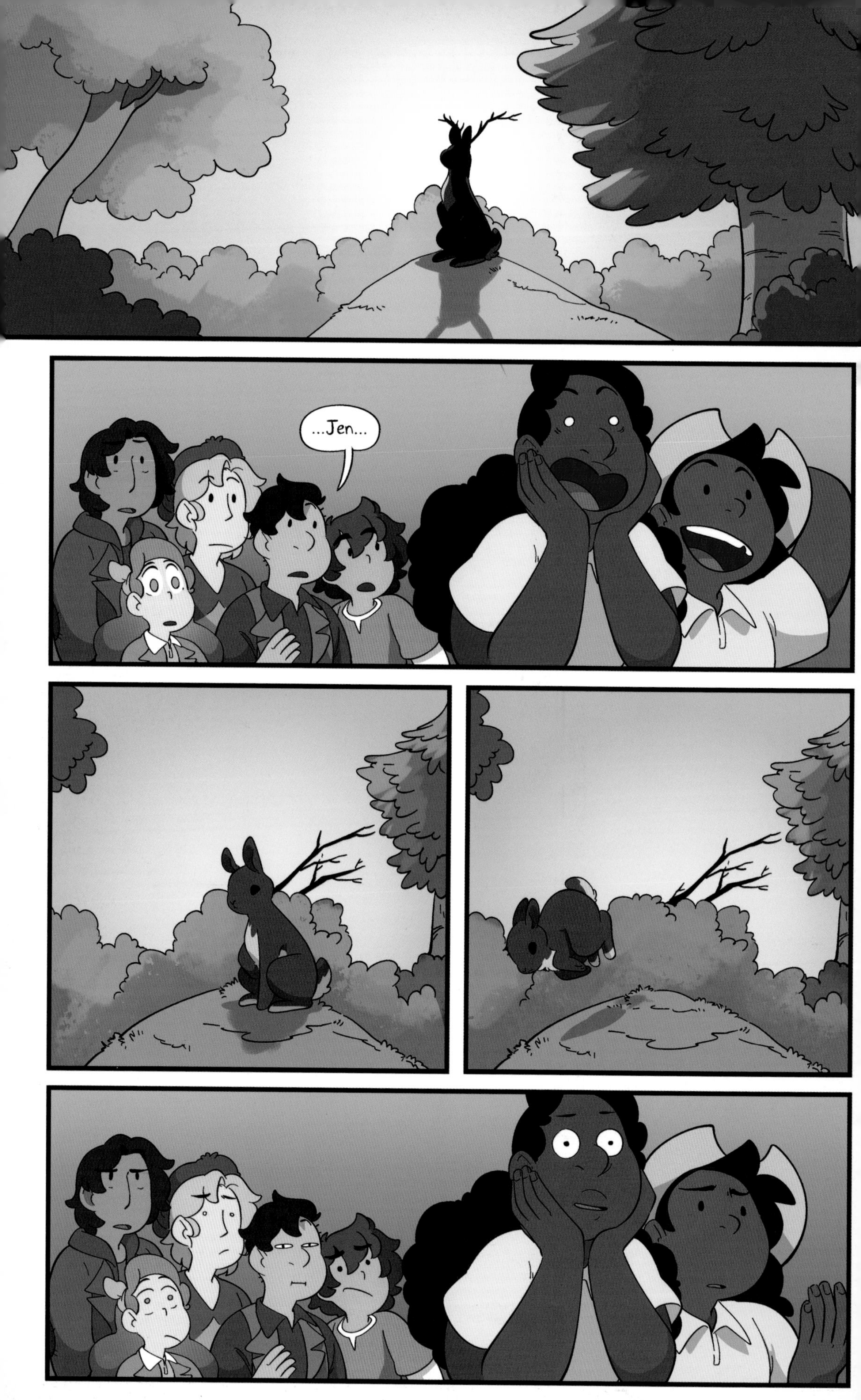
...Jen...

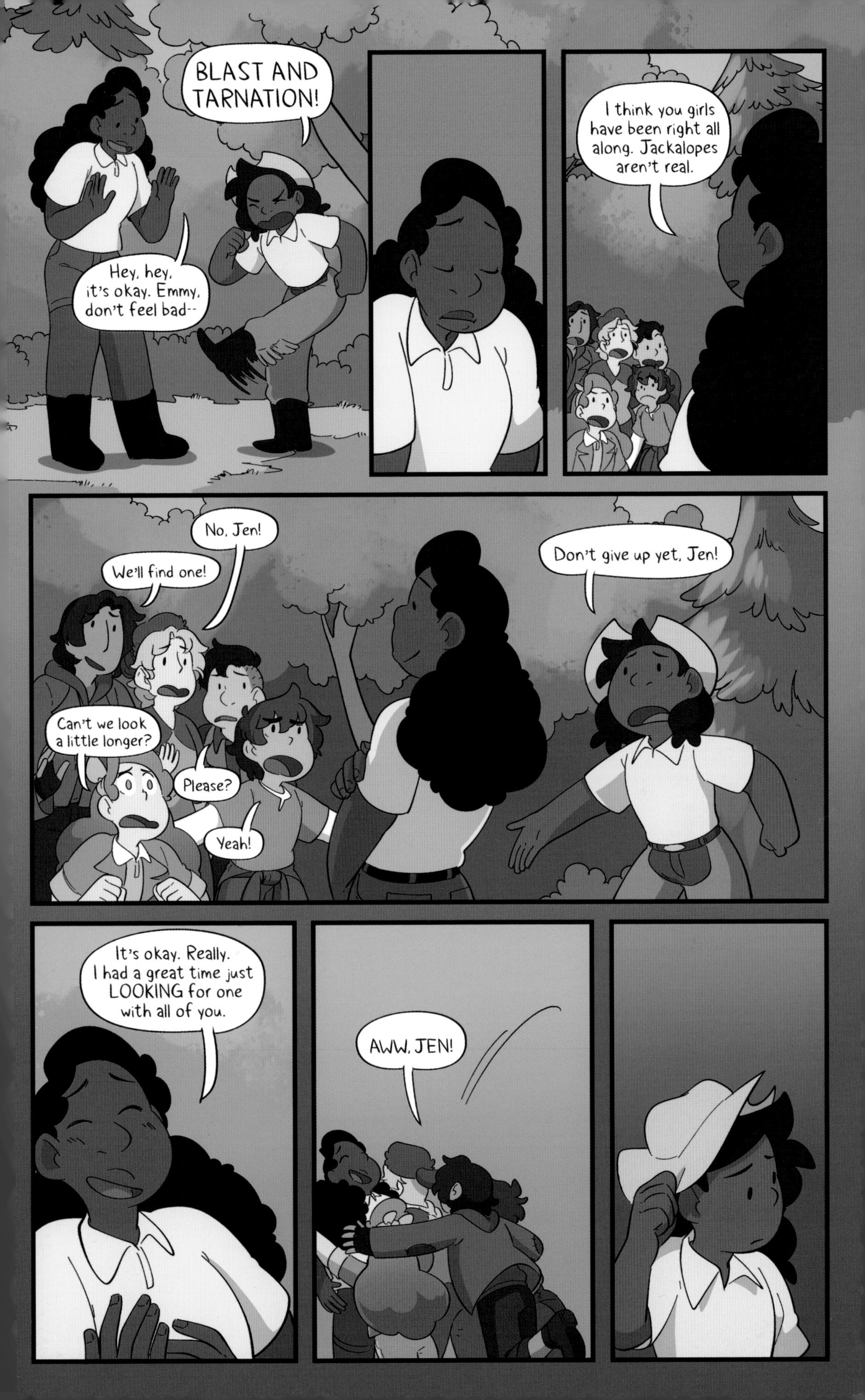
BLAST AND TARNATION!
Hey, hey, it's okay. Emmy, don't feel bad--
I think you girls have been right all along. Jackalopes aren't real.
No, Jen!
We'll find one!
Don't give up yet, Jen!
Can't we look a little longer?
Please?
Yeah!
It's okay. Really. I had a great time just LOOKING for one with all of you.
AWW, JEN!

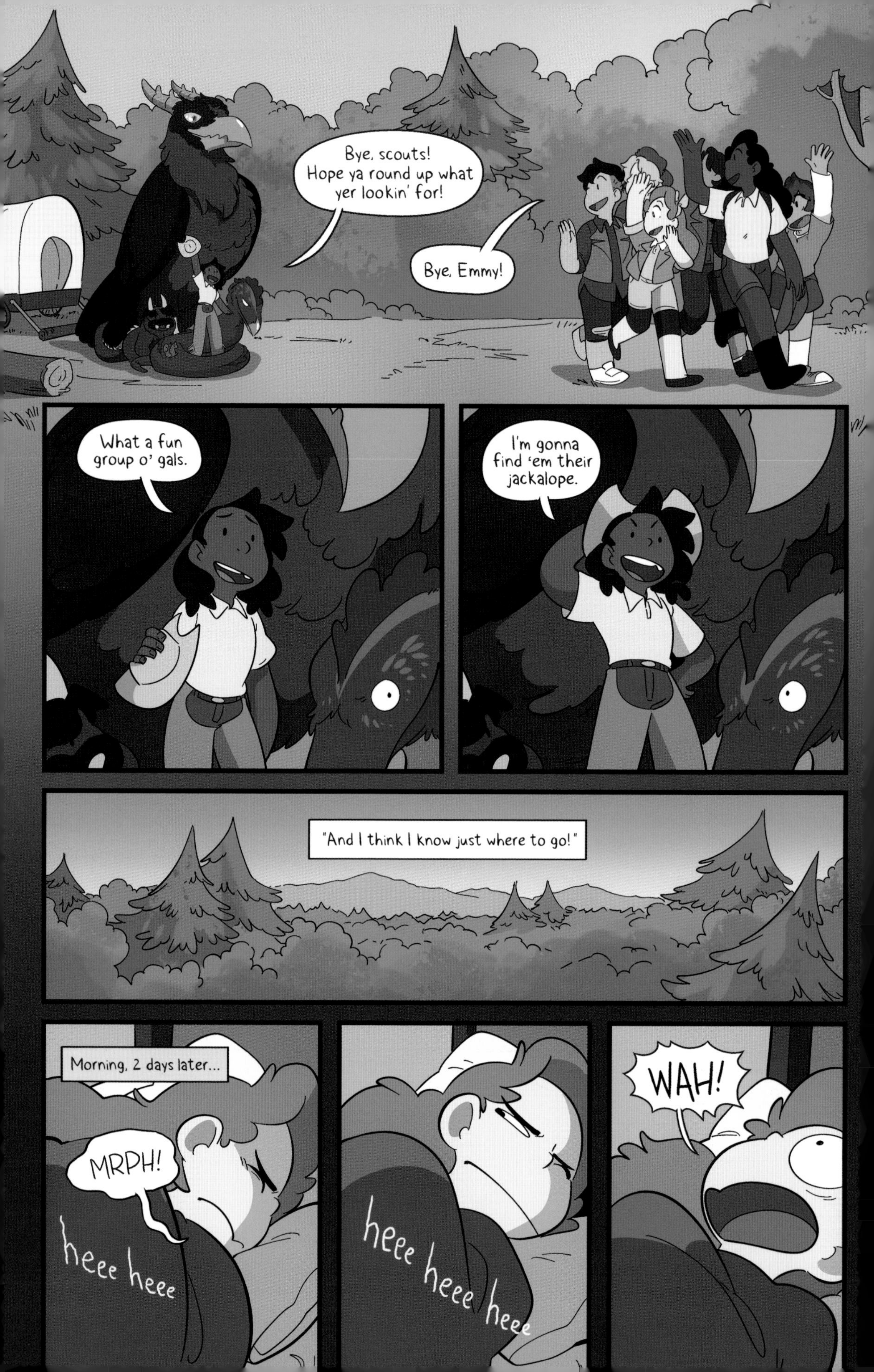
Bye, scouts! Hope ya round up what yer lookin' for!
Bye, Emmy!
What a fun group o' gals.
I'm gonna find 'em their jackalope.
"And I think I know just where to go!"
Morning, 2 days later...
MRPH!
heee heee
heee heee heee
WAH!

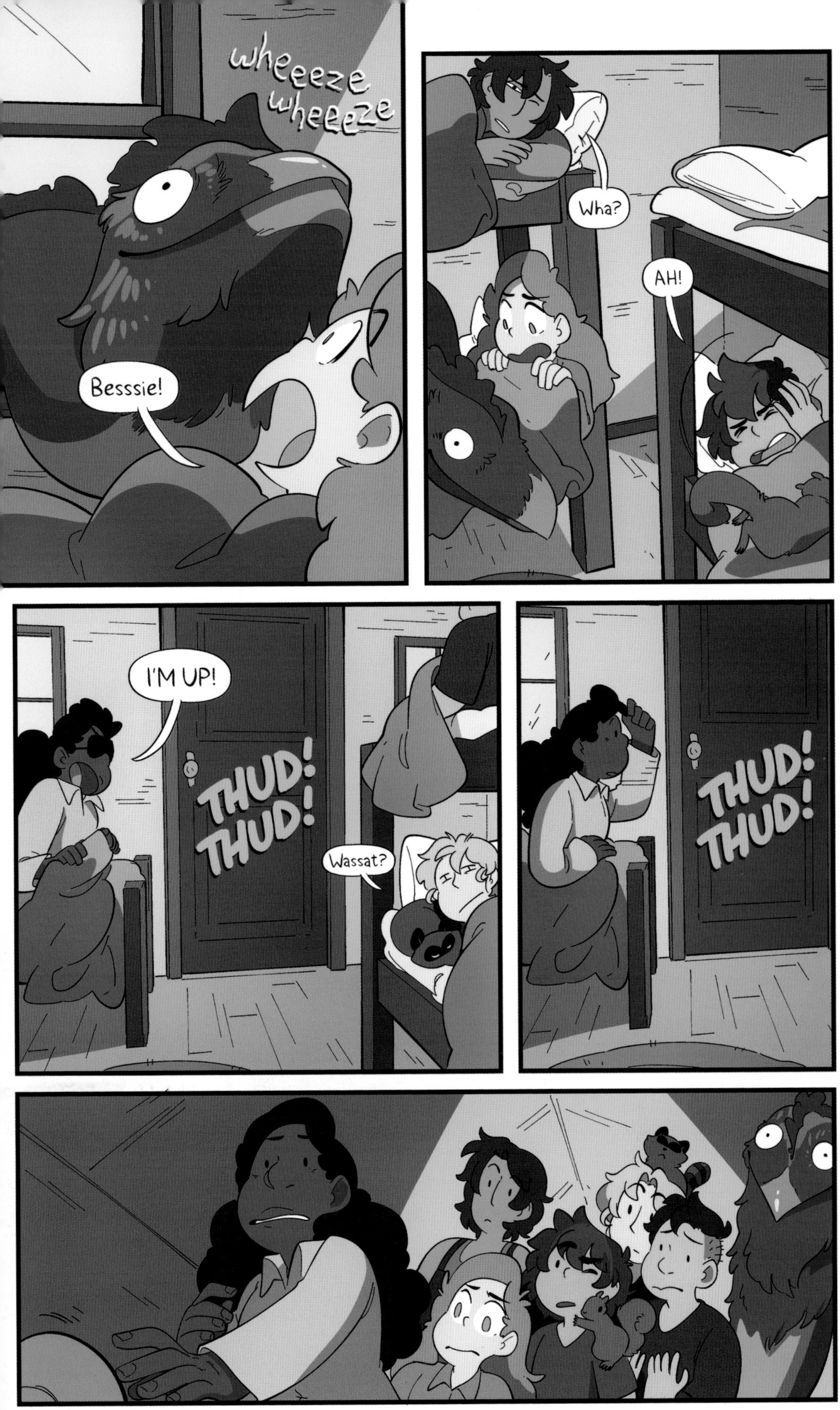
wheeeze
wheeeze
Besssie!
Wha?
AH!
I'M UP!
THUD!
THUD!
Wassat?
THUD!
THUD!

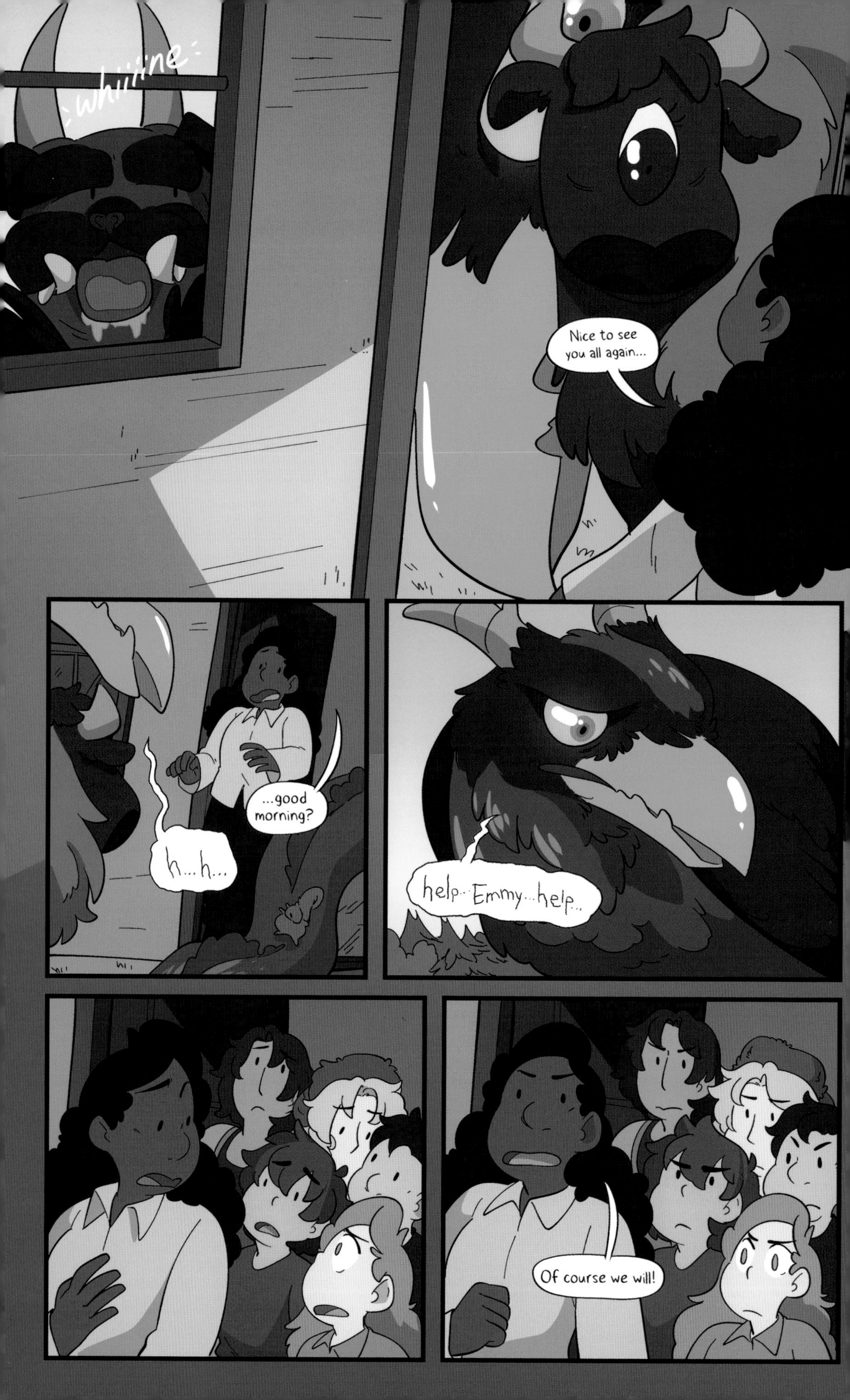
whiiiine
Nice to see you all again...
h...h...
...good morning?
help...Emmy...help...
Of course we will!

will co...
The ur...
It helps...
appearan...
dress fo...
Further...
Lumber...
to have...
part in...
Thiskw...
Hardc...
have o...
thems...

THE UNIFORM

...hould be worn at camp
...events when Lumberjanes
...may also be worn at other
...ions. It should be worn as a
...the uniform dress with
...rect shoes, and stocking or
...ut grows her uniform or
...ther Lumberjane.
...signia she has
...her
...her

HOLY SMOKES!

HERD YOU WERE LOOKING FOR US!

WE GOT THIS!

The...
yellow, sho...
emb...
the w...
choose...
slacks,...
made o...
out-of-do...
green bere...
the colla...
Shoes ma...
heels, round...ings or
socks should...with the shoes or wit...
the uniform. Ne...es, bracelets, or other jewelry do...
belong with a Lumberjane uniform.

HOW TO WEAR THE UNIFORM

To look well in a uniform demands first of...
uniform be kept in good condition—clean...
pressed. See that the skirt is the right length for your own
height and build, that the belt is adjusted to your waist,
that your shoes and stockings are in keeping with the
uniform, that you watch your posture and carry yourself
with dignity and grace. If the beret is removed indoors,
be sure that your hair is neat and kept in place with an
inconspicuous clip or ribbon. When you wear a
Lumberjane uniform you are identified as a member of
this organization and you should be doubly careful to
conduct yourself in a way that will show everyone that
courtesy and thoughtfulness are part of being a
Lumberjane. People are likely to judge a whole nation by
the selfishness of a few individuals, to criticize a whole
family because of the misconduct of one member, and to
feel unkindly toward an organization because of the

The unifor...
helps to cre...
in a group...
active life th...
another bond...
future, and pr...
in order to b...
Lumberjane pr...
Penniquiqul Thi...re Lady
Types, but m...es will wish to have one. They
can either b...e uniform, or make it themselves from
materials available at the trading post.

LUMBERJANES FIELD MANUAL

CHAPTER
FORTY-SEVEN

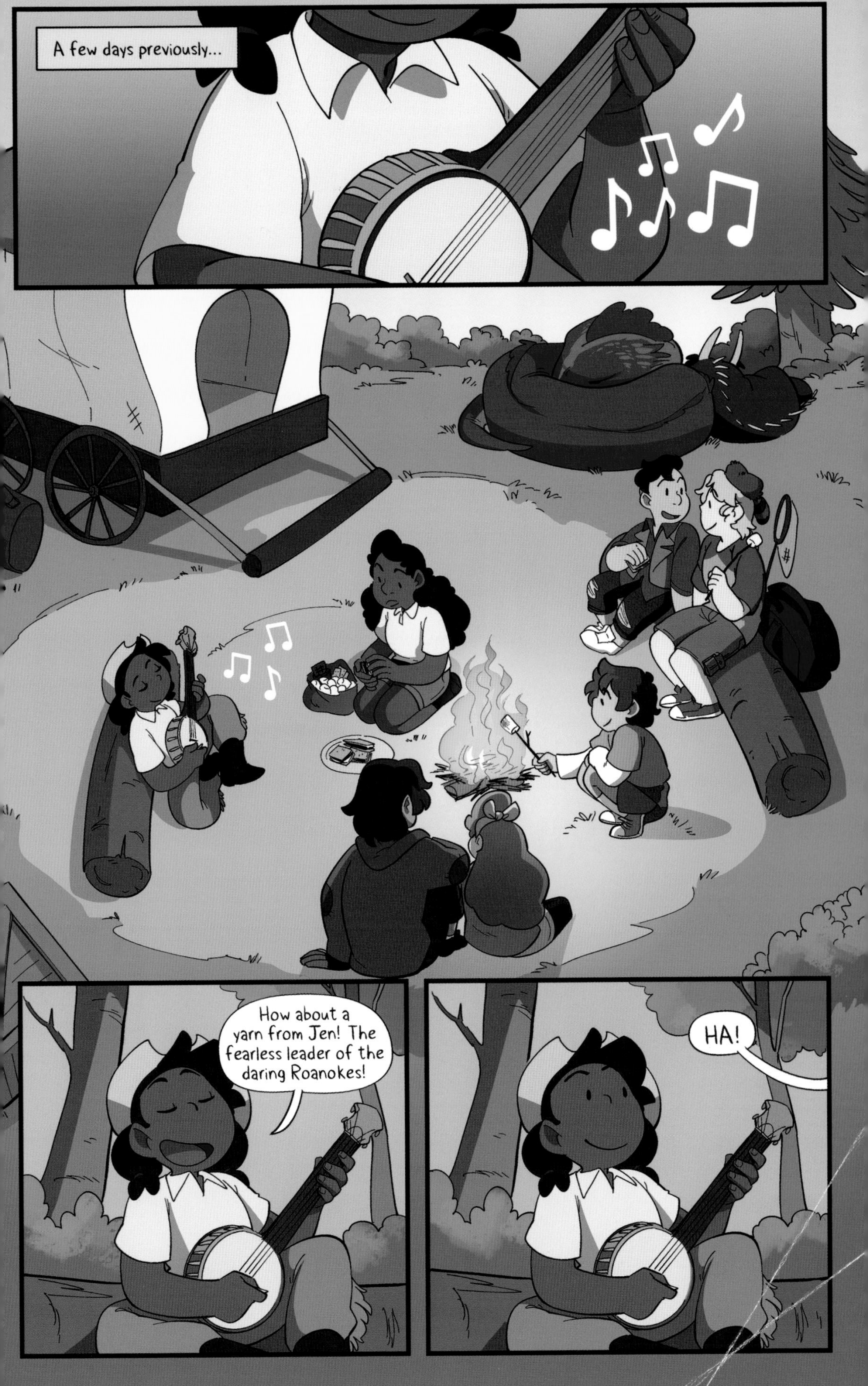
A few days previously...
How about a yarn from Jen! The fearless leader of the daring Roanokes!
HA!

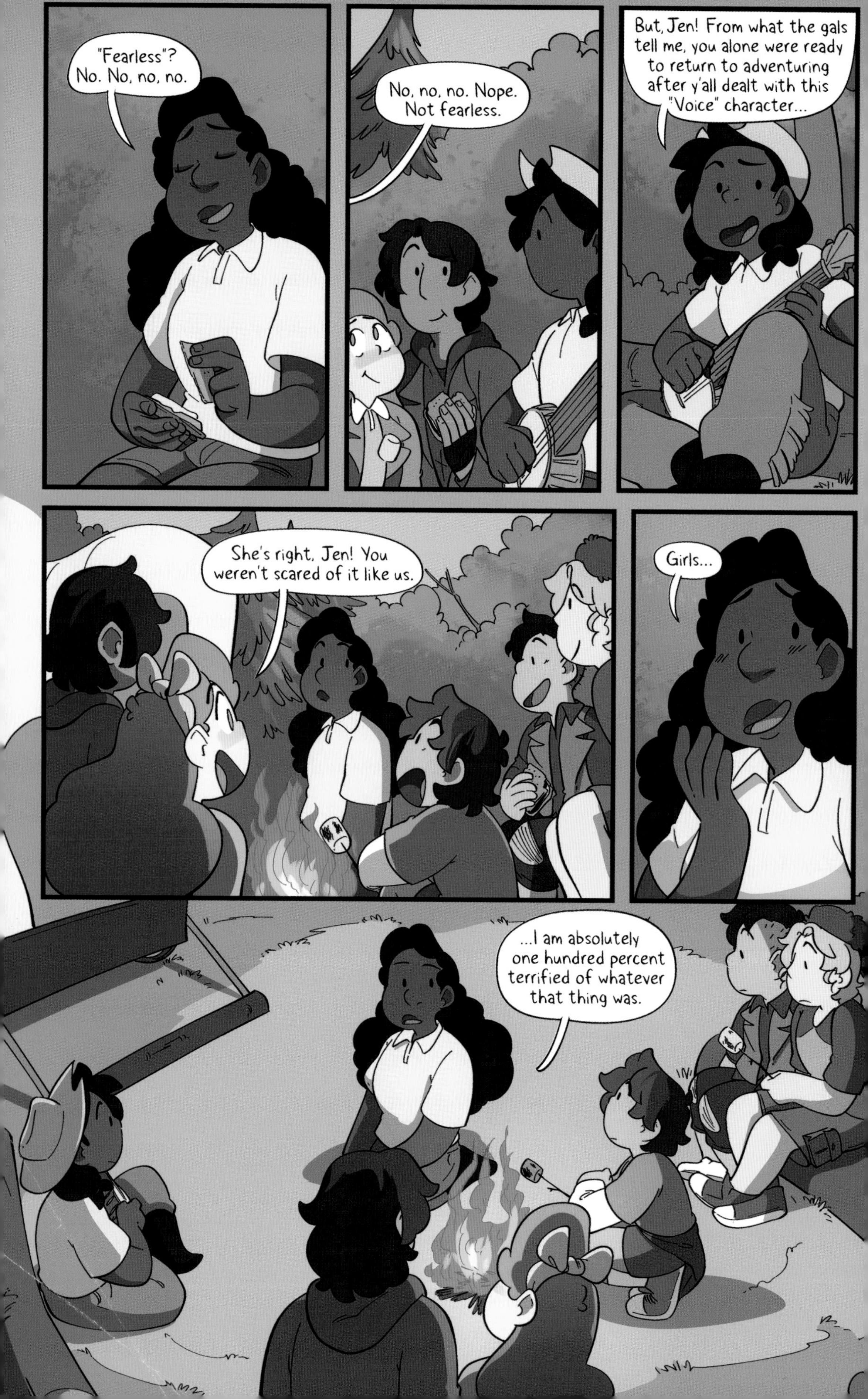
"Fearless"? No. No, no, no.
No, no, no. Nope. Not fearless.
But, Jen! From what the gals tell me, you alone were ready to return to adventuring after y'all dealt with this "Voice" character...
She's right, Jen! You weren't scared of it like us.
Girls...
...I am absolutely one hundred percent terrified of whatever that thing was.

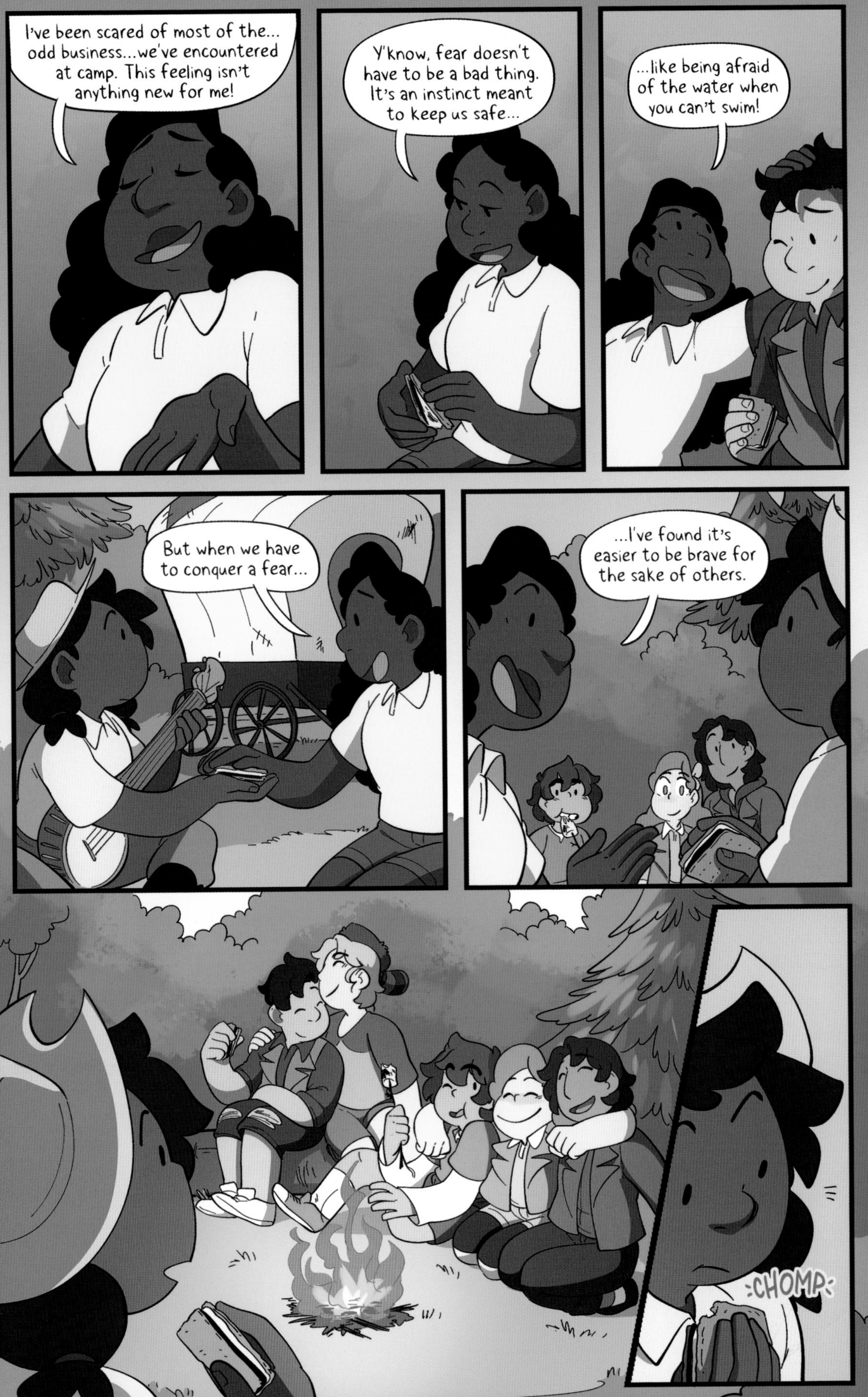
I've been scared of most of the... odd business...we've encountered at camp. This feeling isn't anything new for me!
Y'know, fear doesn't have to be a bad thing. It's an instinct meant to keep us safe...
...like being afraid of the water when you can't swim!
But when we have to conquer a fear...
...I've found it's easier to be brave for the sake of others.
CHOMP

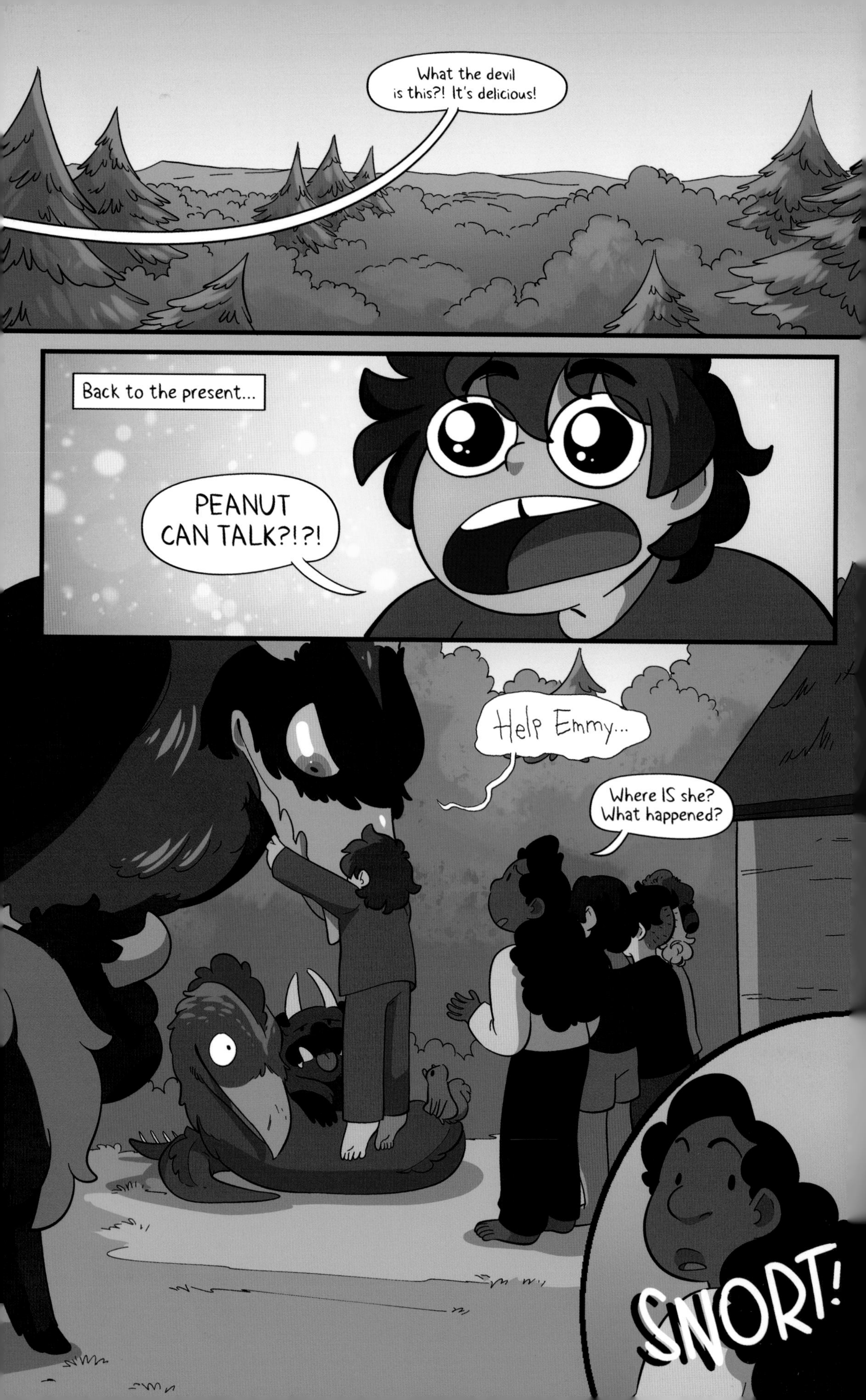
What the devil is this?! It's delicious!
Back to the present...
PEANUT CAN TALK?!?!
Help Emmy...
Where IS she? What happened?
SNORT!

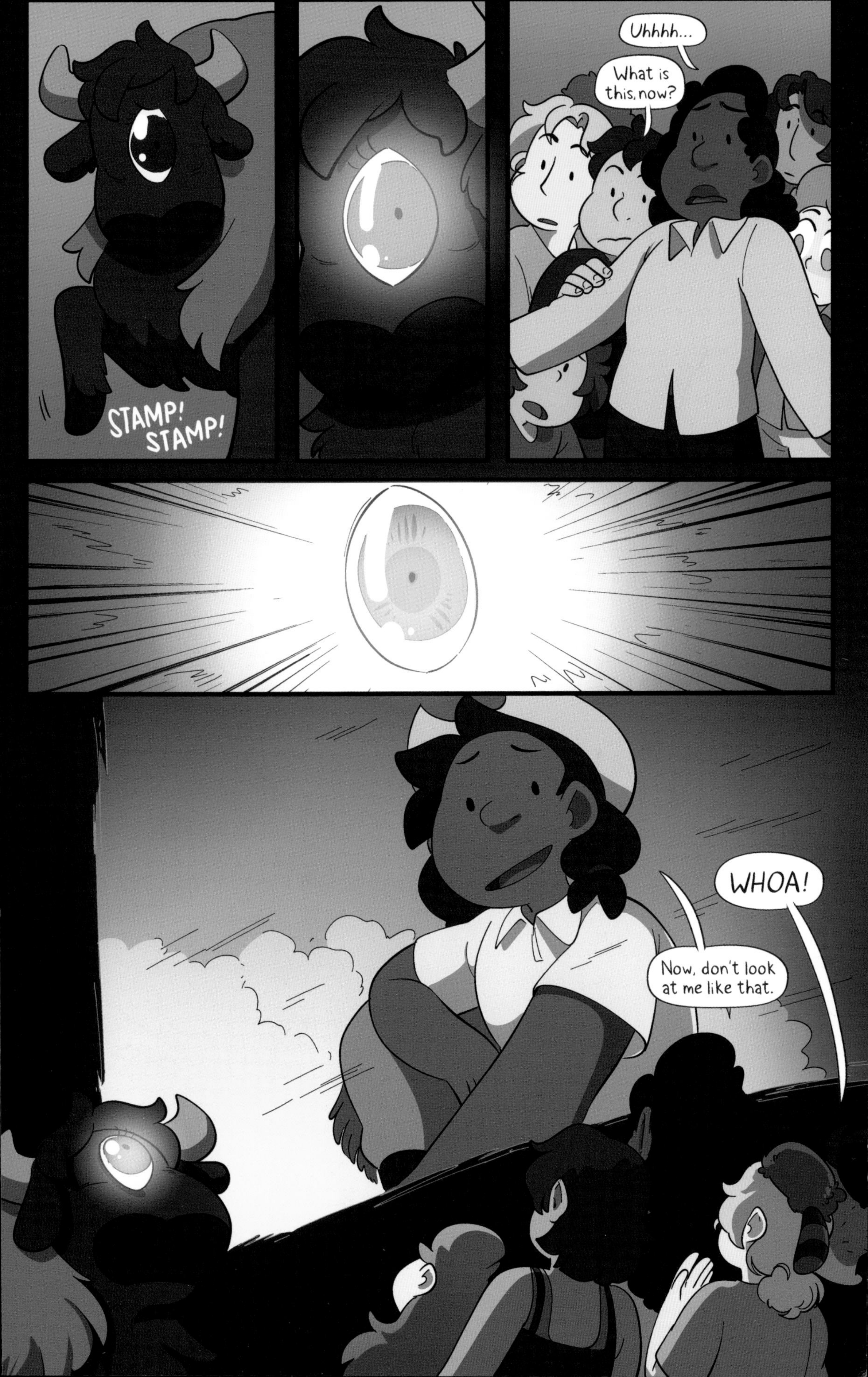
STAMP!
STAMP!
Uhhhh...
What is this, now?
WHOA!
Now, don't look at me like that.

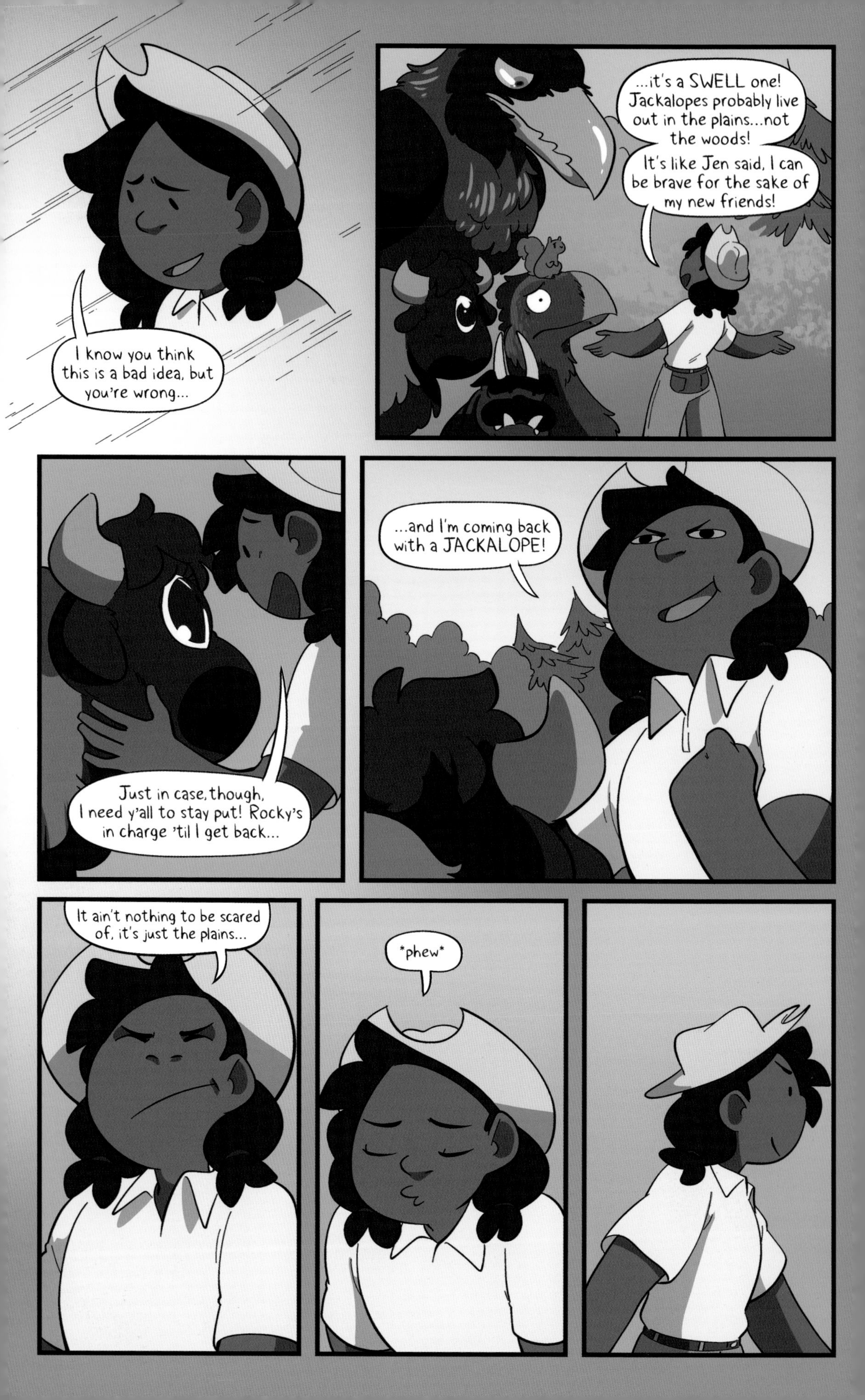
I know you think this is a bad idea, but you're wrong...
...it's a SWELL one! Jackalopes probably live out in the plains...not the woods!
It's like Jen said, I can be brave for the sake of my new friends!
Just in case, though, I need y'all to stay put! Rocky's in charge 'til I get back...
...and I'm coming back with a JACKALOPE!
It ain't nothing to be scared of, it's just the plains...
phew

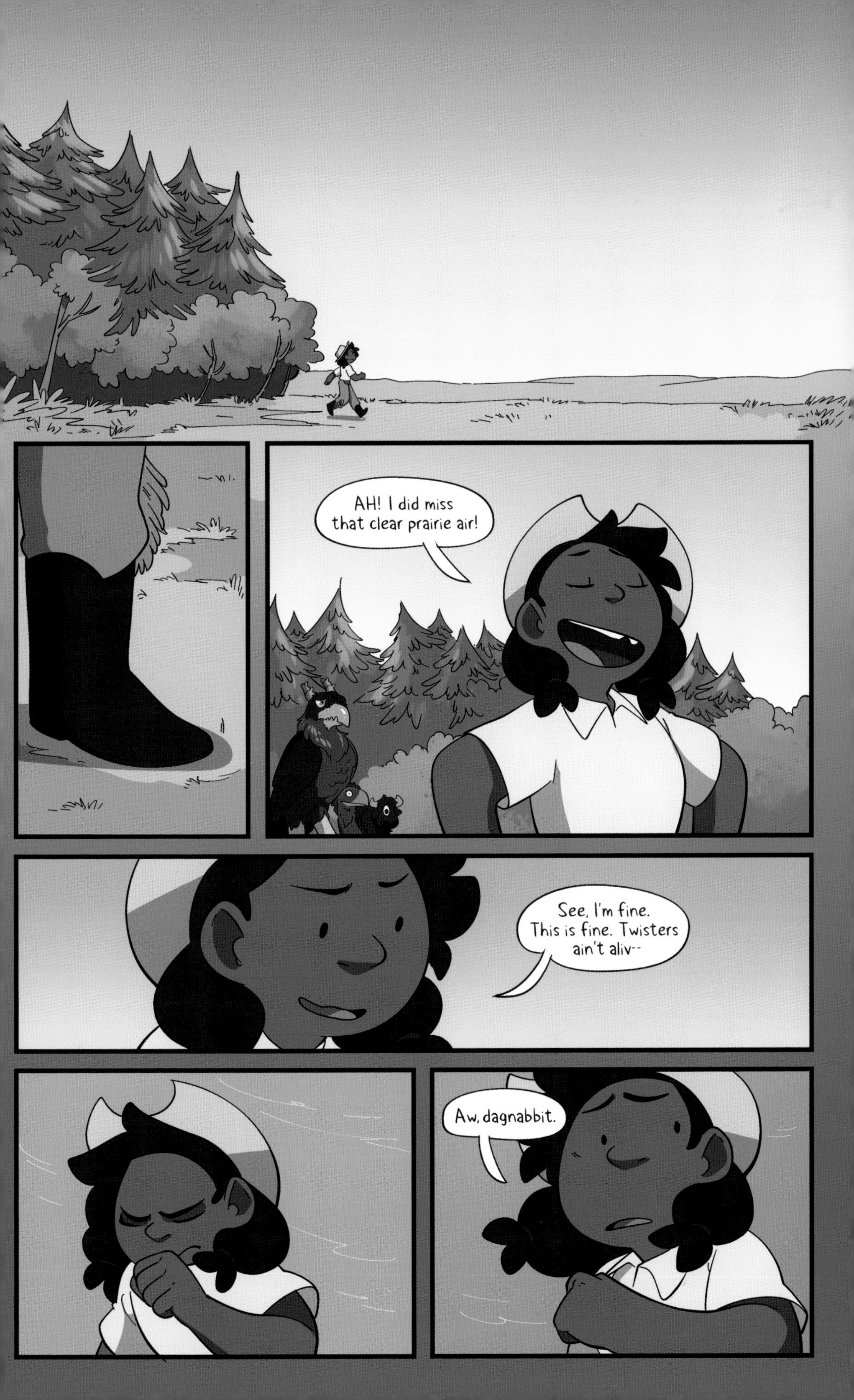
AH! I did miss that clear prairie air!
See, I'm fine. This is fine. Twisters ain't aliv--
Aw, dagnabbit.

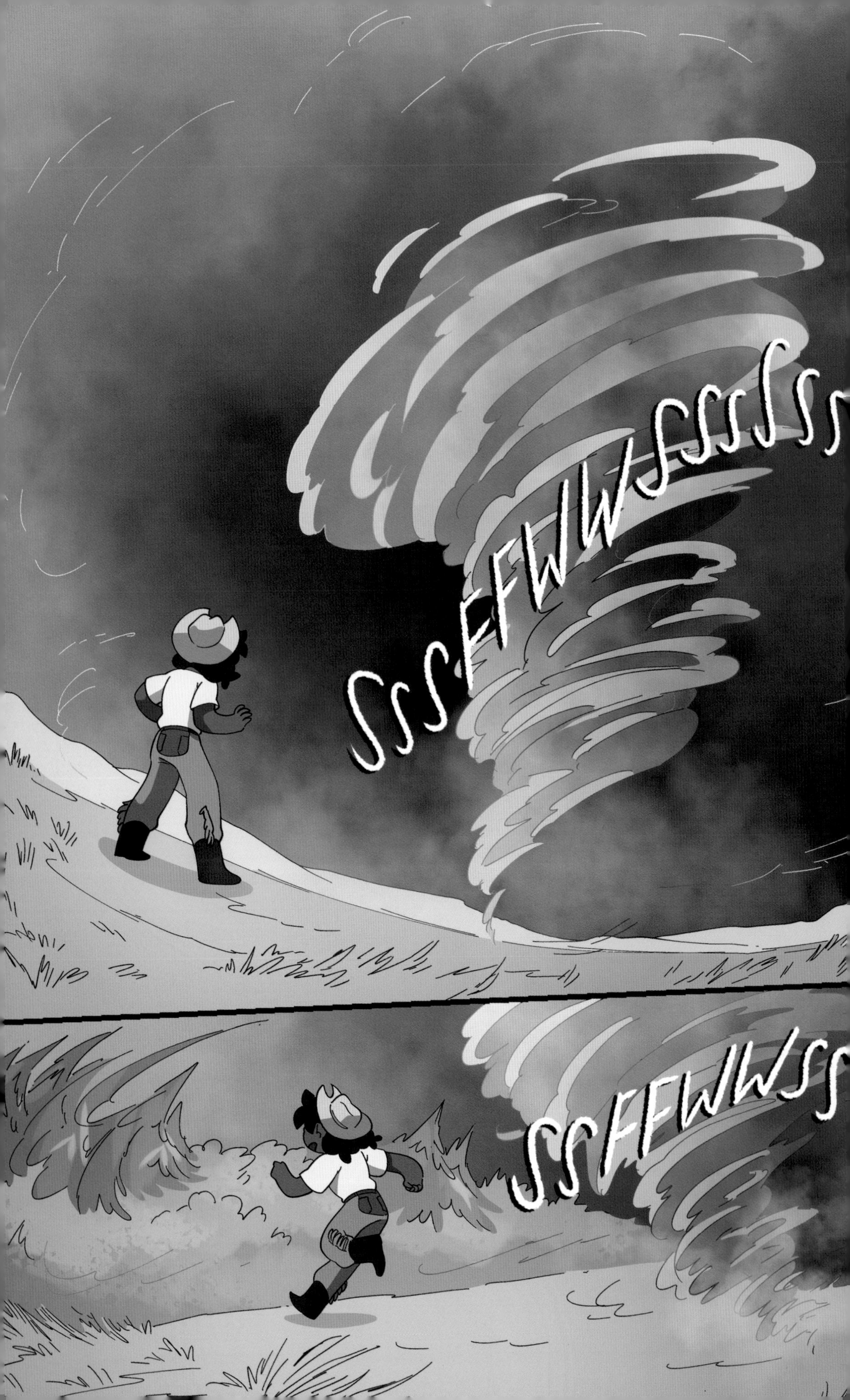
SSSFFWWSSSSSS
SSSFFWWSS

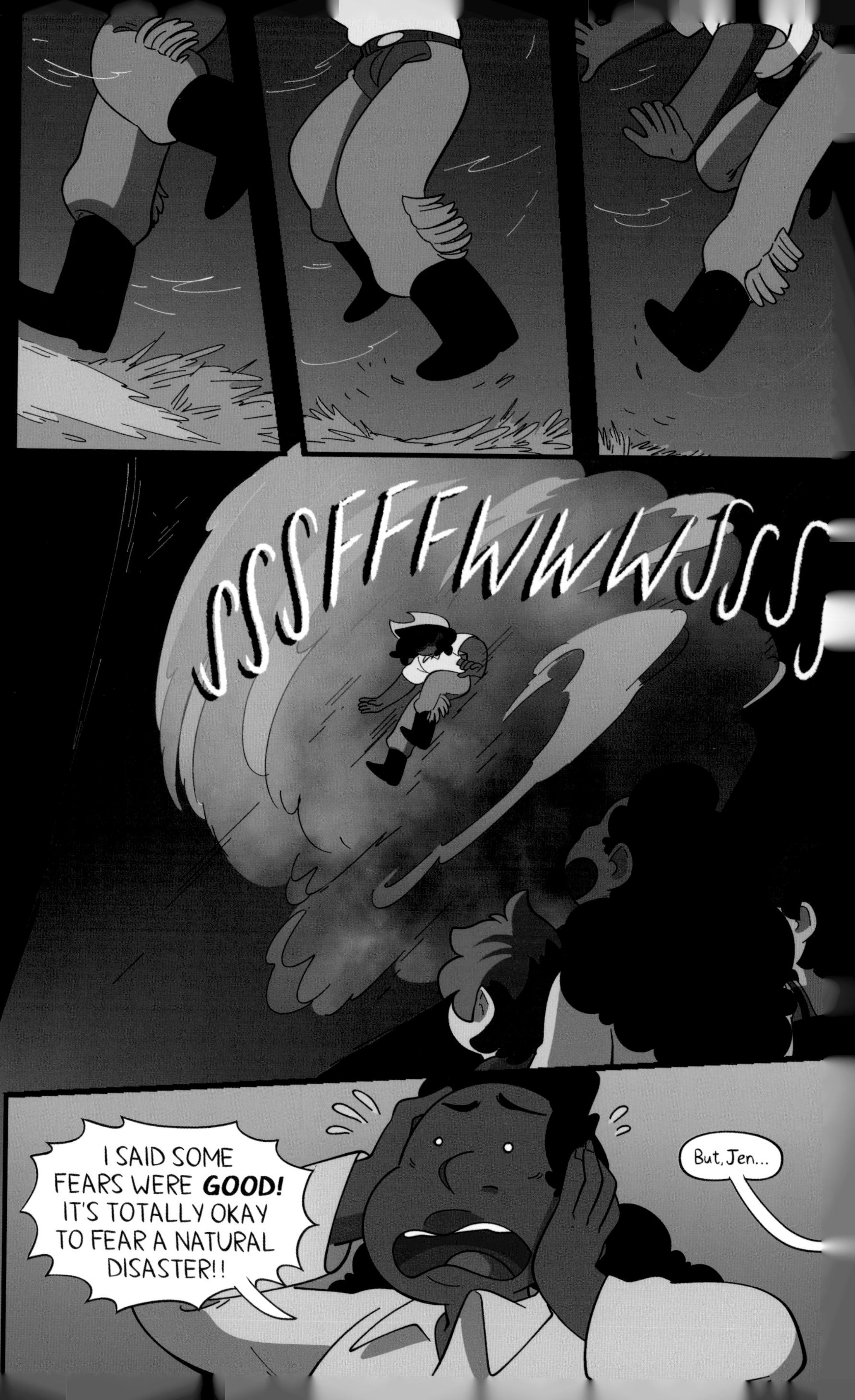
SSSFFFWWWSSS
I SAID SOME FEARS WERE **GOOD!** IT'S TOTALLY OKAY TO FEAR A NATURAL DISASTER!!
But, Jen...

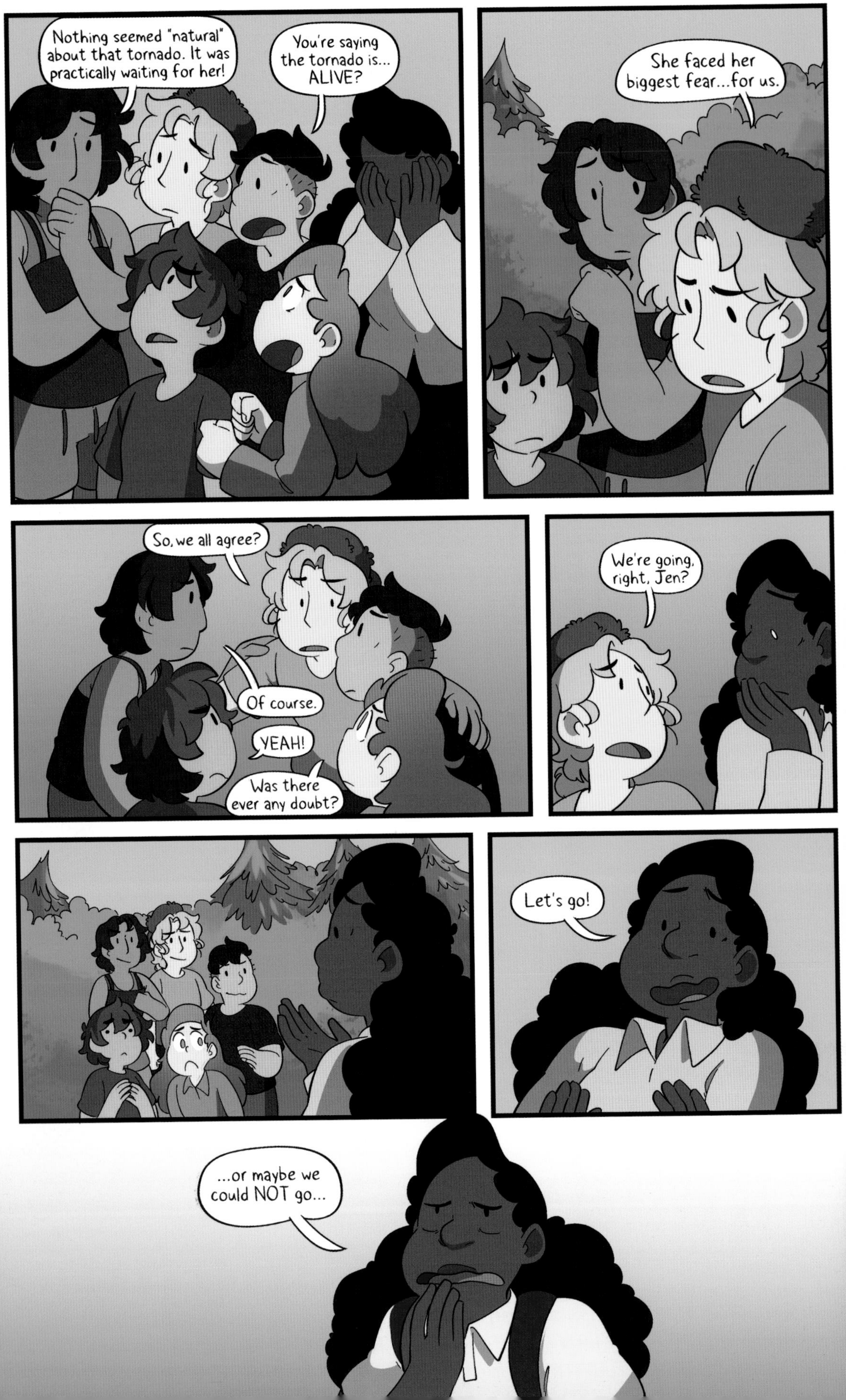
Nothing seemed "natural" about that tornado. It was practically waiting for her!
You're saying the tornado is... ALIVE?
She faced her biggest fear...for us.
So, we all agree?
Of course.
YEAH!
Was there ever any doubt?
We're going, right, Jen?
Let's go!
...or maybe we could NOT go...

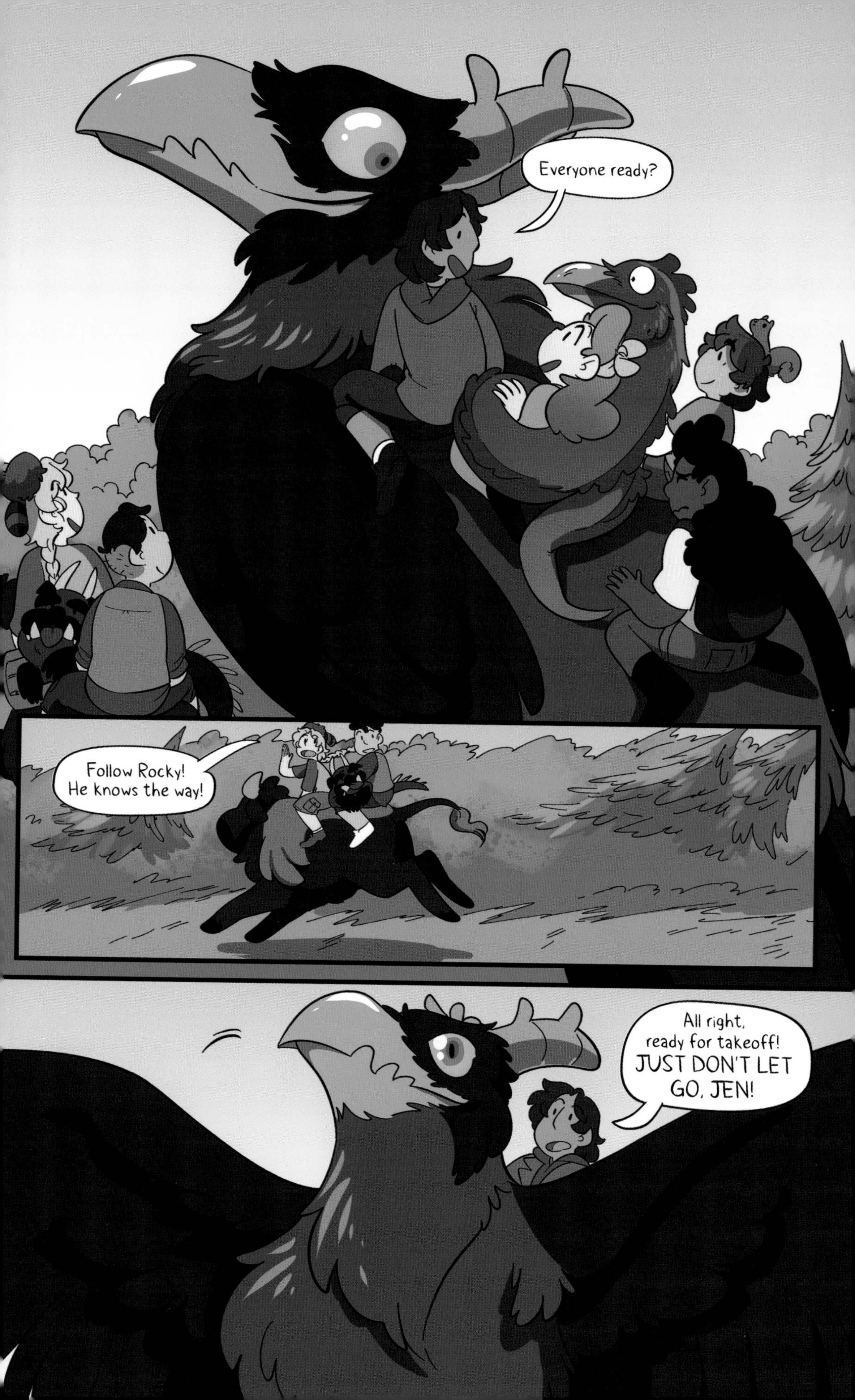
Everyone ready?
Follow Rocky! He knows the way!
All right, ready for takeoff! JUST DON'T LET GO, JEN!

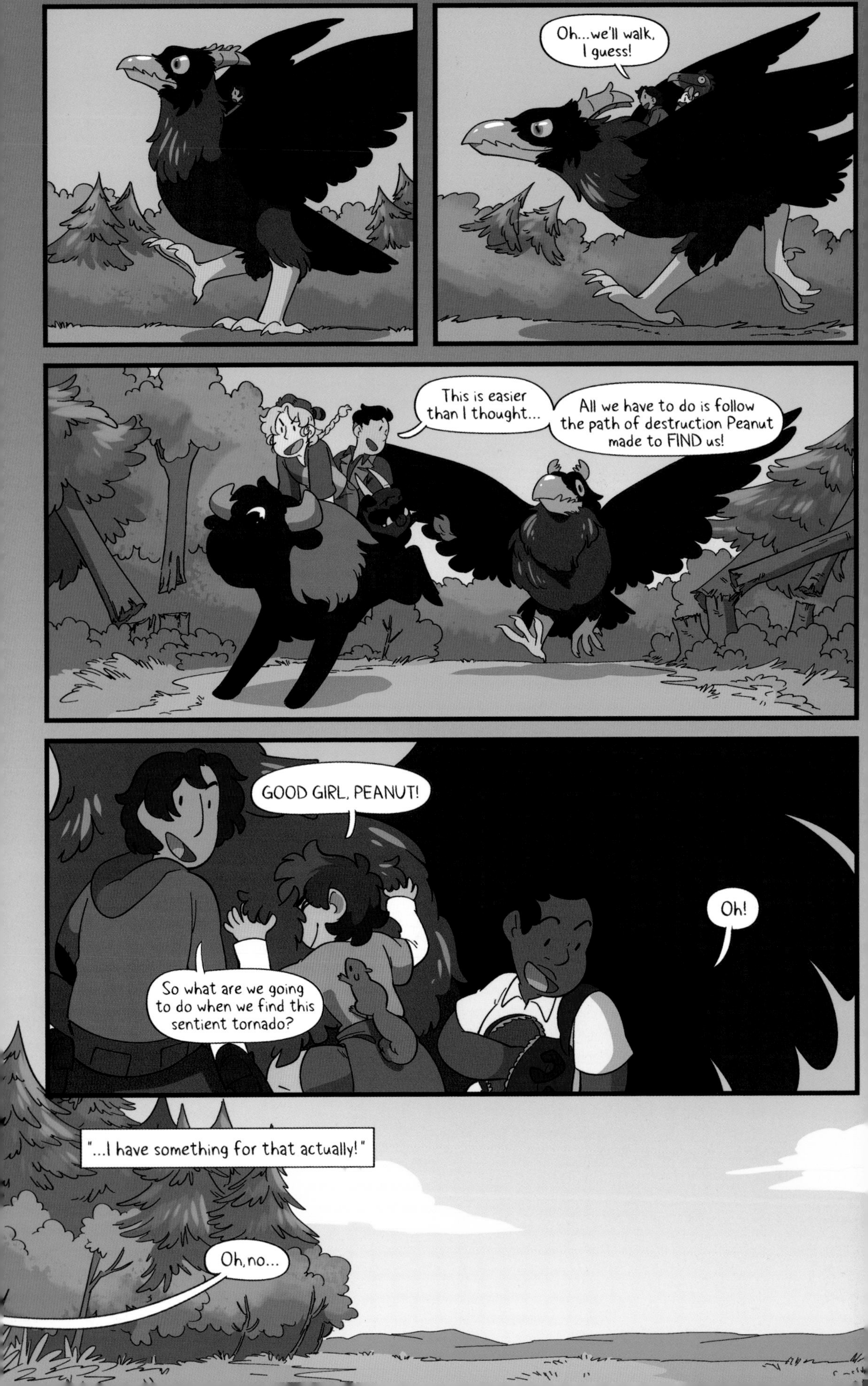
Oh...we'll walk, I guess!
This is easier than I thought...
All we have to do is follow the path of destruction Peanut made to FIND us!
GOOD GIRL, PEANUT!
So what are we going to do when we find this sentient tornado?
Oh!
"...I have something for that actually!"
Oh, no...

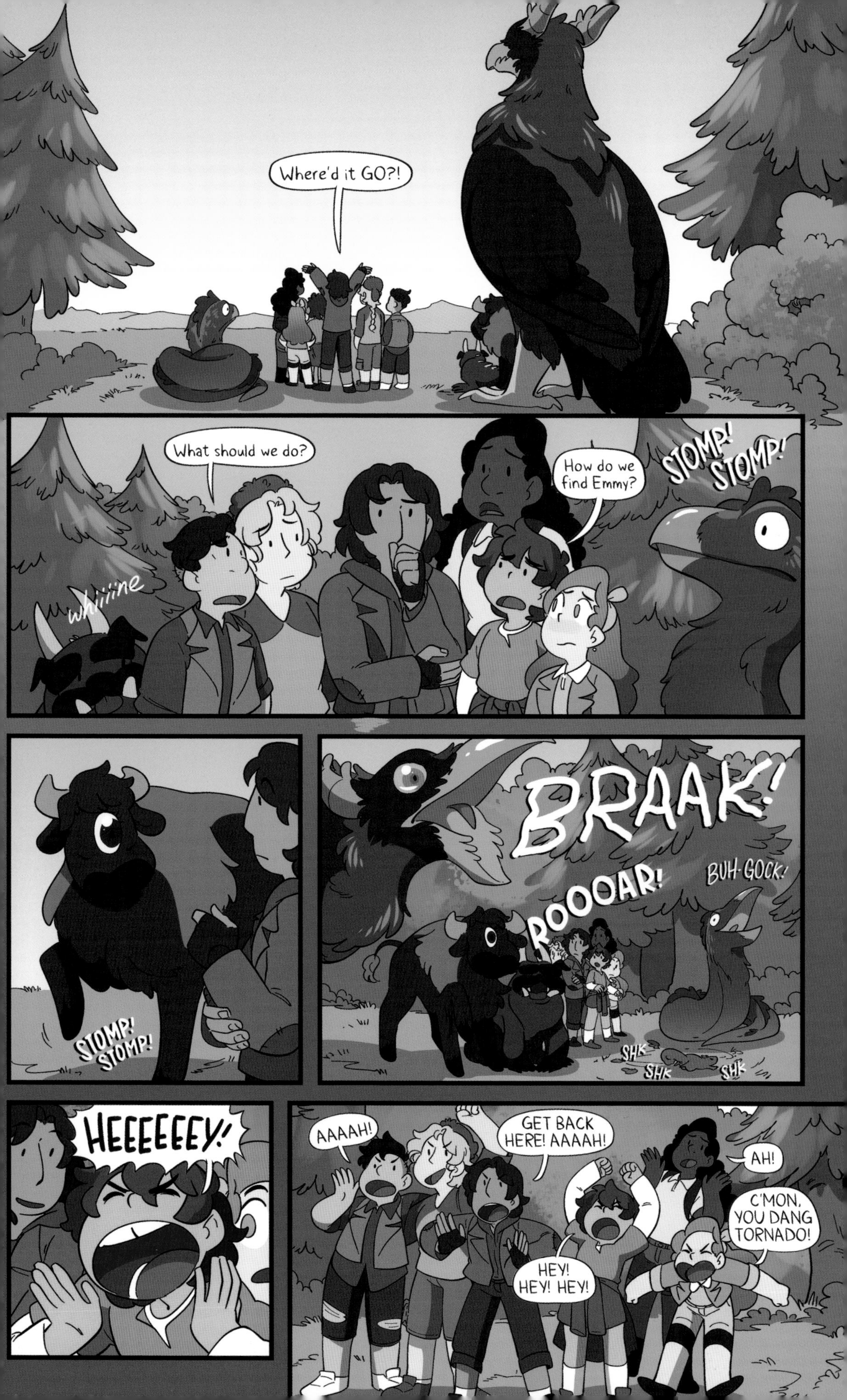

Where'd it GO?!
What should we do?
How do we find Emmy?
STOMP! STOMP!
whiiiine
STOMP! STOMP!
BRAAK!
ROOOAR!
BUH-GOCK!
SHK SHK SHK
HEEEEEEY!
AAAAH!
GET BACK HERE! AAAAH!
AH!
C'MON, YOU DANG TORNADO!
HEY! HEY! HEY!

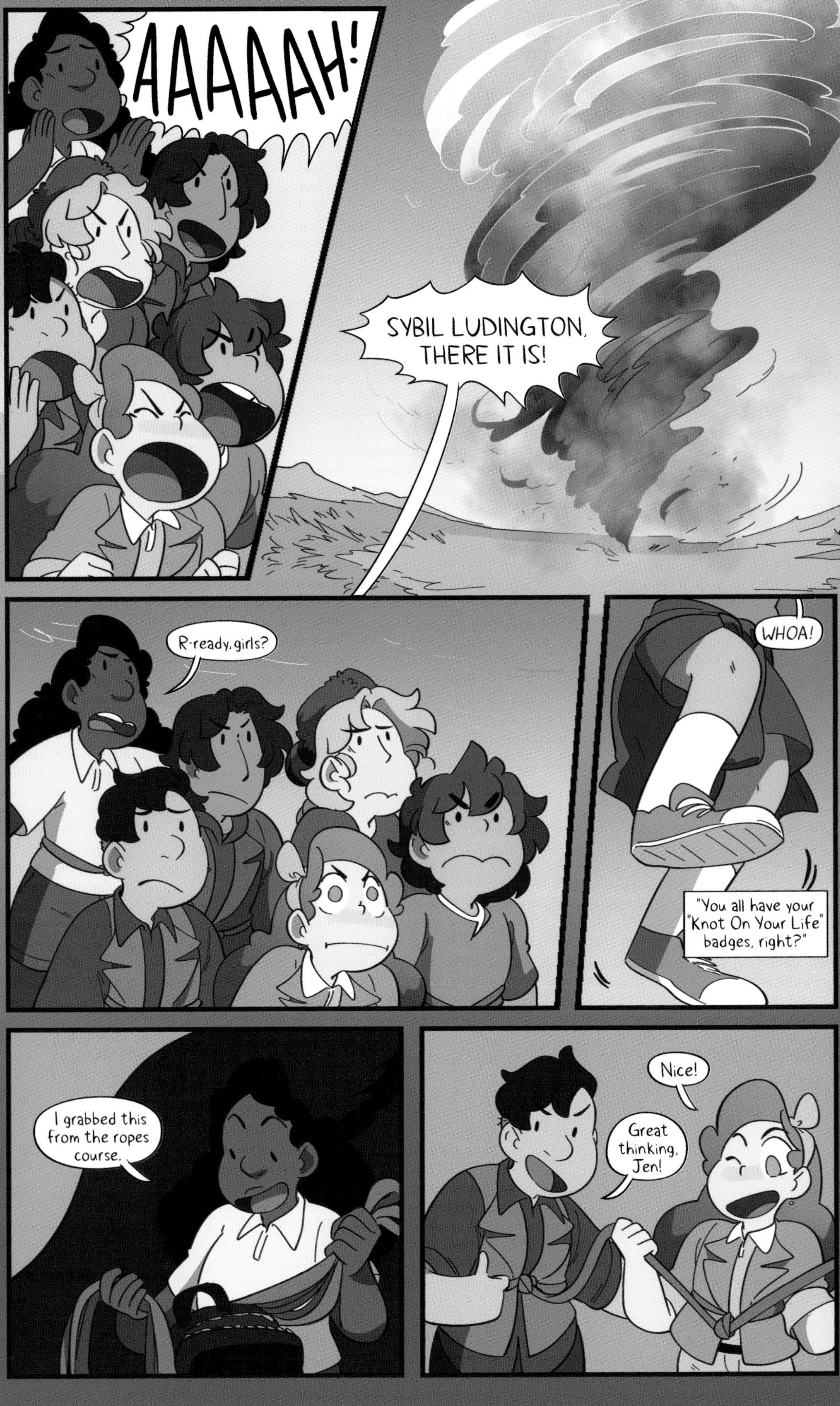
AAAAAH!
SYBIL LUDINGTON, THERE IT IS!
R-ready, girls?
WHOA!
"You all have your "Knot On Your Life" badges, right?"
I grabbed this from the ropes course.
Nice!
Great thinking, Jen!

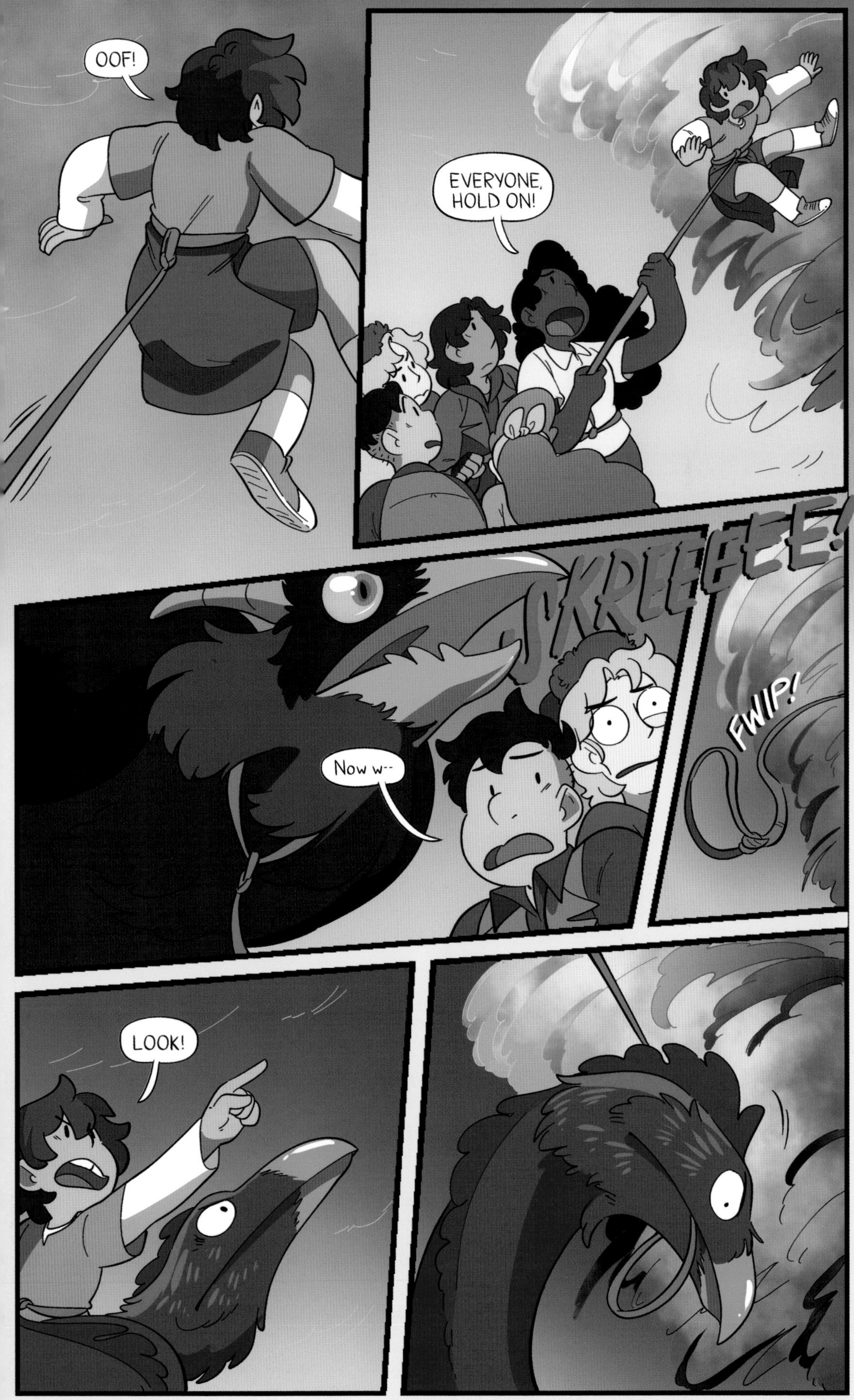
OOF!
EVERYONE, HOLD ON!
SKREEEEEE!
Now w--
FWIP!
LOOK!

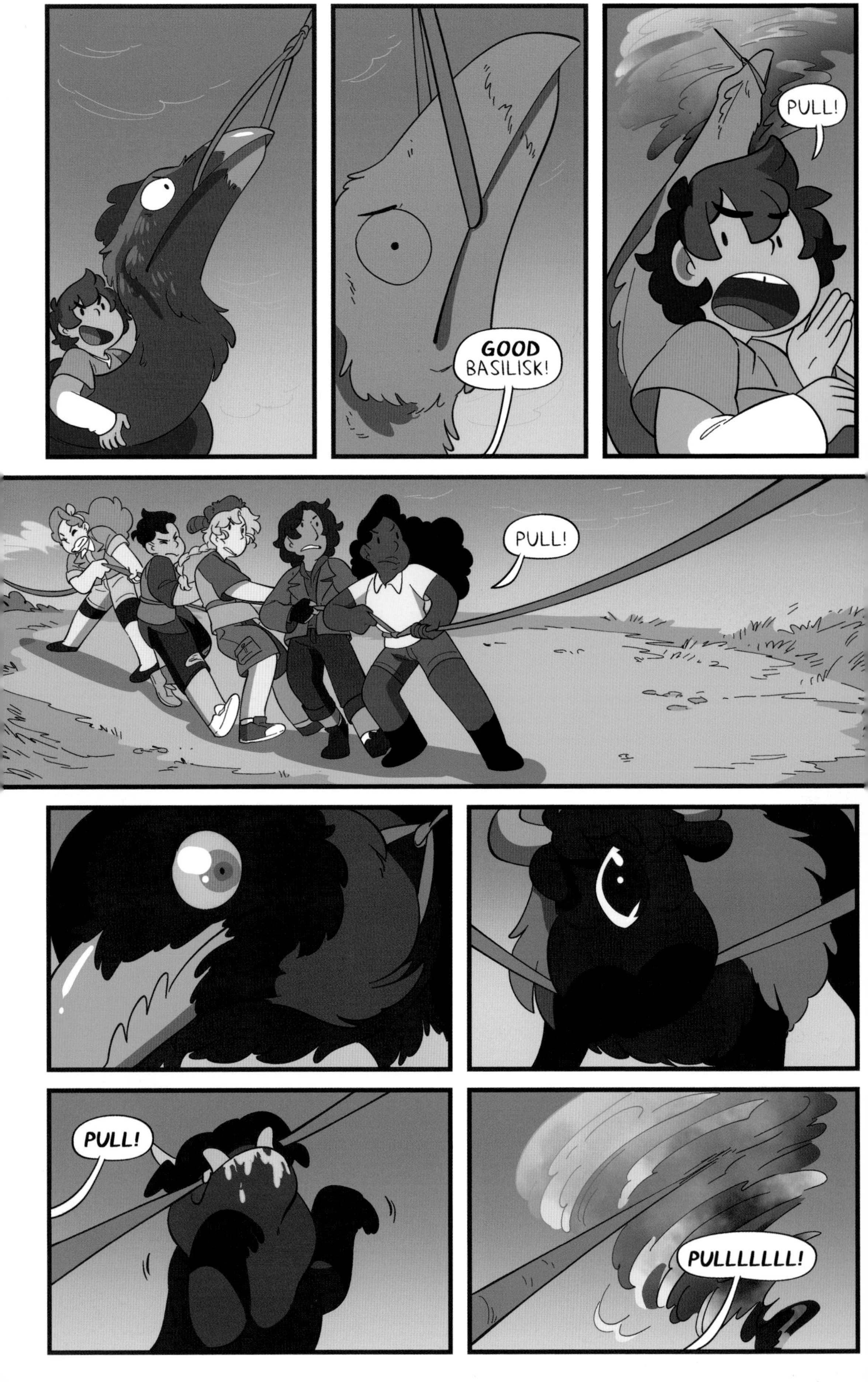
GOOD BASILISK!
PULL!
PULL!
PULL!
PULLLLLLL!

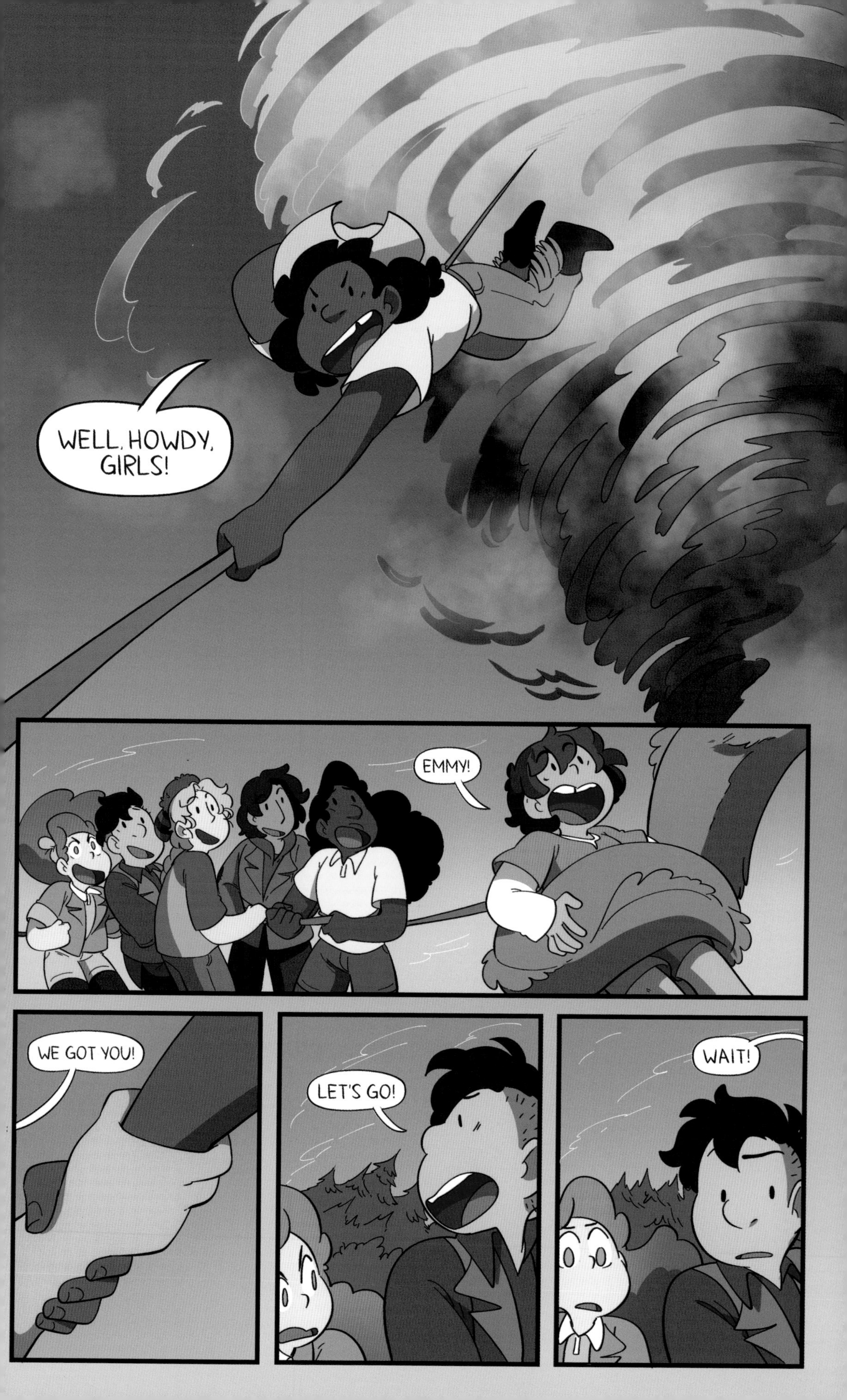
WELL, HOWDY, GIRLS!
EMMY!
WE GOT YOU!
LET'S GO!
WAIT!

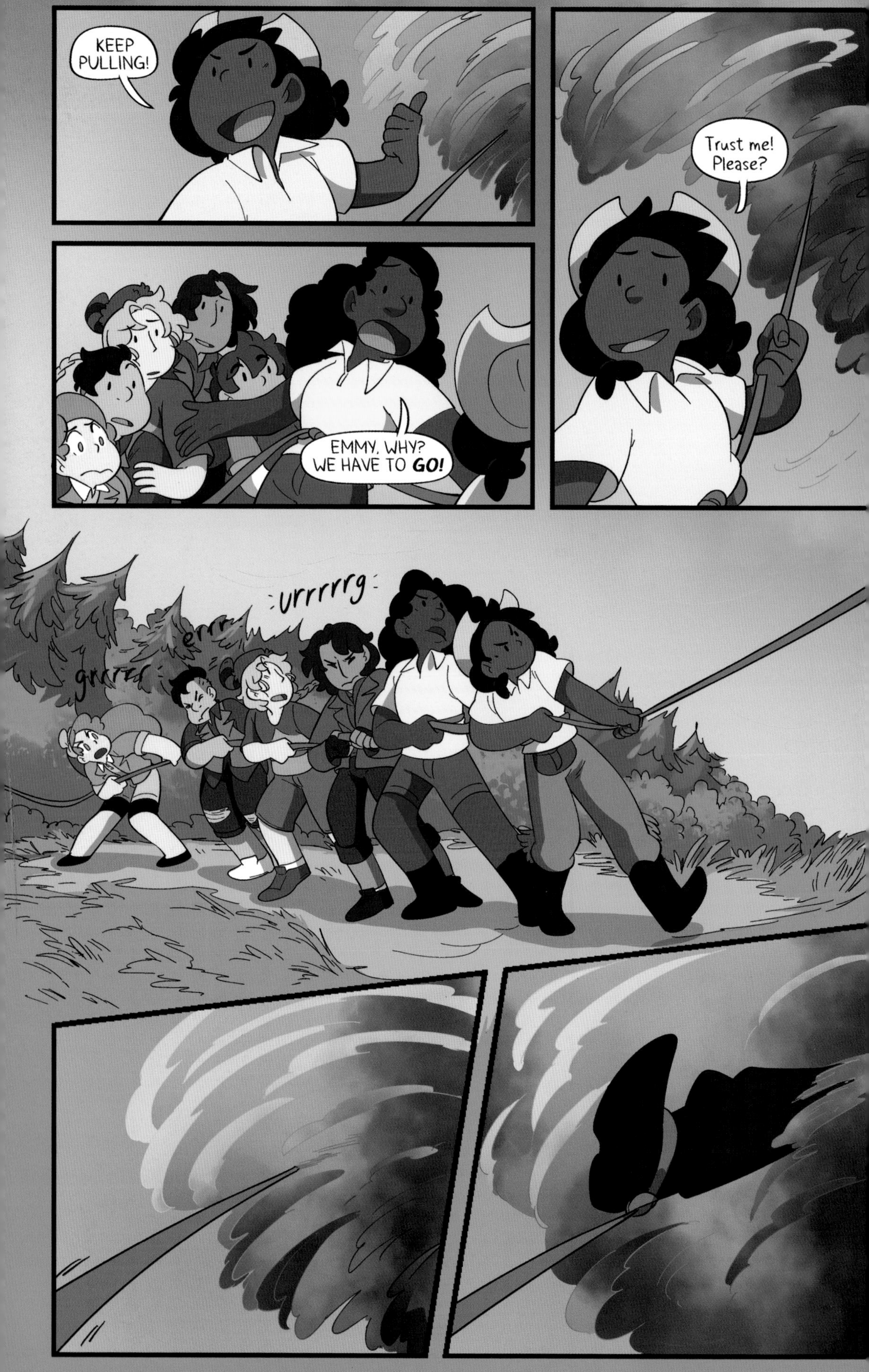
KEEP PULLING!
Trust me! Please?
EMMY, WHY? WE HAVE TO **GO!**
urrrrg
errr
grrrrr

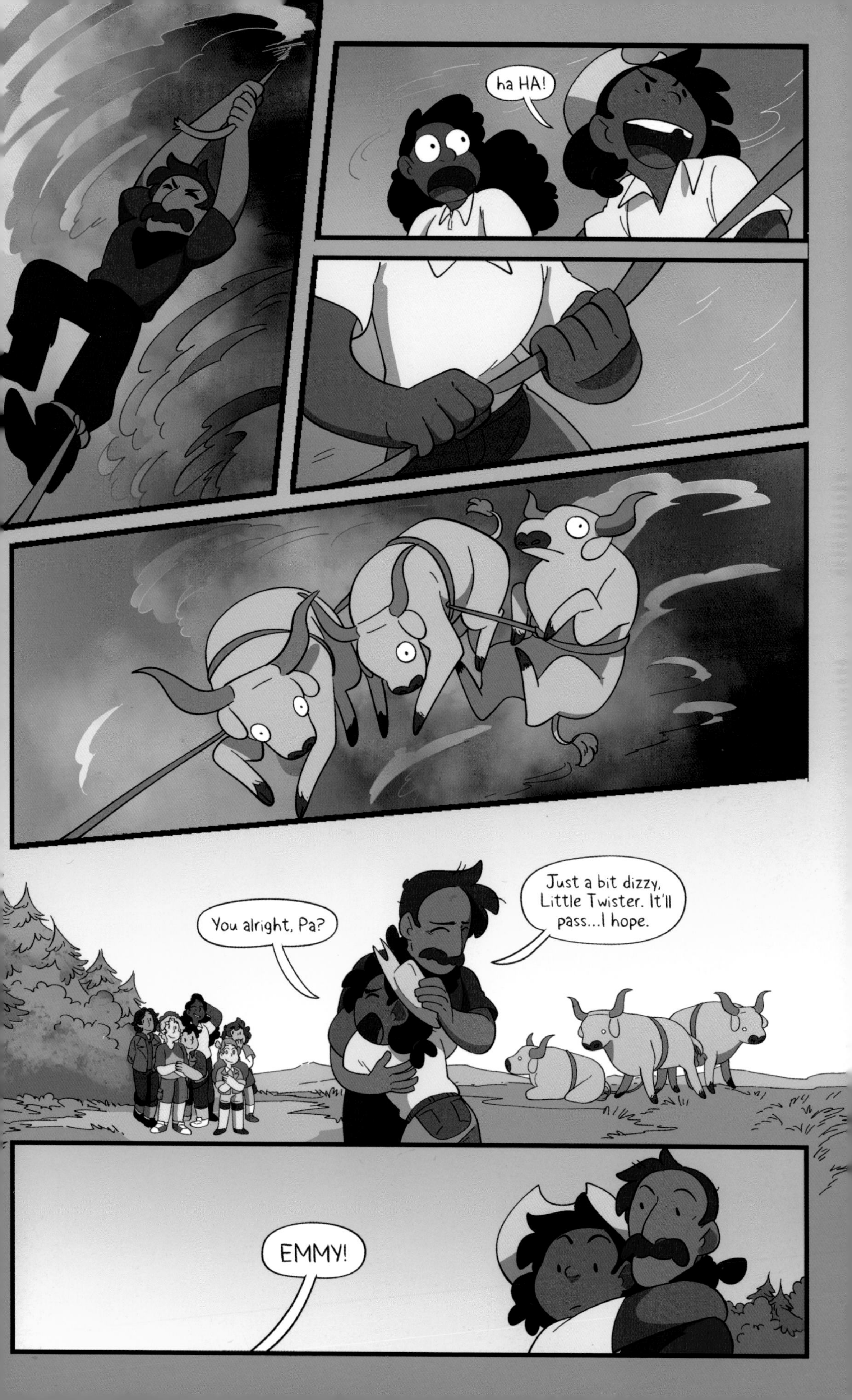
ha HA!
You alright, Pa?
Just a bit dizzy, Little Twister. It'll pass...I hope.
EMMY!

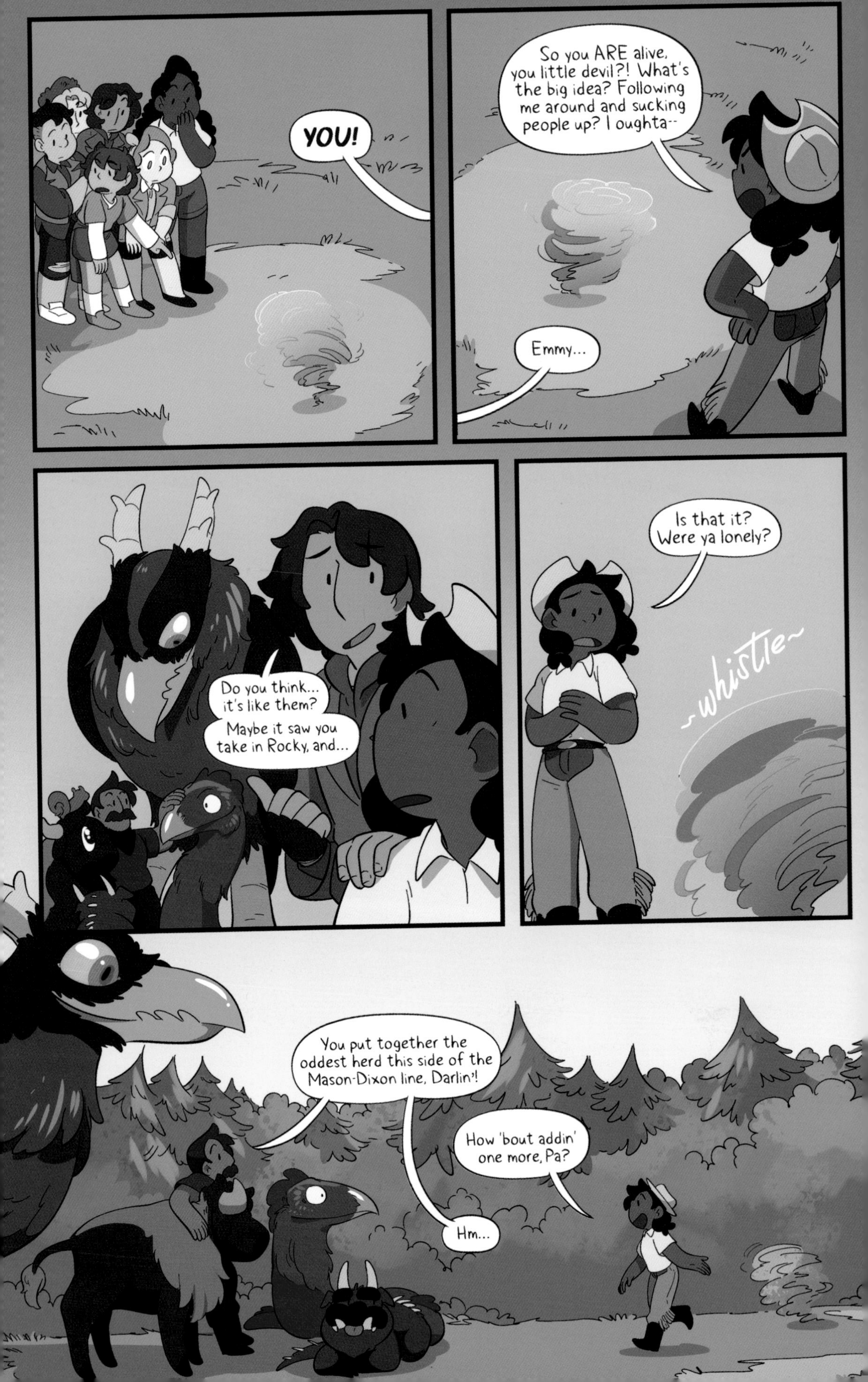
YOU!
So you ARE alive, you little devil?! What's the big idea? Following me around and sucking people up? I oughta--
Emmy...
Do you think... it's like them?
Maybe it saw you take in Rocky, and...
Is that it? Were ya lonely?
~whistle~
You put together the oddest herd this side of the Mason-Dixon line, Darlin'!
How 'bout addin' one more, Pa?
Hm...

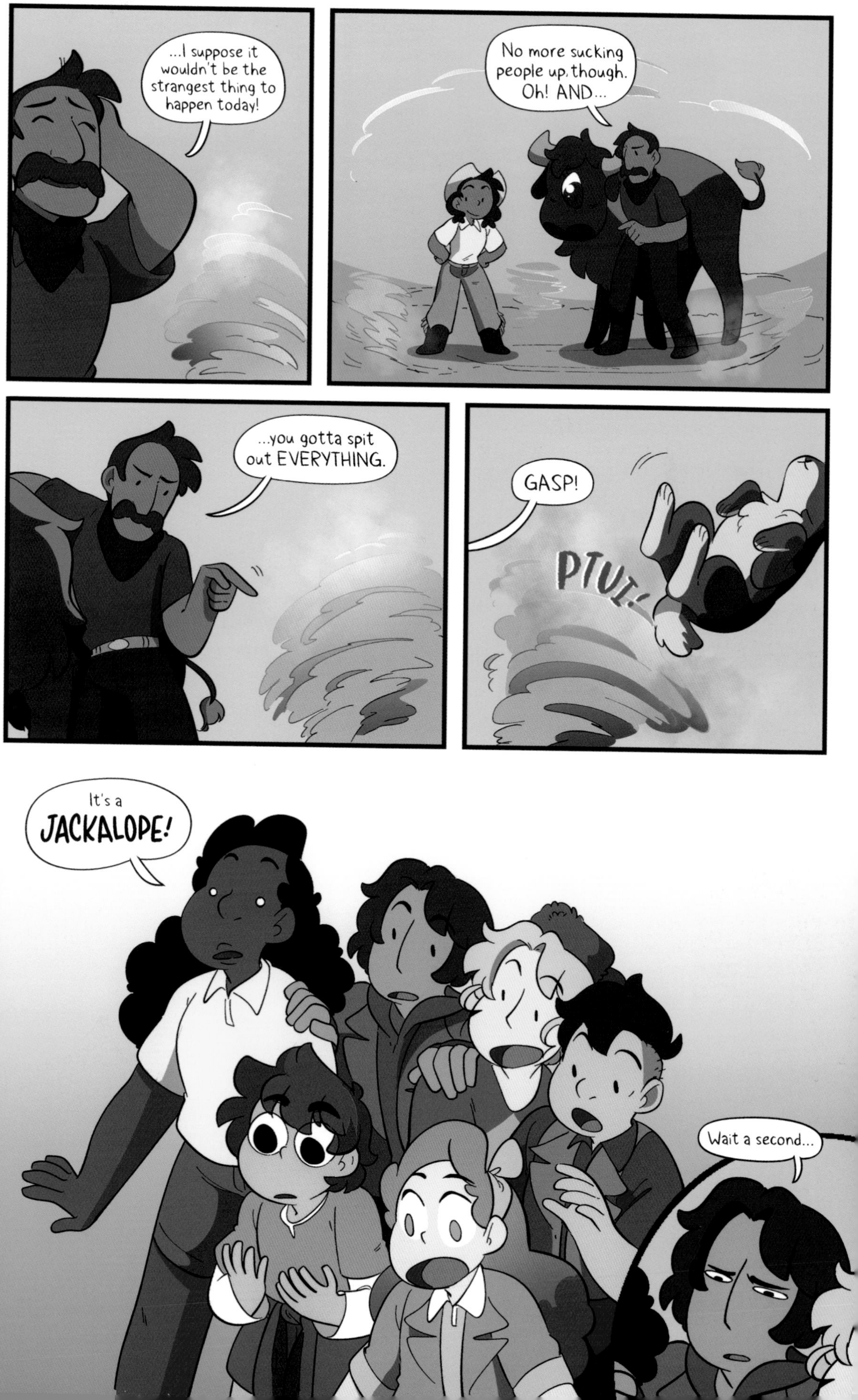
...I suppose it wouldn't be the strangest thing to happen today!
No more sucking people up, though. Oh! AND...
...you gotta spit out EVERYTHING.
GASP!
PTUI!
It's a JACKALOPE!
Wait a second...

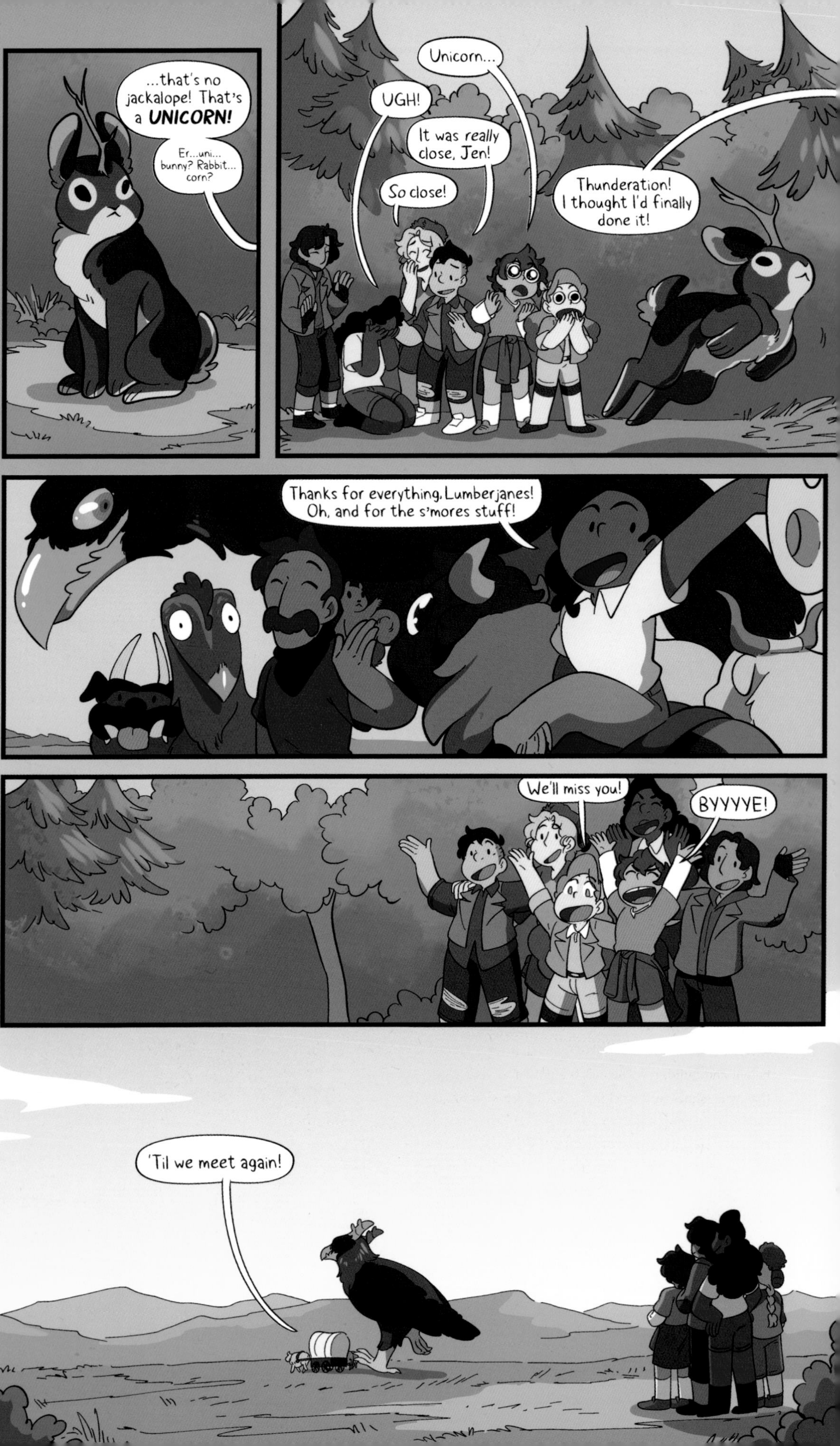
...that's no jackalope! That's a UNICORN!
Er...uni... bunny? Rabbit... corn?
Unicorn...
UGH!
It was really close, Jen!
So close!
Thunderation! I thought I'd finally done it!
Thanks for everything, Lumberjanes! Oh, and for the s'mores stuff!
We'll miss you!
BYYYYE!
'Til we meet again!

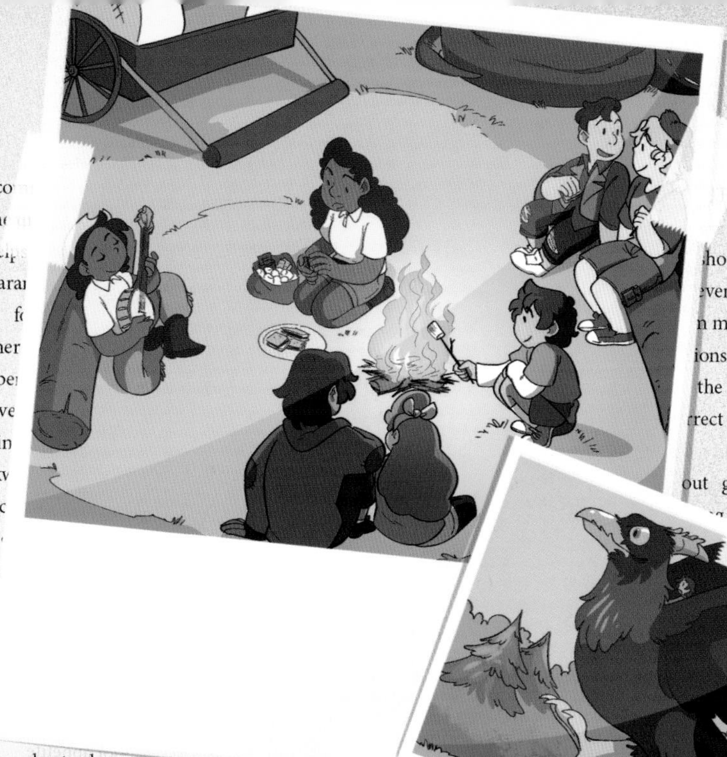

will co

The

It he

appeara

dress f

Further

Lumbe

to have

part in

Thiskv

Hardc

have

them

...E UNIFORM

...hould be worn at camp ...events when Lumberjanes ...n may also be worn at other ...ions. It should be worn as a ... the uniform dress with ...rrect shoes, and stocking or

... out grows her uniform or ...ther Lumberjane. ...ia she has ... her ... her

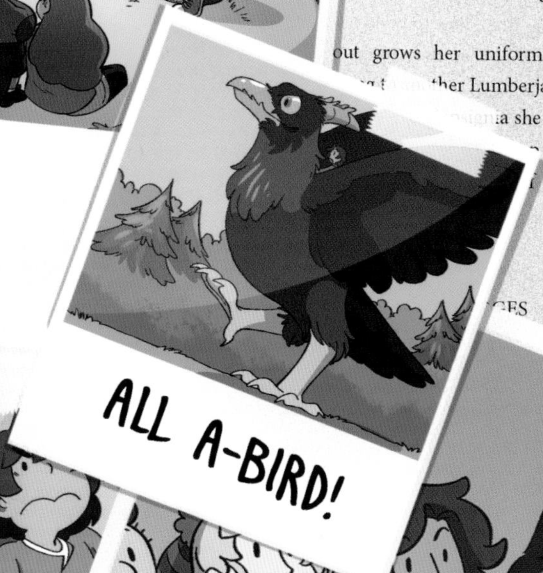
ALL A-BIRD!

The

yellow, short sl

emb

the w

choos

slacks,

made o

out-of-dc

green bere

the colla

Shoes ma

heels, rou ... kings or

socks shou ... th the shoes or wi

the uniform. Ne... ces, bracelets, or other jewelry do

belong with a Lumberjane uniform.

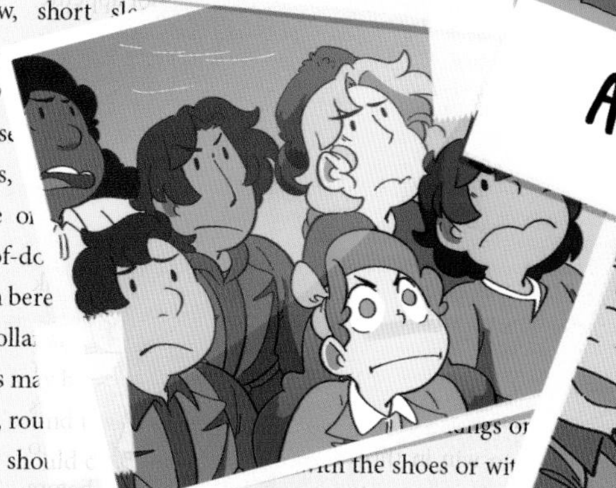

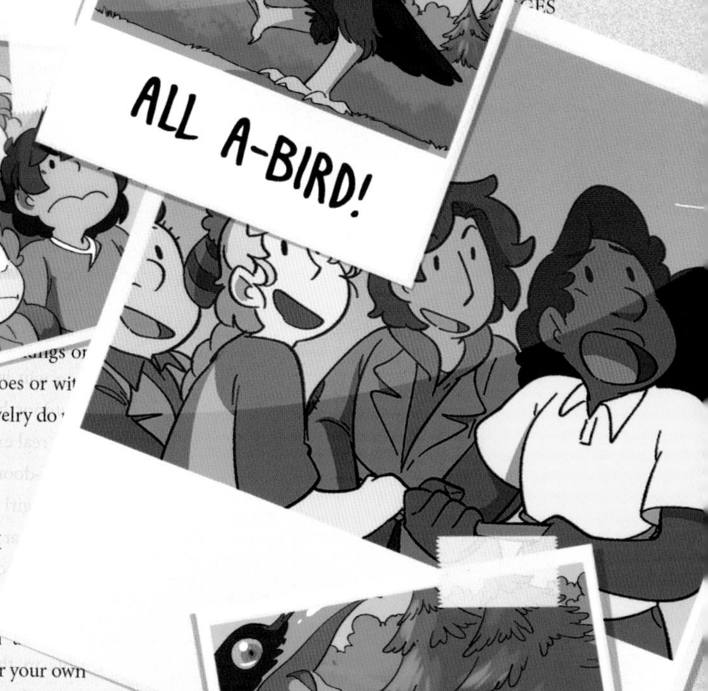

...GES

HOW TO WEAR THE UNIFORM

To look well in a uniform demands first of ... uniform be kept in good condition—clean ... pressed. See that the skirt is the right length for your own height and build, that the belt is adjusted to your waist, that your shoes and stockings are in keeping with the uniform, that you watch your posture and carry yourself with dignity and grace. If the beret is removed indoors, be sure that your hair is neat and kept in place with an inconspicuous clip or ribbon. When you wear a Lumberjane uniform you are identified as a member of this organization and you should be doubly careful to conduct yourself in a way that will show everyone that courtesy and thoughtfulness are part of being a Lumberjane. People are likely to judge a whole nation by the selfishness of a few individuals, to criticize a whole family because of the misconduct of one member, and to feel unkindly toward an organization because of the

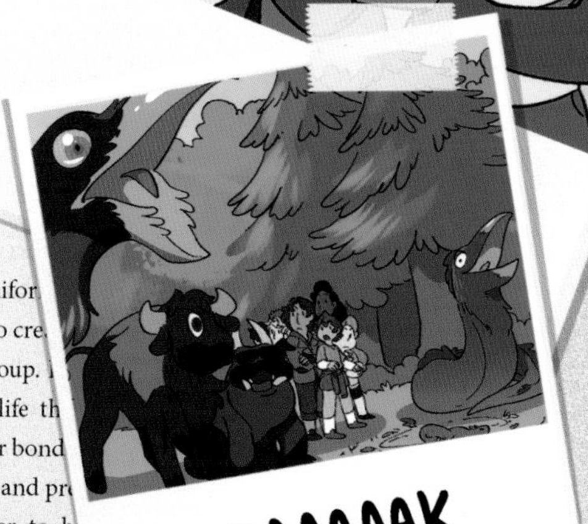
BRAAAAK

The unifor ... helps to cre ... in a group. ... active life th ... another bond ... future, and pr ... in order to b ... Lumberjane pr ... Penniquiqul Thi ... ore Lady Types, but m ... s will wish to have one. They can either bu ... , or make it themselves from materials available at the trading post.

LUMBERJANES FIELD MANUAL

CHAPTER FORTY-EIGHT

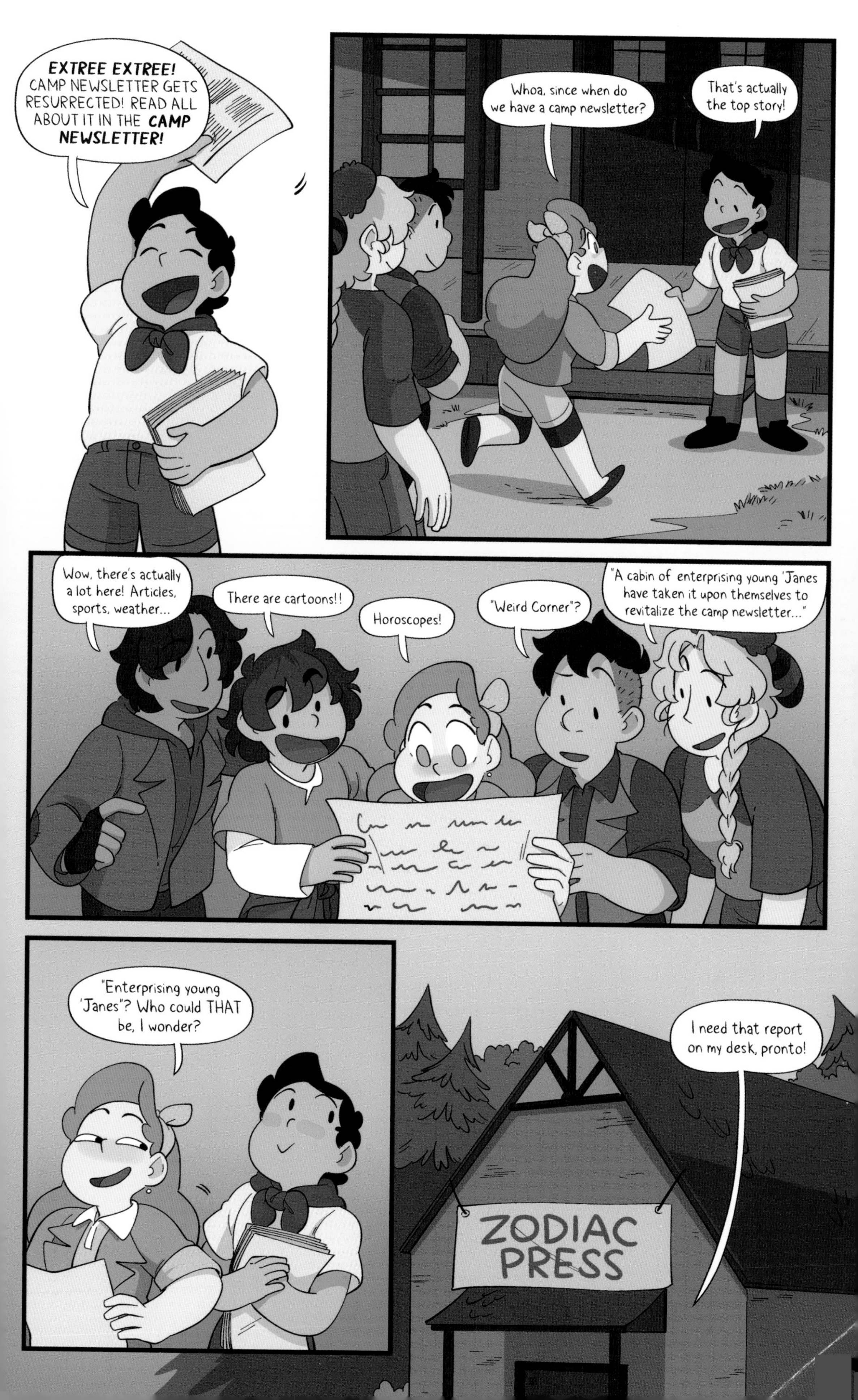
EXTREE EXTREE! CAMP NEWSLETTER GETS RESURRECTED! READ ALL ABOUT IT IN THE CAMP NEWSLETTER!
Whoa, since when do we have a camp newsletter?
That's actually the top story!
Wow, there's actually a lot here! Articles, sports, weather...
There are cartoons!!
Horoscopes!
"Weird Corner"?
"A cabin of enterprising young 'Janes have taken it upon themselves to revitalize the camp newsletter..."
"Enterprising young 'Janes"? Who could THAT be, I wonder?
ZODIAC PRESS
I need that report on my desk, pronto!

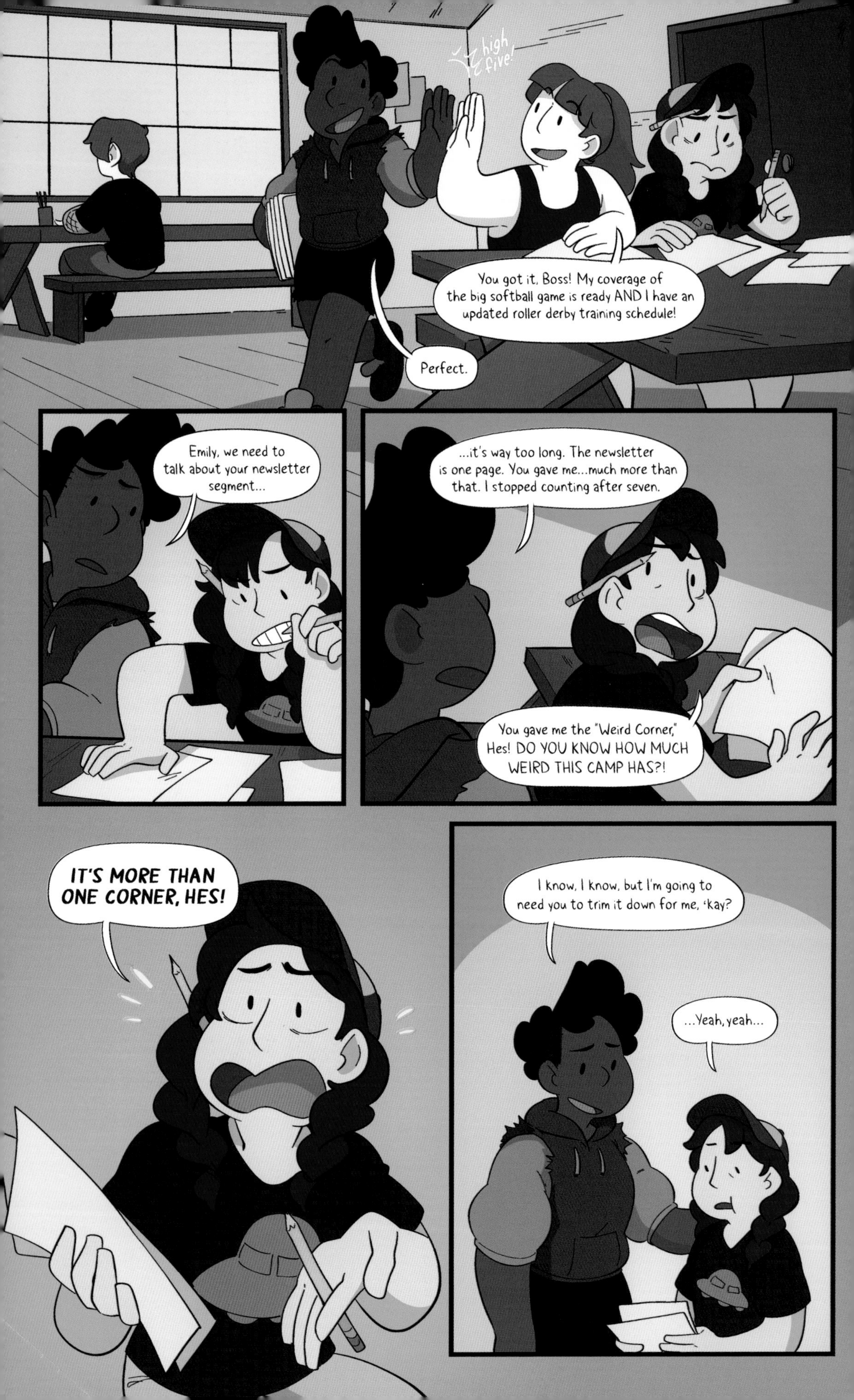
high five!
You got it, Boss! My coverage of the big softball game is ready AND I have an updated roller derby training schedule!
Perfect.
Emily, we need to talk about your newsletter segment...
...it's way too long. The newsletter is one page. You gave me...much more than that. I stopped counting after seven.
You gave me the "Weird Corner," Hes! DO YOU KNOW HOW MUCH WEIRD THIS CAMP HAS?!
IT'S MORE THAN ONE CORNER, HES!
I know, I know, but I'm going to need you to trim it down for me, 'kay?
...Yeah, yeah...

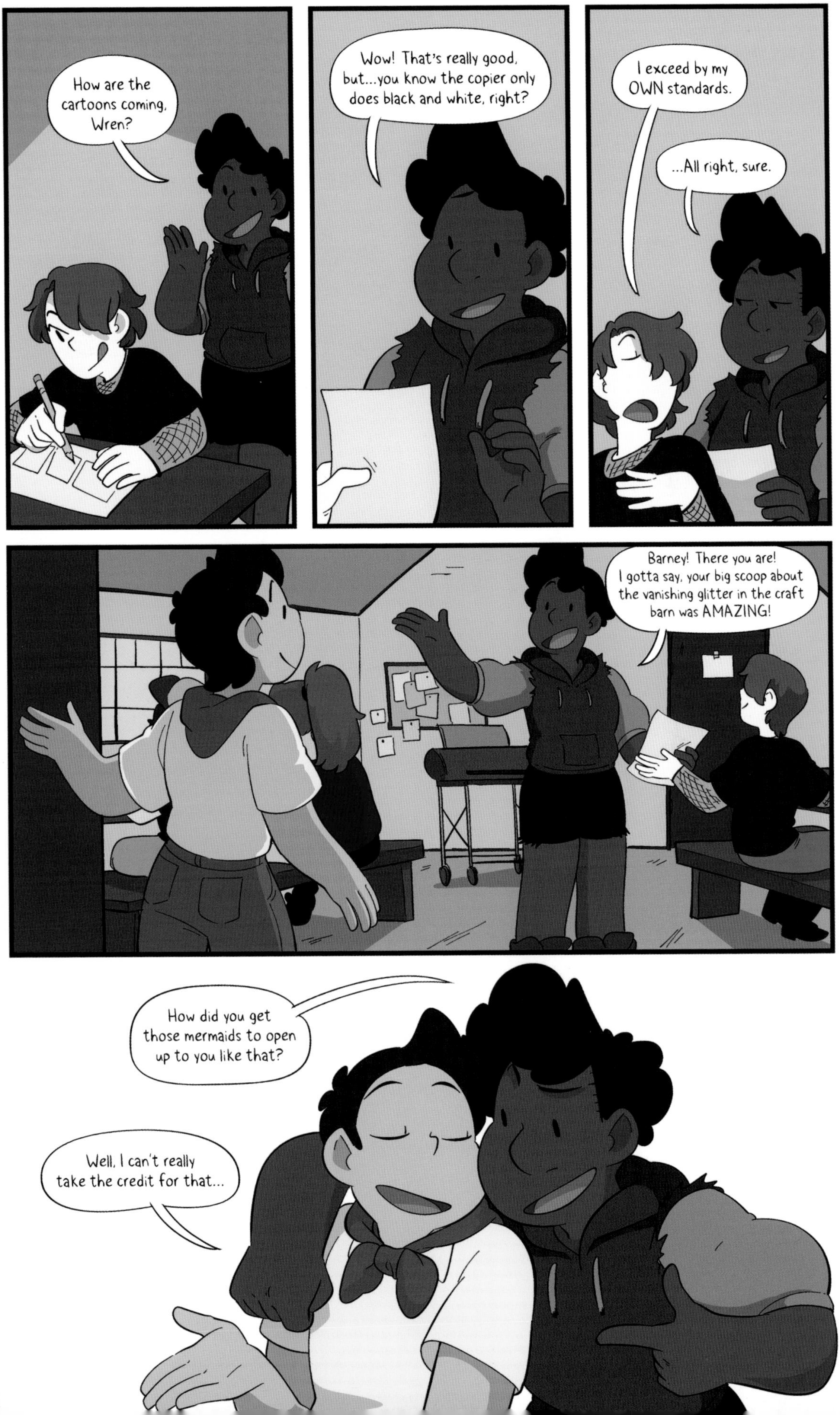
How are the cartoons coming, Wren?
Wow! That's really good, but...you know the copier only does black and white, right?
I exceed by my OWN standards.
...All right, sure.
Barney! There you are! I gotta say, your big scoop about the vanishing glitter in the craft barn was AMAZING!
How did you get those mermaids to open up to you like that?
Well, I can't really take the credit for that...

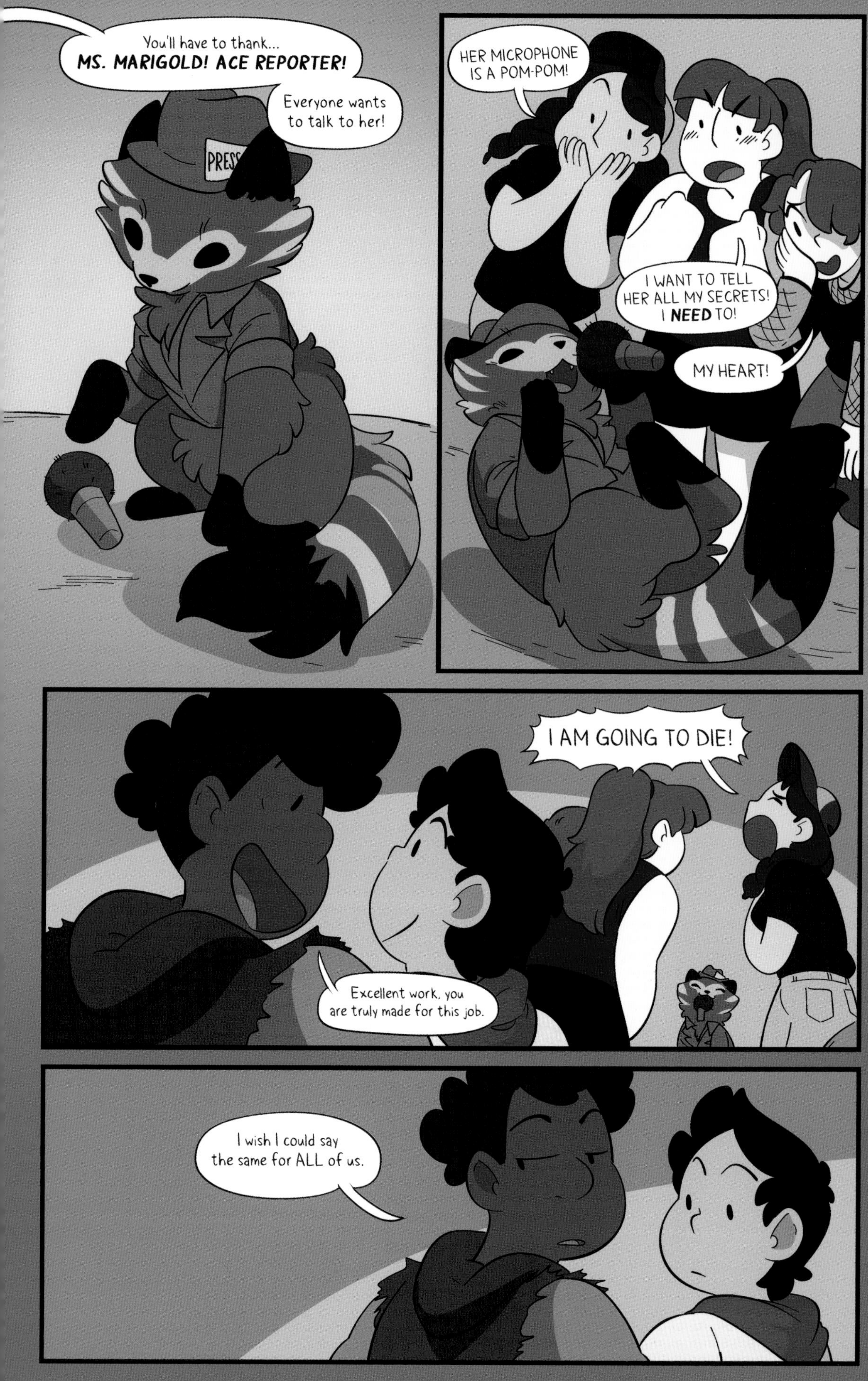
You'll have to thank...
MS. MARIGOLD! ACE REPORTER!
Everyone wants to talk to her!
HER MICROPHONE IS A POM-POM!
I WANT TO TELL HER ALL MY SECRETS! I NEED TO!
MY HEART!
I AM GOING TO DIE!
Excellent work, you are truly made for this job.
I wish I could say the same for ALL of us.

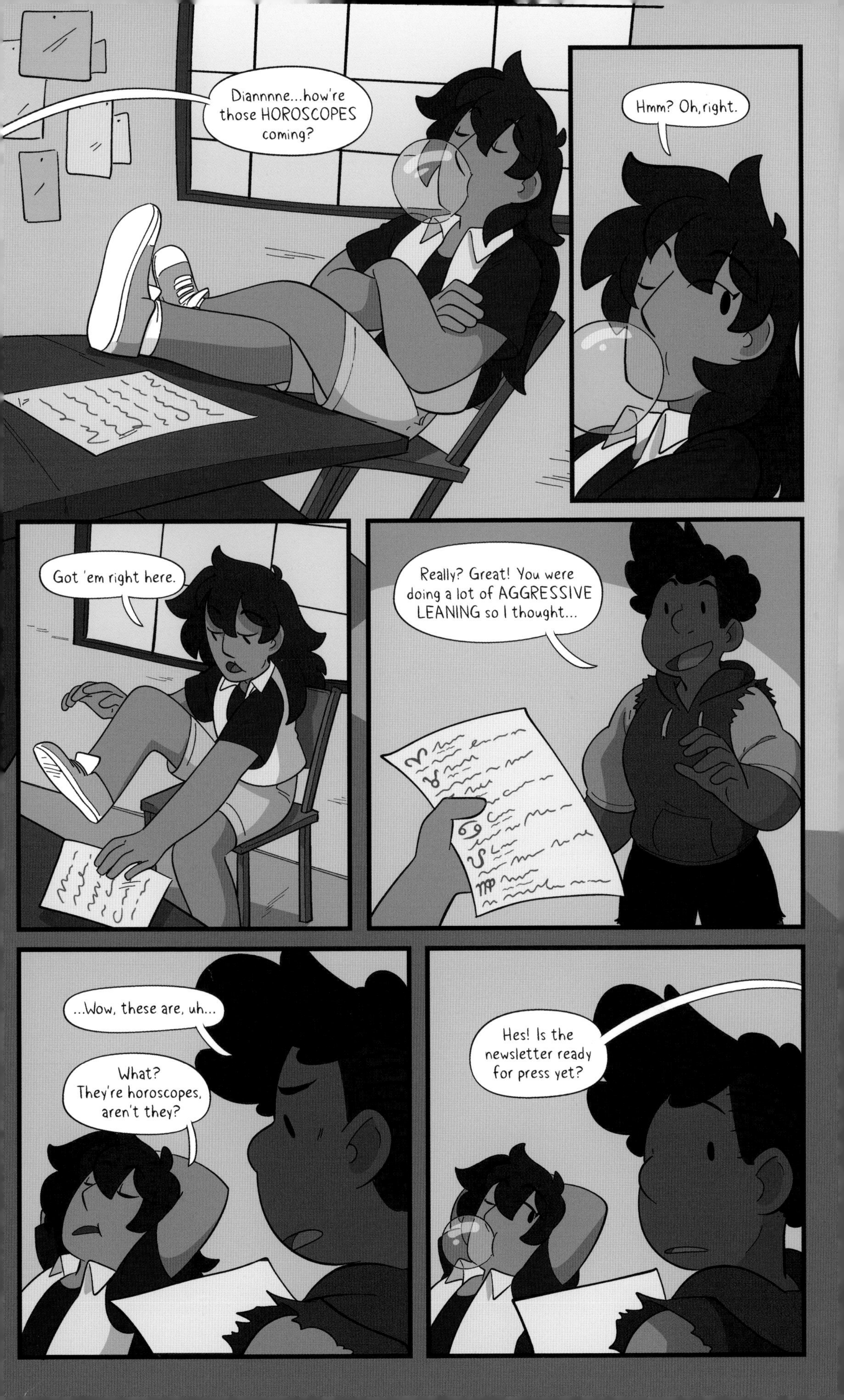
Diannnne...how're those HOROSCOPES coming?
Hmm? Oh, right.
Got 'em right here.
Really? Great! You were doing a lot of AGGRESSIVE LEANING so I thought...
...Wow, these are, uh...
What? They're horoscopes, aren't they?
Hes! Is the newsletter ready for press yet?

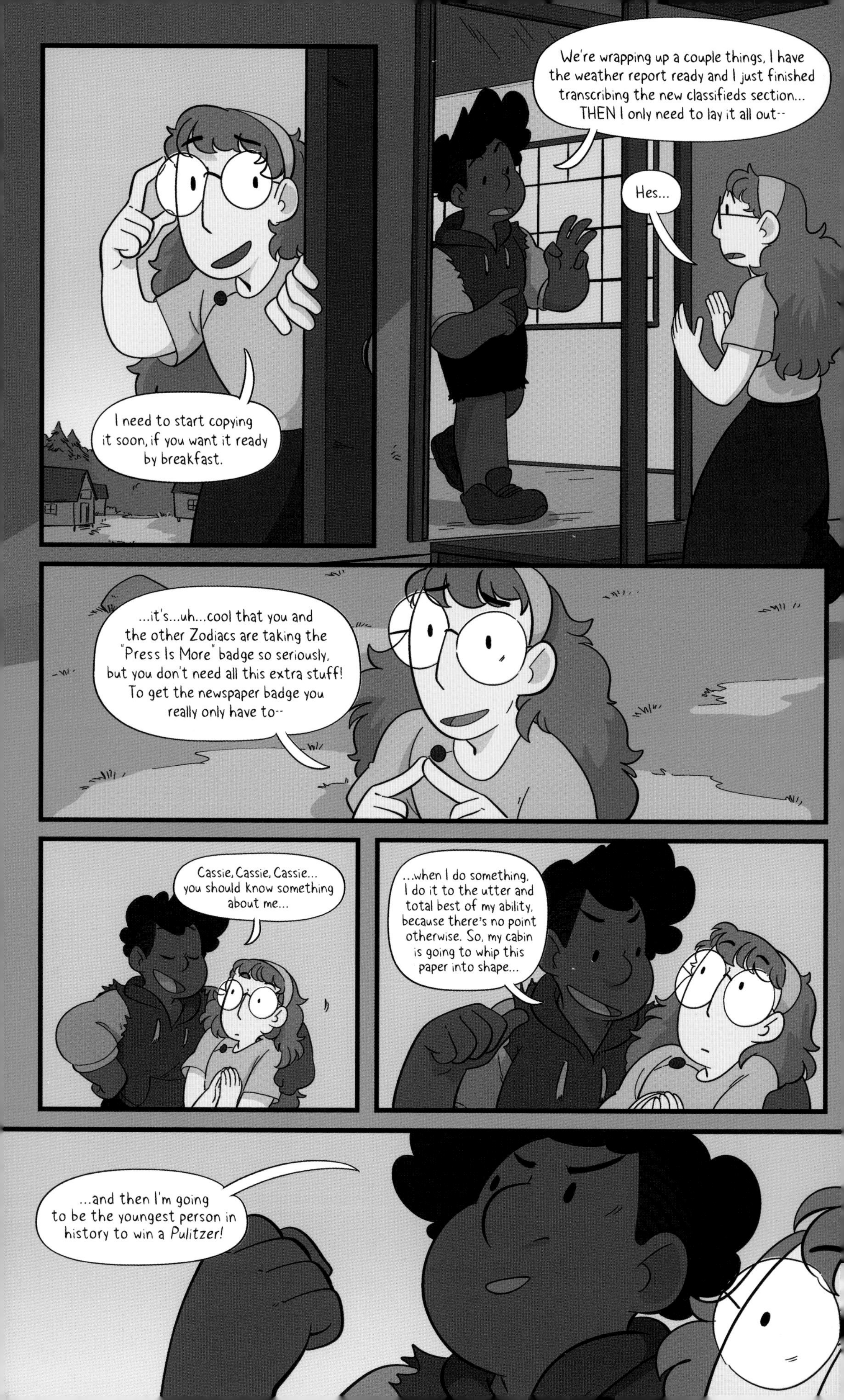
I need to start copying it soon, if you want it ready by breakfast.
We're wrapping up a couple things, I have the weather report ready and I just finished transcribing the new classifieds section... THEN I only need to lay it all out--
Hes...
...it's...uh...cool that you and the other Zodiacs are taking the "Press Is More" badge so seriously, but you don't need all this extra stuff! To get the newspaper badge you really only have to--
Cassie, Cassie, Cassie... you should know something about me...
...when I do something, I do it to the utter and total best of my ability, because there's no point otherwise. So, my cabin is going to whip this paper into shape...
...and then I'm going to be the youngest person in history to win a *Pulitzer*!

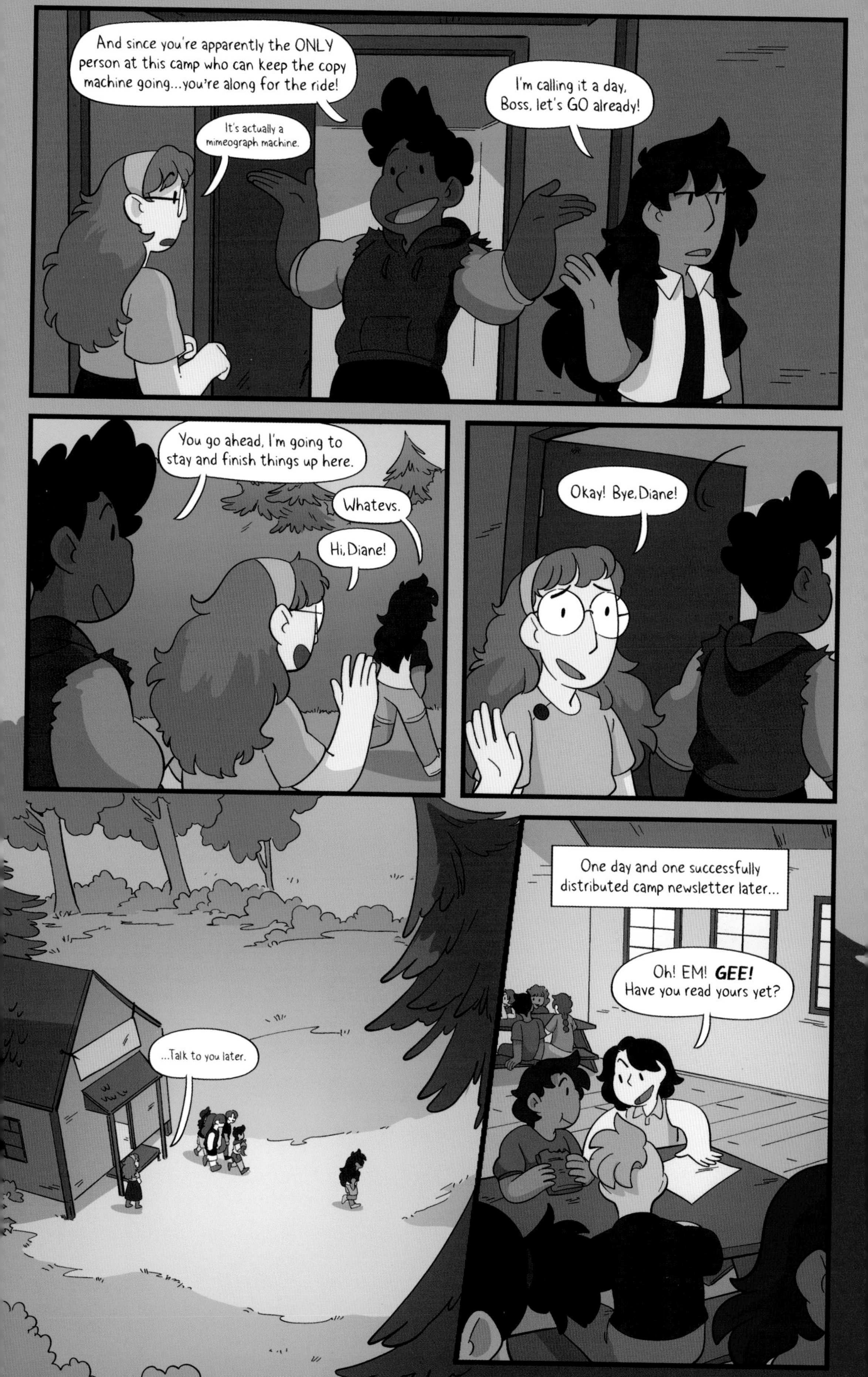
And since you're apparently the ONLY person at this camp who can keep the copy machine going...you're along for the ride!
It's actually a mimeograph machine.
I'm calling it a day, Boss, let's GO already!
You go ahead, I'm going to stay and finish things up here.
Whatevs.
Hi, Diane!
Okay! Bye, Diane!
...Talk to you later.
One day and one successfully distributed camp newsletter later...
Oh! EM! **GEE!** Have you read yours yet?

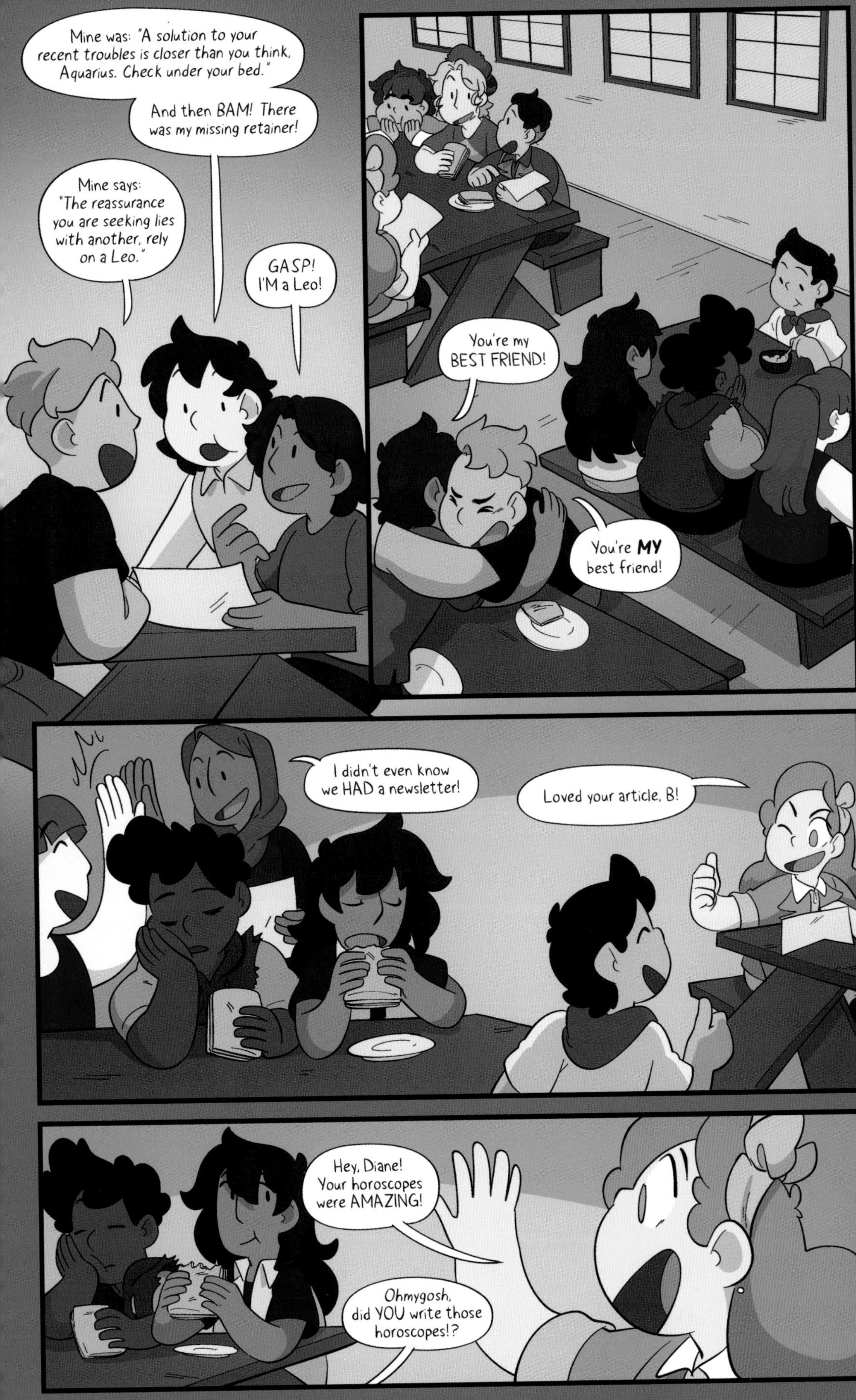
Mine was: "A solution to your recent troubles is closer than you think, Aquarius. Check under your bed."
And then BAM! There was my missing retainer!
Mine says: "The reassurance you are seeking lies with another, rely on a Leo."
GASP! I'M a Leo!
You're my BEST FRIEND!
You're MY best friend!
I didn't even know we HAD a newsletter!
Loved your article, B!
Hey, Diane! Your horoscopes were AMAZING!
Ohmygosh, did YOU write those horoscopes!?

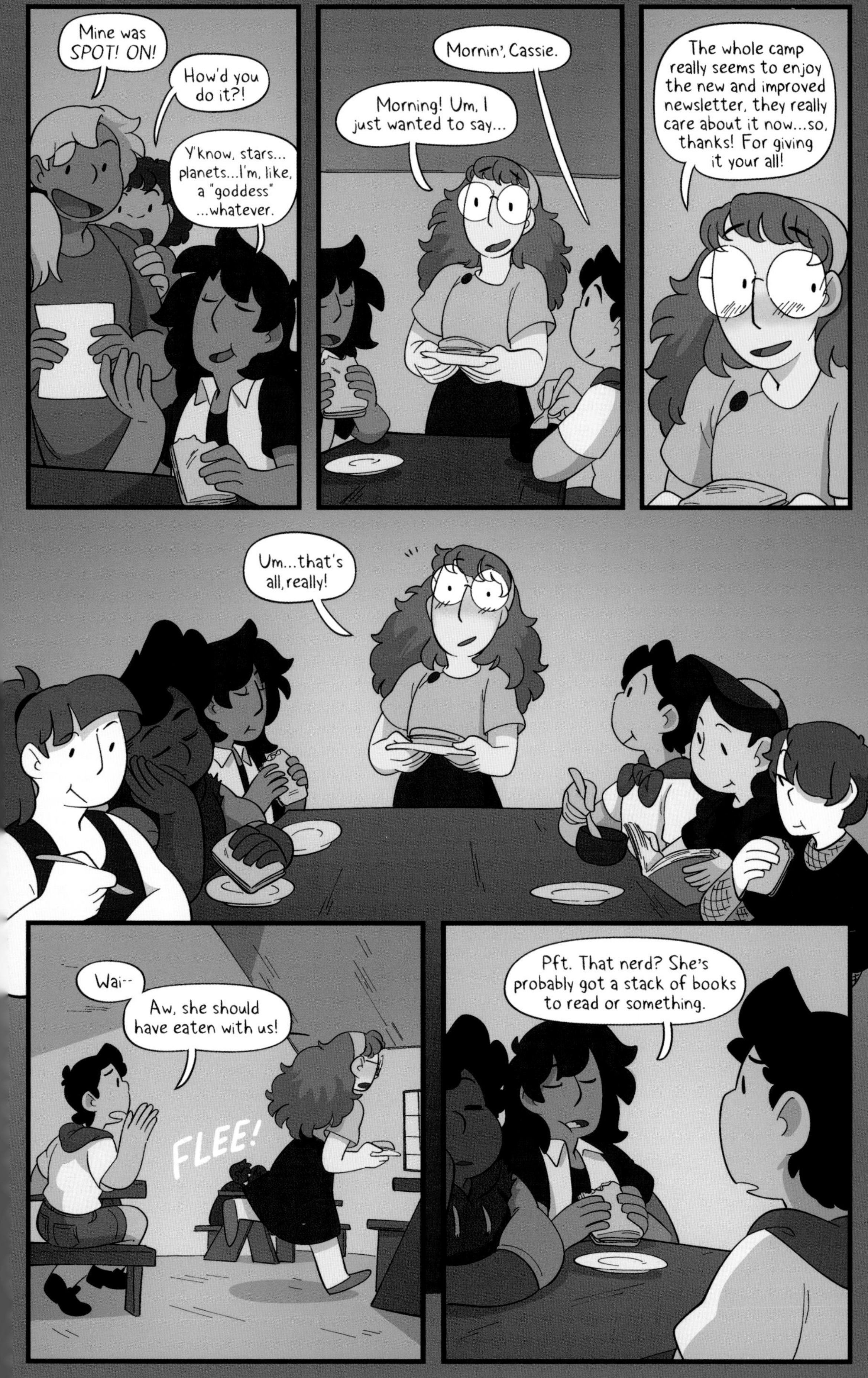
Mine was SPOT! ON!
How'd you do it?!
Y'know, stars... planets...I'm, like, a "goddess" ...whatever.
Mornin', Cassie.
Morning! Um, I just wanted to say...
The whole camp really seems to enjoy the new and improved newsletter, they really care about it now...so, thanks! For giving it your all!
Um...that's all, really!
Wai--
Aw, she should have eaten with us!
FLEE!
Pft. That nerd? She's probably got a stack of books to read or something.

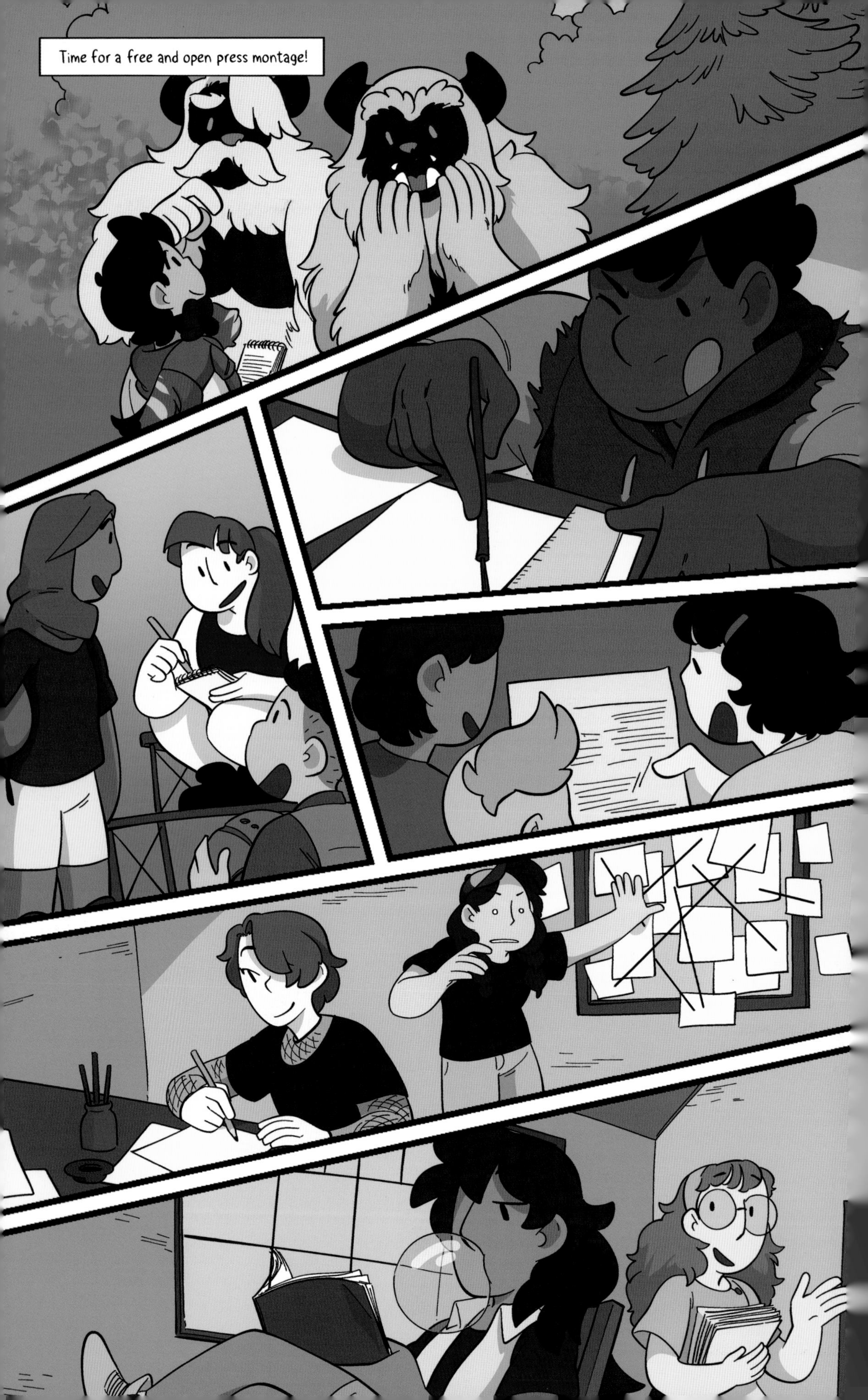
Time for a free and open press montage!

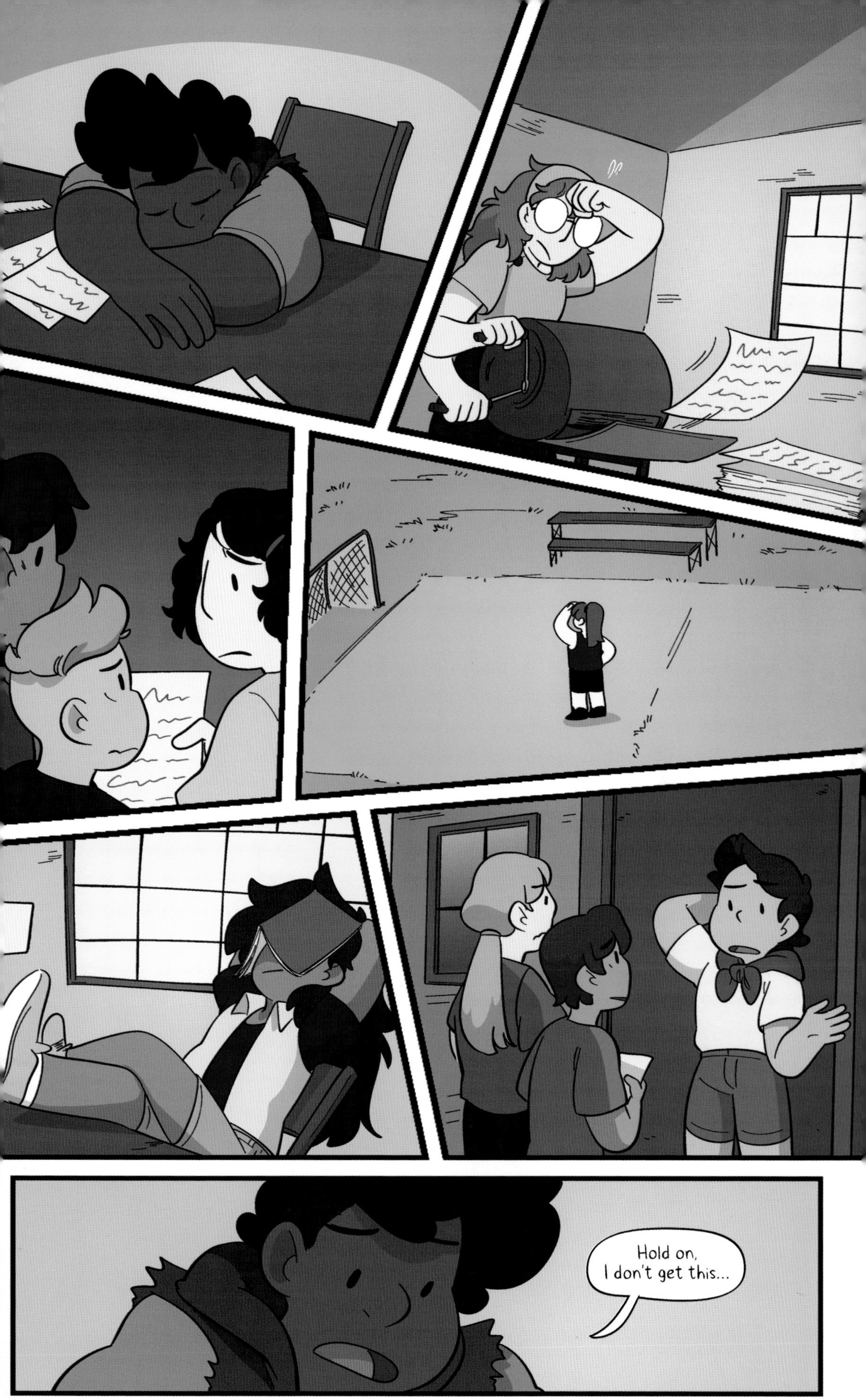
Hold on,
I don't get this...

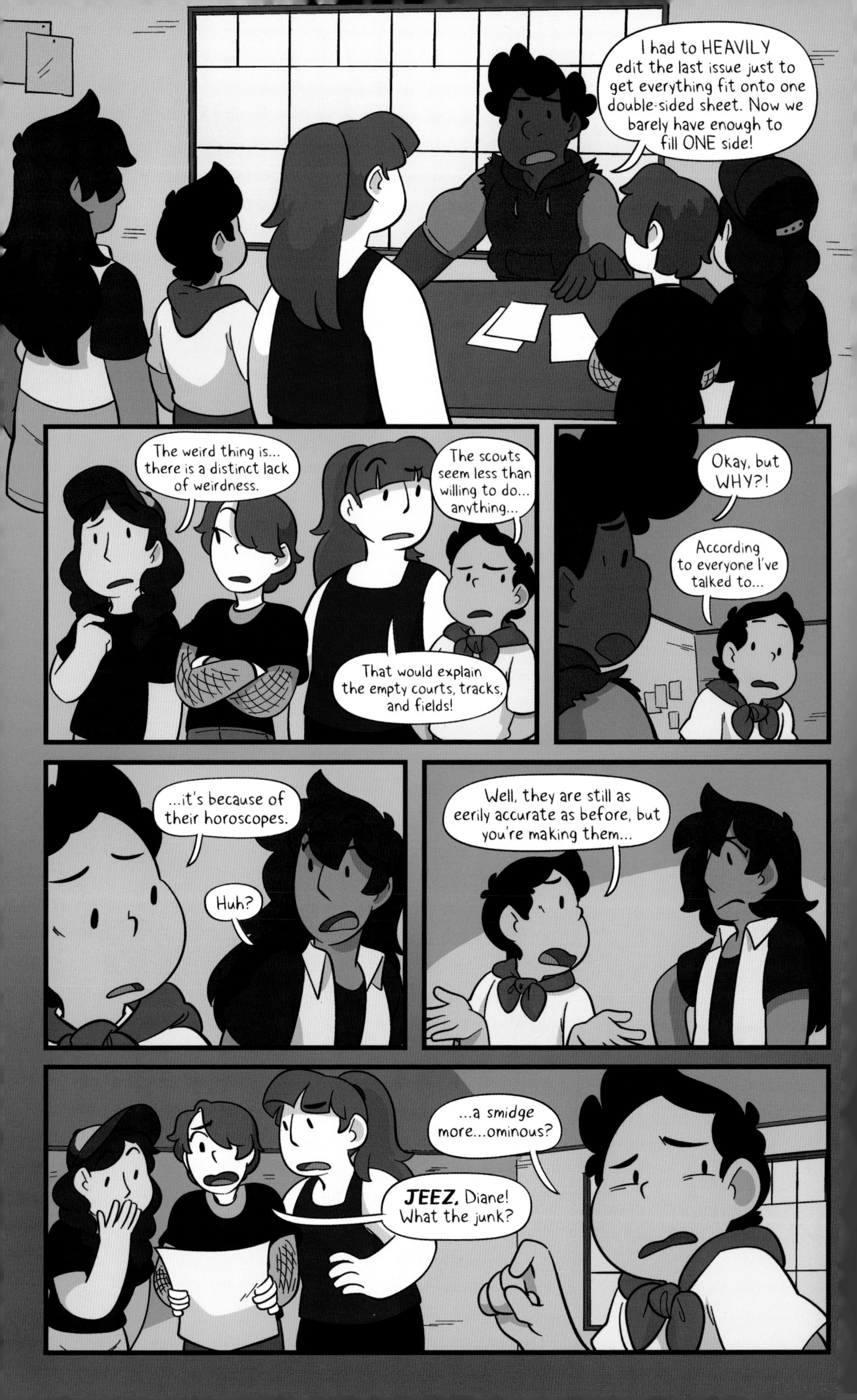
I had to HEAVILY edit the last issue just to get everything fit onto one double-sided sheet. Now we barely have enough to fill ONE side!
The weird thing is... there is a distinct lack of weirdness.
The scouts seem less than willing to do... anything...
That would explain the empty courts, tracks, and fields!
Okay, but WHY?!
According to everyone I've talked to...
...it's because of their horoscopes.
Huh?
Well, they are still as eerily accurate as before, but you're making them...
...a smidge more...ominous?
JEEZ, Diane! What the junk?

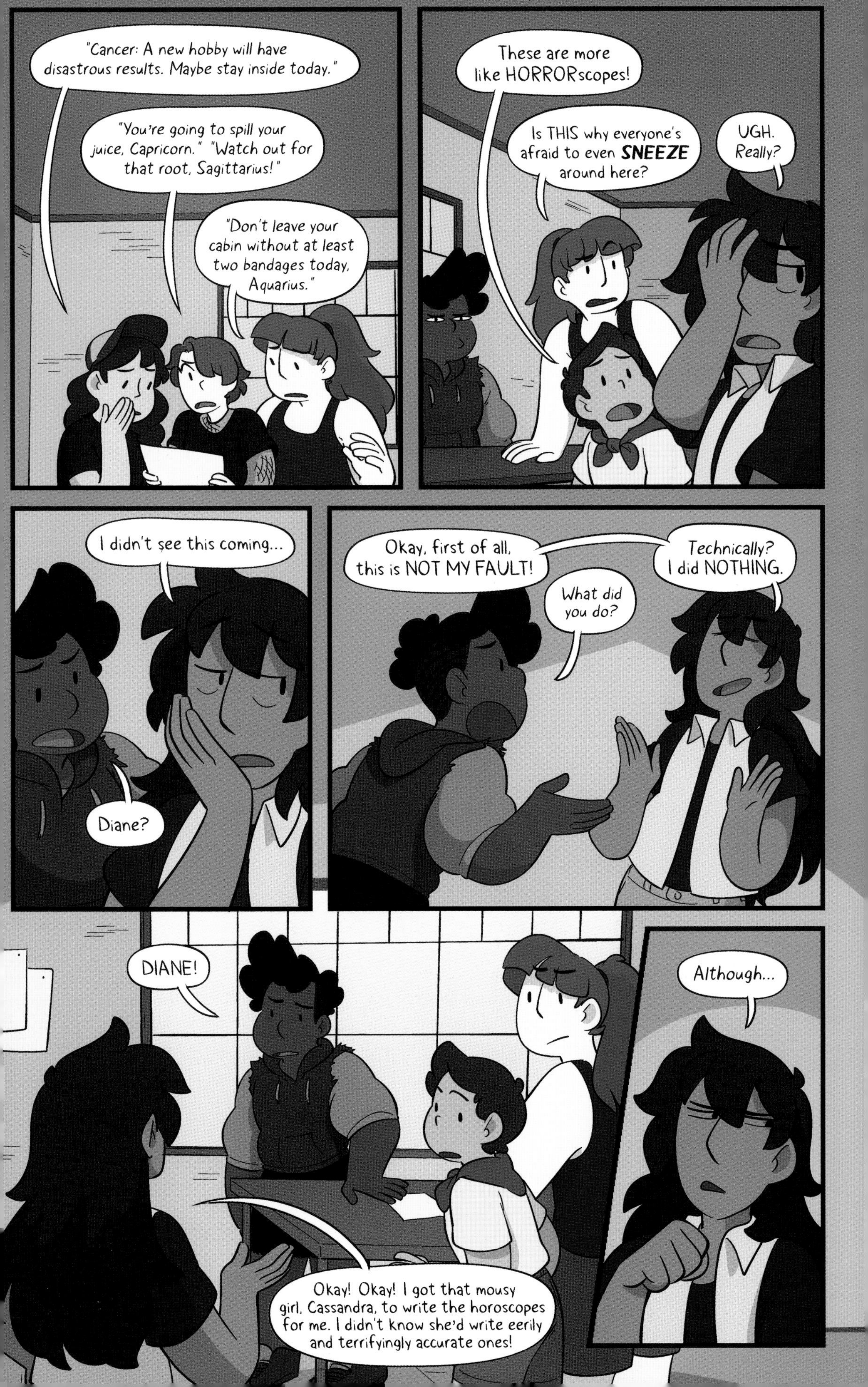
"Cancer: A new hobby will have disastrous results. Maybe stay inside today."
"You're going to spill your juice, Capricorn." "Watch out for that root, Sagittarius!"
"Don't leave your cabin without at least two bandages today, Aquarius."
These are more like HORRORscopes!
Is THIS why everyone's afraid to even **SNEEZE** around here?
UGH. Really?
I didn't see this coming...
Diane?
Okay, first of all, this is NOT MY FAULT!
Technically? I did NOTHING.
What did you do?
DIANE!
Although...
Okay! Okay! I got that mousy girl, Cassandra, to write the horoscopes for me. I didn't know she'd write eerily and terrifyingly accurate ones!

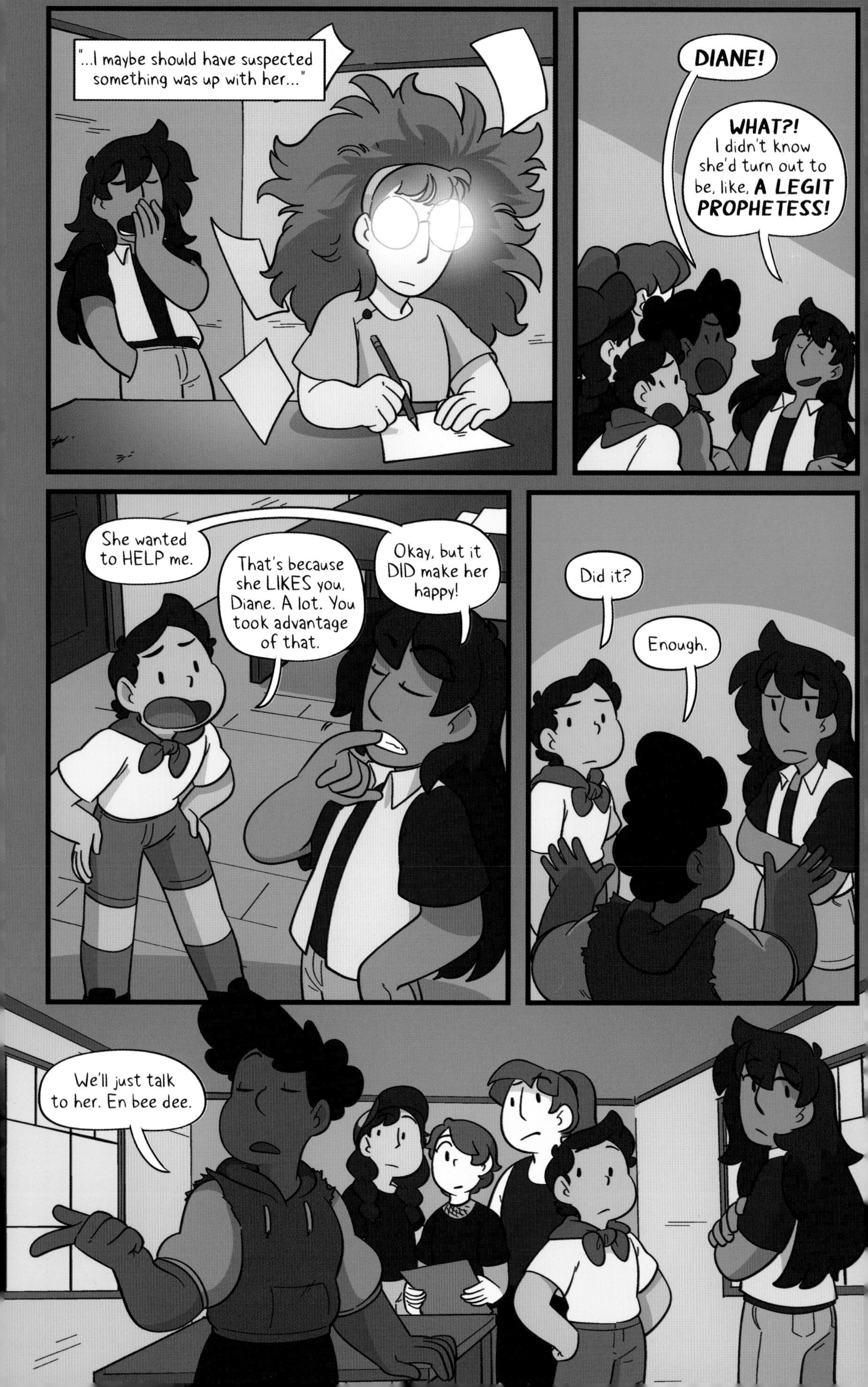
"...I maybe should have suspected something was up with her..."
DIANE!
WHAT?! I didn't know she'd turn out to be, like, A LEGIT PROPHETESS!
She wanted to HELP me.
That's because she LIKES you, Diane. A lot. You took advantage of that.
Okay, but it DID make her happy!
Did it?
Enough.
We'll just talk to her. En bee dee.

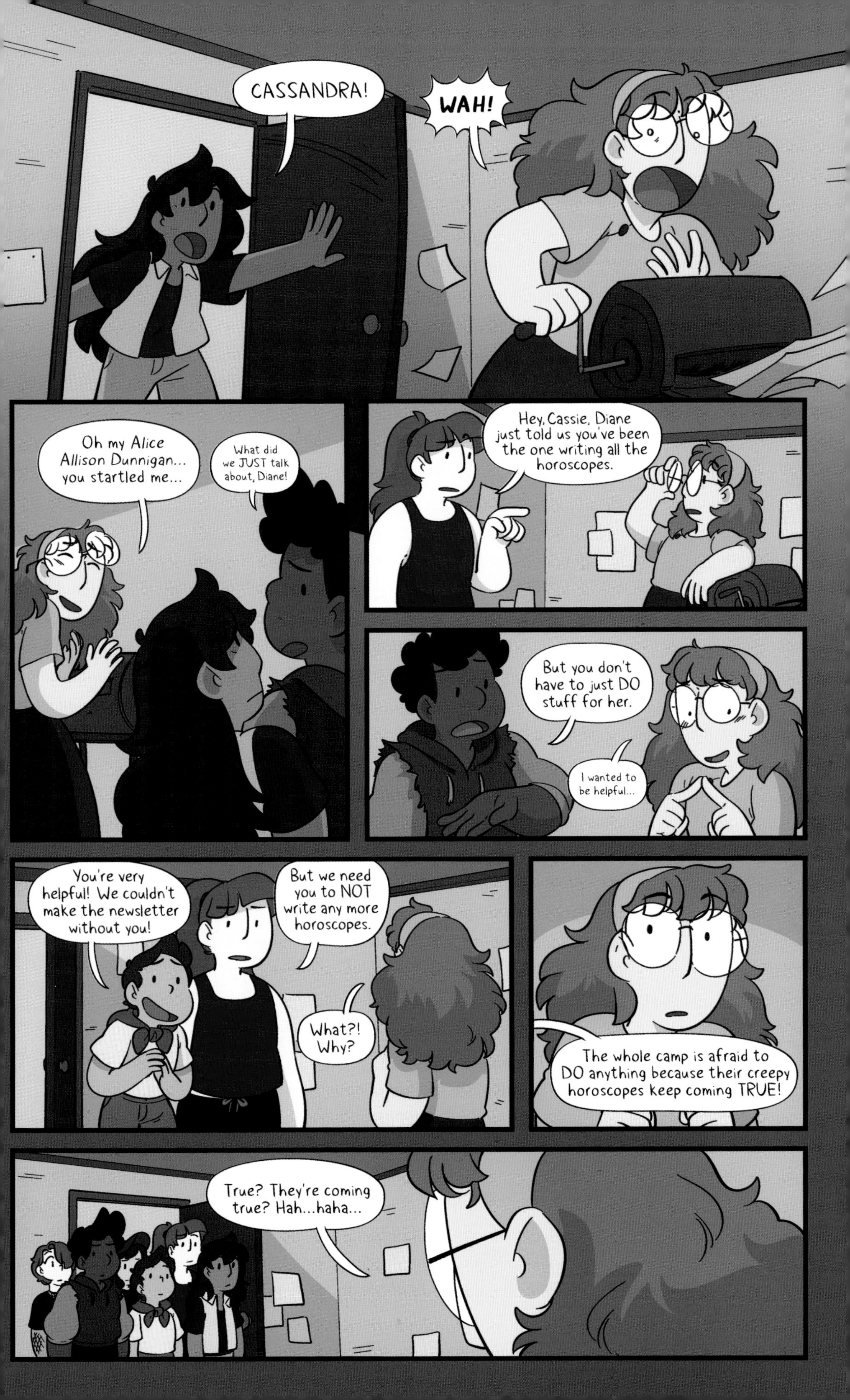
CASSANDRA!
WAH!
Oh my Alice Allison Dunnigan... you startled me...
What did we JUST talk about, Diane!
Hey, Cassie, Diane just told us you've been the one writing all the horoscopes.
But you don't have to just DO stuff for her.
I wanted to be helpful...
You're very helpful! We couldn't make the newsletter without you!
But we need you to NOT write any more horoscopes.
What?! Why?
The whole camp is afraid to DO anything because their creepy horoscopes keep coming TRUE!
True? They're coming true? Hah...haha...

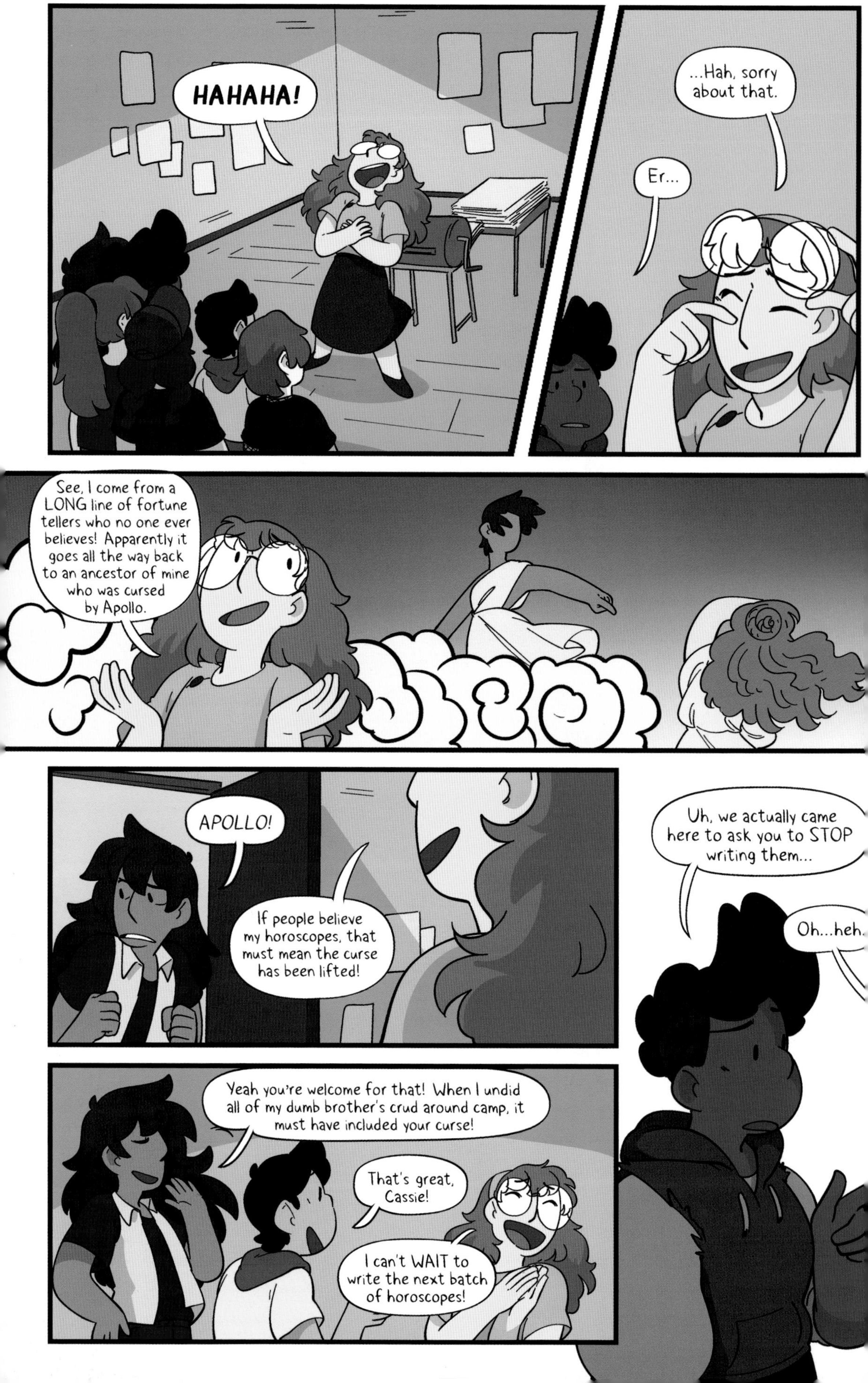
HAHAHA!
...Hah, sorry about that.
Er...
See, I come from a LONG line of fortune tellers who no one ever believes! Apparently it goes all the way back to an ancestor of mine who was cursed by Apollo.
APOLLO!
If people believe my horoscopes, that must mean the curse has been lifted!
Yeah you're welcome for that! When I undid all of my dumb brother's crud around camp, it must have included your curse!
That's great, Cassie!
I can't WAIT to write the next batch of horoscopes!
Uh, we actually came here to ask you to STOP writing them...
Oh...heh.

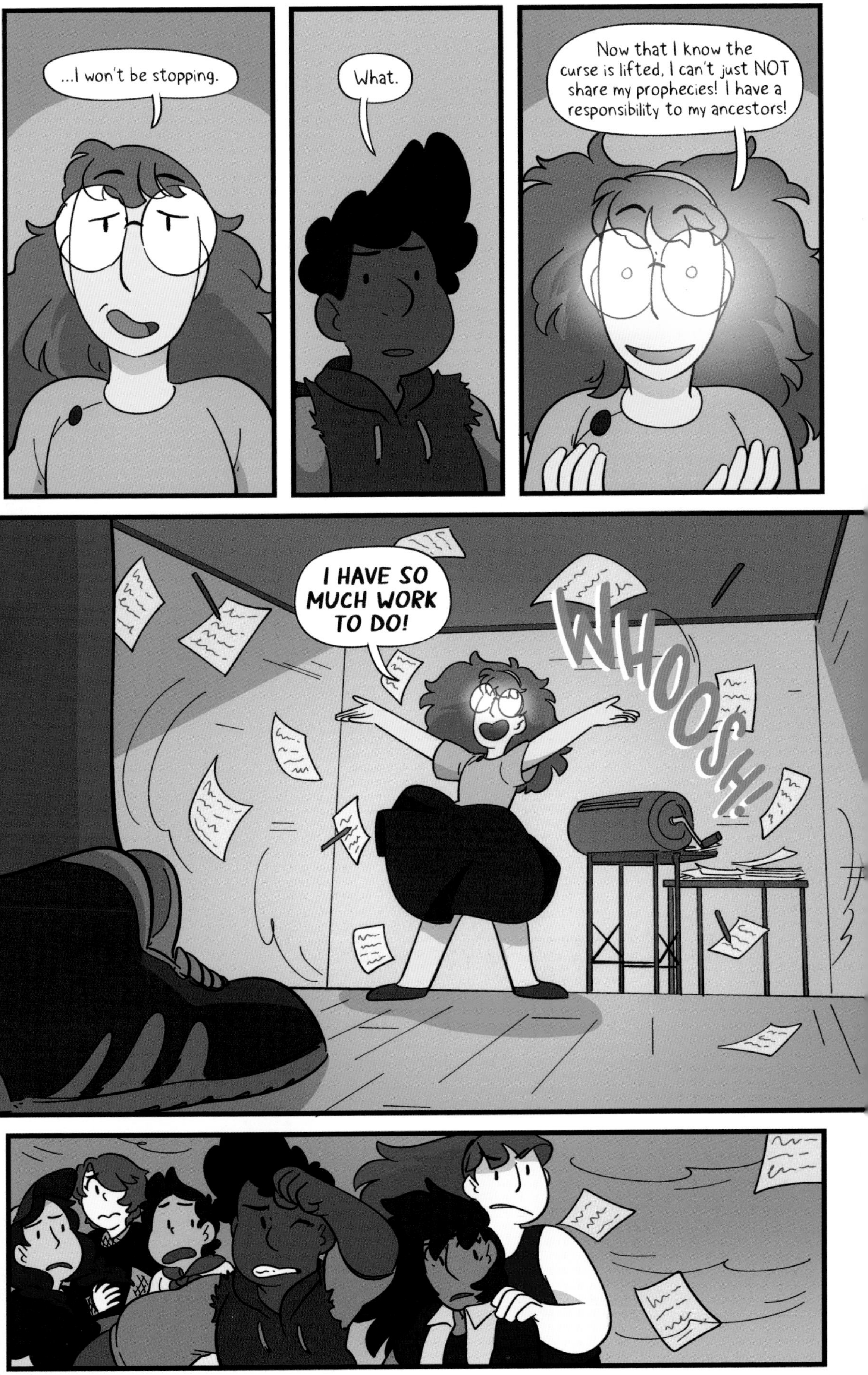
...I won't be stopping.
What.
Now that I know the curse is lifted, I can't just NOT share my prophecies! I have a responsibility to my ancestors!
I HAVE SO MUCH WORK TO DO!
WHOOSH!

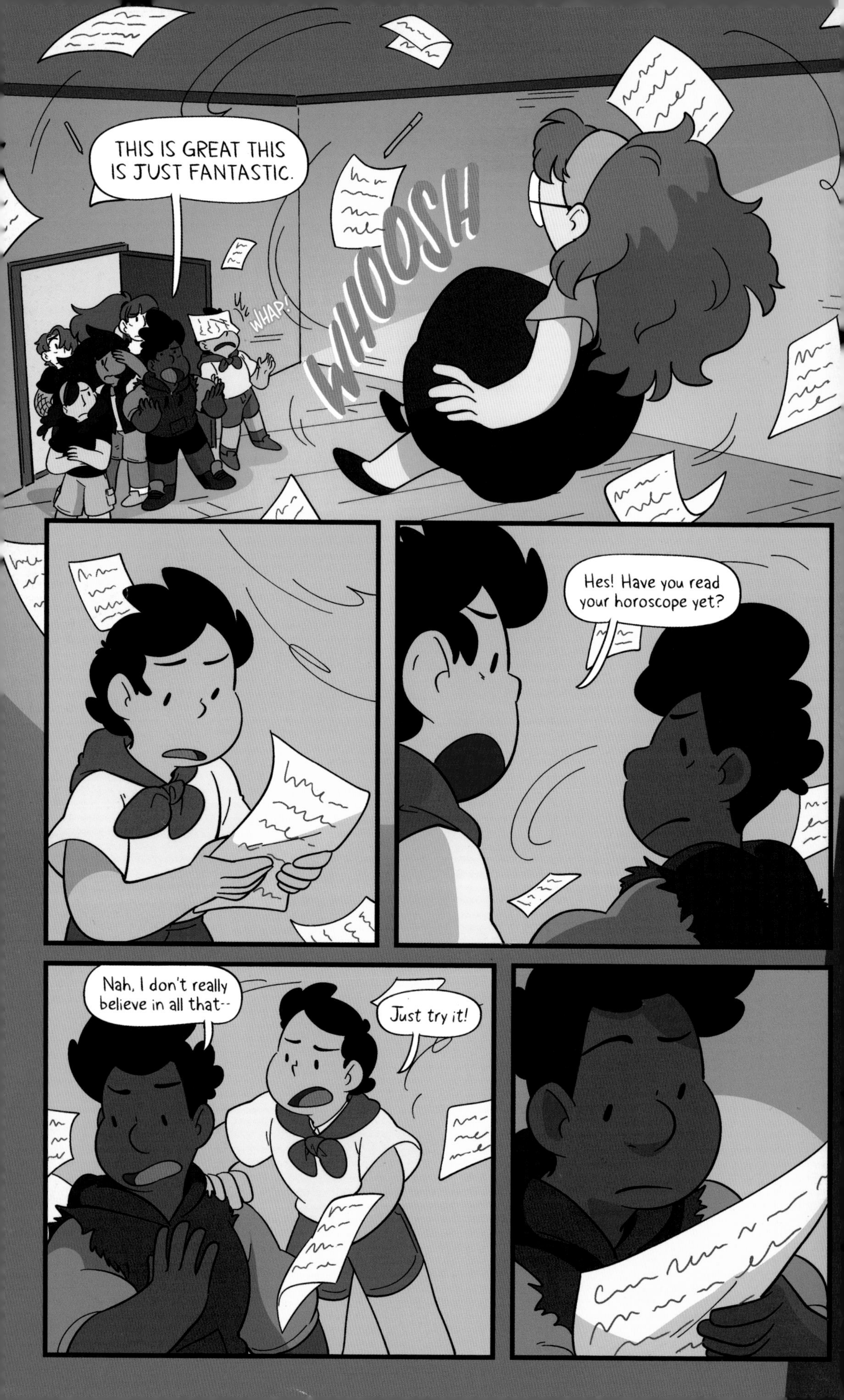
THIS IS GREAT THIS IS JUST FANTASTIC.
WHAP!
WHOOSH
Hes! Have you read your horoscope yet?
Nah, I don't really believe in all that--
Just try it!

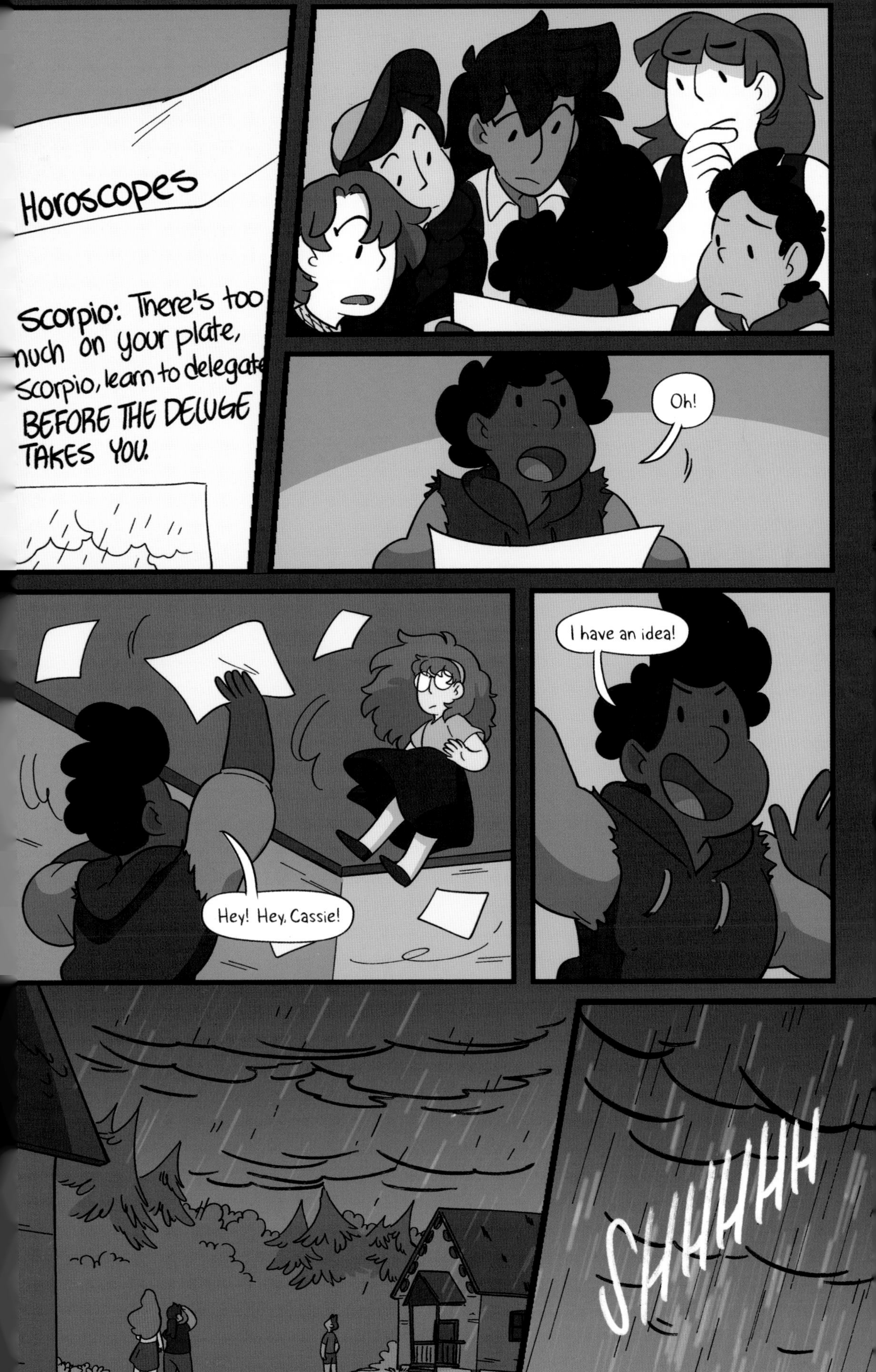
Horoscopes
Scorpio: There's too much on your plate, scorpio, learn to delegate BEFORE THE DELUGE TAKES YOU.
Oh!
Hey! Hey, Cassie!
I have an idea!
SHHHHH

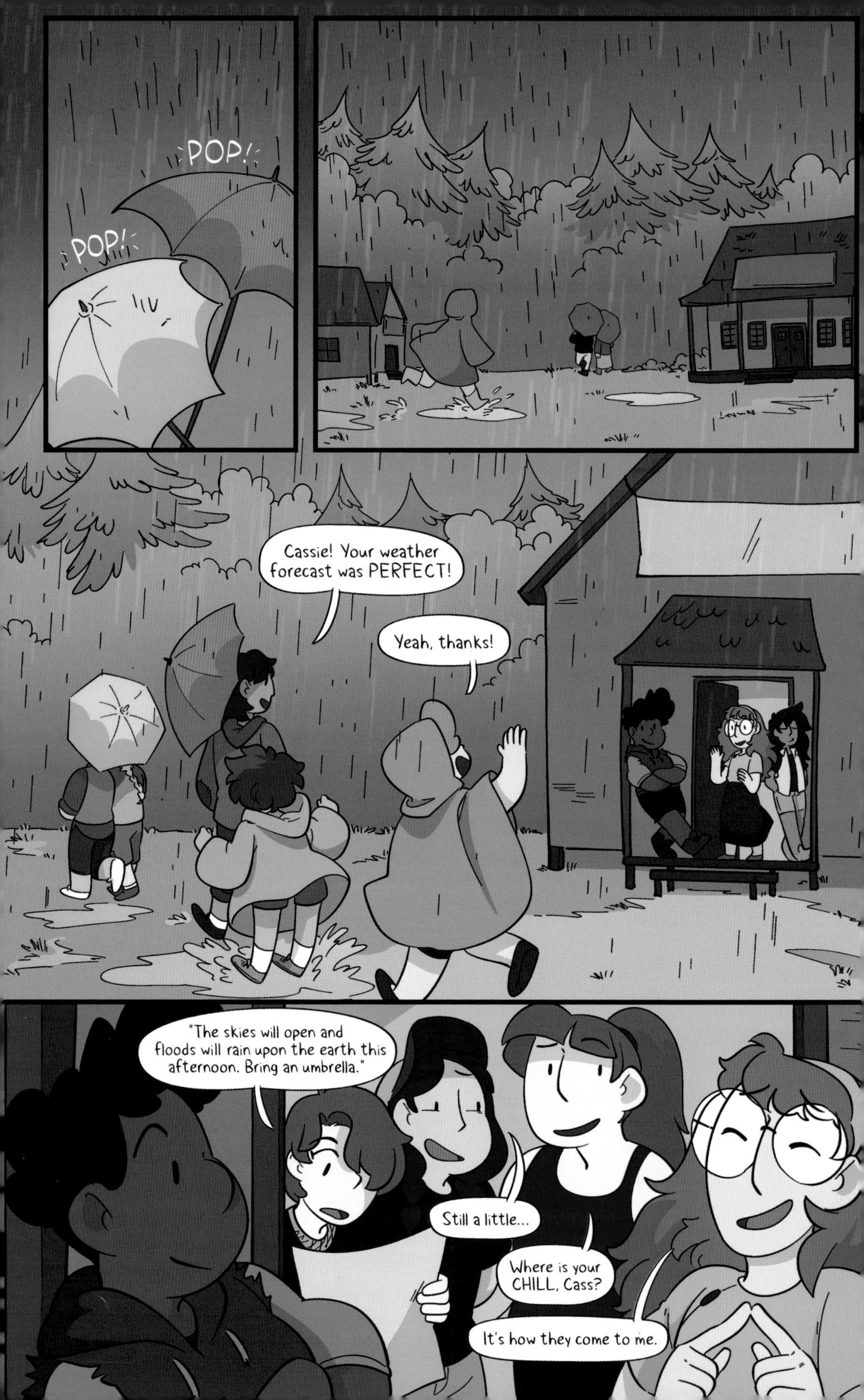
POP!
POP!
Cassie! Your weather forecast was PERFECT!
Yeah, thanks!
"The skies will open and floods will rain upon the earth this afternoon. Bring an umbrella."
Still a little...
Where is your CHILL, Cass?
It's how they come to me.

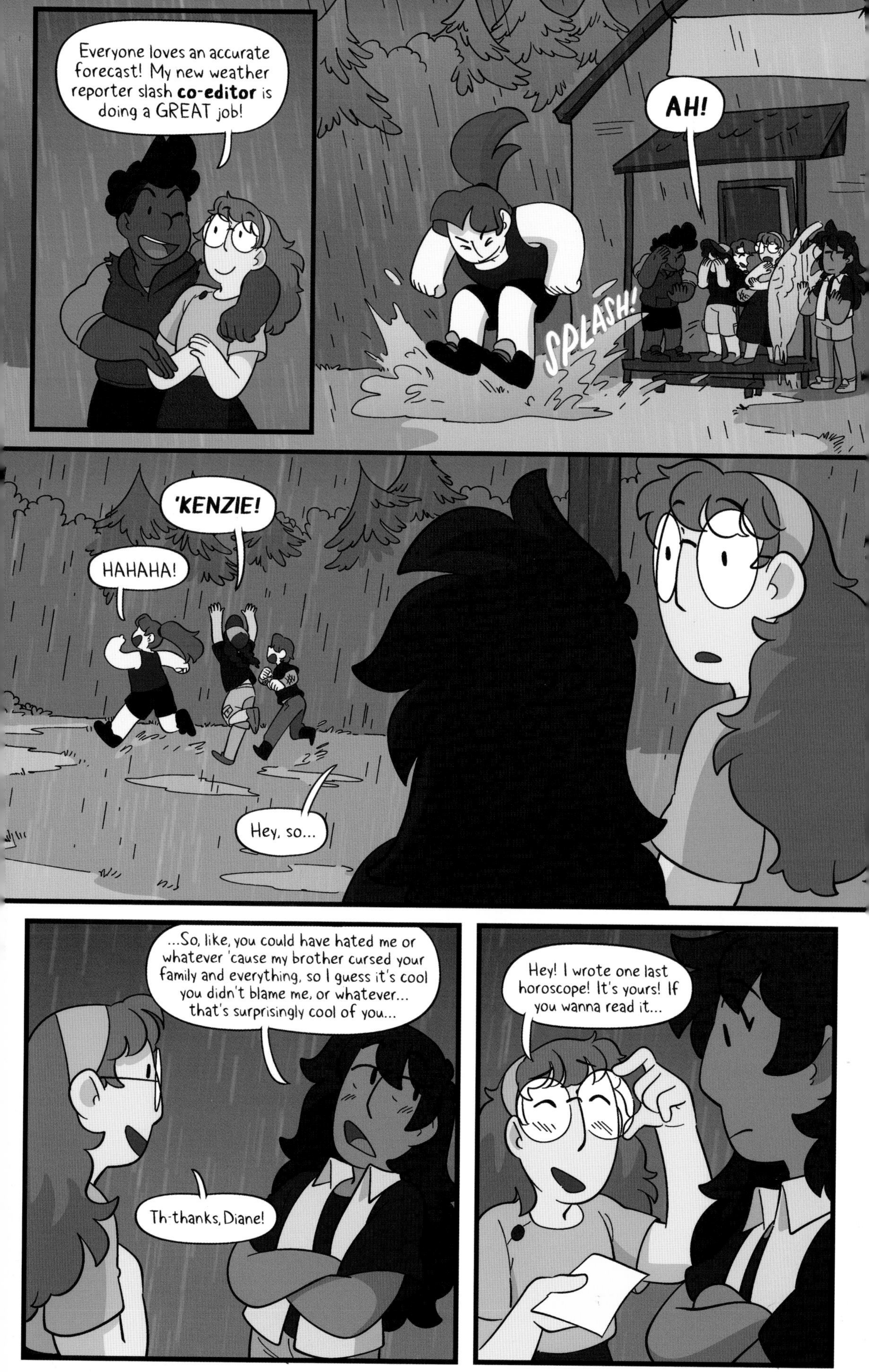
Everyone loves an accurate forecast! My new weather reporter slash **co-editor** is doing a GREAT job!
AH!
SPLASH!
HAHAHA!
'KENZIE!
Hey, so...
...So, like, you could have hated me or whatever 'cause my brother cursed your family and everything, so I guess it's cool you didn't blame me, or whatever... that's surprisingly cool of you...
Th-thanks, Diane!
Hey! I wrote one last horoscope! It's yours! If you wanna read it...

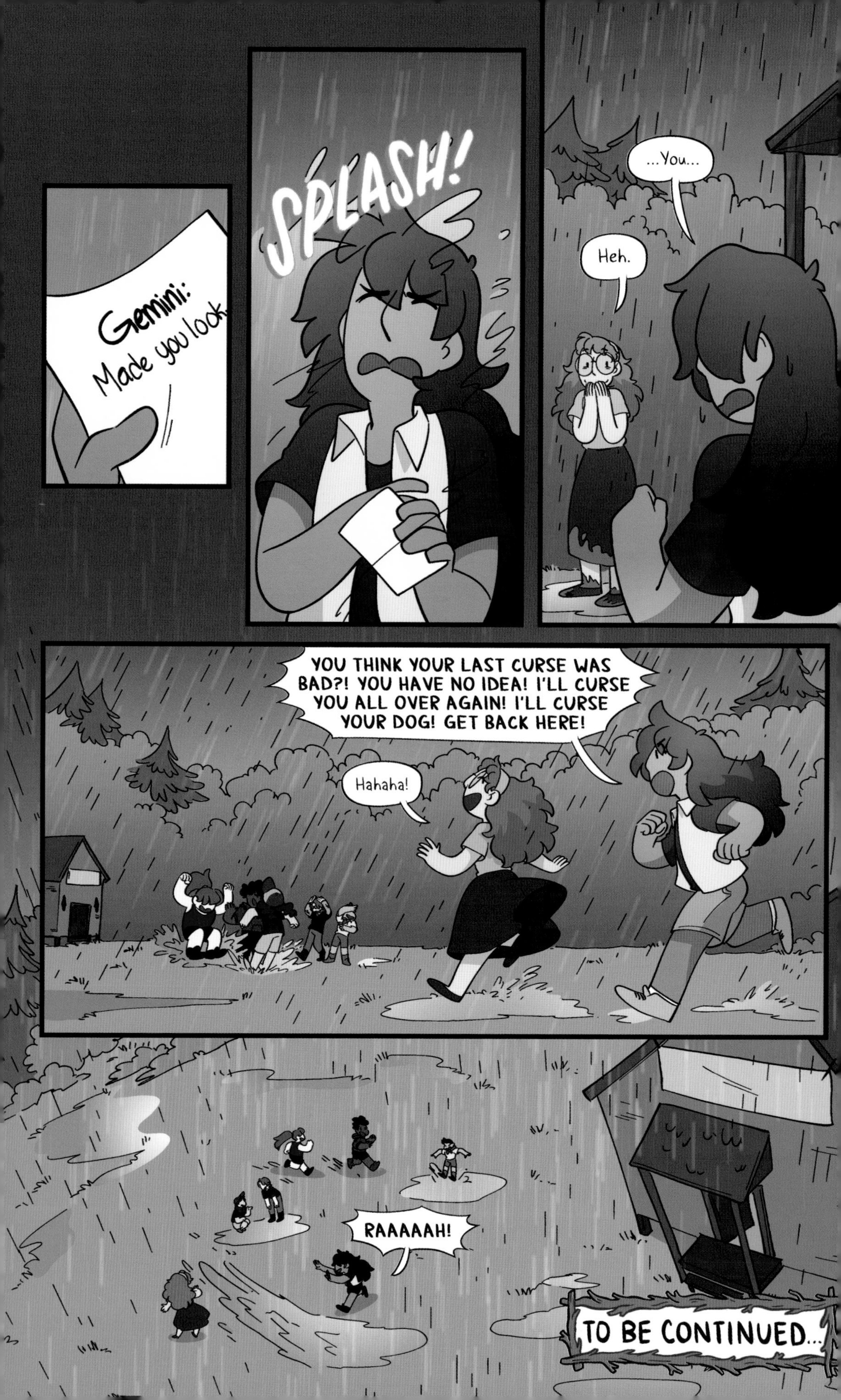
Gemini:
Made you look
SPLASH!
...You...
Heh.
YOU THINK YOUR LAST CURSE WAS BAD?! YOU HAVE NO IDEA! I'LL CURSE YOU ALL OVER AGAIN! I'LL CURSE YOUR DOG! GET BACK HERE!
Hahaha!
RAAAAAH!
TO BE CONTINUED...

will co

The

It help

appearar

dress f

Further

Lumbe

to have

part in

Thiskv

Hardc

have

them

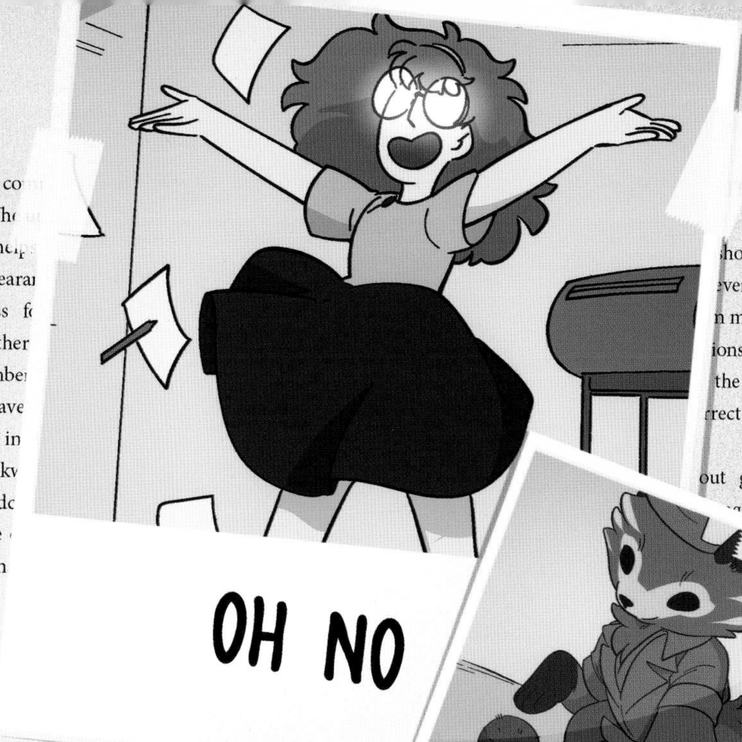
OH NO

HE UNIFORM

should be worn at camp
events when Lumberjanes
n may also be worn at other
ions. It should be worn as a
the uniform dress with
rrect shoes, and stocking or

out grows her uniform or
ther Lumberjane.
a she has
her
her

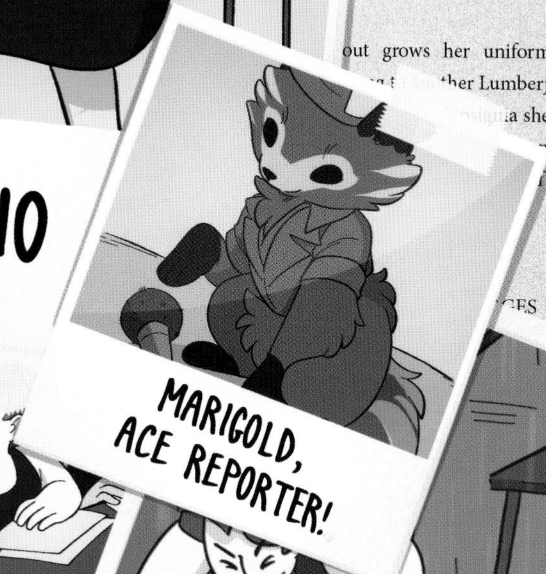
MARIGOLD,
ACE REPORTER!

The

yellow, short sl

emb

the w

choose

slacks,

made o

out-of-dc

green bere

the colla

Shoes ma

heels, rou

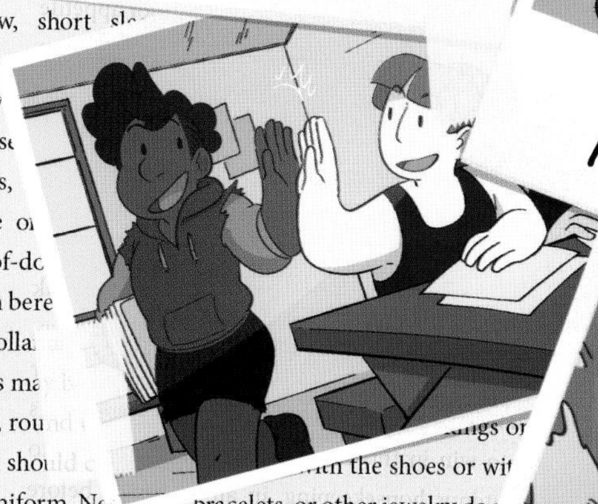

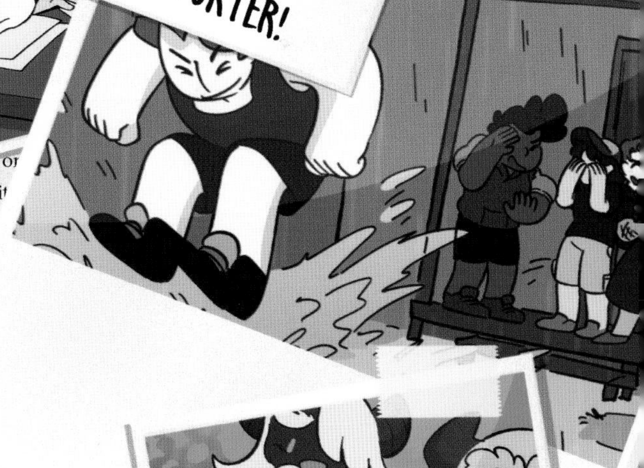

ings or

socks shou with the shoes or wi

the uniform. Ne es, bracelets, or other jewelry do

belong with a Lumberjane uniform.

HOW TO WEAR THE UNIFORM

To look well in a uniform demands first of uniform be kept in good condition—clean pressed. See that the skirt is the right length for your own height and build, that the belt is adjusted to your waist, that your shoes and stockings are in keeping with the uniform, that you watch your posture and carry yourself with dignity and grace. If the beret is removed indoors, be sure that your hair is neat and kept in place with an inconspicuous clip or ribbon. When you wear a Lumberjane uniform you are identified as a member of this organization and you should be doubly careful to conduct yourself in a way that will show everyone that courtesy and thoughtfulness are part of being a Lumberjane. People are likely to judge a whole nation by the selfishness of a few individuals, to criticize a whole family because of the misconduct of one member, and to feel unkindly toward an organization because of the

The unifor

helps to cre

in a group.

active life th

another bond

future, and pr

in order to b

Lumberjane pr

Penniquiqul Thi ore Lady

Types, but m es will wish to have one. They

can either bu the uniform, or make it themselves from

materials available at the trading post.

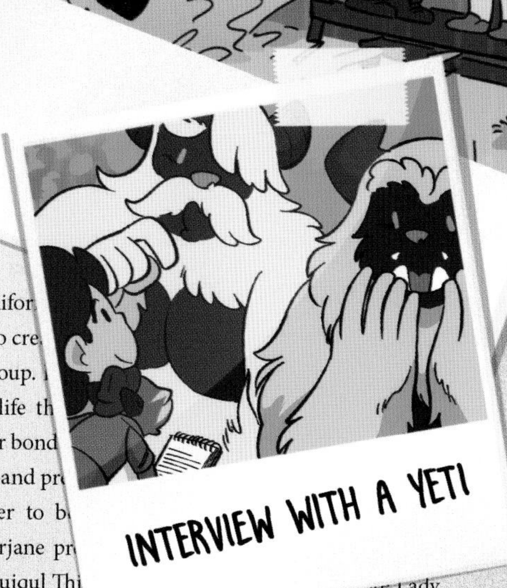
INTERVIEW WITH A YETI

BROOKLYN ALLEN

COVER GALLERY

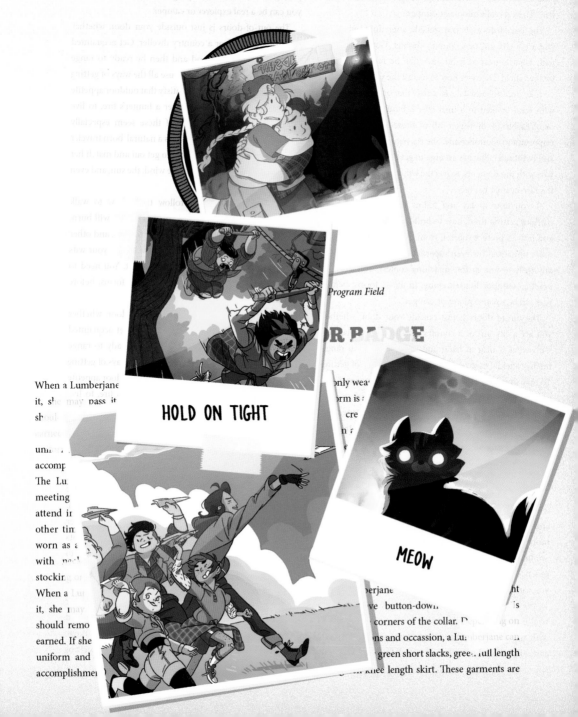

HOLD ON TIGHT

MEOW

Issue Forty-One
KAT LEYH

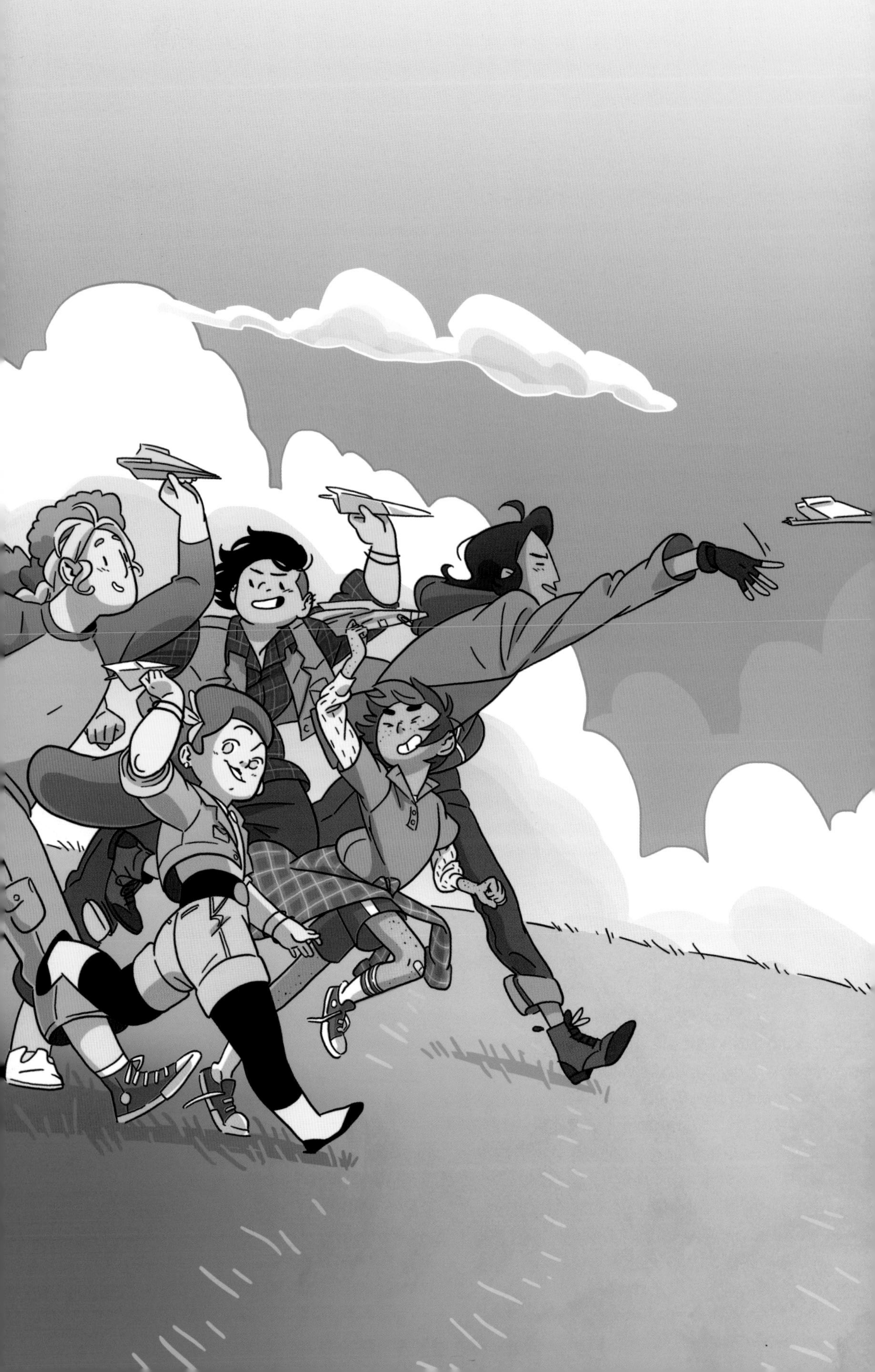

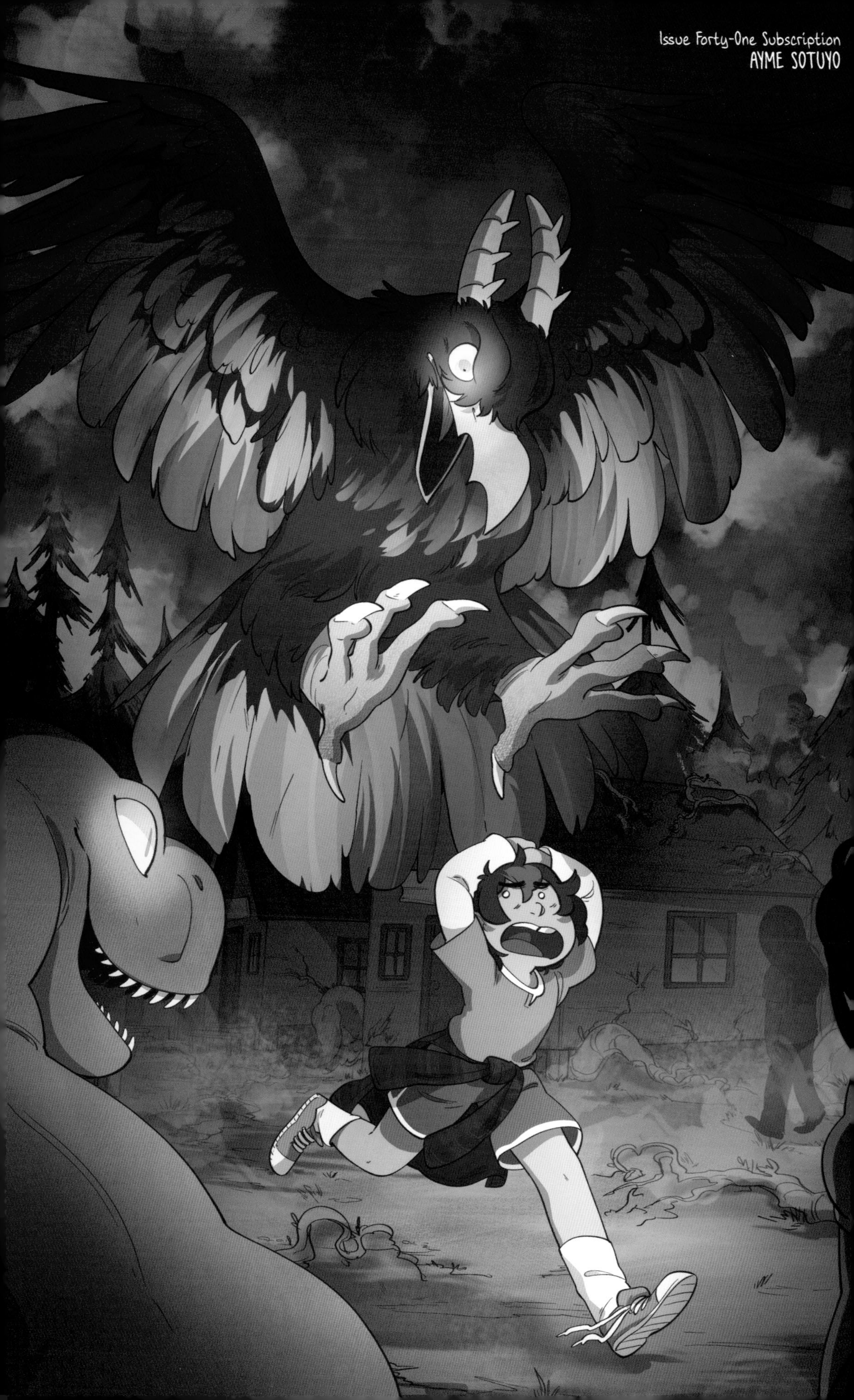

Issue Forty-One Subscription
AYME SOTUYO

Issue Forty-Two
KAT LEYH

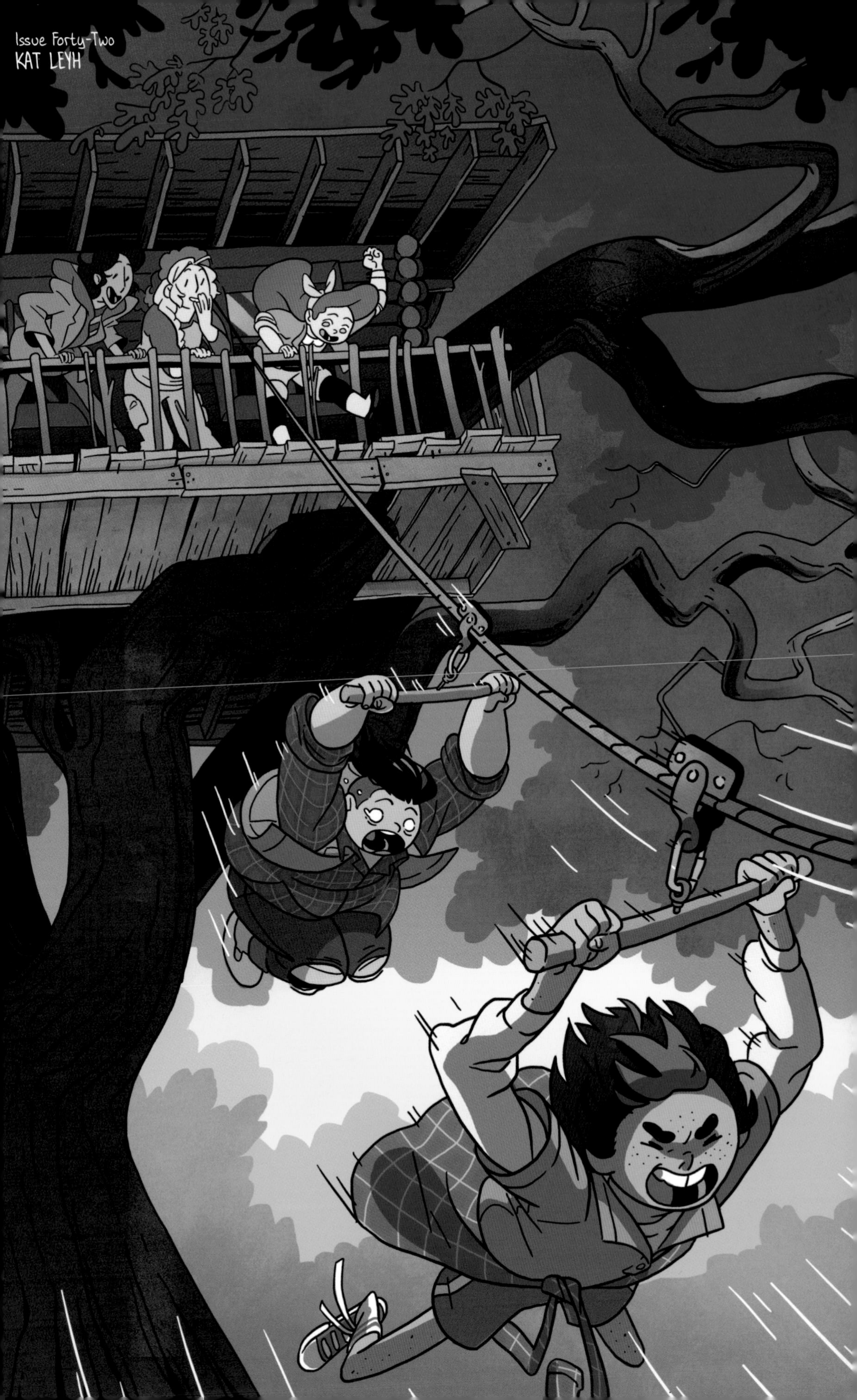

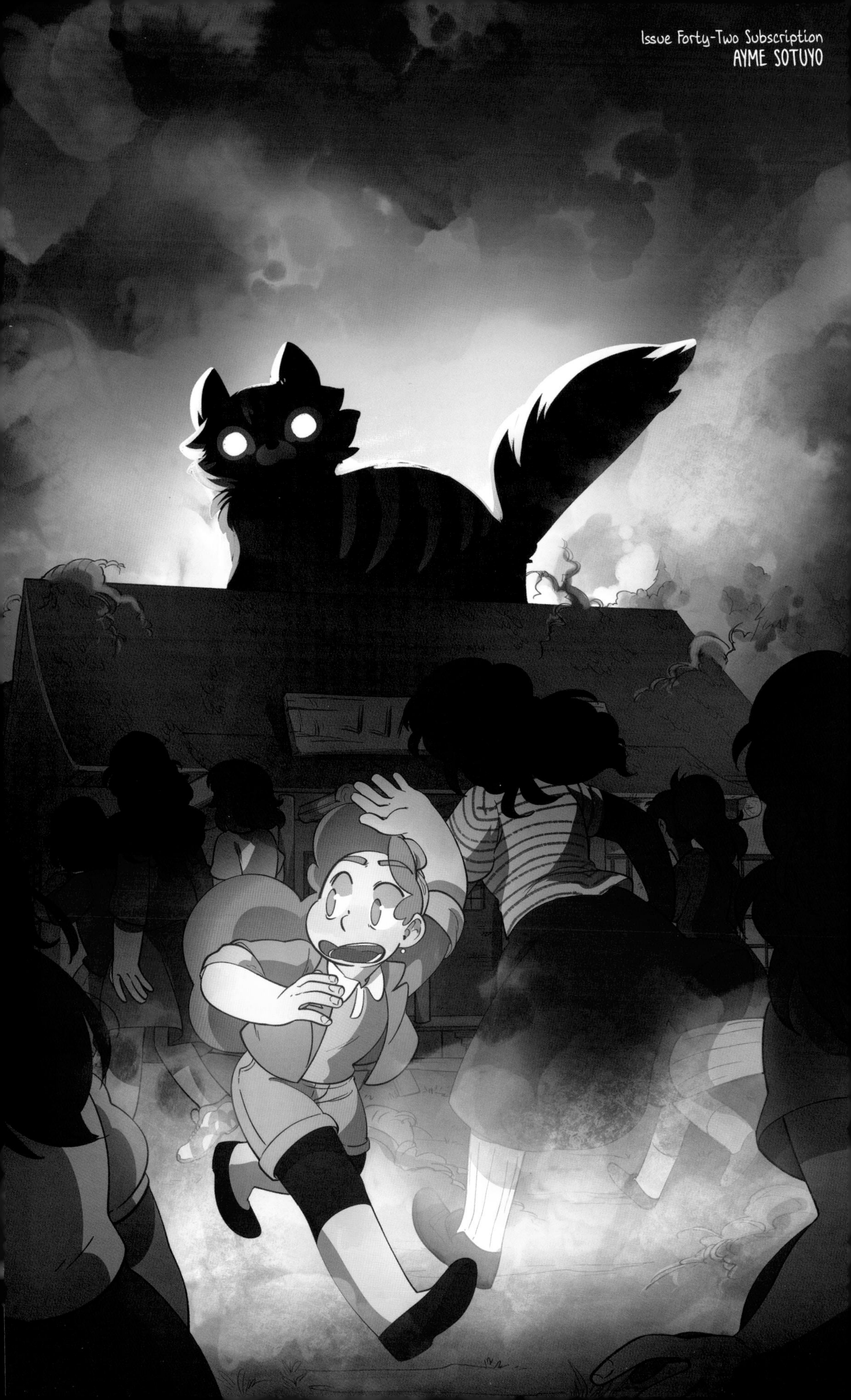
Issue Forty-Two Subscription
AYME SOTUYO

Issue Forty-Two Rose City Comic Con Variant
AYME SOTUYO

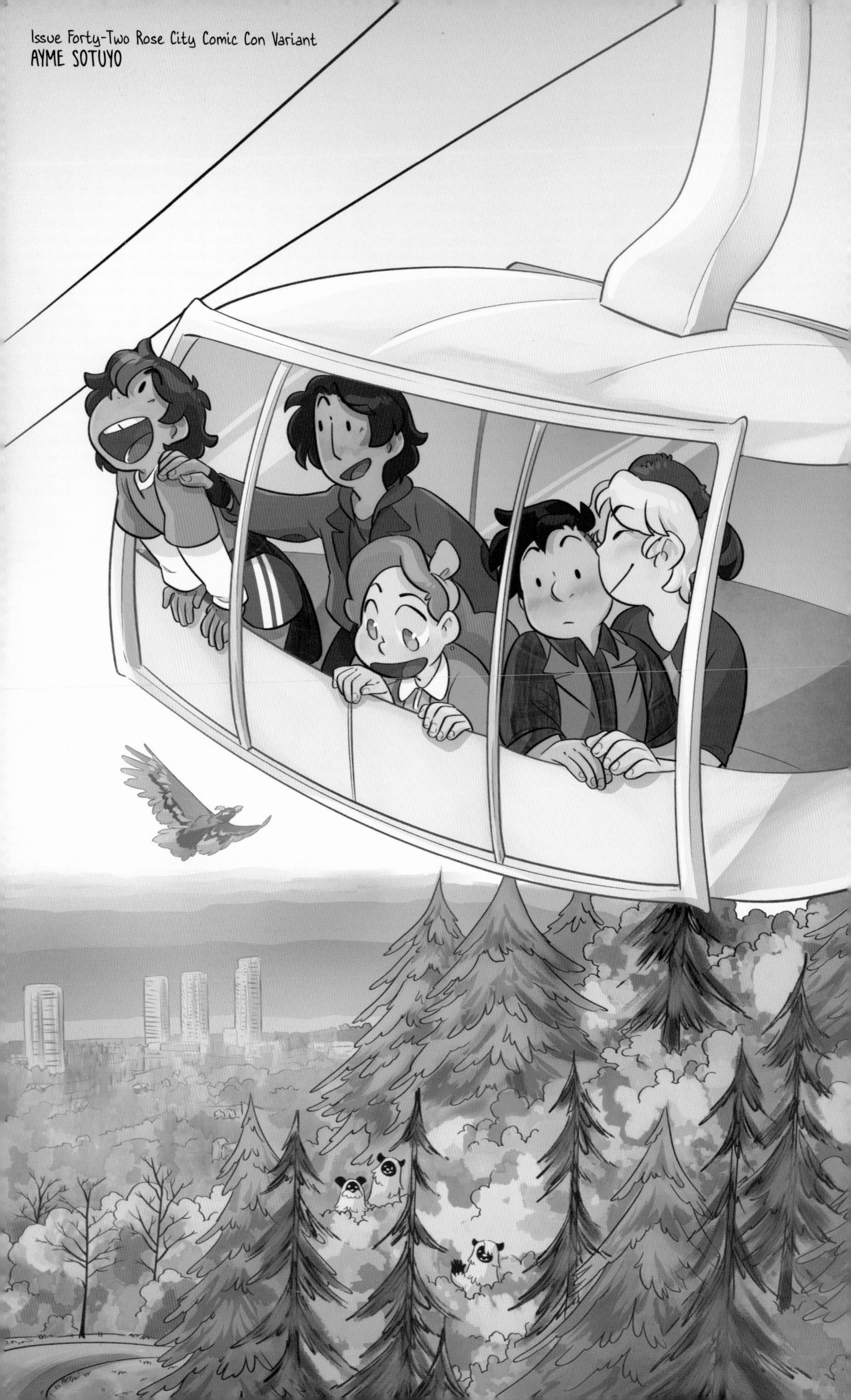

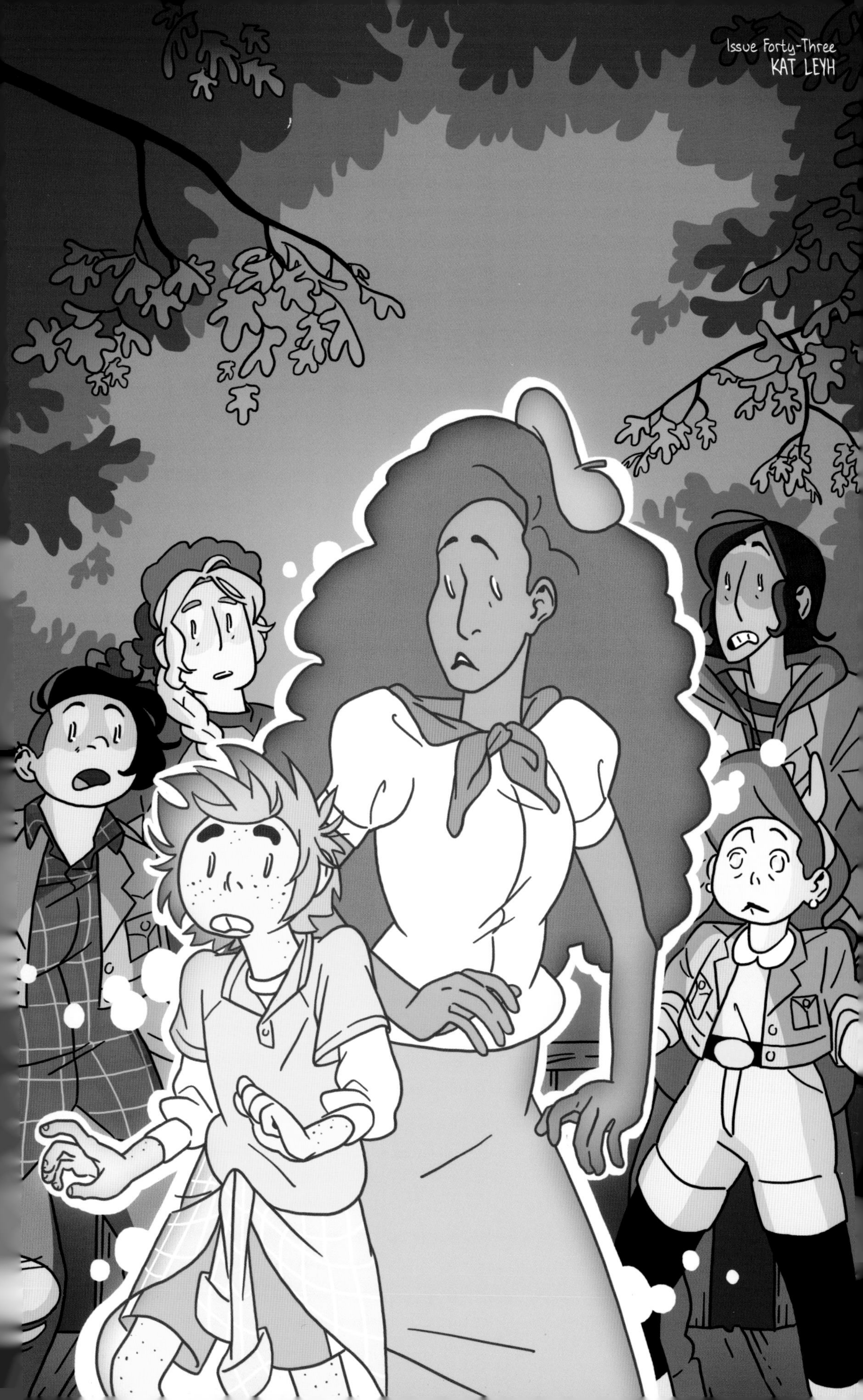
Issue Forty-Three
KAT LEYH

Issue Forty-Three Subscription
AYME SOTUYO

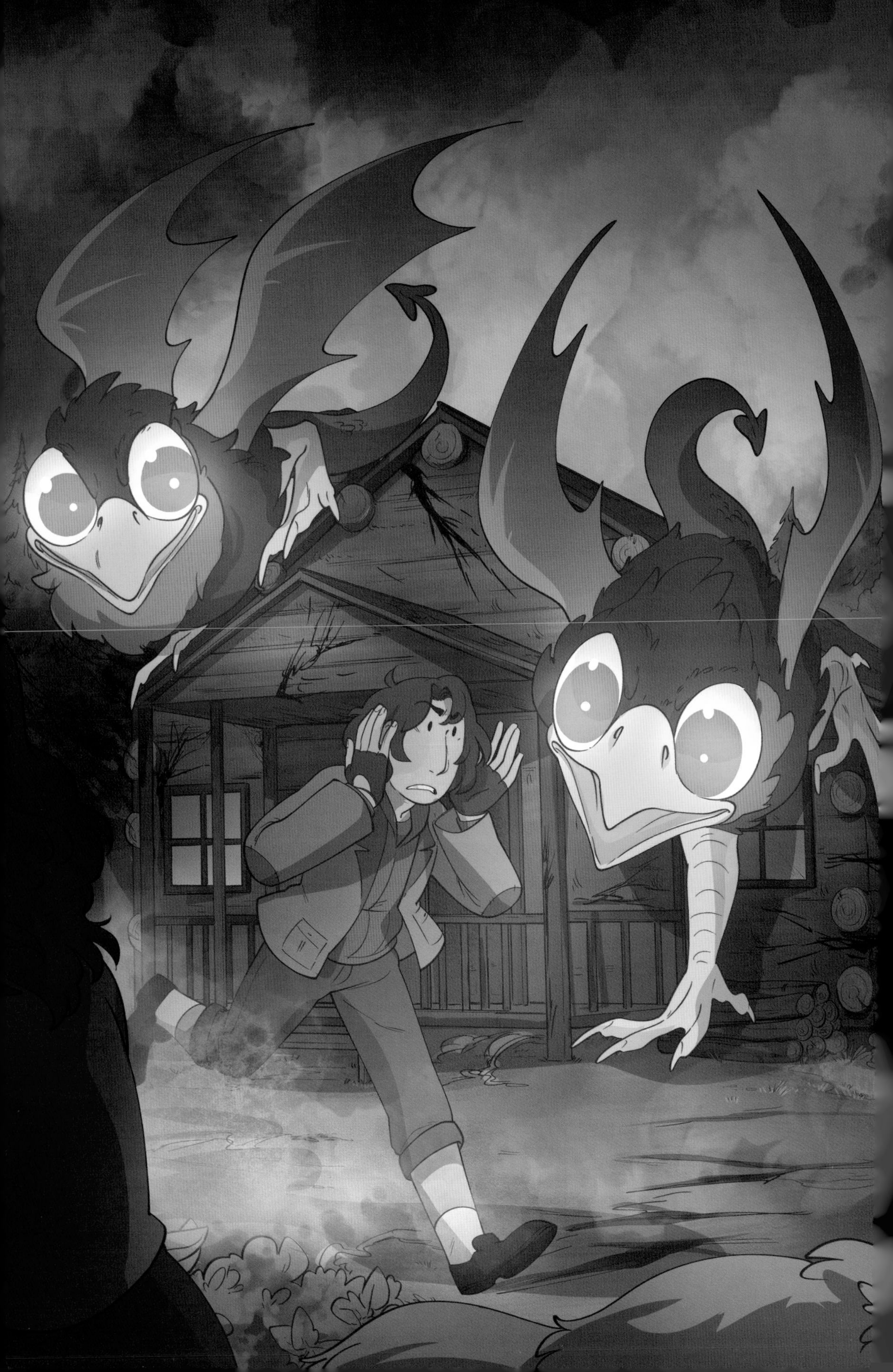

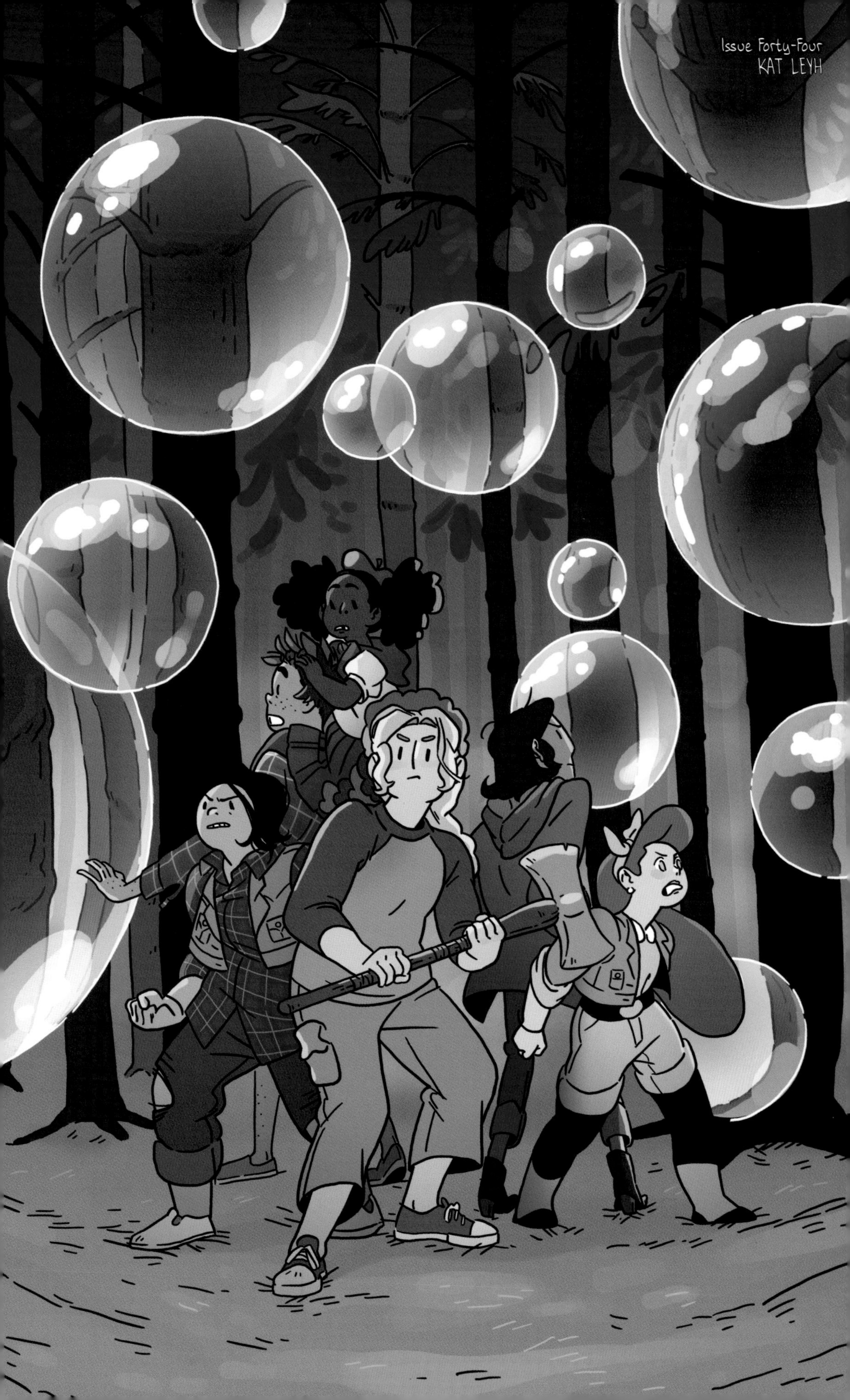
Issue Forty-Four
KAT LEYH

Issue Forty-Four Subscription
AYME SOTUYO

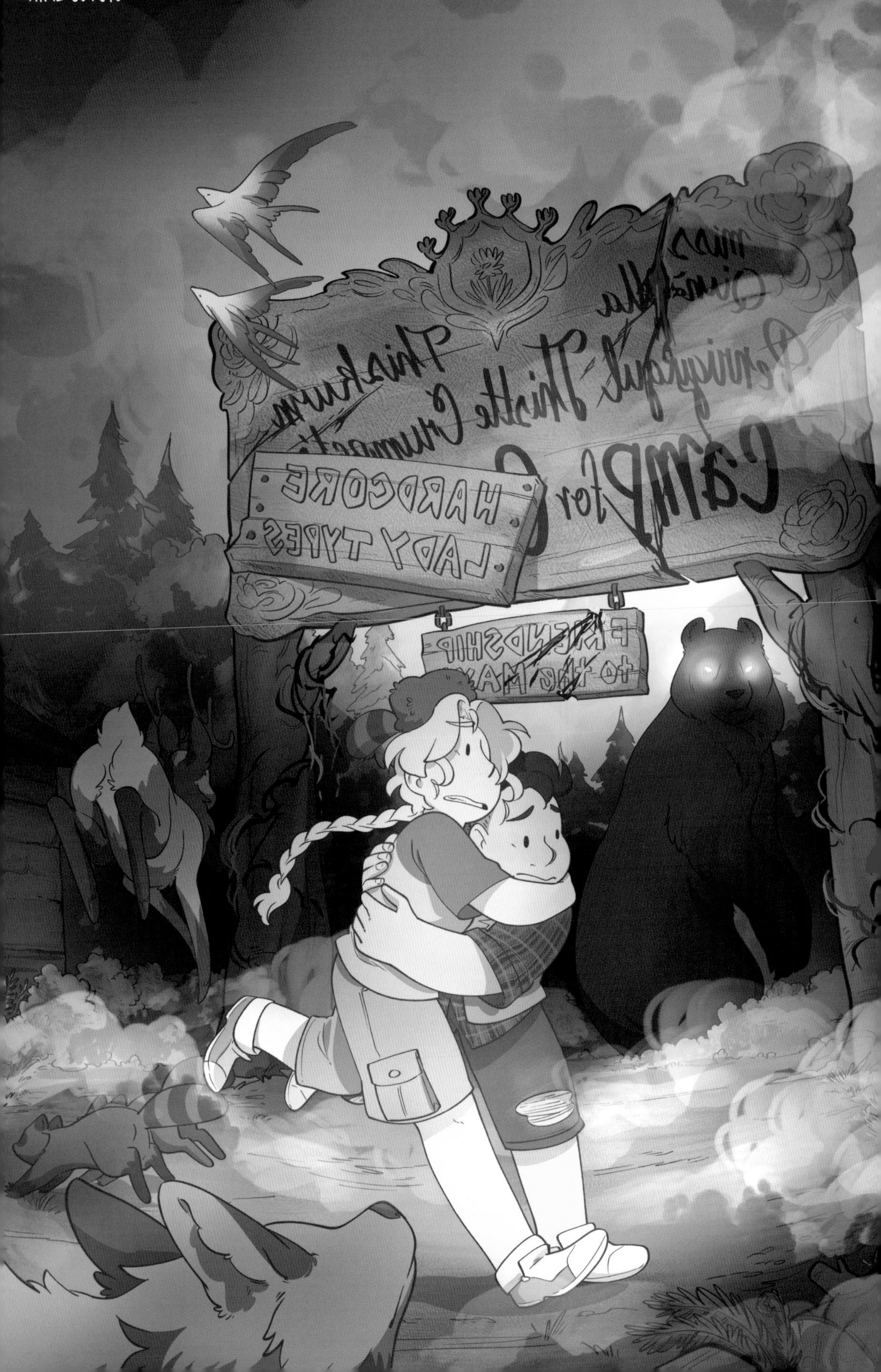
HARDCORE
LADY TYPES

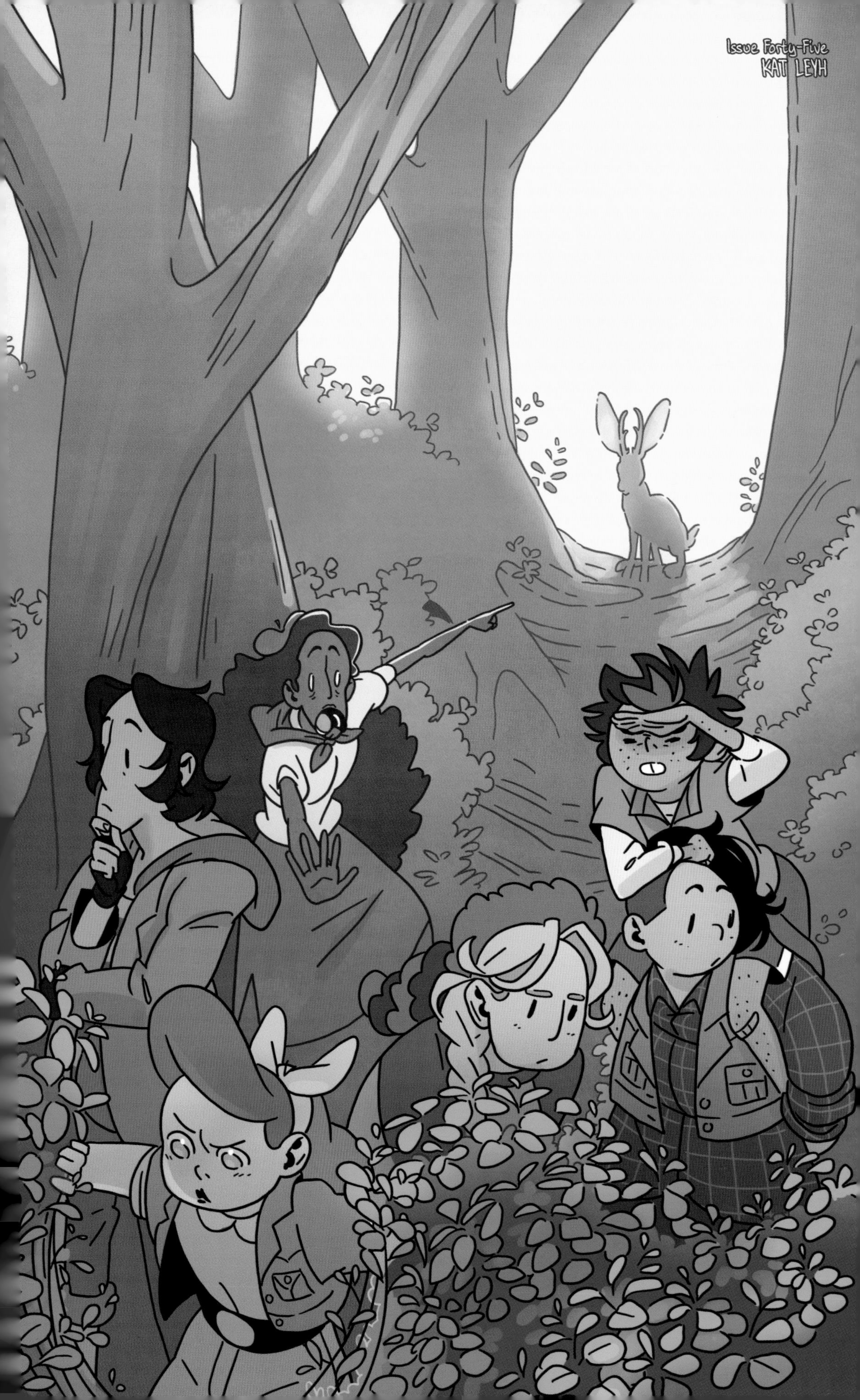
Issue Forty-Five
KAT LEYH

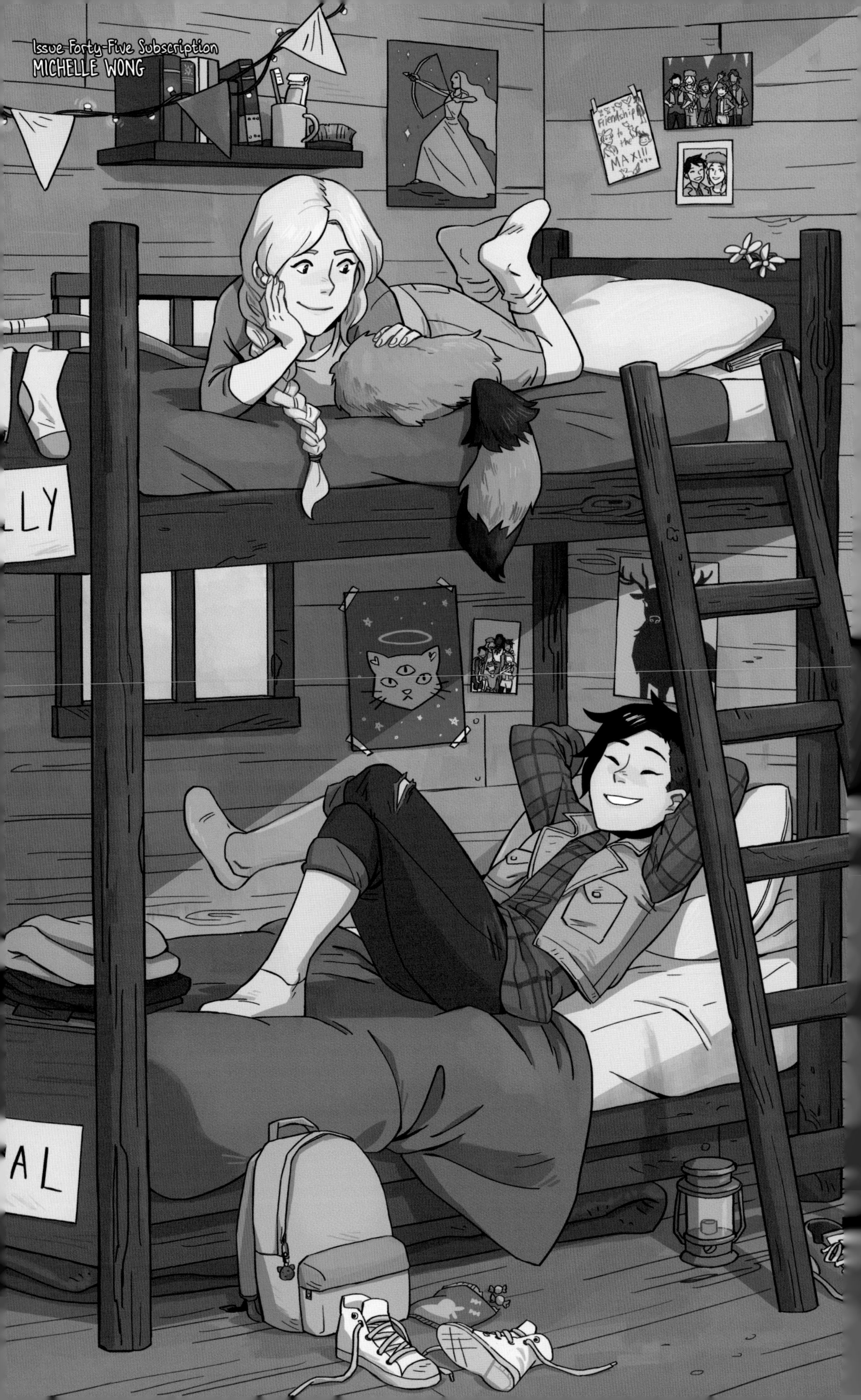
Issue Forty-Five Subscription
MICHELLE WONG
Friendship to the MAX!!!
LLY
AL

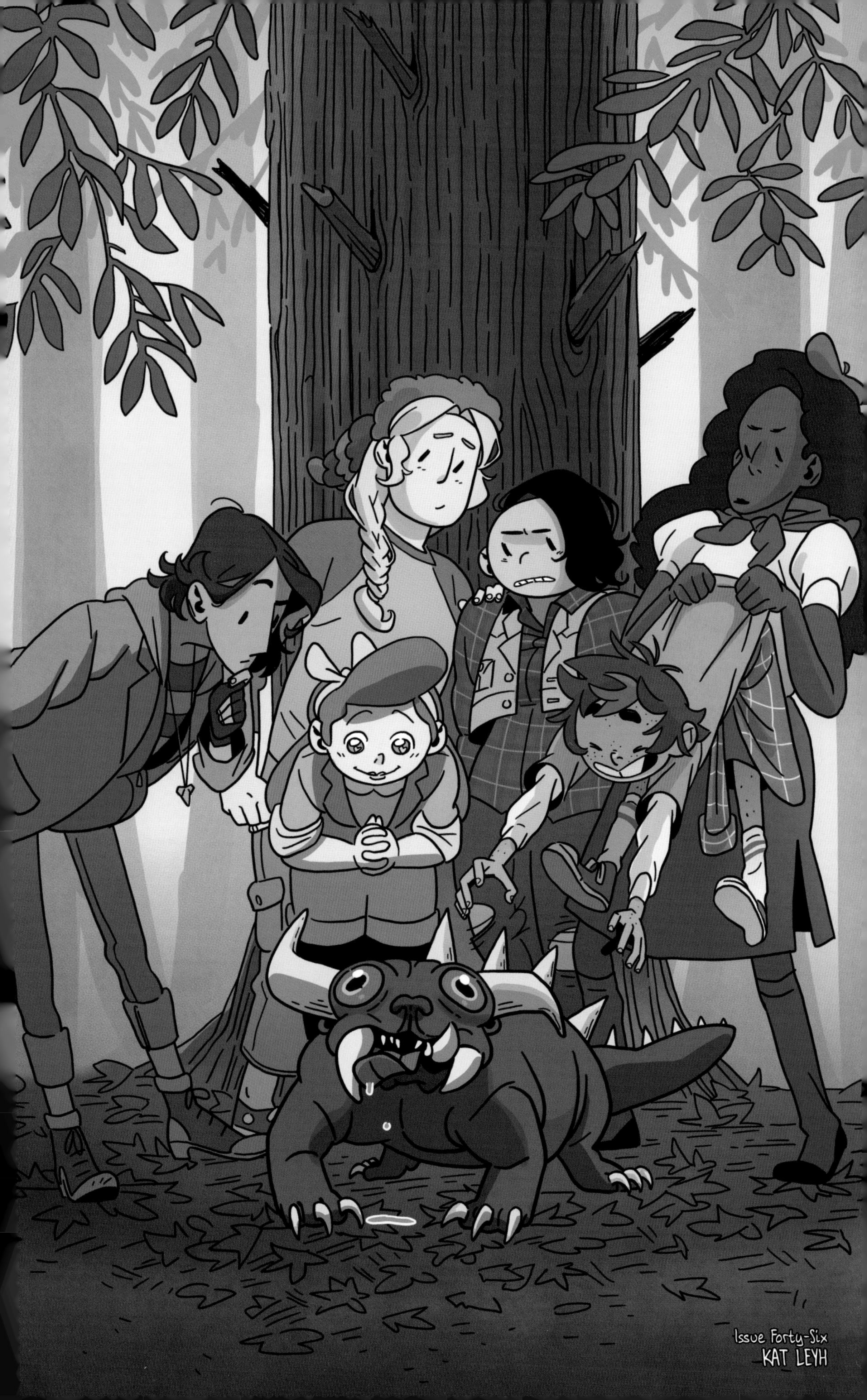
Issue Forty-Six
KAT LEYH

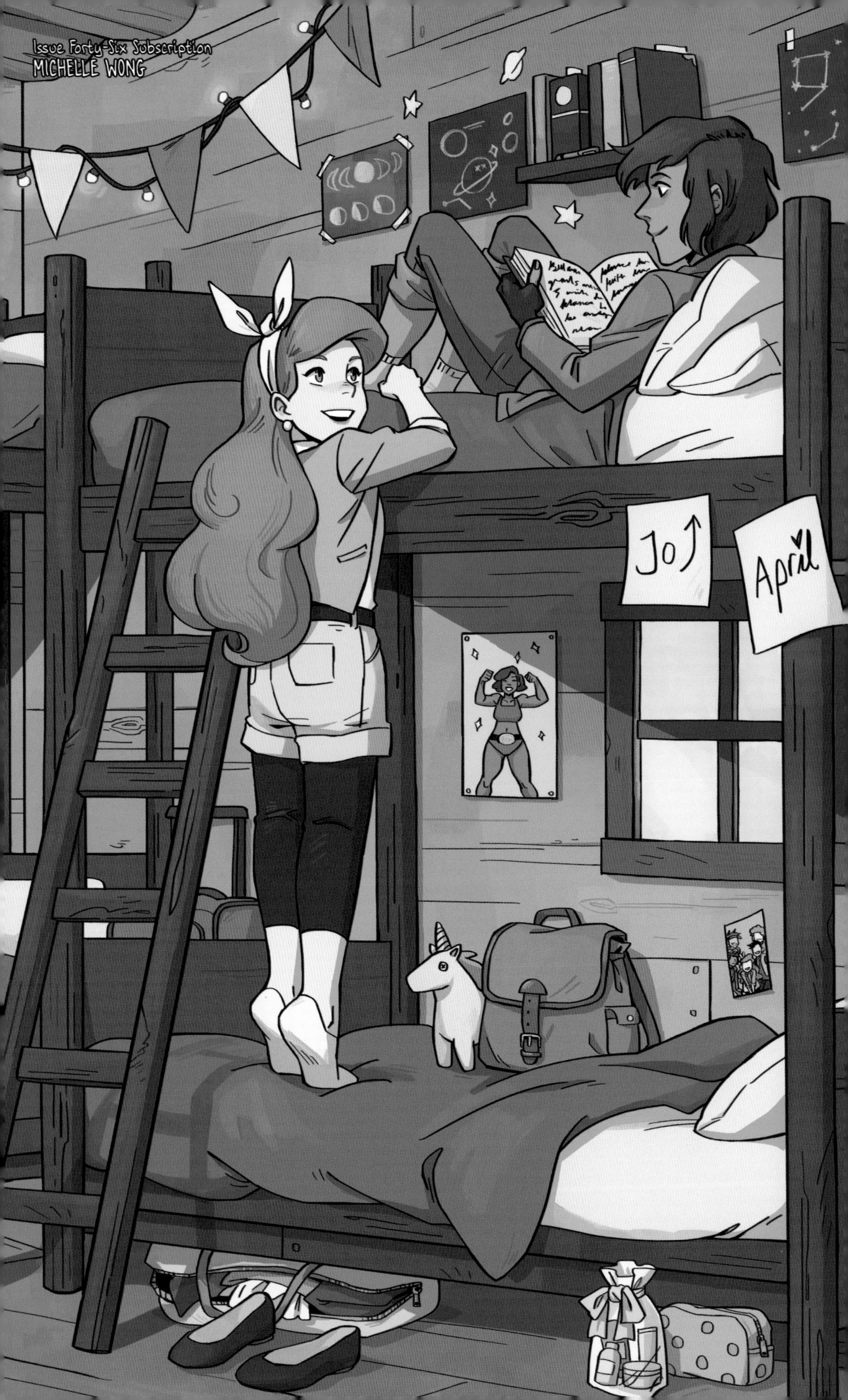
Issue Forty-Six Subscription
MICHELLE WONG
Jo
April

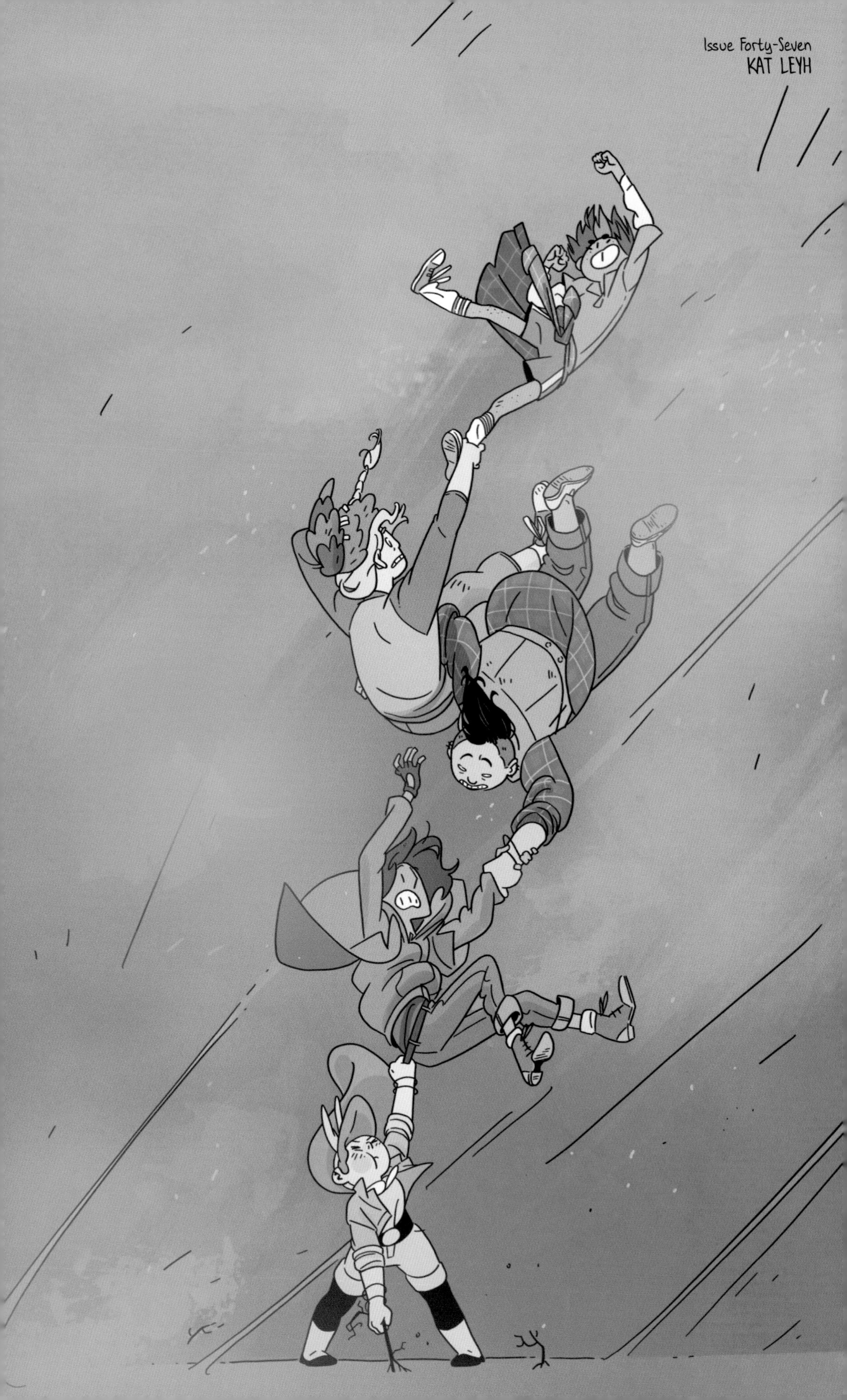
Issue Forty-Seven
KAT LEYH

Issue Forty-Seven Subscription
MICHELLE WONG

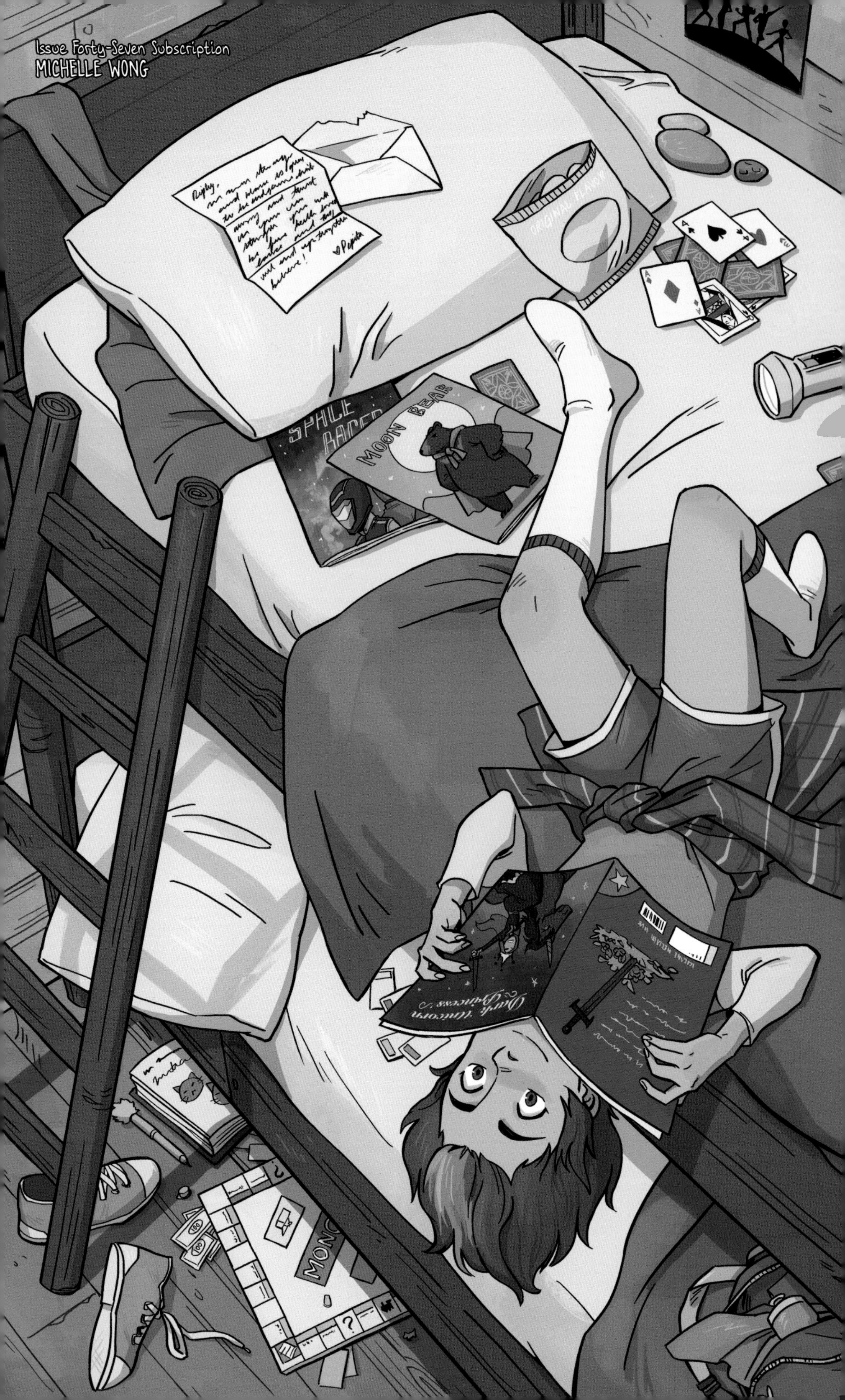
SPACE RACER
MOON BEAR
ORIGINAL FLAVOR
Dark Unicorn Princess

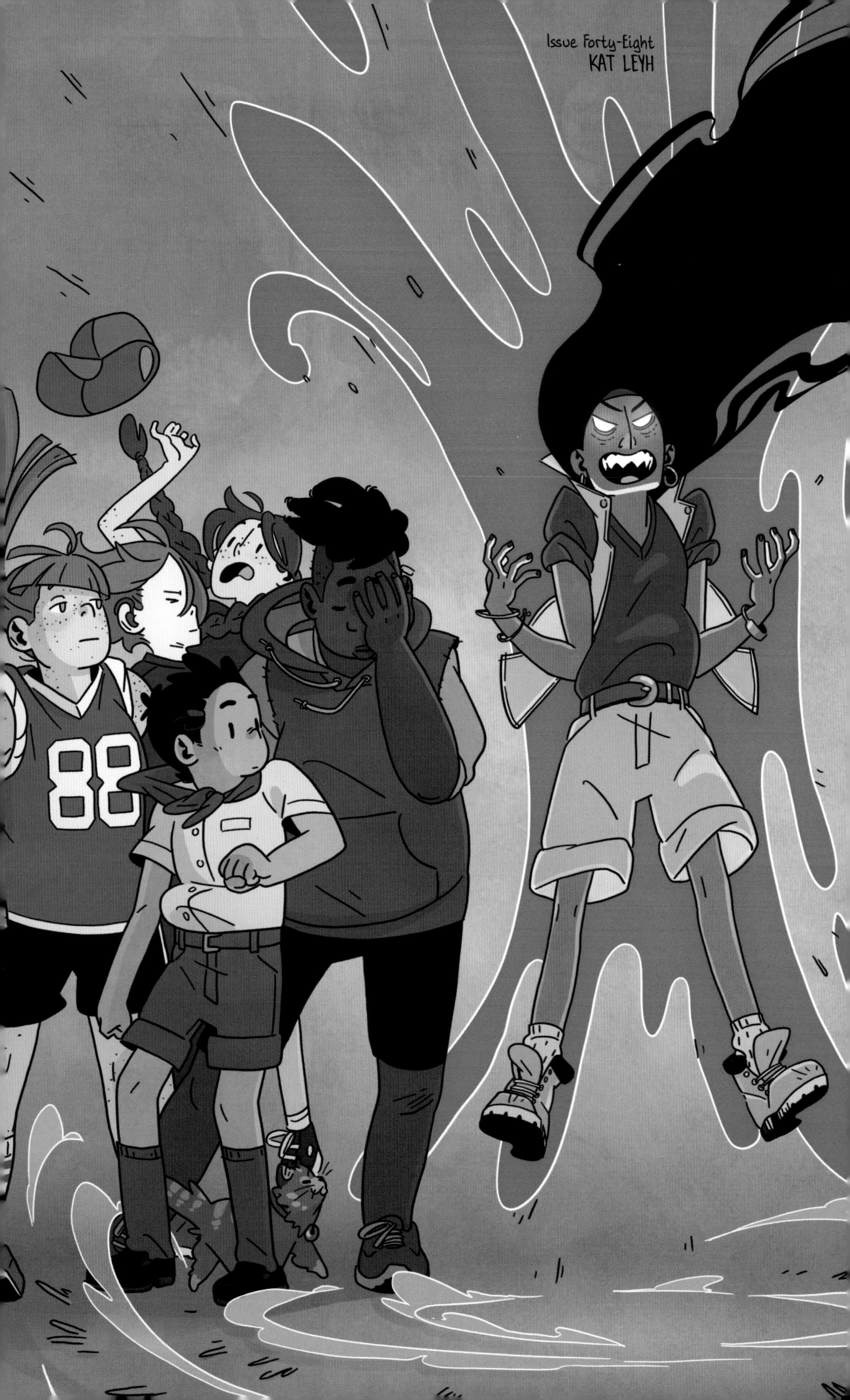
Issue Forty-Eight
KAT LEYH
88

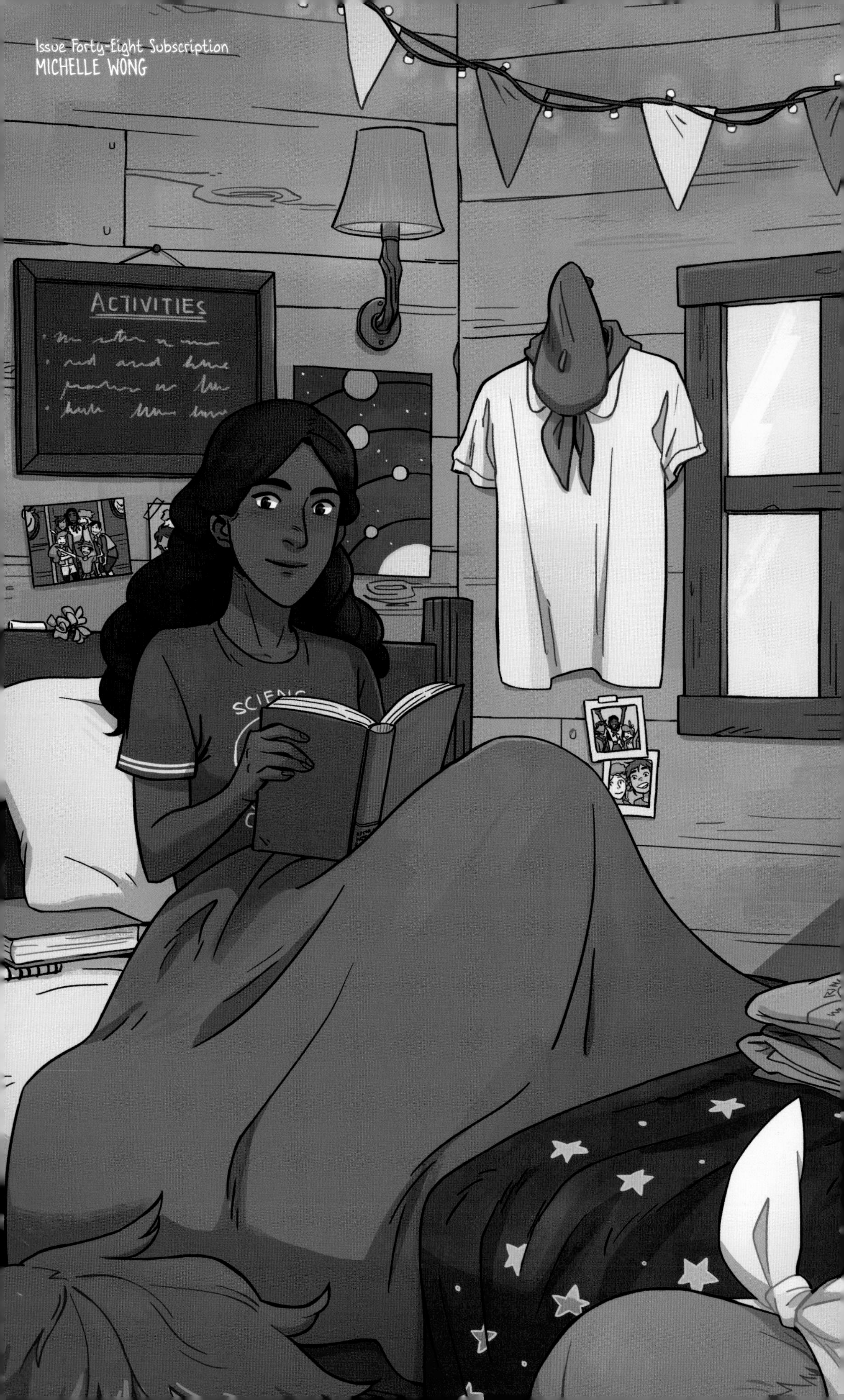
ACTIVITIES

Issue Forty-Eight Subscription
MICHELLE WONG

WHERE DID IT COME FROM? WHERE DID IT GO?!

BUNK BUDS!

WHAT A VIEW

HOW TO WEAR THE UNIFORM

To look well in a uniform demands first of all that the uniform be kept in good condition—clean and pressed. See that the skirt is the right length for your own height and build, that the belt is adjusted to your waist, that your shoes and stockings are in keeping with the uniform, that you watch your posture and carry yourself with dignity and grace. If the beret is removed indoors, be sure that your hair is neat and kept in place with an inconspicuous clip or ribbon. When you wear a Lumberjane uniform you are identified as a member of this organization and you should be doubly careful to conduct yourself in a way that will show everyone that courtesy and thoughtfulness are part of being a Lumberjane. People are likely to judge a whole nation by the selfishness of a few individuals, to criticize a whole family because of the misconduct of one member, and to feel unkindly toward an organization because of the

Types, but many of these will wish to have one. They can either buy the uniforms, or make it themselves from materials available at the trading post.

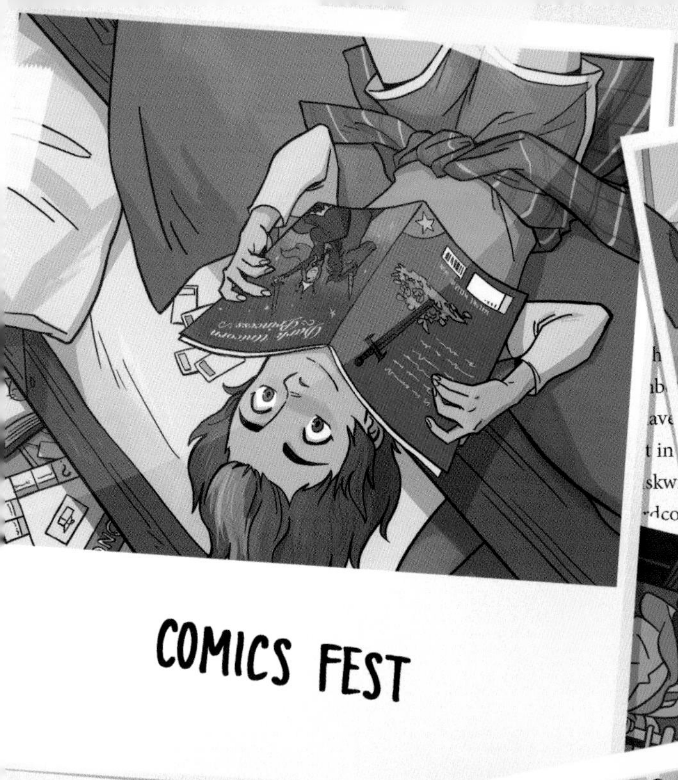

COMICS FEST

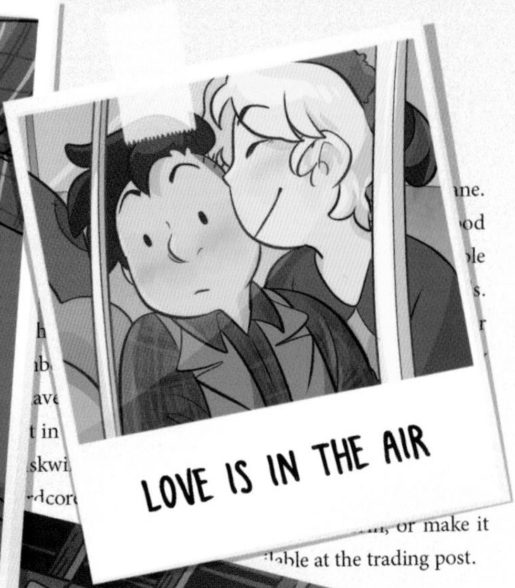

LOVE IS IN THE AIR

ine.
ood
ple
s.
r
h
ab
ave
t in
skwi
rdcor
..., or make it
...able at the trading post.

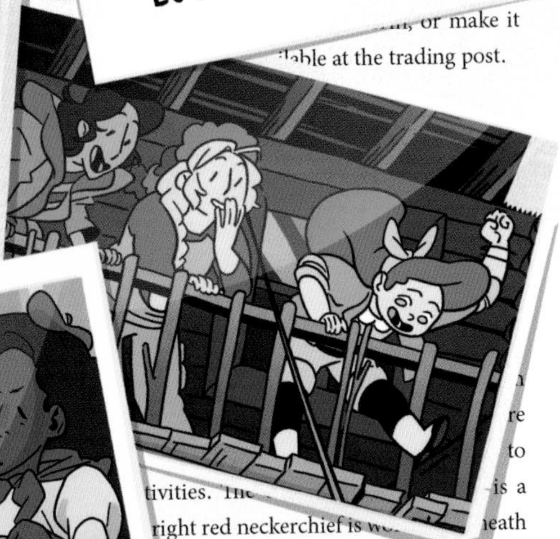

The Lumberjane uniform sh...
meeting...

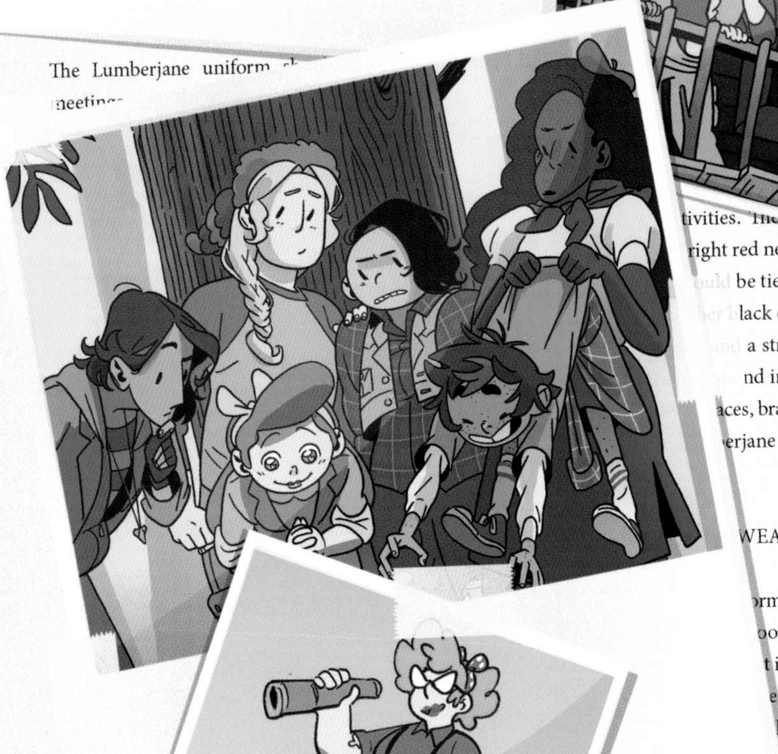

n
re
to
tivities. The ... is a
right red neckerchief is wo... neath
...ould be tied in a simple friendship knot.
...her black or brown and should have flat
...and a straight inner line. Stockings or
...nd in color with the shoes or with
...aces, bracelets, or other jewelry do not
...erjane uniform.

...WEAR THE UNIFORM

...orm demands first of all that the ...ood condition—clean and well ... it is the right length for your own ... belt is adjusted to your waist, ... kings are in keeping with the ... our posture and carry yourself ... dignity and grace. If the beret is removed indoors, ... e sure that your hair is neat and kept in place with an inconspicuous clip or ribbon. When you wear a Lumberjane uniform you are identified as a member of this organization and you should be doubly careful to conduct yourself in a way that will show everyone that courtesy and thoughtfulness are part of being a Lumberjane. People are likely to judge a whole nation by the selfishness of a few individuals, to criticize a whole family because of the misconduct of one member, and to feel unkindly toward an organization because of the

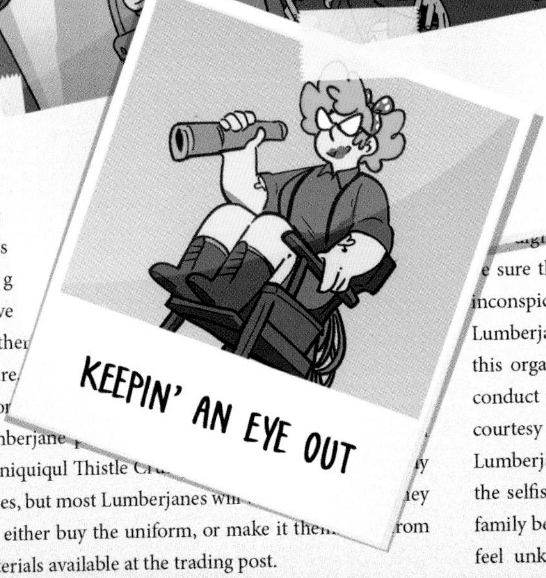

KEEPIN' AN EYE OUT

The
helps
in a g
active
another
future.
in or
Lumberjane p...
Penniquiqul Thistle Cru... ...ny
Types, but most Lumberjanes wi... ...ney
can either buy the uniform, or make it them... ...rom
materials available at the trading post.

SKETCHBOOK

ILLUSTRATIONS BY **AYME SOTUYO**

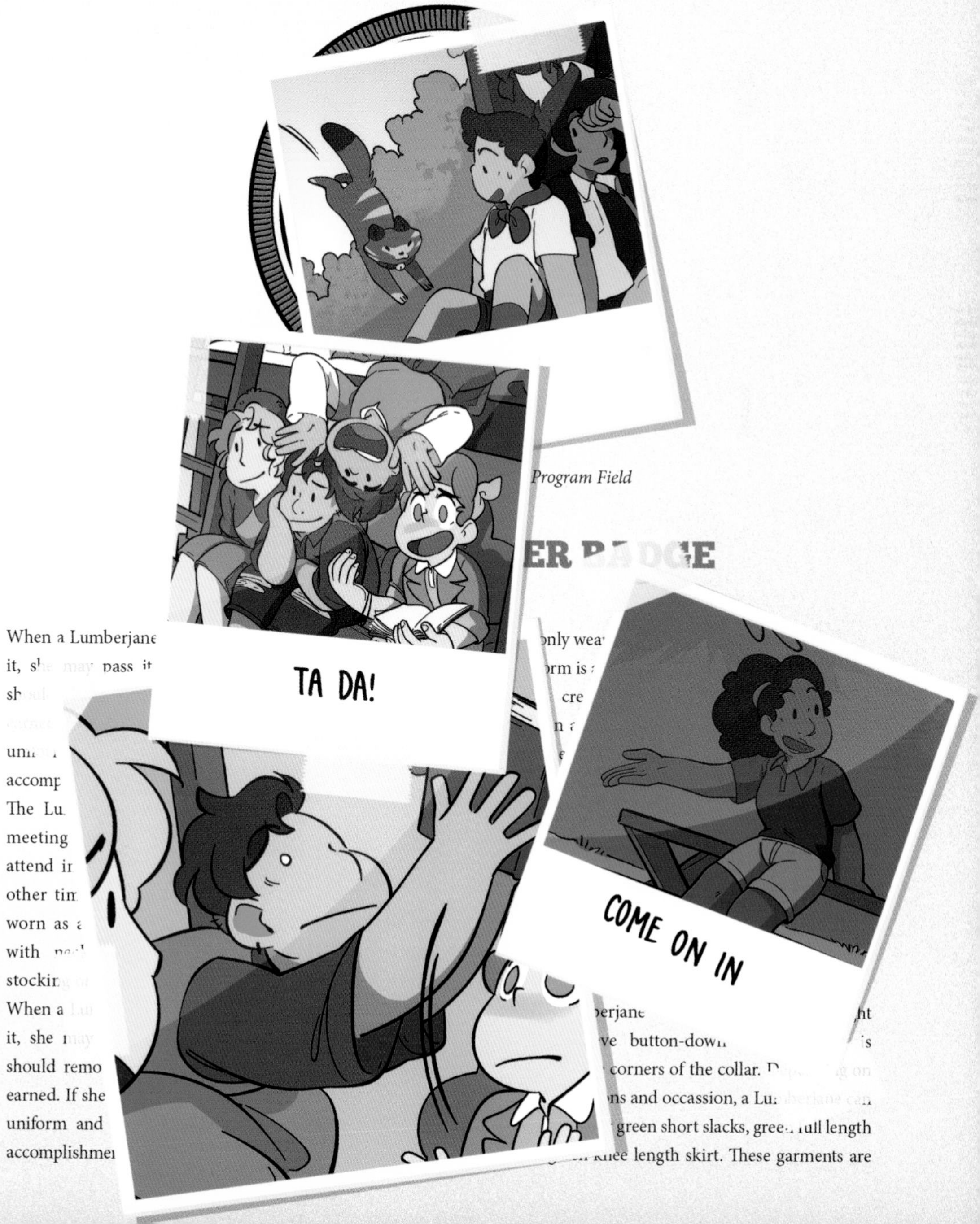
TA DA!
COME ON IN

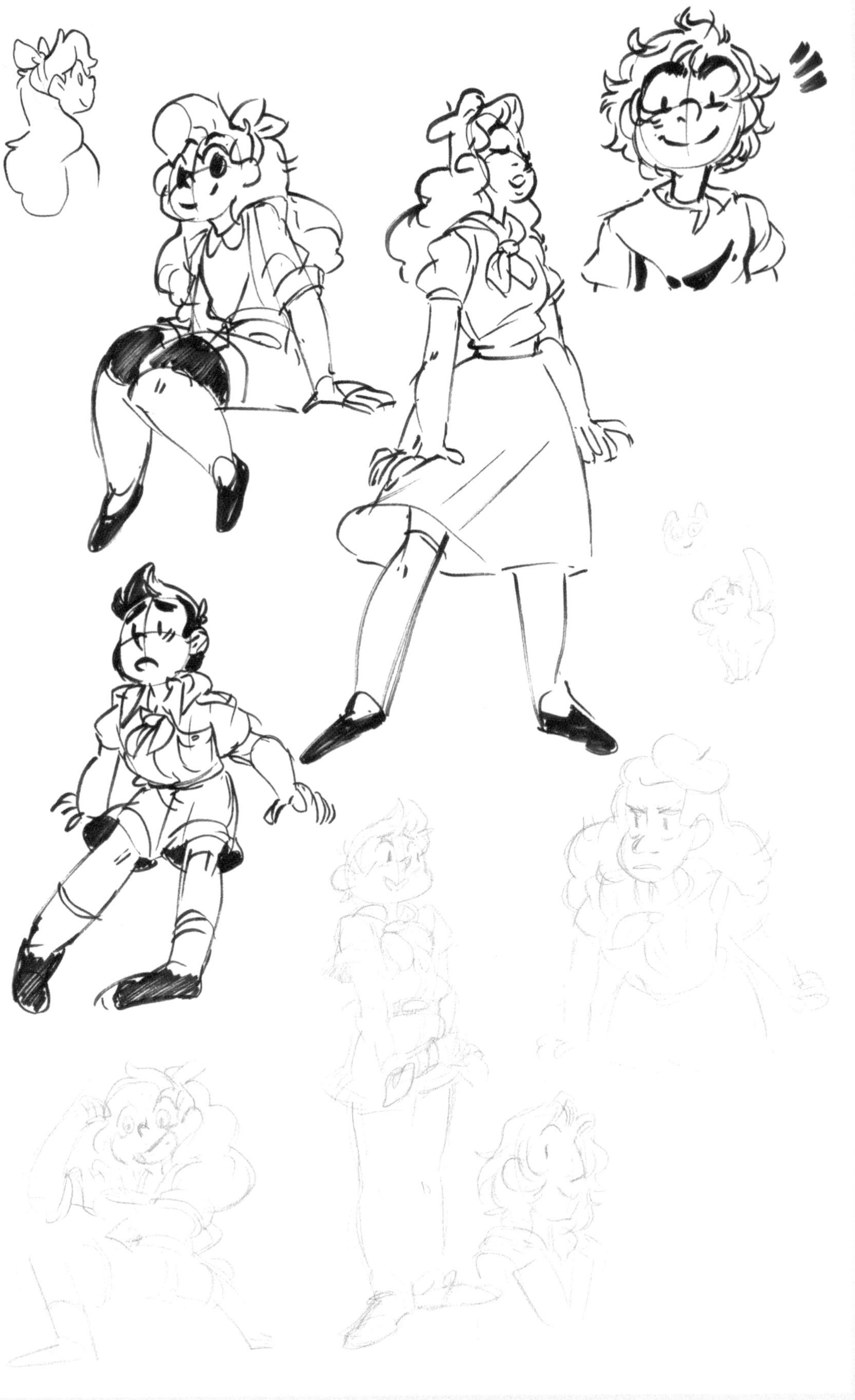

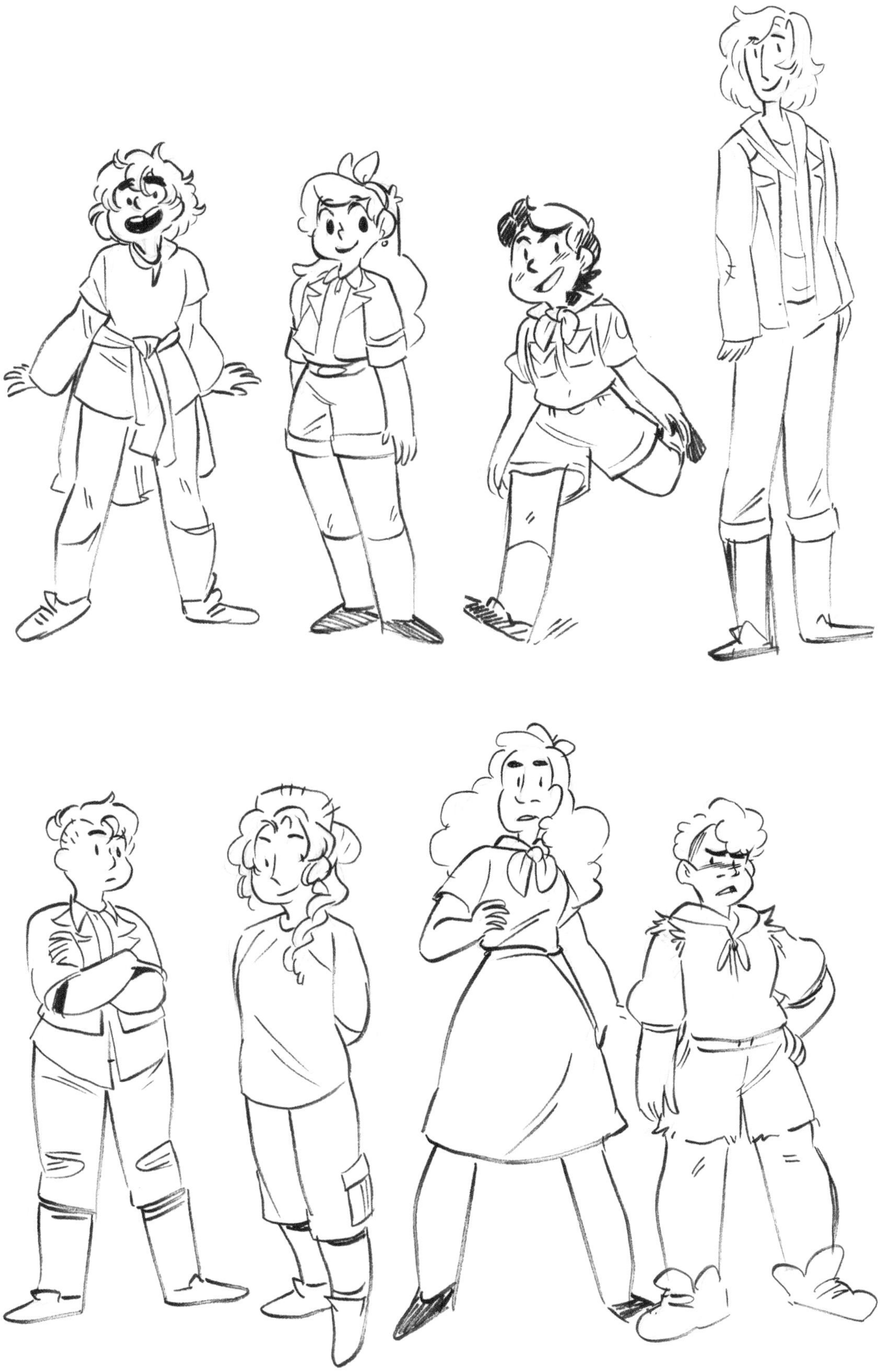

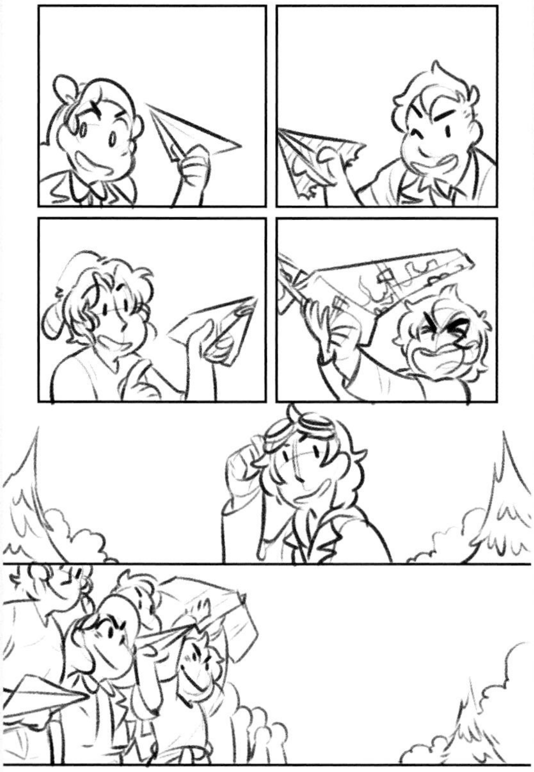

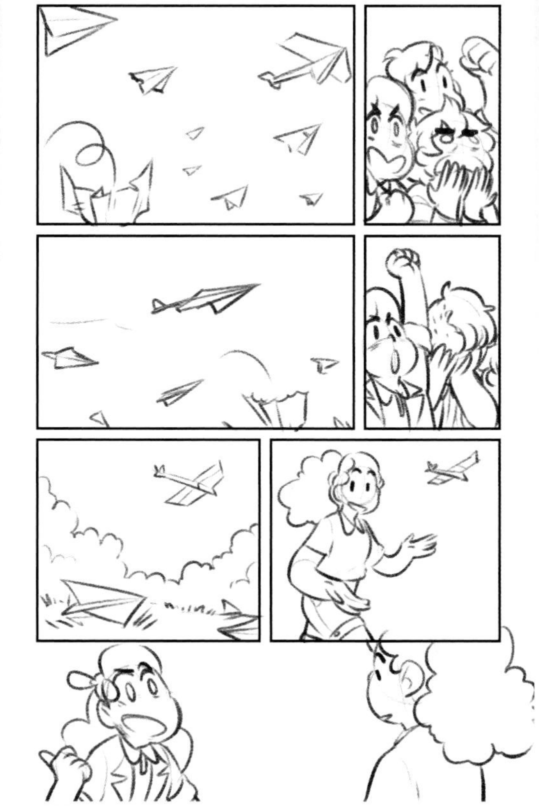

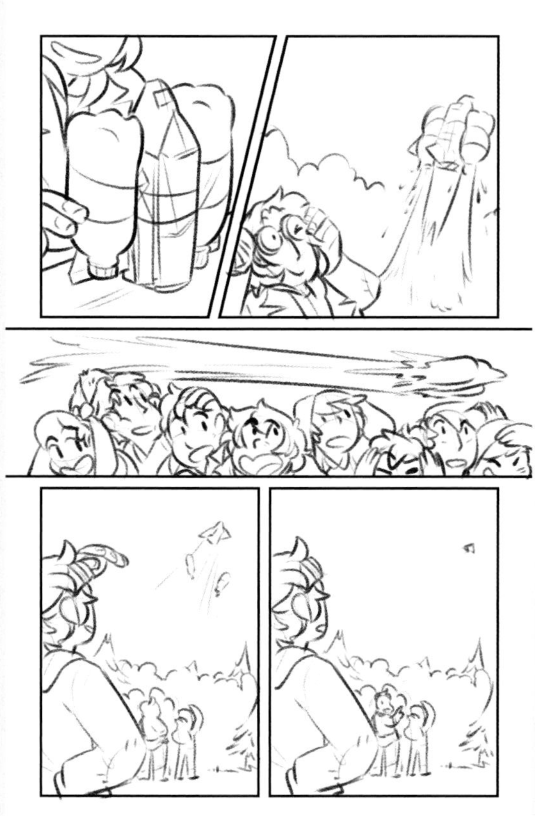

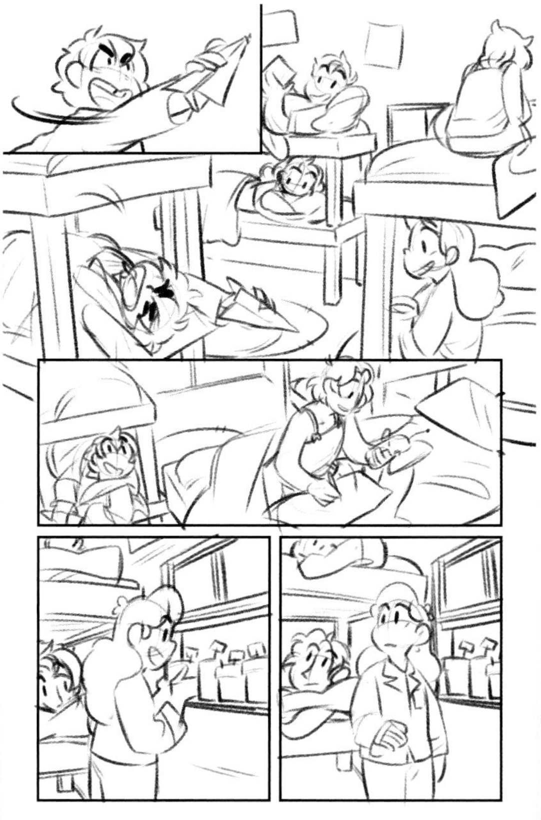

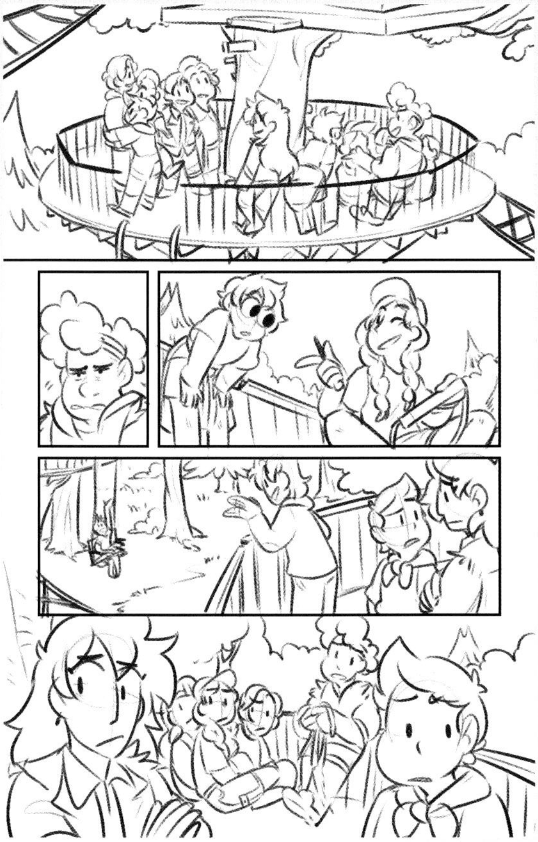

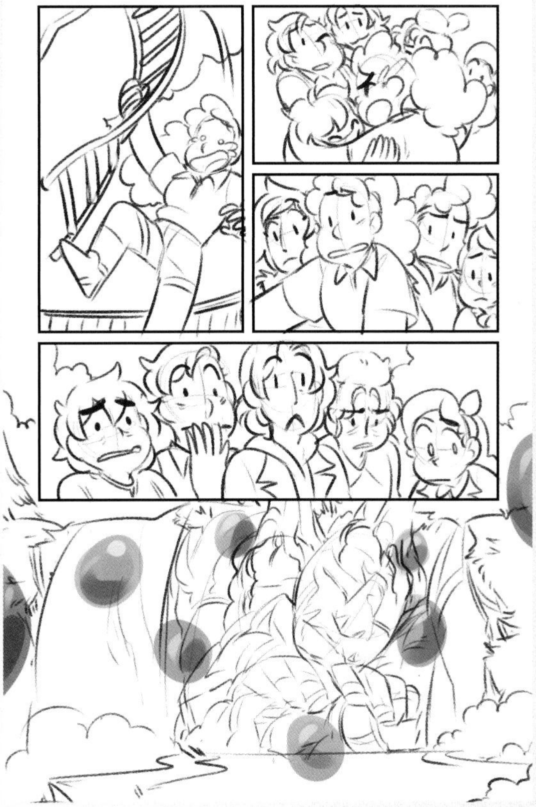

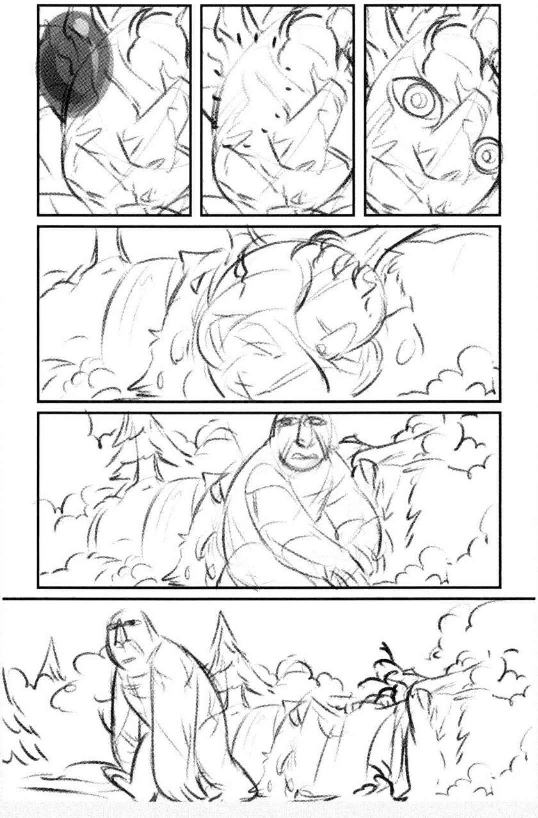

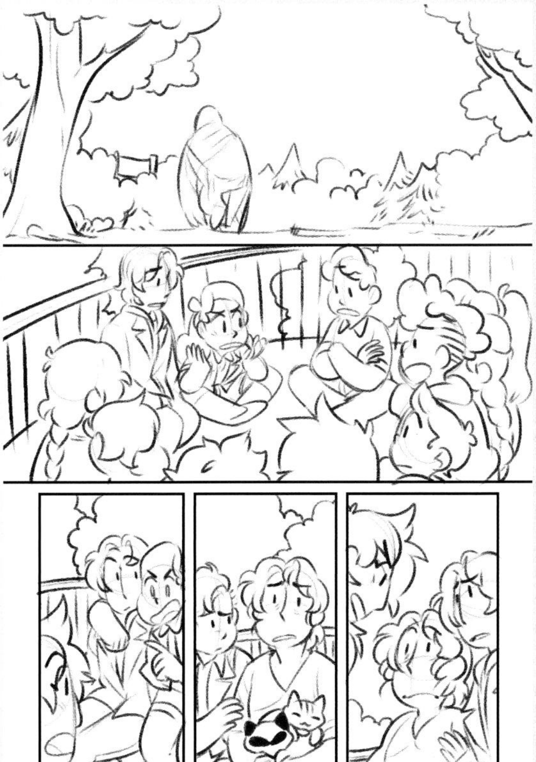

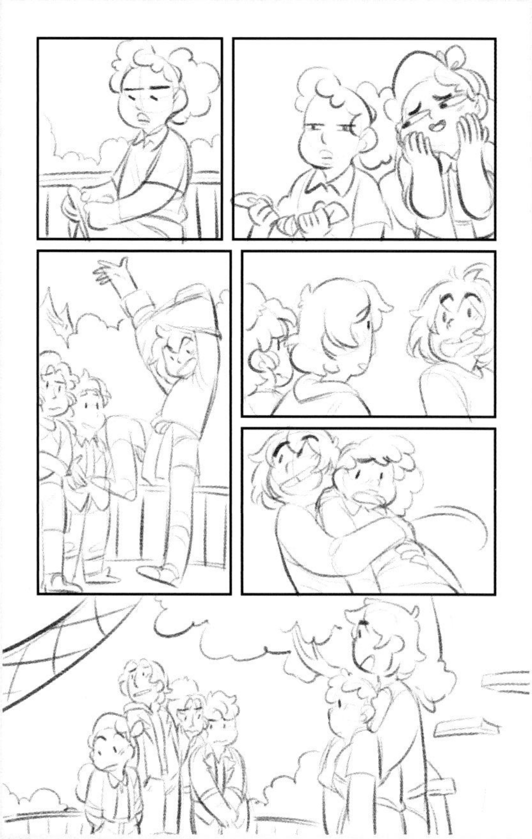

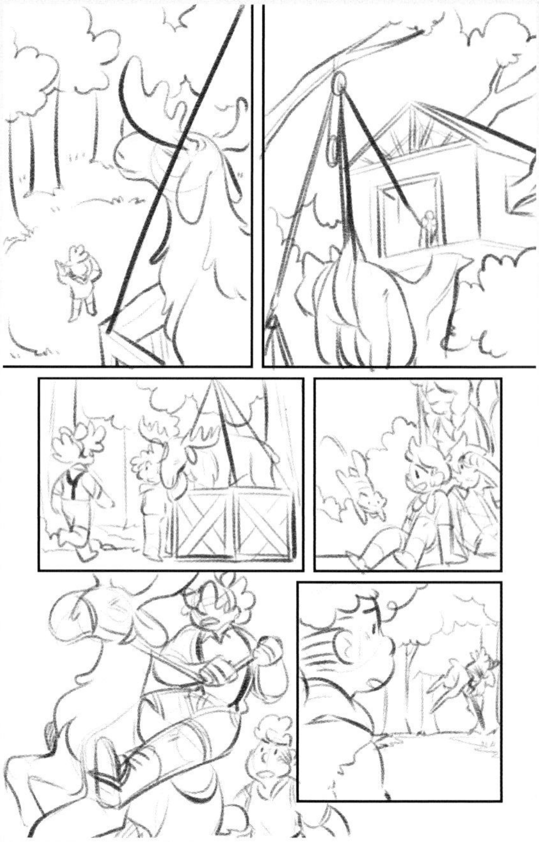

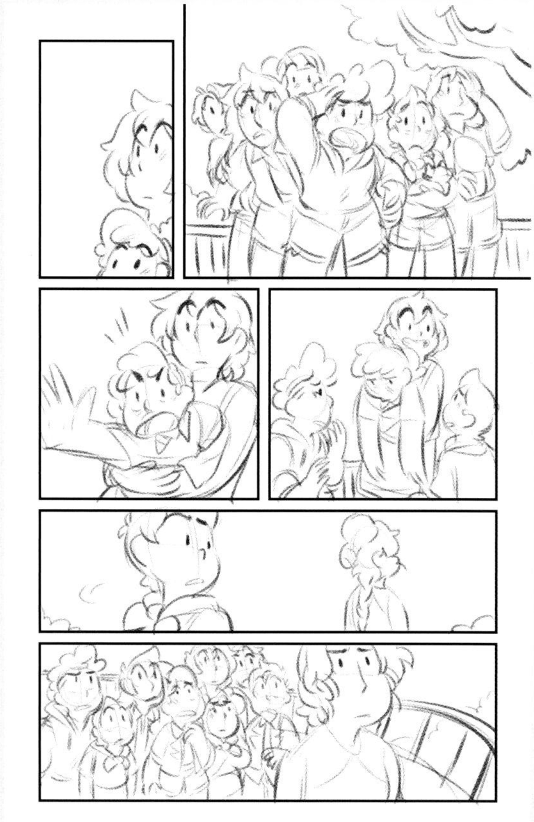

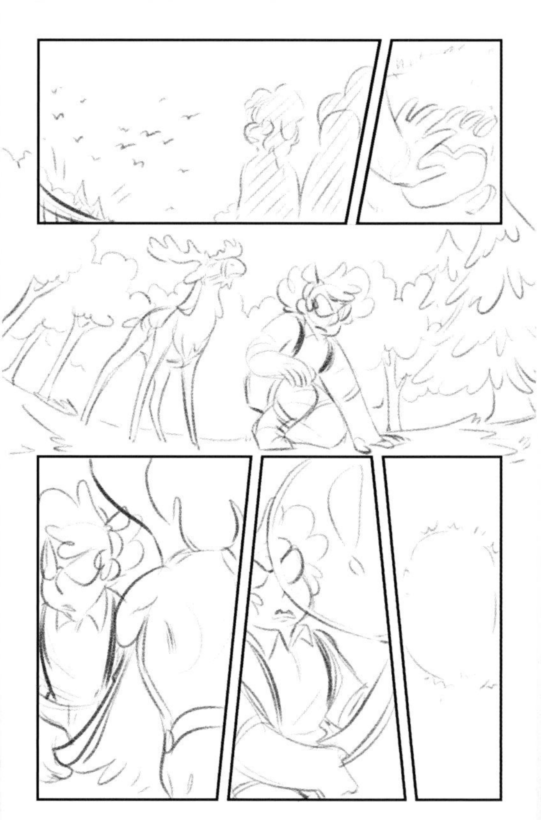

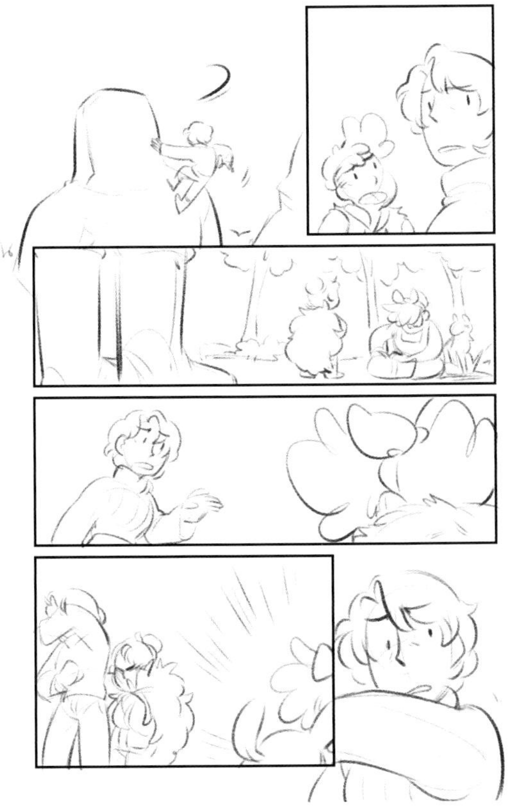

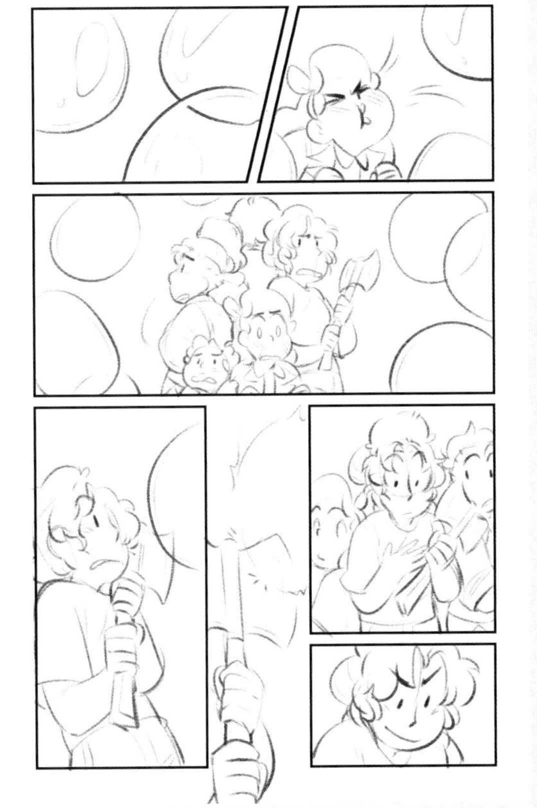

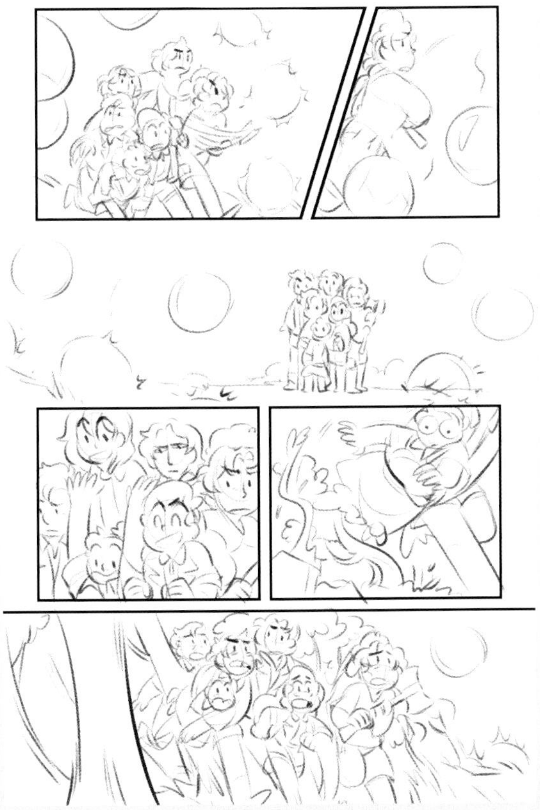

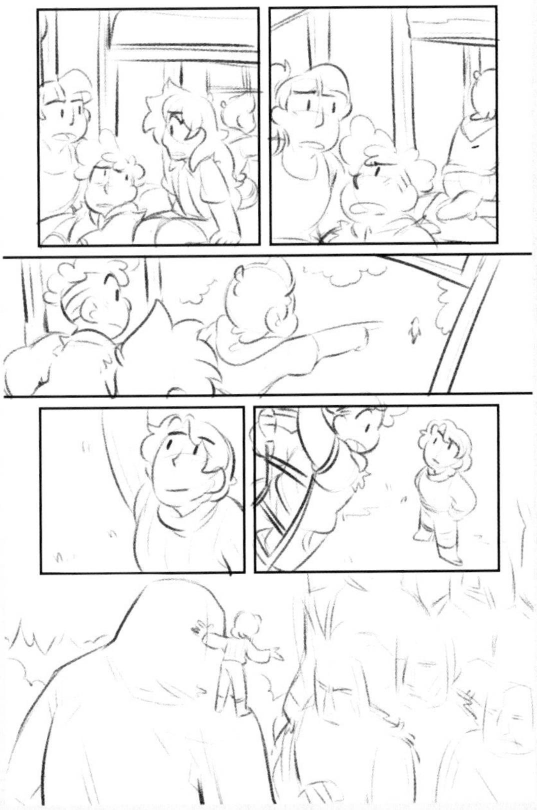

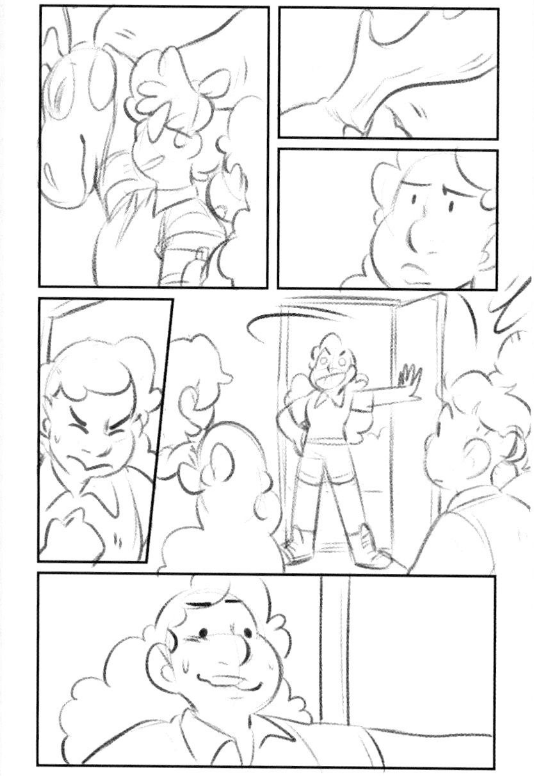

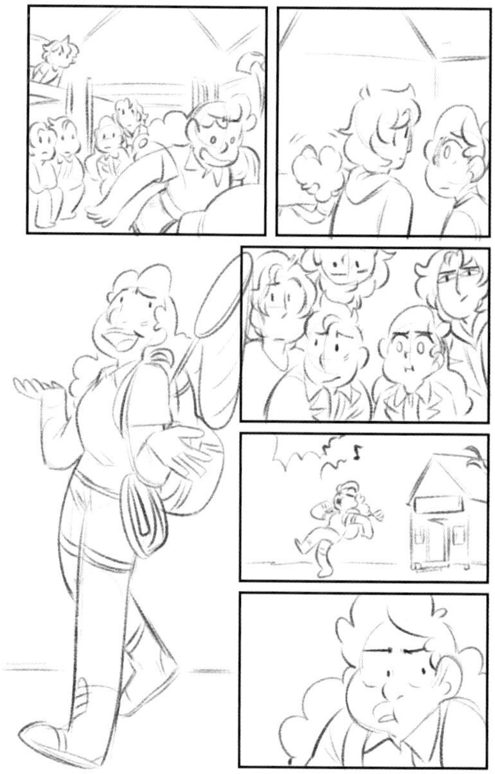

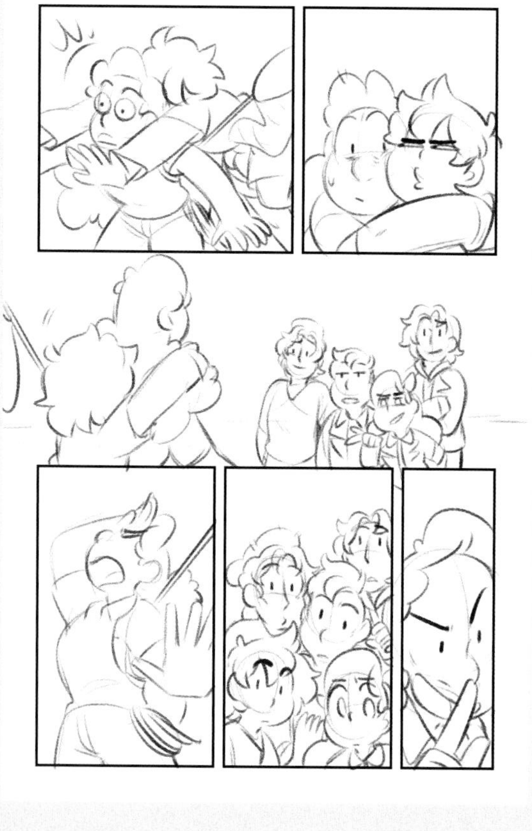

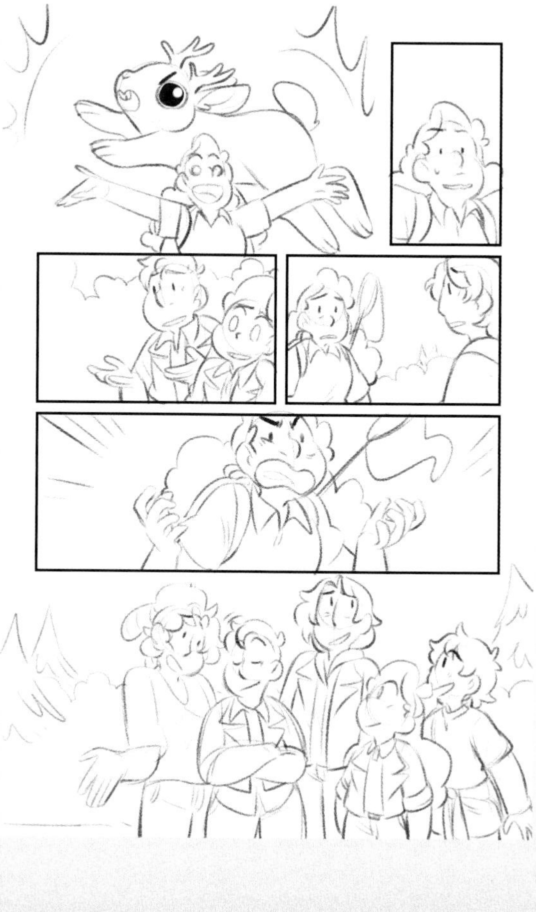

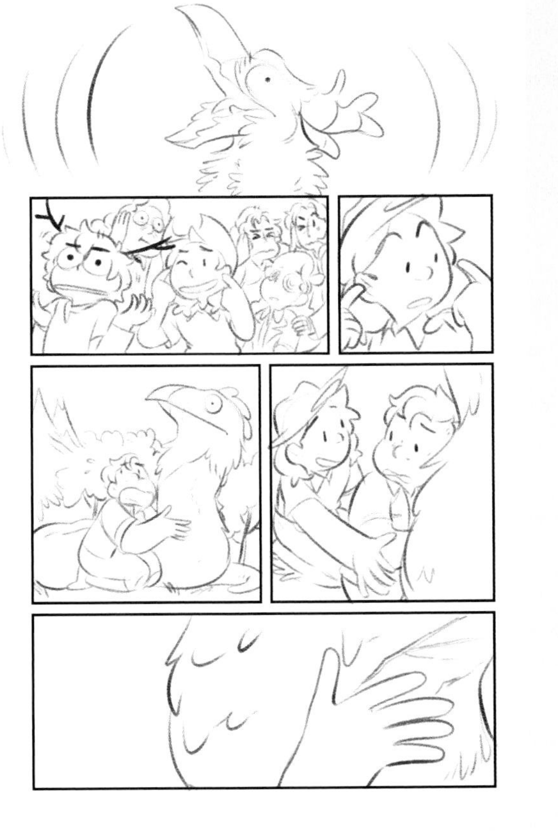

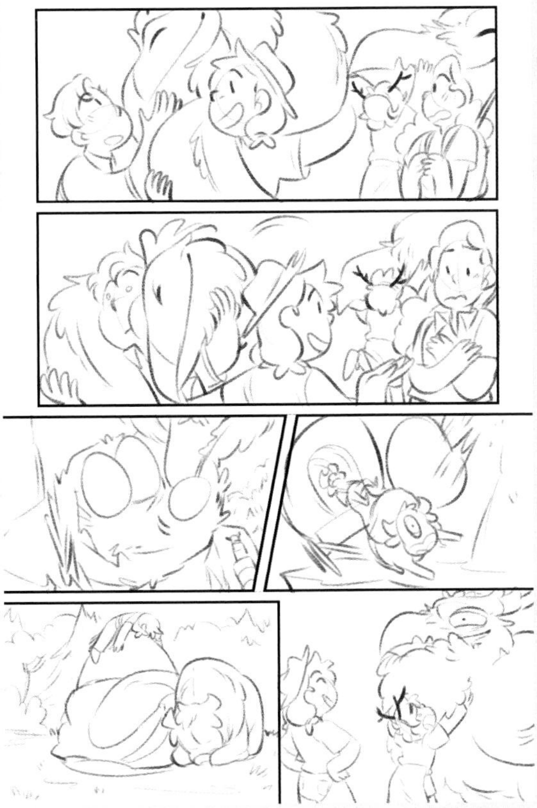

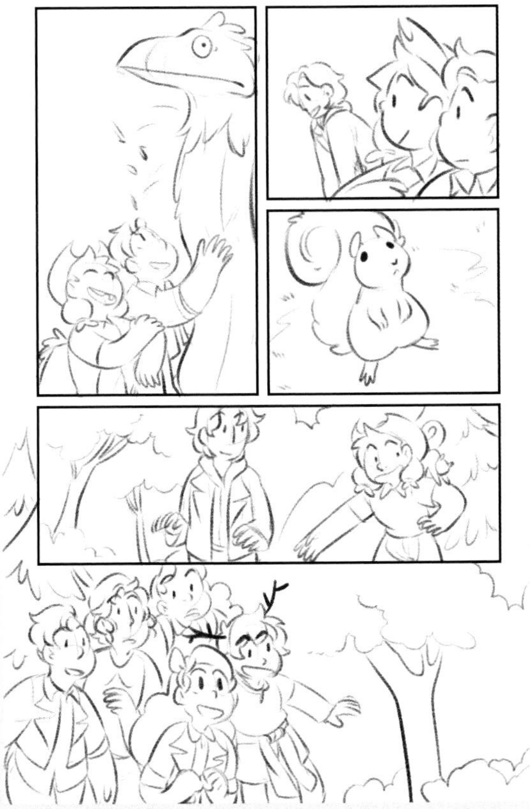

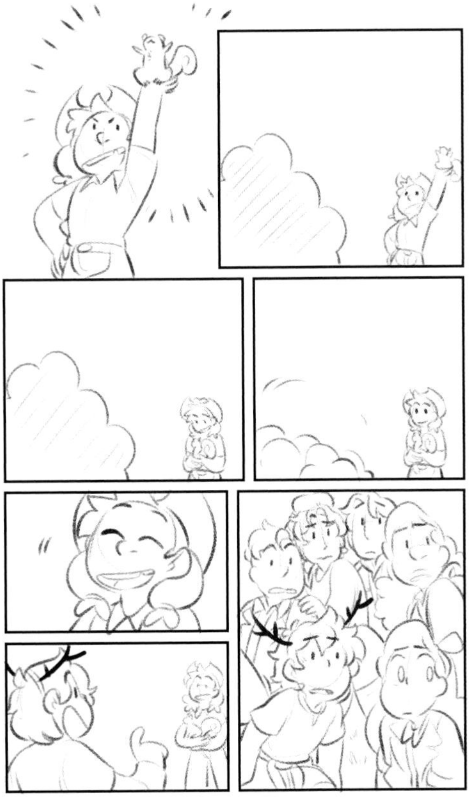

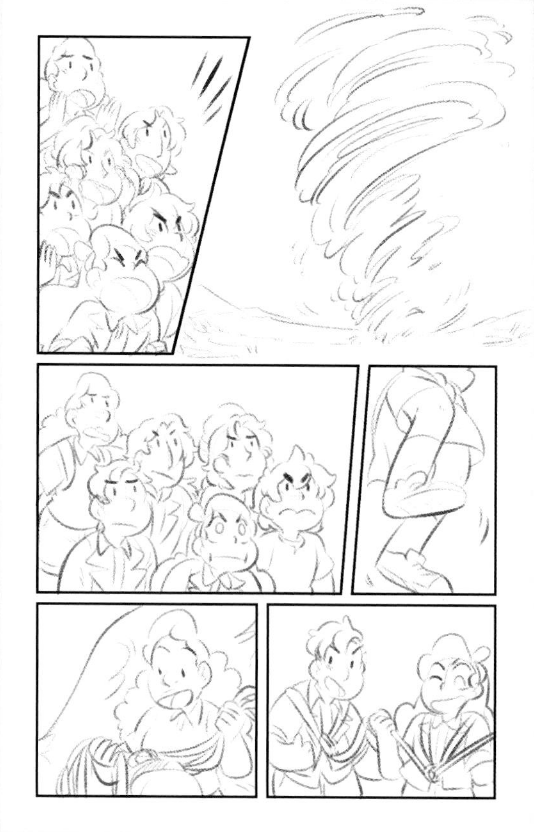

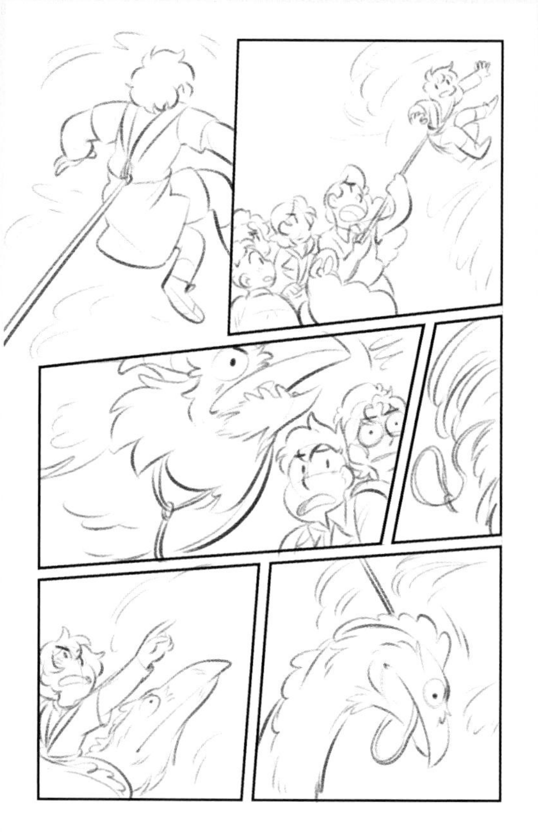

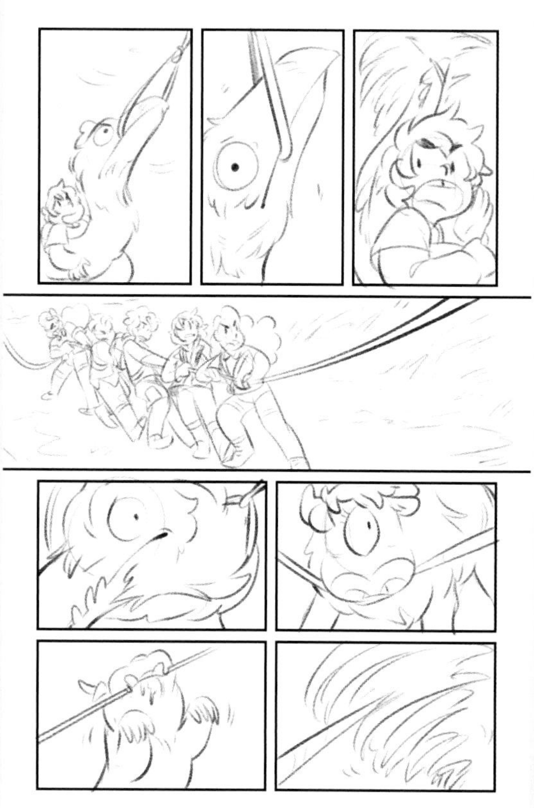

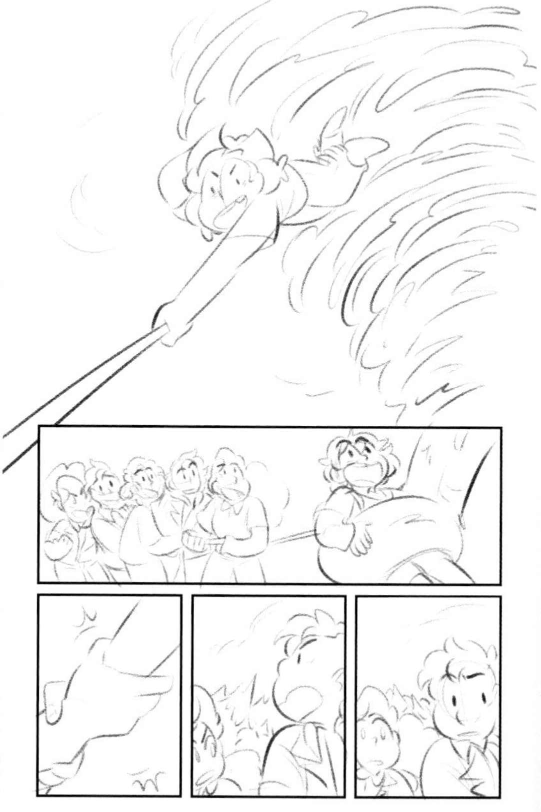

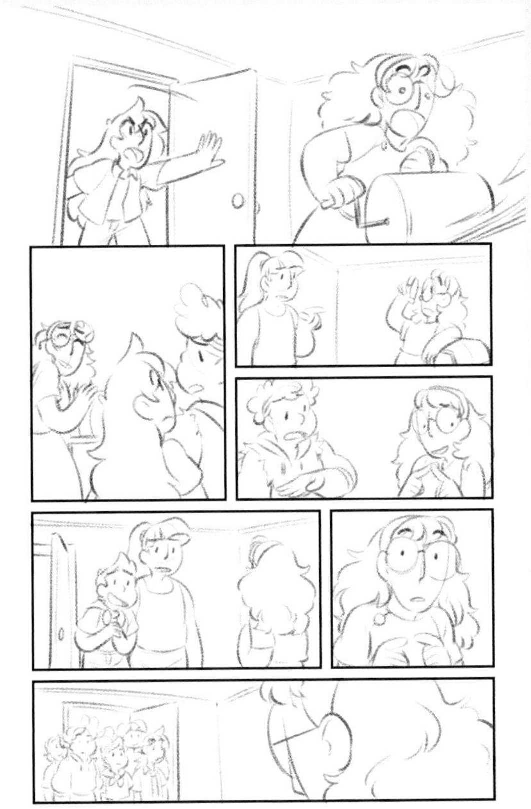

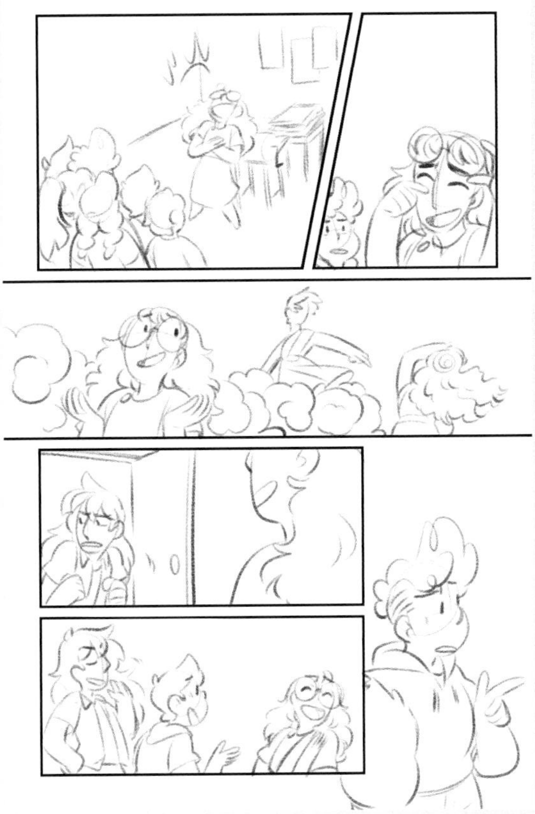

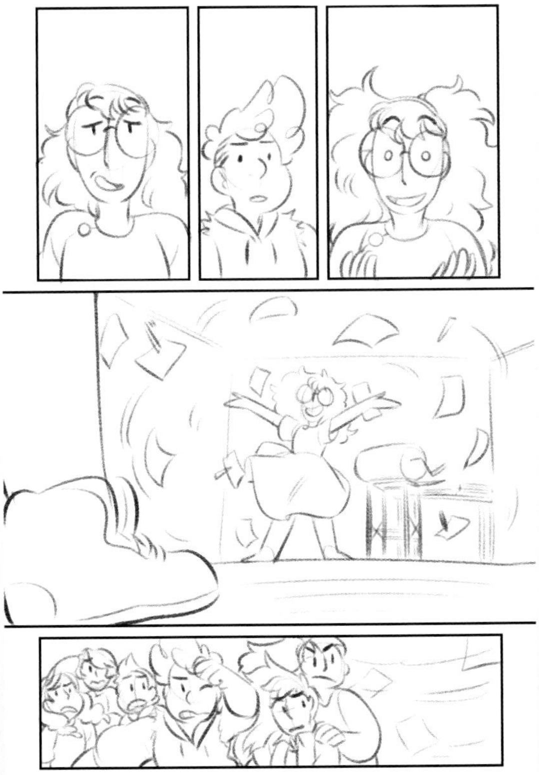

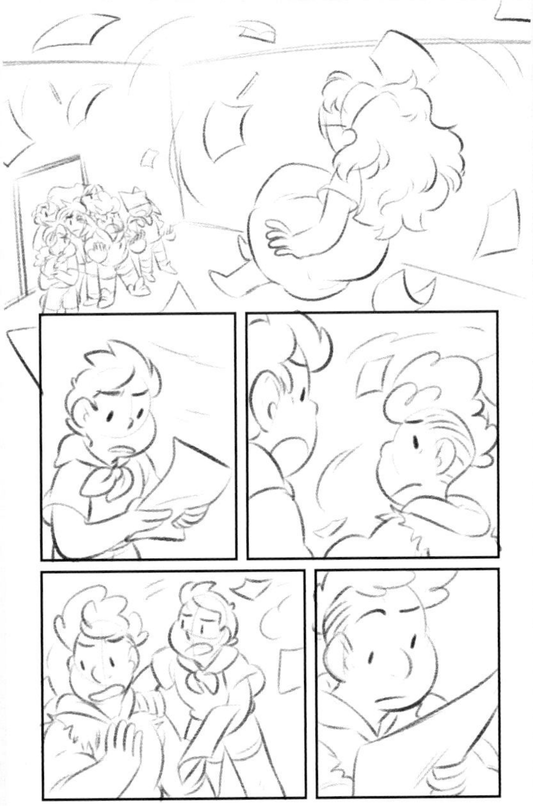

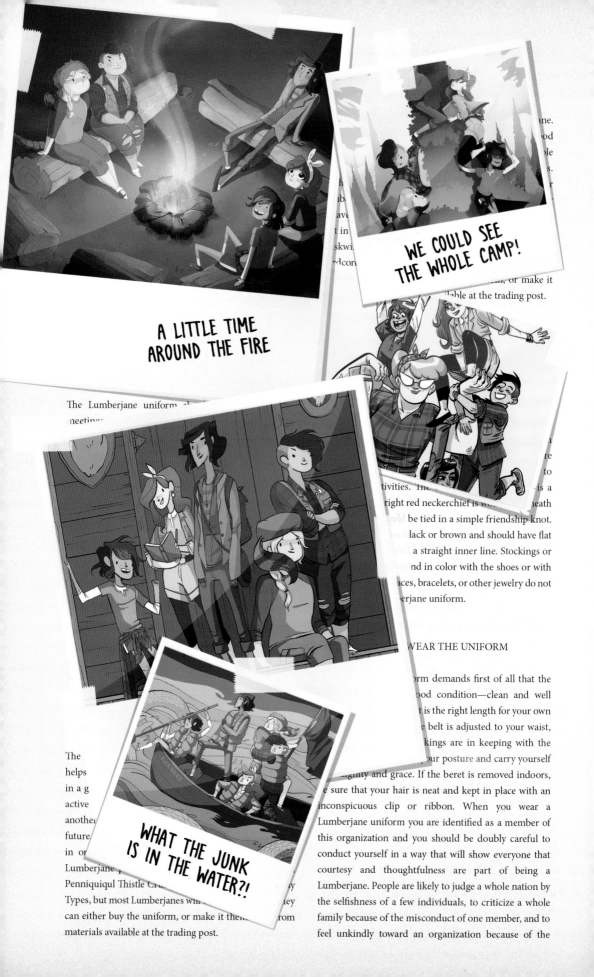

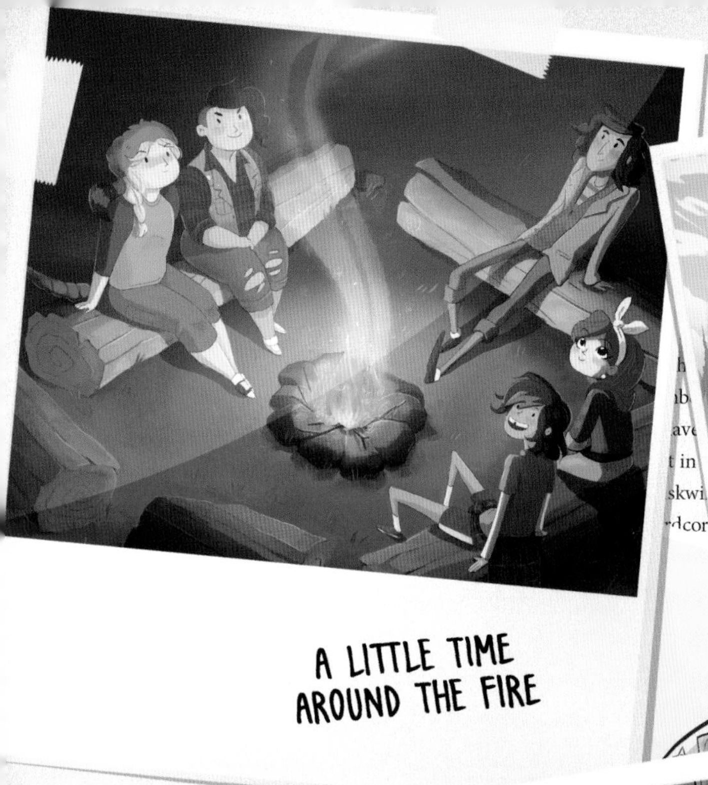
A LITTLE TIME
AROUND THE FIRE

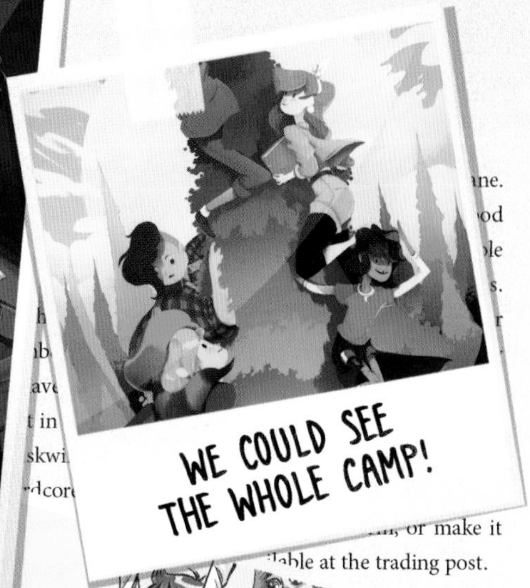
WE COULD SEE
THE WHOLE CAMP!

ane.
ood
ple
s.
r
b
ave
t in
skwi
dcore
, or make it
ilable at the trading post.

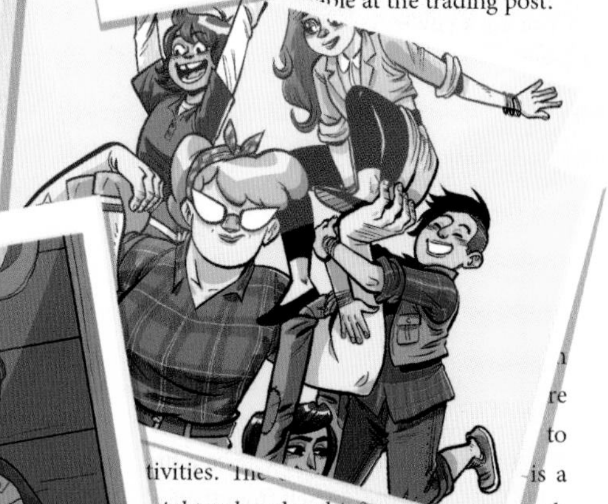

The Lumberjane uniform
meetings

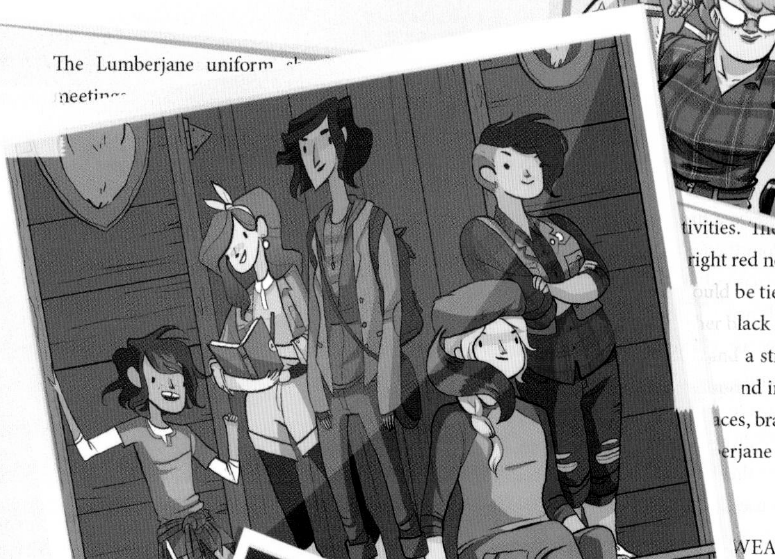

n
re
to
tivities. The — is a
right red neckerchief is w... neath
uld be tied in a simple friendship knot.
lack or brown and should have flat
a straight inner line. Stockings or
nd in color with the shoes or with
aces, bracelets, or other jewelry do not
erjane uniform.

WEAR THE UNIFORM

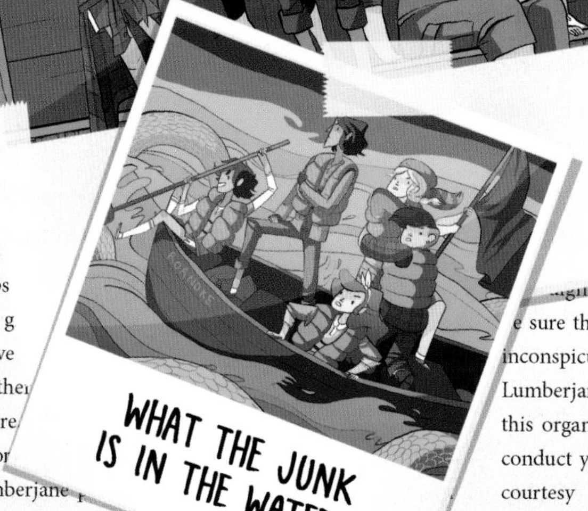
WHAT THE JUNK
IS IN THE WATER?!

The
helps
in a g
active
another
future
in or
Lumberjane
Penniquiqul Thistle Cr... y
Types, but most Lumberjanes wi... ey
can either buy the uniform, or make it the... rom
materials available at the trading post.

orm demands first of all that the
ood condition—clean and well
t is the right length for your own
e belt is adjusted to your waist,
kings are in keeping with the
our posture and carry yourself
dignity and grace. If the beret is removed indoors,
e sure that your hair is neat and kept in place with an inconspicuous clip or ribbon. When you wear a Lumberjane uniform you are identified as a member of this organization and you should be doubly careful to conduct yourself in a way that will show everyone that courtesy and thoughtfulness are part of being a Lumberjane. People are likely to judge a whole nation by the selfishness of a few individuals, to criticize a whole family because of the misconduct of one member, and to feel unkindly toward an organization because of the

SCRIPT TO PAGE

NEW FRIENDS!

WE ARE NOT AMOOSED!

Program Field

ER BADGE

When a Lumberjane...
it, she may pass it...
should...
un...
accomp...
The Lu...
meeting...
attend in...
other tim...
worn as...
with...
stockin...
When a Lu...
it, she may...
should remo...
earned. If she...
uniform and...
accomplishme...

only wea...
orm is...
cre...
n a...

...berjane...
...ve button-down...
...corners of the collar. D...
...ns and occassion, a Lu...
...green short slacks, gree...ull length
...knee length skirt. These garments are

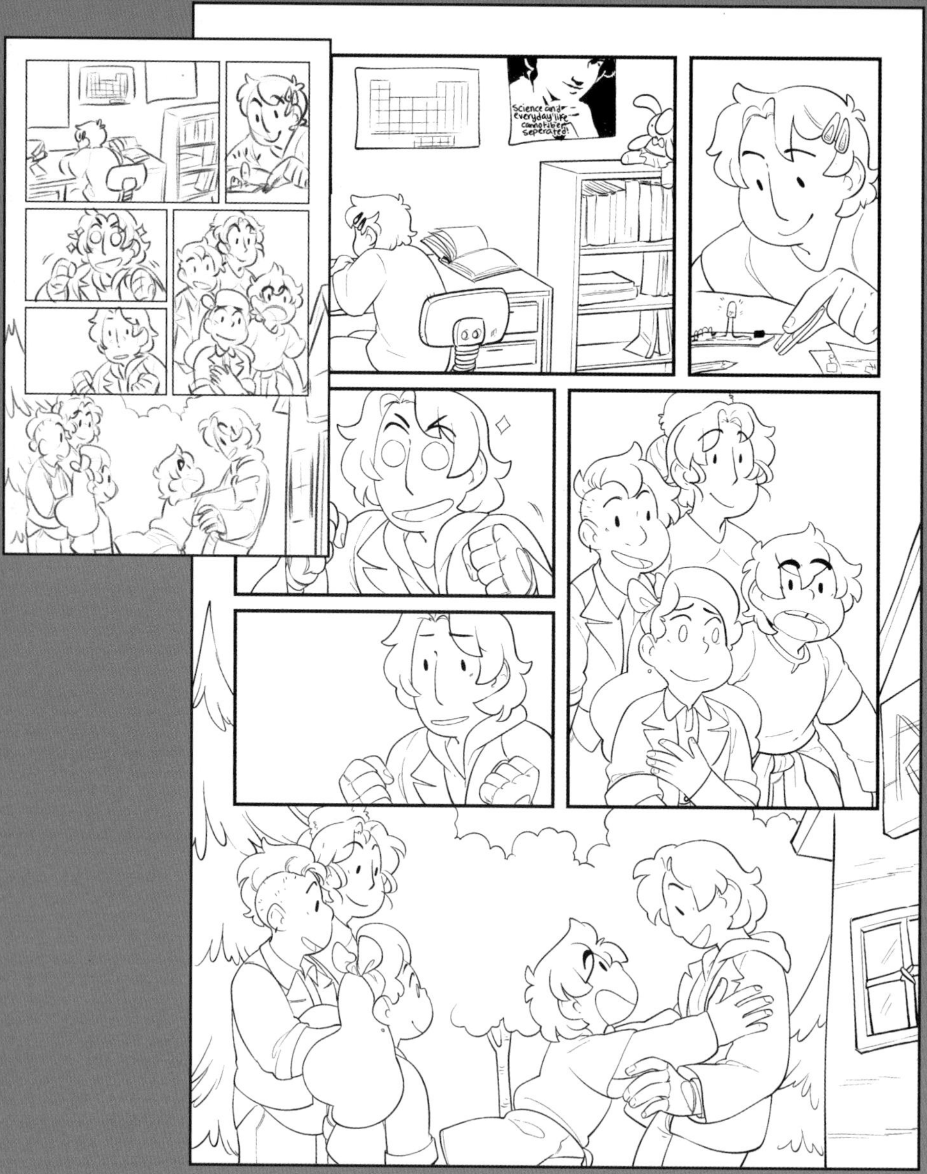
Science and everyday life cannot be seperated!

Issue Forty-One, Page Five

Panel 1: Flashback scene of young Jo, at a worktable in her room, fiddling with diodes and circuit boards. On her walls are Marie Curie and Rosalind Franklin quote posters: "We must have perseverance and above all confidence in ourselves. We must believe that we are gifted for something and that this thing must be attained." – Marie Curie; "Science and everyday life cannot and should not be separated." – Rosalind Franklin.

JO: (caption) "Science is THE BEST. It solves problems, answers questions…

Panel 2: Closer shot of little Jo. Her face is lighting up as the diode lights up.

JO: (caption) "…and the best part is when you find MORE questions that you didn't even *KNOW TO ASK…"*

Panel 3: Out of the flashback. Jo is starry eyed.

JO: …And this place has given me more questions than anything else ever has! I want to DO something about it!

Perseverance and above all, confidence
Science and everyday life cannot be seperated!

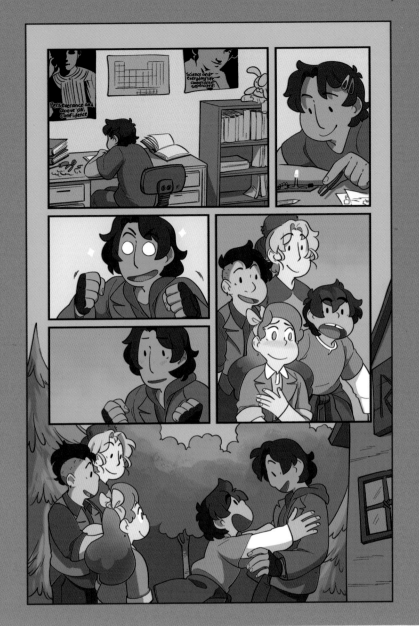

Panel 4: Small panel. She's looking over at the others, unsure.

JO: …Does that make sense?

Panel 5: The other Roanokes are looking at her. They are captivated. She's inspired them.

MAL: That is straight-up amazing, Jo.

RIPLEY: Oooo!

Panel 6: Group shot. Ripley looks fired up.

RIPLEY: I wanna experiment! Can I do…A SCIENCE?

JO: Well…THIS experiment still has to collect data before we learn anything…BUT…

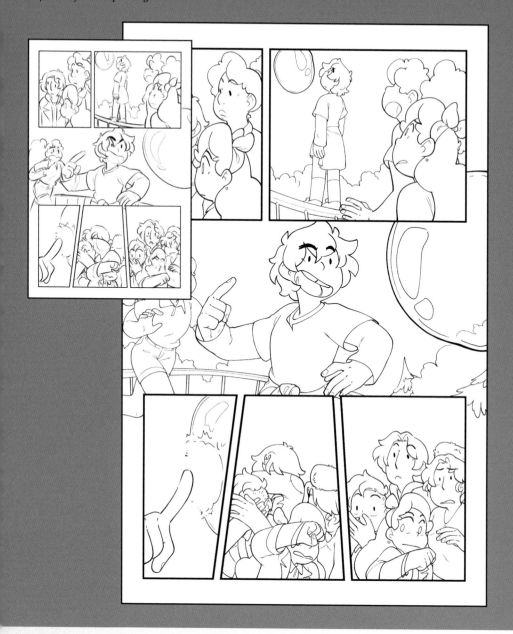

Issue Forty-Two, Page Twenty-One

Panel 1: The others glance over.

     RIPLEY: (off panel) Hey, guys! Check out this HUGE BUBBLE!

Panel 2: Ripley is standing on the rail, watching this bubble float lazily in front of her.

     APRIL: *WHOA,* that is a big bubble…

     JEN: Ripley! Get DOWN from there!

Panel 3: Ripley reels back with her finger point, dramatically poised to pop this bub. Jen is moving towards her, hand outstretched towards Ripley's.

     RIPLEY: ***AHM GONNA POP IT!***

     JEN: Get down!

Panel 4: Ripley's finger pops the balloon.

    SFX: Pip!

Panel 5: The Roanokes shield their eyes from the bright light.

Panel 6: Everyone's reaction shot. They are all dumbstruck by what they're looking at.

    JEN:(off panel) Girls?

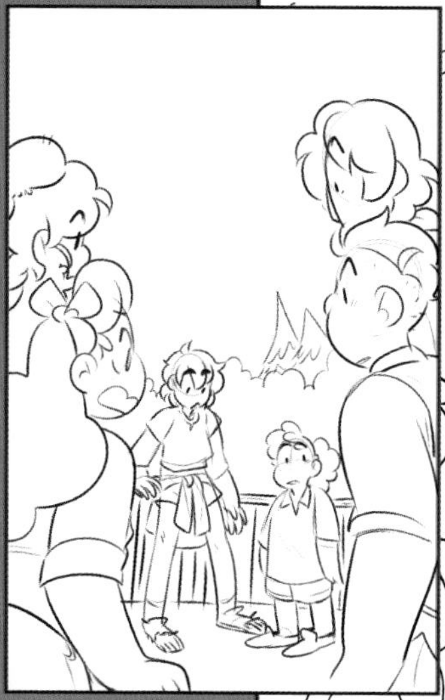

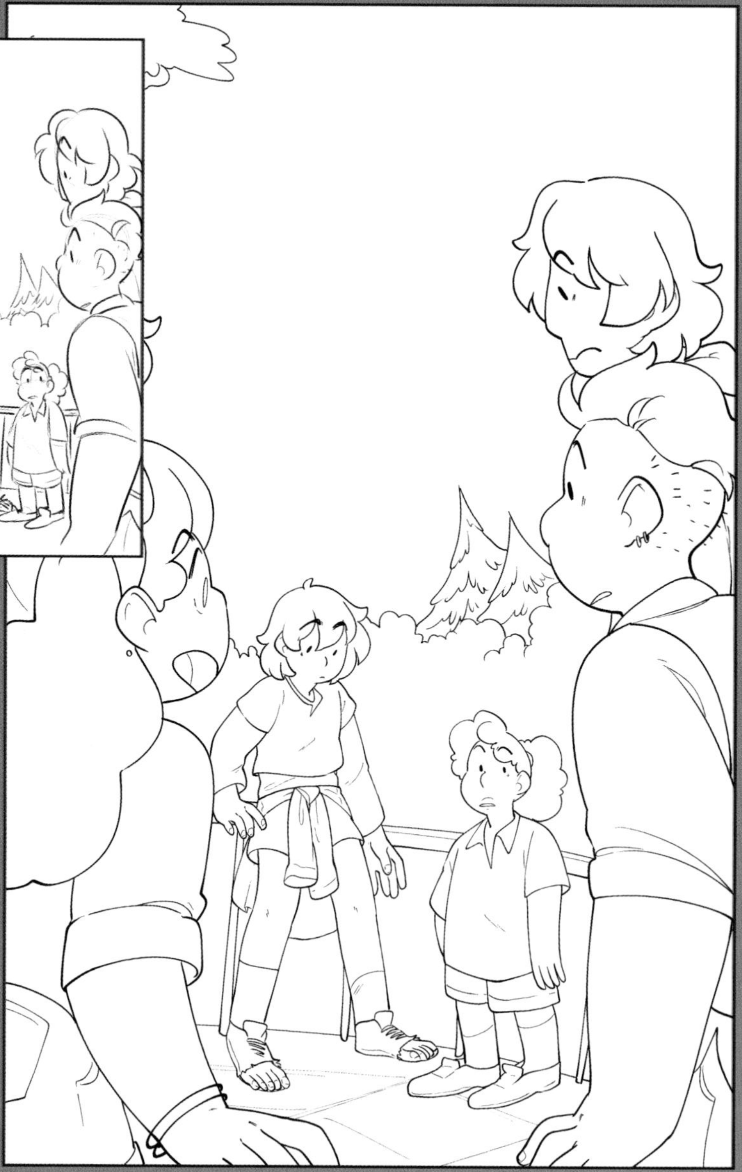

Issue Forty-Two, Page Twenty-Two

Panel 1: Full page. Ripley and Jen have swapped ages. Ripley's clothes are small on her and her feet pop out of her shoes. She is a tall string bean. Jen looks adorable in her oversized counselor uniform. Everyone is STUNNED.

JEN: What? What is it?

To Be Continued!

Issue Forty-Three, Page Fourteen

Panel 1: A stoic-looking Abigail, slingshot in hand, steps into the light. She's on a tree branch. Her ammunition is a pouch of rocks at her hip. (A general art note for Abigail: she favors her right arm--it didn't heal quite right from her last appearance.)

     JEN: (off panel) ***ABIGAIL?!?!***

Panel 2: Abigail dramatically repels down from the branch with a sweet grappling hook.

Panel 3: She lands on the ground and fires another rock. The Sentry is between her and the group at the elevator and is moving away from her and towards the elevator.

     JO: It's turning back this way!

     SFX: PLNK!

Panel 4: The girls at the elevator are moving towards the Sentry with the rope.

Panel 5: They hook it!

     SFX: CLICK!

Panel 6: Hes yells up.

     HES: *NOW!*

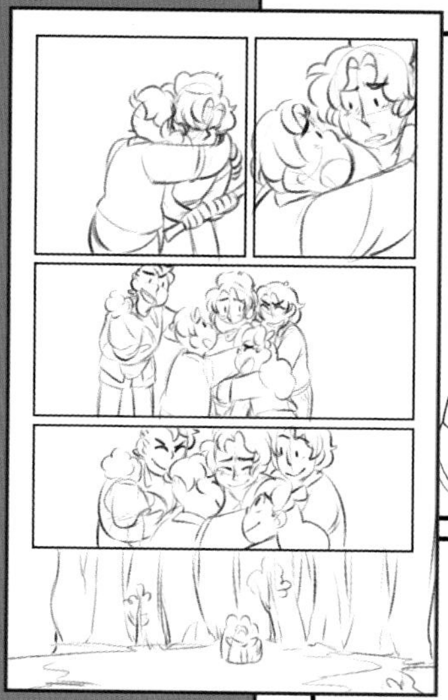

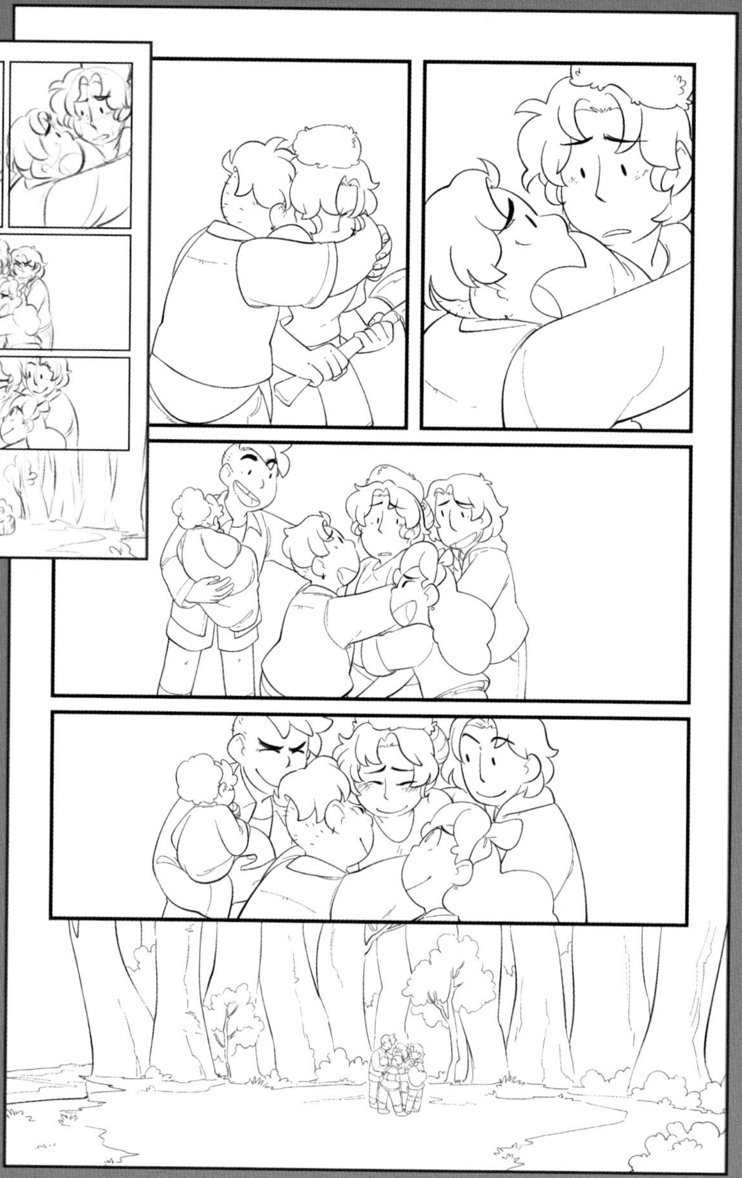

Issue Forty-Four, Page Fourteen

Panel 1: Mal crushes Molly in a hug.

MAL: (small) I'm sorry you don't want to go home. I'm sorry your parents aren't nice…

Panel 2: Shot of Mal's face as she pulls back a bit from the hug to look in Molly's eyes.

MAL: But…*you're* nice! You're the greatest! And I…*WE*…can all see that!

Panel 3: The other Roanokes join in the hug.

RIPLEY: YEAH! And there are more of US than there are of THEM!

APRIL: And we'll always be your friends! We'll be just a call away.

JO: Just try and stop us!

MAL: No matter where or when you are or whatever, that won't change!

Panel 4: Closer shot of the group huddled together. Molly smiles.

    APRIL: We LOVE you!

    RIPLEY: *YEAH!*

    MAL: Yeah.

Panel 5: Wide shot. The Roanokes are small in this panel, still in their group hug.

    MOLLY: Thanks…

    SFX: *THUD!*

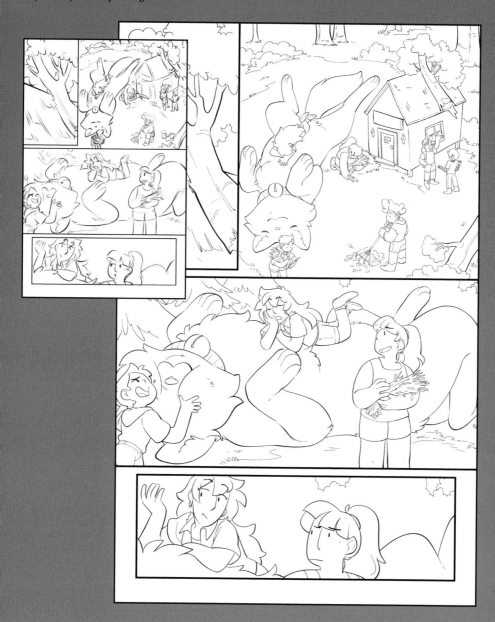

Issue Forty-Five, Page One

Panel 1: Shot of a very large tree bough on a cabin roof. This is fallout from the previous arc.

    MACKENZIE: (from below) C'mon, let's just pull it down! We're tough!

Panel 2: Zoom out to reveal the Zodiac's cabin. The Zodiacs are all outside. They are cleaning up around their cabin. Marigold is giant and sleeping on her back in a sunbeam. Diane is laying on her belly, napping in the same sunbeam. Hes is raking up detritus.

    EMILY: It could scrape off half the shingles! Or, y'know, crush us.

    WREN: Can't Marigold just bring it down, Barney? She's helped us carry huge things before!

Panel 3: Barney nuzzles Marigold's face. Diane continues to lie on top of her.

    BARNEY: Yes, she has! She is my big, strong, beautiful girl. But also, a very sleepy girl.

WREN: (from off panel) What about you, Diane? Why don't YOU help?

DIANE: I refuse to use my UNFATHOMABLE GODDESS POWERS on a stupid branch.

MACKENZIE: (from off panel) HOW ABOUT HELPING LIKE A NORMAL **PERSON** THEN!

DIANE: Uuuuuuh. No.

Panel 4: The Zodiacs all turn towards the voice from off panel. Diane and Mackenzie pause mid scuffle.

OFF PANEL: Can I help?

Issue Forty-Six, Page Two

Panel 1: Shot of Emmy placing Besssie around her shoulders and scratching Besssie's head affectionately.

     SFX: BA-GOK!

     EMMY: Nothing to worry about friends! Besssie here was only saying hello!

Panel 2: Group shot of Emmy with her critters. Now they look decidedly NOT ominous. Besssie and Hodag look especially ridiculous and stupid.

     EMMY: This is my herd!

Panel 3: April cautiously approaches the Hodag.

     EMMY: (off panel) Go ahead! He's harmless!

     SFX: (the Hodag panting) huff huff huff

Panel 4: Same shot as previous. The Hodag flops over, April grins.

Panel 5: Same shot as previous, April scratches its belly, making its leg shake.
 EMMY: (off panel) That's it!

Issue Forty-Seven, Page Eighteen

Panel 1: Emmy is pulling the rope fastened around her waist, which is still leading back into the twister.

    EMMY: KEEP PULLING!

Panel 2: The Roanokes look unsure. Jen is stern.

    JEN: EMMY, WHY? WE HAVE TO GO!

Panel 3: Emmy looks back at them, the twister in the background, being ominous. Emmy grins.

    EMMY: Trust me! Please?

Panel 4: The group all pulls together again, with Emmy at the front.

Panel 5: Shot of where the rope disappears in the tornado.

Panel 6: Same shot as previous. A boot emerges, the rope tied around it.

Issue Forty-Eight, Page Ten

Panel 1: Start of a newsletter creating montage! Barney is interviewing the Yetis with Marigold on their shoulders. The Yetis have starry eyes as they coo over Marigold.

Panel 2: Hes is working with an X-acto blade and ruler, her tongue sticking out as she concentrates.

Panel 3: Kenzie writing notes as she speaks with Mal and Feryal in their roller derby gear.

Panel 4: Some Lumberjanes gather round reading the newsletter eagerly.

Panel 5: Wren sits, drawing in the newsroom, behind her Emily sits surrounded by messy notes, perhaps a classic conspiracy board.

Panel 6: Diane reads a magazine and blows a bubble with her gum. Behind her, Cassandra waves at her as she passes by, but Diane doesn't acknowledge her.

LUMBERJANES FIELD MANUAL

ABOUT THE AUTHORS

SHANNON WATTERS

Shannon Watters is an editor lady by day and the co-creator of *Lumberjanes*...also by day. She helped guide KaBOOM!—BOOM! Studios' all-ages imprint—to commercial and critical success, and oversees BOOM! Box, an experimental imprint created "for the love of it." She has a great love for all things indie and comics, which is something she's been passionate about since growing up in the wilds of Arizona. When she's not working on comics she can be found watching classic films and enjoying the local cuisine.

ART BY BROOKLYN ALLEN

GRACE ELLIS

Grace Ellis is a writer and co-creator of *Lumberjanes*. She is currently writing *Moonstruck*, a comic about lesbian werewolf baristas, as well as scripts for the animated show *Bravest Warriors*. Grace lives in Columbus, Ohio, where she co-parents a preternaturally smart cat, even though she's usually more of a dog person.

NOELLE STEVENSON

Noelle Stevenson is the *New York Times* bestselling author of *Nimona*. She's been nominated for Harvey Awards, and was awarded the Slate Cartoonist Studio Prize for Best Web Comic in 2012 for Nimona. A graduate of the Maryland Institute College of Art, Noelle has worked on shows like Disney's *Wander Over Yonder* and *She-Ra*, and she has written for Marvel and DC Comics. She lives in Los Angeles. In her spare time she can be found drawing superheroes and talking about bad TV.
www.gingerhaze.com

ART BY **BROOKLYN ALLEN**

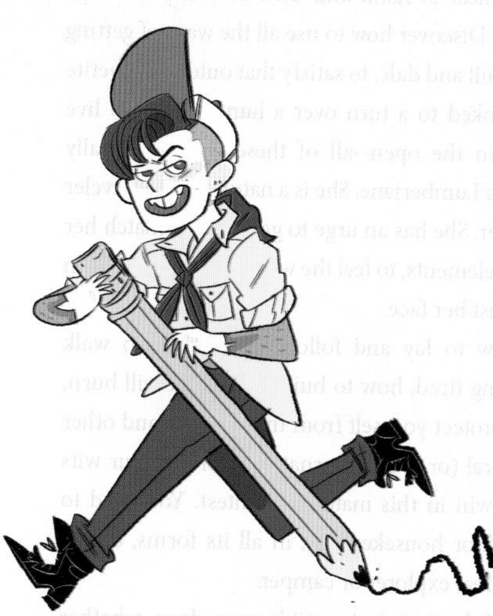

BROOKLYN ALLEN

Brooklyn Allen is the co-creator and the artist for *Lumberjanes* and when he is not drawing, then he will most likely be found with a saw in his hand making something rad. Currently residing in the "for lovers" state of Virginia, he spends most of his time working on comics with his not-so-helpful assistant Linus...his dog.

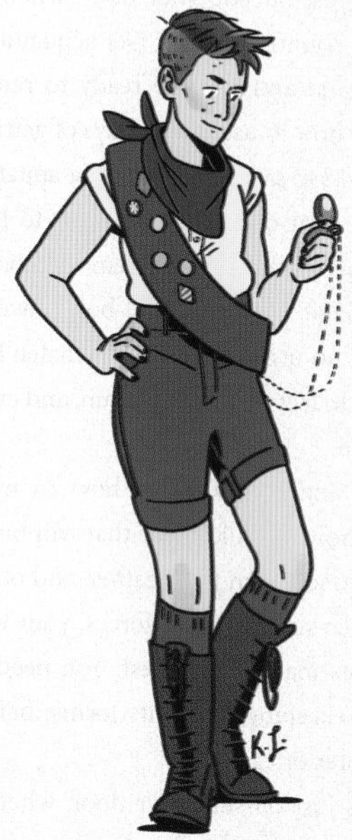
K.T.

KAT LEYH

Kat Leyh has been co-writer of *Lumberjanes* since issue 18 and cover artist since issue 24. Growing up in the woods, attending 4-H camp in the summers, and creating comics about supernatural queer characters have all led to her feeling right at home with the Lumberjanes! She's done various short comics for series like *Adventure Time* and *Bravest Warriors*, and her own series, *Supercakes*; and upcoming graphic novel, *Roadkill Witch*. When not making comics, she loves to cook, travel and explore!

ART BY BROOKLYN ALLEN AND KAT LEYH

AYME SOTUYO

Ayme Sotuyo is a Cuban freelance comic artist currently residing in the Pacific Northwest and finally seeing snow for the first time. She grew up in south Florida and attended Savannah College of Art and Design. A good chunk of her time is spent drawing her webcomic *[un] Divine*, being yelled at by her cat for attention, and watching old anime.

MAARTA LAIHO

Maarta Laiho spends her days and nights as a comic colorist, where her work includes BOOM! Studio's *Lumberjanes*, and *Adventure Time*; Oni Press's *The Mighty Zodiac*; and the graphic novel adaptation of the *Wings of Fire* series from Scholastic. When she's not doing that, she can be found hoarding houseplants and talking to her cat.

www.PencilCat.net

AUBREY AIESE

Aubrey Aiese is an illustrator and hand letterer from Brooklyn, New York currently living in Portland, Oregon. She loves eating ice cream, making comics, and playing with her super cute corgi pups, Ace and Penny. She's been nominated for a Harvey Award for her outstanding lettering on *Lumberjanes* and continues to find new ways to challenge herself in her field. She also puts an absurd amount of ketchup on her french fries.

www.lettersfromaubrey.com

ART BY **BROOKLYN ALLEN**